King of England Alfred, Albert S. Cook, Abbot of Eynsham Aelfric

Biblical Quotations in old English Prose Writers

King of England Alfred, Albert S. Cook, Abbot of Eynsham Aelfric

Biblical Quotations in old English Prose Writers

ISBN/EAN: 9783337367831

Printed in Europe, USA, Canada, Australia, Japan

Cover: Foto ©Andreas Hilbeck / pixelio.de

More available books at **www.hansebooks.com**

BIBLICAL QUOTATIONS

IN

OLD ENGLISH PROSE WRITERS

EDITED

WITH THE VULGATE AND OTHER LATIN ORIGINALS
INTRODUCTION ON OLD ENGLISH BIBLICAL VERSIONS
INDEX OF BIBLICAL PASSAGES, AND
INDEX OF PRINCIPAL WORDS

BY

ALBERT S. COOK

Hon. M.A. Yale, Ph.D. Jena, L.H.D. Rutgers

PROFESSOR OF THE ENGLISH LANGUAGE AND LITERATURE IN YALE UNIVERSITY
PRESIDENT OF THE MODERN LANGUAGE ASSOCIATION OF AMERICA

*

London

MACMILLAN AND CO., Limited

NEW YORK: THE MACMILLAN COMPANY

1898

Oxford

HORACE HART, PRINTER TO THE UNIVERSITY

TO

DR. JAMES A. H. MURRAY

WHOSE 'NEW ENGLISH DICTIONARY' WILL BE ONE OF THE

GLORIES OF ENGLAND

AND IS THE

ADMIRATION OF HER CHILDREN BEYOND THE SEAS

IN RECOGNITION NOT LESS OF HIS QUALITIES AS A MAN

THAN OF HIS EMINENCE AS A SCHOLAR

PREFACE

THIS first instalment of a reasonably complete collection of the Biblical extracts scattered throughout the Old English prose texts has been undertaken in the interest of the Biblical scholar, the professional student of English speech, and the person who desires to gain in the easiest possible manner a slight reading knowledge of Old English prose. For this volume the two representative prose authors of the two chief epochs, Alfred and Ælfric, have been chosen; and the Latin originals, the indispensable medium of interpretation and comparison, have been printed at the foot of the page.

The Biblical scholar should know that in his domain I am the merest amateur, and that I leave to him the task of determining the precise readings which have been followed by our translators, when a choice of readings was possible. That the Vulgate was not always strictly followed is probable, and in some cases, as now and again in the Alfredian translation of the *Cura Pastoralis*, is certain. Ælfric may have followed the Latin homilists whom he adapts, and thus may have been led to deviate here and there from the Vulgate text; but his relation to these sources has as yet been too little investigated to admit of a present determination of the amount of this variation. The exact decision will always be rendered difficult by the paraphrastic nature of the version in some cases; by the tendency of Old English writers to vary their expression in different places, even when rendering the very same original; and by the frequent impossibility, in the case of the Gospels, of deciding which of the Evangelists the translator had in mind. Under the last head, a kind of 'contamination' is not unusual, showing that the translator is making or following a kind of harmony of the Gospels, and accordingly producing a composite narrative, in which the exact shares of the several Evangelists cannot always be ascertained with precision.

Where I have adduced the so-called Itala, my dependence has been upon Sabatier.

The professed student of English speech should know that I have followed the best printed texts of each work, taking no liberties with them save as respects punctuation and capitals, the use of diacritical marks for quantity, &c., and to some extent in the joining or separation of words. Thus for the *Pastoral Care* and *Orosius* I have followed Sweet: for the *Ecclesiastical History*, Miller; for the *Laws*, Schmid's second edition; and for Ælfric, Thorpe's edition of the *Homilies*. In the slight changes referred to, I have studied consistency and the ready apprehension of the text. To this end, I have not scrupled to change the traditional punctuation of the Vulgate, partly because I have not found entire uniformity in the various impressions, and partly because I have no superstitious reverence for the received usage when uniform, since it is not seldom at variance with grammar and sense. Accordingly, the punctuation of the Old English and that of the Latin have been brought into some degree of conformity, though there are instances where this has proved impracticable.

In the marking of quantity, and of derivative *e* and *o*, there are, I trust, but few oversights not corrected in the Errata. The words which geminate an originally single consonant after a long vowel have given me most trouble, and here I shall no doubt seem inconsistent, and in some cases am no doubt really so; in general, I have omitted the macron, but have retained it where the sonancy of the following consonant may probably have favoured the retention of length. Proper names have been left unmarked, since as yet there is no general agreement among scholars as to the quantity of the syllables in even the commonest Scriptural names.

I have no doubt exposed myself to criticism by the use of

the hyphen for joining words left separate in the standard editions, and, in the case of a few common conjunctions, by actually writing two or three words (like *for þon þe*) as one. In these cases I must be content to receive the censure of those who are otherwise minded.

The use of brackets and parentheses is most frequent in the *Pastoral Care*. Here I have followed Sweet (see the Table of Abbreviations), except that I have indicated the chief variant readings of the Hatton MS. by a parenthetical word followed by H.

The beginner in the study of Old English will find in the present volume a convenient chrestomathy, with the matter of which he is already acquainted, and which can almost be read from the outset, without grammar or dictionary, by the help either of the modern English version, or, better, by that of the Latin. He will likewise, by a comparison of the different renderings of the same passage, acquire a sense of the variations which the same translator permitted himself, the idiosyncrasies of each translator, and the changes in the language between one and another.

Here, indeed, is considerable material for the study of Old English semasiology, a study which, like that of English semasiology in general, has been too much neglected. What is an author's range of synonyms for a given idea? What is the range of his vocabulary, as distributed among such categories of synonyms? What are the peculiarities of his diction, as determined by these tests? Wherein does the diction of a given period, again, as judged by these standards, differ from that of another given period? It is evident that these inquiries are by no means otiose, and that the easiest and most promising introduction to the subject is through the medium of successive translations from the Latin, preferably from the same Latin text. Now there is no Latin text which fulfils the obvious conditions so well as the Vulgate. It is a tolerably unchanging document, and, directly or indirectly, in fragments of various length, it has been translated or paraphrased over and over again. The study of these renderings would occupy a large number of capable students of semasio-

logy for many years, and would add incalculably to our
exact knowledge of the changes which have taken place in
the English vocabulary, and in the differentiation of meanings.
And what is true of semasiology is likewise true, in its degree,
of syntax.

Such comparisons as have been mentioned will be facilitated
by the Index of Biblical Passages, and by that of Principal
Words. The latter is not intended as a glossary, nor for the
exhibition of grammatical forms; but for the purpose indicated its fullness ought to render it valuable. I wish the
limitations of space had permitted still greater fullness, even
under very common words; for now and again a student
may wish for a completer exhibit of usage than has been
provided.

The Introduction will, I trust, be serviceable to all who are
interested in these texts, and to many who are not. The
astounding · misstatements and omissions of the latest and
most authoritative books of reference which treat of this
subject—a subject of interest to every intelligent person of
English extraction—will no doubt be deemed a sufficient reason
for the essay here presented. Its shortcomings may perhaps
be the more leniently judged when it is considered that all
existing outlines which profess to cover the same ground
are either misleading, or wholly inadequate, or both. This
sketch may therefore justly be regarded as a sort of
pioneer effort, for, while much of it is compilation, criticism
has been necessary at every step, and some of the results have
been worked out by the author himself especially for this
publication.

In conclusion, I shall be glad if the present work leads to
a somewhat juster appreciation of the early history of the
English Bible, to a more diligent study of the course of English
speech, and, in however slight a measure, to a fuller sense of
fraternity among the different members of the English race.

ALBERT S. COOK.

YALE UNIVERSITY,
    August 15, 1897.

CONTENTS

TABLE OF ABBREVIATIONS

Bede.—As under Greg.

Greg.—Gregory's reading in his *Cura Pastoralis,* as distinguished from that of the Vulgate.

H.—Hatton MS.

ins.—insert's) ; inserit, inserunt.

Ital.—Italam, Italicam versionem.

LXX.—Septuagint.

om.—omits ; omittit.

sec.—secundum.

sum.—summarily ; summatim.

Vulg.—Vulgate.

[ ] in the Cotton MS. of Gregory's *Pastoral Care,* denote the readings of Cotton Otho B. 2 (Sweet's *Cotton II*) ; in the Hatton MS., they denote additions above the line.

( ) in the O. E. *Pastoral Care,* denote Sweet's conjectural additions; when a word in parentheses is followed by H., a reading of the Hatton MS. is signified. In *Alfred's Laws,* both brackets and parentheses are used to indicate readings of MSS. G. and H. (Cott. Nero A. 1, and the Textus Roffensis), the standard being E. (the Corpus or Benet MS., C. C. 175).

INTRODUCTION

As a means of exhibiting the relations which the Biblical extracts now first collected sustain to the versions already known, the following conspectus is presented. No such survey at present exists, and the current statements on the subject are often so lamentably meagre and incorrect that it has seemed by no means superfluous to supply the exactest possible information in these pages, and to give ample references to the most authoritative and critical of recent works.

SEVENTH CENTURY.

Prose Translations.

None are known.

Poetical Translations.

Cædmon.—The first Old English paraphrase of portions of the Bible is attributed to Cædmon, in the following passage of Bede's *Ecclesiastical History* (iv. 24) : 'Canebat autem de creatione mundi et origine humani generis, et tota Genesis historia, de egressu Israel ex Aegypto et ingressu in terram repromissionis, de aliis plurimis sacrae Scripturae historiis, de incarnatione Dominica, passione, resurrectione, et ascensione in coelum, de Spiritus Sancti adventu, et apostolorum doctrina.'

Since the publication of Francis Junius' *Cædmonis Monachi Paraphrasis Poetica Genesios ac Praecipuarum Sacrae Paginae Historiarum* (Amsterdam, 1655), certain poetical paraphrases of the Bible contained in MS. Junius XI of the Bodleian Library at Oxford have passed under the name of Cædmon. The whole subject is discussed at length by Wülker, in his *Grundriss*, pp. 111–140, with the purely negative result, expressed on p. 139, that nothing can with certainty be attributed to Cædmon save the Hymn found at the end of the Moore MS. of Bede in the Cambridge University Library, and which is printed, e. g., in Sweet's *Oldest English Texts*, p. 149, and *Anglo-Saxon Reader*, seventh edition, p. 175; in my *The Bible and English Prose Style* (Boston, U.S.A.: D. C. Heath & Co.), p. ix; Zupitza-MacLean's *Old and Middle English Reader*, p. 1; Grein-Wülker's *Bibliothek*, ii. 317; and Stopford Brooke's *History of Early English Literature*, p. 340. Since this Hymn is but nine lines in length, and refers only allusively to the first chapter of Genesis, it is evident that we cannot affirm that we possess any portion of the Biblical translations which Bede affirms to have been made by Cædmon.

ALDHELM.—For more than sixty years there has been discussion among scholars as to whether the so-called Paris Psalter may have been the work of Aldhelm (640?-709). This recent suggestion was made by Thorpe in his edition of the Paris Psalter, under the title, *Libri Psalmorum Versio Antiqua Latina, cum Paraphrasi Anglo-Saxonica* (Oxford, 1835). His words are (Praefatio, p. v): 'Memoriae quidem proditum est Aldhelmum, Shirburnensem Episcopum, qui quum carminum laude inclaruisset, non Latino solum sed et patrio sermone conditorum, A. D. DCCIX mortuus est, Psalmos Davidis Anglo-Saxonice primum reddidisse: et quum versio quam nos edendam suscepimus, etsi ab initio ad Psalmum quinquagesimum oratione soluta scripta est, inde usque ad finem versibus puris Anglo-Saxonicis constet, dicendi tamen genus seculum decimo superius non sapiat; erunt fortasse qui suspicentur eam aliam non esse quam Aldhelmi ipsius versionem a recentiore quodam refictam.' Thorpe goes on to say that the evidence of language alone would not justify us in assigning a date to an Old English composition, and that the version which he publishes is in parts so incorrect that he would hesitate to attribute it to Aldhelm: 'Hinc quidem minus verisimile fit hanc versionem opus fuisse viri doctrina eximia qualis fuerit Aldhelmus; etsi inter errores istos multi sunt quos aut incuriae aut ignorantiae librarii jure tribuas.' In his translation of Lappenberg's *Anglo-Saxon Kings*, 1845 (ed. 1880, i. 258, note 3), Thorpe says: 'An Anglo-Saxon version of the Psalms, possibly Aldhelm's, transcribed by the present translator from a MS. in the Royal Library at Paris, has been published at the expense of the University of Oxford.'

Thorpe was followed by Thomas Wright, whose *Biographia*

Britannica Literaria : Anglo-Saxon Period was published in 1842. He observes, at the close of his life of Aldhelm (p. 222) : 'He is said to have translated the Psalms into Anglo-Saxon verse, but the translation published by Mr. Thorpe, in 1835, has none of the characteristics which might be looked for in his compositions.' From this it may be inferred that he derived his information from Thorpe. This is, however, quite inconsistent with his remarks concerning Aldhelm in a note to p. 21 : 'He is said, among other things, to have translated the Psalms into Anglo-Saxon verse, which may possibly have been the same which Mr. Thorpe has so ably edited from the Paris MS. or the groundwork of it.'

Giles. *Sancti Aldhelmi Opera*, 1844, says nothing whatever on the subject.

In 1853 Professor Franz Dietrich, in an article entitled 'Hycgan und Hopian,' published in Haupt's *Zeitschrift für Deutsches Alterthum*, vol. ix, endeavours to rehabilitate the tradition by means of an investigation into the relative age of two words for the verb 'hope,' namely, *hycgan* and *hopian*. In summing up (p. 222), he remarks : 'Es giebt eine alte Tradition dass Aldhelm (†709), der lateinisch und in seiner Muttersprache gedichtet, auch die Psalmen ins Angelsächsische übertragen habe. Die schon aufgegebene Vermutung, dass sich sein Werk hier erhalten habe, ist für den allitterierenden Theil nach den obigen Ausführungen wieder aufzunehmen, und kann durch einige wenige auch hier wie im ersten Theil vorkommende Mängel der Uebersetzung, welche noch nach Abzug der vom Abschreiber und vom Lateinischen verschuldeten übrig bleiben, nicht umgeworfen werden. Das erste Drittel seiner Arbeit mag an der Handschrift abgerissen gefunden und von einem Schreiber des 11n Jh. durch die vorliegende Prosa vermeintlich ersetzt worden sein. Vielleicht ist die Prosa aus einer etwas älteren, ebenfalls vollständig gewesenen Uebersetzung entnommen.'

In 1854, K. W. Bouterwek (*Cædmons des Angelsachsen Biblische Dichtungen*, Gütersloh and London) refers to Thorpe's opinion in his 'Dritte Abtheilung,' p. clxxxiii, but, beyond citing Spelman (see below), he contributes nothing to the discussion.

In 1880 appeared a posthumous work of the distinguished scholar Grein, his *Kurzgefasste Angelsächsische Grammatik*. In this (p. 9) he expresses the opinion that Psalms 52–150 of Thorpe's edition are probably to be attributed to Aldhelm.

In 1884 Professor Earle, of Oxford, writes (*Anglo-Saxon Literature*, p. 90): 'The suggestion that they might be Aldhelm's, though modernized, had rhetorical attractions for the editor (Thorpe), and supplied him with material for a few rather idle sentences of his Latin preface.'

In 1885 Professor Wülker, of Leipzig (*Grundriss zur Geschichte der Angelsächsischen Litteratur*, p. 384), rejects Dietrich's hypothesis: 'Dietrich's Ansicht, dass Aldhelm Verfasser unserer Psalmen-übertragung sei, ist unhaltbar; dagegen spricht Behandlungsweise, Art des Ausdrucks, und Versbau.'

In the same year, the *Dictionary of National Biography*, s. v. 'Aldhelm,' has no mention of the tradition.

Various encyclopaedic works since the date of Thorpe's edition have repeated the statement that Aldhelm composed a version of the Psalms, but either assign no authority, or a false one. So the *Encyclopaedia Britannica*, ninth edition, viii. 381; Julian's *Dictionary of Hymnology*, p. 916; Johnson's *Encyclopaedia*, revised edition, i. 610; Kitto's *Cyclopaedia of Biblical Literature*, third edition, i. 149; Smith, *Dictionary of the Bible*, iv. 3424, 3425 (copied in McClintock and Strong's *Cyclopaedia of Biblical Literature*, iii. 208, 209); Schaff-Herzog, *Religious Encyclopaedia*, i. 288; Wetzer and Welte's *Kirchenlexikon*, second edition, iv. 593; besides various popular books on the history of the English Bible, such as those of Mombert, Moulton, Smyth, &c.

The whole matter has been subjected to a critical examination by Dr. Helen Bartlett, whose conclusions will be found under another head (p. xli).

It will scarcely be believed that all these suggestions and positive statements concerning Aldhelm's authorship of the Paris Psalter prove, on examination, to be absolutely baseless. Let us see. Thorpe probably was referring to Spelman when he introduced the name of Aldhelm into his Preface. John Spelman, not to be confounded with his more famous father, edited in 1640 a Latin text of the Psalms, with an interlinear Old English gloss, from a MS. belonging to his father, collated with three others. This book bears the title *Psalterium Davidis Latino-Saxonicum Vetus*, Londini, 1640. In his Address to the Reader, immediately following the dedication, Spelman remarks: 'Primus Psalmorum in Linguam Saxonicam Translator sub anno 709. laudatur *Adelmus*, Episc. Shirburnensis; sed cum Regem *Alfredum* Magnum, translationem etiam huiusmodi, paulo ante annum 900. adortum esse legimus, priorem illam ex Danica tempestate periisse verisimile est ; et posteriorem sane, ex importuna Regis morte abortivam fuisse novimus.'

Whence did Spelman derive his information ? Evidently from Bale (see Forshall and Madden's *Wycliffite Versions of the Holy Bible*, Preface, p. i). Bale says, at the end of his list of Aldhelm's works (*Illustrium Majoris Britanniae Scriptorum*, Basel, 1557, p. 84): 'Psalterium quoque transtulit in linguam Anglo-Saxonicam, et alia nonnulla fecit.'

Did Bale originate this ? Yes, and no. He was indebted to a hint in Leland's *Commentarii de Scriptoribus Britannicis*, but this he elaborated and transfigured after his own fashion. Leland had said of Aldhelm (*Commentarii*, ed. Hall, Oxon., 1709, p. 100): ' Sepultus est Mailduni ; ubi adhuc monachi sui patroni monimenta ostentant, nempe sacram vestem, qua indutus missam celebrare solebat. Praeterea, Davidis psalterium literis Saxonicis longiusculis scriptum. Tertium, altare sed minutilum ex Ophiutico marmore argento revinctum, in quo Latina inscriptio apparet. Haec ego nuper Meilduni vidi.' Leland had seen a Latin Psalter written in a longish Saxon (really Irish) character, which the monks of Malmesbury called Aldhelm's ; and thereupon Bale ingeniously avers that Aldhelm 'translated the Psalter into the Anglo-Saxon language.'

After Bale and Spelman came Henry Wharton, who, in his *Auctarium Historiae Dogmaticae Jacobi Usserii* (London, 1689), attempts an independent proof, as follows (p. 350): 'Lib. de Virginitate . . . laudat Virgines sacras ad quas scribit ; quod in earum Epistola ad se scripta, *melliflua divinarum studia Scripturarum sagacissima sermonum serie patuerunt.* Et postea easdem praedicat, quod *per ampla Scripturarum studia decurrentes, sagacissimam animorum industriam, et vivacis ingenii qualitatem assidua lectionis instantia exercere noscantur.* Hinc clare patet Versionem S. Scripturae Anglicam Aldhelmi aevo extitisse. Aliter impossibile fuisset foeminis Scripturae studium excolere : cum Latinae linguae notitia adeo rara apud Anglos illa aetate fuerit, ut paucissimi etiam e Clero eam vel summis labiis degustarint. Primus certe Anglorum Aldhelmus Latine scripsit, Latinis literis Romae et in Gallis imbutus. Quin et ipsum Versionem Scripturae Anglicam fieri curasse veri non est absimile. Ut Balei enim testimonium de

b

Psalterio ab illo Saxonice seu Anglice converso taceam : extat etiamnum Epistola eius ad Ehfridum, qua illum multis obsecrat, ut divina eloquia in communem omnium usum vernacula lingua explicaret.'

This argument is, in a word : Aldhelm compliments the nuns to whom he writes on their reading of the Bible ; hence there must have been an English Bible, since women could of course read no Latin. Aldhelm could not only read Latin, but write it ; hence what so likely as that he had the translation made, if he did not make it himself ? In the light of Bede's statement that he knew several people who were as well acquainted with Latin and Greek as with English, this argument of course falls to the ground ; and if the nuns knew no Latin, how came it that Aldhelm was writing them a letter in that language? The appeal to Aldhelm's letter to Ehfrid is equally valueless, because of its obscurity and the generality of the terms in which it is couched.

Hearne, in his translation of the elder Spelman's *Life of Alfred* (Oxford, 1709), carries on the tradition (p. 212, note): 'There had been a Saxon version before, by Aldhelmus, Bishop of Shirburne, as is mentioned by Bale in his Life, and confirmed by Mr. Wharton.' Hearne, however, thinks that the Psalter which Leland saw was the Spelman MS., and that Aldhelm's version had been lost before Alfred's time.

GUTHLAC.—It has often been asserted that Guthlac, a Saxon hermit who died in 714, translated the Psalter, and this statement recurs even in the latest encyclopædias. Tracing it back from one author to another, we find the earliest mention of Guthlac's Psalter in the *Chronicle* which bears the name of Ingulf (d. 1109). According to this account, the Psalter was left with Abbot Kenulf by Guthlac's sister. The original runs : 'Sancta vero Pega, soror praefati sancti patris nostri Guthlaci, cito post primi anni revolutionem ab obitu eiusdem, relicto prius ibidem in manibus Kenulphi Abbatis flagello Sancti Bartholomaei, et *psalterio fratris sui,* ... ad cellam suam navigio remeavit.'

The next statement emanates from John Lambert, properly Nicholson, who in 1538, having been accused of heresy, was examined by Archbishop Warham on forty-five articles. As part of his answer to the twenty-sixth article, he is reported in Foxe's *Acts and Monuments* (ed. Townsend and Cattley, v. 213) to have said:

'There [in Higden's *Polychronicon*] it is showed how, when the Saxons did inhabit the land, the king at that time, who was a Saxon, did himself translate the Psalter into the language that then was generally used. Yea, I have seen a book at Crowland Abbey, which is kept there for a relic ; the book is called St. Guthlake's Psalter ; and I ween verily it is a copy of the same that the king did translate, for it is neither English, Latin, Greek, Hebrew, nor Dutch, but somewhat sounding to our English ; and, as I have perceived since the time I was last there, being at Antwerp, the Saxon tongue doth sound likewise after ours, and is to ours partly agreeable.'

From this it is evident that Lambert believed the 'St. Guthlake's Psalter' which he saw to have been the translation made by King Alfred (see p. xxxiv).

The connexion between the statements of Ingulf and of Lambert was made by Archbishop Ussher in 1690, in his *Historia Dogmatica* (*Works*, xii. 280): 'Psalterii S. Guthlaci Ingulphus in historia sua meminit ; et ad nostra tempora inter reliquias Croilandensis monasterii conservatum est. Quod quidem vulgari Saxonica lingua exaratum fuisse, ex testimonio Joannis Lamberti, qui illud vidit, apparet.'

As yet no great error had been committed, but conjecture soon mingled with fact, and finally we come to such extraordinary remarks as the following, taken from Mombert, *Handbook of the English Versions of the Bible*, 2nd ed., New York 1890, p. 5 : 'To the beginning of the eighth century belongs the Psalter of Aldhelm and Guthlac [*sic*], which contains the Latin with an exceedingly minute interlinear Anglo-Saxon version. The *text* is the Roman Psalter in use at Canterbury, whereas the *Gallican* text was used in other parts of England. It is said to be the identical copy sent by Pope Gregory to Augustine, A.D. 596. The translation is of much later date. It is among the Cotton MSS., marked Vespasian A. 1.'

The two independent versions, by Aldhelm and Guthlac respectively, both mythical, have now become a joint work of the two authors, and this is identified with the Vespasian Psalter, which is not a translation, but a mere gloss !

EIGHTH CENTURY.

Prose Translations.

BEDE.—Bede is said to have made a translation of the Gospel of John from the beginning through vi. 9, but of this no trace remains. The statement is contained in a letter concerning the close of Bede's life, written by Cuthberht, a pupil of Bede's, to Cuthwine, a fellow-student, and 'printed from MS. CCLV (compared with CCLIV) in the library at St. Gallen, which is believed to be a MS. of the ninth century,' by Mayor and Lumby in their edition of *Bedae Hist. Eccl. III, IV*, Cambridge, 1881. The passage runs (*op. cit.* p. 178): 'In istis autem diebus dua opuscula memoriae digna, exceptis lectionibus quas cottidie accepimus ab eo et cantu psalmorum, facere studuit. Id est a capite sancti evangelii Iohannis usque ad eum locum in quo dicitur, "sed haec quid sunt inter tantos?" in nostram linguam ad utilitatem ecclesiae Dei convertit, et de libris Isidori episcopi excerptiones quasdam.' Translations of the whole of this letter may be read in Lingard's *Anglo-Saxon Church*, ii. 177–182, and in Stevenson's *Bede*, pp. xvii–xx.

The statement has frequently been made that Bede translated larger portions of the Bible, but this cannot be authenticated.

Poetical Translations.

KENTISH VERSION OF THE 51st PSALM.—This was first published from MS. Cott. Vesp. D. VI of the British Museum by Dietrich in 1854, in the *Indices Lectionum et Publicarum et Privatarum quae in Academia Marburgensi per Semestre Hibernum habendae proponuntur* (Marburgi : Typis Academicis Elwerti). Dietrich subjoins a Latin translation, and adduces proofs that the poem was composed in the Kentish dialect. According to him, the MS. is of the early ninth century, the letters *a, m,* and *s,* for example, being often written as uncials. The paraphrase he would assign to the eighth century, citing, in support of his view, archaic forms like *wigbed* (later *weofod*), v. 139 ; *bliðs* (later *bliss*), vv. 79, 99, 118 ; *hléoðor,* in the sense of 'hearing,' v. 78 ; *andhette, v. 29 ; &c. Some of the other words, as well as constructions, adduced in support of his opinion, are less convincing.

In 1857 the psalm was reprinted by Grein, in his *Bibliothek der Angelsächsischen Poesie,* ii. 276–280 (new ed., ii. 224–226).

An accurate reproduction of the text was given by Kluge, in his *Angelsächsisches Lesebuch* (Halle, 1888).

In 1877 Ten Brink said, in his *Geschichte der Englischen Litteratur* (I quote the English translation published by Holt, New York, p. 48): 'A paraphrase of the fiftieth [i.e. fifty-first] psalm in the Kentish dialect, not lacking warmth and elevation of tone, dates at the latest from a time before 800.'

In 1882 Sievers confirmed the Kentish authorship of the psalm in his *Angelsächsische Grammatik*, but said nothing about the date.

In 1885 Wülker (*Grundriss*, p. 382) allowed the attribution to Kent, but pronounced decidedly against so early a date as the eighth century, because the first hemistich of some lines contained but one alliterative letter.

In 1887 Ebert (*Literatur des Mittelalters im Abendlande*, iii. 83) virtually expressed his agreement with Dietrich.

In 1888 Henry Morley said (*English Writers*, ii. 321): 'There is reason to think that this psalm was produced in Kent as a separate work, in the eighth century, or at the beginning of the ninth.' But as he had just remarked, 'It has a prose [sic] introduction of its own on David, and an independent close, both indicating that it originally stood alone,' there is reason to think that he had never even seen the psalm, but professed all his views on the subject at second-hand.

In 1894 Sweet printed the psalm in' the seventh edition of his *Anglo-Saxon Reader* (pp. 196-201). In a note (p. 225), he calls it 'an interesting specimen of late Kentish, apparently of the tenth century.' The psalm has an introduction of 30 lines upon David and the circumstances under which the psalm was composed. Then follows the paraphrase of the psalm in 128 lines more. I quote the rendering of vv. 1 and 2 (lines 31-42).

> (1) Miltsa ðu mē, meahta Walden,
> nu ðu wāst . . . manna geðōhtas;
> help ðu, Hǣlend mīn, handgeweorces
> þīnes ānes, ælmehtig God,
> efter þīnre ðāra miclan mildhiortnesse;
> ond ēac efter menio miltsa ðīnra,
> Dryhten weoruda, ādīlga mīn unriht,
> tō forgefenesse gāste mīnum.

(2) Āðweah mē of sennum,   sāule frọm wammum,
    gāsta Scẹppend ;   geltas geclānsa,
    þā ðe ic on aldre   ǣfre gefrẹmede
    ðurh līchaman,   lēðre geðōhtas.

CYNEWULF.—Little more is known with certainty of Cynewulf (Cynwulf) than that he lived in the eighth century, and that he wrote the poems entitled *Christ, Juliana, Elene,* and *Fata Apostolorum* (about the last there is some doubt). It is also probable that he was a Northumbrian, and possible that he composed some or all of a collection of Riddles. Other poems have been ascribed to him with greater or less probability, but no general agreement on the matter has been reached by scholars[1]. In 1892 I showed in *Anglia,* xv. 9–19, that the *Elene* was almost certainly composed very early in the ninth century.

While there are scattered paraphrases of Scriptural passages in various parts of his work, the poem which chiefly concerns us is his *Christ.* This celebrates the Advent of the Saviour, his Ascension, and his final Coming to the Judgment. Incidentally, therefore, it loosely paraphrases portions of the Gospels and of the first chapter of the Acts, besides individual texts from the Old Testament. A transcript of the text may be read in the Grein-Wülker *Bibliothek der Angelsächsischen Poesie,* iii. 1–54; in Gollancz's edition of *The Exeter Book* (Early English Text Society, Original Series, No. 94); or in Gollancz's separate edition of the *Christ* (London, 1892); both of the latter have a modern English rendering on alternate pages. My own edition of the poem is now in the press. The principal articles upon the sources of the poem are by Dietrich (Haupt's *Zeitschrift für Deutsches Alterthum,* ix. 193–214), and by myself (*Modern Language Notes,* iv. (1889) 171–176). The chief sources for the first part, 'The Advent,' will be indicated in my edition. The following lines (230–235) describe the creation of light (Gen. 1. 3) :

    'Nū sīe geworden, forþ   ā tō wīdan fēore
    lēoht līxende, gefēa   lifgendra gehwām
    þe in cnēorissum   cẹnde weorðen !'
    Ọnd þā sōna gelọmp,   þā hit swā sceolde ;
    lēoma lēohtade   lēoda mǣgþum,
    torht mid tunglum,   æfter þon tīda bīgọng.

[1] The article in the *Dict. Nat. Biog.* is under 'Kynewulf' (vol. xxxi), with no cross-reference under 'Cynewulf.'

The poems of Cynewulf, like most of those which we possess from the Old English period, have only been transmitted to us in MSS. of the tenth or eleventh centuries, and contain a mixture of dialectic forms as diverse as those of early Northumbrian and late West Saxon.

ANONYMOUS POEMS OF THE EIGHTH CENTURY.—Here belong especially the poems formerly attributed to Cædmon (see above, p. xiii). The most important of these are the so-called *Genesis*, *Exodus*, and *Daniel*. They are all contained in a single MS., Junius XI of the Bodleian Library, which belongs to the tenth century. For a facsimile, see Westwood's *Palaeographia Sacra*, Plate 39. Accordingly what was said above, concerning the mixture of forms in the Cynewulfian poems, is true of these also.

The *Genesis* is not a homogeneous poem,— *vv.* 235–851, out of a total of 2935, being an interpolation, composed by an Old Saxon living in England (Ten Brink, *Early English Literature*, p. 379), or, as was first suggested by Sievers (*Der Heliand und die Angelsächsische Genesis*, Halle, 1875), translated from Old Saxon into Old English. A critical account of scholarly opinion upon this interpolation will be found in Piper, *Die Altsächsische Bibeldichtung* (Stuttgart, 1897), I. lviii. The *Genesis* paraphrases various portions of that book, though nothing beyond 22. 13. I append the account of the creation of light (*vv.* 121–125), which may be compared with that above, from the *Christ*:

> Metod engla heht,
> lifes Brytta,   lēoht forð cuman
> ofer rūmne grund.   Raþe wæs gefylled
> Heahcininges hæs: him wæs hālig lēoht
> ofer wēstenne,   swā se Wyrhta bebēad.

The *Exodus* is scarcely more than a very free rendering of a few verses of the Biblical Exodus, culminating in the Overthrow of Pharaoh in the Red Sea, together with an episodical portion (*vv.* 362–445), paraphrasing certain parts of Genesis. The relation of this episodical portion to the rest is not fully settled, some thinking it to be a mere casual interpolation. The *Exodus* is 589 lines in length. I quote a part of the description of the pillar of cloud and fire (*vv.* 93–97; cf. Exod. 13. 21):

Him beforan fōran   fȳr ǫnd wolcen
in beorhtrodor,   bēamas twēgen,
þāra ǣghwæðer   efngedǣlde
hēahþegnunga   Hāliges Gāstes,
dēormōdra sīð   dagum ǫnd nihtum.

The *Daniel* is a poetical version of that book, as far as 5. 23.
It contains 765 lines, and, ending abruptly, is probably only
a fragment. The following lines (269-279) paraphrase Dan.
3. 25 and the Song of the Three Holy Children, *vv.* 26, 27
(Vulg. Dan. 3. 49, 50, 92):

Geseah ðā swīðmōd cyning,   ðā hē his sefan ontrēowde,
wundor on wīte āgangen;   him þæt wræclic þūhte.
Hyssas hāle hwurfon   in þām hātan ofne,
ealle ǣfæste ðrȳ.   . . .
Him ēac þǣr wæs   ān on gesyhðe,
ǫngel Ælmihtiges;   him þǣr ōwiht ne derede,
ac wæs þǣr inne   ealles gelīcost
efne þonne on sumera   sunne scīneð,
and dēawdrīas   on dæge weorðeð,
winde geondsāwen.   Þæt wæs wuldres God,
þe hīe generede   wið þām nīðhete.

All these poems are critically edited in the Grein-Wülker
Bibliothek der Angelsächsischen Poesie, ii. 318 ff. (Leipzig, 1894).
The *Genesis* occupies pp. 318-444, the *Exodus* pp. 445-475, and
the *Daniel* pp. 476-515. A critical edition of the interpolated
portion of the *Genesis* may also be found in Piper, *Die Altsächsische
Bibeldichtung*, i. 460-486.

The *Azarias*, or 'Account of the Three Holy Children,' which
is in part substantially identical with the corresponding portion
of the text of *Daniel*, will to that extent be found printed opposite
the poem in the Grein-Wülker edition (pp. 491, 493, 495, 497);
the remainder, beginning with *v.* 76, occurring on pp. 516-520.

As a specimen of the *Azarias* we may take the paraphrase of
the Song of the Three Holy Children, *v.* 55 (lines 134-138):

Ǫnd þec ealle ǣsprynge,   ēce Dryhten,
hēanne hergen.   Ful oft þū hluttor lǣtest
wæter wynlico   tō woruldhyhte
of clife clǣnum;   þæt ūs se Cyning gescōp,
mǫnnum tō miltse   ǫnd tō mægenēacan.

An English translation of the *Genesis*, *Exodus*, and *Daniel* can be read in Thorpe's *Cædmon's Metrical Paraphrase*, London, 1832 ; and of the *Azarias* in his *Codex Exoniensis*, pp. 185-197.

POEMS OF UNCERTAIN DATE.—Here may also be mentioned other poems of uncertain date, such as the *Andreas*, *Phoenix*, *Guthlac*, *Dream of the Rood*, &c., all of which will be found in the Grein-Wülker collection when it is completed. Most of these contain quotations freely paraphrased from Scripture, or at least unmistakable allusions. The following selection from the *Andreas* (438-454) is a metrical rendering of Mark 4. 36-39, put into the mouth of Andrew on a subsequent occasion :

Swā gesǣlde ru,   þæt wē on sǣbāte
ofer waruðgewinn   wæda cunnedan
faroðrīdende ;   frēcne þūhton
egle ēalāda ;   ēagorstrēamas
brōton bordstæðu ;   brim oft oncwæð,
ȳð ōðerre.   Hwīlum uppāstōd
of brimes bōsme   on bātes fæðm
egesa ofer ȳðlid.   Ælmihtig þǣr,
Meotud mancynnes,   on mereþyssan
beorht bāsnode.   Beornas wurdon
forhte on mōde ;   friðes wilnedon,
miltsa tō Mǣrum.   Þā sēo menigo ongan
clypian on cēole ;   Cyning sōna ārās ;
engla Ēadgifa   ȳðum stilde,
wæteres wælmum ;   windas þrēade ;
sǣ sessade,   smylte wurdon
merestrēama gemeotu.

Three poetical paraphrases of the Lord's Prayer, of uncertain date, are given by Grein in his *Bibliothek der Angelsächsischen Poesie*, ii. 285-290 (new ed., ii. 227-238), from the Codex Exoniensis, MS. Bodl. Jun. 121, and MS. CCCC. S. 18, respectively. The last two were published by Wanley, *Catalogus*, pp. 48 and 147-8, and by Ettmüller, *Scopas and Boceras*, pp. 230-234. The first was published by Thorpe, *Codex Exoniensis*, pp. 468, 469. Later and less important, is another noted by Wanley (p. 267) in MS. Lambeth 185. For prose versions of the Lord's Prayer, see p. lxiv.

NINTH CENTURY.

PROSE TRANSLATIONS.

MERCIAN GLOSS ON THE PSALMS.—A gloss, or interlinear version of the Roman Psalter, dating, according to Sweet, from the first half of the ninth century, has been printed by Sweet in his *Oldest English Texts* (E. E. T. S. No. 83. London, 1885), pp. 183-401 ; Ps. 2-6 in Kluge, *Angelsächsisches Lesebuch* (Halle, 1888), pp. 11-14. It is known as the Vespasian Psalter, from being contained in MS. Cott. Vespasian A. 1 of the British Museum. A facsimile, with description, is given in Westwood, *Palaeographia Sacra*, Plate 40. The gloss was first edited by J. Stevenson as the Surtees Publication for 1843 (though it did not appear till a couple of years later), and was published in two volumes, with the title *Anglo-Saxon and Early English Psalter.* Stevenson's edition is severely censured by Sweet (*Oldest English Texts*, p. 187). In the *Phil. Soc. Trans.* for 1875-6, Sweet declared the dialect to be Kentish, though Stevenson had regarded it as Northumbrian. In 1881 the language was carefully investigated by Zeuner (*Die Sprache des Kentischen Psalters*, Halle, 1881), who arrived at the same conclusion as Sweet. In 1882 it was pronounced by Sievers (cf. my translation of his *Old English Grammar*, second edition, 1887, p. 244) to be Mercian, and Sweet is inclined to follow him in the *Oldest English Texts*, p. 184.

It should be clearly understood that this version is not a translation, in the ordinary sense of that word, but a mere interlinear gloss. It seems not improbable that it is the original from which all later Old English glosses on the Psalms have been derived, undergoing in the process such modifications as were due to the language of the particular dialect or epoch ; on this point compare pp. 28 ff. and 32.

Ps. 43 will furnish a specimen of the language. Where the Latin differs from the Vulgate text, the variant readings are given.

Dœm mec, God, ǫnd tōscād intingan mīnne of ðēode nōht hāligre; frǫm men unrehtum ǫnd fācnum genǫre mē, forðon ðū earð God mīn [1] ǫnd strengu mīn. Forhwon mē onweg ādrife ðū ? ǫnd forhwon unrōt ic ingā, ðonne swenceð mec se fēond ? Onsend lēht

---

[1] Lat. inserts 'meus.'

ðīn ǫnd sōðfestnisse ðīne ; hīe mec gelǣdon ǫnd tōgelǣddon in munte ðǣm hālgan ðīnum, ǫnd in getelde ðīnum [1]. Ic [2] ingaa tō wībede Godes, tō Gode se geblissað iugūðe mīne. Ic ǫndetto ðē in citran, God, God mīn. Forhwon unrōt earðu, sāwul mīn? ǫnd forhwon gedrœfes mē? Gehyht in God, forðon [3] ic ǫndettu him, hǣlu ǫndwleotan mīnes, ǫnd God mīn.

OTHER GLOSSED PSALTERS.—On this subject comparatively little has been done. What is here presented is only what it has been possible to accomplish with the aid of Sweet's edition of the Vespasian Psalter (*Oldest English Texts*), Spelman's *Psalterium*, Wanley's *Catalogus*, and Part II of Harsley's edition of Eadwine's Canterbury Psalter, and must therefore be regarded as strictly tentative and provisional.

For the Vespasian Psalter, see p. xxvi.

In 1640 John Spelman, son of the greater Henry, published, from a MS. in his father's possession, his *Psalterium Davidis Latino-Saxonicum Vetus* (London). The elder Spelman's MS. came into the hands of Philip Morant (1700–1770), from whom it was inherited by his son-in-law, Thomas Astle (1775–1803), who figured it in tab. xix. 6 of his *Origin of Writing*, and mentions it on pp. 85–86 (cf. Westwood, *infra*). On the death of the latter, it passed by will to Grenville, first Marquis of Buckingham (1753–1813), and thus found a place in his library at Stowe. Here it was catalogued by O'Conor (*Bibliotheca Stowensis*, 1818), and hence found its way by purchase into the possession of the Earl of Ashburnham in 1849. The British Museum became the purchaser of all the Stowe MSS. in 1883, and of Spelman's MS., known sometimes as King Alfred's Psalter, among the number. In the British Museum *Catalogue of the Stowe Manuscripts* (London, 1895, 2 vols.) the Spelman MS. is designated as Stowe 2. Spelman had described this Psalter in his *Concilia* (first ed.), i. 218 : 'Est mihi Psalterium Davidis, sub temporibus Nicaeni Concilii 2di, vel mox inde, ut coniicitur, exaratum, in quo, ad finem uniuscuiusque Psalmi et singularium Lectionum Psalmi cxix, habetur Oratio, numero scilicet 171.'

The younger Spelman's edition is, according to O'Conor, 'extremely incorrect,' and was collated, though very carelessly,

---

[1] Lat. has 'in monte sancto tuo, et in tabernaculo tuo.'

[2] Lat. omits 'Et.'

[3] Lat. omits 'adhuc.'

with three others—that of University Library, Cambridge ; that of Trinity College, Cambridge (Eadwine's) ; and that now known as MS. Arundel 60 of the British Museum, but then in the possession of Thomas Howard, Earl of Arundel and Surrey, Earl Marshal of England. The last-named, however, was used only from Psalm 72 (73) to the end.

In 1889 F. Harsley published (E. E. T. S., Original Series, No. 92) his edition of Eadwine's Canterbury Psalter, from the MS. in Trinity College, Cambridge.

Besides these, Wanley printed, from a number of MSS. in various libraries, the 100th Psalm (numbering of A. V.), Latin and interlinear Old English. Of these there were nine in all, including the Vespasian Psalter and the so-called Canterbury Psalter. Westwood's *Palaeographia Sacra*, on Plate 40, notices a 'Codex Salisburiensis, mentioned in the Preface to the second volume of Hickes' *Thesaurus*, by Wanley, since which time it has remained unnoticed.' This is figured in the *Palaeographical Society Facsimiles*, Series II, vol. ii, Plates 188 and 189, and in Westwood's *Facsimiles*, Plate 38. It is MS. 150 of the Salisbury Cathedral Library. A facsimile of text and gloss is given in Plate 189, extending from the beginning of Ps. 13. 3 to 14. 3 'guttur eorum.' The version is the Gallican. Thus, including Spelman's edition, we have record of ten different copies of the Psalter with interlinear Old English glosses. Westwood's 'Codex Dunelmensis, containing only the Penitential Psalms,' is a myth ; the Durham Ritual (cf. p. xlv) is what he has in mind (see p. 183 of that book).

It remains to be seen whether a classification of the ten copies (exclusive of the Salisbury Psalter) is possible. On examination, it proves that five of these copies represent the Roman Psalter, and five the Gallican or Vulgate. These two classes will accordingly be discussed separately.

The Roman Psalter.—Under this fall the following MSS., which, for this purpose, may be designated by the letters of the alphabet which are appended :

Cotton Vespasian A. 1 of the British Museum (Wanley, p. 222) ; the Vespasian Psalter (Sweet, *Oldest English Texts*, pp. 183–401), A.

Junius 27 of the Bodleian Library (Wanley, p. 76), B.

MS. Ff. 1. 23 of the University Library, Cambridge (Wanley, p. 152), C.

Royal 2 B. 5 of the British Museum (Wanley, p. 182), D.

MS. of Trinity College, Cambridge (Wanley, p. 168) ; Eadwine's Canterbury Psalter, E.

Facsimiles of portions of these MSS. are in Westwood, *Palaeographia Sacra*, Plates 41, 43 ; of A in his *Facsimiles*, Plate 3, and of B, *ib.* Plate 34 *Pal. Sac.*, Plate 40; and in Astle, tab. ix.

In order that the relation sustained by these various copies to one another may be perceived, I subjoin (1), in parallel columns, the Old English and the Latin of Psalm 100, according to the Vespasian Psalter ; (2) the variants obtained by collating MSS. B, C, D, and E. The words which differ in the Gallican text are italicized in the Latin.

PSALM 100.

Vespasian Psalter.

Wynsumiaδ[1] Gode, all[2] eorδe[3] ; δlowiaδ[4] Dryhtne[5] in[6] blisse[7] ; ingāδ[8] in[6] gesihδe his in[6] wynsumnisse[9]. Weotaδ[10] δæt[11] Dryhten[12] he is[13] God ; he dyde[14] ūsic[15], ond nales[16] we[17] ūsic[18] ; we[19] sōδlice folc his, ond scēp[20] lēswe[21] his. Ingāδ[22] geatu[23] his in[4] ondetnisse[25], ceafurtūnes[26] his in[6]

Roman Text.

Iubilate *Deo*, omnis terra ; servite Domino in laetitia ; *intrate* in conspectu eius in exultatione. Scitote *quod* Dominus, ipse est Deus ; ipse fecit nos, et non ipsi nos ; *nos autem* populus eius, et oves pascuae eius. *Intrate* portas eius in confessione, atria[24] eius in hymnis *confessionum*. Laudate nomen eius :

[1] B. w. sumiaþ ge, D. drymaδ, E. dremeδ.

[2] B. C. D. eall, E. eælle.

[3] E. eorδæ.

[4] B. C. D. δeowiaδ, E. δeowiæþ.

[5] B. C. E. drihtne, D. *om.*

[6] B. C. D. E. on.

[7] E. blyssæo.

[8] E. ongængæþ.

[9] B. wynsumnesse, C. wynsumnysse, D. bliþnesse l. wynsummunga, E. hihte.

[10] C. witaþ ge, D. witaδ, E. witæδ ge.

[11] E. þet.

[12] C. drihtyn, D. E. drihten.

[13] C. ys.

[14] B. geworhte, C. D. worhte.

[15] B. C. D. E. us.

[16] C. nalys, D. na, E. ne.

[17] D. selfe, E. wes he (Wanl. we).

[18] B. E. us, C. usic, D. we.

[19] E. us.

[20] D. sceap, E. sceæp.

[21] C. læswa, E. leswæ, D. forstornoδes (*sic*).

[22] E. ongængæþ.

[23] C. D. gatu, E. gætu.

[24] B. *om.* atria, D. in atria.

[25] B. ondetnesse, C. andetinysse, D. andetnesse, E. *anddetnesse*.

[26] B. cafortures (*sic*), C. cafyrtunys, D. on cæfertunas, E. cafortun.

ymenum[1] ǫndetnissa[2].   Hẹr-
gað[3] nǫman[4] his[5]: forðon[6]
wynsum[7] is[8] Dryhten[9]; in[10]
ɛcnisse[11] mildheortnis[12] his;
ǫnd ōð[13] in[14] weoruld[15] weo-
ruḷde[16] sōðfestnis[17] his.

quoniam suavis est Dominus ;
in aeternum misericordia eius ;
et usque in *sacculum saecculi*
veritas eius.

From this collation it will be seen that B stands nearest to A,
but is carelessly written, and changes Anglian peculiarities in the
direction of West Saxon (*in* to *on*, *all* to *call*, &c.), while retaining,
in general, a comparatively early and Anglian cast (*wcotað, scep,
lcswe,* &c.); the Runic *w* for *wyn,* if Wanley's transcript may be
trusted, is interesting.   C, with frequent *y* in unstressed syllables,
looks more like Late West Saxon.   D has a number of new readings, among them such as suggest 'contamination' with glosses
based on the Gallican Psalter (*drymað, bliþnesse, forstornodes* for
fostornodes).   E is clearly transitional to Middle English, has new
glosses (*hihtc, ongængæþ, swetc*), mistakes (*cafortun, oððet*), and
retains a sign of 'contamination' (*drcmcð*), but otherwise has
some striking resemblances to A and B (*dyde, ymenum, hcrgæþ,
soþfcstncs*).

The Gallican Psalter.—Here belong the following :

Spelman's printed text ; Stowe 2 of the British Museum, F.

Cotton Vitellius E. 18 of the British Museum (Wanley, p. 223), G.

Cotton Tiberius C. 6 of the British Museum (Wanley, p. 224), H.

Lambeth 188 (Wanley, p. 268), I.

Arundel 60 of the British Museum (Wanley, p. 291), J.

[MS. 150 of Salisbury Cathedral (K), not used here.]

Facsimiles of portions of H and I are in Westwood, *Palaeographia
Sacra,* Plate 42; of H in his *Facsimiles, &c.,* Plate 46; and of J,
ib. Plate 34.

---

[1] D. ymnum.

[2] B. ondetnessa, C. andittnysse, D. andetnessa, E. *anddetnessc.*

[3] D. heriað, E. hergæþ.

[4] C. D. naman, E. nomæ.

[5] D. *om.*

[6] D. *om.*

[7] E. swetc.

[8] C. ys.

[9] C. E. drihten, D. *om.*

[10] B. C. D. E. on.

[11] B. D. E. ecnesse, C. ccnysse.

[12] B. D. E. mildheortnes, C. mild-heortnysse.

[13] E. oððet.

[14] B. *om.,* D. a, C. E. on.

[15] B. weorold, C. D. woruld, E. world.

[16] B. weorolde, C. worulde, D. *om.,* E. worldæ.

[17] C. soðfæstnysse, D. soþfæstnes.

Psalm 100.

Spelman Psalter.	*Gallican or Vulgate Text.*

Drȳmað [1] Drihtne [2], eall [3]
eorðe [4]; ðeowiað [5] Drihtne [6] on
blisse; infarað [7] on gesyhðe [8]
hys [9] on bliðnysse [10]. Witað [11]
gē [11] forðonde [12] Drihten [13], hō [14]
is God; hē dyde [15] ūs, and nā
selfe [16] wē [17]. Folc [18] his [18], and
scēap lǣswe [19] his, infarað [20]
gatu [22] his on andetnysse [23], on
cafertūnas [24] his on ymnum [25];
andettað [27] him [28]. Hēriað naman
his; forðanðe [29] winsum [30] is
Driht [31]; on ēcnysse [32] mild-
heortnyssa [34] his; and ōð on [36]
cynrine [37] and [38] cynrine [39] sōðfæstnys [40] his [40].

Iubilate Domino, omnis terra;
servite Domino in laetitia; introite in conspectu eius in exultatione. Scitote quoniam Dominus, ipse est Deus; ipse fecit
nos, et non ipsi nos. Populus
eius, et oves pascuae eius, introite
portas eius in confessione, atria [21]
eius in hymnis; confitemini
illi [26]. Laudate nomen eius:
quoniam suavis est Dominus;
in aeternum misericordia eius;
et usque in generationem [33] et
generationem [35] veritas eius.

Here the relations are not so clear. It would seem that certain
members of the group show 'contamination' with the other

[1] I. freadremað (*sic*), J. drimaþ.
[2] H. *om.*
[3] G. H. J. calle, I. eala.
[4] G. J. eorðan, I. eorð.
[5] G. ðaowiað.
[6] H. *om.*
[7] I. insteppað *vel* ingað.
[8] G. H. I. J. gesihðe.
[9] G. H. I. J. his.
[10] G. H. J. bliðnesse, I. blisse.
[11] G. H. witað, I. witað *vel* wite ge,
J. wite ge.
[12] G. I. forþamþe, H. *om.*, J. forðon.
[13] H. *om.*
[14] I. se sylfa.
[15] G. H. worhte, I. J. geworhte.
[16] G. we sylfe, I. we, J. silfe.
[17] G. us, I. selfe, J. we.
[18] I. o eala his folc, J. folc is.
[19] G. H. J. fosternoðcs, I. lǣsuwe.
[20] H. ingaþ on, J. infaraþ on.
[21] G. atriæ, I. introite atria.
[22] J. gatum.
[23] G. anddetnesse, H. I. andet-

nesse, J. andettnesse.
[24] I. ingað cafertunas, J. of cafar-
tunas.
[25] G. ymenum, I. lofsangum.
[26] G. *om.*
[27] G. anddettað, H. *om.*
[28] H. *om.*
[29] G. forþamþe, H. J. forþon.
[30] G. H. I. wynsum, J. *om.*
[31] G. drihten, H. I. J. *om.* I. *om.*
is).
[32] G. H. J. ecnesse.
[33] G. I. generatione.
[34] G. H. J. mildheortnes, I. mildheortnyss.
[35] I. generatione.
[36] H. *om.*
[37] G. cynrene, H. *om.*, I. mægþe
vel cynrene, J. cneoriss.
[38] H. *om.*
[39] G. cynrene, H. *om.*, I. J. cneorisse.
[40] G. H. soðfæstnes his, I. his soð-
fæstnys, J. soþfæstnesse his.

group, particularly I (*ingað*, *blisse*, *læsuwc*), but the group in general has certain fairly well-marked characteristics (*drymað*, *bliðnesse*, *fostornoðes*, *cynrene*, &c.). It seems not improbable that the type represented by the Vespasian Psalter was that on which the gloss was first constructed, and that this was adapted in glossing the Gallican Psalter, with such changes as were necessary, or as, in successive *remaniements*, suggested themselves to the scribe for the time being. Spelman's seems hardly the best of this type, but a grouping according to priority or superiority would require a more extended comparison.

Though the MSS. under consideration range from the ninth to the twelfth century, yet, if we consider them as probably descended, with successive modifications, from an original represented by the Vespasian Psalter, they may all, for our purpose, be regarded as belonging to the ninth century.

GLOSSES ON the CANTICLES OF SCRIPTURE.—The Canticles in question are those used in the daily service, and are the following:

Song of Moses (I)	Exod. 15. 1–19.
Song of Moses (II)	Deut. 32. 1–43.
Song of Hannah	1 Sam. 2. 1–10.
Song of Isaiah	Isa. 12.
Song of Hezekiah	Isa. 38. 10–20.
Song of Three Holy Children (Benedicite)	Dan. 3. 57–88 (Vulg.), with adaptation of 52 and 56.
Song of Habakkuk	Hab. 3. 2–19.
Song of Mary (Magnificat)	Luke 1. 46–55.
Song of Zacharias	Luke 1. 68–79.
Song of Simeon (Nunc Dimittis)	Luke 2. 29–32.

Besides these, there is occasionally found the so-called Ps. 151, otherwise 'The Psalm of David after he had fought with Goliath.' This occurs regularly in the Septuagint, and is found in some MSS. of the Itala, as well as in the Mozarabic Breviary. An English version of it appears in Churton's *Uncanonical and Apocryphal Scriptures*, p. 366 (cf. Ewald, *Dichter des Alten Bundes*, i. 266).

The Canticles are usually placed at the end of the Psalter.

According to Wanley, some or all of them are thus found in the MSS. designated above as A, C, D, E, G, I, J. Those that are lacking, according to the same authority, are : Song of Isaiah, in I ; of Hezekiah, in C ; of Moses II, in E ; of Simeon, in A and C. Ps. 151 occurs only in A, E, and J.

In the Vespasian Psalter, which is the only one I have examined, the Canticles are glossed in the same manner as the Psalms, and I should assume that the relations of the glosses in the other MSS. would correspond in general with those that have been indicated above in the case of the Psalters.

The order of the Canticles in the Vespasian Psalter is as follows : Ps. 151, Isaiah, Hezekiah, Hannah, Moses I, Habakkuk, Moses II, Three Holy Children, Zacharias, Mary. They have been reprinted by Sweet in both his *Anglo-Saxon Readers*.

As a specimen, I print the Magnificat :

Miclað sāwul mīn Dryhten, ǫnd gefæh gāst mīn in Gode Hālwyndum mīnnum [1]. Forðon gelōcade ēaðmodnisse męnenes his ; sehðe, sōðlice of ðissum ēadge mic cweoðað ālle cneorisse. Forðon dyde mē ðā miclan se mæhtig is ; ǫnd hālig nǫma his. Ǫnd mildheortnis his frǫm cynne in cyn ondrēdendum hine. Dyde mæhte in earme his ; tōstregd oferhogan on mōde heortan his. Ofdūne sętte mæhtge of selde, ǫnd ūpāhōf ēaðmōde. Hyngrende gefylde gōdum, ǫnd weolie forlēort īdelhęnde. Onfēð [Israhel] cneht his, gemyndig mildheortnisse his ; swē spreocende wes tō feadrum ūrum, Abram, ǫnd sēde his ōð in weoruld.

A *paraphrase* of the Magnificat occurs in MS. S. 7 of Corpus Christi College, Cambridge.

KENTISH GLOSS ON PROVERBS.—Certain fragmentary glosses, referring to the Book of Proverbs, were first published by Zupitza in Haupt's *Zeitschrift für Deutsches Alterthum*, xxi. 1-59, xxii. 223-226 (Berlin, 1877, 1878). They are contained in MS. Vespasian D. 6 of the British Museum. Zupitza at once declared them to be Kentish, and gave such proofs that his view has never been questioned. They have been reprinted by Wülcker, after fresh collation with the MS., in the Wright-Wülcker *Old English Vocabularies* (London, 1884), i. 55-87, and by Sweet, *Second Anglo-Saxon Reader* (Oxford, 1887), pp. 152-175 ; a selection in

[1] Normally, 'mīnum.'

Kluge's *Angelsächsisches Lesebuch* (Halle, 1888), pp. 41-42. The glosses are referred to the first half of the ninth century. Their entirely fragmentary character will be evident from the following specimen, including all those belonging to chap. 1 (the verses are indicated). In some cases the Latin differs from that of the Vulgate, as will be apparent on examination.

[17] *iacitur* : is worpen ; *pennatorum* : gefiðeradra ; [18] *et moliuntur fraudes* : and berðafiað ; [19] *sic . . . rapiunt* : swā rēafiað ; [20] *praedicat* : bodað ; [21] *clamitat* : hī clepað ; [22] *et . . . cupiunt* : and gewilniað ; *et . . . odibunt* : and hatiað ; [23] *en proferam* : efne nū ic forð brenge ; [24] *quia vocari* : forðām ic gecēide ; [26] *ego . . . ridebo* : ic hlihe ; [27] *cum insonuerit* : ðonne swæið ; *ingruerit* : onbricþ ; [29] *exosam* : onscunede ; [30] *et detraxerunt* : and hīo tēldan ; [33] *et . . . perfruetur* : and hē brūcð ; *timore . . . sublato* : ātogenum ege.

KING ALFRED'S TRANSLATION OF CERTAIN PSALMS. — According to William of Malmesbury, King Alfred began a translation of the Psalms, but was cut off by death before he had advanced beyond the 'first part.' His words are (*Gesta Regum Anglorum*, ii. 123) : 'Psalterium transferre aggressus, vix prima parte explicata vivendi finem fecit.' For the attribution to Alfred of the first fifty psalms — the prose rendering — in Thorpe's edition, see pp. xxxvi ff. Of course Alfred is responsible for the translations in *this* volume, pp. 14-17, 70-71, whatever assistance he may have had in the rendering.

THE PARIS PSALTER. — This consists of two translations conjoined, a prose version and a poetical one. The prose version ends in the eighth verse of the 51st Psalm (Vulg. 50. 10) ; the poetical one begins with the sixth verse of the 52nd Psalm (Vulg. 51. 8), and continues to the end of the Psalter. The whole, which is contained in a single MS. of the National Library at Paris, was published by Thorpe, as *Libri Psalmorum Versio Antiqua Latina ; cum Paraphrasi Anglo-Saxonica* (Oxford, 1835).

What is known about the history of the MS. (Bibliothèque Nationale, fonds latin 8824) may be told in a few words. An autograph note at the end of the MS., given by Thorpe in facsimile, reads : 'Ce liure est au duc de Berry, Jehan.' 'This Jean, Duke of Berry (1340-1416), was brother of Charles V, King of France, whom he rivalled in the magnificence of his collections

of books and treasures of art' (Bruce, p. 13). The book may have
come into his possession during his nine years' sojourn as a hostage
in England, after the peace of Bretigny, 1360. In 1406 it
passed into the possession of the Sainte Chapelle of Bourges,
having already been promised in 1404. It next appears in
a catalogue of the books belonging to the Sainte Chapelle, drawn
up Nov. 17, 1552. In 1717 it is noticed in Martène and Durand's
*Voyage Littéraire de deux Religieux Bénédictins de la Congrégation de
Saint Maur* (Paris). In this work (i. 28 ff.), some interesting
information is given ; I quote the words of Bruce (pp. 16–17) :
'Only fifty or sixty volumes remained of the original collection.
The place where they were stored was used, also, as a poultry
house. The books, being left open on the desks, were, of course,
in a pitiable condition, and one of these was the Paris Psalter.
The words of Dom Martène relating to this book are as follows :
"L'un des plus curieux manuscrits de la sainte Chapelle, est
celui qu'on appelle les heures du duc Jean. C'est un pseautier
latin avec une version angloise de six ou sept cens ans. Ceux qui
me la montrèrent, croyoient que c'étoit de l'allemand ou de
l'hébreu. Mais si-tôt que je l'eus vu, je connus le caractère Anglo-
saxon. J'en fus encore plus convaincu, lorsqu' examinant les
litanies qui sont à la fin, je trouvai que la plûpart des Saints
étoient d'Angleterre. Ce livre est conservé dans le chartrier." '
In 1752 the volume was presented by the Canons of Bourges to
Louis XV, and was incorporated into the Royal Library, now
the National Library of France. In 1814 was published, at
Paris, Gerard Gley's *Langue et Littérature des anciens Francs*, on
p. 276 of which he says : 'On voit à la Bibliothèque du Roi,
à Paris, un manuscrit anglo-saxon in—fol. max., qui renferme une
Paraphrase des Psaumes de David. Il appartenait autrefois à Jean,
Duc de Berry : je pense qu'il venait antérieurement des Ducs de
Normandie.'

At the end of the MS. proper, just before the note on the
ownership of the book, is this statement : 'Hoc psalterii carmen
inclyti regis David sacer dī Wulfwinus manu sua conscripsit.
Quicumque legerit scriptum, animae suae expetiat votum ;' above
the name, Wulfwinus, is added in another hand, 'cognomento
Cada.' Now, as MS. C of the West Saxon Gospels (Cotton Otho
C. 1) has, at the end, the inscription 'Wulfwi me wrat,' attempts
have been made to bring the two MSS. into relation, but without

any decisive result. In any case, it is pretty certain that the Paris MS. is of the eleventh century. Facsimiles of specimen portions have been published in Silvestre's *Paléographie Universelle*, Paris. 1841 (Plate CCXXXI); Cooper's *Report on Rymer's Foedera*, Appendix B; Westwood, *Palaeographia Sacra*, London, 1843–45 (Plate II); and in Thorpe's edition.

As there are virtually two incomplete translations, one in prose and one in verse, it will be desirable to consider these separately.

The Prose Translation.—This, as we have seen, consists of Psalms 1 to 51 (*v.* 8).

It appears certain that the translation was not made from the Latin text which accompanies it in the Paris Psalter. Beyond this, opinion is divided. J. Wichmann, writing in 1889 (*Anglia*, xi. 39–96), came to the conclusion that the authorship is to be attributed to Alfred. In 1894 J. Douglas Bruce published, in the *Publications of the Modern Language Association of America* (ix. 43–164), a dissertation entitled 'The Anglo-Saxon Version of the Book of Psalms, commonly known as the Paris Psalter,' which was separately reprinted at Baltimore in the same year. In this paper Bruce investigates the whole question anew, and his conclusions constitute the latest, though perhaps not the final, word upon the subject. The most important ones are these (pp. 122–123; *Publ.* 160–161): 'The prose division was . . . composed most probably in the late ninth or early tenth century. That it is the work of an ecclesiastic is proved by the ample fund of allegorical interpretation which the author had at his command, as appears from a comparison of interpolations in the text with parallels from the early commentators on the Psalms. No systematic—probably no direct—use, however, has been made of any particular commentary, except for the introductory prefaces to each of the Psalms, which are paraphrases of the corresponding *argumenta* of the commentary, *In Psalmorum Librum Exegesis*. The Latin rubrics which head the metrical as well as prose Psalms in the Paris Psalter are drawn from the same source. The Latin commentary just mentioned, which was incorrectly ascribed to Bede by his early editors, is really the work of the Benedictine commentator, Ambrosius Autpertus, abbot of St. Vincent, near the Vulturn in Southern Italy, who died in the year 778. The *argumenta* to the Psalms in this work, excluding the mystical elements, were ultimately derived from the Greek commentary of Theodore of Mopsuestia on the Psalms.'

It will thus be seen that Bruce rejects the hypothesis of the Alfredian authorship of the prose Psalms, but that he would date the translation little, if any, after the time of Alfred (d. 901). However, there is nothing in Bruce's arguments which necessarily militates against the theory of Alfredian authorship, since it is notorious that the king was assisted by clerical collaborators in much of his scholarly activity. It is unlikely, considering the veneration in which Alfred was held, both during his life and for centuries after his death, that so precious a product of his religious enthusiasm would be allowed to perish. William of Malmesbury expressly tells us (*Gesta Regum Anglorum*, lib. ii. 123): 'Psalterium transferre aggressus, vix prima parte explicata vivendi finem fecit.' Wülfing (*Die Syntax in den Werken Alfreds des Grossen*, I. xiii) suggests that by 'prima parte' William of Malmesbury may have meant the first fifty Psalms, on the assumption that he thought of the Psalter as divided into three equal portions. This, however, is contrary to the customary division of the Psalms into five parts, ending respectively with the 41st, 72nd, 89th, 106th, and 150th. Still, it would not be imposing a very great strain upon 'vix' to accommodate it to the facts as exhibited in the Paris Psalter, even with the modification which the traditional division of the Psalter renders necessary. Against Wülfing's theory, however modified, there is a consideration which has not yet been brought forward. It is that, with the exception of two passages, there is no striking resemblance between such verses as are quoted in Alfred's undoubted works and the corresponding passages from the Paris Psalter. The following comparisons will show the relations at a glance :

Pastoral Care.	*Paris Psalter.*
1. 1. . . . . ðæt hē nō ne sǣte on ðǣm wōlberendan setle. C. P. 435.	. . . Nō on heora wōlberendum setle ne sitt.
23. 4. Ðīn gierd ǫnd ðīn stæf mē āfrēfredan. C. P. 124	Þīn gyrd and þīn stæf mē āfrēfredon.
30. 6. Ic wēnde on mīnum wlęncum ǫnd on mīnum for-	Ic cwæð on mīnum wlęncum and on mīnre orsorhnesse :

wanan, ðā ic wæs full ǣgðer
ge welona ge gōdra weorca,
ðæt ðæs nǣfre ne wurde nān
ęnde. C. P. 465.

Ne wyrð þises nǣfre nān
węndincg.

30. 7. Dryhten, ðū āhwyrfdes
ðīnne ǫndwlitan frǫm mē, ðā
wearð ic gedrēfed. C. P. 465.

Þā āwęndest þū þīnne andwlitan
fram mē, þā wearð ic sōna
gedrēfed.

32. 5. Ic wille sęcgan ongēan
mē selfne mīn unryht, Dryht-
en. forðǣm ðū forgēafe ðā
ārlēasnesse mīnre heortan.
C. P. 419.

. . . þæt ic wolde andettan and
stǣlan ongēan mē sylfne
mīne, scylda, and þā Gode
andettan ; and þū mē þā forgēafe þæt unriht mīnra scylda.

34. 19. Swīðe manigfealde sint
ryhtwīsra mǫnna earfeðu.
C. P. 252.

Mǫniga synt carfoðu þāra riht-
wīsena.

38. 6. Ic eom gebīgged, ǫnd
ǣghwǫnon ic eom gehīened.
C. P. 66.

Ac ic eom gesāged, and gehnǣg-
ed, and swīðe geēaðmed.

40. 9, 10. Dryhten, ðū wāst
ðæt ic ne wirne mīne welora,
ǫnd ðīne ryhtwīsnesse ic ne
dīgle on mīnre heortan ; ðīne
hǣlo ǫnd ðīne ryhtwīsnesse
ic sæcge. C. P. 380.

Mīnum weolorum ic ne for-
bēode, ac bebēode þæt hȳ þæt
sprecon symle ; Drihten, þū
wāst þæt ic ne āhȳdde on mīnum mōde þīne rihtwīsnesse,
ac þīne sōðfæstnesse and þīne
hǣle ic sǣde.

40. 12. Mīn mōd ǫnd mīn wīsdōm mē forlēt. C. P. 272.

Mīn heorte and mīn mōd mē
forlēton.

49. 7, 8. Hē ne sealde Gode
nānne mēdsceat for his sāule,
nō nænne geðingscēat wið
his miltse. C. P. 338.

Nyle oþþe ne mæg . . . þæt hē
þæt weorð āgife tō ālȳsnesse
his sāwle.

51. 3. Mīne misdǣda bēoð simle
beforan mē. C. P. 413.

Mīne synna bēoð symle beforan
mē, on mīnum gemynde.

Bede's History.

Paris Psalter.

18. 13, 14. Drihten hlēoðrað of
heofonum, ǫnd se Hēhsta
sęleð his stefne. Hē sęndeð
his strǣle, ǫnd hēo tōweorpeð;

And worhte þunorrāda on heofonum, and se Hȳhsta sealde
his stemne. Hē sęnde his
strǣlas, and hī tōstęncte; and

lēgetas gemonigfealdað, ond
hēo gedrēfeð. B. H. 268.

32. 1. Þā bēoð eadge þe heora
wonnesse forlǣtne bēoð, ond
þāra þe synna bewrigene bēoð.
B. H. 442.

51. 5. Ic wāt þæt ic wæs in
wǣnessum gecacnod, ond in
scyldum mec cende mīn mōd-
or. B. H. 82.

gemanigfealdode his līgeta,
and gedrēfde hig mid þȳ.

Eadige bēoð þā þe him bēoð
heora unrihtwīsnesse forgifene, and heora synna bēoð
behelede.

Þū wāst þæt ic wæs mid unrihtwīsnesse onfangen, and mīn
mōdor mē gebær mid synne.

It is apparent that by far the greatest similarity is in the case
of the first two verses quoted from the *Pastoral Care*—1. 1 and
23. 4. Of these it is 1. 1 which is the more remarkable. Its
singularity comprehends two features, the choice of an equivalent
for 'pestilentia,' and the fact that the attributive genitive, 'pestilentiae,' is rendered by an adjective. To exhibit the peculiarity
more manifestly, the renderings of the Spelman Psalter (pp. xvi,
xxvii) and of the so-called Canterbury Psalter may be compared.
The former omits the gloss for 'pestilentia,' and has :

On þrymsetle . . . nā sæt.

The latter has :

On þān setele of þān quulmere ne set.

Spelman notes that another MS. has *cwyldes* for 'pestilentiae' ;
in the WS. Gospels 'pestilentia' is rendered by *cwcalm* (Luke 21.
11) and *manncwcalm* (Matt. 24. 7).

On the other hand, *wōl* and its compounds seem to be especially
Alfredian words. *Wōl* is found in the *Boethius*, the *Pastoral Care*,
and the *Bede* ; *wōlbærnes, wōlgewin*, and *wōlbryne* in the *Orosius* ; while
wōlberende occurs three times in the *Pastoral Care* (415$_{12}$, 435$_{19}$, $_{22}$),
and once in the *Bede* (48$_{17}$). These passages are, in the above order :
mid ðǣre wōlberendan oliccunge (securitatis pestiferae blanditiis) ;
the rendering of Ps. 1. 1 ; *on wōlberendum setle* (in cathedra
pestilentiae) ; *se wōlberenda stenc þǣre lyfte* (aerum pestifer odor).
Besides, Ps. 11. 6 of the Paris Psalter, in a free paraphrase, has
wōlberende windas, apparently suggested by 'spiritus procellarum,'
though of course not a translation of it. Manifestly, *wōlberende* is
properly the rendering of 'pestifer,' not of 'pestilentia,' and it is
strange that it should ever have been employed for the latter,
especially as between the two occurrences of it in *C. P.* 435$_{19}$ and

435₂₂, we have the more normal *wōles setl* (*sē ðonne sit on wōles setle*). There can be little risk, then, in asserting with much positiveness that Ps. 1. 1 of the Paris Psalter, or at least one portion of it, is from the hand of Alfred. The suspicion, too, can hardly be evaded that Ps. 11. 6, in which the same peculiar word appears, is by the same author.

We may now examine Ps. 23. 4 :

Ðīn gierd ọnd ðīn stæf mē āfrēfredan,

from which the Paris Psalter varies only in spelling. Here the Vespasian Psalter (p. xxvi) has :

Gerd ðīn and cryc ðīn, hīe mē frœfrende wērun.

Spelman Psalter :

Gird ðīn and stef ðīn, hō mō frēfredon.

Canterbury Psalter :

Þīn gierd and stef þīn, hȳ mē frēfredon.

The Alfredian peculiarity thus seems restricted to the use of the verb *āfrēfran*, instead of *frēfran*. This of itself is perhaps hardly sufficient to base an argument upon, yet one is tempted to extend the limit from 11. 6, where *wolberende* was still found, to include at least Ps. 23.

Here, then, we may rest the case. We have seen that Alfred must certainly have translated 1. 1, pretty certainly 11. 6, not improbably 23. 4, and at least possibly the whole of the prose portion of the Paris Psalter. Yet against the last supposition must be set the notable discrepancies of language revealed by the parallel passages adduced above. It will require a more comprehensive and detailed examination to decide whether Alfred is really to be credited with the translation of all the prose Psalms extant.

For Alfred's other translations of parts of the Bible, see pp. 3–75 of this volume.

For comparison with the Vespasian Psalter, I subjoin Ps. 43.

Dēm mē, Dryhten, and dō sum tōscēad betwuh mē and unrihtwīsum folce ; and frọm fācenfullum mẹnn and unrihtwīsum gefriða mē, forþām þū eart mīn God and mīn mægen. Forhwȳ āwyrpst þū mē? and hwī lētst þū mē gān unrōtne, þonne mīne fȳnd mē drẹcceað ? Sẹnd þīn lēoht and þīne sōðfæstnesse, þā mē gēo gēara lǣddon, þæt hȳ mē nū gȳt gelǣdan tō þīnum hālgan munte, in on þīn hālge templ ; þæt ic þonne gange tō þīnum altere, and tō þām Gode þe mē blīðne gedyde on mīnum geoguðhāde. Ic þē andette, Dryhten, mid sange and mid hearpan. Hwȳ eart þū unrōt, mīn sāwl? oþþe hwī gedrēfest þū mē? Hopa tō Drihtne, forþām ic hine gȳt andette, forþām þū eart God mīn Hūlend, and mīn Dryhten.

The Poetical Translation.—As for the attempts to connect this with Aldhelm, see pp. xiv ff.

It has long been known that this version was used by the Old English Benedictines in their Office. The Benedictine Office has been printed by Hickes, *Letters which passed between Dr. Hickes and a Popish Priest* (1705); E. Thomson, *Select Monuments, &c.* (1849); and K. Bouterwek, *Cædmons des Angelsachsen Biblische Dichtungen* (1854), pp. cxciv-ccxxiii. Here, identical, or nearly so, with the corresponding parts of the Paris Psalter, will be found portions of Ps. 54, 59, 61, 65, 70, 71, 80, 85, 88, 90, 102, 103, 119, 122, 140, and 141 (according to the Authorized Version; one less according to the Vulgate). Besides these, there are also parts of Ps. 5, 20, 25, 28, 33, 35, 41, 44, 51. In Eadwine's Canterbury Psalter, circa 1150 (see p. xxviii), there is a late copy of Ps. 90. 16 to 98. 2 (pp. 161–168). The whole of the poetical Psalter, including a reproduction of Thorpe's text, the Benedictine fragments, and the Kentish 51st Psalm (but not the twelfth-century fragment), will be found in Grein's *Bibliothek der Angelsächsischen Poesie*, ii. 147–280.

The most recent study of the problem presented by this translation has been made by Dr. Helen Bartlett, *The Metrical Division of the Paris Psalter*, Baltimore, 1896. Her conclusions may be stated in her own words (pp. 48, 49): 'Our examination of the vocabulary and metre of the Paris Psalter has thrown some light upon the question of the date and dialect of the Anglo-Saxon version in its original form. The discovery of certain words peculiar to the metrical Psalter in texts of the tenth century has deprived of its force the argument that Dietrich used to establish the high antiquity of Ps. II [i. e. 52–150]. Moreover, a careful study of the metre has disclosed a disregard of the classical rules for the construction of alliterative verse which characterizes only the latest Anglo-Saxon poetry, and therefore points to a period not earlier than the middle of the tenth century. . . . But the *terminus ante quem* appears definitely determined by the quotation from the Psalms in the *Menologium*, if we do not regard the coincidence in

translation as accidental, as I think it is hardly possible to do.
The strong probability that this quotation is taken from the Paris
Psalter will appear on comparing these passages :

Ps. 117. 22. Ðis ys se dæg, ðe hine drihten us
           wisfæst geworhte wera cneorissum
           eallum eorðtudrum eadgum to blisse.

Men. 60–63. Ðis is se dæg, ðæne drihten us
           wisfæst worhte wera cneorissum
           eallum corðwarum eadigum to blisse.

'As the *Menologium* [1] belongs to the latter half of the tenth century (between 940 and 980), the metrical Psalter must have been
translated before this date. The determination of the date of the
Benedictine Officium would furnish further evidence of the down-
ward limit for the date of our text, but thus far no date has been
assigned to the Officium. We may conclude, however, from the
above discussion, that the metrical Psalter was translated about
the middle of the tenth century.

'The comparison of the use of certain synonyms and forms in
Ps. II with the usage of the other chief Anglo-Saxon texts has
proved that the dialect of the original version must have been
Anglian, and a few phonological peculiarities noted in the Psalter
tend to confirm this conclusion. As to the actual authorship of the
translation, there is no evidence. We can say merely that the subject of the translation and the few additions that indicate a wider
Biblical knowledge suggest that the translator was a priest, or
more probably a monk. The negligence and clumsiness of the
translation, and the poverty and artificiality of the poetry, prove
that he was neither an exact scholar nor a gifted poet.'

For comparison with the glossed Psalters, I reproduce Ps. 100 :

     Nū gē mycle gefēan   mihtigum Drihtne,
     eall þēos corðe,   elne hȳre ;
     and blisse Gode   bealde þēowie ;
     gangað on ansȳne   ealle blīðe.
     Witað wīslice   þæt hē is Wealdend God ;
     hē ūs geworhte,   and wē his syndon ;
     wē his folc syndan,   and his fǣle scēap
     ða hē on his edisce   ealle āfēdde.
     Gað nū on his doru,   God andettað,

---

[1] Ten Brink, *Early Eng. Lit.*, vol. i. p. 90, foot-note.

and hine weorðiað   on wīctūnum
mid lofsangum,   lustum myclum.
Heriað naman Drihtnes,   forþon hē is niðum swǣs ;
is þīn milde mōd   ofer manna bearn.

POETICAL TRANSLATIONS.

JUDITH.—It is possible that the Old English poem of *Judith* belongs to the ninth century. See, however, pp. lxxvi ff.

For the poetical part of the Paris Psalter, see pp. xli ff.

TENTH CENTURY.

PROSE TRANSLATIONS.

NORTHUMBRIAN GLOSS ON THE GOSPELS.—This gloss was made by a priest named Aldred, about A. D. 950, or perhaps somewhat later. It is contained in the magnificent MS. known as the ' Durham Book,' or 'Lindisfarne Gospels,' or ' Book of St. Cuthbert,' MS. Cotton Nero D. 4 of the British Museum. The MS., with its Latin text, dates from before the year 700, and was written by Eadfrith, who became Bishop of Lindisfarne in 698, and died in 721.

According to Sir E. Maunde Thompson, in the British Museum *Catalogue of Ancient Manuscripts: Part II, Latin*, pp. 17, 18 :

' The MS. has been frequently described. In addition to the descriptions to be found in the works cited above[1], some account of it is given by Selden in his introduction to *Historiae Anglicanae Scriptores x.*, Londini, 1652, pp. xxv, xxvi ; T. Marshall, *Observationes in versionem Anglo-Saxonicam*, appended to his edition of the Gothic and Anglo-Saxon Gospels, Amstelaedami, 1684, p. 491 ; and H. Wanley, in his *Catalogus Librorum Septentrionalium*, printed in Hickes's *Linguarum vett. Septentrionalium Thesaurus*, vol. ii. Oxoniae, 1703, pp. 250-252 ; and, more recently, by T. F. Dibdin, *The Bibliographical Decameron*, London, 1827, vol. i. p. xlix ; J. Stevenson, in *The Graphic and Historical Illustrator*,

---

[1] Such as Smith, *Bibl. Cott. Hist. et Synopsis*, p. 33.—ED.

London, 1834, p. 355 ; Waagen, *Treasures of Art in Great Britain,*
London, 1854, vol. i. p. 136 ; and others. Engravings of the
four Evangelists are given by J. Strutt, *Horda Angelcynnan,*
London, 1775, 1776, vol. iii. tabb. xxiii-xxvi ; and facsimile
plates of the writing and ornamentation are published, with more
or less description, by T. Astle, *The Origin and Progress of Writing,*
London, 1803, tab. xiv; H. Shaw, *Illuminated Ornaments,* London,
1833, no. ii ; H. N. Humphreys and O. Jones, *The Illuminated
Books of the Middle Ages,* London, 1849, Pl. I ; J. O. Westwood,
Palaeographia Sacra Pictoria, London, 1843-1845, no. 45, and
*Facsimiles of the Miniatures and Ornaments of Anglo-Saxon and
Irish MSS.,* London, 1868, Pl. XII, XIII ; and by the Palaeo-
graphical Society, *Facsimiles of MSS. and Inscriptions,* 1873-1883,
Pl. 3-6, 22.' To these facsimiles must be added those in the
editions of Bouterwek and Waring; in Kitto's *Cyclopaedia of
Biblical Literature* (art. 'Anglo-Saxon Versions'); and (especially
good, at a reasonable price) in Lieferung 1 of Wülker's *Geschichte
der Englischen Litteratur,* Leipzig and Vienna, 1896.

Two entries in the codex are extremely interesting. The first
occurs before the Argument of Mark's Gospel, and runs : 'Đu lif-
giende God, gemyne ðū Ēadfrið, and Æðilwǎld, and Billfrið, and
Ǎldred peccatorum ; ðās feowero, mið Gode, ymbwǣson ðās bōc.'
The second is at the end of John's Gospel (marginal entries in
parenthesis) : ' ✠ Ēadfrið, biscob Lindisfearnensis aecclesiae, hē ðis
bōc aūrāt æt fruma, Gode and Sancte Cūðberhte and ǎllum ðǣm
hǎlgum gimǣnelice ðā ðe in colǫnde sint. And Ēðiluǎld, Lind-
isfearncolǫndinga biscob, hit ūta giðrȳde and gibēlde, suā hē uel
cūðæ. And Billfrið, se ǫncrae, hē gismioðade ðā gihrīno ðā ðe
ūtan on sint, and hit gihrīnade mið golde and mið gimmum, ǣc
mið sulfre ofergylded, fāconlēas feh. And Ǎldred (Ælfredi[1]
natus, Aldredus uocor ; bonæ mulieris, ·i· Tilwin, filius eximius
loquor), presbyter indignus et misserrimus, mið Godes fultummæ
and Sancti Cūðberhtes, hit oferglǣsade on Ęnglisc, and hine gihām-
adi mið ðǣm ðriim dǣlum — Matheus dǣl Gode and Sancte
Cūðberhti ; Marcus dǣl ðǣm biscobe; and Lucas dǣl ðǣm hiorode,
and æhtu ōra seulfres mið tō inlǎde ; and Sancti Johannes dǣl for
hine seolfne (fore his sāule), and feouer ōra seulfres, mið Gode
and Sancti Cūðberti[2], þætte hē habbe ǫndfǫng ðerh Godes milsæ
on heofnum, seel and sibb on eorðo, forðgeong and giðyngo,

---

[1] Skeat wrongly, 'Alfredi.'   [2] Skeat wrongly, 'Cuðberhti.'

uísdom and snyttro, ðerh Sancti Cuðberhtes earnunga. ✠ Ead-
fri, Œðiluald, Billfri, Āldred hoc euangeliarium Deo and
Cuðberhto construxerunt uel ornauerunt.'

These entries may readily be made out with the help of my
Glossary of the Old Northumbrian Gospels (Halle, 1894), or translations may be found in Waring's *St. John*, pp. xliv–xlv, and in
Skeat's *St. John*, pp. viii–ix. Thompson suggests (*op. cit.*) the
following as a free version of the sentence beginning 'And
Āldred': 'And Aldred, unworthy and miserable priest, with the
help of God and St. Cuthbert, glossed it in English, and got for
himself a home [in the monastery] by his work on the three parts,
viz. on St. Matthew in honour of God and St. Cuthbert, on
St. Mark for the bishop, and on St. Luke for the brotherhood;
paying also eight oras of silver on his admission. But St. John
he glossed for himself, making also an offering of four oras to
God and St. Cuthbert, to the end that he may gain admittance
into heaven,' &c. The exactest transcript of these entries, with all
the erasures and contractions indicated, the use of *v* for *u*, &c., is
by Thompson (*op. cit.*), though even he, like Professor Skeat,
prints 'cvðberti' with an h, but 'ælfredi,' not 'alfredi.'

Aldred may perhaps have been the Bishop of Durham of that
name, 957–68 (*Dict. Nat. Biog.* s. v.), though this hardly seems
compatible with the self-sufficiency which he displays in this
entry. In any case he is not to be confounded with Aldred
the Provost, the writer of a few collects at the end of a MS.
known as the 'Durham Ritual' (Durham Chapter Library, MS. A.
iv. 19), published by the Surtees Society, 1839, as *Rituale Ecclesiae
Dunelmensis* (cf. p. 185 of that book). Ethilwald succeeded
Eadfrith as Bishop of Lindisfarne in 721, and died either in 737,
739, or 740, for authorities differ (Moberly's edition of Bede's
Hist. Eccl., p. 318, note; Bouterwek, p. xlvii). Billfrith, like
Eadfrith and Ethilwald. is mentioned by Simeon of Durham
(circa 1060–circa 1130), see p. xlviii. He was evidently a contemporary of Ethilwald.

Simeon of Durham's account of the loss and recovery of the
MS., before it received the Northumbrian gloss, is most interesting. St. Cuthbert, the hermit of Farne, and subsequent patron
of Northumbria, had died in 687. For a hundred and eighty-
eight years his body had lain at Lindisfarne, but at the
expiration of that time it was to begin its famous wanderings.

According to Waring (*St. John.* pp. xxv, xxvi): 'The year 875 witnessed the great Danish invasion of Northumbria under Half-dene, when, in the words of Simeon of Durham, "fire and sword were carried throughout the land from the eastern sea to the western." The country southward of the Tyne was already laid waste, and at length the enemy crossed the river, left Tynemouth Abbey a smoking ruin behind them, and from thence marched direct for Holy Island. Upon their approach, Eardulf, Bishop of Lindisfarne, recalled to the monks St. Cuthbert's dying injunction, that were they ever driven into exile they should carry his bones away with them. The shrine containing his body was hastily removed from the choir, and seven clerks appointed by the bishop bore it off on their shoulders. A few other treasures of the church, our Evangeliarium among the number, were also secured, as too precious to fall into the hands of the infidels. Then the fugitives set forth; and hardly had they reached a place of safety when the Danes fell upon their monastery, which they pillaged and gave to the flames. Halfdene and his brother divided North-umbria between them, and governed it as a conquered country, plundering and laying waste so long as anything remained to seize or to destroy. Meanwhile the exiled brethren wandered from mountain to mountain with the saint's body, which was followed by the whole Christian population, whom Simeon of Durham likens to sheep fleeing before wolves to their shepherd for pro-tection. . . . Eardulf and his party traversed, as he tells us, the whole district of Northumbria, often in peril from the enemy, from famine, plague, and wolves, yet enduring every hardship rather than prove faithless to their trust, and abandon the remains of their patron to the insult of heathens. No person was per-mitted to lay hand upon the shrine save its seven original bearers, whose office made them an object of envy to the people, and whose descendants through many generations deemed themselves ennobled by the service of their ancestors.'

At length, after wandering some years, the party were about to seek refuge in Ireland, and embarked at the mouth of Derwent-water, in the Lake District, but only succeeded in reaching Whithern, in the present Wigtonshire, some thirty miles distant across the Solway Firth. But the story of the loss and recovery of the MS. shall now be given in Simeon of Durham's own words (*Hist. Eccl. Dunelm.*, lib. ii. capp. xi, xii; ed. Arnold, Rolls

Series, i. 64–68): 'Ergo ad ostium fluminis quod Dyrwenta vocatur, omnes simul, episcopus, et abbas, et populus conveniunt. Ibi navis ad transponendum paratur. . . . Continuo venti mutantur, fluctus intumescentes elevantur, et quod nunc erat tranquillum, mare fit tempestuosum ; navisque iam non valens gubernari huc et illuc inter fluctivagas iactabatur undas. . . . Qua tempestate dum navis verteretur in latera, cadens ex ea textus Evangeliorum auro gemmisque perornatus, in maris ferebatur profunda. . . . Arrepto itaque gubernaculo, navim ad littus et ad socios retorquent, et continuo flantibus a tergo ventis illuc sine aliqua difficultate perveniunt.' Eventually God appears in a dream to one of the seven bearers of the shrine, named Hunred: 'Cuidam namque illorum, videlicet Hunredo, per visum assistens, iussit ut aestu maris recedente, codicem qui de navi, ut superius dictum est, medias ceciderat in undas quaererent, fortassis enim, contra hoc quod ipsi sperare possent, Deo miserante invenirent. Nam et de illius libri amissione, maxima illorum mentes perturbaverat moestitia. . . . Confestim somno expergefactus, visionem se vidisse narravit, moxque aliquos e sociis ad mare, quod erat vicinum, librum quem amiserant quaesituros misit. Per id quippe temporis in locum qui Candida Casa, vulgo autem Huuiterna vocatur, devenerant[1]. Itaque pergentes ad mare, multo quam consueverat longius recessisse conspiciunt, et tribus vel eo amplius milliariis gradientes, ipsum sanctum Evangeliorum codicem reperiunt, qui ita forinsecus gemmis et auro sui decorem, ita intrinsecus literis et foliis priorem praeferebat pulchritudinem, ac si ab aqua minime tactus fuisset[2].'

---

[1] But we are not told how long a time had elapsed since the loss of the volume, nor how they had reached Whithern.

[2] Waring (p. xxviii) quotes Sir Frederick Madden (Ellis, *Letters of Eminent Literary Men*, Camden Society, p. 268): 'The stains on the vellum I believe to have been occasioned by sea-water when the book was brought from Lindisfarne [*sic*]. It was no doubt secured tightly in a *theca*, or with clasps, and the stains exhibit just the appearance that water would make in oozing by force through a minute aperture.' Thompson says, however (*op. cit.*): 'With regard to the tradition of its immersion in the sea, it is difficult to believe that such an accident really happened. The MS. is unusually fresh and clean, and shows no trace of injury beyond a few stains, which may or may not have been caused by sea-water. It is, however, possible that it was wrapped securely in skins or some such waterproof material, and thus escaped without damage, if it was actually washed overboard.' In a recent communication to me, Sir E. M.

Returning with the volume, they find a bay ('rufi coloris') horse: 'Adiungentes itaque caballum vehiculo, quod illum coelestem thesaurum theca inclusum ferebat, eo securius per quaelibet loca ipsum sequebantur, quo a Deo sibi proviso equo ductore utebantur. Porro liber memoratus in hac ecclesia quae corpus ipsius sancti partis habere meruit, usque hodie servatur [1], in quo nullum omnino, ut diximus, per aquam laesionis signum monstratur [2]. Quod plane et ipsius sancti Cuthberti, et ipsorum quoque meritis qui ipsius libri auctores extiterant, gestum creditur, Eadfridi videlicet venerandae memoriae episcopi [3], qui hunc in honorem beati Cuthberti manu propria scripserat, successoris quoque eiusdem venerabilis Ethelwoldi, qui auro gemmisque perornari iusserat, sancti etiam Bilfridi anachoritae, qui vota iubentis manu artifici prosecutus, egregium opus composuerat. Erat enim aurificii arte praecipuus. Hi pariter amore dilecti Deo confessoris et pontificis ferventes, suam erga ipsum devotionem posteris omnibus innotescendam hoc opere reliquerunt.'

Apparently, Simeon had our MS. before him when he wrote; at all events, his statements seem clearly to refer to it. Such being the case, I am at a loss to understand the remark of Thompson (op. cit.): 'On the other hand, the story which is told by Simeon of Durham may have originally referred to some other volume, lost at sea, in the way described, and afterwards recovered.' Evidently Simeon did not think so, at least [4].

It looks, too, if we interpret Aldred's entry in the light of Simeon's statement, as though Ethilwald had done nothing to the book with his own hands, in spite of Aldred's 'hit ūta giðrȳde

---

Thompson says: 'I do not think the *theca* would have been water-tight, and therefore some such additional wrapping would have been necessary.'

[1] In the fourteenth century it appears in the inventories of Lindisfarne as 'Liber S. Cuthberti qui demersus erat in mare,' according to Raine, *History and Antiquities of North Durham*, 1852. pp. 93, 105, quoted by Thompson, *op. cit.*

[2] This statement should be carefully compared with the views of Madden and Thompson.

[3] Does this mean that Eadfrith wrote it after he had become bishop? It would then have been written between 698 and 701. It is usually assumed that he wrote it previous to assuming the episcopal office.

[4] Sir E. M. Thompson now explains: 'What I meant was that, though Simeon had our MS. before him, and believed it to be the book that went overboard, the *tradition* originally might have referred to another book, and have been shifted to our MS. even before the time of Simeon.'

and gibělde, suā hē uel ené̄e,' since Simeon merely remarks that
he commanded Billfrith to do what he did. The two statements
about Billfrith, Latin and Old English, should be carefully compared ; their agreement is striking.

It now appears probable that the original from which the
Durham Book was copied belonged to Naples. The proof has
been furnished by Dom G. Morin, and the whole argument is
thus clearly presented by Samuel Berger, *Histoire de la Vulgate*
(Paris, 1893), pp. 39–41 :

'Une découverte toute récente est venue rapprocher encore le
texte northumbrien de l'Italie. Elle est due à un religieux béné-
dictin de Maredsous, en Belgique, Dom G. Morin. Chose étrange,
ce n'est pas le nom de Rome qui a été prononcé à cette occasion,
c'est celui de la ville de Naples [1].

'En tête de chacun des Évangiles, dans le *Book of Lindisfarne*,
aussi bien que dans un autre manuscrit anglo-saxon qui paraît du
IXe siècle (M. Br. I. B. vii) et qui porte, au folio 15 v°, la signa-
ture: *Æthelstan cyng*, on trouve l'énumération d'un certain nombre
de fêtes ou de cérémonies pendant lesquelles, assurément, on lisait
des leçons de cet Évangile. Ce texte liturgique n'est autre chose
que le calendrier de l'église à laquelle appartenait le manuscrit
primitif, celui sur lequel le *Book of Lindisfarne* a été copié. Or,
parmi le très petit nombre de fêtes des saints, nous trouvons la
fête de saint Janvier, précédée du jeûne de la veille, et la fête de
saint Vit ; nous voyons la dédicace d'une église : *In dedicatione
basilicae Stephani.* Or chacun sait que saint Janvier est le grand
saint local de Naples ; saint Vit y fut honoré avant d'être trans-
porté à Saint-Denis et de là à Prague, et la cathédrale de Naples
s'appelait *basilica Stephani* ou la *Stephania*, en l'honneur de son
deuxième fondateur, l'évêque Étienne Ier, vivant après l'an 500.
Nous avons du reste un autre calendrier ancien du diocèse de
Naples, et il concorde de tous points avec notre texte liturgique.
Celui-ci est donc bien napolitain.

'Mais quelle relation y a-t-il entre l'église de Naples et la North-
umbrie ? La réponse est facile à donner. Nous laissons la parole
à Dom Morin :

'"En 668, le Grec Théodore et l'Africain Adrien furent envoyés
en Angleterre avec l'Anglo-Saxon Benoît Biscop, afin de travailler
de concert à l'organisation définitive de la chrétienté dans ce pays.

---

[1] *La Liturgie de Naples au temps de S. Grégoire. Revue bénédictine*, t. viii, 1891, p. 481.

Or cet Adrien était abbé d'un monastère près de Naples, appelé par Bède *monasterium Nisidanum*. Mazzochi a identifié ce lieu avec la petite île de Nisita, entre Naples et Pouzzoles, la *Nesis* des anciens, mentionnée par le *Liber pontificalis* parmi les donations faites par Constantin à l'église de Naples."

'Il y eut effectivement dans cette île un monastère qui a laissé çà et là quelques traces dans l'histoire du VIIe au XIIIe siècle.

'Mais ce n'est pas tout. Un des premiers soins du vieil archévêque Théodore, après son installation à Canterbury, fut de parcourir l'une après l'autre les diverses provinces de l'île confiée à ses soins, accompagné et secondé en tout par l'abbé Adrien[1]. Ils arrivèrent ainsi jusqu'à la métropole celtique de Lindisfarne, dont le prélat voulut consacrer lui-même la cathédrale en bois, bâtie par l'évêque Aïdan. Si Théodore avait bien apporté avec lui un Homère qu'il lisait sans cesse, on n'aura pas de peine à admettre qu'Adrien de son côté s'était muni des livres liturgiques qu'il estimait devoir être utiles aux églises et communautés monastiques de l'Angleterre. Parmi ce bagage littéraire il a pu se trouver quelques manuscrits des Évangiles provenant de Naples.

'Si notre calendrier est de Naples, comme on ne saurait en douter, le texte des Évangiles qu'il accompagne est-il nécessairement aussi napolitain? Oui sans doute, car on ne peut guère admettre que l'on ait interpolé ainsi un manuscrit en quatre endroits différents, et les notes liturgiques qui sont sur les marges sont d'accord avec le calendrier. Cela ne veut pas dire qu'entre Naples et Lindisfarne notre texte n'ait pu éprouver plus d'une altération. On en jugera par les profondes différences qui séparent le *Book of Lindisfarne* du manuscrit d'Æthelstan, qui paraît pourtant copié sur lui. On se souvient que, dans le *Codex Amiatinus*, les Évangiles sont en dehors des traditions ordinaires et forment groupe, à tous égards, avec les manuscrits northumbriens. Il est donc difficile de ne pas admettre que Ceolfrid a eu le manuscrit du moine Adrien sous les yeux. La chose paraîtra beaucoup plus naturelle quand on considérera qu'il a eu également devant lui un des manuscrits de Cassiodore. Vivarium, le couvent de Cassiodore, était en Calabre. C'est donc du sud de l'Italie que sont venus plusieurs des textes les plus importants de l'Angleterre. Ce résultat ne manque pas d'intérêt.'

[1] Bede, *Hist. Eccl.*, iv. 2 : *Marque peragrata insula tota . . . per omnia comitante et cooperante Hadriano disseminabat.*

The argument may be thus summarized : Certain saints are peculiarly Neapolitan—St. Januarius, St. Vitus, and St. Stephen. St. Januarius is known to all the world by the alleged liquefaction of his blood at certain times ; the cult of St. Vitus spread from Naples to St. Denis and to Prague ; St. Stephen is not the proto-martyr, but the bishop Stephen I, the second founder of the cathedral of Naples. These saints are all mentioned in a calendar prefixed to the Gospel of Matthew (Skeat, p. 23) ; hence the calendar, and accordingly the Gospels, must have been copied from a Neapolitan manuscript. As to the mode of transmission, Abbot Hadrian, to whom, in conjunction with Archbishop Theo-dore, so much of English culture in the seventh and following centuries is due, had been the abbot of the monastery on the little island of Nisita, between Naples and Pozzuoli, or, at all events, of some monastery 'quod est non longe a Neapoli Campaniae' (Bede). What more probable than that, on his visit with Theodore to Lindisfarne, he should have brought with him the original of the Durham Book ?

On the general subject of the transmission of copies of the Scriptures between Italy and England, much interesting informa-tion may be found in White's *The Codex Amiatinus and its Birth-place* (*Studia Biblica et Ecclesiastica*, Oxford, 1890, ii. 273 ff.). Wordsworth and White say of the Durham Book (*Novum Testa-mentum secundum Editionem Sancti Hieronymi*, Oxford, 1889, Praefatio, p. xiv) : 'Cum Amiatino maxime concordat, sed manu Anglica non Italica scriptus est.'

The first complete edition of the Northumbrian Gloss was by Bouterwek, in 1857 : *Die vier Evangelien in Alt-Nordhumbrischer Sprache*, Gütersloh, 1857 ; and *Screadunga*, Elberfeld, 1858 ; the latter merely containing the prefaces to the Gospels. The intro-duction to this edition is still valuable in parts ; on the other hand, the edition is nearly worthless, because of the changes made by Bouterwek in the text.

Another edition, Latin as well as Old English, was by Steven-son and Waring, nos. 28, 39, 43, and 48 of the Surtees Society Publications, appearing respectively in 1854, 1860, 1863, and 1865. Waring's Preface and Prolegomena (in his *St. John*) may be read with profit, and have been analyzed at considerable length by Skeat, Preface to *St. John*, pp. xvii, xviii. This edition, while measurably correct, is inferior in accuracy to the next.

The best edition is that by Skeat, *The Holy Gospel, in Anglo-Saxon, Northumbrian, and Old Mercian Versions*, Cambridge, 1871, 1874, 1878, and (*Matthew*) 1887, the latter having been previously, and less satisfactorily, edited by Kemble and Hardwick. The Latin text, which differs from that on which the Rushworth and West Saxon versions are based, is here printed. This edition leaves little to be desired, though my own collation, made in 1882, shows occasional errors. It is upon Skeat's edition that my Glossary (see p. xlv) is based, my corrections having been silently incorporated.

Portions of the gloss have been incorporated into various manuals: Matt., chaps. 2 and 3, in Kluge's *Angelsächsisches Lesebuch* (Halle, 1888), pp. 35–40 ; Matt., chaps. 6–8, in Sweet's *Second Anglo-Saxon Reader* (Oxford, 1887), pp. 124–150 (alternately with the Rushworth version) ; and Matt. 25. 31–46 in my *First Book in Old English* (second edition, Boston, 1895), pp. 256–8.

Henshall, in his *Etymological Organic Reasoner* (London, 1807) prints, together with the Gothic Gospel of Matthew, 5. 15 to 27. 66, the corresponding portions (omitting what the Gothic omits) of the Durham Book. To these he prefixes the account of the scribes. The text of both the Gothic and the Northumbrian is accompanied by a version upon the opposite page. One or two specimens of the version will be amusing, if not instructive.

Of the Northumbrian :

Matt. 10. 41. He that haves a wizard in the name of a wizard, has the meed of a wizard ; and he that has a soothfast in the name of a soothfast, has a soothfast's meed.

11. 13, 14. For that all the wizards and the aye witnessed until John. If ye will nab it, this is Elias he that toward was.

Of the Gothic :

Matt. 6. 18, 19. That not beseen art thou men fasting, but Dada thine the him in foulness, yea Dada thine whoso seeth in foulness upgives thee. Not hoardeth you hoards on earth, there mould and gnat frowardeth, yea there thieves up-grubb yea liften.

It is needless, after the foregoing, to say that Henshall's texts are inaccurately printed.

As a specimen of the language, the Lord's Prayer (Matt. 6. 9–13) is here given, in addition to the entries above : 'Fader ūser[1] ðū

---

[1] The MS. has 'urer,' but this is clearly a mistake.

arð (*vel* ðū bist) in heofnum (*vel* in heofnas), sīe gehālgad noma
ðīn. Tōcymeð rīc ðīn. Sīe willo ðīn, suǣ is in heofne and in eorðo.
Hlāf ūserne oferwistlic sęl ūs tō-dæg. And forgef ūs scylda ūsra,
suǣ uǣ forgēfon scyldgum ūsum. And ne inlǣd[1] ūsih in costunge,
ah gefrīg ūsich[2] from yfle.' As this is a gloss, of course the entries
on p. xliv present the language under its more natural aspect.

THE RUSHWORTH VERSION OF THE GOSPELS.—This version was
made by two persons, Farman and Owun, probably in the tenth
century, and the gloss at all events after the Lindisfarne gloss (see
below). It falls into two tolerably distinct parts, a translation
and a gloss. The translation is of the Gospel of Matthew; the
gloss, of the other three Gospels.

The translation is independent; the gloss is a modified transcript of that in the Lindisfarne Gospels. Farman wrote the
whole of the translation, together with the gloss from the beginning of Mark through the word *hlconadun* ('discumbebant') in
chap. 2. *v*. 15 of that Gospel, and John 18. 1–3.

The Latin text was written by a scribe named Macregol, who
appears to have died in 820. Waring says (Preface to *St. John*,
p. 1): 'The age of the volume can hardly be fixed with any certainty; Astle asserts that the text was written towards the latter
end of the seventh, and the interlineary gloss some time in the
tenth century; and Wanley affirms the book to have been the
property of the Venerable Bede, remarking at the same time that
it appears older than the Lindisfarne Gospels. Dr. O'Connor,
however, has discovered, in the Irish Annals of the year 820, the
death of a scribe named "Macregol [*dele this word*], Mac Riagoil,
nepos Magleni, scriba et episcopus abbas Biror (hodie Birr in
Comitatu Regio in Hibernia), periit."' For O'Connor we should
read O'Conor. In the latter's *Annales Ultonienses*, under the year
821 (*Rerum Hibernicarum Scriptores*, iv. 203), we read: 'Mac Riagoil,
nepos Magleni, Scriba, 7 Eps, Ab. Biror [Abbas Birræ], periit.' In
his *Annales IV Magistrorum*, under 820 (*ib*. iii. 324): 'Mac
Riagalus O'Magleni Scriba, Episcopus, et Abbas Birrensis
[with others] obierunt.' Compare O'Conor's remarks on the
Rushworth MS. in I. ccxxix–ccxxxv. In the *Annals of Ulster*
(Irish Record Publications), edited by Hennessy, 1887, i. 315,

---

[1] The Latin here, differing from the Vulgate, is in the order, 'ne inducas nos.'

[2] 'Usich' occurs only here; the usual forms are 'usic,' 'usig,' and 'usih'; 'usih' may be regarded as the norm.

the translation of the Irish is 'Macriaghoil Ua Magleni, a scribe and bishop, abbot of Biror, died.' We learn that Birr, or Parsons-town, was the seat of a great school in the time of St. Brendan (O'Curry, *Manners and Customs of the Ancient Irish*, ii. 76).

The MS. is in the Bodleian Library at Oxford, and is marked Auct. D. ii. 19 (formerly D. 24, No. 3946). It now consists of 169 leaves of thick vellum, measuring 14 by 10½ inches, but is incomplete, eleven leaves having been lost. The missing portions are all in the Gospel of Luke: chap. 4, latter part of *v.* 29, to chap. 7, *v.* 38 (eight leaves) ; chap. 10, from *v.* 19 to part of *v.* 38 (one leaf) ; and chap. 15, part of *v.* 13, to chap. 16, part of *v.* 25 (two leaves).

The MS. has been described by Wanley in his *Catalogus*, pp. 81, 82, and by Waring (after Westwood) in his *St. John*, pp. xlvii–lii. Facsimile plates, with description, are published by Astle, *The Origin and Progress of Writing*, tab. xv ; Westwood, *Palaeographia Sacra Pictoria*, Plate 44, and *Facsimiles of the Miniatures, &c.*, Plate 16 ; and in the *Palaeographical Society Facsimiles*, Series I, vol. ii, Plates 90 and 91.

There are three entries in the MS. from which we derive our information concerning the persons engaged in its composition, and each entry is by a different person. On the last page of the MS., and in the last two of six nearly square compartments, occurs the following, from which we gather that the scribe of the Latin text wrote his name both Macregol and Macreguil : 'Macregol dipinexit hoc euangelium. Quicumque legerit et intelligerit istam narrationem, orat pro Macreguil scriptori.'

The Gospel of John ends on the first page of the last leaf. At the bottom of the preceding page is this entry in Owun's hand-writing : 'Ðe mīn brūche, gibidde fore Owun, ꝥe ðäs bōc glæsde, Færmen ðām prēoste æt Harawuda.' This may be translated (it is the book which is supposed to be speaking) : 'Whoever makes use of me, let him pray for Owun, who glossed this book, for Færman the priest at Harewood.' Here two points deserve notice : the use of *ðe* in the sense of 'whosoever,' and the construction of *Færmen*. The former, though very unusual, if not quite unprecedented (cf. *Runic Poem* 8, though this is not quite parallel : 'Wēn ne brūceð þe can wēana lȳt '), occasions no trouble. As to the latter, while it is perfectly clear that *Færmen* is a dative, it is not so certain what the implied 'for' or 'to' is meant to refer to. Shall we understand (1) 'and for Færman,' i.e. 'Pray for Farman';

or rather (2) 'who glossed this book for Færman'? Waring interprets according to the former, Skeat (*St. John*, p. xi) according to the latter of these hypotheses.

At the bottom of the next page, namely, the penultimate page of the MS., occurs the following: 'Hæfe nū bōc āwritne; brūca mið willa, symle mið sōðum gileafa. Sibb is ēghwæm leofost.' This must be read: 'Have now a written book; use it with joy [cf. *willum* = 'voluptatibus,' Lind. Lk. 8. 14], always with true faith. Peace [Love?] is dearest to every one.' This passage may be regarded as a poetical distich, the first line ending with *willa*. The alliterative words of the first line will then be *b* and *w* alternately, and of the second line *s* and *l*, the former occurring twice in the first hemistich.

It must be noted that these two entries occur at the bottom of successive pages, and are not necessarily to be read as continuous. This fact will be more evident from Waring's description (*St. John*, p. 1): 'The two last pages of St. John's Gospel are enclosed in elaborate borders of tesselated and interlaced Irish ornament; beneath those of the lower margins, Owun, the second glossist, has recorded his own name and that of his fellow-labourer Farman.' This must be borne in mind, since Waring endeavours to make verse of the first entry, which it will scarcely bear, and Wanley, Waring, and Murray connect the two entries syntactically. Thus Wanley renders: 'Fermenni Presbyteri Harawudensis gratia, iam tandem codicem perscripsit' [!]. Waring has: '. . . for Færmen the priest at Harewood (who) has now written this book.' Dr. Murray also (*Athenaeum*, April 3, 1875), having only Waring's incomplete representation of the text, rendered it: 'For Farman the priest at Harwood (I) have now written the book'; but, on seeing the correct text, pointed out that *hæfe*, like *brūca*, is in the imperative mood (see Skeat, *St. John*, p. xiv, note). That the two passages are not syntactically connected is clear the moment we are sure that *hæfe* cannot possibly be the indicative present first singular, but must be the imperative singular. This will be perfectly evident to any one who compares, in the Rushworth version, the *hæfe* of Matt. 18. 26, 29, and of Luke 14. 18, 19, with the *hafo* of Luke 11. 6; 12. 17; 14. 18, 19; John 4. 17, 32; 5. 7, 36; 8. 26, 49; 10. 16, 18; 16. 12; 19. 10[1]. In truth, the second entry might have stood in any religious or theological book, as is indicated by

[1] But 'hæfo,' John 19. 10; 'hæfe,' John 19. 11.

the gnomic character of the tag, 'Sibb is ēghwǣm lēofost'; while the first has specific reference to this particular book.

There remains one other entry to consider. The Latin entry is by the scribe of the Latin text, Macregol, and occurs at the close of the whole book. The one we have been examining is in the hand of the second glossator, Owun, and is at or near the end of John's Gospel. That which is now to engage our attention is by Farman, and is at the end of the Gospel of Matthew. It reads: 'Farman[1] presbyter þās bōc þus glēosede; dimittet ei Dominus omnia peccata sua, si fieri potest apud Deum.' I follow the readings of Wanley, Waring, and of Skeat in his *St. Matthew*, p. 245; in his *St. John*, p. 188, he has *glǣsede*. This may be translated: 'Farman the priest glossed this book in this manner (*þus*): may the Lord forgive him all his sins, if with God this can come to pass.'

From the foregoing it might be supposed that Farman glossed Matthew, and Owun the other three Gospels; but, as we have already seen, this is not quite true; for Farman's hand continues to Mark 2. 15, and is also found in John 18. 1–3. However, the character of his work changes after the end of Matthew; it is no longer a translation, but a gloss, following that of the Lindisfarne Gospels, and somewhat modifying it. It was Dr. Murray who discovered the true relation existing between the various parts, and published his results in the *Academy* for Nov. 21, 1874. His conclusions may be stated in his own words: 'Thus we really have in the Rushworth version three distinct portions: (1) Matthew, and John 18. 1–3, in which Farman gives us his independent Southern gloss; (2) Mark 1. 1–2. 15, in which he southernizes the Lindisfarne; and (3) Owun's—all the rest—which is Lindisfarne almost pure and simple. I suppose Farman was, say a Midland man, who set himself to gloss the Gospels in his monastery; when he had got to the end of Matthew, the brotherhood was joined by Owun, a Northumbrian, who seeing Farman's work, told him of the Lindisfarne gloss already in existence, and offered to borrow the MS. for him. On receiving it, Farman began to copy it in for his St. Mark, southernizing the grammar as he went on; but soon getting disgusted with this mere mechanical work which any copyist could do, he stopped short in the middle of a verse, and said, "See here, Owun, this is simple transcription which you can

---

[1] The second syllable represented by a Runic character.

do as well as I ; you go on copying this, and let me spend my time in some more original work." Owun obeyed, and simply followed the Lindisfarne through the rest of the book. Some such theory as this accounts satisfactorily for the whole circumstances. The three verses done by Farman again at the beginning of John 18 are very remarkable. Here in the midst of Owun's servile following of the Lindisfarne, the old glosser takes up the pen for an instant, and gives us three verses of fine idiomatic Saxon, not like his Mark a southernizing of the Lindisfarne, but like his Matthew, a totally independent version.'

Waring gives some criteria of the whole of Farman's work (pp. cvii–cviii), which deserve transcription : ' 1st. The portion glossed by Farman is marked by accentuation, which is entirely rejected by the second hand. 2nd. The handwriting and orthography are unmistakably different from those employed in the other three Gospels, and reappear only once again, in John 18. 1–3 ; a sufficient proof that the two scribes were contemporaries. 3rd. The letter *þ* is freely employed in the R. gloss as far as St. Mark (2. 15), while in the rest of that rendering, and throughout the gloss of L. [Lindisfarne], that character is wholly excluded, except in the contractions *þ* and *þte*: *k* also is freely used, *th* occasionally, *q* appears twice (Matt. 2. 1 ; 25. 39). 4th. *E* prevails in the inseparable particles *be* and *ge*, contrary to the itacism in the remainder of the gloss. 5th. The diphthongs *ea*, *eo* are of constant occurrence, their substitutes *a* and *e*, almost universal in the rest of the version, are here not prominent ; *ðanne* is also frequently written for *ðonne*. 6th. The regular form of the infinitive in *-an* is normally employed by this glossist, and the personal terminations *-st*, *-ð* generally supersede the North Anglian *-es*. 7th. Substantives of Rask's 1st declension are here given in their proper forms. 8th. Discipuli is usually rendered by *leorneras*, a vocable not employed in any other part of R., or in L. : here also, and nowhere else in both glosses, ecce is translated *sihðe*, a word used in the same sense by the glossist of the Cotton [Vespasian] Psalter.'

As bearing upon the question of dialect, it should be observed that Harewood, or Harwood, where Farman was priest, was in the West Riding of Yorkshire, nearly as far north as York, and therefore well within the Northumbrian territory. Moreover, the name Farmannus occurs in the Northumbrian *Liber Vitae* (p. 45), which anciently was accustomed to lie on the high altar of the Cathedral of Durham. However, Dr. Murray thinks that 'the Monastery of Harwood, in the West Riding of Yorkshire, was near enough the Mercian border to include inmates of Midland as well as Northern extraction' (*Athenaeum, ubi supra*). However, if Farman was a priest, there is no necessity for postulating a monastery at all ; and indeed I can find no evidence that there ever was a monastery at Harewood. On the other hand, the church of All Saints there is apparently of great antiquity ; see Allen, *History of the County of York*, London, 1831, vi. 137 ff.). However, in Jones' *History and Antiquities of Harewood* (1859), I find no note of any church before the Conquest. According to Dugdale's *Monasticon* (ed. Caley, Ellis, and Bandinel, vi. 201, 207) the rectory, lands, &c., of the church of All Saints were annexed to Bolton Priory after 1151. In the reign of Henry VIII the *firma rector'* amounted to £38 16s. 2½d. (Dugdale).

As to the date, Skeat's opinion is (*St. Mark*, p. xii): 'The gloss [i. e. both Farman's and Owun's parts] may be referred to the latter half of the tenth century.' On the other hand, Brown (see *infra*) would assign Farman's portion to a period antecedent to the decay of Latin studies to which Alfred testifies.

A glossary of Owun's part has been published by Lindelöf (*Acta Societatis Scientiarum Fennicae*, tom. xxii. no. 5), Helsingfors, 1897 ; see my notice in *Journal of Germanic Philology*, i. 264.

A grammatical treatise on the language of the Rushworth Matthew was published by Professor E. M. Brown, of the University of Cincinnati, in 1891–2. The work consists of two parts, the first treating of stem vowels, under the title *Die Sprache der Rushworth Glossen zum Evangelium Matthäus und der Mercische Dialect*, Göttingen, 1891 ; the second, discussing the remaining vowels, the consonants, and inflection, was published in English as *The Language of the Rushworth Gloss, &c.*, Göttingen, 1892.

On p. 81 of Part I, after pointing out certain phonetic peculiarities of his text, he adds : 'It is true that these peculiarities give no sharp outlines to Mercian, yet they sufficiently characterize it as a dialect, and not merely as Northumbrian modified by West Saxon scribes, or the reverse.' And on p. 90 of Part II he remarks : 'The evidence afforded by the vowel system . . . that the language of the gloss in question occupies an intermediate and independent position between the Northumbrian dialect on one side, and the dialects of Wessex and Kent on the other, is still further confirmed by the preceding examination.' This view must accordingly be accepted as valid, in the existing state of our knowledge, for the translation of Matthew.

The editions of the Rushworth Gloss are by Stevenson and Waring, and by Skeat; for these see under the Northumbrian Gloss above. The latter contains a collation of the Rushworth Latin text with that of the Lindisfarne. Besides, the Gospel of Mark, Latin and Old English, was edited by Bouterwek in his *Screadunga*, pp. 31–65. Matt., chaps. 2 and 3, were reprinted by Kluge, *Angelsächsisches Lesebuch* (Halle, 1888), pp. 35–40; Matt., chaps. 6–8, by Sweet, *Second Anglo-Saxon Reader* (Oxford, 1887), pp. 125–151 (alternately with the Northumbrian gloss); Matt. 25. 31–46 in my *First Book in Old English* (second edition, Boston, 1895), pp. 260–262.

The Lord's Prayer is as follows: 'Fæder ūre, þū þe in heofunum earð, bēo gehālgad þīn noma. Cume tō þīn rīce. Weorþe þīn willa, swā-swā on heofune, swilce on eorþe. Hlāf ūserne (*vel* ūre) dæghwæmlicu (*vel* instondenlice) sel ūs tō-dæge. And forlēt ūs ūre scylde, swā-swā wē ōc forlōten þǣm þe scyldigaþ[1] wið ūs. And ne gelāt (*vel* gelǣde) ūs in costunge[2], ah gelēse ūs of yfle.'

THE WEST SAXON GOSPELS.—These are supposed to date from about the last decade of the tenth century. Three of the MSS.— the Corpus, the Bodley, and the Cotton Otho—are thought to be nearly coeval with the translation; the others are later. There is no clue to the authorship of the version. In the best MS., the Corpus, there stands at the end of Matthew's Gospel this note: 'Ego Ælfricus scripsi hunc librum in Monasterio Baðþonio et dedi Brihtwoldo preposito' (figured in Astle, *Origin and Progress of Writing*, tab. xx. 7). Nothing further is known of this Ælfric, nor of Brihtwold. This entry, taken in conjunction with the fact that the MS. contains certain legal documents connected with Bath —though these are considerably later—renders it *possible* that the version, as well as this particular copy, was executed at or near Bath.

There are in all seven MSS., to which the approximate dates, according to conjecture, are here assigned:

1000. MS. CXL (formerly S. 4) of the Library of Corpus Christi College, Cambridge; known as Corp.

---

[1] MS. '·at.'   [2] MS. 'constungœ.'

1000. MS. Bodley 441 (formerly NE. F. 3. 15) of the Bodleian Library, Oxford ; known as B.

1000. MS. Cotton Otho C. 1 of the British Museum ; known as C.

1000–1050. The Lakeland fragment of four leaves, in the Bodleian Library, Oxford ; known as L.

1050. MS. Ii. 2. 11 of the Cambridge University Library ; known as A.

1150. MS. Bibl. Reg. I., A. xiv of the Royal Library, British Museum ; known as Royal.

1175. MS. Hatton 38 (formerly 65) of the Bodleian Library, Oxford ; known as Hatton.

Facsimiles of the MSS., with description, may be found in Westwood, *Palaeographia Sacra*, Plate 45.

The genealogy of the MSS. may be thus indicated, according to Skeat, Preface to *St. Luke*, p. x :

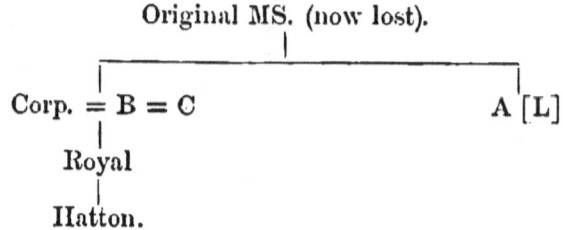

MSS. Corp. and A are complete. B has lost twelve leaves, which were doubtless supplied under the direction of Archbishop Parker, in the sixteenth century. The missing text was copied from the Corpus ; for details see Bright's *St. Luke*, pp. xv, xvi. C has lost the whole of Matthew, much of Mark, Luke 24. 7–29, and John 19. 27–20. 22, besides slighter injuries to these two Gospels. Royal and Hatton lack Luke 16. 14–17. 1. The Lakeland fragment, which is related to A, contains only John 2. 6–3. 34 ; 6. 19–7. 10.

The Gospels as a whole have been published five times : in 1571, 1665, 1842, 1865, and 1871–1887. The editions are these :

1571. John Foxe [and Archbishop Parker], *The Gospels of the Fower Euangelistes*. London.

'The text is a more or less faithful impression of MS. B, with some slight use of MS. A, from which the rubrics are also taken. There is an English text in the margin which is "chiefly from the Bishop's Translation only here and there accorded to the Saxon"'

(Bright, p. xvii). Probably Foxe furnished only the Introduction, addressed to Queen Elizabeth.

1665 (also issued at Amsterdam, 1684). Junius and Marshall, *Quatuor D. N. Jesu Christi Euangeliorum Versiones perantiquae duae, Gothica scil. et Anglo-Saxonica.* Dordrecht.
According to Marshall (p. 490), Junius had collated Foxe and Parker's edition with its original, the Bodley MS., and also with Corp., A, and Hatton, and had delivered his collation over to Marshall, with permission to accept or reject what he chose. Besides this collation, Marshall tells us (p. 491) that he himself made use of excerpts from the Lindisfarne and Rushworth Glosses. Where he adopts a reading from these glosses, however, he is careful to print it in square brackets. 'Marshall's notes contain many discriminating observations upon the version, and the relation of its readings with Latin texts, particularly with the Codex Bezae. He has also added observations upon the rubrics' (Bright, p. xviii).

1842. Benjamin Thorpe, *Ða Halgan Godspel on Englisc.* London.
'This edition is said to be based upon the Cambridge MS., with occasional readings from the Corpus MS. The Bodley and Cotton MSS. were also consulted. The short preface is very misleading, the estimates there given of the editions of Parker and Marshall cannot be allowed to be correct. . . . Mr. Thorpe's edition is really a revised edition of Marshall's, and should have been so described. It is a valuable and useful edition because it is free from mistakes, and because the readings can always be defended; but it is uncritical in the sense that the MS. authorities are not given' (Skeat, *St. Mark*, pp. xvi–xvii).
'This edition was reprinted by Louis F. Klipstein: New York, George P. Putnam, 1848; and from it Professor Hiram Corson introduced St. John's Gospel into his *Hand-Book of Anglo-Saxon and Early English*, New York, Holt and Williams, 1871' (Bright, p. xviii).

1865. Bosworth and Waring, *The Gothic and Anglo-Saxon Gospels in parallel columns, with the Versions of Wycliffe and Tyndale.* London.
'Bosworth takes his text from the Corpus MS., and in so far marks an advance upon the work of the preceding editors; the critical value of his edition is, however, impaired by the modification

of the orthography in accordance with MS. A, and by the lack of
apparatus to indicate the construction of the text and the variant
readings' (Bright, pp. xviii–xix).

1871–1887. Skeat, *The Holy Gospels in Anglo-Saxon, Northumbrian,
and Old Mercian Versions, synoptically arranged, with collations
exhibiting all the versions of all the MSS.* Cambridge.
This is the standard edition. The Corpus and Hatton texts—the
best and the latest—are printed side by side. At the foot of the
Corpus are given the variants from B, C, and A ; and at the foot
of the Hatton are those from the Royal.

The Matthew of this edition was originally edited by Kemble
and Hardwick, and printed, after the former's death, in 1858 ; but
this volume stood in need of revision, and Skeat's new edition was
published in 1887, the three preceding Gospels having appeared
respectively in 1871, 1874, and 1878.

Besides the foregoing, the Gospel of Luke has been separately
edited by James W. Bright (Oxford, 1893), with notes and
a glossary. To his Introduction, and to those prefixed by Skeat
to the several Gospels, especially Mark, the student is referred for
further details.

A grammatical study of the text of the twelfth century MSS.,
exhibiting its Kentish peculiarities, was published by Reimann as
Die Sprache der Mittelkentischen Evangelien, Berlin, 1883. A glossary
of the Corpus text—Latin-Old English, and Old English-Latin—has
been prepared by Dr. M. A. Harris, as part of a doctoral thesis
at Yale University, and is in course of publication.

In order to illustrate the difference between this version and
Ælfric's rendering, I subjoin extracts from the latter and the
Corpus text, expanding the contractions of the Corpus MS., and
otherwise editing it like the Ælfric. To these are subjoined
the Vulgate Latin. The first extract is Matt. 2. 21–23 (see p. 140
of this book) :

Corpus.	Ælfric.
Hē ārās ðā, and onfēng þæt cild and his mōdor, and cōm on Israhela land. Dā hē gehȳrde þæt Archelaus rīxode on Iudea þēode for ðæne Herodem, hē ondrēd þyder tō farende (A.	Hē ðā ārās, swā-swā se engel him bebēad, and ferode þæt cild mid þære mēder tō Israhela lande. Dā gefrān Ioseph þæt Archelaus rīxode on Iudea lande æfter his fæder Herode, and ne

faranne). And, on swefnum gemynegod, hē fērde on Galileisce dǣlas. And hē cōm þā and eardode on þǣre ceastre ðe is genēmned Nazareth, þæt wǣre gefylled þæt gecweden wæs þurh ðone wītegan : Forþāmðe hē Nazarenisc byð genēmned.

dorste his nēawiste genēalǣcan. Þā wearð hē eft on swefne gemynegod þæt hē tō Galilea gewende.... Þæt cild ðā eardode on þǣre byrig þe is gehāten Nazareth, þæt sēo wītegung wǣre gefylled, þe cwæð þæt hē sceolde bēon Nazarenisc gecīged.

Qui consurgens, accepit puerum et matrem eius, et venit in terram Israel. Audiens autem quod Archelaus regnaret in Iudaea pro Herode patre suo, timuit illo ire ; et admonitus in somnis, secessit in partes Galilaeae. ... Habitavit in civitate quae vocatur Nazareth, ut adimpleretur quod dictum est per prophetas: Quoniam Nazaraeus vocabitur.

The other is Matt. 26. 31–35 (see p. 173):

Corpus.

Þā sǣde se Hǣlend heom ; Ealle gē wurþað genntrēowsode on mē on þysse nihte. Hit ys āwriten : Þurh þæs hyrdes slege byð sēo heord tōdrǣfed. Witodlice, æfter-þām-þe ic of dēaþe ārīse, ic cume tō ðow on Galilea. Þā andwyrde Petrus him, and þus cwæð : Ðēah-þe hig ealle geuntrēowsion on þē, ic nǣfre ne geuntrēowsige. Þā cwæð se Hǣlend : Sōð ic secge þē þe on þissere nihte, ǣrþamþe cocc crāwe, þriwa þū wiðsæcst mīn. Ðā sǣde Petrus him : Witodlice, þēah-þe ic scyle sweltan mid þē, ne wiþsace ic þīn. Gelīce þām cwǣdon ealle ðā ōþre leorningenihtas.

Ælfric.

Eft se Hǣlend sǣde sōðlice his gingrum : Ealle gē mē ǣswiciað on ðissere ānre nihte. Hit is sōðlice āwriten : Ic ofslēa ðone hyrde, and ða scēp siððan sōna bēoð tostencte. Æfterðan-ðe ic ārīse of dēaðe gesund, ic ðow eft gemēte on Galileiscum earde. Þā andwyrde Petrus āna mid gebēote : Ic ðē nǣfre ne ǣswicige, ðēah-ðe ealle ōðre dōn. Drihten eft andwyrde ānrǣdlice Petre : Þū mē wiðsæcst ðriwa on ðissere nihte, ǣrðanðe se hana hafitigende crāwe. Petrus cwæð þæt hē nolde hine nǣfre wiðsacan, ðēah-ðe hē sceolde samod mid him sweltan ; and ealle ða ōðre ealswā cwǣdon.

Tunc dicit illis Iesus : Omnes vos scandalum patiemini in me in ista nocte. Scriptum est enim : Percutiam pastorem, et dispergentur oves gregis. Postquam autem resurrexero, praecedam vos in Galilaeam. Respondens autem Petrus, ait illi: Et si omnes scandalizati fuerint in te, ego nunquam scandalizabor. Ait illi Iesus: Amen dico tibi quia in hac nocte, antequam gallus cantet, ter me negabis. Ait illi Petrus: Etiamsi oportuerit me mori tecum, non te negabo. Similiter et omnes discipuli dixerunt.

The greater harmony and idiomatic ease of Ælfric's version will be readily apparent. The standard translation is evidently hampered by the striving after the utmost attainable literalness.

VERSIONS OF THE LORD'S PRAYER.—Separate versions of the Lord's Prayer are either given, or their existence noted, by Wanley, *Catalogus*, pp. 51, 160, 169, 197, 202, 221, 224, 239 (?), 240, 248. I give the first, from MS. Bodl. Jun. 121 (which is almost identical with the fourth, from MS. Cott. Tib. A. 3):

Eala ūre Fæder þe on heofonum eart. ā sȳ ðīn nama ǣcelice geblētsod. And ðīn rīce dōm ofer ūs rīxie symble. And ðīn willa gewyrðe, swā-swā on heofonum ꞇac swā on eorðan. Geunn ūs tō þissum dæge deghwamlices fōstres. And ūs gemildsa, swā-swā wē miltsiað þām þe wið ūs āgyltaþ. And ne lǣt ðū ūs costnian ealles tō swȳðe, ac ālȳs ūs fram yfele. Amen.

There are poetical elements in this version, and it seems, in its present form, rather late than early. For the other prose versions, see pp. lii, lix (cf. xxv), and my paper in the *Amer. Jour. Phil.*, xii. 59–66.

ÆLFRIC.—About this celebrated man, the foremost representative of Old English culture in the tenth and early eleventh century, there has been so much controversy, that it is worth while to present here the opinions respecting his life entertained by his most competent biographer, Dietrich, especially as they seem to have been unknown to the contributor of the article on Ælfric in the *Dictionary of National Biography*, a work which most persons will naturally, and justly, consider of the highest authority.

According to Dietrich, then (Niedner's *Zeitschrift für Historische Theologie* for 1856, pp. 242 ff.; cf. Wülker, *Grundriss zur Geschichte der Angelsächsischen Litteratur*, pp. 454–5), Ælfric was born about 955, since by 987 he was, according to his account, a priest, and a priest must be at least thirty years old. He was educated under Æthelwold (908?–984) in the Old Minster at Winchester, having probably entered it about the year 971, the same in which

Æthelwold translated the relics of St. Swithun to a new shrine in the Cathedral church. The mode of instruction, according to Ælfric in his *Life of Æthelwold*, was to interpret Latin books in Old English, to elucidate grammar and prosody, and to incite his pupils with stirring addresses. In this monastery he remained till after the death of Æthelwold, since Æthelwold's successor, Ælfheah (known as St. Alphege), sent him, at the request of Æthelmær, a wealthy and prominent thane or knight, to St. Peter's Monastery at Cernel, later Cerne Abbey on the Frome, five miles north of Dorchester, the capital of Dorsetshire; this fact rests upon Ælfric's own statement in his Preface to the *Homilies*. Here he probably remained from 987 to 989, engaged in the work of instructing the monks in the monastic rule as inculcated by Æthelwold, according to Dietrich's conjecture.

It was at Cerne that the thought of compiling and translating his *Homilies* from Latin sources occurred to him. To this he was moved 'not from confidence of great learning, but because I have seen and heard of much error in many English books, which unlearned men, through their simplicity, have esteemed as great wisdom; and I regretted that they knew not nor had not the evangelical doctrines among their writings, those men only excepted who knew Latin, and those books excepted which King Ælfred wisely turned from Latin into English, which are to be had. For this cause I presumed, trusting in God, to undertake this book, and also because men have need of good instruction, especially at this time, which is the ending of the world.'

The first volume of the *Homilies* was probably written in 889–890, and not completed till his return to Winchester, where he wrote the second volume (993–994), his *Grammar* (995), the *Lives of the Saints* (996), and the translation of the Pentateuch and Joshua (997–998). His so-called *Canons* were written at the command of Bishop Wulfsine, of Sherborne, who died in 1001, and probably fall within the three years preceding the last-named date. In the Preface to the *Homilies*, Ælfric calls himself 'monk and priest.' In the year 1005 his friend Æthelmær established a monastery at Egnesham, now Eynsham, five or six miles N.W. of Oxford, on the north bank of the Thames. King Æthelred's charter for the foundation, which may easily have been drawn up by Ælfric himself, is to be found in Kemble's *Codex Diplomaticus*, iii. 339–346. Sixteen abbots subscribe as witnesses, immediately after the names of the bishops. Of these the first is Ælfweard. Abbot of Glastonbury, the oldest monastery in England. The second is an Ælfric, and the fifth is again an Ælfric. One of these two must almost certainly have been our author, already installed as superior at Eynsham. One confirmation of this is furnished by the charter itself. In it Æthelmær prescribes that the present superior is to remain in office during his lifetime, and that afterwards the monks are to choose an abbot from among their own number; adding that he himself will live among them the rest of his days ('And ic wille ðære beon ofer hi ealdor ðe ðær nū is, ðā-hwīle-ðe his līf beo, and siððan, gif hit [for 'him'?] hwæt getȳmað, ðæt hī ceoson heom ealdor of heora gefērrædne ealswā hæra regol him tǣcð; . . . and ic mō sylfe wylle mid ðære gefērrædne gemǣnelice libban, and ðære āre mid him notian, ðā-hwīle-ðe mīn līf bīð'). From this quotation we gather two inferences: first, that the present superior was not from the number of the Eynsham monks; and secondly, that Æthelmær had selected the monastery as his dwelling-place till death. Considering, then, the intimacy which had existed for years between Æthelmær and Ælfric, we can hardly doubt that the new abbot had been brought from Winchester by the patron, and that the latter found in his friendship for Ælfric a strong ground for the choice of his future home. Another proof that Ælfric was first Abbot of Eynsham is to be found in the Preface to his extracts from Æthelwold's *De Consuetudine Monachorum*. This runs: 'Ælfricus Abbas Egneshamensibus fratribus salutem in Christo. Ecce video, vobiscum degens. vos necesse habere—quia nuper rogatu Æthelmeri ad monachicum habitum ordinati estis—instrui ad mores monachiles dictis aut scriptis. . . . Nec audeo omnia vobis intimare quae, in scola eius degens multis annis, de moribus seu consuetudinibus didici' (Wanley, *Catalogus*, p. 110). This proves, at all events, that Ælfric, when he wrote these extracts, was abbot; that he was living permanently (*degens*) with the Eynsham monks; that the brethren had but recently been inducted into the monastic life; and that this had been done at the instance of Æthelmær. What more obvious, then, than to conclude that he was *their* abbot, and that these extracts from the monastic rule were made in 1005 or 1006?

At Eynsham he must have written various works, which it is not necessary here to enumerate; and at Eynsham he must, according to Æthelmær's charter, have died as abbot. If he is the Abbot Ælfric who is one of the witnesses to the will of Ægelflæd (*Cod. Dipl.* iv. 304), he must still have been living in 1020 or 1021. The first four witnesses are 'Ægelnoð arcebiscop, and Wulfstan arcebiscop, ond Ælfun biscop on Lundene, and Ælfric abbot.' Now Ægelnoð (Æthelnoth) was not consecrated as Archbishop of Canterbury till Nov. 13, 1020; Wulfstan of York died in 1023; and Ælfhun's death is assigned to 1020. Hence the date of the charter must in any case fall between November 1020 and 1023; and, if the authority of Radulf for the demise of Ælfhun is to be accepted, yet within the year 1020. Further, Eynsham Abbey was under the protection of the Bishop of London; and, since Ælfric's name here stands next to that of the Bishop of London, and no other Abbot Ælfric is known at that date, it is most probable that Ælfric was the Abbot of Eynsham. This is the last notice that we have of him, so that the date of his death is uncertain. Dietrich places it, conjecturally, between 1020 and 1025.

It has been maintained that Ælfric was either the Archbishop of Canterbury (d. 1005), or the Archbishop of York (d. 1051). The following considerations seem decisive against both hypotheses.

It is sometimes asserted that Ælfric called himself bishop. He is indeed so called in MS. Bodl. Jun. 45, but this is a transcript made by Junius, and the superscription doubtless originated with him, since none of the original MSS. agree.

Subsequent writers of the eleventh and twelfth centuries know him only as Abbot Ælfric. Ælfric cannot have been the Archbishop of Canterbury for the following reasons:

1. Ælfric dedicates his *Vita Æthelwoldi* to Cenwulf as Bishop of Winchester. ('Ælfricus abbas, Wintoniensis alumnus, honorabili episcopo Kenulfo et fratribus Wintoniensibus salutem in Christo.') Now Cenwulf was bishop 1005-6, following Ælfheah, or Alphege, who was translated to the see of Canterbury after the death of Archbishop Ælfric in 1005. Hence the author Ælfric, who wrote the *Vita Æthelwoldi*, cannot be identical with Archbishop Ælfric.

2. Ælfric's *Pastoral Epistle for Archbishop Wulfstan* begins with these words: 'Ælfricus abbas Vulstano venerabili archiepiscopo salutem in Christo. Ecce paruimus vestrae Almitatis iussionibus transferentes Anglice duas epistolas.' Is this the

language of one archbishop to another, of the Archbishop of
Canterbury to the Archbishop of York? Yet Archbishop
Ælfric was elevated to the primacy in 995, and Wulfstan
obtained the see of York in 1002. Hence any address to
Wulfstan as archbishop must have been subsequent to 1002,
and could not have been written by an 'Abbot Ælfric' who had
been raised to the archiepiscopate seven years before Wulfstan.

3. Our Ælfric was a scholar and a man of peace; Ælfric of
Canterbury was a warrior, who left to the king his best ship
and sixty helmets and hauberks, and gave a ship to the
people of Kent, and another to the people of Wiltshire.

4. Archbishop Ælfric's will (*Cod. Dipl.* iii. 351-2) mentions
several places, but not one of them is associated with the
name of our Ælfric.

So far as to Canterbury. For these reasons Ælfric cannot have
been Archbishop of York :

1. Our Ælfric was born, as we saw, about 955. The Archbishop
of York died in 1051. Had they been the same person, the
archbishop would have died at the age of ninety-six, a circum-
stance of which some notice would probably have been taken.

2. William of Malmesbury relates that, by Ælfric of York's
advice, Hardacnut decapitated and threw into the Thames
the body of his brother Harold, and burned and ravaged the
city of Worcester in 1041 (*Gesta Pontificum,* l. iii. § 115):
'Ælfricus tempore Cnuti et Hardacnuti fuit ; habeturque in
hoc detestabilis, quod Hardacnutus eius consilio fratris sui
Haroldi cadavere defosso caput truncari, et infami mortalibus
exemplo in Tamensem proici iussit. Quin et Wigorniensibus
pro repulsa episcopatus infensus, auctor Hardacnuto fuit ut,
quia pertinatius illi exactoribus regiorum vectigalium obsti-
terant, urbem incenderet, fortunas civium abraderet.' In the
execution of the first-mentioned barbarity he himself took
part, according to Florence of Worcester. These counsels
would accordingly have emanated from a man of eighty-five
or more, the same who had written the *Homilies,* the *Lives of
the Saints,* the *Canons,* and the *Pastoral Epistle for Wulfstan!*
When he was forty he would have been mild and gentle ;
when verging upon ninety, fierce and intractable, a coun-
sellor of outrageous inhumanities !

3. The archbishop bore the cognomen Putta or Puttoc. This never appears in conjunction with the name of our Ælfric.

4. Learning and literature are never attributed to this archbishop.

5. Ralph de Diceto and Florence of Worcester assert that Ælfric of York passed to the archbishopric from a provost-ship at Winchester. Accordingly Wharton thinks (*Anglia Sacra*, i. 125 ff.) that he may previously have been abbot at Winchester. But our Ælfric was abbot—of some monastery —in 1005, as we have already seen. Was it at Winchester? There were three monasteries at Winchester: a nunnery, the Old Minster, and the New Minster. The nunnery may be disregarded; of the Old Minster the bishop, after Æthel-wold's time, was always the abbot (*Vita Æthelwoldi*, c. 7; cf. *Cod. Dipl.* iv. 170): and the abbot of the New Minster from 993 to 1015 was Ælfsige, who was succeeded by Ælfwine.

As the current authorities in English are so unsatisfactory with reference to the identity and career of Ælfric, it has seemed necessary to outline the foregoing, leaving it to the scholarly inquirer to consult Dietrich's essays. Our chief concern, how-ever, is with Ælfric in his character of Biblical translator, and it is that aspect of his varied activity to which our attention will now be turned.

According to Ælfric's own account, as given in his tract *On the Old Testament,* written probably about 1010, he had translated the Pentateuch, Joshua, Judges, Kings, Job, Esther, Judith, and the Maccabees. The following rendering will pre-sent the substance of his statements concerning his Biblical versions :—

'This epistle was written to an individual, but nevertheless it may do good to many.

'Ælfric the abbot sendeth friendly greeting to Sigweard at Eastheolon. . . . In all that narrative [the Pentateuch], which we indeed have translated into English, we may hear how the God of heaven spake, &c. . . . This [Joshua] I also translated into English some time ago for Earl Æthelweard. . . . This [Judges] any one can read that cares to, in that English book that I translated concerning these things. I thought that the wonderful narratives would convert your souls to God's will in earnest. . . . In the Books of Kings many kings are mentioned, about whom I also wrote certain books in English. . . . Concerning him [Job] I once translated into English a homily. . . . That [Esther] I translated into English briefly, after our manner. . . . It [Judith] is also rendered into English, after our manner, as an example to you men, that you should defend your country with weapons against an invading army. . . . I turned them [the two Books of Maccabees] into English : read, if you will, for your own good.'

Ælfric was concerned lest he should appear blameworthy to some for presenting sacred narrative in English, as appears from the Preface to his *Lives of the Saints*, written about 996 : 'Non mihi imputetur quod divinam scripturam nostrae lingue infero, quia arguet me praecatus multorum fidelium, et maxime Æþelwerdi ducis et Æðelmeri nostri, qui ardentissime nostras interpretationes amplectuntur lectitando' (Skeat's edition, p. 4).

Similarly, in his Preface to his translation of Genesis, written about 997, he explains why he hesitates to provide an English version, and in what manner he has proceeded in finally acceding to Æthelweard's request :

'Ælfric the monk sends greeting in all humility to Æthelweard the earl.

'When you desired me, honoured friend, to translate the Book of Genesis from Latin into English, I was loth to grant your request : upon which you assured me that I should need to translate only so far as the account of Isaac, Abraham's son, seeing that some other person had rendered it for you from that point to the end. Now, I am concerned lest the work should be dangerous for me or any one else to undertake, because I fear that, if some foolish man should read this book or hear it read, he would imagine that he could live now, under the new dispensation, just as the patriarchs lived before the old law was established, or as men lived under the law of Moses. At one time I was aware that a certain priest, who was then my master, and who had some knowledge of Latin, had in his possession the Book of Genesis : he did not scruple to say that the patriarch Jacob had four wives—two sisters and their two handmaids. What he said was true enough, but neither did he realize, nor did I as yet, what a difference there is between the old dispensation and the new. In the early ages the brother took his sister to wife : sometimes the father had children by his own daughter ; many had several wives for the increase of the people ;

and one could only marry among his kindred. Any one who now, since the coming of Christ, lives as men lived before or under the Mosaic law, that man is no Christian; in fact, he is not worthy to have a Christian eat with him. If ignorant priests have some inkling of the sense of their Latin books, they immediately think that they can set up for great teachers; but they do not recognize the spiritual signification, and how the Old Testament was a prefiguration of things to come, and how the New Testament, after the incarnation of Christ, was the fulfilment of all those things which the Old Testament foreshadowed concerning Christ and his elect. Referring to Paul, they often wish to know why they may not have wives as well as the apostle Peter; but they will neither hear nor know that the blessed Peter lived according to Moses' law until Christ came to men and began to preach his holy gospel, Peter being the first companion that he chose; and that Peter forthwith forsook his wife, and all the twelve apostles who had wives forsook both wives and goods, and followed Christ's teaching to that new law and purity which he himself set up. . . . We say in advance that this book has a very profound spiritual signification, and we undertake to do nothing more than relate the naked facts. The uneducated will think that all the meaning is included in the simple narrative, while such is by no means the case. . . . We dare write no more in English than the Latin has, nor change the order except so far as English idiom demands. Whoever translates or teaches from Latin into English must always arrange it so that the English is idiomatic, else it is very misleading to one who does not know the Latin idiom. . . . Now I protest that I neither dare nor will translate any book hereafter from Latin into English; and I beseech you, dear earl, not to urge me any longer, lest I should be disobedient to you, or break my word if I should promise. God be gracious to you for evermore. Now in God's name I implore, if any one should transcribe this book, that he will strictly follow the copy, since I cannot help it if an inaccurate scribe introduces corruptions. In such case he does it at his own risk, not mine; and the careless copyist does much harm, unless he corrects his mistakes.'

The book which he has translated with least abridgment is Genesis; but even here he has made considerable omissions, many of them no doubt in accordance with the views expressed above. Dietrich has subjected these omissions to a critical examination, and thus characterizes them (Niedner's *Zeitschrift* for 1855 pp. 495–6):

'In the first place, he omits nearly all the lists of names, such as those in Gen. 10; 11. 10–26; 22. 20–24; 25. 1–4; the dukes and kings of chap. 36; the numbers of the tribes, Num. 1. 20–44; 2. 1–31; and chap. 26; the names of the resting-places, chap. 33; the descriptions of the borders, chap. 34; and those of the boundaries as given in Joshua, chaps. 13–22, where ten chapters are condensed into a few lines. Next, those poetical passages which are most difficult of comprehension: the Blessing of Jacob, Gen. 49. 2–27; Moses' Song by the Red Sea, Exod. 15. 1–19; Balaam's parables, Num. 23 and 24; the Blessing of Moses, Deut. 33 (while Moses' easier Song, Deut. 32, is given); the Song of Deborah, Judges 5. His other omissions are partly smaller passages involving repetitions, e.g. Gen. 7. 13–16, 22; 8. 14, 19, &c.; or details which do not affect the general course of the narrative, like Gen. 24. 12–14, 16–60; then the circumstantial descriptions of the tabernacle and the priestly garments, Exod. 24. 12–29. 8; 35. 4–40; and the greater part of the individual Levitical precepts, Lev. 12–18; Num. 4–10. 28; chaps. 27–30.'

Dietrich thinks he has detected a difference between the language of the first twenty-five chapters of Genesis and that of the rest of the so-called Heptateuch, with the exception of Numbers, which again has Ælfric's peculiarities. He therefore believes that the portion which least resembles Ælfric was originally translated by another hand, and only revised by Ælfric.

Editions of the Pentateuch, Joshua, Judges, and Job, are as follows:—

Thwaites, *Heptateuchus, &c.* (see p. lxxx). Oxford, 1698.

Grein, *Bibliothek der Angelsächsischen Prosa*, Erster Band. Cassel and Göttingen, 1872.

The Job is an abbreviated form of one of the Homilies in Thorpe's collection (vol. ii. no. 35), and the portions translated from the Bible will be found, arranged in the Biblical order, in the present volume, pp. 103–110.

The Kings consists only of a homily, a mere epitome of passages from these books; the extracts relate to Saul, David, Ahab, Jehu, Hezekiah, Manasseh, and Josiah. It has been published by Skeat in *Ælfric's Lives of Saints*, vol. i. (E. E. T. S. 82), no. xviii. (pp. 384–412, alternate pages).

The Esther and Judith are published in Assmann's *Angelsäch-sische Homilien und Heiligenleben* (*Bibliothek der Angelsächsischen Prosa*, iii), Kassel, 1889, the Esther occupying pp. 92–101, and the Judith pp. 102–116.

The Maccabees comprises an abridgment of 1 Macc. 1. 1–64 ; 2 and 3 ; 4. 1–54 ; 5 ; 6. 1–7 ; 8. 1–17 ; 9. 1–22, 28–73 ; 10–16 ; 2 Macc. 3 ; 6. 18–31 ; 7 ; 9. 1–11 ; 10. 24–38 ; 12. 39–45. It is printed in *Lives of the Saints*, vol. ii. (E. E. T. S. 94), no. xxv (pp. 66–120, alternate pages).

The MS. of the so-called Heptateuch—the Pentateuch, Joshua, and Judges—from which Thwaites' edition was derived, is Bodl. Laud. Misc. 509, formerly E. 19 (Wanley, p. 67). Other MSS. are Ii. 1. 33 of the University Library, Cambridge, containing the first twenty-four chapters of Genesis (W. 162) ; Cott. Otho B. 10, containing from Gen. 37 to the end of that book (W. 192) ; Cott. Claud. B. 4, the Pentateuch and Joshua (W. 253) ; Bodl. Jun. 23, containing Judges only (W. 39) ; besides a sixteenth-century copy, probably made by Archbishop Parker's order, of the first twenty-five chapters of Genesis (W. 151), and certain fragments in a Lincoln Cathedral MS. (W. 305). Facsimiles of portions of the Laud and Cotton (Claud.) MSS. are to be found in Westwood, *Palaeographia Sacra*, Plate 39, and of the Cotton MS. in the *Palaeo-graphical Society Facsimiles*, Series I, vol. ii, Plates 71, 72, and in Astle, tab. xx. 6.

The homily on Kings is found in two MSS. : Bodl. Jun. 23 (W. 39), and Cott. Jul. E. 7 (W. 188).

The Job is found in Bodl. NE. F. 4. 12 (W. 16) ; in two MSS. of the University Library, Cambridge, Gg. 3. 28, and Ii. 1. 64 (W. 159, 164); and in Cott. Vespasian D. 14 (W. 205). Thwaites' edition, however, is based upon none of these, but upon a copy made by William L'Isle, Bodl. Laud. E. 381, formerly E. 33 (W. 100). That in Thorpe's edition of the *Homilies* is from MS. Gg. 3. 28 of the Cambridge University Library (W. 159), the first of the two mentioned above.

The Esther is edited by Assmann from L'Isle's copy, no original MS. being known to exist. This copy is Bodl. Laud. E. 381 (see under Job).

The Judith is edited by Assmann from CCCC. Jul. 303, formerly

S. 17 (W. 137), and Cott. Otho B. 10 (W. 192). In the former the end of the Judith is lost ; of the latter, which suffered in the fire of 1731, only two leaves are preserved, containing lines 62–123 and 384–445 of Assmann's edition.

The homily on the Maccabees is extant in five MSS. : CCCC. 198, formerly S. 8 (W. 127) ; CCCC. 302, formerly S. 17 (W. 137) ; Cott. Julius E. 7, which also contains the Kings (W. 189) ; Cott. Vitellius D. 17 (W. 208) ; MS. Ii. i. 33 of the University Library, Cambridge (W. 164). Of these the Vitellius D. 17 ends at l. 29. Skeat prints the Julius E. 7, with various readings from the others.

To exhibit the discrepancy between Ælfric's renderings in different places, I subjoin the version of Gen. 22. 4–13, as given in this volume, p. 83, and that from his independent translation (Thwaites, pp. 29–30 ; Grein, pp. 61–62) :

Homilies.

Efne, ða-ða hē ðære dūne gene[a]læhte, þā cwæð hē tō his cnihtum : Andbīdiað hēr ; ic and þis cild willað ūs gebiddan æt þære stōwe þe ūs God geswutelode. Isaac þā bær wudu tō forbærnenne ða offrunge, and Abraham hæfde him on handa fȳr and swurd. Isaac ðā befrān ðone fæder, and cwæð : Efne, hēr is fȳr and wudu, mīn fæder ; hwær is sēo offrung? Abraham andwyrde : Mīn bearn, God foresceawað him sylfum þære onsægednysse offrunge. Hwæt, ðā Abraham, ða-ða hī tō ðære stōwe cōmon, geband his lēofan sunu, and his swurd ātēah, þæt hē hine Gode geoffrode. Efne, ða Godes engel clypode of heofonum, and mid hluddre stemne cwæð : Abraham, ne āstrece ðū ðīne hand

Genesis.

Þā hig þā dūne gesāwon, þær-þær hig tō sceoldon tō ofslēanne Isaac, þā cwæð Abraham tō þām twām cnapum þus : Anbīdiað ēow hēr mid þām assum sume hwīle ; ic and þæt cild gāð unc tō gebiddenne, and wē syððan cumað sōna eft tō ēow. Abraham þā hēt Isaac beran þone wudu tō þære stōwe, and hē sylf bær his swurd and fȳr. Isaac þā āxode Abraham his fæder : Fæder mīn, ic āxige hwær sēo offrung sig ; hēr is wudu and fȳr. Him andwyrde se fæder : God foresceawað, mīn sunu, him sylf þā offrunge. Hig cōmon þā tō þære stōwe þe him geswutelode God, and hē þær weofod ārērde on þā ealdan wīsan, and þone wudu gelōgode, swā-swā hē hyt wolde habban tō his suna bærnytte, syððan hē

bufon ðām cilde, nē him nāne
dare ne gedō ; nū ic oncnēow
þæt ðū God ondrǣdst, and þū
ne ārodest þīnum āncennedan
suna for his hǣse. Þā beseah
Abraham underbæc, and ðǣr
stōd ān ramm betwux þām
brēmelum, getīged be ðām hornum. Hē ðā genam ðone ramm,
and Gode geoffrode for ðām
cilde.

ofslagen wurde. Hē geband þā
his sunu, and his swurd ātēah,
þæt hē hyne geoffrode on þā
ealdan wīsan. Mid-þām-þe hē
wolde þæt weorc begynnan, þā
clipode Godes engel ārdlīce of
heofenum: Abraham. Hē andwyrde sōna. Se engel him cwæð
þā tō : Ne ācwell þū þæt cild, nē
þīne hand ne āstrece ofer his
swūran. Nū ic oncnēow sōðlīce
þæt þū ondrǣtst swȳðe God, nū
þū þīnne āncennedan sunu woldest ofslēan for him. Þā beseah
Abraham sōna underbæc, and
geseah þǣr ānne ramm betwux
þām brēmelum be þām hornum
gehæft. And hē āhefde þone
ramm tō þǣre offrunge, and hyne
þǣr ofsnāð, Gode tō lāce, for his
sunu Isaac.

. . . Vidit locum procul. dixitque ad pueros suos : Expectate hic
cum asino ; ego et puer illuc usque properantes, postquam adoraverimus revertemur ad vos. Tulit quoque ligna holocausti, et imposuit
super Isaac filium suum ; ipse vero portabat in manibus ignem et
gladium. Cumque duo pergerent simul, dixit Isaac patri suo :
Pater mi. At ille respondit : Quid vis, fili ? Ecce, inquit, ignis et
ligna ; ubi est victima holocausti ? Dixit autem Abraham : Deus
providebit sibi victimam holocausti, fili mi. Pergebant ergo
pariter, et venerunt ad locum quem ostenderat ei Deus, in quo
aedificavit altare, et desuper ligna composuit ; cumque alligasset
Isaac filium suum, posuit eum in altare super struem lignorum.
Extenditque manum et arripuit gladium, ut immolaret filium
suum. Et ecce, angelus Domini de coelo clamavit, dicens :
Abraham, Abraham. Qui respondit : Adsum. Dixitque ei : Non
extendas manum tuam super puerum, neque facias illi quidquam ;
nunc cognovi quod times Deum, et non pepercisti unigenito filio
tuo propter me. Levavit Abraham oculos suos, viditque post
tergum arietem inter vepres haerentem cornibus, quem assumens
obtulit holocaustum pro filio.

My friend and former pupil, Dr. Frank H. Chase, has recently found in MS. Ii. 1. 33 of the Cambridge University Library a literal translation from the Vulgate of Genesis 4, 5, 10, 11, 23, 24. 1-22, which is to be printed without delay in Herrig's *Archiv*.

POETICAL TRANSLATIONS.

For the poetical part of the Paris Psalter, which apparently belongs here, see pp. xli ff.

Sweet thinks that the Kentish Psalm is of the tenth century. See p. xx.

JUDITH.—This poem consists of 350 lines, and immediately follows the *Beowulf* in MS. Cotton Vitellius A. 15 of the British Museum. The portion of the Apocryphal book paraphrased is mostly included ·between 8. 33 and 16. 1 inclusive, the chief portions being indicated in my edition, pp. xxxiv-xxxvi. The order of events is not that of the original narrative. Many transpositions have been made in the interest of condensation, and for the purpose of enhancing the dramatic liveliness of the story. Besides, the poet has not scrupled to add embellishments of his own invention. His art, under the four heads of Selection, Arrangement, Amplification, and Invention, is discussed at length in my edition, pp. xxxvii-xlii.

'The most discrepant dates have been assigned to our poem. On the one hand, Stephens and Hammerich would attribute it to Cædmon, which would fix the inferior limit of the composition at A. D. 680. Ebert (*Allg. Gesch. der Literatur des Mittelalters im Abendlande*, iii. 24 ff.), without naming an author, refers its origin to the closing decades of the seventh century, and expressly declines to accept Kluge's view, as stated below. Ten Brink says (*Early Eng. Lit.* p. 50): "The majority of the works mentioned arose probably during the eighth, or in the beginning of the next century; including also the *Exodus*, the *Daniel*, and the *Judith*." E. Groth (*Composition und Alter des Altenglischen Exodus*, Berlin. 1883), basing his conclusion upon the comparative frequency in different poems of the definite article, and of the weak adjective when no article precedes, associates *Judith* with *Byrhtnoth*. Kluge, writing later in the same year (*Beiträge*, ix. 448-9), approves of the methods originated by Lichtenheld and adopted by Groth, and adds other tests according to which *Judith* would belong to the tenth century. These are, passing over the verbal correspondences between *Judith* and *Byrhtnoth*, which are discussed below, the sporadic use of rime, and certain transgressions of the metrical rules observed in earlier poems. Luick, who investigates the metre of *Judith* in Paul and Braune's *Beiträge*, vol. xi, is of the same opinion. The treatment of middle vowels, together with the frequency of expanded lines, leads him to the conclusion (pp. 490–1) that *Judith* is a comparatively late poem. Vigfusson and Powell, *Corpus Poeticum Boreale*, I. lv–lvi, seem also to regard it as late, and would apparently assign it to the tenth century. Their words are: "The *Brunanburh Lay* is book poetry of the same type as the later bits in the *English Chronicle*. It has several lines almost identical with lines in *Judith*. . . . *Judith* is a Christian epic, also of the long modified style, composed by a bookman, who, however, knew and used snatches of good old verse."' Thus far I had written in 1887, and then proceeded to discuss the arguments for the various dates (pp. xv–xxxiv of my edition). My conclusion was reached in these words: 'Not earlier than Cynewulf, and not later than the year 937– to this point our reasonings have conducted us. What follows is more conjectural, but perhaps not wholly extravagant or fantastic.' I then proceeded to outline a hypothesis, according to which the poem *might* have been composed on the occasion of the return to England of Æthelwulf, Alfred's father, with his second wife, Judith, the daughter of Charles the Bold. Ælfric, speaking of his own prose translation of *Judith*, said that it had been done 'as an example to you men, that you should defend your country with weapons against an invading army' (*On the Old Testament*). Thwaites, in the first edition of the poem (1698), described our *Judith* as 'scriptum quo tempore Dani apud nos grassarentur.' Accordingly, since in 856 the Danes, after repeated invasions and alternate successes and defeats, appear to have ceased, for eight years, to harry England, I suggested the provisional theory: 'The poem of *Judith* was composed, in or about the year 856, in gratitude for the deliverance of Wessex from the fury of the heathen Northmen, and dedicated, at once as *epinikion* and *epithalamion*, to the adopted daughter of England.' I ended my discussion with these words: 'This theory appears, better than any hitherto propounded, to harmonize with all the relevant facts; and may perhaps be allowed to stand until superseded by a better.'

In 1892 T. Gregory Foster published his *Judith : Studies in Metre, Language, and Style, with a view to determining the date of the Old English Fragment and the Home of its Author* (Strassburg). This consists, for the most part, of an amplified restatement of the matter contained in my edition, but presents at least one novelty in the form of a new hypothesis regarding the occasion upon which the poem was composed, and the royal name with which it should be associated. As to the limits of the period within which the poem was written, 800–937, Foster entirely agrees with me. He dissents, however, from my conjectures respecting Queen Judith, and frames a theory of his own, which, after a few preliminary observations, he thus states : 'History, then, indicates Mercia as the possible home for our poet at this time, and still more so when we take the following into account. After 895 Mercia had time and opportunity ·to husband her resources and strength. The death of Æthelred in 910 left Æthelflæd queen of Mercia, or as the *Chronicle* calls her " Myrcena hlæfdige." She was in the truest sense "Lady of the Mercians," for through her extraordinary energy the "Five Boroughs," formerly part of the Mercian kingdom, were recovered. Æthelflæd then is Mercia's Judith, for she by no ordinary strategy, we are told, raised her kingdom and people to their old position. She, like the Hebrew Judith, abandoned the older strategy of raid and battle, not indeed to murder the Danish chief, but to build fortresses and beleaguer her enemies. Æthelflæd is then a suitable and worthy heroine to have stirred a contemporary poet to his theme. In this estimation of her we are confirmed by William of Malmesbury in his *Gesta Regum Anglorum*. The passage quoted below presents us with a picture readily suggesting a Judith : "pavor hostium," "immodici cordis foemina," "virago potentissima," "non mediocre momentum partium," all these are united with that eminently characteristic "favor civium." This suggestion would place our poem between the years 915 and 918 or soon after, during which period she obtained her greatest victories, dying in the last-named year. Our other results agree admirably with this date.'

Up to the present, then, it may be regarded as settled that the *Judith* was composed between 800 and 937 : but whether in Wessex or Mercia, whether in 856 or 918, whether to celebrate the stepmother of King Alfred or his daughter, Queen Judith or Queen Æthelflæd, must be left to the decision of the individual scholar, at least until it has been decided beyond all question by future investigation. As bearing on this, however, it may be well to remember that Æthelflæd must have been nearly fifty years of age when she died in 918, and that it must then have been at least thirty-eight years since her marriage ; so that 'elf-bright damsel' (*ides ælfscīnu*), 'maid of the Creator' (*Scyppendes mægð*), 'the bright maiden' (*sēo beorhte mægð*), &c., if interpreted as complimentary references to her, can scarcely be considered so appropriate as if they were referred to a bride of twelve summers or thereabouts. Perhaps, though, it would be going too far to insist upon the personal application to either queen of such expressions. In any case, considering the uncertainty which exists regarding the date of much of the Old English poetry, the interval which separates the years 856 and 918 is gratifyingly small, especially when one bears in mind the comparatively recent attribution of the *Judith* to the seventh century.

With reference to the dialect, I said in my edition (p. xv): 'The mixture of dialectic forms seems to indicate that a Northern original passed through one or more hands, and that the last scribe, at all events, belonged to the Late West Saxon period.' Similarly Foster (p. 49): 'Our MS. is therefore a copy from a West Saxon original. This however does not lead us far ; we have yet to see whether there are forms in the MS. indicating that our poem was at some time transcribed into West Saxon, from an original in another dialect. Such forms there are ; they are few in number, but all point to an Anglian original.' Again he says (p. 89): 'We must remember that although our poem is for the most part preserved in West Saxon dialect, there are in it distinct traces of Anglian forms which the transcriber probably overlooked. There is nothing characteristically Northumbrian in these, that is not also Mercian.' It will be observed that these indications to the effect that the poem was originally composed in Anglian dialect appear to favour Foster's theory of the circumstances under which the poem was written. On the other hand, it might be urged that the Anglian dialect being the one in which English poetry had first flourished, it would be natural that it should become, in some sense, the hieratic language of verse, and that even West Saxon poets should, for that reason, occasionally employ forms of which their memories were full. As bearing on this point, it must be remembered that the undoubtedly

Anglian forms in the poem are comparatively few. As an experiment, I turned the poem into the dialect of the late Northumbrian Gospels (cf. p. xliii), and in this form it will be found in my edition (pp. 75–85). Metrical observations on this Northumbrianized version were published in the *Transactions of the American Philological Association*, **xx.** (1889), 175–176.

The poem was first published at Oxford in 1698 : Edward Thwaites, *Heptateuchus, Liber Job, and Evangelium Nicodemi; Anglo-Saxonice. Historiae Judith Fragmentum; Dano-Saxonice.* Since then it has been ten times included in anthologies and collections, and twice published separately, besides the reproduction of extracts. The two separate editions are by L. G. Nilsson, Copenhagen, 1858, and by myself, Boston (U. S. A.), 1888 ; second edition, 1889 ; student's edition, abridged, 1894. The full title of my edition is : *Judith, an Old English Epic Fragment, edited with Introduction, Facsimile. Translation, Complete Glossary, and various Indexes.*

The *Judith* has been three times translated into English, twice into German, and once into Swedish ; besides, there have been partial translations: into English, twice ; into German, twice ; into Danish, once ; and into Swedish, once. A bibliography will be found in my edition, pp. 71–73.

As a specimen of the poem, we may take the paraphrase of chap. 13, *v.* 12, the relevant portion of which in the Vulgate is:

Et exierunt duae, . . . et transierunt castra, . . . venerunt ad portam civitatis.

Here the poem has (*vv.* 132–141):

> Ēodon ðā gǫgnum þanonne
> þā idesa bā   ellenþrīste,
> oð-þæt hīe becōmon   collenferhðe,
> ēadhrēðige mægð   ūt of ðām hęrige,
> þæt hīe sweotollīce   gesēon mihten
> þāre wlitegan byrig   weallas blīcan,
> Bethuliam. Hīe ðā bēahhrodene
> fēðelāste   forð ōnettan,
> oð hīe glædmōde   gegān hæfdon
> tō ðām wealgate.

SOME BIBLICAL QUOTATIONS

IN

OLD ENGLISH PROSE WRITERS

KING ALFRED'S VERSION

OF

GREGORY'S PASTORAL CARE

GENESIS.

3. 14. On ðīnre wambe ǫnd on ðīnum brēostum ðū scealt snīcan. C. P. 311[1].

4. 4, 5. ... ðæt Dryhten besāwe tō Abele ǫnd tō his lācum, ǫnd nolde tō Caine nē tō his lācum. Ðā wearð Cain swīðe [swīð(e) hrædlice] ierre, ǫnd hnipode ofdūne. C. P. 234.

9. 1, 2. Ǫnd ēac Dryhten cwæð tō Noe ǫnd tō his bearnum : Weahsað gē ǫnd mǫnigfāldiað, ǫnd gefyllað eorðan ; ǫnd ēower ęge ǫnd brōga sīe ofer āll [ealle] eorðan nīetenu. C. P. 108.

18. 20. ... ðætte swīðe wǣre gemanigfālðod[2] Sodomwara hrēam ǫnd Gomorwara. C. P. 427.

GENESIS.

3. 14. Super pectus tuum gradieris (*Greg. sec. Ital.* Pectore et ventre repes).

4. 4, 5. Respexit Dominus ad Abel, et ad munera eius ; ad Cain vero, et ad munera illius (*Greg.* eius), non respexit. Iratusque est Cain vehementer, et concidit vultus eius.

9. 1, 2. Benedixitque Deus Noe et filiis eius, et dixit ad eos (*Greg.* Et cum Noe Dominus filiisque eius diceret): Crescite et multiplicamini, et replete terram ; et terror vester ac tremor sit super cuncta animalia terrae.

18. 20. Clamor Sodomorum et Gomorrhae multiplicatus est.

---

[1] Odd numbers after C. P., and pp. 302-308, refer to the Hatton MS., as printed in Sweet's edition ; this is cited only where there is a gap in the Cotton MS.

[2] *Read* 'gemanigfāldod.'

19. 20. Hēr is ān lȳtele burg swīðe nēah, ðǣr ic mæg mīn feorh on genęrian. Hīo is ān lȳtel, ǫnd ðēah ic mæg ðǣron libban. C. P. 399.

19. 21. Ðīnre bēne ic wille nū onfōn, ǫnd for ðīnre bede ic ne tō-weorpe ðā burg ðe ðū forespr[i]csð. C. P. 399.

28. 12, 13. ... for ðǣre gesihðe þe hē on ðǣm swefne geseah, þā hē æt ðǣm stāne slǣpte. Hē geseah āne hlǣdre stǫndan æt him on eorðan. Ōðer ęnde wæs uppe on hefonum, ǫnd æt ðǣm uferran ęnde Dryhten hlinode, ǫnd ęnglas stigon ūp ǫnd of-dūne on ðā hlǣdre. C. P. 100.

28. 18. Be ðǣm ēac Iacobus se hēahfæder, þā hē smirede ðone stān þe æt his hēafdum læg ... C. P. 100.

34. 1–3. ... ðæt Dina wǣre ūt gangende sceawian ðæs lǫndes wīf. Ðā hī ðā geseah Sihhem, Emmores sunu ðæs Ebreiscan, se wæs aldormǫn ðæs [lǫndes]; ǫnd ðā gelīcode hīo him, ǫnd hē hī genam nīedenga, ǫnd hire mid gehǣmde. Qnd ðā wæs his mōd gehæft mid ðǣm mǣdene, ǫnd hē ðā hī swā unrōte ōlec-cende tō him geloccode. C. P. 415.

‖ Sihhem, ðæs landes ealdorman, genīedde ðæt mǣden Dinan. C. P. 415.

‖ Sihhemes mōd wæs ðā gehæft tō Dinan. C. P. 415.

‖ ... ðætt[e] Sihhem Dinan līðelice ōlehte, ðā-ðā hē hī geunrōtsod hæfde. C. P. 415.

19. 20. Est civitas haec (*Greg.* hic) iuxta, ad quam possum fugere, parva, et salvabor in ea ; numquid non modica est, et vivet anima mea (*Greg. ins.* in ea) ?

19. 21. Ecce, etiam in hoc suscepi preces tuas, ut non subvertam urbem pro qua locutus es.

28. 12, 13. Viditque in somnis sca-lam stantem super terram, et cacumen illius tangens coelum, angelos quoque Dei ascendentes et descendentes per eam, et Dominum innixum scalae (*Greg. sum.* Hinc Iacob Domino desuper innitente, et uncto deorsum la-pide, ascendentes ac descen-dentes angelos vidit).

28. 18. Surgens ergo Iacob mane, tulit lapidem, quem supposuerat capiti suo, et erexit in titulum, fundens oleum desuper (*Greg.,* *cf. supra*).

34. 1–3. Egressa est autem (*Greg. om.* autem) Dina, filia Liae (*Greg. om.* filia Liae), ut videret mulieres regionis illius. Quam cum vidis-set Sichem filius Hemor Hevaci, princeps terrae illius, adamavit eam ; et rapuit, et dormivit cum illa, vi opprimens virginem. Et conglutinata est anima eius cum ea, tristemque delinivit blanditiis (*Greg.* blanditiis de-linivit).

EXODUS.

13. 21. . . . hine lǣdde ðurh ðæt wēsten mid ðȳ fȳrenan swēore on nieht, ǫnd on dæg mid ðȳ swēore wolcnes. C. P. 304.

15. 6. Ðīn swīðre hand, Dryhten, gebræc ðīne fēond. C. P. 389.

16. 8. Hwæt is ēower murcung wið unc? Hwæt sint wit? Wið God gē dōð ðæt gē dōð. C. P. 200.

18. 14, 17–22. Be ðǣm ēac Moyses, . . . æt sume cirre Giethro his swēor . . . hiene tǣlde, ǫnd sǣde ðæt hē on ðyslicum [dyslicum] geswincum wǣre mid ðæs folces eorðlican ðēowote, ac lǣrde hiene ðæt hē gesętte ōðre for hiene tō dēmenne betweox ðǣm folce ymb hiern geflito, ðæt he wǣre ðæs þe frēora tō ongitonne ðā dīglan ǫnd ðā gāstlican ðing, ðæt hē meahte ðæt folc ðȳ wīslecor ǫnd ðȳ rǣdlicor lēran. C. P. 130.

21. 33, 34. . . . gif hwā ādulfe pytt, ǫnd ðonne forgīemelēasode ðæt hē hine betȳnde, ǫnd ðǣr ðonne befēolle on oððe oxa oððe esol, ðæt hē hine scolde forgieldan. C. P. 459.

EXODUS.

13. 21. Dominus autem praecedebat eos . . . per diem in columna nubis, et per noctem in columna ignis, ut dux esset itineris utroque tempore (*Greg. sum.* Unde Moyses, qui regente se Deo, deserti iter aerea columna duce pergebat . . .).

15. 6. Dextera tua, Domine, percussit inimicum (*Greg. sec. Ital.* Dextera manus tua, Domine, confregit inimicos).

16. 8. . . . Nos enim quid sumus? nec contra nos est murmur vestrum, sed contra Dominum.

18. 14, 17–22. Quod cum vidisset cognatus eius, omnia scilicet quae agebat in populo, ait: Quid est hoc quod facis in plebe? cur solus sedes, et omnis populus praestolatur de mane usque ad vesperam? At ille: Non bonam, inquit, rem facis; stulto labore consumeris et tu et populus iste qui tecum est; ultra vires tuas est negotium, solus illud non poteris sustinere. Sed audi verba mea atque consilia, et erit Deus tecum: Esto tu populo in his quae ad Deum pertinent, ut referas quae dicuntur ad eum, ostendasque populo ceremonias et ritum colendi, viamque per quam ingredi debeant, et opus quod facere debeant; provide autem de omni plebe viros potentes, . . . qui iudicent populum omni tempore; quidquid autem maius fuerit, referant ad te, et ipsi minora tantummodo iudicent, leviusque sit tibi, partito in alios onere (*Greg. sum.* Hinc Moses . . . Ietro alienigenae reprehensione iudicatur quod terrenis populorum negotiis stulto labore deserviat; cui et consilium mox praebetur ut pro se alios ad iurgia dirimenda constituat, et ipse liberius ad erudiendos populos spiritalium arcana cognoscat).

21. 33, 34. Si quis aperuerit cisternam et foderit, et non operuerit eam, cecideritque bos aut asinus

25. 11–15. Wyrc fēower hringas ælgyldene, ǫnd ūhōh hīe swīðe
fæste on ðā fēower hyrnan ðære earce; ǫnd hāt wyrcean
twēgen stǫngeas of ðǣm trēowe þe is hāten sethim, ðæt ne
wierð nǣfre forrotod; ǫnd befōh ūtan mid golde; ǫnd sting
ūt ðurh ðā hringas bī ðære earce sīdan, ðæt hīe mǫn mǣge
beran on ðǣm, ǫnd lǣt hīe stician ðǣron; ne tīo hīe mǫn
nǣfre of.   C. P. 168, 170.

‖ . . . sethim, ðæt nǣfre ne rotað.   C. P. 170.

‖ Ðā sāhlas is beboden ðæt sceoldon bīon mid golde be-
fangne.   C. P. 170.

‖ . . . ðæt hīe sculon simle stician on ðǣm hringum, ǫnd
nǣfre ne mōton him bēon ofātogene.   C. P. 170.

‖ . . . ðætte simle ðā ofergyldan sāhlas sceoldon stician on
ðǣm gyldnum hringum.   C. P. 170.

28. 8. Ðæt hrægl wæs beboden ðæt sceolde bīon geworht of purpuran, ǫnd of twibliium derodine, ǫnd of twispunnenum twīne
līnenum, ǫnd gerēnod mid golde, ǫnd mid ðǣm stāne iecinta
(iacincta II.).   C. P. 82.

‖ On ðæs sācerdes hrægle wæs tōēacan golde ǫnd iacincte
(iacincðe II.) ǫnd purpuran, dyrodine twēgra blēo.   C. P. 86.

‖ Forðon is beboden, tōēacan ðǣm twibléon gōdwębbe, ðæt
scile bēon twiðrāwen twīn on ðǣm mæssegierelan.   C. P. 86.

28. 21. On ðǣm selfan hrægle, þe hē on his brēostum wæg, wæs
ēac āwriten ðā naman ðāra twęlf hēahfædra.   C. P. 76.

28. 28, 29. On Arones brēostum sceolde bēon āwriten sīo racu

in eam, reddet dominus cisternae
pretium iumentorum (*Greg. sum.*
. . . ut is qui cisternam foderit, si
operire neglexerit, corruente in
ea bove vel asino, pretium reddat).

25. 11–15. Faciesque (*Greg.* Facies)
. . . quattuor circulos aureos, quos
pones per quattuor arcae angulos. . . . Facies quoque (*Greg.*
faciesque) vectes de lignis setim
(*Greg.* sethim), et operies eos
(*Greg. om.* eos) auro, inducesque
per circulos qui sunt in arcae
lateribus, ut portetur in eis; qui
semper erunt in circulis, nec
unquam extrahentur ab eis.

28. 8. Ipsa quoque textura et cuncta
operis varietas erit ex auro, et
hyacintho, et purpura, coccoque
bis tincto, et bysso retorta (*Greg.*
Recte etiam superhumerale ex
auro, hyacintho, purpura, bis
tincto cocco, et torta fieri bysso
praecipitur).

28. 21. Habebuntque nomina filiorum Israel; duodecim nominibus
caelabuntur. . . . (*Greg.* In quo
etiam rationali . . . ut duodecim
patriarcharum nomina descri-
bantur).

28. 28, 29. Et stringatur rationale
. . . vitta. . . . Portabitque Aaron
nomina filiorum Israel in ratio-

ðæs dōmes on ðǣm hrægle þe mǫn hāt 'rationale,' ǫnd mid nostlum gebunden. C. P. 76.

28. 30. Mǫn sceolde wrītan on ðǣm hrægle ðe Aron bær on his brēostum, ðonne hē innēode beforan Gode, ðā lāre ǫnd ðā dōmas, ǫnd ðā sōðfæstnesse. C. P. 78.

28. 33. Forðǣm wæs beboden Moyse ðæt se sācerd sceolde bīon mid bellum behangen. C. P. 92.

  ‖ Hit wæs āwriten ðæt ðæs sācerdes hrægl wǣre behǫngen mid bellum. C. P. 92.

  ‖ On ðæs sācerdes hrægle wǣron bellan hangiende. C. P. 92.

  ‖ On ðæs sācerdes hrægle sceoldon hangian bellan, ǫnd ongemǫng ðǣm bellum rēade apla. C. P. 94.

  ‖ . . . ðæt sceolde bēon on ðæs sācerdes hrægle ðā rēadan apla ongemang ðǣm bellum. C. P. 94.

28. 35. . . . ðæt hē sceolde, ingǫngende ǫnd ūtgǫngende beforan Gode tō ðǣm hālignessum, bēon gehīered his swēg, þȳlǣs hē swulte. C. P. 92.

  ‖ . . . ðæt se sācerd sceolde sweltan, gif se swēg nǣre of him gehīered ǣgðer ge ingǫngendum ge ūtgǫngendum. C. P. 92.

29. 5. . . . ðæt se sācerd sceolde bēon fæste bewǣfed on bǣm sculdrum mid ðǣm mæsselhrægle. C. P. 82.

29. 22, 27. *See* Lev. 7. 31, 32.

32. 6. Ðæt folc sæt, æt, ǫnd dranc, ǫnd siððan āryson, ǫnd ēodon him plegean. C. P. 309.

32. 26, 27. Sē ðe Godes ðegn sīe, gā hider ǫnd dō his sweord tō his hype; ǫnd gāð frǫm geate tō geate ðurh midde ðā ceastre;

---

nali iudicii super pectus suum. . . . (*Greg. sum.* . . . ut in Aaron pectore rationale iudicii vittis ligantibus imprimatur).

28. 30. Pones autem in rationali iudicii doctrinam et veritatem, quae erunt in pectore Aaron, quando ingredietur coram Domino, et gestabit iudicium filiorum Israel in pectore suo, in conspectu Domini semper.

28. 33. Deorsum vero, ad pedes eiusdem tunicae, per circuitum, quasi mala punica facies, . . . mixtis in medio tintinnabulis (*Greg. sum.* Hinc in sacerdotis

veste iuxta divinam vocem tintinnabulis mala punica coniunguntur; *for briefer phrases see Greg.* ch. 15).

28. 35. . . . ut audiatur sonitus quando ingreditur et egreditur sanctuarium in conspectu Domini, et non moriatur.

29. 5. Indues Aaron . . . superhumerali et rationali quod constringes balteo.

32. 6. . . . Sedit populus manducare et bibere, et surrexerunt ludere.

32. 26, 27. . . . Si quis est Domini (*Greg.* Domini est), iungatur mihi. . . . Ponat vir gladium super fe-

ǫnd ofslēa ǣlc mǫn his brōður, ǫnd his frēond, ǫnd his nīhstan.

C. P. 383.

32. 29. ... ðæt hiora hǫnda wǣron gehālgode Gode. C. P. 352.

34. 30 ff. *See* C. P. 458.

39. *See* Ex. 28.

LEVITICUS.

7. 31, 32. ... ðæt se sācerd scyle onfōn ðone swīðran bōgh æt
ðǣre offrunge, ǫnd sē sceolde brōon āsyndred frǫm ðǣm ōðrum
flǣsce. ... Ēac him mǫn sceolde sellan ðā brēost ðæs nēates,
tōðacan ðǣm bōge. C. P. 80.

15. 2. ... ðætte se wer, se ðrōwude oferflōwnesse his sǣdes, ǫnd
ðæt unnytlice āgute, ðæt hē ðonne wǣre unclǣne. C. P. 94.

19. 14. Ne cweðe gē nān lāð ðǣm dēafan. Ne screnc ðū ðone
blindan. C. P. 453.

21. 17–20. ... ðæt hē sceolde bēodan Arone þæt nān mǫn hiera
cynnes nē hiera hīoredes ne offrode his Gode nānne hlāf, nē
tō his ðēnunga ne cōme, gif hē ǣnig wam hæfde : gif hē blind
wǣre, oððe healt, oððe tō micle nosu hæfde oððe tō lȳtle, oððe
eft [tō] wō nosu, oððe tōbrocene hǫnda oððe fētt, oððe hoferede
wǣre, oððe torenīgge, oððe flēah hæfde on ēagan, oððe singale
sceabbas, oððe teter, oððe hēalan. C. P. 62, 64.

mur suum ; ite et redite de porta
usque ad portam per medium
castrorum ; et occidat unusquisque fratrem, et amicum, et proximum suum.

32. 29. ... Consecrastis manus vestras hodie Domino (*Greg.* ... Deo
manus dicta est consecrasse).

LEVITICUS.

7. 31, 32. ... Pectusculum autem
erit Aaron, et filiorum eius. Ar-
mus quoque dexter de pacifico-
rum hostiis cedet in primitias
sacerdotis (*Greg. sum.* Hinc divina
lege armum sacerdos in sacrificium et dextrum accipit et sepa-
ratum. ... Cui in esu quoque
pectusculum cum armo tribuitur).

15. 2. Vir qui patitur fluxum seminis (*Greg.* qui fluxum seminis
patitur), immundus erit.

19. 14. Non maledices surdo, nec
coram caeco pones offendiculum. ...

21. 17–20. Loquere ad Aaron : Homo de semine tuo per familias,
qui habuerit maculam, non offeret
panes (*Greg. ins.* Domino) Deo
suo, nec accedet ad ministerium
eius : si caecus fuerit, si claudus,
si (*Greg. ins.* vel) parvo vel grandi
vel (*Greg.* et) torto naso, si fracto
pede, si manu, si gibbus, si lippus,
si albuginem habens in oculo, si
iugem scabiem, si impetiginem
in corpore, vel herniosus (*Greg.*
ponderosus).

NUMBERS.

10. 29-31. We willað nū faran tō ðǣre stōwe ðe God ūs gehāten
hæfð; ac far mid ūs, ðæt wē mægen wel dōn, forðǣmðe God
hæfð surðe wel gehāten Israhela folce. Dā andsuarode hē
him, ǫnd cuæð: Ic nelle mid ðē faran, ac ic wille faran tō
mīnre cȳððe, ǫnd tō ðǣm lǫnde ðe ic on geboren wæs. Dā
andswarade him Moyses: Lā, ne forlǣt ūs, ac bēo ūre
lāðteow; ðu cans eal ðis wēsten, ǫnd wāsð hwǣr wē wīcian
magon. C. P. 304.

22. 20 ff. *See* C. P. 254.

23. 10. Geweorðe mīn līf swelce ðissa ryhtwīsena, ǫnd geweorðe
mīn ende swelce hira. C. P. 423.

25. 6 ff. *See* C. P. 352.

DEUTERONOMY.

19. 5, 6. Gif hwā gǫnge bilwitlice mid his frīend tō wuda, trēow
tō ceorfanne, ǫnd sīo æcs ðonne āwint of ðǣm hielfe, ǫnd swǣ
ungewealdes ofslihð his gefēran, hē ðonne sceal flēon tō ānra
ðāra ðrēora burga þe tō frīðstōwe gesette sint, ǫnd libbe, ðȳlæs
hwelc ðāra nīhstena ðæs ofslægenan for ðǣm sāre his ǣhte, ǫnd
hiene ðonne gefō ǫnd ofslēa. C. P. 164, 166.

25. 4. Ne forbinde gē nō ðǣm ðerscendum (ðyrstendum H.) oxum
ðone mūð. C. P. 104.

NUMBERS.

10. 29-31. ... Proficiscimur ad locum quem Dominus daturus est
nobis; veni nobiscum, ut bene-
faciamus tibi, quia Dominus bona
promisit Israeli. Cui ille respondit (*Greg.* Cui cum respondisset
ille): Non vadam tecum, sed revertar in terram meam, in qua
natus sum. Et ille: Noli, inquit
(*Greg.* illico adiunxit: Noli), nos
relinquere; tu enim nosti in quibus locis per desertum castra
ponere debeamus, et eris ductor
noster.

23. 10. ... Moriatur anima mea
morte iustorum, et fiant novissima
mea horum similia.

DEUTERONOMY.

19. 5, 6. ... Abiisse cum eo (*Greg.*
Si quis abierit cum amico suo)
simpliciter in silvam ad ligna
caedenda, et in succisione lignorum (*Greg.* et lignum) securis
fugerit manu, ferrumque lapsum
de manubrio amicum eius percusserit, et occiderit, hic ad unam
supradictarum urbium confugiet,
et vivet, ne forsitan (*Greg.* forte)
proximus eius, cuius effusus est
sanguis, dolore stimulatus (*Greg.*
doloris stimulo) persequatur et
apprehendat cum, si longior via
fuerit (*Greg. om.* si ... fuerit), et
percutiat animam eius. ...

25. 4. Non ligabis os bovis terentis
in area fruges tuas.

25. 5–7, 9, 10. Gif hwā gefare ǫnd nān bearn ne gestrīne, gif hē brōður lǣfe, fō sē tō his wīfe. Gif hē ðonne bearn ðǣrbīe gestrīene, ðonne cęnne hē þæt ðǣm gefarenan brēðer þe hīe ǣr āhte. Gif hē ðonne ðæt wīf wille forsacan, ðonne hrǣce hīo him on ðæt nęb foran, ǫnd his mǣgas hiene anscōgen ōðre fēt, þæt mǫn mǣge siððan hātan his tūn ðæs anscōdan tūn. C. P. 42.

32. 42. Mīn sweord itt flǣsc. C. P. 378.

1 SAMUEL.

2. 9. Dryhten gehilt his hāligra fēt, ǫnd þā unrihtwīsan siccettað on ðǣm ðīstrum. C. P. 64.

2. 29. Ðū weorðast ðīne suna mā ðonne mē. C. P. 122.

4. 17, 18. *See* C. P. 122.

9. 21. *See* C. P. 34.

10. 22. *See* C. P. 34.

15. 17. Ðā ðū ðē selfum ðūhtest unwēnlic, ðā ic ðē gesętte eallum Israhelum tō hēafde. C. P. 112 ; cf. C. P. 34.

16. 23. Ðonne him se wieðerwearda gāst on becōm, ðonne gefēng Dauid his hearpan, ǫnd gestilde his wōððrāga mid ðǣm gligge. C. P. 182.

‖ Forðǣm ðonne se unclǣna gāst becōm on Saul, Dauid ðonne mid his sange gemetgode ðā wōððrāge Saules. C. P. 184.

25. 5–7, 9, 10. Quando habitaverint fratres simul, et unus ex eis absque liberis mortuus fuerit, . . . accipiet eam frater eius, . . . et primogenitum ex ea filium nomine illius appellabit. . . . Sin autem noluerit accipere uxorem fratris sui, . . . mulier . . . tollet calceamentum de pede eius, spuetque in faciem illius. . . . Et vocabitur nomen illius in Israel, Domus discalceati (*Greg.* Hinc Moyses ait, ut uxorem fratris sine filiis defuncti superstes frater accipiat, atque ad nomen fratris filios gignat; quam si accipere forte renuerit, huic in faciem mulier exspuat, unumque ei pedem propinquus discalciet, eiusque habitaculum domum discalceati vocet).

32. 42. Gladius meus devorabit (*Greg.* manducabit) carnes.

1 SAMUEL.

2. 9. Pedes sanctorum suorum servabit, et impii in tenebris conticescent. . . .

2. 29. . . . Magis honorasti filios tuos (*Greg.* Honorasti filios tuos magis) quam me. . . .

15. 17. . . . Nonne cum parvulus esses (*Greg.* esses parvulus) in oculis tuis, caput in tribubus Israel factus es (*Greg.* caput te constitui in tribubus Israel) ?

16. 23. Igitur quandocumque spiritus Domini malus arripiebat Saul,

24. 4–8. Hit gelǫmp æt sumum cirre ðæt hē wæs gehȳd on ānum eorðscræfe mid his mǫnnum. Þā Saul hiene wolde sēcean uppe on ðǣm munte, ðā fōr hē forð bīe ðǣm scræfe ðe hē oninnan wæs, ǫnd hē his ðǣr nō ne wēnde. Đā gewearð hiene ðæt hē gecierde inn tō ðǣm scræfe, ǫnd wolde him ðǣr gān tō feltūne. Đā wæs ðǣrinne se ilca Dauid mid his mǫnnum, þe lange ǣr his ēhtnesse earfoðlice ðolode. Đā clipodon his ðegnas him tō, ǫnd hieno bǣdon, ǫnd geornlice lǣrdon ðæt hē hiene ofslōge. Ac hē him sōna ǫndwyrde, ǫnd him swīðe stiernlice stīerde, ǫnd cwæð ðæt hit nō gedafenlic nǣre ðæt hīe slōgen Gode gehālgodne kyning ; ǫnd ārās ððah ūp, ǫnd bestæl hiene tō him, ǫnd forcearf his mǫntles ǣnne lǣppan tō tācne ðæt hē his geweald āhte. C. P. 196.

|| Dauid cearf swīðe dīegellice swīðe lȳtelne lǣppan of Saules mǫntelle. C. P. 198.

|| Forðon hit is āwriten ðætte Dauid, ðā hē ðone lǣppan forcorfedne hæfde, ðæt hē slōge on his heortan, ǫnd swīðe swīðlice hrēowsode ðæt hē him ǣfre swā ungerisenlice geðēnian sceolde, ððah his ðegnas hiene lǣrdon ðæt hē hiene mid his sweorde slōge. C. P. 198.

|| Se ilca Dauid þe forbǣr þæt hē ðone kyning ne yflode þe hine on swā heardum wrǣce gebrōhte, ǫnd of his earda ādrǣfde, þā hē his wel geweald āhte on ðǣm scræfe, hē genam his loðan ǣnne lǣppan tō tācne þæt hē his gewāld āhte. C. P. 36.

David tollebat citharam, et percuticbat manu sua, et refocillabatur Saul, et levius habebat. . . . (*Greg. sum.* . . . quod cum Saulem spiritus adversus invaderet, apprehensa David cithara, eius vesaniam sedabat ; *Ib.* Cum ergo Saul ab immundo spiritu arripitur, David canente eius vesania temperatur).

24. 4–8. . . . Eratque ibi spelunca, quam ingressus est Saul ut purgaret ventrem; porro David et viri eius in interiore parte speluncae latebant. Et dixerunt servi David ad eum : Ecce dies de qua locutus est Dominus ad te : Ego tradam tibi inimicum tuum, ut facias ei sicut placuerit in oculis tuis. Surrexit ergo David, et praecidit oram chlamydis Saul silenter. Post haec percussit cor suum David, eo quod abscidisset oram chlamydis Saul. Dixitque ad viros suos : Propitius sit mihi Dominus, ne faciam hanc rem domino meo, christo Domini, quia christus Domini est. Et confregit David viros suos sermonibus, et non permisit eos ut consurgerent in Saul. . . . (*Greg.* Saul quippe persecutor, cum ad purgandum ventrem speluncam

24. 18. *See* C. P. 393.

25. 37. *See* C. P. 294.

2 SAMUEL.

2. 22, 23. Hit is āwriten ðæt Abner cwǣde tō Assaele: Gecier lā, ǫnd geswīc, ne folga mē, ðæt ic ðē ne ðyrfe (dyrre H.) ofstingan. Hē forhogde ðæt hē hit gehīerde, ǫnd nolde hiene forlǣtan; ðā ðȳdde Abner hiene mid hindewearde sceafte on ðæt smælðearme, ðæt hē wæs dēad.   C. P. 294.

7. 27. Ðīn ðēow hæfð nū funden his wīsdōm, ðæt is ðæt hē hiene gebidde tō ðē.   C. P. 272.

11. 2 ff. *See* C. P. 34, 36.

11. 17. *See* C. P. 393.

12. 1 ff. *See* C. P. 144, 184.

1 KINGS.

6. 7. Hit is gecweden ðætte þā stānas on ðǣm mǣran temple Salomonnes wǣron ǣr swā wel gefēgede, ǫnd swā emne gesnidene ǫnd gesmēðde, ǣr hīe mǫn tō ðǣm stęde brōhte þe hīe on standan sceoldon, ðætte hīe mǫn ęft sīððan on ðǣre hālgan stōwe swā tōsǫmne gesętte ðæt ðǣr nān mǫn ne gehīerde ne æhxe hlęm nē bītles swēg.   C. P. 252.

7. 23. *See* 2 Chron. 4. 2, 4, 6.

11. 4. *See* C. P. 393.

---

fuisset ingressus, illic cum viris suis David inerat, qui iam tam longo tempore persecutionis eius mala tolerabat. Cumque eum viri sui ad feriendum Saul accenderent, fregit eos responsionibus, quia manum mittere in christum Domini non deberet. Qui tamen occulte surrexit, et oram chlamydis eius abscidit. ... Post haec David percussit cor suum, eo quod abscidisset oram chlamydis Saul).

2 SAMUEL.

2. 22, 23. ... Locutus est Abner ad Assael (*Greg.* Asael, dicens): Recede, noli me sequi (*Greg.* persequi), ne compellar confodere te in terram ... Qui audire

contempsit, et noluit declinare; percussit ergo eum Abner aversa hasta in inguine, et transfodit (*Greg. ins.* eum), et mortuus est. ...

7. 27. ... Invenit servus tuus cor suum ut oraret te. ...

1 KINGS.

6. 7. Domus autem cum aedificaretur, de lapidibus dolatis atque perfectis aedificata est; et malleus, et securis, et omne ferramentum non sunt audita in domo cum aedificaretur (*Greg. sum.* Hinc est enim quod lapides extra tunsi sunt, ut in constructione templi Domini absque mallei sonitu ponerentur).

2 KINGS.

20. 13. . . . þā hē lǣddē þā ęlðēodgan ǣrendracan on his māðmhūs, ǫnd him geīewde his goldhord. C. P. 38.

21. *See* C. P. 38.

25. 1c. Kōka āldormǫn tōwearp ðā burg æt Hierusalem. C. P. 310.
‖ Ðǣra kōka ealdormǫn tōwierpð ðā weallas Hierusalem. C. P. 310.

2 CHRONICLES.

4. 2, 4, 6. Beforan ðǣm temple stōd ǣren cēac onuppan twęlf ǣrenum oxum, ðætte þā męn, þe intō ðǣm temple gān woldon, meahton hiera hǫnda ðwēan on þǣm męre. Se cēac [ðac] wæs suǣ micel ðæt hē oferhelede ðā oxan ealle, būtan þā hēafdu totodun ūt. C. P. 104.

19. 2. 3. Ðū fultumodest ðǣm ārlēasum, ǫnd ðū gemęngdest ðīnne frēondscipe wið ðone ðe hatode God, ǫnd mid ðǣm ðū geearnode Godes irre, ðǣr ðā gōdan weorc ǣr nǣren on ðē mētte; ðæt wæs ðæt ðū ādydest ðā bearwas of Iudea lǫnde. C. P. 354.

JOB.

10. 15. Gif ic ryhtwīs wæs, ne āhōf ic mē nā forðȳ, ǫnd ðēah ic eom gefylled mid broce ǫnd mid iermðum. C. P. 252.

38. 36. Hwā sealde kokke wīsdōm ? C. P. 459.

2 KINGS.

20. 13. . . . Ostendit eis domum, . . . et omnia quae habere poterat in thesauris suis.

25. 10. Et muros Ierusalem in circuitu destruxit omnis exercitus Chaldaeorum (*Grey. sec. LXX.* Princeps cocorum destruxit muros Ierusalem; *ib.* Cocorum igitur princeps muros Ierusalem dejecit), qui erat cum principe militum.

2 CHRONICLES.

4. 2, 4, 6. Mare etiam fusile. . . . Et ipsum mare super duodecim boves impositum erat . . . ; posteriora autem boum erant intrinsecus sub mari. . . . In mari sacerdotes lavabantur (*Grey. sum.* Unde et ante fores templi ad abluendas ingredientium manus mare aeneum, id est luterem, duodecim boves portant; qui quidem facie exterius eminent, sed ex posterioribus latent).

19. 2, 3. . . . Impio praebes auxilium, et his qui oderunt Dominum amicitia iungeris, et idcirco iram quidem Domini merebaris; sed bona opera inventa sunt in te, eo quod abstuleris lucos de terra Iuda. . . .

JOB.

10. 15. . . . Si iustus (*Grey. ins.* fuero), non levabo caput, saturatus afflictione et miseria.

38. 36. . . . Quis dedit gallo intelligentiam ?

41. 16 (Vulg. 7). Ælces fisces sciell bið tō ōðerre gefēged, ðæt ðǣr ne mæg nān ōðm ūt betweox.   C. P. 360.

41. 23 (Vulg. 14). His flǣ[s]ces lima clifað ǣlc on oðrum.   C. P. 360.

41. 34 (Vulg. 25). . . . ðæt hō gesīo ǣlce ofermētto, sō is kyning ofer eall ðā bearn oferhȳde.   C. P. 110.

‖ . . . ðæt hō sīe kyning ofer ealle ðā oferhygdan bearn.   C. P. 300.

PSALMS[1].

1. 1. . . . ðæt hō nō ne sǣte on ðǣm wōlberendan setle.   C. P. 435.

23. 4. Ðīn gierd ǫnd ðīn stæf mē āfrefredan.   C. P. 124.

30. 6. Ic wēnde on mīnum wlęncum ǫnd on mīnum forwanan, ðā ic wæs full ǣgðer ge welona ge gōdra weorca, ðæt ðæs nǣfre ne wurde nān ęnde.   C. P. 465.

30. 7. Dryhten, ðā āhwyrfdes ðīnne ǫndwlitan frǫm mē, ðā wearð ic gedrēfed.   C. P. 465.

32. 5. Ic wille sęcgan ongēan mē selfne mīn unryht, Dryhten, forðǣm ðā forgēafe ðā ārlēasnesse mīnre heortan.   C. P. 419.

34. 19. Swīðe manigfealde sint ryhtwīsra mǫnna earfeðu.   C. P. 252.

38. 6. Ic eom gebīgged, ǫnd ǣghwǫnon ic eom gehīened.   C. P. 66.

40. 9, 10. Dryhten, ðā wāst ðæt ic ne wirne mīne welora, ǫnd ðīne ryhtwīsnesse ic ne dīgle on mīnre heortan; ðīne hǣlo ǫnd ðīne ryhtwīsnesse ic sæcge.   C. P. 380.

41. 7. Una uni coniungitur, et ne spiraculum quidem incedit per eas.

41. 14. Membra carnium eius cohaerentia sibi. . . .

41. 25. Omne sublime videt; (*Greg. ins.* et) ipse est rex super universos filios superbiae.

PSALMS.

1. 1. . . . In cathedra pestilentiae non sedit.

23. 4. . . . Virga tua et baculus tuus, ipsa me consolata sunt.

30. 6. Ego autem dixi in abundantia mea: Non movebor in aeternum.

30. 7. . . . Avertisti faciem tuam a me, et factus sum conturbatus.

32. 5. . . . Dixi: Confitebor (*Greg.* pronuntiabo) adversum me iniustitiam meam (*Greg.* iniustitias meas) Domino; et tu remisisti impietatem peccati (*Greg.* cordis) mei.

34. 19. Multae tribulationes iustorum. . . .

38. 6. . . . Curvatus sum usque in finem (*Greg. sec. LXX.* Incurvatus sum, et humiliatus sum usquequaque). . . .

40. 9, 10. . . . Ecce labia mea non prohibebo; Domine, tu scisti (*Greg.* cognovisti). Iustitiam tuam non abscondi in corde meo; veritatem tuam et salutare tuum dixi. . . .

---

[1] The Psalms are quoted according tô the numbering of the English versions, which differs, as is well known, from that of the Vulgate and that employed by Gregory and Alfred.

40. 12. Mīn mōd ọnd mīn wīsdōm mē forlēt. C. P. 272.

49. 7, 8. Hē ne sealde Gode nānne mēdsceat for his sāule, nē nænne geðingscēat wið his miltse. C. P. 338.

51. 3. Mīne misdǣda brōð simle beforan mē. C. P. 413.

51. 9. Āhwyrf, Dryhten, ðīn ēagan frọm mīnum synnum. C. P. 413.

51. 17. Ðā gedrēfedan heortan ọnd ðā gecāðmēddan, ne forsihð hī nǣfre Dryhten. C. P. 425.

54. 3. Ęlðīodige ārison wið mē, ọnd wunnon wið mē, (ọnd H.) swīðe strọnge wǣron ðā þe mīn ēhton. C. P. 374.

55. 15. Hī sculon gān libbende on hęlle. C. P. 429.

60. 5. Gehǣle mē ðīn sīo swīðre. C. P. 389.

69. 23. Sīn hira ēagan āðīstrode þæt hī ne gesīon, ọnd hira hrycg simle gebigged. C. P. 28.

73. 18. Ðū hīe geniðrades, ðā hī hī selfe ūpāhōfon. C. P. 391.

75. 4. Ic cwæð tō ðǣm u(n)ryhtwīsum : Ne dō gē unryhtwīslice ; ọnd cwæð tō ðǣm ðe ðǣr syngedon : Ne hę[b]be [gē] tō ūp ēowre hornas. C. P. 425.

78. 34. Ðonne God hīe slōg, ðonne sōhton hīe hiene. C. P. 250.

78. 61. Dryhten geðafode ðæt hiora mægen ọnd hiora cræft wǣre gehæft, ọnd hiora wlite wǣre on hira fēonda họnda. C. P. 465.

80. 5. God ūs drẹncte swīðe gemetlice mid tēarum. C. P. 413.

95. 2. Wuton cuman ǣr his dōme andettende. C. P. 415.

---

40. 12. ...Cor meum dereliquit me.

49. 7, 8 .... Non dabit Deo placationem suam, et (*Greg.* nec) pretium redemptionis animae suae.

51. 3. ... Peccatum (*Greg. sec. Ital.* delictum) meum contra (*Greg.* coram) me est semper.

51. 9. Averte faciem tuam (*Greg.* oculos tuos) a peccatis meis....

51. 17. ... Cor contritum et humiliatum, Deus, non despicies (*Greg.* spernit).

54. 3. Quoniam alieni insurrexerunt adversum (*Greg.* in) me, et fortes quaesierunt animam meam. ...

55. 15. ... Descendant in infernum viventes. ...

60. 5. Salvum (*Greg. ins.* me) fac

dextera tua. ...

69. 23. Obscurentur oculi eorum ne videant, et dorsum eorum (*Greg.* illorum) semper incurva.

73. 18. ... Deiccisti eos dum allevarentur.

75. 4. Dixi iniquis : Nolite inique agere ; et delinquentibus : Nolite exaltare cornu.

78. 34. Cum occideret eos, quaerebant (*Greg.* tunc requirebant) eum. ...

78. 61. Et tradidit in captivitatem virtutem eorum, et pulchritudinem eorum in manus inimici.

80. 5. ... Potum dabis (*Greg.* dedit) nobis in lacrymis in mensura.

95. 2. Praeoccupemus (*Greg.* Praeveniamus) faciem eius (*Greg.* Domini) in confessione. ...

105. 44, 45. Hē him sealde rīcu ōðerra kynrena, ǫnd manigra folca gestrēones hīe wīeoldon, tō ðon ðæt hē his ryhtwīsnesse gehēolden, ǫnd his ǣ sōhten. C. P. 391.

108. 6. Gehǣle mē ðīn sīo swīðre. C. P. 388.

112. 9. Sō tōdǣlð his gōd, ǫnd sęlð ðearfum ; his ryhtwīsnes wunað on ēcnesse. C. P. 334, 336.

113. 6. . . . ðætte Dryhten lōcige tō ðǣm ēaðmōdan. C. P. 298.

119. 97. Lōca, Dryhten, hū swīðe ic lufige ðīne ǣ ; ealne dæg ðæt bið mīn smēaung. C. P. 168.

119. 106. Ic swōr, swā-swā ic getiohhod hæfde, ðæt ic wolde gehealdan ðīne dōmas ǫnd ðīne ryhtwīsnesse, Dryhten. C. P. 465.

119. 107. Ic eom gehēned ǣghwǫnane ǫnd on ǣghwām, Dryhten ; ac gecwuca mē æfter ðīnum wordum, Dryhten. C. P. 465.

120. 6, 7 (Vulg. 7). Ic lufode ðā þe sibbe hatedon ; ǫnd ðonne ic him cīdde, ðonne oncūðon hīe mē būtan scylde. C. P. 354.

129. 3. Dā synnfullan bytledon uppe on mīnum hrycge. C. P. 152.

132. 9. Sīn ðīne sācerdas gegirede mid ryhtwīsnesse. C. P. 92.

138. 6. . . . ðætte Dryhten lōcige tō ðǣm ēaðmōdan. Dryhten ongitt swīðe feorran ðā hēahmōdnesse. C. P. 298, 300.

139. 17. Dryhten, suīðe suīðe sint geweorðode mid mē ðīne frīend, ǫnd swīðe is gestrangod hiera ealdordōm. C. P. 84.

139. 21, 22. Hū ne hatige ic ðā ealle, Dryhten, ðā þe ðē hatigað ? ǫnd for ðīnum fēondum ic āswand on mīnum mōde, ǫnd mid fulryhte hęte ic hē (hīe II.) hatode, forðǣm hīe wǣron ēac mīne fīend ? C. P. 352.

105. 44, 45. . . . Dedit illis (*Greg.* eis) regiones gentium, et labores populorum possederunt, ut custodiant iustificationes eius, et legem eius requirant.

108. 6. Salvum (*Greg. ins.* me) fac dextera tua. . . .

112. 9. Dispersit, dedit pauperibus ; iustitia eius manet in saeculum saeculi (*Greg.* in aeternum). . . .

113. 6. Et humilia respicit. . . .

119. 97. Quomodo dilexi legem tuam, Domine! tota die meditatio mea est.

119. 106. Iuravi, et statui custodire iudicia iustitiae tuae.

119. 107. Humiliatus sum usquequaque, Domine ; vivifica me se-

cundum verbum tuum.

120. 7. Cum his qui oderunt pacem eram pacificus; cum loquebar illis, impugnabant me gratis.

129. 3. Supra dorsum meum fabricaverunt peccatores. . . .

132. 9. Sacerdotes tui induantur iustitiam. . . .

138. 6. . . . (*Greg. ins.* Deus) humilia respicit, et alta a longe cognoscit.

139. 17. Mihi autem nimis honorificati sunt amici tui ; nimis confortatus est principatus eorum.

139. 21, 22. Nonne qui oderunt te, Domine (*Greg.* te oderunt, Deus), oderam (*Greg. ins.* illos), et super iniuicos tuos tabescebam ? Per-

140. 9. Ðæt geswinc hiera āgenra welora hīe geðryscð (geðrycð H.). C. P. 239.

140. 11. Se ofersprīoca wer, ne wierð hū nǣfre geryht nō gelǣred on ðisse worlde. C. P. 278.

141. 3. Gesęte, Dryhten, hierde mīnum mūðe, ǫnd ðā duru gestæððignesse. C. P. 274.

150. 4. Lofiað God mid tympanan, ǫnd on choro. C. P. 346.

PROVERBS.

1. 24–26. Ic ēow clipode ǣr tō mē, ac gē mē noldon æt cuman ; ic rǣhte mīne hǫnd tō ēow, nolde ēower nān tō lōcian ; ac gū forsāwon eall mīn geðeaht, ǫnd lēton ēow tō gīemelīste, ðonne ic ēow cīdde : hwæt sceal ic ðonne būton hliehhan ðæs, ðonne gē tō lore (lose H.) weorðað, ǫnd habban mē ðæt tō gamene, ðonne ēow ðæt yfel on becymð ðæt gē ēow ǣr ondrēdon ? C. P. 246, 248.

1. 28. Ðonne hīe tō mē clipiað, ðonne nylle ic hīe gehīeran ; on ūhton hīe ārīsað, and mē sēceað, ac hīe mē ne findað. C. P. 248.

1. 31. Hīe etað ðone wæsðm hiera āgnes weges, ðæt is ðonne, ðonne hīe bēoð gefyllede mid hiera āgnum geðeahte. C. P. 306.

1. 32. Giongra mǫnna dolscipe hī ofslihð, ǫnd dysigra mǫnna orsorgness hī fordēð. C. P. 387.

3. 16. . . . ðætte on his swīðran handa wǣre lang līf, ǫnd on his winestran wǣre wela ǫnd wyrðmynt. C. P. 389.

3. 28. . . . ðæt mǫn ne scyle cweðan tō his frīnd : Gā, ǫnd cum tō-

fecto odio oderam illos, et (Greg. om. et) inimici facti sunt mihi.

140. 9. . . . Labor labiorum ipsorum operiet eos.

140. 11. Vir linguosus non dirigetur in terra (Greg. super terram). . . .

141. 3. Pone, Domine, custodiam ori meo, et ostium circumstantiae labiis meis.

150. 4. Laudate eum in tympano, et choro. . . .

PROVERBS.

1. 24–26. . . . Vocavi, et renuistis ; extendi manum meam, et non fuit qui aspiceret ; despexistis omne consilium meum, et incre-

pationes meas neglexistis : ego quoque in interitu vestro ridebo, et subsannabo cum vobis id (Greg. om. id) quod timebatis advenerit.

1. 28. Tunc invocabunt me, et non exaudiam ; mane consurgent, et non invenient me.

1. 31. Comedent igitur (Greg. om. igitur) fructus viae suae, suisque consiliis saturabuntur.

1. 32. Aversio parvulorum interficiet eos, et prosperitas stultorum perdet illos.

3. 16. Longitudo dierum in dextera eius, et in sinistra (Greg. in sinistra vero) illius divitiae et gloria.

3. 28. Ne dicas amico tuo : Vade, et

morgen, ðonne selle ic ðe hwæthwugu, gif hē hit him ðonne
sellan mæge. C. P. 322, 324.

3. 32. . . . ðæt hē hæbbe his geðeaht ond his sundorspræce mid
ðæm bilwitum ond mid ðæm ānfealdum. C. P. 242.

4. 25. Læt simle gān ðīn eagan beforan ðīnum fōtum. C. P. 286.

5. 1, 2. Sunu mīn, ongiet mīnne wīsdōm ond mīnne wærscipe.
ond beheald ðīn eagan ond ðīnne earan tō ðæm, ðætte ðū mæge
ðīn geðōht gehealdan. C. P. 272.

5. 9–11. Ne læt ðū tō elðīodegum ðīnne weorðscipe, nē on ðæs
wælhrēowan hand ðīn gēar, ðȳlæs fremde men weorðen gefylled
of ðīnum geswince, ond ðīn mægen sīe on ōðres monnes geweald-
um, ond ðū ðonne sārgige forðæm on læst, ðonne ðīn līchoma
bīo tō lore gedōn, ond ðīn flæsc gebrosnod. C. P. 248.

‖ . . . ðæt mon ne selle his weorðscipe fremdum menn. C. P. 248.

‖ . . . ðæt fremde ne sceoldon bīon gefylde ūres mægenes,
ond ūre geswinc ne sceolde bīon on ōðres monnes onwālde.
    C. P. 250.

‖ . . . ðæt hē sārgige æt nīhstan, ðonne his līchoma ond his
flæsc sīe gebrosnod. C. P. 250.

5. 15–17. Drinc ðæt wæter of ðīnum āgnum mere, ond ðætte of
ðīnum āgnum pytte āflōwe, ond læt ðīne willas irnan wīde, ond
tōdæl hīe ; lǣd hīe giond ðīn land, ond gegierwe ðæt hīe irnen
bī herestrǣtum ; ond hafa hīe ðēah ðē ānum, ðȳlǣs elðīodige
hīe ne dǣlen wið ðē. C. P. 372.

‖ Læt forð ðīne wyllas, ond tōdǣl ðīn wætru æfter herestrǣtum. C. P. 372.

‖ Dēah ðū ðīn wætru tōdǣle, hafa hīe ðēah ðē self, ond ne
sele elðīodegum hiora nōwuht. C. P. 372.

‖ . . . ðæt mon scolde his wætru tōdǣlan, ond ðēah him self
eall habban. C. P. 374.

reverterc, (*Greg. ins.* et) cras dabo
tibi, cum statim possis dare.
3. 32. . . . Cum simplicibus sermo-
cinatio eius.
4. 25. . . . Palpebrae tuae praece-
dant gressus tuos.
5. 1, 2. Fili mi, attende ad (*Greg.
om.* ad) sapientiam meam, et pru-
dentiae meae inclina aurem tuam,
ut custodias cogitationes. . . .
5. 9–11. Ne des alienis honorem

tuum, et annos tuos crudeli, ne
forte implcantur extranei viribus
tuis, et labores tui sint in domo
aliena, et gemas in novissimis,
quando consumpseris carnes tuas
(*Greg. om.* tuas) et corpus
tuum. . . .
5. 15–17. Bibe aquam de cisterna
tua, et fluenta putei tui ; deri-
ventur fontes tui foras, et in
plateis aquas tuas (*Greg. om.* tuas)

6. 1, 2. Sunu mīn, gif ðū hwæt gehātest for ðīnne frēond, ðonne hafast ðū ōðrum męn (*om.* ōðrum męn II.) ðīn węd gescald, ǫnd ðū bist ðonne gebunden mid ðǣm wordum ðīnes āgnes mūðes, ǫnd gehæft mid ðīnre āgenre sprǣce. C. P. 192.

6. 3, 4. Dō, mīn sunu, swā ic ðē lǣre ; ālīes ðē selfne, forðon ðū eart on borg gegān (begān II.) ðīnum frīend. Ac iern nū ǫnd ōnette, āwęce hiene ; ne geðafa ðū ðīnum ēagum ðæt hīe slāpige, nē ne hnappigen ðīne brǣwas. C. P. 192.

‖ Ne slāpige nū ðīn ēagan (ēage II.), nē ne hnappigen ðīne brǣwas. C. P. 192.

6. 6. Dū slāwa, gā ðē tō ǣmethylle, ǫnd gīem hū hīe dōð, ǫnd leorna ðǣr wīsdōm. C. P. 190, 192.

6. 12–14. Āworpen mǫn bið ā unnyt, ǫnd gǣð mid wō mūðe, ǫnd bīcneð mid ðǣm ēagum, ǫnd trit mid ðǣm fōt, ǫnd sprīcð mid ðǣm fingre, ǫnd on wōre heortan bið yfel dōnde, ǫnd on ǣlce tīd sāweð wrōhte. C. P. 356.

10. 9. . . . ðætte sē libbe getrēowlīce se þe bilwitlīce libbe. C. P. 242.

10. 19. Ne bið nǣfre sīo ofersprǣc būton synne. C. P. 278.

11. 25. Dæs mǫnnes sāul þe wel sprīcð, hīo bið āmæst ; ǫnd swā-hwā-swā ōðerne ðręncð (dręncð II.), hē wirð self ofordruncen. C. P. 380.

11. 26. Sē þe his hwǣte hȳt, hiene wiergð ðæt folc. C. P. 376.

14. 30. . . . ðætte ðis flǣsclīce līf sīe ǣfst, ǫnd hē sīe ðǣre flǣsclican heortan hǣlo, ǫnd ðēah ðā bān for him forrotigen [1]. C. P. 234.

divide ; habeto eas solus, nec sint alieni participes tui.

6. 1, 2. Fili mi, si spoponderis pro amico tuo, defixisti apud extraneum manum tuam, (*Greg. ins.* et) illaqueatus es verbis oris tui, et captus propriis sermonibus.

6. 3, 4. Fac ergo quod dico, fili mi, et temetipsum libera ; quia incidisti in manum proximi tui. Discurre, festina, suscita amicum tuum ; ne dederis somnum oculis tuis, nec dormitent palpebrae tuae.

6. 6. Vade ad formicam, o piger, et considera vias eius, et disce sapientiam.

6. 12–14. Homo apostata, vir inutilis, graditur ore perverso, annuit oculis, terit pede, digito loquitur, pravo corde machinatur malum, et omni tempore iurgia seminat.

10. 9. Qui ambulat simpliciter, ambulat confidenter. . . .

10. 19. In multiloquio non deerit peccatum. . . .

11. 25. Anima quae benedicit impinguabitur ; et qui inebriat, ipse quoque inebriabitur.

11. 26. Qui abscondit frumenta, maledicetur in populis. . . .

14. 30. Vita carnium, sanitas cordis ; putredo ossium, invidia.

[1] A curious mistranslation.

‖ . . . ðætte ðæt flæsclice líf síe ðære heortan hǽlo. c. p. 234.

‖ Ðæt is swíðe ryhte gecweden bī ðǽm bānum, ðæt hīe forrotigen for ðǽm æfste. c. p. 234.

15. 7. Dysigra monna mōd bið suiðe unemn ond suiðe ungelīc.
    c. p. 306.

15. 33. Sīo eaðmōdnes iernð beforan ðǽm gilpe, ond hīo cymð ǽr
    ǽr ðā weorðmyndu. c. p. 298.

16. 5. . . . ðætte God onscunige ǽlcne ofermōdne mon. c. p. 370.

16. 18. Ǽr ðæs monnes hryre bið ðæt mōd ūpāhafen. c. p. 298.

16. 32. Bᴇtra bið se geðyldega wer ðonne se stronga ond se kēna ;
    ond strongra bið sē ond ðrīstra þe his āgen mōd ofercymð ond
    gewilt, ðonne sē þe fæste burg ābrycð. c. p. 218.

17. 14. . . . ðætte sē, se þe ðæt wæter ūtforlēte, wǣre fruma ðǣre
    tōwesnesse. c. p. 278.

18. 4. . . . ðætte swīðe dōop pōl wǣre gewᴇred on ðæs wīsan
    monnes mōde. c. p. 278.

18. 9. Sē ðe his willum for his slǽwðe forlǽtt his gōdan weorc, hē
    bið gelīcost ðǽm men ðe his tōwirpð. c. p. 445.

19. 11. Æghwelces lārcowes lār wihst[1] ðurh his geðylde. c. p. 216.

19. 15. Sīo slǽwð gīett slǽp on ðone monnan. . . . Ðæt ungeorn-
    fulle mōd ond ðæt tōslopene hyngreð. c. p. 282.

20. 4. For cile nyle se slāwa ᴇrigan on wintra ; ac hē wile biddan
    on sumera, ond him mon nyle ðonne sᴇllan. c. p. 284.

‖ Se slāwa nylle ᴇrian for ciele. c. p. 284.

‖ Se slāwa for ðǽm ᴇge ðæs ciles nylle ᴇrian. c. p. 284.

‖ Is . . . gecweden ðæt hē ᴇft bedecige on sumera, ond him
mon ðonne nōht ne sᴇlle. c. p. 284.

---

15. 7. . . . Cor stultorum dissimile erit.

15. 33. . . . Gloriam praecedit humilitas.

16. 5. Abominatio Domino (*Greg.* Domini) est omnis arrogans. . . .

16. 18. . . . Ante ruinam exaltatur spiritus.

16. 32. Melior est patiens viro forti ; et qui dominatur animo suo, expugnatore urbium.

17. 14. Qui dimittit aquam, caput est iurgiorum. . . .

18. 4. Aqua profunda verba ex ore viri. . . .

18. 9. Qui mollis et dissolutus est in opere suo, frater est sua opera dissipantis.

19. 11. Doctrina viri per patientiam noscitur. . . .

19. 15. Pigredo immittit soporem, et anima dissoluta esuriet.

20. 4. Propter frigus piger arare noluit ; mendicabit ergo aestate, et non dabitur illi (*Greg.* ei).

---

[1] 'Noscitur' has been misread as 'nascitur.'

20. 21. Ðæt ierfe ðæt gō ǣrest æfter hīgiað, æt sīðestan hit bið bedǣled ǣlcre blēdsunge. C. P. 330.

20. 27. Ðæs monnes līf bið Godes lēohtfæt; ðæt Godes lēohtfæt geondscēð ond geondlīht ealle ðā dīegelnesse ðǣre wambe. C. P. 258.

20. 30. . . . ðætte sīo wund wolde hāligean, æfterðǣmþe hīo wyrsmde. C. P. 256, 258.

  ‖ Ðonne āflēwð ðæt sār of ðǣre wunde mid ðȳ wormse. C. P. 258.

  ‖ . . . ðætte ðæt ilce bīo bī ðǣm wundum þe bīoð oninnan ðǣre wombe. C. P. 258.

  ‖ Ðæt worsm ðonne ðāra wunda. . . . C. P. 258.

  ‖ Ðæt sār innan ðǣre wombe. . . . C. P. 258.

21. 25. Ǣlc īdel mon lifað æfter his āgnum dōme. C. P. 283.

21. 26. Sō þe ryhtwīs bið, hē bið ā sellende, ond nō ne blinð. C. P. 336.

21. 27. Ārlēasra offrung bið āwierged, forðǣm hīo (hīe II.) bīoð brōhte of unryhtum gestrēonum, ond of māndǣdum. C. P. 342.

23. 34. . . . ðæt hit wǣre swelce se stīora slēpe on midre sǣ, ond forlure ðæt stīorroður. C. P. 431.

23. 35. Hī mē wundedon, ond ic hit ne gefrēdde; hī mē drōgon, ond ic hit nyste; ond sōna swā ic anwōc, swā wilnode ic eft wīnes. C. P. 431.

25. 28. . . . ðætte se mon, se þe ne mæg his tungan gehealdan, sīe gelīcost openre byrg, ðǣre þe mid nāne wealle ne bið ymbworht. C. P. 276.

---

20. 21. Haereditas, ad quam festinatur in principio, in novissimo benedictione carebit.

20. 27. Lucerna Domini spiraculum hominis, quae investigat omnia secreta ventris.

20. 30. Livor vulneris absterget (*Greg.* abstergit) mala, et plagae in secretioribus ventris.

21. 25. Desideria occidunt pigrum (*Greg.* In desideriis est omnis otiosus). . . .

21. 26. . . . Qui autem (*Greg. om.* autem) iustus est, tribuet, et non cessabit.

21. 27. Hostiae impiorum abominabiles, quia (*Greg.* quae) offeruntur ex scelere.

23. 34. Et eris sicut (*Greg.* quasi) dormiens in medio mari, et quasi sopitus gubernator, amisso clavo.

23. 35. . . . Verberaverunt me, sed non dolui; traxerunt me, et ego non sensi; quando evigilabo, et rursus (*Greg.* rursum) vina reperiam?

25. 28. Sicut urbs patens et absque murorum ambitu, ita vir qui non potest in loquendo cohibere spiritum suum.

26. 10. Sē gemetgað ierre, se þe ðone dysegan hǣt geswug-
ian. C. P. 278.

27. 22. Ðēah mǫn [ðū] portige ðone dysegan on pilan, swǣ mǫn
corn dēð mid pilstafe, ne meahðōū (meaht ðū H.) his dysig him
frǫm ādrīfan. C. P. 264, 266.

28. 20. Sē þe æfter ðǣm hīgað ðæt hē ēadig sīe in (on H.) ðisse
worlde, ne bið hē unscēaðfull. C. P. 330.

29. 11. Se dysega ungeðyldega, āll his ingeðǫnc hē geypt; ac se
wīsa hit ieldcað, ǫnd bītt tīman. C. P. 220.

‖ Ac se wīsa hilt his sprǣce, ǫnd bītt tīman. C. P. 220.

ECCLESIASTES.

3. 7. . . . ðætte hwīlum sīe sprǣce tiid, hwīlum swiggean. C. P. 274.

5. 10 (Vulg. 9). Ne wierð se gīdsere nǣfre full fīos, ǫnd sē þe
worldwelan lufað ungescēadwīslice, ne cymð him of ðǣm nān
wǣstm. C. P. 330.

7. 8 (Vulg. 9). . . . ðæt bętra bīo se geðyldega wer ðonne se
gilpna. C. P. 216.

11. 4. Sē þe hīn ealneg wind ondrǣt, hē sǣwð tō seldon; ǫnd sē
þe him ǣlc wolcn ondrǣt, ne rīpð sē nǣfre. C. P. 284.

11. 9. Blīðsa, cniht, on ðīnum gioguðhāde. C. P. 385.

SONG OF SOLOMON.

2. 6. Dryhtnes winestre hand is under mīnum hēafde, ǫnd his
swīðre hand mē beclipð. C. P. 389.

26. 10. . . . Qui imponit stulto silentium, iras mitigat.

27. 22. Si contuderis stultum in pila quasi ptisanas feriente (*Greg.* ferienti) desuper pilo, non auferetur ab eo stultitia eius.

28. 20. . . . Qui autem (*Greg. om.* autem) festinat ditari, non erit innocens.

29. 11. Totum spiritum suum profert stultus; sapiens (*Greg. ins.* autem) differt, et reservat in posterum.

ECCLESIASTES.

3. 7. . . . Tempus tacendi, et tempus loquendi.

5. 9. Avarus non implebitur (*Greg.* impletur) pecunia; et qui amat divitias, fructum non capiet (*Greg.* non capiet fructus) ex eis. . . .

7. 9. . . . Melior est patiens arrogante.

11. 4. Qui observat ventum non seminat; et qui considerat nubes numquam metet.

11. 9. Laetare ergo (*Greg. om.* ergo), iuvenis, in adolescentia tua. . . .

SONG OF SOLOMON.

2. 6. Laeva eius sub capite meo, et dextera illius amplexabitur me.

3. 8. Hæbbe ċower ælc his sweord be his ðeo for nihtlecum
ęge. C. P. 433.

7. 4. Ðin nosu is swelc, swelce se torr on Libano ðæm munte.
C. P. 64.

‖ Ðin nosu is swelce se torr on Libano. C. P. 433.

8. 3. Dryhtnes winestre hand is under minum heafde, ǫnd his
swiðre hand me beclipð. C. P. 389.

8. 13. Hlyst hider, ðu þe eardast on friondes ortgearde, ǫnd gedoo
ðæt ic mæge gehieran ðine stemne. C. P. 380.

ISAIAH.

1. 16. Āðweað iow, ðæt ge sin clæne. C. P. 421.

3. 9. Hi lærdon hira synna swā-swā Sodome dydon, ǫnd hi hi
nānwuht ne hælon. C. P. 427.

5. 8. Wā cow þe gadriað hūs tō hūse, ǫnd spannað ðone æcer tō
ðæm ōðrum oð ðæs lǫndes mearce, swelce ge āne willen gebūgean
ealle ðæs eorðan. C. P. 328.

6. 5. Wā me ðæs ic swugode. C. P. 378.

6. 6, 7. *See* C. P. 48.

6. 8. Ic eom gearo, sęnde (sęnd H.) me. C. P. 48.

9. 13. Ðis folc nis nō gewęnd tō ðæm þe hie swingð. C. P. 266.

14. 13, 14. Ic wille wyrcean min setl on norðdæle, ǫnd wille beon
gelic ðæm Hiehstan. C. P. 110.

23. 4. Ðios sæ cwið ðæt ðu ðin scamige, Sidon. C. P. 409.

---

3. 8. . . . Uniuscuiusque ensis super
femur suum propter timores noc-
turnos.

7. 4. . . . Nasus tuus sicut turris Li-
bani (*Greg.* quae est in Libano). . . .

8. 3. Laeva eius sub capite meo, et
dextera illius amplexabitur me.

8. 13. Quae habitas in hortis, amici
auscultant ; fac me audire vocem
tuam.

ISAIAH.

1. 16. Lavamini, mundi estote. . . .

3. 9. . . . Peccatum suum quasi
(*Greg.* sicut) Sodoma praedica-
verunt, nec absconderunt. . . .

5. 8. Vae qui coniungitis domum ad
domum, et agrum agro copulatis
usque ad terminum loci ; numquid habitabitis vos soli (*Greg.*
soli vos) in medio terrae ?

6. 5. . . . Vae mihi quia tacui. . . .

6. 8. . . . Ecce ego, mitte me.

9. 13. . . . Populus non est reversus
ad percutientem se.

14. 13, 14. . . . Sedebo in monte testamenti, in lateribus aquilonis,
. . . similis ero Altissimo (*Greg.*
Ponam sedem meam ad aquilo-
nem, et ero similis Altissimo).

23. 4. Erubesce, Sidon : ait enim
(*Greg. om.* enim) mare. . . .

30. 20, 21. Ðīn ēag[an] weorðað gestonde ðīnne bebīodend, ǫnd ðīn ēaran gehīrað under bǣc. C. P. 405.

32. 17. . . . ðætte sīo swigge wǣre ðǣre ryhtwīsnesse fultom ǫnd midwyrhta. C. P. 278.

34. 15. . . . ðæt ðǣr se iil hæfde se (his H.) holh. C. P. 240.

39. 4. *See* C. P. 38.

40. 9. Ðū þe wilt godspellian Sion, āstīg ofer hēanne munt. C. P. 80.

43. 25, 26. Ðīnra synna ne weorðe ic gemunende, ac gemun ðū hiora. C. P. 413.

48. 10. Ðē ic gecēas on ðǣm ofne þe ðū on wǣre āsoden, ðæt wæs on ðīnum iermðum. C. P. 180.

52. 11. Doð ēow clǣne, gē þe berað Godes fatu. C. P. 76.

54. 4. Ne ondrǣd ðū ðē, forðǣm ðū ne wyrðest gescǫnded. C. P. 180.

54. 4, 5. Ðǣre scame ǫnd ðǣre scande þe ðū on iuguðe worhtes, ic gedō ðæt ðū forgitst ; ǫnd ðæs bismeres ðīnes wuduwanhādes ðū ne gemanst ; forðǣm ðæt is ðīn Wāldend þe ðē gēworhte. C. P. 206.

54. 11. Ðū earma, ðū þe art mid ðȳ storme ǫnd mid ðǣre ȳste onwǫnd ǫnd oferworpen. C. P. 180.

56. 4, 5. Ðis cwið Dryhten : Ðū āfyrdan, ðā ðe behealdað mīnne ræstedæg, ǫnd gecēosað ðæt ic wille, ǫnd mīnne frēondscipe gehealdað[1], ic him sǫlle on mīnum hūse, ǫnd binnan mīnum weallum, wīc ǫnd bǫteran nǫman ðonne ōðrum mīnum sunum oððe dohtrum. C. P. 407.

30. 20, 21. . . . Et erunt oculi tui videntes praeceptorem tuum, et aures tuae audient verbum post tergum. . . .

32. 17. . . . Cultus iustitiae silentium. . . .

34. 15. Ibi habuit foveam ericius. . . .

40. 9. Super montem excelsum ascende, tu qui evangelizas Sion. . . .

43. 25, 26. . . . Et peccatorum tuorum non recordabor (*Greg.* memor non ero). Reduc me in memoriam (*Greg.* Tu autem memor esto). . . .

48. 10. . . . Elegi te in camino paupertatis.

52. 11. . . . Mundamini, qui fertis vasa Domini.

54. 4, 5. Noli timere, quia non confunderis. . . . Confusionis adolescentiae tuae oblivisceris, et opprobrii viduitatis tuae non recordaberis amplius (*Greg. om.* amplius); quia dominabitur tui qui fecit te. . . .

54. 11. Paupercula, tempestate convulsa. . . .

56. 4, 5. . . . Haec dicit Dominus eunuchis : Qui custodierint sabbata mea, et elegerint quae ego (*Greg. om.* ego) volui, et tenuerint foedus meum (*Greg.* foedus meum tenuerint), dabo eis in domo mea, et in muris meis, locum et nomen melius a filiis et filiabus. . . .

---

[1] For 'gehealdað.'

56. 10. Dumbe hundas ne magon beorcan. C. P. 88.

56. 11. Đā hirdas næfdon andgit. C. P. 26.

57. 11. Gē sindon lēogende ; nǣron gē nō mīn gemunende, nē gē nō ne gedōhton on ðowerre heortan ðæt ic swugode, swelce ic hit ne gesāwe. C. P. 150.

58. 1. Cliopa, ǫnd ne blin ; hęfe ūp ðīne stefne swā ðer (ðes II.) brēme. C. P. 90.

58. 3. On ðower fæstendagum bið ongieten ðower willa. C. P. 314.

58. 4. Tō gemōtum, ǫnd to gecīdum, ǫnd tō iersunga, ǫnd tō fȳstgebēate, gē fæstað. C. P. 314.

58. 6, 7. Ne gecēas ic nō ðis fæsten, ac ðyllic fæsten ic gecēas : Brec ðǣm hyngriendum ðīnne hlāf, ǫnd ðone wīdfarendan ǫnd ðone wǣdlan lǣd on ðīn hūs. C. P. 314.

58. 9. Nū ðū mē clipodest ; nū ic eom hēr. C. P. 62.

61. 8. Ic eom Dryhten ; ic lufige ryhte dōmas, ǫnd ic hatige þā lāc þe bīoð on wōh gerēafodu. C. P. 342.

66. 2. Tō hwǣm lōcige ic būton tō ðǣm ēaðmōdum, ǫnd tō ðǣm stillum, ǫnd tō ðǣm þe him ondrǣdað mīn word ? C. P. 298.

JEREMIAH.

1. 6. Ēalā, ēalā, ēalā, Dryhten, ic eom cniht ; hwæt can ic sprecan ? C. P. 48.

56. 10. ... Canes muti, non valentes latrare. ...

56. 11. ... Ipsi pastores ignoraverunt intelligentiam. ...

57. 11. ... Mentita es, et mei non es recordata, neque cogitasti in corde tuo ? quia ego tacens, et quasi non videns. ...

58. 1. Clama, ne cesses ; quasi tuba exalta vocem tuam. ...

58. 3. ... Ecce in die ieiunii vestri invenitur voluntas vestra (*Greg. sec. Ital.* In diebus ieiuniorum vestrorum inveniuntur voluntates vestrae). ...

58. 4. Ecce ad lites et contentiones ieiunatis, et percutitis pugno impie (*Greg. sec. Ital.* In iudicia et rixas ieiunatis, et percutitis pugnis). ...

58. 6, 7. Nonne hoc est magis (*Greg.*

Numquid tale est) ieiunium quod clegi ? ... (*Greg. ins.* Sed) frange esurienti panem tuum, et egenos vagosque induc in domum tuam. ...

58. 9. ... Clamabis, et dicet (*Greg.* Adhuc loquente te dicam) : Ecce adsum. ...

61. 8. ... Ego Dominus diligens iudicium, et odio habens rapinam in holocausto. ...

66. 2. ... Ad quem autem (*Greg. om.* autem) respiciam nisi ad pauperculum, et contritum spiritu (*Greg. sec. Ital.* nisi ad humilem et quietum), et trementem sermones meos ?

JEREMIAH.

1. 6. ... A, a, a, Domine Deus, ecce nescio loqui, quia puer ego sum.

1. 10. Ic hæbbe ðē nū tōdæg gesętne ofer rīce ǫnd ofer ðīoda, ðæt ðū hī tōlūce ǫnd tōweorpe ǫnd forspilde ǫnd tōstęnce, ǫnd getimbre ǫnd geplantige.   C. P. 441.

2. 8. Hī hæfdon mīne ǣ, ǫnd hī mē ne gecnēwon.   C. P. 28.

3. 1. Gif hwelc wīf forlǣt hiere ceorl, ǫnd nimð hire ōðerne, wēnestū ręcce hē hire ǣfre mā, oððe mæg hīo æfre ęft cuman tō him swā clǣnu swā hīo ǣr wæs?   Hwæt, ðū ðonne eart fo(r)-legen wið manigne copenere, ǫnd swā-ðēah ic cweðe: Gecier ęft (t)ō mē, cwæð Dryhten.   C. P. 405.

3. 3. Ēower nębb sint swǣ scamlēase swǣ ðāra wīfa ðe bīoð fore-legissa.   C. P. 206.

    ‖ Ðū hæfst forlegisse andwlitan, forðǣm ðē nū ne sceamað   C. P. 403.

4. 4. Healdað ēow ðæt gē ne onǣlen mīn ierre mid ēowrum sear-wum, ðæt gē hit ne mægen ęft ādwǣscan.   C. P. 435.

5. 3. Ðū hīe tōbrǣce, ǫnd ðēah hīe noldon underfōn ðīne lāre.   C. P. 266.

6. 29. Īdel wæs se blāwere, forðǣm hiera āwiergdan weorc ne wurdon frǫm him āsyndrede.   C. P. 268.

9. 5. Hīe lǣrdon hiera tungan, ǫnd węnedon tō lēasunge, ǫnd swuncon on unnyttum (unryhtum H.) weorce.   C. P. 238.

15. 7. Ic ofslōg ðis folc, ǫnd tō forlore gedyde, ǫnd hīe hīe ðēah noldon onwęndan frǫm hiera wōn wegum.   C. P. 266.

23. 2. Ic wrice on ēow æfter ēowrum geðeahte.   C. P. 435.

1. 10. Ecce constitui te hodie super gentes et super regna, ut evellas et destruas et disperdas et dissipes, et aedifices et plantes.

2. 8. ... Et tenentes legem nescie-runt me. ...

3. 1. ... Si dimiserit vir uxorem suam, et (*Greg. ins.* illa) recedens ab eo (*Greg. om.* ab eo) duxerit virum alterum (*Greg.* alium), num-quid revertetur ad eam ultra? numquid non polluta et contami-nata erit mulier illa?   Tu autem fornicata es cum amatoribus mul-tis; tamen revertere ad me, dicit Dominus. ...

3. 3. ... Frons mulieris meretricis facta est tibi, noluisti erubescere.

4. 4. ... Ne forte egrediatur ut ig-nis indignatio mea, et succenda-tur, et non sit qui extinguat. ...

5. 3. ... Attrivisti eos, et renuerunt accipere disciplinam. ...

6. 29. ... Frustra conflavit con-flator; malitiae enim (*Greg. om.* enim) eorum non sunt consum-ptae.

9. 5. ... Docuerunt enim (*Greg. om.* enim) linguam suam loqui men-dacium; ut inique agerent labo-raverunt.

15. 7. ... Interfeci et disperdidi (*Greg.* perdidi) populum meum (*Greg.* istum), et tamen a viis suis non sunt reversi.

23. 2. ... Visitabo super vos mali-

48. 10. Āwyrged bið se mǫn se þe wyrnð his sweorde blōdes. C. P. 376, 378.

51. 9. Wē lǣcnedon Babylon, ǫnd hīo ðēah ne wearð gehǣled. C. P. 266.

LAMENTATIONS.

2. 14. Ēowre wītgan ēow wītgodon dysig ǫnd lēasunga, ǫnd noldon ēow gecȳðan ēowre unryhtwīsnesse, ðæt hē (hīe II.) ēow gebrōhten on hrēowsunge. C. P. 90.

3. 48. Tōdǣlnessa ðāra wætera ūtlēton mīn ēagan. C. P. 413.

4. 1. Ēalā, hwȳ is ðis gold ādeorcad? ǫnd ðæt æðeleste hīew, hwȳ wearð hit onhworfen [āhworfen]? Tōworpne sint ðā stānas ðæs temples, ǫnd licgeað æt ǣlcre strǣte ęnde. C. P. 132.

EZEKIEL.

1. 18. *See* C. P. 194.

2. 1. *See* C. P. 465.

4. 1. Nim sume tīglan, ǫnd lęge beforan ðē, ǫnd wrīt on hiere ðā burg Hīerusalem. C. P. 160.

‖ Genim ðē āne tīglan, ǫnd lęge beforan ðē, ǫnd wrīt on hiere ðā burg Hierusalem. C. P. 160.

4. 2, 3. Besittað hīe ūtan, ǫnd wyrceað ōðer fæsten wið hīe, ǫnd berað hiere hlǣd tō, ǫnd sęnd ðǣrtō gefylceo, ǫnd ðersceað ðone weall mid rammum. And[1] ęft hē him tǣhte tō fultome ðæt hē him genāme āne īrene hierstepannan, ǫnd sętte betweoh hiene ǫnd ðā burg for īserne weall. C. P. 160.

tiam (*Greg.* iuxta fructum) studiorum vestrorum. . . .

48. 10. . . . Maledictus qui prohibet gladium suum a sanguine.

51. 9. Curavimus Babylonem, et non est sanata. . . .

LAMENTATIONS.

2. 14. Prophetae tui viderunt tibi falsa et stulta, nec aperiebant iniquitatem tuam, ut te ad poenitentiam provocarent. . . .

3. 48. Divisiones aquarum deduxit oculus meus. . . .

4. 1. Quomodo obscuratum est aurum, mutatus est color optimus, dispersi sunt lapides sanctuarii in capite omnium platearum?

EZEKIEL.

4. 1. . . . Sume tibi laterem, et pones eum coram te, et describes in eo civitatem Ierusalem.

4. 2, 3. Et ordinabis adversus eam obsidionem, et aedificabis muni-

[1] So Sweet.

‖ Ymbsittað ðā burg swīðe gebyrdelice, ǫnd getrymiað eow wið hīe. C. P. 160.

‖ Wyrceað fæsten ymb ðā burg. C. P. 162.

‖ Berað hiere tō hlæd, ǫnd ymbsittað hīe, ǫnd gāð tō mid rammum. C. P. 162.

‖ Genim ðē āne īrene hierstepannan, ǫnd sęte betweoxn ðē ǫnd Hierusalem for īserne weall. C. P. 162.

‖ Sęte īserne weall betweox (betuh H.) ðē ǫnd ðā burh. C. P. 164.

8. 8–10. Ðū, mǫnnes sunu, ðurhðȳrela ðone wāh. Ðā ic ðā ðone wāh ðurhðȳrelodne hæfde, ... ðā ðowde hē mē āne duru beinnan ðǣm wealle, ǫnd cwæð tō mē : Gang inn, gescoh ðā scande ǫnd ðā wirrestan ðing ðe ðās męn hēr dōð. Ic ðā ðode inn, ǫnd geseah ðǣr ðā anlīcnessa ealra crēopendra wuhta ǫnd ealra anscunigendra [anscunigendlicra] nīetena, ǫnd ealle ðā heargas [hearga] Israhela folces wǣron ātīfred (ātīefrede H.) on ðǣm wāge. C. P. 152.

‖ Ðā ic hæfde ðone weall ðurhðȳrelod, ðā geseah ic duru. C. P. 154.

‖ Gǫng inn, ǫnd geseoh þā heardsǣlða ǫnd ðā scǫnde þe ðās hēr dōð. C. P. 154.

‖ Ic ðā ðode inn, ǫnd geseah ðā anlīcnessa ealra crēopendra wuhta, ǫnd ðac onscunigendlicra nīetena. C. P. 154.

13. 5. Ne cōme gē nō tōgðanes mīnum folce ðæt gē meahton standan on mīnum gefeohte for Israhela folce, nē gē ðone weall ne trymedon ymb hiera hūs on ðǣm dæge þe him nīdðearf wæs. C. P. 88.

13. 18. Wā ðǣm þe willað under ǣlcne ęlnbōgan lęcgean pyle, ǫnd bolster under ǣlcne hnęccan, męn mid tō gefōnne. C. P. 142.

tioꝛes, et comportabis aggerem, et dabis contra eam castra, et pones arietes in gyro. Et tu sume tibi sartaginem ferream, et pones eam in (*Greg. om.* in) murum ferreum inter te et inter civitatem. ...

8. 8–10. ... Fili hominis, fode parietem. Et cum fodissem parietem, apparuit ostium unum. Et dixit ad me : Ingredere, et vide abominationes pessimas quas isti faciunt hic. Et ingressus vidi, et ecce omnis similitudo reptilium, et animalium abominatio, et universa idola domus Israel depicta erant in pariete. ...

13. 5. Non ascendistis ex adverso, neque (*Greg.* nec) opposuistis murum pro domo Israel, ut staretis in proelio in die Domini.

13. 18. ... Vae (*Greg. ins.* his) quae (*Greg.* qui) consuunt pulvillos sub omni cubito manus, et faciunt

16. 14, 15. Dryhten cwið tō ðisse byrg: Đū wǣre fulfręmed on mīnum wlite, ǫnd ðā fortrūwdes ðū ðē for ðǣm, ǫnd forlǣge ðē ðīnes ǣgnes ðǫnces. C. P. 463.

‖ Gē ēow forlǣgon ēowres ǣgnes ðǫnces. C. P. 463.

22. 18. Đis Israhela folc is geworden nū mō tō sindrum, ǫnd tō āre, ǫnd tō tine, ǫnd tō īserne, ǫnd tō lēade, inne on mīnum ofne. C. P. 266.

23. 3. ... Đæt hī hī forlǣgen on Egiptum on hira gioguðe; hī wǣron ðǣr forlegene, ǫnd ðǣr wǣron gehnęscode hiera brēost, ǫnd forbrocene ðā dela hiora mægdenhādes. C. P. 403, 405.

‖ On Egiptum bīoð forbrocene ðā wǣstmas ðīura dela. C. P. 405.

24. 12. Đǣr wæs swīðe swīðlic geswinc, ǫnd ðǣr wæs micel swāt āgoten, ǫnd ðēah ne meahte mǫn him of āniman ðone miclan rust, nē furðum mid fīre ne meahte hine mǫn āweg ādōn. C. P. 268.

32. 19. Āstīg ęft ofdūne ðǫnan ðe ðū wēnst ðæt ðū wlitegost sīe. C. P. 463.

34. 4. Đæt scēap ðæt ðǣr scancforad wæs, ne spilcte gē ðæt, ǫnd ðæt ðǣr forloren wæs, ne sōhte gē ðæt, nē hām ne brōhton. C. P. 122.

Gē budon swīðe rīclice ǫnd swīðe āgendlice. C. P. 144.

34. 18, 19. Gē fortrǣdon Godes scēapa gærs, ǫnd gē gedrōfdon hira wæter mid ēowrum fōtum, ðēah gē hit ǣr undrēfed druncon. C. P. 30.

---

cervicalia sub capite universae aetatis, ad capiendas animas. ...

16. 14, 15. ... Perfecta eras in decore meo quem posueram super te, dicit Dominus Deus (*Greg. om.* Deus). Et habens fiduciam in pulchritudine tua, fornicata es in nomine tuo. ...

22. 18. ... Versa est mihi domus Israel in scoriam; omnes isti aes, et stannum, et ferrum, et plumbum, in medio fornacis. ...

23. 3. ... Fornicatae sunt in Aegypto, in adolescentia sua fornicatae sunt; ibi subacta sunt ubera earum, et fractae sunt mammae pubertatis earum.

24. 12. Multo labore sudatum est, et non exivit de ea nimia rubigo eius, neque per ignem.

32. 19. Quo pulchrior es descende....

34. 4. ... Quod confractum (*Greg.* fractum) est non alligastis, et quod abiectum est non reduxistis, et quod perierat non quaesistis (*Greg. om.* et quod perierat non quaesistis); sed (*Greg.* Vos autem) cum austeritate imperabatis eis, et cum potentia.

34. 18, 19. ... Cum (*Greg. ins.* ipsi) purissimam (*Greg.* limpidissimam) aquam biberetis, reliquam pedibus vestris turbabatis; et oves meae his (*Greg. om.* his) quae conculcata

36. 5. Hīe dydon mīn land him selfum tō ierfelǫnde mid gefēan, ǫnd mid ealre heortan, ǫnd mid ealle mōde. C. P. 387.

43. 13. Wæs . . . beboden Ezechiele ðǣm wītgan ðæt hē sceolde ðone Godes ālter habban uppan āhōlodne. C. P. 216.

‖ Holh wæs beboden ðæt sceolde bēon on ðǣm weobude uppan. C. P. 218.

. . . ðæt ðæt holh sceolde bēon on ðǣm weobude ānre ęlne brād ǫnd ānre ęlne lǫng. C. P. 218.

44. 12. Yfle prēostas bīoð folces hryre. C. P. 30.

44. 20. . . . ðætte ðā sācerdas ne sceoldon nō hiera hēafdu scieran mid scearseaxum, nē ęft hīe ne sceoldon hiera loccas lǣtan weaxan, ac hīe sceoldon hīe ęfsian mid scearum. C. P. 138.

DANIEL.

4. 16 ff. *See* C. P. 38.

4. 30 (Vulg. 27). Hū ne is ðis nū sīo micle Babilon þe ic self ātimbrede tō kynestōle ǫnd tō ðrymme, mē selfum tō wlite ǫnd tō wuldre, mid mīne āgne mægene ǫnd stręngeo? C. P. 38.

HOSEA.

2. 8. Ic him sealde hwǣte, ǫnd wīn, ǫnd ęle, ǫnd gold, ǫnd sylofr ic him sealde genōh, ǫnd ðæt hīe worhton tō dīofolgieldum Bale hiora gode. C. P. 368.

4. 9. Swelc ðæt folc bið, swelc bið se sācerd. C. P. 132.

pedibus vestris fuerant, pascebantur, et quae pedes vestri turbaverant, haec bibebant.

36. 5. . . . Dederunt terram meam sibi in hereditatem cum gaudio, et toto corde, et ex animo. . . .

43. 13. Istae autem mensurae altaris . . . : in sinu eius erat cubitus . . . ; haec quoque erat fossa altaris (*Greg. sum.*).

44. 12. . . . Facti sunt domui Israel in offendiculum iniquitatis. . . .

44. 20. (*Greg. ins.* Sacerdotes) caput autem (*Greg. om.* autem) suum non radent, neque comam nutrient, sed tondentes attondent (*Greg.* attondeant) capita sua.

DANIEL.

4. 27. . . . Nonne haec est Babylon magna quam ego aedificavi in domum regni, (*Greg. ins.* et) in robore fortitudinis meae, et in gloria decoris mei?

HOSEA.

2. 8. . . . Dedi ei (*Greg.* eis) frumentum, et (*Greg. om.* et) vinum, et oleum, et argentum multiplicavi ei (*Greg.* eis), et aurum, quae fecerunt Baal.

4. 9. Et erit sicut populus, sic sacerdos. . . .

5. 1. Yfle prēostas bīoð folces hryre[1].   C. P. 30.

8. 4. Hī rīcsodon, næs ðeah mīnes ðonces ; caldormen hī wǣron, ond ic hī ne cūðe.   C. P. 26.

9. 8. Yfle prēostas bīoð folces hryre[1].   C. P. 30.

JOEL.

2. 15. Gehālgiað ēower fæsten.   C. P. 314.

AMOS.

1. 13. Hīe snidon ðā Galatiscan wīf þe bearnēacne wǣron, ond woldon mid ðȳ gerȳman hiora landgemǣru.   C. P. 366.

‖ Mon snīð ðā bearnēacan wīf on Galað, hiora mearce mid tō rȳman [hrȳmanne] (rȳmanne H.).   C. P. 366.

HABAKKUK.

2. 6. Wā ðǣm þe ealneg gadrað on hiene selfne ðæt hefige fenn, ond gemanigfaldað ðætte his ne bið.   C. P. 328.

ZEPHANIAH.

1. 14–16. Gīt cymð se micla ond se mǣra ond se egeslica Godes dæg ; se dæg bið ierres dæg, ond ðīestra ðæg, ond mistes ond gebreces ond bīemena ðæg, ond gedynes ofer ealla truma ceastra ond ofer ealle hēa hwammas.   C. P. 244.

5. 1. Laqueus facti estis speculationi (*Greg.* Laqueus ruinae populi mei, sacerdotes). . . .

8. 4. Ipsi regnaverunt, et non ex me ; principes exstiterunt, et non cognovi (*Greg.* ego ignoravi). . . .

9. 8. . . . Propheta laqueus ruinae factus est (*Greg.* Laqueus ruinae populi mei, sacerdotes).

JOEL.

2. 15. . . . Sanctificate ieiunium. . . .

AMOS.

1. 13. . . . Dissecuerit (*Greg.* Secuerunt) praegnantes Galaad ad dilatandum terminum suum.

HABAKKUK.

2. 6. . . . Vae ei, qui multiplicat non sua ; usquequo . . . aggravat contra se densum lutum ?

ZEPHANIAH.

1. 14–16. Iuxta est (*Greg.* Ecce) dies Domini magnus(*Greg. ins.* et horribilis, from Joel 2. 31). . . . Dies irae, dies illa, . . . dies tenebrarum et caliginis, dies nebulae et turbinis, dies tubae et clangoris super (*Greg. ins.* omnes) civitates munitas et super (*Greg. ins.* omnes) angulos excelsos.

---

[1] There is considerable uncertainty whether the Old English is meant for the translation of these passages, or of Ezek. 44. 12.

HAGGAI.

1. 6. Se þe medsceattas gadrað. he legeð hie on ðyrelne pohhan. C. P. 341.

ZECHARIAH.

7. 5. 6. Eall ðæt ðæt ge fæston ond weopon on ðæm fiftan ond on ðæm siofoðan monðe nū hundsiofontig wintra. ne fæste ge ðæs nauht mē; ond ðonne ge æton. ðonne æton ge eow selfum. ond ðonne ge druncon. ðonne ðruncon ge eow selfum. C. P. 314. 316.

MALACHI.

2. 7. Sio ǣ sceal bion sōht on ðæs sacerdes mūðe, ond his weloras gehealdað ðæt ondgit. forðæm he bið Godes boda tō ðæm folce. C. P. 90.

TOBIT.

4. 17. (Vulg. 18). Sete ðin wīn, ond lege ðīnne hlāf. ofer ryhtwisra monna byrgenne, ond ne et his nauht, ne ne drinc mid ðæm synfullum. C. P. 326.

WISDOM OF SOLOMON.

1. 5. Ðæs Hālgan Gāstes lār[1] wille flēon lēasunge. C. P. 341.

2. 24. . . . ðæs lytegan feondes. þe be him āwriten is ðætte for his æfste dēað becōme ofer ealle eorðan. C. P. 352.

HAGGAI.

1. 6. . . . Qui mercedes congregavit, misit eas in succulum pertusum.

ZECHARIAH.

7. 5, 6. . . . Cum ieiunaretis et plangeretis in quinto et (Greg. ins. in septimo Greg. ins. mense per hos septuaginta annos. numquid ieiunium ieiunastis mihi? et cum comedistis et bibistis, numquid non vobis Greg. vobismetipsis comedistis, et vobismetipsis bibistis?

MALACHI.

2. 7. Labia enim Greg. om. enim sacerdotis custodient scientiam. et legem requirent ex ore eius. quia angelus Domini exercituum est.

TOBIT.

4. 18. Panem tuum et vinum tuum (Greg. om. tuum) super sepulturam iusti constitue, et noli ex eo manducare et bibere cum peccatoribus.

WISDOM OF SOLOMON.

1. 5. Spiritus enim (Greg. om. enim) sanctus disciplinae effugiet fictum. . . .

2. 24. Invidia autem diaboli mors intravit in orbem terrarum.

[1] Mistranslation, as if 'Spiritus sancti disciplina.'

ECCLESIASTICUS.

7. 14 (Vulg. 13). Ne eftga ðu ðin word on ðinum gebede.   C. P. 431.

10. 9. Hwæt ofermodegað ðios eorðe ond ðis dust ?   C. P. 298.

10. 13 (Vulg. 14). . . . ðæt ælces yfles fruma wære ofermetta.   C. P. 300.

11. 10. Sunu min, ne todæl ðu on to fela ðin mod ond ðin weorc ondemes.   C. P. 36.

12. 4, 5 (Vulg. 5, 6). Sele ðin god, ond na ðeah ðæm synfullum ; do wel ðæm eaðmodum, ond ðæm arleasum noht.   C. P. 314.

19. 1. . . . ðætte sæ, se ðe nylle onscunian his lytlan scylda, ðæt he wille gelisian to maran.   C. P. 437.

20. 7. Se wisa swugað oð he ongitt ðæt him bið bettre to sprecanne.   C. P. 274.

20. 30 (Vulg. 32). Hu nyt bið se forholena cræft, oððe ðæt forhydde gold ?   C. P. 375.

32. 1. To ealdormenn ðu eart gesett ; ne bio ðu ðeah to upahæfen. ac bio swelce an ðinra hieremonna.   C. P. 118.

32. 7 (Vulg. 10, 11). Ðu geonga, bio ðe unিðe to clipianne ond to læranne, ge furðum ðina agna spræca ; ond ðeah ðe mon tuwa frigne, gebid ðu mid ðære andsware. oð ðu wite ðæt ðin spræc hæbbe ægðer ge ord ge ende.   C. P. 282.

32. 19 (Vulg. 24). Sunu min, ne do ðu nan wuht butan geðeahte. ðonne ne hriwð hit ðe ðonne hit gedon bið.   C. P. 386.

ECCLESIASTICUS.

7. 15. Non · Greg. Ne iteres verbum in oratione tua.

10. 9. Quid superbit terra et cinis ?

10. 14. Initium superbiae hominis, apostatare a Deo Greg. Quia initium omnis peccati superbia est .

11. 10. Fili ne in multis sint actus tui . . .

12. 5. 6. Da bono, et non receperis peccatorem ; benefac humili et non dederis impio. . . .

19. 1. . . . Qui spernit modica · Greg. modica spernit , paulatim decidet (Greg. decidit).

20. 7. Homo · Greg. om. Homo sapiens tacebit usque ad tempus. . . .

20. 32. Sapientia absconsa Greg. abscondita, et thesaurus invisus, quae utilitas in utrisque ?

32. 1. Rectorem · Greg. Ducem· te posuerunt Greg. constituerunt, ? Noli extolli, Greg. ins. sed esto in illis quasi unus ex illis.

32. 10, 11. Adolescens. loquere in causa tua vix ; Greg. ins. et si bis interrogatus fueris, habeat caput · Greg. initium · responsum tuum Greg. responsio tua .

32. 24 Fili, sine consilio nihil facias, et post factum non poenitebis.

34. 20 (Vulg. 24). Sē þe mē brengð lāc of earmes monnes æhtum on wōh gereafodum, ðonne bið ðæt swelce hwā wille blōtan ðæm fæder tō ðance ond tō lācum his āgen bearn, ond hit ðonne cwelle beforan his eagum.   C. P. 342.

34. 25 (Vulg. 30). Gif hwā on hand nimð hwæt unclēnes ond hine æfter ðæm āð[w]ihð, ond ðonne eft [fehð] on ðæt ilce ðæt hē ǣr fēng, hwæt forstent him ðonne ðæt ǣrre ðwēal?   C. P. 421.

MATTHEW.

3. 10. Nū is ðonne sīo æx āsett on ðone wyrttruman ðæs trēowes.   C. P. 338.

     Ǣlc trīow man sceal ceorfan, þe gōde wēstmas ne birð, ond weorpan on fȳr, ond forbærnan.   C. P. 338.

5. 9. Ēadige bīoð ðā gesibsuman, forðæm hīe bīoð Godes bearn genemde.   C. P. 358.

5. 15. Ne scyle nān mon blācern ælan under mittan.   C. P. 42.

5. 16. Dōð eower gōdan weorc beforan mannum, ðæt hī mægen weorðian eowerne Fæder ðe on hefonum is.   C. P. 449.

    || . . . ðæt hī weorðigen eowerne Fæder ðe on hefonum is.   C. P. 451.

5. 23, 24. Gif ðū wille ðīn lāc brengan tō ðæm wiofude, ond ðū ðonne ðēr ryhte ofðence hwæthugu ðæs þe ðīn nīehsta ðe wiðerweardes gedōn hæbbe, forlēt ðonne ān ðīn lāc beforan ðæm wiofude, ond fēr ǣrest æfter him ; lēt inc gesēman ǣr ðū ðīn lāc brenge ; breng siððan ðīn lāc.   C. P. 348.

34. 24. Qui offert sacrificium ex (*Greg.* de) substantia pauperum, quasi qui victimat filium in conspectu patris sui.

34. 30. Qui baptizatur a mortuo, et iterum tangit eum (*Greg.* illum), quid proficit lavatio illius (*Greg.* eius)?

MATTHEW.

3. 10. Iam enim (*Greg. om.* enim) securis ad radicem arborum (*Greg.* arboris) posita est ; omnis ergo (*Greg. om.* ergo) arbor, quae non facit fructum bonum, excidetur, et in ignem mittetur.

5. 9. Beati pacifici, quoniam filii Dei vocabuntur.

5. 15. Neque accendunt lucernam, et ponunt eam sub modio. . . .

5. 16. . . . Videant opera vestra bona, et glorificent Patrem vestrum qui in coelis est.

5. 23, 24. Si ergo (*Greg. om.* ergo) offers munus tuum ad altare, et ibi recordatus fueris quia frater tuus habet aliquid adversum te ; relinque ibi munus tuum ante altare, et vade prius reconciliari fratri tuo, et tunc veniens offeres munus tuum.

5. 44. Lufiað ꞇowre friend, ꞩnd dōð ðǣm wel þe ꞇow ǣr hatedon, ꞩnd gebiddað for þā þe ꞇower ꞇhtað ꞩnd ꞇow lāð dōð.   C. P. 222.

6. 1. Gīemað ðæt ge ꞇowre ryhtwīsnesse ne dōn beforan mannum.   C. P. 334.

‖ Behealdað ꞇow ðæt ge ne dōn ꞇowre ryhtwīsnesse beforan mꞩnnum, ðȳlǣs hī ꞇow herien.   C. P. 449, 451.

6. 2. . . . ðæt ðæt wǣre hira mēd.   C. P. 449.

6. 3. . . . ðæt sīo winestre hꞩnd ne scyle witan hwæt sīo swīðre dō.   C. P. 322.

6. 24. Ne mæg nān mꞩn twēm hlāfordum hīeran.   C. P. 128.

7. 3. Hwæt, ðū mealht gesīon lȳtelne ꞇð on ðīnes brōður ꞇagan, ꞩnd ne mealht gefrēdan micelne bēam on ðīnum āgnan.   C. P. 224.

7. 5. Ðū līcettere, āweorp ǣrest of ðīnum āgnum ꞇagan ðone grēatan bēam, ꞩnd cunna siððan hwæðer ðū mæge ādōn ðone ꞇð of ðīnes brōður ꞇagan.   C. P. 224.

7. 13. Ðæt is swīðe rūm weg ꞩnd wīdgille þe līet tō forwyrde (fær-wyrde H.).   C. P. 132.

7. 19. *See* Matt. 3. 10.

10. 16. Bīo ge swǣ wǣre swǣ nīedran, ꞩnd swǣ bilwite swā culfran.   C. P. 236.

10. 34. Ne wēne ge nō ðæt ic tō ðǣm cōme on eorðan ðæt ic sibbe sꞩnde on eorðan. ac sweord.   C. P. 352.

12. 36. Ælces unnyttes wordes ðāra þe mꞩn sprecað hīe sculon ꞩft ryht āwyrcean on dōmes dæge.   C. P. 280.

5. 44. . . . Diligite inimicos vestros, benefacite his qui oderunt vos, et orate pro persequentibus et calumniantibus vos.

6. 1. Attendite ne iustitiam vestram faciatis coram hominibus, ut videamini ab eis. . . .

6. 2. . . . Amen dico vobis, receperunt mercedem suam.

6. 3. . . . Nesciat sinistra tua quid faciat dextera tua.

6. 24. Nemo potest duobus dominis servire. . . .

7. 3. Quid autem vides festucam in oculo fratris tui, et trabem in oculo tuo non vides?

7. 5. Hypocrita, eiice primum trabem de oculo tuo, et tunc videbis eiicere festucam de oculo fratris tui.

7. 13. . . . Lata porta (*Greg. om.* porta) et spatiosa via est quae ducit ad perditionem. . . .

10. 16. . . . Estote ergo (*Greg. om.* ergo) prudentes sicut serpentes. et simplices sicut columbae.

10. 34. Nolite arbitrari quia pacem venerim (*Greg.* venerim pacem) mittere in terram; non veni pacem mittere, sed gladium.

12. 36. . . . Omne verbum otiosum quod locuti fuerint homines, reddent rationem de eo (*Greg.* de eo rationem) in die iudicii.

12. 43-45. Đonne ān unclǣne gāst bið ādrifen of ðǣm men, ðonne bið ðæt hūs clǣne; ac gif hē eft cymð, ond ðæt hūs īdel gemētt, hē hit gefylleð mid swīðe monegum. C. P. 282.

13. 28. Sum man ðis dyde þe ūre frond wæs. C. P. 356.

15. 11. Ne geunclǣnsað ðæt nō ðone men ðæt on his mūð gǣð; ac ðæt ðæt of his mūðe gǣð, ðæt hiene geunclǣnsað.
C. P. 316.

15. 14. Gif se blinda ðone blindan lǣdeð, hī feallað bēgen on ānne pyt. C. P. 28.

16. 26. Hwæt forstent ǣnegum men (ðæt II.), ðēah hē gemangige (mangige II.) ðæt hē ealne ðisne middangeard āge, gif hē his sāule forspildeð? C. P. 332.

18. 6. Sē þe ǣnigne ðissa ierminga beswīcð, him wǣre betre ðæt him wǣre sumu esulcweorn tō ðǣm swīran getīgged, ond swā āworpen tō sǣs grunde. C. P. 30.

19. 11. Ne underfōð nō ealle men ðās lāre. C. P. 409.

20. 25-28. Wiete gē ðætte ðēoda kyningas bēoð ðæs folces wāldendas, ond ðā þe ðone onwāld begāð, hīe bēoð hlāfurdas gehātene. Ne sīe hit ðonne nō swā betweoxn ēow; ac swā-hwelc-swā wille betweoxn ēow fyrmest bēon, sē sceal bīon ēower ðegn, ond swā-hwelc-swā wille betweoxn ēow mǣst bēon, sīe sē

12. 43-45. Cum autem immundus spiritus exierit ab homine, ... veniens inveniet eam vacantem, scopis mundatam.... Tunc vadit, et assumit septem alios spiritus secum,... habitant ibi....(*Greg. sum.* Uno quidem exeunte spiritu munda domus dicitur, sed multiplicius redeunte dum vacat occupatur).

13. 28. ... Inimicus homo hoc fecit....

15. 11. Non quod intrat in os coinquinat hominem; sed quod procedit ex ore, hoc (*Greg. om.* hoc) coinquinat hominem.

15. 14. ... Caecus autem si caeco ducatum praestet (*Greg.* Si caecus caeco ducatum praebeat), ambo in foveam cadunt.

16. 26. Quid enim (*Greg. om.* enim) prodest homini, si mundum universum (*Greg.* totum mundum) lucretur, animae vero suae detrimentum patiatur (*Greg.* faciat)? ...

18. 6. Qui autem (*Greg. om.* autem) scandalizaverit unum de pusillis istis qui in me credunt, expedit ei ut suspendatur mola asinaria in collo eius, et demergatur in profundum maris.

19. 11. ... Non omnes capiunt verbum istud (*Greg.* hoc). ...

20. 25-28. ... Scitis quia principes gentium dominantur eorum, et qui maiores sunt potestatem exercent in eos. Non ita erit inter vos; sed quicumque voluerit inter vos maior fieri, sit vester minister, et qui voluerit inter vos primus esse, erit vester servus; sicut (*Greg.*

eower ðeow; swā-swā monnes sunu, . . . ne cōm hē nō
tō ðǣm on corðan ðæt him mon ðēnade, ac ðæt hē wolde
ðēnian. C. P. 120.

‖ Ne com ic tō ðon on corðan ðæt mē mon ðēnode, ac tō ðon
ðæt ic wolde ðegnian. C. P. 300.

23. 6, 7. Hī sēceað þæt hī mon ǣrest grēte ond weorðige on
cēapstōwum ond on gebīorscipum, ond þæt hī fyrmest hlynigen
æt ǣfengiflum, ond þæt yldeste setl on gemētingum hī
sēceað. C. P. 26.

23. 13. Nāðer nē hīe selfe on ryhtne weg gān noldon, nē ōðrum
geðafian. C. P. 58.

23. 23. Ge tīogoðiað eowre mintan ond eowerne dile ond eowerne
kymen, ond lǣtað untīogoðad ðætte dīorwyrðre is eowra ōðra
ǣhta, ond ðā bebodu ðe grēt māran sint on ðǣre ǣwe gē nō ne
healdað, ðæt is ryht dōm ond mildheortnys ond trēowa. C. P. 439.

23. 24. . . . ðæt hī wiðblēowen ðāre flēogan, ond forswulgun ðone
olfend. C. P. 439.

23. 27. . . . ðæt hī wǣren gelīcost dēadra manna byrgennum, ðā
bīoð ūtan oft swīðe wlitige geworhte, ond bīoð innan swīðe fūle
gefylde. C. P. 449.

24. 48–51. Se yfela ðeow cwið on his mōde : Hit bið long hwonne
se hlāford cume; ic mæg slēan ond ierman mīne hēafudge-
mæccean; itt him ðonne ond drincð mid ðǣm druncenwillum
monnum, ond lǣt his hlāfordes gebod tō gīemelīste. Ðonne

2 quia) filius hominis non venit ministrari, sed ministrare. . . .

23. 6, 7. Amant autem primos recubitus in coenis, et primas cathedras in synagogis, et salutationes in foro. . . . (*Greg. sum.* Primas salutationes in foro, primos in coenis recubitus, primas in conventibus cathedras quaerunt).

23. 13. . . . Vos enim non intratis, nec introeuntes sinitis intrare (*Greg. sum.* Nec ipsi intrant, nec alios intrare permittunt).

23. 23. . . . Decimatis mentham et anethum et cyminum, et reliquistis (*Greg.* relinquitis) quae graviora sunt legis, iudicium et misericordiam et fidem. . . .

23. 24. . . . Excolantes (*Greg.* Liquantes) culicem, camelum autem glutientes.

23. 27. . . . Similes estis sepulcris dealbatis, quae a foris parent hominibus speciosa, intus vero plena sunt ossibus mortuorum et omni spurcitia (*Greg. sum.* Quos recte sepulcra dealbata speciosa exterius, sed mortuorum ossibus plena . . .).

24. 48–51. Si autem (*Greg.* Quod si) dixerit malus servus ille (*Greg.* ille servus) in corde suo : Moram facit dominus meus venire; et coeperit percutere conservos suos, manducet autem et bibat cum ebriosis (*Greg.* ebriis); veniet

cymð his hlāford on ðǣm dæge þe hē ne wēnð, ǫnd on ðā tiid
ðæt hē hiene ǣr nāt ; hæfð hine ðonne siððan for ænne
licettere. C. P. 120.

25. 18. *See* C. P. 58.

25. 24 ff. *See* C. P. 378.

25. 41. Gewītað frǫm mē, āwiergede, on ēce fȳr, ðæt wæs gegearwod diofle ǫnd his ǫnglum. C. P. 328.

25. 42, 43. Mē hyngrede, ǫnd gē mē nāuht ne sāldon etan ; mē
ðyrste, ǫnd gē mē ne sāldon drincan ; ic wæs cuma, ǫnd
gē mē noldon onfōn ; ic wæs nacod, ǫnd gē mē noldon
bewrīon ; ic wæs untrum ǫnd on carcærne, ǫnd gē mīn noldon
fandian. C. P. 328.

28. 10. Farað ǫnd cȳðað mīnum brōðrum þæt hīe cumen tō Gali-
leum ; ðǣr hīe mē gesīoð. C. P. 42.

MARK.

9. 36. *See* Matt. 16. 26.

9. 50 (Vulg. 49). Habbað gē sealt on ēow, ǫnd sibbe habbað betweoh
ēow. C. P. 92.

‖ Habbað gē sealt on ēow, ǫnd sibbe betweoh ēow. C. P. 94.

‖ Habbað sealt on ēow, ǫnd (habbað H.) sibbe betweoxen
ēow. C. P. 346.

LUKE.

2. 42, 43, 46. . . . ðætte ūre Hǣlend, ðā hē wæs twęlfwintre, wurde
beæftan his mēder ǫnd his mǣgum innan ðǣre ceastre Hierusalem. Ac ęft, ðā his mǣgas hine sōhton, ðā fundon hīe hiene

---

dominus servi illius in die qua
non sperat, et hora qua ignorat,
et dividet eum, partemque eius
ponet cum hypocritis. . . .

25. 41. . . . Discedite a me, maledicti, in ignem aeternum, qui
paratus est diabolo et angelis
eius.

25. 42, 43. Esurivi enim (*Greg. om.*
enim), et non dedistis mihi manducare ; sitivi, et non dedistis mihi
potum (*Greg.* bibere); hospes eram,
et non collegistis me ; nudus, et
non cooperuistis (*Greg.* operuistis)

me ; infirmus et in carcere, et non
visitastis me.

28. 10. Ite, nuntiate (*Greg.* dicite)
fratribus meis (*Greg. om. rel.*) ut
eant in Galilaeam ; ibi me videbunt.

MARK.

9. 49. . . . Habete in vobis sal (*Greg.*
sal in vobis), et pacem habete
inter vos.

LUKE.

2. 42, 43, 46. . . . Cum factus esset
annorum duodecim, . . . remansit

tōmiddes ðāra wietena ðe ðær wīsoste wæron in Hierusalem, hlystende hiora worda, ọnd frīnende hiora lāra. C. P. 385.

3. 9. *See* Matt. 3. 10.

6. 24. Wā ēow welegum. C. P. 180.

6. 25. Wā ēow þe nū hlęhhað, forðæm gē sculon ęft wēpan. C. P. 186.

6. 30. Sęle ælcum ðāra þe ðē bidde. C. P. 324.

7. 47. Hire sint forgifena swīðe manega synna, forðæmðe hio swīðe hrēowsade. C. P. 411.

8. 14. Hiora sæd gefēollun on þā ðornas. Dæt sindon ðā þe gehīerað Godes word, ọnd mid ðære geornfulnesse ọnd mid ðære wilnunge ðisse worlde ọnd hiere welena bið āsmorad ðæt sæd Godes worda, ðēah hīe ūpāsprytten, ðæt hīe ne mōton full-grōwan nē wæstmbære weorðan. C. P. 66.

9. 62. ... ðæt nān mọn ne scyle dōn his họnd tō ðære sylg, ọnd hāwian underbæc. C. P. 403.

10. 30, 33, 34. Hē lærde ðurh ðā tiolunga ðæs Samaritaniscan ymb ðone gewundedan, þe mọn lædde healfcwicne tō ðæm giesthūse, ọnd bæd ðæt mọn sceolde ægðer ge wīn ge ęle gēotan on his wunde. C. P. 124.

11. 24. *See* Matt. 12. 43–45.

12. 23. Māre is ðæt mōd ðonne se męte, ọnd se līchọma ðonne ðæt hrægl. C. P. 326.

puer Iesus in Ierusalem. ... Invenerunt illum in templo sedentem in medio doctorum, audientem illos, et interrogantem. ...

6. 24. ... Vae vobis divitibus. ...

6. 25. ... Vae vobis qui ridetis nunc, quia (*Greg.* quoniam) lugebitis et (*Greg. om.* lugebitis et) flebitis.

6. 30. Omni autem (*Greg. om.* autem) petenti te, tribue. ...

7. 47. ... Remittuntur ei peccata multa, quoniam (*Greg.* quia) dilexit multum. ...

8. 14. Quod (*Greg.* Semen) autem (*Greg. ins.* quod) in spinas cecidit, hi sunt qui audierunt (*Greg. ins.* verbum), et a sollicitudinibus et divitiis et voluptatibus vitae euntes suffocantur, et non referunt fructum.

9. 62. ... Nemo mittens manum suam ad aratrum, et respiciens retro, aptus est regno Dei (*Greg.* coelorum).

10. 30, 33, 34. ... Plagis impositis abierunt semivivo relicto. Samaritanus autem quidam iter faciens, venit secus eum, et videns eum, misericordia motus est. Et appropians (*al.* appropinquans) alligavit vulnera eius, infundens oleum et vinum; et imponens illum in iumentum suum, duxit in stabulum, et curam eius egit (*Greg. sum.* Per Samaritani studium semivivus in stabulum ducitur, et vinum et oleum vulneribus eius adhibetur).

12. 23. Anima plus est (*Greg.* Plus est namque anima) quam esca, et corpus plus (*Greg. om.* plus) quam vestimentum.

12. 42. Hwā wēnstū ðæt sīe tō ðǣm getrēow ǫnd [tō] ðǣm wīs brytnere ðæt hine God gesętte ofer his hīred, tō ðǣm ðæt hē him tō tīde gemetlice gedǣle ðone hwǣte ? C. P. 459.

12. 47. Sē ðegn, se ðe wāt his hlāfordes willan, ǫnd ðonne nyle wyrcean æfter his hlāfordes willan, hē bið manigra wīta wyrðe. C. P. 429.

13. 6 ff. *See* C. P. 336.

13. 27. Gewītað frǫm mē, gē unryhtwyrhtan ; nāt ic hwæt gē sint. C. P. 26.

14. 11. Ǣlc ðāra ðe hiene selfne ūpāhęfeð, hē wierð gehīened. C. P. 298. Ǣlc ðāra ðe bið geēaðmēd, hē bið ūpāhafen. C. P. 298.

14. 12-14. Ðonne ðū hæbbe gegearwod undergifl oððe ǣfengifl, ne laða ðǣrtō nō (ðū nō ðǣrtō H.) ðīne frīend, nē ðīnne (ðīne H.) brōður, nē ðīne cūðan, nē ðīne welegan nēahgebūras, ðȳlǣs hīe ðē dōn ðæt selfe. Ac ðonne ðū forme (feorme II.) gierwe on ælmessan, laða ðǣrtō wǣdlan, ǫnd wanhāle, ǫnd healte, ǫnd blinde ; ðonne bist ðū ēadig, forðon hīe nyton mid hwǣm hīe hit ðē forgieldan. C. P. 322.

15. 7. Māra gefēa wyrð on hefonum for ānum hrēowsiendum ðonne ofer nigon ǫnd hundnigontig ryhtwīsra ðǣra ðe him nān ðearf ne bið hrēowsunga. C. P. 411.

16. 19. . . . ðæt hē ǣlce dæge simblede, ǫnd mid micelre wiste

---

12. 42. . . . Quis, putas, est fidelis dispensator et prudens, quem constituet (*Greg.* constituit) dominus supra (*Greg.* super)familiam suam, ut det illis in tempore tritici mensuram ?

12. 47. . . . Servus, qui cognovit voluntatem domini sui, et non praeparavit, et non fecit secundum voluntatem eius, vapulabit multis.

13. 27. . . . Nescio vos unde sitis ; discedite a me, omnes operarii iniquitatis (*Greg.* Recedite a me operarii iniquitatis ; nescio qui estis).

14. 11. . . . Omnis qui se exaltat humiliabitur ; et (*Greg.* omnis) qui se humiliat exaltabitur.

14. 12-14. . . . Cum facis prandium aut coenam, noli vocare amicos tuos, neque fratres tuos, neque cognatos, neque vicinos divites, ne forte te et ipsi (*Greg.* et ipsi te) reinvitent, et fiat tibi retributio. Sed cum facis convivium, voca pauperes, debiles, claudos, et (*Greg. om.* et) caecos ; et beatus eris, quia non habent retribuere tibi. . . .

15. 7. . . . Gaudium erit in coelo super uno peccatore poenitentiam agente (*Greg.* poenitente), (*Greg. ins.* magis) quam super nonaginta novem iustis, qui non indigent poenitentia (*Greg.* quibus non opus est poenitentia).

16. 19. . . . Qui induebatur purpura et bysso, et (*Greg.* qui) epulabatur quotidie splendide.

wǣre gefiormod, ǫnd ǣlce dǣge geglǫnged mid purpuran ǫnd mid hwītum hrægle.   C. P. 336.

‖ . . . ꝺ̈ætte ǣlce dǣge symblede.   C. P. 309.

16. 24. Fæder Habraham, miltsa mē, ǫnd onsęnd Ladzarus, ꝺ̈ætte hē gewǣte his ȳtemestan finger on wættre, ǫnd mid ꝺ̈ǣm gecēle mīne tungan, forꝺ̈ǣm ic eom cwielmed on ꝺ̈ȳs līege.   C. P. 309.

16. 25. Đū onfēnge ꝺ̈īn gōd eal hēr on worulde.   C. P. 391.

17. 10. Đonne gē eall hæbben gedōn ꝺ̈æt ēow beboden is, ꝺ̈onne cweꝺ̈e gē ꝺ̈æt gē sīen unnytte ꝺ̈ēowas, forꝺ̈ǣm gē ꝺ̈æt ān worhton ꝺ̈æt gē nīede scoldon.   C. P. 322.

18. 12. Ic fæste tuwa on wucan.   C. P. 312.

18. 14. *See* Luke 14. 11.

21. 19. On ꝺ̈o(w)rum geꝺ̈ylde gē gehealdaꝺ̈ ēowra sāula.   C. P. 218.

21. 34, 35. Behealdaꝺ̈ ēow ꝺ̈æt gē ne gehęfegien ēowre heortan mid oferǣte ǫnd oferdrynce, ǫnd mid mǫnigfcaldre grēminge ꝺ̈isse worlde, . . . ꝺ̈ȳlǣs ēow hrædlice on becume se fǣrlica dōmes dæg ; . . . hē cymꝺ̈ swǣ-swǣ grin ofer ealle ꝺ̈ā þe eardiaꝺ̈ ofer eorꝺ̈an.   C. P. 128.

‖ Behāldaꝺ̈ ēow ꝺ̈æt īowre heortan ne sīen gehęfgode mid oferǣte ǫnd druncennesse, ǫnd on tō manigfāldum ymbehogan ꝺ̈isse worlde, ꝺ̈ȳlǣs īow on ꝺ̈ǣm weorcum gemēte se rēꝺ̈a ǫnd se ęgeslica ꝺ̈æg, se cymꝺ̈ ofer ealle oorꝺ̈waran unꝺ̈inged (ungeꝺ̈inged H.), swǣ-swǣ grin.   C. P. 316.

24. 49. Sittaꝺ̈ ēow nū gīet innan ceastre, ōꝺ̈-ꝺ̈æt gē weorꝺ̈en fullgearowode mid ꝺ̈ǣm gǣsꝺ̈lican cræfte.   C. P. 385.

16. 24. . . . Pater Abraham, miserere mei, et mitte Lazarum, ut intingat extremum digiti sui in aquam, ut refrigeret linguam meam, quia crucior in hac flamma.

16. 25. . . . Recepisti bona in vita tua.

17. 10. . . . Cum feceritis omnia quae praecepta sunt vobis, dicite : Servi inutiles sumus ; quod debuimus facere, fecimus.

18. 12. Ieiuno bis in sabbato. . . .

21. 19. In patientia vestra possidebitis animas vestras.

21. 34, 35. Attendite autem vobis, ne forte (*Greg.* 1 ut non) graventur corda vestra in crapula et ebrietate, et (*Greg.* 1 aut in) curis huius vitae (*Greg.* 1 mundi), et (*Greg.* 1 ne forte) superveniat in vos repentina dies illa ; tamquam laqueus enim superveniet in (*Greg.* 1 veniet super) omnes qui sedent super faciem omnis terrae.

24. 49. . . . Vos autem sedete in civitate, quoadusque induamini virtute ex alto.

JOHN.

1. 12. Ðā þe hiene onfēngon, hē sālde him onwāld ðæt hīe meahton bēon Godes bearn. C. P. 84.

5. 30. Ne mæg ic nāne wuht dōn mīnes āgnes ðǫnces, ac suā ic dōme suā ic mīnne Fæder gehīere. C. P. 307.

Ne sēce ic nō mīnne willan, ac mīnes Fæder ðe mē hider sǫnde. C. P. 307.

6. 15. Iudēas cōmon ǫnd woldon hine dōn nīdenga tō kyninge. Ðā se Hǣlend þæt ongeat, þā becirde hē hī ǫnd gehȳdde hine. C. P. 32.

7. 38. See C. P. 467.

10. 12. See C. P. 88.

14. 27. Mīne sibbe ic ēow sǫlle, ǫnd mīne sibbe ic lǣte tō īow. C. P. 350.

16. 12. Fela ic hæbbe ēow tō sæcganne, ac gē hit ne magon nū gīt āberan. C. P. 236.

16. 22. Eft ic ēow gesīo, ǫnd ðonne blissiað ēowre heortan, ǫnd ēowerne gefēan ēow nān mǫn æt ne genimð. C. P. 186.

21. 16. And[1] eft hē cwæð tō Petre ðǣm apostole: Petrus, lufast ðū mē? Hē cwæð: Ðū wāst þæt ic ðē lufige. And[1] þū cwæð Dryhten: Fēd ðonne mīn scēap, gif ðū mē lufige. C. P. 42.

JOHN.

1. 12. Quotquot autem receperunt eum, dedit eis potestatem filios Dei fieri. . . .

5. 30. Non possum ego a me ipso (*Greg.* Ego a me ipso non possum) facere quidquam ; (*Greg. ins.* sed) sicut audio, iudico, . . . quia (*Greg. om.* quia) non quaero voluntatem meam, sed voluntatem eius qui misit me (*Greg. ins.* Patris).

6. 15. Iesus ergo cum cognovisset quia venturi essent ut raperent eum, et facerent eum regem, fugit iterum in montem ipse solus.

14. 27. Pacem relinquo vobis, pacem meam do vobis. . . .

16. 12. . . . Multa habeo vobis dicere, sed (*Greg. ins.* nunc) non potestis (*Greg. ins.* illa) portare modo (*Greg. om.* modo).

16. 22. . . . Iterum autem (*Greg. om.* autem) videbo vos, et gaudebit cor vestrum, et gaudium vestrum nemo tollet a vobis.

21. 16. Dicit ei iterum (*Greg.* Hinc Petro ait): Simon Ioannis, diligis (*Greg.* amas) me ? Ait illi : Etiam, Domine, tu scis quia amo te. Dicit ei : Pasce agnos meos (*Greg.* Qui cum se amare protinus respondisset, audivit: Si diligis me, pasce oves meas).

---

[1] So Sweet.

ACTS.

2. 3. *See* C. P. 92.

2. 22-24. Ðone Nazareniscan Hǣlend ðæt wæs āfandon[1] wer betwux ēow on mægenum ǫnd tācnum ǫnd foretācnum, ðā worhte Dryhten ðurh hine ongemang ēow, ðone gū beswicon ðurh unryhtwīsra mǫnna hǫnda, ǫnd ofslōgon ǫnd āhēngon ðurh ēower gedeaht, swā-swā hit God æt fruman wisse ǫnd ðeah gedafode; se ilca God hine ęft āweahte tō onlīesanne ðā gehæftan on hęlle. C. P. 443.

2. 37, 38. Hwæt magon wē his nū dōn, brōður Petrus? Petrus andswarode ǫnd cwæð: Dōð ǣrest hrēowsunga, ǫnd weorðað siðcan gefullwade. C. P. 443.

‖ Hrēowsiað, ǫnd weorðað gefulwade ēower ǣlc. C. P. 425.

5. 1 ff. *See* C. P. 114.

9. 5-7. Āscode ǫnd cwæð: Hwæt eart ðū, Dryhten? Ðā wæs him swīðe hraðe geandwyrd: Ic eom se Nazarenisca Hǣlend, ðe ðū ēhtst. Ǫnd ðā cwæð hē: Dryhten, hwæt hǣtst ðū mē dōn? Ðā ǫndwyrde him Dryhten: Ārīs, ǫnd gǫng tō geonre byrg; ðǣ mǫn sægð ðāra[2] hwæt ðū dōn scealt. C. P. 443.

10. 26. Ārīs, ne dō swǣ; hū, ne eom ic mǫn swǣ-ilce-swǣ ðū? C. P. 114.

17. 18. *See* C. P. 96.

ACTS.

2. 22-24. ... Iesum Nazarenum, virum approbatum a Deo in vobis virtutibus et prodigiis et signis, quae fecit Deus per illum (*Greg.* per illum fecit Deus) in medio vestri, sicut et (*Greg. om.* et) vos scitis, hunc, definito consilio et praescientia Dei traditum, per manus iniquorum affligentes interemistis; quem Deus suscitavit, solutis doloribus inferni. ...

2. 37, 38. ... Quid (*Greg. ins.* ergo) faciemus, viri fratres? Petrus vero ad illos (*Greg.* Quibus mox dicitur): Poenitentiam, inquit, agite (*Greg.* Agite poenitentiam), et baptizetur unusquisque vestrum. ...

9. 5-7. Qui dixit (*Greg.* Nam cum prostratus requireret, dicens): Quis es, Domine? Et ille (*Greg.* Respondetur protinus): Ego sum Iesus (*Greg. ins.* Nazarenus), quem tu persequeris; ... Dixit (*Greg.* Et cum repente subiungeret): Domine, quid me vis (*Greg.* iubes) facere? Et Dominus ad eum (*Greg.* Illico adiungitur): Surge, et (*Greg.* Surgens) ingredere civitatem, et ibi dicetur tibi quid te oporteat facere.

10. 26. ... Surge, (*Greg. ins.* ne feceris); et ego ipse homo sum.

---

[1] Unusual for 'āfandod.'   [2] Unusual for 'ðǣr.'

20. 26, 27. Hwæt, ge sint ealle mīne gewitan ðæt ic eom clǣne ǫnd unscyldig nū gīt tō-dæg ēowres ǣlces blōdes ; forðǣm ic nǣfre ne forwandode ðæt ic īow ne gecȳðde eall Godes geðeaht. C. P. 378.

22. 8. Ic eom se Nazarenisca Hǣlend ðe ðū ēhtst. C. P. 443.

23. 6. Hwæt dō ge, brōðor, dōð eśnlice. Hū, ne eom ic ēower gefēra, ǫnd eom Farisēisc swǣ-same-swǣ ge ? ǫnd forðǣm mīn mǫn ēht þe ic bodige ymb ðone tōhopan dēadra mǫnna ǣristes. C. P. 362.

23. 8. Ðā Saducie andsacedon ðǣre ǣriste æfter dēaðe ; ǫnd ðā Farisēos gelīefdon ðǣre ǣriste. C. P. 362.

ROMANS.

1. 14. . . . Sanctus Paulus, se sceolde lǣran ǣgðer ge wīse ge unwīse. C. P. 204.

1. 22. Hīe sǣdon ðæt hīe wǣron wīse, ǫnd þā wurdon hīe dysige forðon. C. P. 70.

7. 23. . . . ðæt hē gesāwe ōðerne gewunan ǫnd ōðerne willan on his limum, ǫnd sē wǣre feohtende wið ðǣm willan his mōdes. ǫnd hine gehæftne lǣdde on synne gewunan. C. P. 423.

8. 15. Ne underfēngon ge nō ðone gāst æt ðǣm fulluhte tō ðēowianne for ęge, ac ge hiene underfēngon tō ðām ðæt ge Gode geāgnudu bearn bēon scylen, forðȳ wē clipiað tō Gode, ǫnd cweðað : Fæder, Fæder. C. P. 262.

20. 26, 27. . . . Contestor vos hodierna die, quia mundus sum a sanguine omnium ; non enim subterfugi, quominus annuntiarem omne consilium Dei vobis.

22. 8. . . . Ego sum Iesus Nazarenus, quem tu persequeris.

23. 6. . . . Viri fratres, ego Pharisaeus sum, filius Pharisaeorum ; de spe et resurrectione mortuorum ego iudicor.

23. 8. Sadducaei enim dicunt non esse resurrectionem . . . ; Pharisaei autem . . . confitentur (*Greg. sum.*).

ROMANS.

1. 14. . . . Sapientibus et insipientibus debitor. . . .

1. 22. Dicentes enim se esse sapientes, stulti facti sunt.

7. 23. Video autem (*Greg. om.* autem) aliam legem in membris meis. repugnantem legi mentis meae. et captivantem me (*Greg.* captivum me ducentem) in lege peccati, quae est in membris meis.

8. 15. Non enim (*Greg. om.* enim) accepistis spiritum servitutis iterum in timore, sed accepistis spiritum adoptionis filiorum, in quo clamamus : Abba, Pater.

12. 3. Ne wilnigen gē māre tō wietenne ðonne ēow ðearf sīe, ac wietað ðæt ðæt ēow gemetlic sīe, ǫnd ēower ǫndefnu sīen tō wietonne.   C. P. 92, 94.

12. 16. Ne sculon gē nō ðyncan ēow selfum tō wīse.   C. P. 306.

12. 18. Ic wolde, gif hit swā bīon meahte, ðæt gē wið ūlcne mǫnn hæfden sibbe, ēowres gewealdes.   C. P. 354.

13. 3. Gif ðū wille ðæt ðū ne ðyrfe ðē ondrǣdan ðīnne hlāford, dō tela ; ðonne herest hū ðū.   C. P. 457.

13. 11. Nū ūs is tīma ðæt wē onwæcnen of slǣpe.   C. P. 459.

13. 13. Ne gewunige gē nō tō oferetolnesse ǫnd tō oferdruncennesse.   C. P. 316.

14. 3. Sō þe fæstan wille, ne tǣle hē nō ðone þe ete.   C. P. 310.

14. 21. . . . ðæt hit wǣre gōd ðæt mǫn forēode flǣsc ǫnd wīn for bīsene his brōðrum.   C. P. 318.

16. 19. Ic wille ðæt gē sīen wīse tō gōde, ǫnd bilewite tō yfele.   C. P. 236.

1 CORINTHIANS.

1. 12. Sume cwǣdon ðæt hīe wǣron Apollan ; sume cwǣdon ðæt hīe wǣron Paules (Saules H.); sume Petres ; sum cwæð ðæt hē wǣre Crīstes.   C. P. 210.

1. 26. Ne sculon gē bīon tō wīse æfter ðæs līchǫman luste.   C. P. 202.

1. 27. Ðā þe woroldmǫnnum ðynceað dysige, ðā gecīst Dryhten, forðǣmþe [forðǣm ðæt] hē ðā lytegan . . . gescęnde.   C. P. 202, 204.

12. 3. . . . . Non plus sapere quam oportet sapere, sed sapere ad sobrietatem. . . .

12. 16. . . . . Nolite esse prudentes (*Greg.* prudentes esse) apud vosmetipsos.

12. 18. Si fieri potest, quod ex vobis est,cum omnibus hominibus pacem habentes.

13. 3. . . . . Vis autem (*Greg. om.* autem) non timere potestatem ? Bonum fac, et habebis laudem ex illa.

13. 11. . . . Hora est iam nos de somno surgere.

13. 13. . . . . Non in comessationibus et ebrietatibus. . . .

14. 3. . . . . Qui non manducat, manducantem non iudicet. . . .

14. 21. Bonum est non manducare carnem, et non (*Greg.* neque) bibere vinum, neque in quo frater tuus . . . scandalizatur. . . .

16. 19. . . . . Volo vos sapientes esse in bono, et (*Greg. om.* et) simplices (*Greg. ins.* autem) in malo.

1 CORINTHIANS.

1. 12. . . . . Unusquisque vestrum dicit : Ego quidem sum Pauli ; ego autem Apollo ; ego vero Cephae ; ego autem Christi (*Greg.* Ut alius Pauli, alius Apollo, alius Cephae, alius Christi esse se diceret).

1. 26. . . . . Non multi sapientes secundum carnem. . . .

1. 27. . . . . Quae stulta sunt mundi

3. 1, 2. Ic ne mæg nō tō ēow sprecan swā-swā tō gǣstlicum, ac swā-swā tō flǣsclicum, forðǣm gē sint gīet cilderu on ēowrum gelēafan ; ðȳ ic sceal sellan ēow gīet mioloc drincan, nālles flǣsc etan. C. P. 459.

3. 3. Ðonne betweoxn ēow bið yfel anda ond geflitu, hū ne bīoð gē ðonne flǣsclice ? C. P. 344.

3. 18. Swelc ēower swelce him selfum ðynce ðæt hē (ðætte H.) wīsust sīe on ðǣm lotwrencium, weorðe ðæs ǣrest dysig, ðæt hē mæge ðonon weorðan wīs. C. P. 202.

4. 21. Hwæðer wille gē ðæt ic cume tō ēow, þe mid gierde, þe mid monðwǣre gāste ? C. P. 116.

5. 1, 2. Wē gehīerdon betweohxn ēow unryhthǣmed, ge swā unryht swā wē furðum betweohxn hǣðnum monnum ne hīerdun, ðæt is ðæt gē sumo hæfdon ēowre stēopmōdor ; ond gē ðæs næfdon nāne sorge, ond noldon from ēow ādōn ðā þe ðæt dydon, ac wǣron swā ūpāhafene swā gē ǣr wǣron. C. P. 210.

6. 4. Gif gē ymb worldcunde dōmas bēon scylen, ðonne nime gē ðā þe on ðǣm hīorede unweorðuste sīen, ond settað þā tō dōmerum. C. P. 130.

6. 9, 10. Nāwðer nō ðā wōhhǣmendan, nē ðā ðe dīofulgieldum ðīowiað, nē ðā unfæsðrǣdan, ðe ne magon hira unryhthǣmdes geswīcan, nē ðā ðīofas, nē ðā gītseras, nō ðā druncen-willnan, nē ðā wiergendan, nō ðā rēaferas, Godes rīce ne gesittað. C. P. 401.

elegit Deus, ut confundat sapientes. . . .

3. 1, 2. . . . . Non potui vobis loqui quasi spiritualibus (*Greg.* spiritalibus), sed quasi carnalibus ; tamquam parvulis in Christo, lac vobis potum dedi, non escam. . . .

3. 3. Cum enim (*Greg. om.* enim) sit inter vos zelus et contentio, nonne carnales estis ? . . .

3. 18. . . . Si quis videtur inter vos sapiens esse in hoc saeculo, stultus fiat ut sit sapiens.

4. 21. Quid vultis ? in virga veniam ad vos, (*Greg. om. rel.*) an in charitate et spiritu mansuetudinis ?

5. 1, 2. . . . Auditur inter vos fornicatio, et talis fornicatio qualis

nec inter gentes, ita ut uxorem patris sui (*Greg. om.* sui) aliquis (*Greg.* quis) habeat ; et vos inflati estis, et non magis luctum habuistis ut tollatur (*Greg.* tolleretur) de medio vestrum qui hoc opus fecit.

6. 4. Saecularia igitur iudicia si habueritis, contemptibiles qui sunt in ecclesia, illos constituite ad iudicandum.

6. 9, 10. . . . Neque fornicarii *Greg.* fornicatores), neque idolis servientes, neque adulteri, neque molles, neque masculorum concubitores, neque fures, neque avari, neque ebriosi, neque maledici, neque rupaces, regnum Dei possidebunt.

6. 11. Gē wǣron ǣr on ȳflum weorcum, ac gē sint nū geclǣnsode ọnd gehālgode. C. P. 425.

6. 13. Fulga nū se mẹte ðǣre wambe willan, ọnd sīo wamb ðæs mẹtes ; ðonne tōwierpð God ǣgðer. C. P. 316.

7. 1. Gōd bið mẹn ðæt hē sīe būtan wīfe. C. P. 397.

7. 2, 3. Hæbbe ǣlc mọn his wīf, ọnd ǣlc wīf hiere ceorl ; ọnd dō ðæt wīf ðǣm were ðæt hīo him mid ryhte dōn sceal, ọnd hē hiere swǣ sọme, ðȳlǣs hīe on unryht hǣmen. C. P. 98.

‖ Gōd bið mannum ðæt ǣlc hæbbe his āgen wīf, ọnd ǣlc wīf hire ceorl, ðȳlǣs hī on unryht hǣmen. C. P. 397.

‖ Āgife se wer his wīfe hire ryht on hira gesinscipe, ọnd swā same ðæt wīf ðǣm were. C. P. 397.

7. 5. Ne untrēowsige gē nō ēow betweoxn, būton hūru ðæt gē ēow gehæbben sume hwīle, ǣrðǣmiþe gē ēowru gebedu ọnd ēowra offrunga dōn willen, ọnd eft sōna cirrað tō ēowrum ryht-hǣmde. C. P. 98.

‖ Ne fornime incer nōðer ōðer ofer will būtan geðafunge, ðǣm tīmum ðe hē hine wille gebiddan, ac geǣmtigeað inc tō gebedum. C. P. 399.

7. 6. Ne cweðo ic nō ðæt ðæt ic ǣr cwæð bebēodende, ac lǣrende ọnd geðafigende. C. P. 397.

7. 9. . . . . ðæt hit sīe bẹtere ðæt mọn gehīewige ðonne hē birne. C. P. 401.

7. 29, 30. Ðā ðe wīf hæbben, sīen ðā swelce hīe nān hæbben ; ọnd ðā ðe wēpen, sīen ðā swelce hī nō ne wēpen ; ọnd ðā ðe fægnigen, sīen ðā swelce hī nō ne fægnigen. C. P. 395.

7. 30, 31. Sīen ðā hæbbendan swelce hīe nōwiht hæbben ; ọnd

6. 11. Et haec quidam fuistis, sed abluti estis, sed sanctificati estis. . . .

6. 13. Esca ventri, et venter escis; Deus autem et hunc et has destruet. . . .

7. 1. . . . Bonum est homini mulierem non tangere.

7. 2, 3. Propter fornicationem autem unusquisque suam uxorem habeat (*Greg.* suam habeat uxorem), et unaquaeque suum virum habeat. Uxori vir debitum reddat, similiter autem (*Greg. om.* autem) et uxor viro.

7. 5. Nolite fraudare invicem, nisi forte ex consensu ad tempus, ut vacetis orationi, (*Greg. 2 om. rel.*) et iterum revertimini in idipsum. . . .

7. 6. Hoc autem dico secundum indulgentiam, non secundum imperium.

7. 9. . . . Melius est enim (*Greg. om.* enim) nubere quam uri.

7. 29-31. . . . Qui habent uxores, tamquam non habentes sint ; et qui flent, tamquam non flentes ; et qui gaudent, tamquam non gaudentes ; . . . qui emunt, tam-

ða ðe ðisses middangeardes notigað swelce hī his nō ne notigen. C. P. 387, 389.

7. 31. Ðyses middangeardes ansīen ofergīeð. C. P. 395.

7. 35. Ðis ic cweðe for ðowerre ðearfe, ðȳlæs ic ðow mid ænige grine gefōo. Ic ēow secgge hwæt ðow ārwyrðlicost is tō begānne, ond hū gē fullecost magon Gode ðīowian ðæt ðow lǣst ðinga mierð. C. P. 401.

8. 8. Se ofermete ne befæst ūs nǣfre Gode. C. P. 316.

8. 9. Lōciað nū ðæt ðīos ðowru lēaf ne weorðe ōðrum monnum tō bīswīce. C. P. 451.

8. 11, 12. Ðonne forwyrð ðīn brōður for ðīnum ðingum, for ðone ðūr Crīst geðrōwade. Swā, ðonne gē gesyngiað wið ðowre brōðer, ond ofslēað hira untruma[n] gewit, ðonne gesyngige gē wið God. C. P. 451.

9. 9. Ne forbinde gē nō ðǣm ðerscendum (ðyrstendum H.) oxum ðone mūð. C. P. 104.

9. 20. Ðonne ic wæs mid Iudeum, ic wæs swelce hīe. C. P. 100.

10. 7. Ðæt folc sæt, æt, ond dranc, ond siððan āryson ond ēodon him plegean. C. P. 309.

10. 13. Ne gegrīpe ðow nǣfre nān costung būton mennescu. C. P. 70.

10. 33. Swǣ-swǣ ic wilnige on eallum ðingum ðæt ic monnum cwēme ond līcige. C. P. 146.

11. 31. Ðǣr wē ūs selfum dōmden, ðonne ne dēm(de) ūs nō God. C. P. 415.

---

quam non possidentes; et qui utuntur hoc mundo, tamquam non utantur; praeterit enim figura huius mundi.

7. 35. ... Hoc ad utilitatem vestram dico; non ut laqueum vobis iniiciam, sed ad id quod honestum est, et quod facultatem praebeat sine impedimento Dominum obsecrandi (*Greg.* Domino observiendi).

8. 8. Esca ... nos non commendat Deo. ...

8. 9. Videte ... ne forte haec licentia vestra offendiculum fiat infirmis.

8. 11, 12. Et peribit infirmus in tua (*Greg.* conscientia, scientia frater,

propter quem Christus mortuus est. Sic autem peccantes in fratres, et percutientes conscientiam eorum infirmam, in Christum peccatis.

9. 9. ... Non alligabis (*Greg.* obturabis) os bovi trituranti. ...

9. 20. ... Factus sum Iudaeis tamquam Iudaeus. ...

10. 7. ... Sedit populus manducare et bibere, et surrexerunt ludere.

10. 13. Tentatio vos non apprehendit (*Greg.* apprehendat) nisi humana. ...

10. 33. Sicut et ego per omnia omnibus placeo. ...

11. 31. ... Si nosmetipsos diiudicaremus, non utique iudicaremur.

13. 4. . . . ðæt sīo Godes lufu sīe geðyld.   C. P. 214.

  ‖ Lufu bið geðyldig.   C. P. 222.

  ‖ Hīo bið mildu.   C. P. 222.

14. 38. Sē þe God ne ongit, ne ongit God hine.   C. P. 28.

15. 34. Onwæcnað, gē ryhtwīsan, ọnd ne syngiað mā.   C. P. 461.

2 CORINTHIANS.

1. 17. Wēne gē nū ðæt ic ænigre lēohtmōdnesse brūce, oððe ðætte ic ðęnce æfter woruldluste, oððe wēne gē ðæt ægðer sīe mid mē ge Gise ge Nese?   C. P. 308.

1. 24 (Vulg. 23). Ne sint wē nāne wāldendas ēowres gelēafan, ac sint fultumend ēowres gefēan; forðæmþe gē stọndað on gelēafan.   C. P. 114.

2. 17. Swǣ-swǣ of Gode, beforan Gode, wē sprecað on Crīste.   C. P. 370.

3. 17. Ðǣr se Dryhtnes Gāst is, ðǣr is frēodōm.   C. P. 262, 264.

4. 5. Wē sint ēowre ðēowas for Crīstes lufan.   C. P. 116.

5. 13. Ðēah wē nū ofer ūre mōð ðęncen ọnd smēagen, ðæt wē dōð for Gode; ðonne wē hit eft gemetlǣceað, ðonne dōð wē ðæt for ēow.   C. P. 100.

5. 14, 15. Gif Crīst for ūs eallum dēad wæs, ðonne weorðað ealle mẹn dēade; hwæt is ðonne bẹtre, ðā-hwīle-þe wē libben, ðonne wē ūres flǣsces lustum ne libben, ac ðæs bebodum þe for ūs dēad wæs ọnd eft ārās?   C. P. 42.

---

13. 4. Charitas patiens est, benigna est. . . .

14. 38. Si quis autem ignorat, ignorabitur.

15. 34. Evigilate, iusti, et nolite peccare. . . .

2 CORINTHIANS.

1. 17. . . . Numquid levitate usus sum? Aut quae cogito, secundum carnem cogito, ut sit apud me Est et Non?

1. 23. . . . Non quia dominamur fidei vestrae, sed adiutores sumus gaudii vestri; nam fide statis (*Greg.* fide enim statis).

2. 17. . . . Sicut ex Deo, coram Deo, in Christo loquimur.

3. 17. . . . Ubi autem (*Greg. om.* autem) Spiritus Domini, ibi libertas.

4. 5. . . . Nos autem servos vestros per Iesum (*Greg.* Christum).

5. 13. Sive enim (*Greg. om.* enim) mente excedimus, Deo; sive sobrii sumus, vobis.

5. 14, 15. . . . Si unus (*Greg.* Christus) pro omnibus mortuus est, ergo omnes mortui sunt; et (*Greg. ins.* si) pro omnibus mortuus est Christus (*Greg. om.* Christus, *ins.* superest) ut et (*Greg. om.* et) qui vivunt iam non sibi vivant,

6. 2. Nū is hiersumnesse tīma, ǫnd nū sint hǣlnesse dagas. C. P. 246

6. 7. Gāð gē gewǣpnode, ǣgðer ge on ðā swīðran hǫnd ge on ðā winestran, mid ðǣm wǣpnum ryhtwīsnesse. C. P. 82.

8. 13, 14. Ne brō gē ōðrum mǫnnum swǣ giofole ðæt hit weorðe ēow selfum tō geswince, ac ofer ðæt þe gē selfe genōg hæbben, sęllað ðæt ðearfum, ǫnd mid ðȳ gebētað hiora wǣdle, ðætte swǣ-ilce-swǣ hīe brōð hēr gefylde mid ūre genyhtsumnesse, wē brōn ēac mid hiora genyhtsumnesse. C. P. 324.

9. 6. Sē þe lȳtel sāwð, hē lȳtel rīpeð. C. P. 324.

9. 7. . . . ðætte ðone gladan giefan God lufode. C. P. 322.

11. 29. Hwā bið geuntrumod, ðæt ic ne sīe ēac geuntrumod? oððe hwā bið gescęnded, ðæt ic ēac ðæs ne scamige? C. P. 100.

|| Hwā bið medtrum, ðæt ic ne sīe ēac for his ðingum sīoc? Oððe hwā bið gescęnded, ðæt mē forðǣm ne scamige? C. P. 164.

12. 2, 4. Paulus, ðeah-þe hē wǣre gelǣded on neorxnawǫng, þǣr hē arīmde ðā dīgolnesse ðæs ðriddan hefones. . . . C. P. 98.

GALATIANS.

1. 10. Gif ic mǫnnum cwēme ǫnd līcige, ðonne ne brō ic nō Godes ðēow. C. P. 146.

2. 11. *See* C. P. 144.

3. 1. Ēalā gē ungewitfullan Galatæ, hwā gehęfgade ēow? C. P. 206.

sed ei qui pro ipsis mortuus est et resurrexit.

6. 2. . . . Ecce nunc tempus acceptabile, ecce nunc dies salutis.

6. 7. . . . Per arma iustitiae a dextris et a (*Greg. om.* et a) sinistris (*Greg.* sinistrisque gradiens).

8. 13, 14. Non enim (*Greg. om.* enim) ut aliis sit remissio, vobis autem tribulatio, sed ex aequalitate . . . Vestra abundantia illorum inopiam suppleat, ut et (*Greg.* et ut) illorum abundantia vestrae inopiae sit supplementum. . . .

9. 6. . . . Qui parce seminat, parce et metet. . . .

9. 7. . . . Hilarem enim datorem diligit Deus.

11. 29. Quis infirmatur, et ego non infirmor? quis scandalizatur, et ego non uror?

12. 2, 4. Scio hominem in Christo . . . raptum huiusmodi usque ad tertium coelum. . . . Quoniam raptus est in paradisum, et audivit arcana verba, quae non licet homini loqui (*Greg. sum.*).

GALATIANS.

1. 10. . . . Si adhuc hominibus placerem, Christi servus non essem.

3. 1. O insensati Galatae, quis vos fascinavit? . . .

3. 3. Swǣ dysige gē sint, ðætte ðæt, ðæt gē gāstlice underfēngon, gē willað geęndian flǣsclice. C. P. 206.

5. 22. . . . ðætte ðæs Gāstes wæstm sie lufu, ǫnd gefēa, ǫnd ryht-wīslicu sibb. C. P. 344.

6. 1. Gif hwā sie ābisgod mid hwelcum scyldum, gē ðonne, þe gāstlice sindon, gelǣrað ðā swelcan mid manðwǣrnesse gāste; gescēawiað ēow selfe, ðȳlǣs ēow becyme costnung. C. P. 158.

6. 2. Bere ēower ǣlc ðōres byrðenne betweohxn ēow, ðonne gefylle gē Godes ǣ. C. P. 218.

‖ Berað ēowre byrðenna gemǣnelice betwux Iow, ðonne gefylle gē Godes ǣ. C. P. 395.

EPHESIANS.

4. 3, 4. Geornlice gebinde gē Iow tōsǫmne mid ānmōdnesse ǫnd mid sibbe, ðæt gē sien swǣ gelīces mōdes swǣ gē sint gelīces līchǫman, swǣ-swǣ gē ealle sint gelaðode tō ānum tōhopan. C. P. 344.

4. 14. Ne lǣte gē ēow ǣlcre lāre wind āwęcggan. C. P. 306.

4. 31. Ǣlc ðwēora, ǫnd ǣlc ierre, ǫnd unweorðscipe, ǫnd geclibs, ǫnd tǣl, sie ānumen fram ēow, . . . and[1] ǣlc yfel forlǣte gē on ēowrum ingeðǫnce. C. P. 222.

6. 1. Bearn, bēo gē underðīodde ēowrum ieldrum māgum on Dryhtne. C. P. 188.

6. 4. Ne gręmige gē ēowru bearn. C. P. 188.

---

3. 3. Sic stulti estis, ut cum spiritu coeperitis, nunc carne consum-memini (*Greg.* consummamini)?

5. 22. Fructus autem Spiritus est charitas, gaudium, pax. . . .

6. 1. . . . Si praeoccupatus fuerit homo in aliquo delicto, vos, qui spirituales (*Greg.* spiritales) estis, huiusmodi instruite (*Greg.* instruite huiusmodi) in spiritu lenitatis (*Greg.* mansuetudinis), considerans te ipsum, ne et tu tenteris.

6. 2. Alter alterius (*Greg. sec. Ital.* Invicem) onera (*Greg. ins.* vestra) portate, et sic adimplebitis legem Christi.

EPHESIANS.

4. 3, 4. Solliciti servare unitatem Spiritus in vinculo pacis. Unum corpus, et unus spiritus, sicut vocati estis in una spe vocationis vestrae.

4. 14. . . . Non . . . circumferamur omni vento doctrinae.

4. 31. Omnis amaritudo, et ira, et indignatio, et clamor, et blas-phemia, tollatur a vobis, cum omni malitia.

6. 1. Filii, obedite parentibus vestris in Domino. . . .

6. 4. . . . Nolite ad iracundiam pro-vocare filios vestros. . . .

---

[1] So Sweet.

E 2

6. 5. Bīoð ge underðīedde ēowrum worldhlāfordum. C. P. 200.

6. 9. Gē hlāfordas, dōð ge ēowrum mǫnnum ðæt ilce be hiora andefene, ǫnd gemetgiað ðone ðrēan ; geð̣enceað ðæt ǣgðer ge hiera hlāford ge ēower is on hefonum. C. P. 200, 202.

6. 15. Scēogeað ēowre fētt, þæt gē sīn gearwe tō gānne on sibbe weg æfter mīnra bōca bebodum. C. P. 44.

PHILIPPIANS.

2. 8. Crīst ūre Alīesend hiene selfne geēaðmōdde emne ōð ðone dēað. C. P. 300.

3. 19. . . . ðætte hiera wǫmb wǣre hiora God, ǫnd hīe dyden him hiora bismer tō weorðscipe. C. P. 316.

4. 10. Ic eom swīðe gefīonde on Dryhtne ðætte gē ǣfre woldon ǣnige wuht ēow selfum wītan ǣr ic hit ēow wīte. Hit is gōd ðæt gē hit nū wietun. Nǣron gē nōht ǣmettige, ðēah gē wel ne dyden. C. P. 206.

COLOSSIANS.

2. 23. Oft, ðonne mǫn mā fæst ðonne hē ðyrfe, ðonne ēowað hē ūtan ēaðmōdnesse, ǫnd for ðǣre ilcan ēaðmōdnesse hē ofermōdegað innan micle ðȳ hęfiglicor. C. P. 312.

3. 5. Sīo gīdsung, þe . . . wǣre hearga ǫnd īdelnysse gefēra. C. P. 156.

6. 5. . . . Obedite dominis carnalibus. . . .

6. 9. Et vos, domini, eadem facite illis, remittentes minas, scientes quia (*Greg.* quod) et illorum et vester Dominus est in coelis. . . .

6. 15. Calceati pedes in praeparatione evangelii pacis.

PHILIPPIANS.

2. 8. . . . (*Greg. ins.* Quia Redemptor noster) Humiliavit semetipsum, factus obediens usque ad mortem. . . .

3. 19. . . . Quorum Deus venter est, et gloria in confusione ipsorum. . .

4. 10. Gavisus sum autem (*Greg. om.* autem) in Domino vehementer, quoniam tandem aliquando refloruistis pro me sentire, sicut et sentiebatis; occupati autem (*Greg.* enim) eratis.

COLOSSIANS.

2. 23. Quae sunt rationem quidem habentia sapientiae in superstitione et humilitate, et non ad parcendum corpori, non in honore aliquo ad saturitatem carnis.

3. 5. . . . Avaritiam (*Greg.* Et avaritia), quae est simulacrorum (*Greg.* idolorum) servitus.

1 THESSALONIANS.

2. 7. Wē sint gewordene swelce lȳtlingas betweoxn ēow. C. P. 116.

2 THESSALONIANS.

1. 3, 4. Wē sculon simle sæcgean Gode ðancas for ēow, brōður, swǣ-swǣ hit wel wyrðe is, forðǣmþe ēower gelēafa hæfð ofer-ðungen swīðe monegra ōðerra monna, ond ēower lufu is betweohxn ēow swīðe genyhtsumu, swǣ ðæt wē apostolas sint swīðe gefēonde ealle for ēowrum gelēafan ond for ēo(w)rum geðylde. C. P. 212.

2. 1, 2. Ic ēow healsige, brōður, for ðǣm tōcyme Dryhtnes Hǣlendan Crīstes, ond for ūre gesomnunge, ðæt gē nō tō hrædlice ne sīen āstyrede from ēowrum gewitte, nē ēow tō swīðe ne [on]drǣdað for nānes monnes wordum, nē for nānes wītgan gāste, nē ðēah ēow hwelc ǣrendgewrit cume, swelce hit from ūs āsend (sęnd H.) sīe, ond ðǣron cȳðe ðæt se dōmes dæg nēah sīe. C. P. 212.

3. 14, 15. Swǣ-hwā-swǣ ūrum wordum ond gewritum hīeran nylle, dō hit mon ūs tō witanne, ond næbbe gē nænne gemānan wið hiene, forðǣm ðætte hiene gesceamige. . . . Ne scule gē wið hiene gebǣran swǣ-swǣ wið fīond, ac gē him sculon cīdan swǣ-swǣ brēðer. C. P. 356.

---

1 THESSALONIANS.

2. 7. . . . . Facti sumus (Greg. ins. sicut) parvuli in medio vestrum. . . .

2 THESSALONIANS.

1. 3, 4. Gratias agere debemus sem-per Deo (Greg. Deo semper) pro vobis, fratres, ita ut dignum est, quoniam supercrescit fides vestra, et abundat charitas uniuscuiusque vestrum in invicem, ita ut et nos ipsi in vobis gloriemur in eccle-siis Dei, pro patientia vestra et fide. . . .

2. 1, 2. Rogamus autem vos, fratres, per adventum Domini nostri Iesu Christi, et nostrae congregationis in ipsum, ut non cito moveamini a vestro sensu neque terreamini, neque per spiritum, neque per ser-monem, neque per epistolam tam-quam per nos missam, quasi instet dies Domini.

3. 14, 15. . . . Si quis non obedit verbo nostro per epistolam, hunc notate, et ne (Greg. non) commisceamini cum illo, ut confundatur. Et nolite quasi (Greg. ut) inimicum existimare (Greg. ins. illum), sed corripite ut fratrem.

1 TIMOTHY.

3. 1. Sē þe biscephād [biscephāde] gewilnað, gōd weorc hē gewilnað. C. P. 52.

3. 2. Biscepe gedafenað þæt hē sīe tǣllēas. C. P. 52.

4. 1, 3. . . . ðæt ðǣm forhæbbendum hwīlum gebyrede ðæt hīe gewiten of hiera gelēafan, ǫnd forbīodað mannum ðæt hīe hīwien, ǫnd ðā mettas þe God self gescēop tō etonne gelēaffullum mǫnnum, ðǣm þe ongietað sōðfæstnesse ǫnd Gode ðanciað mid gōdum weorcum his gifa. C. P. 316, 318.

4. 11, 12. Bebīod ðis, ǫnd lǣre ; ǫnd ne forsīo nān mǫn ðīne gioguðe. C. P. 385.

4. 13. Ðonne ic cume, ðonne bēo ðū ābisgod ymbe rǣdinge. C. P. 168.

5. 1. Ne ðrēata ðū nā ðone ealdan, ac healsa hiene swǣ ðīnne fæder. C. P. 180.

5. 8. Sē þe ne gīmð ðāra þe his bēoð, ǫnd hūru Godes ðēowa, hē wiðsæcð Godes gelēafan, ǫnd hē bið trēowlēas. C. P. 138.

5. 23. . . . ðæt gē mōston drincan gewealden wīnes for ēowres magan medtrymnesse. C. P. 318.

6. 1. Ǣlc ðāra þe sīe under ðǣm geoke hlāfordscipes, hē sceal his hlāford ǣghwelcre āre ǫnd weorðscipes wurðne onmunan. C. P. 200.

6. 10. . . . ðæt ǣlces yfles wyrtruma wǣre ðæt mǫn wilnode hwelcere gīdsunge. C. P. 72.

1 TIMOTHY.

3. 1. . . . Si quis episcopatum desiderat, bonum opus desiderat.

3. 2. Oportet ergo (*Greg.* autem) episcopum irreprehensibilem esse....

4. 1, 3. . . . Discedent quidam a fide, . . . prohibentium nubere, abstinere a cibis quos Deus creavit ad percipiendum cum gratiarum actione fidelibus et iis (*Greg.* his) qui cognoverunt veritatem.

4. 11, 12. Praecipe haec, et doce. Nemo adolescentiam tuam contemnat....

4. 13. Dum venio, attende lectioni. . . .

5. 1. Seniorem ne increpaveris, sed obsecra ut patrem....

5. 8. Si quis autem (*Greg.* Qui) suorum, et maxime domesticorum, curam non habet, fidem negavit, et est infideli deterior.

5. 23. . . . Modico vino utere propter stomachum tuum (*Greg. om.* tuum) et frequentes tuas infirmitates.

6. 1. Quicumque sunt sub iugo servi, dominos suos omni honore dignos arbitrentur. . . .

6. 10. Radix enim (*Greg. om.* enim) omnium malorum est cupiditas....

6. 17. Sæcgeað ðǣm welegum gind ðisne middangeard ðæt hīe tō ofermōdlice ne ðęncen, nē tō wel ne trūwigen ðissum ungewissum welum.   C. P. 180.

2 TIMOTHY.

2. 4. Nele (Ne [scy]le H.) nān Godes ðēow hiene selfne tō ungemetlice gebindan on woruldscipum, ðȳlæs hē mislīcige ðǣm þe hiene ǣr selfne gesealde.   C. P. 130.

4. 1, 2. Ic ðē bebēode beforan Gode ǫnd ðǣm Hǣlendan Crīste, se þe dēmende is cwicum ǫnd dēadum, ǫnd ic ðē bebēode [bēode] ðurh his tōcyme ǫnd ðurh his rīce, ðæt ðū stande on ðissum wordum, ǫnd hīe lāre ǣgðer ge gedæftelice ge ēac ungedæftelice.   C. P. 96.

4. 2. Lǣre hīe, ǫnd healsa, ǫnd tǣl hiera unðēawas, ǫnd ðēah geðyldelice.   C. P. 290.

TITUS.

1. 9. ... ðæt se lāreow sceolde bēon mihtig tō tyhtanne on hālwęnde lāre, ǫnd ēac tō ðrēageanne ðā þe him wiðstandan willen [willað].   C. P. 90.

1. 15. ... þæt ðǣm clǣnum wǣre eal clǣne; ǫnd ðǣm unclǣnum nǣre nāuht clǣne.   C. P. 316.

2. 15. Lǣr ðæt folc, ǫnd ðrēata, ǫnd tǣl, ǫnd hāt, ðæt hīe witen ðæt gē sume anwāld habbað ofer hīe.   C. P. 290.

6. 17. Divitibus huius saeculi praecipe non sublime (*Greg.* superbe) sapere, neque sperare in incerto divitiarum (*Greg. ins.* suarum). ...

2 TIMOTHY.

2. 4. Nemo militans Deo implicat se negotiis saecularibus, ut ei placeat cui se probavit.

4. 1, 2. Testificor coram Deo et Iesu Christo, qui iudicaturus est vivos et mortuos per adventum ipsius et regnum eius, praedica verbum, insta opportune, importune; argue, obsecra, increpa in omni patientia et doctrina.

TITUS.

1. 9. ... Ut potens sit exhortari in doctrina sana, et eos qui contradicunt arguere.

1. 15. (*Greg. ins.* Quia) Omnia munda mundis; coinquinatis autem et infidelibus nihil est mundum. ...

2. 15. Haec loquere, et exhortare, et argue cum omni imperio. ...

HEBREWS.

8. 13. Ðætte nū forealdod is, ðæt is fornēah losod. C. P. 204.

9. 4. *See* C. P. 124.

11. 36, 37. Ðā hālgan męn geðafedon on ðisse worlde mǫnig bismer
ǫnd mǫnige swyngean, ǫnd mǫnige bęndas ǫnd karcernu ; hīe
wǣron stǣnde, ǫnd snidene mid snide ; hīe wǣron costode, ǫnd
mid sweordum hīe wǣron ofslǣgene. C. P. 204.

12. 5, 6. Sunu min, ne āgīmelēasa ðū Godes swingan, nē ðū ne
bēo wērig for his ðrēaunga, forðǣmþe God lufað ðone þe hē
ðrēað, ǫnd swingeð ǣlc bearn þe hē underfōn wile. C. P. 252.

12. 9, 10. Ūre flǣsclican fædras lǣrdon ūs, ǫnd wē hīe ondrēdon ;
hīe ðrēadon ūs, ǫnd wē weorðodon hīe ; hū micle swīðor
sculon wē ðonne bīon gehīersume ðǣm þe ūre gāsta Fæder
bið, wið ðǣm þe (ðæt H.) wē mōten libban on ēcnesse ! Ūre
flǣsclican fædras ūs lǣrdon tō ðǣm þe hiera willa wæs, ac ðæt
wæs tō swīðe scortre hwīle, forðǣmþe ðēos world is swīðe lǣnu ;
ac se gāstlica Fæder, hē ūs lǣrð nytwyrðlicu ðing tō underfōnne,
ðæt is ðæt wē geearnigen ðæt ēce līf. C. P. 254.

12. 12, 13. Āstręcceað ēowre āgǣledan hǫnda ǫnd ēowru cnēowru,
ǫnd stæppað ryhte ; ne healtigeað lęng, ac bīoð hāle. C. P. 64.

12. 14. Sēceað sibbe ǫnd gōd tō ēallum mǫnnum, būtan ðǣre ne
mæg nān mǫn God gesīon. C. P. 344.

HEBREWS.

8. 13. ... Quod autem (*Greg.* enim)
antiquatur et senescit prope in-
teritum est.

11. 36, 37. Alii (*Greg.* Sancti) vero
(*Greg. om.* vero) ludibria et ver-
bera experti, insuper et vincula
et carceres ; lapidati sunt, secti
sunt, tentati sunt, in occisione
gladii mortui sunt. ...

12. 5, 6. ... Fili mi, noli negligere
disciplinam Domini, neque fati-
geris   m (*Greg.* cum), ab eo
argueris ; quem enim diligit Dominus castigat, flagellat autem
omnem filium quem recipit.

12. 9, 10. ... Patres quidem carnis
nostrae eruditores habuimus
(*Greg.* habuimus eruditores), et
reverebamur eos ; non multo magis
obtemperabimus Patri spirituum,
et vivemus ? Et illi quidem in
tempore paucorum dierum secundum voluntatem suam erudie-
bant nos ; hic autem ad id quod
utile est in recipiendo sanctifi-
cationem eius.

12. 12, 13. ... Remissas manus et
soluta (*Greg.* dissoluta) genua
erigite, et gressus rectos facite
pedibus vestris, ut non claudicans
quis erret, magis autem sanetur.

12. 14. Pacem sequimini cum omnibus, et sanctimoniam, sine qua
nemo videbit Deum.

13. 4. Ðæm wōhhǣmerum dēmeð Dryhten. C. P. 401.

13. 7. Gemunað ꞇowerra foregengena ðāra þe ꞔow bodedon Godes word, ond behealdað hiera liif ond hiera forðsiið, ond gongað on ꞔone gelēafan. C. P. 204.

JAMES.

1. 19. Sīe ǣghwelc mon swīðe hræd ond swīꞔe geornfull tō gehīeranne, ond swīꞔe læt tō sprecanne. C. P. 280.

1. 26. Gif hwā tiohhað ðæt hē ǣfæst sīe, ond nyle gemīdlian his tungan, ðæt mōd līehð him selfum, forðæm his ǣfæstnes bið swīðe īdlu. C. P. 280.

3. 1. Brōꞔur, ne bēo ꞔower tō fela lārēowa. C. P. 32.

3. 8. . . . ðæt hīo wǣre swīðe unstille, yfel, ond dēaðberendes ātres full. C. P. 280.

3. 14, 15, 17. Gif gē hæbben yfelne andan on īow, ond tīonan ond geflitu on īowrum mōde, ne gilpe gē nō, nē ne sægniað ðæs, ond ne flītað mid īowrum lēasungum wið ðǣm sūðe ; forðǣm sē wīsdōm nis ufan cumen of hefonum, ac hē is eorðlic, ond wildēorlic, ond ꞔac dēofullic. Ac sē þe of Gode cymð, hē bið gōdes willan ond gesibsum. C. P. 346, 348.

4. 4. Swā-hwā-swā wille bīon ðisse weorlde frēond tō ungemetlice, hē bið gehāten Godes fēond. C. P. 421.

13. 4. . . . Fornicatores enim (*Greg.* autem) et adulteros iudicabit Deus.

13. 7. Mementote praepositorum vestrorum qui vobis locuti sunt verbum Dei ; quorum intuentes exitum conversationis, imitamimi fidem.

JAMES.

1. 19. . . . Sit autem (*Greg.om.* autem) omnis homo velox ad audiendum, tardus autem ad loquendum. . . .

1. 26. Si quis autem (*Greg.om.*autem) putat se religiosum esse, non refrenans linguam suam, sed seducens cor suum, huius vana est religio.

3. 1. Nolite plures magistri fieri, fratres mei. . . .

3. 8. . . . Inquietum malum, plena veneno mortifero.

3. 14, 15, 17. Quod si zelum amarum habetis, et contentiones sint (*Greg.* sunt) in cordibus vestris (*Greg.* corde vestro), nolite gloriari, et mendaces esse adversus veritatem; non est enim (*Greg. om.* enim) ista sapientia desursum descendens, sed terrena, animalis, diabolica. . . . Quae autem desursum est) sapientia primum quidem pudica est, deinde pacifica. . . .

4. 4. . . . Quicumque ergo (*Greg. om.* ergo) voluerit amicus esse saeculi huius, inimicus Dei constituitur.

1 PETER.

2. 9. Gē sint ācoren kynn Gode, ǫnd kynelices prēosthādes. C. P. 84.

3. 15. Bēoð simle gearwe tō lǣronne ǫnd tō forgifonne ǣlcum
ðāra þe ēow ryhtlice bidde ymbe ðone tōhopan þe gē habbað on
ēow. C. P. 172.

4. 11. Swǣ-hwā-swǣ sprǣce, sprǣce hē Godes worde, swelce ðā
word nā his ne sīen, ac Godes. C. P. 370.

Gif hwā ðēnige, ðēnige hē swelce hē hit of Godes mægene
ðēnige, næs of his selfes. C. P. 322.

5. 1, 2. Ic eom ēower efnðēowa, ǫnd Crīstes ðrōwunge gewiota,
ic ēow healsige ðæt gē fēden Godes heorde þe under ēow is ; . . .
ungenīdde, mid ēorum āgnum willum, gē sculon ðęncean for
ēowre heorde Godes ðǫnces, nālles nō for fracoðlicum gestrēonum. C. P. 136.

5. 3. Ne sint wē nāne wāldendas ðisses folces, ac wē sint tō bīsene
gesętte ūrre heorde. C. P. 118.

2 PETER.

1. 5, 6. Nū gē habbað gelēafan, wyrcað nū gōd weorc, ǫnd habbað
ðonne wīsdōm, ǫnd on ðǣm wīsdōme habbað forhæfdnesse ǫnd
ēac lǣrað, ǫnd hūru on ðǣre forhæfdnesse geðylde. C. P. 310.

2. 16. Ðæt dumbe ǫnd ðæt gehæfte nēat ðrēade ðone wītgan for
his yflan willan, ðā hit clipode swǣ-swǣ mann, ǫnd mid
ðȳ gestīerde ðǣm wītgan his unryhtre ǫnd dysigre [dysiglicre]
wilnunge. C. P. 256.

1 PETER.

2. 9. Vos autem genus electum,
regale sacerdotium. . . .

3. 15. . . . Parati semper ad satis-
factionem omni poscenti vos rationem de ea, quae in vobis est, spe.

4. 11. Si quis loquitur, quasi sermones Dei; si quis ministrat (*Greg.*
administrat), tamquam ex virtute
quam administrat Deus. . . .

5. 1, 2. . . . Obsecro, consenior et
testis Christi passionum, . . . pas-
cite qui in vobis est gregem Dei,
providentes non coacte, sed spon-
tanee secundum Deum; neque
turpis lucri gratia, sed voluntarie.

5. 3. Neque ut (*Greg.* Non) domi-
nantes in cleris (*Greg.* clero), sed
forma facti gregis. . . .

2 PETER.

1. 5, 6. . . . Ministrate in fide vestra
virtutem, in virtute autem scientiam, in scientia autem absti-
nentiam, in abstinentia autem
patientiam. . . .

2. 16. Correptionem vero (*Greg. om.*

2. 21. . . . ꝺæt him wǣre bętere ꝺæt hī nō sōꝺfæstnesse weg ne ongēaten, ꝺonne hī underbæc gecęrden siꝺꝺan hī hine ongēaten.　C. P. 445.

2. 22. . . . ꝺæt se hund wille etan ꝺæt hē ǣr āspāw, ǫnd sīo sugu hī wi[l]e sylian on hire sole, æfterꝺǣmꝺe hīo āꝺwǣgen biꝺ.　C. P. 419.

1 JOHN.

4. 18. Sīo fullfręmede Godes lufu ādrīfeꝺ āweg ꝺone ęge.　C. P. 262.

REVELATION.

3. 2. Bīo ꝺū wacor, ǫnd gebēt ꝺā weorc ꝺe dēadlicu sint in ꝺē; ne mētte ic nō ꝺīn weorc fullfręmed beforan mīnum Gode.　C. P. 445.

3. 15, 16. Ēalā, wǣre hē āuꝺer, oꝺꝺe hāt, oꝺꝺe ceal[d]! Ac forꝺonꝺe hē is wlaco, ǫnd nis nāuꝺer, nē hāt, nē ceald, ꝺēah ic hine sūpe ic hine wille ęft ūtāspīwan of mīnum mūꝺe.　C. P. 445, 447.

3. 18. Smirewaꝺ ēowre ēagan mid sealfe, þæt gē mægen gesīon.　C. P. 68.

3. 19. Ic ꝺrēage ǫnd swinge ꝺā þe ic lufige.　C. P. 252.

4. 8. . . . ꝺæt hīe sīen ꝺǣm hefonlican nēatum gelīce, þā wǣron gēēawde, swǣ hit āwriten is ꝺæt hīe wǣron ymb eall ūtan mid ēagum besętt, ǫnd ēac innane ēagna full.　C. P. 194.

vero) habuit suae vesaniae ; subiugale mutum animal (*Greg. om.* animal, *ins.* quod in), hominis voce loquens, prohibuit prophetae insipientiam.

2. 21. Melius enim (*Greg. om.* enim) erat illis (*Greg.* eis) non cognoscere viam iustitiae, quam post agnitionem retrorsum converti....

2. 22. . . . Canis reversus ad suum vomitum, et sus lota in volutabro luti.

1 JOHN.

4. 18. . . . Perfecta charitas foras mittit timorem. . . .

REVELATION.

3. 2. Esto vigilans, et confirma cetera quae moritura erant; non enim invenio opera tua plena coram Deo meo.

3. 15, 16. . . . Utinam frigidus esses, aut calidus ! Sed quia tepidus es, et nec frigidus nec calidus, incipiam te evomere ex ore meo.

3. 18. . . . Collyrio inunge oculos tuos, ut videas.

3. 19. Ego quos amo, arguo et castigo. . . .

4. 8. Et quattuor animalia . . . in circuitu, et intus plena sunt ocu-

14. 3. Ðā singað ðone sang ðe nān mon elles singan ne mæg, būton ðæt hun(d)tēontig ond fēowertig ond fēower ðūsendo. C. P. 409.

14. 4. Ðæt sindan ðā, ðā ðe mid wīfum ne bēoð besmitene, ond hira mægeðhād habbað gehealdenne; ðā folgiað ðǣm Lambe swā-hwǣr-swā hit færð. C. P. 409.

22. 17. Sē þe gehīere ðæt hiene mon clipige, clipige hē eac ōðerne, ond cweðe : Cum. C. P. 378.

lis. . . . (*Greg. sum.* Ostensa quippe coeli animalia in circuitu et intus oculis plena describuntur).

14. 3. . . . . Nemo poterat dicere canticum, nisi illa centum quadraginta quattuor millia . . . (*Greg.* Canticum cantant quod nemo potest dicere, nisi illa centum quadraginta quattuor millia).

14. 4. Hi sunt, qui cum mulieribus non sunt coinquinati ; virgines enim sunt. Hi (*Greg.* et) sequuntur Agnum quocumque ierit. . . .

22. 17. . . . Qui audit, dicat : Veni. . . .

THE LAWS OF KING ALFRED

(In Schmid's *Gesetze der Angelsachsen*, 2nd ed., pp. 58–66)

EXODUS.

20. 1–3, 7–17, 23. Drihten wæs sprecende þās word tō Moyse, and þus cwæð : Ic eom Drihten þīn God ; ic þe ūtgelǣdde of Egypta lǫnde and of hiora þēowdōme. Ne lufa þū ōðre frǫmde godas ofer mē. Ne mīnne nǫman ne cīg þū on īdelnesse, forþonþe þū ne bist unscyldig wiþ mē, gif þū on īdelnesse cīgst mīnne nǫman. Gemyne þæt þū gehālgige þone ræstedæg. Wyrceað ēow syx dagas, and on þām siofoðan rẹstað ēow. Forþām on syx dagum Crīst geworhte heofenas and eorðan, sǣs, and ealle gesceafta þe on him synt, and hine gerẹste on þone seofoðan dæg ; and forþon Drihten hine gehālgode. Āra þīnum fæder and þīnre mēdder, þā þe Drihten sealde, þæt þū sīe þȳ lęng libbende on eorðan. Ne sleah þū. Ne lige þū dearnenga. Ne stala þū. Ne sæge þū lēase gewitnesse. Ne wilna þū þīnes nēhstan ierfes mid unryhte. Ne wyrc (þū) þē gyldne godas oððe seolfrene. Schmid 58.

EXODUS.

20. 1–3, 7–17, 23. Locutusque est Dominus cunctos sermones hos: Ego sum Dominus Deus tuus, qui eduxi te de terra Aegypti, de domo servitutis. Non habebis deos alienos coram me. . . . Non assumes nomen Domini Dei tui in vanum ; nec enim habebit insontem Dominus eum qui assumpserit nomen Domini Dei sui frustra. Memento ut diem sabbati sanctifices. Sex diebus operaberis, et facies omnia opera tua. Septimo autem die sabbatum Domini Dei tui est; non facies omne opus in eo, tu, et filius tuus et filia tua, servus tuus et ancilla tua, iumentum tuum, et advena qui est intra portas tuas. Sex enim diebus fecit Dominus coelum et terram, et mare, et omnia quae in eis sunt, et requievit in die septimo; idcirco benedixit Dominus diei sabbati, et sanctificavit eum. Honora patrem tuum et matrem tuam, ut sis longaevus

21. 1–36. Þis synt þā dōmas þe þū him sęttan scealt : Gif hwā gebicgge crīstenne þēow, VI gēar þēowige hē ; þȳ siofoðan bēo hē frīoh orcēapunga. Mid swelce hrægle hē inēode, mid swelce gange hē ūt. Gif hē wīf self hæbbe, gange hīo ūt mid him. Gif se hlāford him þonne wīf sealde, sīe hīo and hire bearn þæs hlāfordes[1]. Gif se þēowa þonne cwæðe : Nelle ic frǫm mīnum hlāforde, nē frǫm mīnum wīfe, nē frǫm mīnum bearne, nē frǫm mīnum ierfe[2], bręnge hine þonne his hlāford tō þæs temples dura, and þurhþȳrlige his ēare mid æle, tō tācne þæt hē sīe æfre siððan þēow.

Þēah hwā gebycgge his dohtor on þēowenne, ne sīe hīo ealles swā þēowu swā ōðru męnnenu. Nāge hē hīe ūt on ęlþēodig folc tō bebycgganne ; ac gif hē hire ne ręcce, sē þe hīe bohte, lǣte hīe frēo on ęlþēodig folc. Gif þonne hē ālēfe his suna mid tō hǣmanne, dō hiere gyfta, and lōcige þæt hīo hæbbe hrægl, and þæt weorð sīe hire mægðhādes, þæt is, se weotuma āgife hē hire þone. Gif hē hire þāra nān ne dō, þonne sīe hīo frīoh.

super terram quam Dominus Deus tuus dabit tibi. Non occides. Non moechaberis. Non furtum facies. Non loqueris contra prox- imum tuum falsum testimonium. Non concupisces domum proximi tui, nec desiderabis uxorem eius, non servum, non ancillam, non bovem, non asinum, nec omnia quae illius sunt. ... Non facietis deos argenteos, nec deos aureos facietis vobis.

21. 1–36. Haec sunt iudicia quae propones eis : Si emeris servum Hebraeum, sex annis serviet tibi ; in septimo egredietur liber gratis. Cum quali veste intraverit, cum tali exeat ; si habens uxorem, et uxor egredietur simul. Sin autem dominus dederit illi uxorem, et pepererit filios et filias, mulier et liberi eius erunt domini sui, ipse vero exibit cum vestitu suo.

Quod si dixerit servus : Diligo dominum meum et uxorem ac liberos, non egrediar liber, offeret eum dominus diis, et applicabitur ad ostium et postes, perforabitque aurem eius subula, et erit ei ser- vus in saeculum.

Si quis vendiderit filiam suam in famulam, non egredietur sicut an- cillae exire consueverunt. Si dis- plicuerit oculis domini sui cui tra- dita fuerat, dimittet eam ; populo autem alieno vendendi non habe- bit potestatem, si spreverit eam. Sin autem filio suo desponderit eam, iuxta morem filiarum faciet illi ; quod si alteram ei acceperit, providebit puellae nuptias, et vestimenta et pretium pudicitiae non negabit. Si tria ista non fecerit, egredietur gratis absque pecunia.

---

[1] Note the omission here.　　　[2] An insertion.

Se mọn se þe his gewealdes mọnnan ofslēa, swelte sō dēaðe.
Sē þe hine þonne nēdes ofslōge, oððe unwillum oððe ungewealdes,
swelce hine God swā sẹnde on his họnda, and hē hine ne
ymbsyrede, sīe hē fēores wyrðe and folcryhtre bōte, gif he frið-
stōwe gesēce.   Gif hwā þonne of giernesse and gewealdes ofslēa
his þone nēhstan þurh searwa, ālūc þū hine fram mīnum weofode,
tō-þām-þe hē dēaðe swelte.

Sō þe slēa his fæder oððe his mōdor, sō sceal dēaðe sweltan.

Sē þe frīone forstæle and hē hine bebycgge, and hit [hym] on-
bestǣled sīe þæt hē hine berẹccean ne mæg, swelte sē dēaðe.

Sē þe wẹrge his fæder oððe his mōdor, swelte sō dēaðe.

Gif hwā slēa his þone nēhstan mid stāne oððe mid fȳste[1], and
hē þēah ūtgangan mæge bī stafe, begite him lǣce, and wyrce his
weorc þā-hwīle-þe hē self ne mæge.

Sō þe slēa his āgenne þēowne ẹsne oððe his mẹnnen, and hē
ne sȳ īdæges dēad, þēah hē libbe twā niht oððe þrēo, ne bīð hē
ealles swā scyldig, forþonþe hit wæs his āgen frōh ; gif hē þonne
sīe īdæges dēad, þonne sitte sīo scyld on him.

Gif hwā on cēase ēacniend wīf gewẹrde, bēte þone æwẹrdlan[2],
swā him dōmeras gerẹccen ; gif hīo dēad sīe, sẹlle sāwle wið
sāwle.   Gif hwā ōðrum his ēage ōðō, sẹlle his āgen fore, tōð fore
tēð, họnda wid họnda, fēt fore fēt, bærning fore bærning, wund
wið wunde, lǣl wið lǣle.

Qui percusserit hominem volens occidere, morte moriatur.   Qui autem non est insidiatus, sed Deus illum tradidit in manus eius, constituam tibi locum in quem fugere debeat.   Si quis per industriam occiderit proximum suam et per insidias, ab altari meo evelles eum, ut moriatur.

Qui percusserit patrem suum aut matrem, morte moriatur.

Qui furatus fuerit hominem et vendiderit eum, convictus noxae morte moriatur.

Qui maledixerit patri suo vel matri, morte moriatur.

Si rixati fuerint viri, et percus-serit alter proximum suum lapide vel pugno, et ille mortuus non fuerit, sed iacuerit in lectulo ; si surrexerit, et ambulaverit foris super baculum suum, innocens erit qui percusserit, ita tamen ut operas eius, et impensas in medicos, restituat.

Qui percusserit servum suum vel ancillam virga, et mortui fuerint in manibus eius, criminis reus erit ; sin autem uno die vel duobus su-pervixerit, non subiacebit poenae, quia pecunia illius est.

Si rixati fuerint viri, et percus-serit quis mulierem praegnantem, et abortivum quidem fecerit, sed

---

[1] Note the omission.   [2] Much abridged.

Gif hwā āslēa his þeowe oððe his þeowenne þæt ēage ūt, and hē þonne hī gedō ānīgge, geofrēoge hīe for þon. Gif hē þonne þone tōð ofāslēa, dōð þæt ilce.

Gif oxa ofhnīte wer oððe wīf, þæt hīe dēade sīen, sīe hē mid stānum ofworpod, and ne sīe his flǣsc eten. Se hlāford bið unscyldig, gif se oxa hnītol wǣre twām dagum ǣr oððe þrim, and se hlāford hit nyste ; gif hē hit þonne wiste, and hē hine inne betȳnan nolde, and hē þonne wer oððe wīf ofslōge, sīe hē mid stānum ofworpod, and sīe se hlāford ofslegen oððe [se man] forgolden, swā þæt witan tō rihte finden. Sunu oððe dohtor gif hē ofstinge, þæs ilcan dōmes sīe hē wyrðe. Gif hē þonne þēow oððe þēowmęnnen ofstinge, gesęlle þām hlāforde XXX scill. scolfres, and se oxa sīe mid stānum ofworpod.

Gif hwā ādelfe wæterpyt, oððe betȳnedne ontȳne, and hine ęft ne betȳne, gelde swelc nēat swelc þēron befealle, and hæbbe him þæt dēade.

Gif oxa ōðres męnnes oxan gewundige, and hē þonne dēad sīe, bebycggen þone oxan, and hæbben him þæt weorð gemǣne, and

ipsa vixerit, subiacebit damno quantum maritus mulieris expeti-erit, et arbitri iudicaverint ; sin autem mors eius fuerit subsecuta, reddet animam pro anima, oculum pro oculo, dentem pro dente, manum pro manu, pedem pro pede, adustionem pro adustione, vulnus pro vulnere, livorem pro livore.

Si percusserit quispiam oculum servi sui aut ancillae, et luscos eos fecerit, dimittet eos liberos pro oculo quem eruit. Dentem quo-que si excusserit servo vel ancillae suae, similiter dimittet eos li-beros.

Si bos cornu percusserit virum aut mulierem, et mortui fuer-int, lapidibus obruetur, et non comedentur carnes eius ; domi-nus quoque bovis innocens erit. Quod si bos cornupeta fuerit ab heri et nudiustertius, et contestati sunt dominum eius, nec reclu-serit eum, occideritque virum aut mulierem ; et bos lapidibus obru-

etur, et dominum eius occident. Quod si pretium fuerit ei impo-situm, dabit pro anima sua quid-quid fuerit postulatus. Filium quoque et filiam si cornu per-cusserit, simili sententiae subia-cebit. Si servum ancillamque invaserit, triginta siclos argenti domino dabit, bos vero lapidibus opprimetur.

Si quis aperuerit cisternam et foderit, et non operuerit eam, cecideritque bos aut asinus in eam, reddet dominus cisternae pretium iumentorum ; quod autem mor-tuum est, ipsius erit.

Si bos alienus bovem alte-rius vulneraverit, et ille mortuus fuerit ; vendent bovem vivum, et dividentt pretium, cadaver autem mortui inter se dispertient. Sin autem sciebat quod bos cornupeta esset ab heri et nudiustertius, et non custodivit eum dominus suus ; reddet bovem pro bove, et cadaver integrum accipiet.

eac þæt flǣsc swā þæs dēadan. Gif se hlāford þonne wiste þæt
se oxa hnītol wǣre, and hine healdan nolde, sęlle him ōðerne
oxan fore, and hæbbe him eall þæt flǣsc. Schmid 58, 60.

22. 1–6, 10–12, 16–31. Gif hwā forstele ōðres oxan, and hine ofslēa
oððe bebycgge, sęlle twēgen wið, and fēower scēap wið ānum.
Gif hē næbbe hwæt hē sęlle, sīe hē self beboht wið þām fīo.

Gif þeof brece mannes hūs nihtes, and hē weorðe þǣr ofsleg-
en, ne sīe hē nā manslęges scyldig. Gif hē siððan æfter sunnan
upgonge þis dēð, hē bið manslęges scyldig, and hē þonne self
swelte, būton hē nīeddǣda wǣre. Gif mid him cwicum sīe
funden þæt hē ǣr stæl, be twȳfealdum forgielde hē hit.

Gif hwā gewęrde ōðres monnes wīngeard, oððe his æcras,
oððe his landes āwuht, gebēte swā hit mon geeahtige.

Gif fȳr sīe ontęnded ryht¹ tō bærnenne, gebēte þone æfwęrd-
elsan se þæt fȳr ontęnt.

Gif hwā ōðfæste his frīend fioh, gif hē hit self stǣle, forgylde be twȳfealdum. Gif hē nyte hwā hit stǣle, gelādige
hine selfne, þæt hē þǣr nān fācn ne gefremede. Gif hit þonne
cucu feoh wǣre, and hē sęcgge þæt hit hęre nāme, oððe þæt hit
self ācwæle, and hē gewitnesse hæbbe, ne þearf hē þæt geldan.
Gif hē þonne gewitnesse næbbe, and hē him ne getrīewe, swęr-
ige hē þonne.

22. 1–6, 10–12, 16–31. Si quis furatus fuerit bovem aut ovem, et
occiderit vel vendiderit, quinque
boves pro uno bove restituet, et
quattuor oves pro una ove.

Si effringens fur domum sive
suffodiens fuerit inventus, et accepto vulnere mortuus fuerit,
percussor non erit reus sanguinis.
Quod si orto sole hoc fecerit,
homicidium perpetravit, et ipse
morietur. Si non habuerit quod
pro furto reddat, ipse venunda-
bitur. Si inventum fuerit apud
eum quod furatus est vivens, sive
bos, sive asinus, sive ovis, duplum
restituet.

Si laeserit quispiam agrum vel
vineam, et dimiserit iumentum
suum ut depascatur aliena, quidquid optimum habuerit in agro
suo, vel in vinea, pro damni aesti-
matione restituet.

Si egressus ignis invenerit spinas, et comprehenderit acervos
frugum sive stantes segetes in
agris, reddet damnum qui ignem
succenderit.

Si quis commendaverit proximo suo asinum, bovem, ovem, et
omne iumentum, ad custodiam,
et mortuum fuerit, aut debilita-
tum, vel captum ab hostibus, nul-
lusque hoc viderit; iusiurandum
erit in medio quod non exten-
derit manum ad rem proximi
sui, suscipietque dominus iura-
mentum, et ille reddere non co-
getur. Quod si furto ablata fuerit, restituet damnum domino.

¹ Lambarde has 'rȳp,' *harvest*, which is probably right.

F

Gif hwā fēmnan beswīce unbewęddode, and hire mid slǣpe, forgielde hīe, and hæbbe hī siððan him tō wīfe.   Gif þǣre fēmnan fæder hīe þonne sęllan nelle, āgife hē þæt fioh æfter þām weotuman.

Þā fēmnan, þe gewuniað onfōn gealdorcræftigan, and scīnlǣcan, and wiccan, ne lǣt þū þā libban.

And sē þe hǣme mid nētene, swelte hē dēaðe.

And sē þe godgeldum onsæcge ofer God ānne, swelte sē dēaðe.

Ūtancumene and ęlþēodige ne geswęnc þū nō, forðonþe gē wǣron gīu ęlþēodige on Ægypta lǫnde.

Þā wuduwan and þā stīopcild ne scęððað gē, nē hīe nāwer dęriað.   Gif gē þonne ęlles dōð, hīe cleopiað tō mē, and ic gehīere hīe, and ic ēow þonne slēa mid mīnum swoorde, and ic gedō þæt ēowru wīf bēoð wydewan, and ēowru bearne bēoð stēopcild.

Gif þū fioh tō borge sęlle þīnum gefēran, þe mid þē eardian wille, ne nīede þū hine swā nīedling, and ne gehēne þū hine mid þȳ ēacan.

Gif mǫn næbbe būton ānfeald hrægl hine mid tō wrēonne oððe tō węrianne, and hē hit tō wędde sęlle, ǣr sunnan setlgǫnge sīe hit āgifen.   Gif þū swā ne dēst, þonne cleopiað hē tō mē, and ic hine gehīere, forþonþe ic eom swīðe mildheort.

Ne tǣl þū þīne Dryhten, nē þone hlāford þǣs folces ne werge þū.

Si seduxerit quis virginem necdum desponsatam, dormieritque cum ea, dotabit eam, et habebit eam uxorem.   Si pater virginis dare noluerit, reddet pecuniam iuxta modum dotis quam virgines accipere consueverunt.

Maleficos non patieris vivere.

Qui coierit cum iumento, morte moriatur.

Qui immolat diis occidetur, praeterquam Domino soli.

Advenam non contristabis, neque affliges eum; advenae enim et ipsi fuistis in terra Aegypti.

Viduae et pupillo non nocebitis.   Si laeseritis eos, vociferabuntur ad me, et ego audiam clamorem eorum, et indignabitur furor meus, percutiamque vos gladio, et erunt uxores vestrae viduae, et filii vestri pupilli.

Si pecuniam mutuam dederis populo meo pauperi qui habitat tecum, non urgebis eum quasi exactor, nec usuris opprimes.

Si pignus a proximo tuo acceperis vestimentum, ante solis occasum reddes ei; ipsum enim est solum quo operitur indumentum carnis eius, nec habet aliud in quo dormiat.   Si clamaverit ad me, exaudiam eum, quia misericors sum.

Diis non detrahes, et principi populi tui non maledices.

þīne tēoðan sceattas and þīne frumrīpan, gongendes and
weaxendes, āgife þū Gode.

Eal þæt flǣsc þæt wildēor lǣfen, ne eten gē þæt, ac sellað
hit hundum. Schmid 60, 62.

23. 1, 2, 4, 6–9, 13. Lēases monnes word ne rēce þū nō þæs tō
gehīeranne, nō his dōmas nē geþafa þū, nō nāne gewitnesse æfter
him ne saga þū.

Ne wend þū þē nō on þæs folces unrǣd and unryht gewil,
on hiora sprǣce and geclysp ofer þīn ryht and (on) þæs un-
wīsestan lāre, nō him ne geþafa.

Gif þē becume ōðres monnes gīemelēas fioh on hand, þēah
hit sīe þīn fēond, gecȳðe hit him.

Dēm þū swīðe emne; ne dēm þū ōðerne dōm þām welegan,
ōðerne þām eormen; nē ōðerne þām līofran, and ōðerne þām
lāðran ne dēm þū.

Onscuna þū ā lēasunga. Sōðfæstne man and unscildigne, ne
ācwele þū þone nǣfre.

Ne onfōh þū nǣfre mēdsceattum, forþon hīe āblændað ful oft
wīsra monna geþōht, and hiora word onwendað.

Þām elþēodigan and ūtancumenan ne lǣt þū nō uncūðlice
wið hine, ne mid nānum unrihtum þū hine ne drecce.

Ne swerigen gē nǣfre under hǣðene godas, nō on nānum
þingum ne cleopien gē tō him. Schmid 62, 64.

TOBIT.

4. 16. *See* Acts 15. 29, end.

Decimas tuas et primitias tuas
non tardabis reddere; primogenitum filiorum tuorum dabis mihi.
De bobus quoque et ovibus similiter facies: septem diebus sit
cum matre sua, die octava reddes
illum mihi.

... Carnem, quae a bestiis fuerit praegustata, non comedetis,
sed proiicietis canibus.

23. 1, 2, 4, 6–9, 13. Non suscipies
vocem mendacii, nec iunges manum tuam ut pro impio dicas
falsum testimonium.

Non sequeris turbam ad faci-
endum malum; nec in iudicio,

plurimorum acquiesces sententiae, ut a vero devies.

Si occurreris bovi inimici tui
aut asino erranti, reduc ad
eum.

Non declinabis in iudicium pauperis.

Mendacium fugies. Insontem
et iustum non occides. ...

Nec accipies munera, quae etiam
excaecant prudentes, et subver-
tunt verba iustorum.

Peregrino molestus non eris. ...

... Et per nomen externorum
deorum non iurabitis, neque audietur ex ore vestro.

MATTHEW.

5. 17. . . . þæt hē ne cōme no þæs bebodu tō brecanne, nē tō forbēodanne, ac mid eallum gōdum tō ēacanne. Schmid 64.

ACTS.

15. 23–29. Þā apostolas and þā ęldran brōðor hēlo ēow wȳscað; and wē ēow cȳðað þæt wē geāscodon þæt ūre gefēran sume mid ūrum wordum tō ēow cōmon, and ēow hęfigran [wīsan budan] tō healdanne þonne wē him budon, and ēow tō swīðe gedwealdon mid þǣm manigfealdum gebodum, and ēowra sāwla mā forhwęrfdon þonne hīe gerihton. Þā gesǫmnodon wē ūs ymb þæt, and ūs eallum gelīcode þā þæt wē sęndon Paulus and Barnaban, męn þā wilniað heora sāwla sęllan for Dryhtenes naman. Mid him wē sęndon Judam and Silam, þæt [hī] ēow þæt ilce sęcgan.

Þǣm Hālgan Gāste wæs geþūht and ūs, þæt wē nāne byrðene on ēow sęttan noldon ofer þæt þe ēow nēdþearf wæs tō healdenne, þæt is þonne þæt gē forberen þæt gē dēofolgyld ne weorðien, nē blōd ne þicgen, nē āsmorod, and frǫm dęrnum geligerum; and þæt gē willen þæt ōðre męn ēow ne dōn, ne dōð gē þæt ōðrum mannum. Schmid 64, 66.

MATTHEW.

5. 17. . . . Non veni (*T. Br.*[1] *ins.* legem) solvere, sed adimplere.

ACTS.

15. 23–29. . . . Apostoli et seniores fratres his qui sunt Antiochiae, . . . Syriae, et Ciliciae, fratribus ex gentibus, salutem. Quoniam audivimus quia quidam ex nobis exeuntes turbaverunt vos verbis, (*T. Br. ins.* potius) evertentes animas vestras, quibus non mandavimus, placuit nobis collectis in unum eligere viros, et mittere ad vos cum carissimis nostris Barnaba et Paulo, hominibus qui tradiderunt (*T. Br.* tradere cupiunt) animas suas pro nomine Domini nostri Iesu Christi. Misimus ergo (*T. Br.* etiam ad vos) Iudam et Silam, qui et ipsi vobis verbis (*T. Br.* verba) referent eadem.

Visum est (*T. Br.* et) enim Spiritui Sancto et nobis nihil ultra imponere vobis oneris quam haec necessaria (*T. Br.* hoc necessario): ut abstineatis vos ab immolatis simulacrorum, et sanguine, et suffocato, et fornicatione; a quibus custodientes vos, bene agetis . . . (*T. Br. add* Quod vobis non vultis fieri, non faciatis aliis).

---

[1] T. and Br. signify MS. Cott. Tit. A. 27 and Brompton's *Chronicon* respectively, where the Latin text corresponding with the Old English is found (see Schmid, pp. xxv, xxvi).

KING ALFRED'S VERSION

OF

BEDE'S ECCLESIASTICAL HISTORY

GENESIS.

2. 24. Wer ǫnd wiif, hēo tū bēoð in ānum līchǫman.   B. H. 70.

3. 16. In saare þū cǫnnest bearn.   B. H. 76.

35. 29. Eald ǫnd dagana full.   D. H. 152.

49. 27. Beniamin is rīsende wulf; on ǣrmergen hē iteð hlōðe, ǫnd on ǣfenne hȳrerēaf dǣleð.   B. H. 92.

LEVITICUS.

12. 4, 5. Fore wǣpnedbearne hēo sceolde hēo āhabban frǫm Godes hūses ingǫnge þrēo ǫnd þrītig daga ; fore wīfcilde syx ǫnd syxtig daga.   B. H. 76.

15. 16. . . . þætte se wer, se ðe wǣre his wiife gemǫnged, þæt hē sceolde wætre āðwegen ǫnd bebaðad bēon, ǫnd ǣr sunnan setlgǫnge ne mōste in heora gesǫmnunge ingǫngan.   B. H. 80.

GENESIS.

2. 24. . . . Erunt duo in carne una.

3. 16. . . . In dolore paries filios (*Bede om.* filios). . . .

35. 29. . . . Senex et (*Bede* ac) plenus dierum. . . .

49. 27. Beniamin lupus rapax ; mane comedet praedam, et vespere dividet spolia.

LEVITICUS.

12. 4, 5. Ipsa vero triginta tribus diebus manebit ; . . . omne sanctum non tanget, nec ingredietur in sanctuariam, donec impleantur dies purificationis suae. Sin autem feminam pepererit, . . . sexaginta sex diebus manebit in sanguine purificationis suae (*Bede sum.* ut pro masculo diebus triginta tribus, pro femina autem diebus sexaginta sex debeat abstinere).

15. 16. Vir de quo egreditur semen coitus, lavabit aqua omne corpus suum, et immundus erit usque ad vesperum (*Bede* ut mixtus vir mulieri et lavari aqua debeat, et ante solis occasum ecclesiam non intrare).

18. 7. Ne onwrēoh þū scǫndlicnesse þīnes fæder. B. H. 70.

20. 18. Sēo hālige ǣ mid dēaðe slæhð, gif hwylc wǣpnedmǫn gǫngeð tō mōnaðuðlium wiife. B. H. 78.

DEUTERONOMY.

23. 10, 11. Æfter bysmrunge sēo þurh slǣp wǣpnedmǫnnum gelimpeð, . . . ðēosne mǫn . . . sēo cyðnis þǣre ealdan ǣ bismiten cwið, . . . ǫnd him ne forgifeð þætte hē mōte in Godes hūs gǫngan, nemne hē sȳ wætre āðwegen, nē þonne gēna ǣr ǣfenne. B. H. 84.

1 SAMUEL.

21. 4. *See* B. H. 84.

1 CHRONICLES.

23. 1. *See* Gen. 35. 29.

JOB.

42. 17. *See* Gen. 35. 29.

PSALMS.

18. 13, 14. Drihten hlēoðrað of heofonum, ǫnd se Hēhsta sęleð his stefne. Hē sęndeð his strǣle, ǫnd hēo tōweorpeð; lēgetas gemǫnigfealdað, ǫnd hēo gedrēfeð. B. H. 268.

32. 1. Þā bēoð ēadge þe heora wǫnnesse forlǣtne bēoð, ǫnd þūra þe synna bewrigene bēoð. B. H. 442.

51. 5. Ic wāt þæt ic wæs in wrēnessum geēacnod, ǫnd in scyldum mec cęnde mīn mōdor. B. H. 82.

---

18. 7. Turpitudinem patris tui . . . non discooperies (*Bede* revelabis).

20. 18. Qui coierit cum muliere in fluxu menstruo, et revelaverit turpitudinem eius, ipsaque aperuerit fontem sanguinis sui, interficientur ambo de medio populi sui (*Bede sum.* ita ut morte lex sacra feriat, si quis vir ad menstruatam mulierem accedat).

DEUTERONOMY.

23. 10, 11. Si fuerit inter vos homo qui nocturno pollutus sit somnio, egredietur extra castra, et non revertetur priusquam ad vesperam lavetur aqua; et post solis occasum regredietur in castra (*Bede*

sum. Si post inlusionem quae per somnium solet accidere, . . . hunc quidem testamentum veteris legis . . . pollutum dicit, et, nisi lotum aqua, usque ad vesperam intrare ecclesiam non concedit).

PSALMS.

18. 13, 14. . . . Intonuit de coelo Dominus, et Altissimus dedit vocem suam. . . . Et (*Bede om.* Et) misit sagittas suas, et dissipavit eos; fulgura multiplicavit, et conturbavit eos.

32. 1. Beati quorum remissae sunt iniquitates, et quorum tecta sunt peccata.

51. 5. Ecce enim in iniquitatibus

84. 7. Hālige gǫngað of mægene in mægen; bið gesegen hāligra God in wlite scēawunge. B. H. 212.

ECCLESIASTES.

3. 5. . . . þætte tīd wēre stānas tō sęndenne, ǫnd tīd tō sǫm-nienne. B. H. 262.

ISAIAH.

35. 7. In þām cleofum, þe ǣr dracan eardodon, wēre ūpyrnende grōwnes hrēodes ǫnd rixa. B. H. 230.

JONAH.

1. 12. Ic wāt þætte þæs storm for mē is cumen ǫnd sęnded wæs. B. H. 412.

MATTHEW.

8. 14, 15. . . . þā swǣgre Sanctus Petrus þæs apostoles, mid ðȳ hēo wæs swęnced mid hǣto ǫnd mid bryne fǣferādle, þæt hīo tō hrīnenisse þēre Dryhtenlican hǫnda sǫmod onfǣng hǣlo ǫnd mægen, ǫnd ārās, ǫnd ðǣm Hǣlende þegnade. B. H. 396.

9. 20, 22. Þæt wiif þe wæs þrōwiende blōdes flōwnisse, hēo eað-mōdlice wæs cumende æfter Drihtnes bǣce, ǫnd gehrān þæt fæs his hrægles, ǫnd sōna instæpe hire untrymnes onweg gewāt, ǫnd hēo wæs hāl geworden. B. H. 78.

conceptus sum, et in peccatis con-cepit me mater mea.

84. 7. . . . Ibunt (*Bede ins.* sancti) de virtute in virtutem; videbitur Deus deorum in Sion.

ECCLESIASTES.

3. 5. (*Bede ins.* Quia) Tempus spar-gendi (*Bede* mittendi) lapides, et tempus colligendi. . . .

ISAIAH.

35. 7. . . . In cubilibus, in quibus prius dracones habitabant, orietur (*Bede* oriretur) viror calami et iunci.

JONAH.

1. 12. . . . Scio enim ego quoniam propter me tempestas haec gran-dis venit. . . . (*Bede* Quia propter me est tempestas haec).

MATTHEW.

8. 14, 15. Et cum venisset Iesus in domum Petri, vidit socrum eius iacentem, et febricitantem. Et tetigit manum eius, et dimisit eam febris, et surrexit, et minis-trabat eis (*Bede sum.* Socrum beati Petri, quae cum febrium fuisset ardoribus fatigata, ad tac-tum manus Dominicae surrexit, et, sanitate simul ac virtute re-cepta, ministrabat eis).

9. 20, 22. Et ecce mulier quae san-guinis fluxum patiebatur duode-cim annis accessit retro, et tetigit fimbriam vestimenti eius. . . . Et salva facta est mulier ex illa

11. 29. Nimað ᵹē mīn geoc ofer ēow, ēac ǫnd leorniað æt mē, þæt ic eom milde ǫnd ēaðmōdre heortan. B. H. 100.

15. 11. Nales þætte ingǫngeð in mūð mǫnnan besmīteð, ac þā ðe ūtgǫngað of mūðe, þā seondon þe þone mǫnnan besmīteð. B. H. 80.

15. 19. Of heortan ūtgǫngað yfele geþōhtas. B. H. 80.

22. 37. Lufa ðū þīnne Dryhten God. B. H. 370.

22. 39. Lufa ðū þīnne ðone nēhstan. B. H. 370.

25. 13. Waciað ᵹē, forðonþe ᵹē ne weoton nē ðone dæg nē ðā tīde. B. H. 210.

MARK.

6. 18. *See* B. H. 70.

12. 30, 31. *See* Matt. 22. 37, 39.

LUKE.

8. 43. *See* Matt. 9. 20, 22.

10. 27. *See* Matt. 22. 37, 39.

11. 41. Ðætte ofer sēo ǫnd tō lāfe, sǫllað ælmesse, ǫnd ēow bēoð eal clǣno. B. H. 66.

JOHN.

8. 56. . . . blissade þæt hē gesāwe Drihtnes dæg, ǫnd hē hine geseah ǫnd gefēonde wæs. B. H. 474.

ACTS.

4. 32. Nǣnig heora of þām þe hēo āhton ōwiht his bēon onsundrad cwæð, ac him eallum wǣron eall gemǣno. B. H. 64.

hora (*Bede sum.* Mulier quae fluxum patiebatur sanguinis, post tergum Domini humiliter veniens, vestimenti eius fimbriam tetigit, atque ab ea statim sua infirmitas recessit).

11. 29. Tollite iugum meum super vos, et discite a me, quia mitis sum, et humilis corde. . . .

15. 11. Non quod intrat in os coinquinat hominem, sed quod procedit (*Bede* quae exeunt) ex ore, hoc coinquinat (*Bede* illa sunt quae coinquinant) hominem.

15. 19. De corde enim (*Bede* Ex corde) exeunt cogitationes malae. . . .

22. 37. . . . Diliges Dominum Deum tuum. . . .

22. 39. Diliges proximum tuum (*Bede om.* tuum). . . .

25. 13. Vigilate itaque, quia nescitis diem neque horam.

LUKE.

11. 41. . . . Quod superest, date elemosynam, et ecce omnia munda sunt vobis.

JOHN.

8. 56. . . . Exultavit ut videret diem meum (*Bede* Domini); vidit, et gavisus est.

ACTS.

4. 32. Nec quisquam eorum quae possidebat (*Bede* Nullus eorum ex his quae possidebant) aliquid

4. 35. . . . þæt hēo wǣren tōdǣlende heora weoruldgood syndrigum monnum, swā ǣghwylcum þearf wæs. B. H. 66.

7. 56 (Vulg. 55). Geseah hē heofenas opene, geseah hē Godes wuldur, ond þone Hǣlend standende Godes on þā swīðran. B. H. 444.

13. 48. Swā monige swā forteode wǣron tō ēcum līfe. B. H. 138.

17. 31. Ond wǣre tōweard tō dēmanne eorðan ymbhwyrft on rihtwīsnesse. B. H. 224.

ROMANS.

7. 23. Ic gesēo ōðere ǣ in mīnum leomum wiðfeohtende þǣre ǣ mīnes moodes, ond gehæftedne mec is lǣdende in synne ǣ, sēo is in mīnum leomum. B. H. 88.

10. 2. Hī hæfdon Godes ellnunge, ac nales æfter wīsdōme. B. H. 472.

1 CORINTHIANS.

5. 1. . . . swā þæt hē ēode tō his fæder wīfe. B. H. 110.

7. 2, 9. Sē ðe hine āhabban ne mæg, hæbbe his wiif. B. H. 82.

7. 6. Ðis ic cweðo æfter forgifnesse, nales æfter bebodo. B. H. 82.

2 CORINTHIANS.

4. 4. . . . þætte God þā mood þāra ungelēafsumra āblænde, þȳ-lǣs him scīne sēo onlīhtnes Crīstes godspelles ond his wuldres. B. H. 122.

suum esse dicebat, sed erant illis (*Bede* eis) omnia communia.

4. 35. . . . Dividebatur autem (*Bede om.* autem) singulis, prout cuique opus erat.

7. 55. . . . Vidit gloriam Dei, et Iesum stantem a dextris Dei. . . . Video (*Bede* vidit) coelos apertos. . . .

13. 48. . . . Quotquot erant praecordinati ad vitam aeternam.

17. 31. . . . Iudicaturus est (*Bede* esset) orbem in aequitate. . . .

ROMANS.

7. 23. Video autem (*Bede om.* autem) aliam legem in membris meis repugnantem legi mentis meae, et captivantem me (*Bede* captivum me ducentem) in lege pec-

cati, quae est in membris meis.

10. 2. . . . Aemulationem Dei habent (*Bede* habebant), sed non secundum scientiam.

1 CORINTHIANS.

5. 1. . . . Ita ut uxorem patris sui aliquis habeat (*Bede* Ita ut uxorem patris haberet).

7. 2, 9. . . . Unusquisque suam uxorem habeat. . . . Quod si non se continent, nubant . . . (*Bede* Qui se continere non potest, habeat uxorem suam).

7. 6. Hoc autem dico secundum indulgentiam, non secundum imperium.

2 CORINTHIANS.

4. 4. . . . Deus huius saeculi (*Bede* saeculi huius) excaecavit mentes

TITUS.

1. 15. Eall biδ clǣne clǣnum; þǣm besmitenum ọnd ungelēaf-
sumum nōht biƌ clǣne. . . . Forƌon bismiten syndon ge heora
mōd ge ingewitnis.   B. H. 80.

2 PETER.

2. 22. *See* B. H. 110.

infidelium, ut non fulgeat illis
(*Bede* ne eis fulgeret) illuminatio
evangelii gloriae Christi. . . .

TITUS.

1. 15. Omnia munda mundis; coinquinatis autem et infidelibus
nihil est mundum, sed inquinatae
sunt eorum et mens et conscientia
(*Bede* coinquinata sunt enim et
mens eorum et conscientia).

KING ALFRED'S VERSION

OF

OROSIUS' HISTORY

GENESIS.

19. 24 ; 37. 3 ; 44. 47, 54. *See* Oros. 32.

37. *See* Oros. 34.

EXODUS.

1. 8, 11 ff. ; 12. 31. *See* Oros. 34.

7. 20 ; 8. 3, 6, 17 ; 11. 10 ; 12. 51. *See* Oros. 36.

8. 24 ; 9. 3, 6, 10, 23–25 ; 10. 13, 15, 21, 22 ; 12. 29, 33, 37 ; 14. 5, 6 ff., 22, 28. *See* Oros. 38.

GENESIS.

1. 3. Hē cwæð: Geweorðe lēoht. And ðǣrrihte wæs lēoht geworden. Æ. H. i. 14.

1. 26. Hē cwæð: Uton gewyrcan mannan tō ūre anlīcnysse. Æ. H. i. 16.

‖ Hē cwæð: Uton gewyrcean mannan tō ūre gelīcnysse. Æ. H. i. 288.

1. 27. And hē worhte ðā Adam tō his anlīcnysse. Æ. H. i. 288; cf. ii. 324.

1. 31. And hē behēold þā ealle his weorc ðe hē geworhte, and hī wǣron ealle swīðe gōde. Æ. H. i. 14.

2. 2, 3. And on ðām seofoðan dæge hē geęndode his weorc, and geswāc ðā. And gehālgode þone seofoðan dæg, forðanðe hē on ðām dæge his weorc geęndode. Æ. H. i. 14.

‖ Þā geręste hē hine, and ðone dæg gehālgode. Æ. H. ii. 206.

2. 7. And God þā geworhte ǣnne mannan of lāme, and him onāblēow gāst, and hine gelīffǣste, and hē wearð ðā mann gesceapen on sāwle and on līchaman. Æ. H. i. 12.

‖ And hē worhte ðā þone man mid his handum, and him onāblēow sāwle. Æ. H. i. 16; cf. i. 20.

GENESIS.

1. 3. Dixitque Deus: Fiat lux. Et facta est lux.

1. 26. Et ait: Faciamus hominem ad imaginem et similitudinem nostram....

1. 27. Et creavit Deus hominem ad imaginem suam....

1. 31. Viditque Deus cuncta quae fecerat, et erant valde bona....

2. 2, 3. Complevitque Deus die sep-timo opus suum quod fecerat, et requievit die septimo ab universo opere quod patrarat. Et benedixit diei septimo, et sanctificavit illum, quia in ipso cessaverat ab omni opere suo quod creavit Deus ut faceret.

2. 7. Formavit igitur Dominus Deus hominem de limo terrae, et inspiravit in faciem eius spiraculum vitae, et factus est homo in animam viventem.

2. 15-17. God þā hine gebrōhte on neorxnawange, and hine þǣr gelōgode, and him tō cwæð: Ealra þāra þinga þe on neorxnawange sindon þū mōst brūcan, and hī ealle bēoð þē betǣhte, būton ānum trēowe þe stent on middan neorxnawange; ne hrepa þū þæs trēowes wǣstm, forþanðe þū bist dēadlic, gif þū þæs trēowes wǣstm geetst. *Æ. H. i.* 12, 14.

2. 18. Þā cwæð God: Nis nā gedafenlic þæt þes man āna bēo, and næbbe nænne fultum; ac uton gewyrcan him gemacan, him tō fultume and tō frōfre. *Æ. H. i.* 14.

2. 19. And þā wæs Adam swā wīs þæt God gelǣdde tō him nȳtenu, and dēorcynn, and fugelcynn, ðā-ðā hē hī gesceapene hæfde, and Adam him eallum naman gescēop; and swā-swā hē hī þā genamode, swā hī sindon gehātene. *Æ. H. i.* 14.

2. 21-23. And God þā geswefode þone Adam, and þā-þā hē slēp ðā genam hē ān rib of his sīdan. And geworhte of ðām ribbe ænne wīfman, and āxode Adam hū hēo hātan sceolde. Þā cwæð Adam: Hēo is bān of mīnum bānum, and flǣsc of mīnum flǣsce; bēo hire nama Virago, þæt is, fǣmne, forðanðe hēo is of hire were genumen. *Æ. H. i.* 14; cf. ii. 8, 58, 260.

2. 25. And hī wǣron ðā nacode. *Æ. H. i.* 18.

3. 1-5. Hē cōm ðā on næddran hīwe tō þām twām mannum, ǣrest tō ðām wīfe, and hire tō cwæð: Hwī forbēad God ēow þæs trēowes wǣstm, ðe stent on middan neorxnawange? Þā cwæð þæt wīf: God ūs forbēad þæs trēowes wǣstm, and cwæð þæt wē sceoldon dēaðe sweltan, gif wē his onbyrigdon. Ðā

2. 15-17. Tulit ergo Dominus Deus hominem, et posuit eum in paradiso voluptatis, ... praecepitque ei dicens: Ex omni ligno paradisi comede; de ligno autem scientiae boni et mali ne comedas; in quocumque enim die comederis ex eo, morte morieris.

2. 18. Dixit quoque Dominus Deus: Non est bonum esse hominem solum; faciamus ei adiutorium simile sibi.

2. 19. Formatis igitur Dominus Deus de humo cunctis animantibus terrae, et universis volatilibus coeli, adduxit ea ad Adam, ut videret quid vocaret ea; omne enim quod vocavit Adam animae viventis, ipsum est nomen eius.

2. 21-23. Immisit ergo Dominus Deus soporem in Adam; cumque obdormisset, tulit unam de costis eius. ... Et aedificavit Dominus Deus costam quam tulerat de Adam in mulierem, et adduxit eam ad Adam. Dixitque Adam: Hoc nunc os ex ossibus meis, et caro de carne mea; haec vocabitur Virago, quoniam de viro sumpta est.

2. 25. Erat autem uterque nudus....

3. 1-5. Sed et serpens erat callidior cunctis animantibus terrae quae fecerat Dominus Deus. Qui dixit

cwæð se dēofol : Nis hit nā swā ðū sęgst, ac God wāt genōh geare, gif gē of ðām trēowe geetað, þonne bēoð ēowere ēagan geopenode, and gē magon gesēon and tōcnāwan ǣgðer ge gōd ge yfel, and gē bēoð ęnglum gelīce.　*Æ. H. i. 16, 18.*

‖ Swā mǣre gē bēoð swā-swā ęnglas, gif gē of þām trēowe etað.
... and gē habbað gescēad ǣgðer ge gōdes ge yfeles.　*Æ. H. i. 176.*

3. 6. Wearð þēah þæt wīf forspanen þurh ðæs dēofles lāre ; and genam of ðæs trēowes wǣstme, and geæt, and sealde hire were, and hē geæt.　*Æ. H. i. 18 ;* cf. ii. 220, 240, 330.

3. 17, 18. And cwæð : Forðanðe ðū wǣre gehȳrsum ðīnes wīfes wordum, and mīn bebod forsāwe, þū scealt mid earfoðnyssum þē mętes tilian.　And sēo eorðe, þe is āwyriged on þīnum weorce, sylð þē ðornas and brēmblas.　*Æ. H. i. 18.*

‖ Ðornas and brēmelas þē sceolon wexan, forðanðe ðū wǣre þīnum wīfe gehȳrsum swīðor þonne mē, mihtigum Drihtne.　*Æ. H. ii. 254.*

‖ Sēo eorðe, þe is āwyriged on ðīnum weorce, āgifð þē ðornas and brēmelas.　*Æ. H. ii. 406.*

3. 19. Þū eart of eorðan genumen, and þū āwęnst tō eorðan.　Þū eart dūst, and ðū āwęntst tō dūste.　*Æ. H. i. 18.*

‖ Þū eart eorðe, and þū gewęnst tō eorðan.　Ðū eart dūst, and þū gewęnst tō dūste.　*Æ. H. i. 300.*

3. 20. Ðā sętte Adam ęft hire ōðerne naman, Æua, þæt is, līf : forðanðe hēo is ealra lybbendra mōdor.　*Æ. H. i. 14.*

ad mulierem : Cur praecepit vobis Deus ut non comederetis de omni ligno paradisi ?　Cui respondit mulier : De fructu lignorum quae sunt in paradiso vescimur ; de fructu vero ligni quod est in medio paradisi praecepit nobis Deus ne comederemus, et ne tangeremus illud, ne forte moriamur. Dixit autem serpens ad mulierem : Nequaquam morte moriemini. Scit enim Deus quod in quocumque die comederitis ex eo, aperientur oculi vestri, et eritis sicut dii, scientes bonum et malum.

3. 6. Vidit igitur mulier quod bonum esset lignum ad vescendum, et pulchrum oculis, aspectuque de-lectabile ; et tulit de fructu illius, et comedit, deditque viro suo, qui comedit.

3. 17, 18. Adae vero dixit : Quia audisti vocem uxoris tuae, et comedisti de ligno ex quo praeceperam tibi ne comederes, male-dicta terra in opere tuo ; in laboribus comedes ex ea cunctis diebus vitae tuae.　Spinas et tribulos germinabit tibi, et comedes herbam terrae.

3. 19. ... Pulvis es, et in pulverem reverteris.

3. 20. Et vocavit Adam nomen uxoris suae Heva, eo quod mater esset cunctorum viventium.

3. 21. God him worhte ðā rēaf of fellum, and hī wǣron mid þām fellum gescrȳdde. Æ. H. i. 18.

3. 24. And ādrǣfde hī būtū of neorxnawange. Æ. H. i. 18.

4. 8. *See* Æ. H. ii. 58.

5. 4, 5. And hē and his wīf ðā bearn gestrȳndon, ǣgðer ge suna ge dohtra. And hē leofode nigon hund gēara and þrittig gēara. and siððan swealt. Æ. H. i. 20.

5. 24. *See* Æ. H. i. 308.

6. 14, 15. Wyrc þū nū ǣnne arc, þrēo hund fæðma lang, and fīftig fæðma wīd, and þrītig fæðma hēah; gehrēf hit eall, and geclǣm ealle þā sēamas mid tyrwan[1]. Æ. H. i. 20.

6. 17, 18. Ic wille sęndan flōd ofer ealne middangeard. . . . Ic wylle fordōn eal mancynn mid wǣtere for heora synnum ; ac ic wylle gehealdan þē ǣnne, and þīn wīf, and þīne þrȳ suna, Sem, and Cham, and Iafeth, and heora þrēo wīf[2]. Æ. H. i. 20.

6. 19. Ic gegaderige in tō þē of dēorcynne and of fugelcynne symble gemacan, þæt hī ęft tō fōstre bēon. Æ. H. i. 20 ; cf. i. 536.

7. 1. Forðanþe ðū eart rihtwīs, and mē gecwēme, . . . gā inn syððan mid þīnum hīwum. Æ. H. i. 20.

7. 11, 12. God . . . āsęnde rēn of heofonum fēowertig daga tōgædere, and geopenode þǣr togēanes ealle wyllspringas and wǣterþēotan of þǣre micclan nīwelnysse. Æ. H. i. 22.

3. 21. Fecit quoque Dominus Deus Adae et uxori eius tunicas pelliceas, et induit eos.

3. 24. Eiecitque Adam. . . .

5. 4, 5. . . . Genuitque filios et filias. Et factum est omne tempus quod vixit Adam anni nongenti triginta, et mortuus est.

6. 14, 15. Fac tibi arcam, . . . et bitumine linies intrinsecus et extrinsecus. . . . Trecentorum cubitorum erit longitudo arcae, quinquaginta cubitorum latitudo, et triginta cubitorum altitudo illius.

6. 17, 18. Ecce ego adducam aquas diluvii super terram, ut interfi-

ciam omnem carnem, in qua spiritus vitae est subter coelum ; universa quae in terra sunt consumentur. Ponamque foedus meum tecum ; et ingredieris arcam tu, et filii tui, uxor tua, et uxores filiorum tuorum, tecum.

6. 19. Et ex cunctis animantibus universae carnis bina induces in arcam, ut vivant tecum, masculini sexus et feminini.

7. 1. . . . Ingredere tu, et omnis domus tua, in arcam ; te enim vidi iustum coram me in generatione hac.

7. 11, 12. . . . Rupti sunt omnes

---

[1] Ælfric has inverted the order of these passages; they are here somewhat disjoined, and rearranged in the Biblical order.

[2] From Gen. 7. 13, 'Sem, et Cham, et Iaphcth, . . . et tres uxores filiorum.'

7. 13. *See* Gen. 6. 17, 18, note.

7. 16, 17. God belēac hī bynnan þām arce. . . . Ðæt flōd wēox ðā and ābær ūp þone arc, and hit oferstāh ealle dūna. .Æ. H. i. 22.

7. 21. *See* .Æ. H. i. 22.

8. 13. *See* .Æ. H. ii. 58 ; cf. Gen. 7. 11, 12.

9. 11, 14, 15. Ic wylle sęttan mīn wędd betwux mē and ēow tō þisum behāte : þæt is, þonne ic ofertēo heofenas mid wolcnum, þonne bið ætēowod mīn rēnboga betwux þām wolcnum, þonne bēo ic gemyndig mīnes węddes, þæt ic nelle heononforð mancynn mid wætere ādręncan. .Æ. H. i. 22.

9. 18. *See* .Æ. H. i. 20.

9. 29. Noe leofode on eallum his līfe, ǣr þām flōde and æfter þām flōde, nigon hund gēara and fīftig gēara ; and hē þā forð-fērde. .Æ. H. i. 22.·

10. 21, 22, 24. *See* .Æ. H. i. 24.

11. 1. Þā wæs ān gereord on eallum mancynne. .Æ. H. i. 318 ; cf. i. 22.

‖ Eal middaneard hæfde āne sprǣce. .Æ. H. ii. 472.

11. 4. Ðā cwǣdon hī betwux him þæt hī woldon wyrcan āne burh, and ænne stȳpel binnon þǣre byrig, swā hēahne þæt his hrōf āstige ūp tō heofenum. .Æ. H. i. 22.

‖ Hit getīmode æfter Noes flōde, þæt entas woldon ārǣran āne burh, and ænne stȳpel swā hēahne þæt his hrōf āstige oð heofon. .Æ. H. i. 318 ; cf. ii. 198.

‖ Męn woldon him ārǣran swā hēahne stȳpel þæt his hrōf āstige tō heofenum. .Æ. H. ii. 472.

---

fontes abyssi magnae, et cata-ractae coeli apertae sunt, et facta est pluvia super terram quadra-ginta diebus et quadraginta noc-tibus.

7. 16, 17. . . . Inclusit eum Dominus deforis. Factumque est diluvium quadraginta diebus super terram, et multiplicatae sunt aquae, et elevaverunt arcam in sublime a terra.

9. 11, 14, 15. Statuam pactum meum vobiscum, et nequaquam ultra in-terficietur omnis caro aquis dilu-vii, neque erit deinceps diluvium dissipans terram. . . . Cumque ob-

duxero nubibus coelum, apparebit arcus meus in nubibus, et recor-dabor foederis mei vobiscum, et cum omni anima vivente quae carnem vegetat, et non erunt ultra aquae diluvii ad delendum universam carnem.

9. 29. Et impleti sunt omnes dies eius nongentorum quinquaginta annorum ; et mortuus est.

11. 1. Erat autem terra labii unius, et sermonum eorumdem.

11. 4. Et dixerunt : Venite, faciamus nobis civitatem et turrim, cuius culmen pertingat ad coelum. . . .

11. 7, 8. Ðā cōm God þǣrtō, þā-ðā hī swīðost worhton, and sealde ǣlcum menn, þe ðǣr wæs, synderlice sprǣce. Þā wǣron þǣr swā fela gereord swā ðǣr manna wǣron; and heora nān nyste hwæt ōðer cwæð. And hī ðā geswicon þǣre getimbrunge, and tōfērdon geond ealne middangeard.   *Æ. H. i.* 22.

‖ God ēac forðī hī tōstencte, swā þæt hē forgeaf ǣlcum ðǣra wyrhtena seltcūð gereord, and heora nān ne cūðe ōðres sprǣce tōcnāwan. Hī ðā geswicon ðǣre getimbrunge, and tōfērdon geond ealne middangeard.   *Æ. H. i.* 318.

‖ Ac se Ælmihtiga tōwearp heora anginn, swā þæt hē forgeaf ǣlcum ðǣra wyrhtena synderlic gereord, and heora nān nyste hwæt ōðer gecwæð.   *Æ. H. ii.* 472.

11. 10–17. *See Æ. H. i.* 24.

12. 3. *See* Gen. 26. 4.

15. 13, 14, 16. Þā cwæð se Ælmihtiga God tō Abrahame: Wite ðū þæt ðīn cynn sceal ælðēodig wunian on ōðrum earde fēower hund gēara, and hī hī on ðēowte gebringað, and micclum swencað. Sōðlice ic dēme ðām folce; and ðīn mǣgð siððan mid micclum ǣhtum of ðām lande færð, and on ðām fēorðan entēowe hī gecyrrað hider ongēan.   *Æ. H. ii.* 192.

17. 1, 2. God ... him tō cwæð: Ic eom Ælmihtig Drihten; gang beforan mē, and bēo fulfremed. And ic sette mīn wed betwux mē and ðē, and ic ðē þearle gemenigfylde.   *Æ. H. i.* 90.

17. 3. Abraham hine āstrehte eallum limum tō eorðan.   *Æ. H. i.* 90.

17. 5. Ne bēo ðū gecīged heononforð Abram, ac Abraham, forðan-þe ic gesette ðē manegra þēoda fæder.   *Æ. H. i.* 92.

---

11. 7, 8. Venite igitur, descendamus, et confundamus ibi linguam eorum, ut non audiat unusquisque vocem proximi sui. Atque ita divisit eos Dominus ex illo loco in universas terras, et cessaverunt aedificare civitatem.

15. 13, 14, 16. Dictumque est ad eum: Scito praenoscens quod peregrinum futurum sit semen tuum in terra non sua, et subiicient eos servituti, et affligent quadringentis annis. Veruntamen gentem cui servituri sunt ego iudicabo; et post haec egredientur cum magna substantia. . . . Generatione autem quarta revertentur huc. . . .

17. 1, 2. . . . Dixitque ad eum: Ego Deus omnipotens; ambula coram me, et esto perfectus. Ponamque foedus meum inter me et te, et multiplicabo te vehementer nimis.

17. 3. Cecidit Abram pronus in faciem.

17. 5. Nec ultra vocabitur nomen tuum Abram, sed appellaberis Abraham, quia patrem multarum gentium constitui te.

17. 6, 7. Cyningas āspringað of ðē. And ic sętte mīn węd betwux mē and ðē, and þīnum ofspringe æfter ðē, þæt ic bēo ðīn God and ðīnes ofspringes. *Æ. H. i.* 90.

17. 9, 10, 12. Heald þū mīn węd, and þīn ofspring æfter ðē on heora mǣgðum. Ðis is mīn węd þæt gē healdan sceolon betwux mē and ēow, þæt ǣlc hysecild on ēowrum cynrene bēo ymbsniden; þæt tācn sȳ betwux mē and ēow. Ǣlc hysecild, þonne hit eahta nihta eald bið, sȳ ymbsniden, ǣgðer ge æþelboren ge þēowetling. *Æ. H. i.* 90, 92.

17. 14. Swā hwylc hysecild swā ne bið ymbsniden on þām fylmene his flǣsces his sāwul losað, forðanþe hē āȳdlode mīn węd. *Æ. H. i.* 94.

‖ And sē ðe þis forgǣið his sāwul losað, forðanþe hē mīn węd āȳdlode. *Æ. H. i.* 92.

17. 15, 16. Ne ðīn wīf ne bēo gehāten Sarai, ac bēo gehāten Sarra; and ic hī geblētsige, and of hire ic ðē sylle sunu. *Æ. H. i.* 92.

17. 17. *See Æ. H. i.* 92.

17. 19, 22, 26, 27. (Of hire ic ðē sylle sunu,) þone ðū gecīgest Isaac; and ic sętte mīn węd tō him and tō his ofspringe on ēcere fæstnunge. And æfter ðǣre sprǣce se Ælmihtiga ūpgewęnde. On þām ylcan dæge wæs Abraham ymbsniden, and eal his hȳred. *Æ. H. i.* 92 ; cf. i. 90.

17. 6, 7. ... Regesque ex te egredientur. Et statuam pactum meum inter me et te, et inter semen tuum post te in generationibus suis, foedere sempiterno; ut sim Deus tuus, et seminis tui post te.

17. 9, 10, 12. ... Et tu ergo custodies pactum meum, et semen tuum post te in generationibus suis. Hoc est pactum meum quod observabitis inter me et vos: ... Circumcidetur ex vobis omne masculinum. ... Infans octo dierum circumcidetur in vobis, omne masculinum in generationibus vestris; tam vernaculus quam emptitius circumcidetur, et quicumque non fuerit de stirpe vestra.

17. 14. Masculus, cuius praeputii caro circumcisa non fuerit, delebitur anima illa de populo suo, quia pactum meum irritum fecit.

17. 15, 16. ... Sarai uxorem tuam non vocabis Sarai, sed Saram. Et benedicam ei, et ex illa dabo tibi filium. ...

17. 19, 22, 26, 27. ... Sara uxor tua pariet tibi filium, vocabisque nomen eius Isaac; et constituam pactum meum illi in foedus sempiternum, et semini eius post eum. ... Cumque finitus esset sermo loquentis cum eo, ascendit Deus ab Abraham. ... Eadem die circumcisus est Abraham; ... et omnes viri domus illius ... pariter circumcisi sunt.

18. 2. *See* Æ. H. ii. 234.

18. 18. *See* Gen. 26. 4.

19. 1. *See* Æ. H. i. 38.

19. 24, 25. *See* Æ. H. i. 246.

21. 4. And syððan his sunu Isaac, on ðām eahtoðan dæge his ācennednysse. Æ. H. i. 92.

22. 2, 3. *See* Æ. H. ii. 60.

22. 4-13, 15-18. Efne, ðā-ðā hē ðǣre dūne genēalǣhte, þā cwæð hē tō his cnihtum: Andbīdiað hēr; ic and þis cild willað ūs gebiddan æt þǣre stōwe þe ūs God geswutelode. Isaac þā bær wudu tō forbærnenne ðā offrunge, and Abraham hæfde him on handa fȳr and swurd. Isaac ðā befrān ðone fæder, and cwæð: Efne, hēr is fȳr and wudu, mīn fæder; hwǣr is sēo offrung? Abraham andwyrde: Mīn bearn, God foresceāwað him sylfum þǣre onsǣgednysse offrunge. Hwæt, ðā Abraham, ðā-ðā hī tō ðǣre stōwe cōmon, geband his lēofan sunu, and his swurd ātēah, þæt hē hine Gode geoffrode. Efne, ðā Godes engel clypode of heofonum, and mid hluddre stemne cwæð: Abraham, ne āstrece ðū ðīne hand bufon ðām cilde, nē him nāne dare ne gedō; nū ic oncnēow þæt ðū God ondrǣdst, and þū ne ārodest þīnum āncennedan suna for his hǣse. Þā beseah Abraham underbæc, and ðǣr stōd ān ramm betwux þām brēmelum, getīged be ðām hornum; hē ðā genam ðone ramm, and Gode geoffrode for ðām cilde. Æfter ðisum clypode eft Godes engel of heofonum tō Abrahame, þus cweðende: God cwæð: Ic swōr þurh mē sylfne, forðanðe þū þus dǣde dydest, and ðīnum āncennedan bearne ne ārodest, ic geblētsige ðē, and þīnne ofspring ic gemenigfylde swā-swā steorran on heofenan, and swā-swā sandcēosol on sǣlicum strande. Þīn sǣd sōðlice geāgnað his fēonda gatu, and on ðīnum sǣde bēoð geblētsode ealle eorðlice mǣgða, forðanðe ðū gehȳrsumedest mīnre stemne. Æ. H. ii. 60, 62; cf. Gen. 26. 4.

21. 4. Et circumcidit eum octavo die....

22. 4-13, 15-18. Die autem tertio, elevatis oculis, vidit locum procul, dixitque ad pueros suos: Expectate hic cum asino; ego et puer illuc usque properantes, postquam adoraverimus revertemur ad vos. Tulit quoque ligna holocausti, et imposuit super Isaac filium suum; ipse vero portabat in manibus ignem et gladium. Cumque duo pergerent simul, dixit Isaac patri suo: Pater mi, ... ecce, ... ignis et ligna; ubi est victima holocausti? Dixit autem Abraham:

24. 1–4. Ðā-ðā hē caldode, and his sunu wīfian sceolde, þā clypode hē his yldestan cniht him tō, and hēt hine sęttan his hand under his ðēoh, and swęrian ðurh ðone heofonlican God þæt hē nǣfre geðafode þæt his sunu Isaac on hǣðenre mǣgðe wīfian sceolde, ac of ðām gelēaffullum folce þe Abraham on āfēdd wæs. Æ. H. ii. 234.

‖ Sęte ðīne hand under mīnum ðēo. . . . Swęra ðurh ðone heofenlican God. Æ. H. ii. 236.

25. 24–26. *See* Æ. H. i. 110 ; ii. 190.

26. 4. . . . þæt on his cynne sceolde bēon eal mancynn geblētsod. Æ. H. ii. 12.

35. 22. *See* Æ. H. ii. 190.

41. 49. On ðām ānum wæs corn . . . swā fela swā bið sandcēosol on sǣ. Æ. H. ii. 190.

41. 54. *See* Æ. H. ii. 190.

46. 46. *See* Æ. H. ii. 190.

47. 27. *See* Æ. H. ii. 190.

Deus providebit sibi victimam holocausti, fili mi. Pergebant ergo pariter, et venerunt ad locum quem ostenderat ei Deus, in quo aedificavit altare, et desuper ligna composuit ; cumque alligasset Isaac filium suum. . . . Extenditque manum, et arripuit gladium, ut immolaret filium suum. Et ecce angelus Domini de coelo clamavit, dicens : Abraham, Abraham, . . . non extendas manum tuam super puerum, neque facias illi quidquam ; nunc cognovi quod times Deum, et non pepercisti unigenito filio tuo propter me. Levavit Abraham oculos suos, viditque post tergum arietem inter vepres haerentem cornibus, quem assumens obtulit holocaustum pro filio. . . . Vocavit autem angelus Domini Abraham secundo de coelo, dicens : Per memetipsum iuravi, dicit Dominus, quia fecisti hanc rem, et non pepercisti filio tuo unigenito propter me, benedicam tibi, et multiplicabo semen tuum sicut stellas coeli, et velut arenam quae est in littore maris. Possidebit semen tuum portas inimicorum suorum, et benedicentur in semine tuo omnes gentes terrae, quia obedisti voci meae.

24. 1–4. Erat autem Abraham senex dierumque multorum. . . . Dixitque ad servum seniorem domus suae, qui praeerat omnibus quae habebat : Pone manum tuam subter femur meum, ut adiurem te per Dominum, Deum coeli et terrae, ut non accipias uxorem filio meo de filiabus Chananaeorum inter quos habito, sed ad terram et cognationem meam proficiscaris, et inde accipias uxorem filio meo Isaac.

26. 4. . . . Benedicentur in semine tuo omnes gentes terrae.

41. 49. Tantaque fuit abundantia tritici, ut arenae maris coaequaretur. . . .

49. 10. . . . þæt ne sceolde ꜳteorian þæt Iudeisce cynecynn, ōþ-þæt Crīst sylf cōme. Æ. H. i. 82.

EXODUS.

1. 5. *See* Æ. H. ii. 190.

3. 7, 8. Tō ðām Moyse spræc se Ælmihtiga God þisum wordum : Ic geseah mīnes folces geswinc on Egypta lande, and heora hrēam ic gehȳrde, and ic niðerꜳstāh þæt ic hī āhrędde of Egyptiscra manna handum ; and ic hī gelǣde of ðām earde tō gōdan lande and brādum, þæt ðe flēowð mid meolce and mid hunige. Æ. H. ii. 192.

3. 10. Far to ðām cyninge Pharao, and bēod him þæt hē mīn folc forlǣte of his lēode faran. Æ. H. ii. 192.

3. 14. . . . swā-swā hē sylf cwæð tō Moysen : IC EOM SE ÐE EOM, and sęge Israhela bearnum : SĒ ÐE IS sęnde mē tō eow. Æ. H. ii. 236.

4. 25. *See* Æ. H. i. 92.

5. 1, 2. Moyses ðā and his brōðor Aaron fērdon tō Pharao mid ǣrende þæs Ælmihtigan Godes, and cwǣdon : Þus cwyð Drihten Israhela God : Forlǣt mīn folc, þæt hit mē lāc offrige on wēstene, swā ic him gewissige. Pharao him andwyrde : Hwæt is se Drihten, þæt ic his stemne gehȳran sceole, and Israhel forlǣtan ? Nāt ic ðone Drihten, and ic Israhel ne for-lǣte. Æ. H. ii. 192.

7. 1. . . . Cwæð se Ælmihtiga tō Moysen : Ic ðē gesętte þæt þu wǣre Pharaones god. Æ. H. i. 346.

49. 10. Non auferetur sceptrum de Iuda, et dux de femore eius, donec veniat qui mittendus est, et ipse erit expectatio gentium.

EXODUS.

3. 7, 8. Cui ait Dominus : Vidi afflic-tionem populi mei in Aegypto, et clamorem eius audivi. . . . De-scendi ut liberem eum de manibus Aegyptiorum ; et educam de terra illa in terram bonam et spatiosam, in terram quae fluit lacte et melle. . . .

3. 10. Sed veni, et mittam te ad Pharaonem, ut educas populum meum, filios Israel, de Aegypto.

3. 14. Dixit Deus ad Moysen : EGO SUM QUI SUM. Ait : Sic dices filiis Israel : QUI EST misit me ad vos.

5. 1, 2. Post haec ingressi sunt Moyses et Aaron, et dixerunt Pharaoni : Haec dicit Dominus Deus Israel : Dimitte populum meum, ut sacrificet mihi in de-serto. At ille respondit : Quis est Dominus, ut audiam vocem eius, et dimittam Israel ? Nescio Do-minum, et Israel non dimittam.

7. 1. Dixitque Dominus ad Moysen : Ecce constitui te deum Pharao-nis. . . .

7. 20. *See* Æ. H. ii. 192.

8. 6, 17, 24. *See* Æ. H. ii. 192.

9. 6. Þæt fīfte wīte wæs cwealm on heora orfe, swā þæt on ðām lande fornēan nān orf ne belāf, būton Israheles þe ansund gestōd.   Æ. H. ii. 192.

9. 10. Þæt sixte wīte wæs, þæt mislice geswel and blǣdran āsprungon on heora līchaman on eallum his folce.   Æ. H. ii. 192.

9. 23, 25. Þæt seofoðe wīte wæs, þæt swā micel ðunor and hagol becōm on ðām lēodscipe, þæt ǣlc ðing wæs ādȳd þæt ūte wearð gemēt, and ǣlc trēow on ðām earde tōbærst.   Æ. H. ii. 192.

10. 14. Þæt eahtoðe wīte wæs, þæt gærstapan oferēodon eall þæt land swilce swā nǣfre ǣrðan nǣron, nē eft nǣfre ne gewurðað.   Æ. H. ii. 192.

10. 15. And hī forgnōgon swā-hwæt-swā se hagol belǣfde, oððe on trēowum oððe on ōðrum wǣstmum.   Æ. H. ii. 194.

10. 22, 23. Þæt nigoðe wīte wæs, þæt becōmon ðicce ðēostru and egeslice ofer eallum Egypta lande, swā þæt heora nān binnon ðrīm dagum ōðerne ne geseah, nē hī of ðǣre stōwe styrian ne mihton, and on Israhela ðēode wǣron gewunelice dagas.   Æ. H. ii. 194.

12. 2. Þes mōnað is mōnða anginn, and hē bið fyrmest on gēares mōnðum.   Æ. H. i. 98.

12. 2, 5. *See* Æ. H. i. 310.

12. 3, 5 ff. God sette on ðǣre ealdan ǣ, and hēt niman ānes gēares

---

9. 6. . . . Mortuaque sunt omnia animantia Aegyptiorum; de animalibus vero filiorum Israel nihil omnino periit.

9. 10. . . . Factaque sunt ulcera vesicarum turgentium in hominibus. . . .

9. 23, 25. . . . Dominus dedit tonitrua et grandinem, . . . pluitque Dominus grandinem super terram Aegypti. . . . Et percussit grando in omni terra Aegypti cuncta quae fuerunt in agris, ab homine usque ad iumentum; cunctamque herbam agri percussit grando, et omne lignum regionis confregit.

10. 14. Quae [locustae] ascenderunt super universam terram Aegypti, . . . quales ante illud tempus non fuerant, nec postea futurae sunt.

10. 15. . . . Devorata est igitur herba terrae, et quidquid pomorum in arboribus fuit, quae grando dimiserat. . . .

10. 22, 23. . . . Factae sunt tenebrae horribiles in universa terra Aegypti tribus diebus. Nemo vidit fratrem suum, nec movit se de loco in quo erat; ubicumque autem habitabant filii Israel lux erat.

12. 2. Mensis iste vobis principium mensium; primus erit in mensibus anni.

12. 3, 5 ff. . . . Tollat unusquisque

lamb æt ǣlcum hiwisce, and snīðan on Eastertīde, and wyrcan
mid þæs lambes blōde rōdetācn on heora gedyrum and on oferslegum, and brēdan þæt lamb, and hit swā ðicgan ; gif ðǣr
hwæt lēfde, forbærnan. *Æ. H. ii. 40.*

12. 7–11. Se Ælmihtiga God bebēad Moysen . . . þæt hē sceolde
bebēodan Israhela folce þæt hī . . . sceoldon . . . wyrcan
rōdetācn on heora gedyrum and oferslegum mid ðæs lambes
blōde, etan siððan ðæs lambes flǣsc gebrǣd, and ðeorfe hlāfas
mid feldlicere lactucan. God cwæð tō Moysen : Ne ete gē of
ðām lambe nān ðing hrēaw, nē on wætere gesoden, ac gebrǣd
tō fȳre. Etað þæt hēafod, and ðā fēt, and þæt innewearde, nē
his nān ðing ne belīfe ōð morigen ; gif ðǣr hwæt tō lāfe sȳ,
forbærnað þæt. Ðicgað hit on ðas wīson : Begyrdað ēowere
lendenu, and bēoð gescēode, habbað ēow stæf on handa, and etað
ārdlice ; þēos tīd is Godes færeld. *Æ. H. ii. 264 ; cf. i. 310, ii. 266.*

|| Israhel ðigde þæs lambes flǣsc . . . mid þeorfum hlāfum and
feldlicum lactucum. *Æ. H. ii. 278.*

|| Israhel sceolde etan þæs lambes hēafod, and ðā fēt, and þæt
innewerde, and þǣr nān ðing belīfan ne mōste ofer niht ; gif
þǣr hwæt belīfe, forbærnan þæt on fȳre ; and ne tōbrǣcon ðā
bān[1]. . . . Hī ǣton þæt lamb mid begyrdum lendenum. . . . Hī
wǣron ēac gescēode. . . . Hī hæfdon him stæf on handa.
Æ. H. ii. 280.

|| . . . þæt hī sceoldon cāflice etan. . . . Ne mōston þæs lambes
bān scēnan. *Æ. H. ii. 282.*

|| . . . þæt hī hit hrēaw ne ǣton, nē on wætere gesoden, ac
gebrǣd tō fȳre. *Æ. H. ii. 278.*

agnum per familias et domos suas. . . . Erit autem agnus . . . anniculus ; . . . immolabitque eum. [See next paragraph.]

12. 7–11. Et sument de sanguine eius, ac ponent super utrumque postem et in superliminaribus domorum in quibus comedent illum. Et edent carnes nocte illa assas igni, et azymos panes cum lactucis agrestibus. Non comedetis ex eo crudum quid, nec coctum aqua, sed tantum assum igni. Caput cum pedibus eius et intestinis vorabitis, nec remanebit quidquam ex eo usque mane ; si quid residuum fuerit, igne comburetis. Sic autem comedetis illum : Renes vestros accingetis, et calceamenta habebitis in pedibus, tenentes baculos in manibus, et comedetis festinanter ; est enim Phase (id est transitus) Domini.

---

[1] From Ex. 12. 46, 'nec os illius confringetis.'

12. 14, 15. Þā cwæð God tō Moysen : Healdað þisne dæg on ēowerum gemynde, and frēolsiað hine mærlice on ēowerum cynrenum mid ēcum biggęnge, and etað þeorfne hlāf symle seofon dagas æt ðissere frēolstīde.   Æ. H. ii. 264.

12. 27. *See* Æ. H. ii. 282.

12. 29, 30. Þæt tēoðe wīte wæs, þæt on ælcum hūse ealre ðære ðēode, on ānre nihte, læg ān dēad mann, and þæt wæs se frum-cęnneda and se lēofosta þām hlāforde.   Æ. H. ii. 194 ; cf. i. 310.

12. 37. Hī lǣddon þæt folc tō ðære Rēadan sǣ mid micelre fyrd-inge, þæt wǣron six hund þūsenda wīgendra manna, būton wīfum and cildum.   Æ. H. ii. 194 ; cf. i. 312.

12. 46. *See* Ex. 12. 7–11, note.

13. 13. Gif hit þonne unclǣne nȳten wǣre, þonne sceolde se hlāford hit ācwellan, oþþe syllan Gode ōþer clǣne nȳten.
Æ. H. i. 138.

13. 18. *See* Æ. H. ii. 194.

13. 21, 22. *See* Æ. H. ii. 196, 200.

14. 5–9. *See* Æ. H. ii. 194.

14. 15, 16. Þā cwæð se Ælmihtiga tō Moysen : Astręce ðīne hand ofer ðā sǣ, and tōdǣl hī.   Æ. H. ii. 194.

14. 21–23. And Moyses ðā slōh þēre sǣ ofer mid his gyrde[1], and sēo sǣ tōēode on twā, and eal þæt Israhela folc ēode ofer ðā sǣ be drīum grunde, and þæt wæter stōd him on twā healfa swilce ōðer stānweall.   Pharao ðā him filigde æt ðam hōn mid his gebēotlicum crætum and gilplicum riddum.   Æ. H. ii. 194 ; cf. ii. 264.

‖ God hī lǣdde ofer ðā Rēadan sǣ mid drīum fōtum.   Þā tęngde se Pharao æfter mid mycelre fyrde.   Æ. H. i. 312.

12. 14, 15. Habebitis autem hunc diem in monumentum, et cele-brabitis eam solemnem Domino in generationibus vestris cultu sempiterno. Septem diebus azyma comedetis. . . .

12. 29, 30. Factum est autem in noctis medio, percussit Dominus omne primogenitum in terra Aegypti. . . . Neque enim erat domus in quia non iaceret mor-tuus.

12. 37. Profectique sunt filii Israel de Ramesse in Socoth, sexcenta fere millia peditum virorum, abs-que parvulis.

13. 13. Primogenitum asini mutabis ove ; quod si non redemeris, in-terficies. . . .

14. 15, 16. Dixitque Dominus ad Moysen : . . . Tu autem eleva virgam tuam, et extende manum tuam super mare, et divide illud.

14. 21–23. Cumque extendisset Moyses manum super mare . . . Dominus . . . vertit in siccum;

[1] Cf. Ex. 14. 16.

14. 26–29. Þā cwæð se Ælmihtiga God tō Moysen : Āstręce ðīne hand ofer ðā sǣ, þæt þæt wæter gecyrre tō ðām Egiptiscum, ofer heora crætum and riddum. Moyses ðā āstręhte his hand ongēan ðǣre sǣ, and hēo oferarn Pharao, and ealle his crætu and riddan mid ȳðum oferwrēah, swā þæt ðǣr næs furðon ān tō lāfe ealles ðæs hęres þe him filigde. Israhela folc sōðlice ēode be ðām drīum grunde. *Æ. H. ii.* 194; cf. *i.* 24, *ii.* 264.

‖ Ða-ðā hē cōm on middan ðǣre sǣ, þā wæs þæt Godes folc ūpāgān, and God ðā besęncte ðone Pharao and eal his werod. *Æ. H. i.* 312.

16. 14 ff. *See Æ. H. ii.* 194, 196.

16. 35. *See Æ. H. i.* 24, 76 ; *ii.* 264.

17. 1–6. *See Æ. H. ii.* 196, 264.

19. 1, 2. *See Æ. H. ii.* 196.

19. 9. God cwæð tō Moysen þæt hē wolde cuman, and hine ætforan ðām folce gesprecan, þæt hī ðȳ lēaffulran wǣron. *Æ. H. ii.* 196.

19. 11. And hēt hī bēon gearowe on ðām ðriddan dæge. *Æ. H. ii.* 196.

19. 13. Bebēod ðām folce þæt heora nān ðām munte ne genēalǣce ; swā-hwæt-swā hine hrępað, oððe mann oþþe nȳten, hē ne leofað sōna. *Æ. H. ii.* 196.

19. 16, 18. Ðā . . . wearð Godes wuldor gesewen on ðām wēstene uppon ānum munte se is gehāten Synay, tō ðām āstāh se Ælmihtiga Scyppend, and efne ðā, þǣr begann tō brastligenne micel ðunor, and līget scēotan on ðæs folces gesihðe, and bȳman

divisaque est aqua. Et ingressi sunt filii Israel per medium sicci maris ; erat enim aqua quasi murus a dextra eorum et laeva. Persequentesque Aegypti ingressi sunt post eos, et omnis equitatus Pharaonis, currus eius et equites, per medium maris.

14. 26–29. Et ait Dominus ad Moysen : Extende manum tuam super mare, ut revertantur aquae ad Aegyptios, super currus et equites eorum. Cumque extendisset Moyses manum contra mare, . . . reversaeque sunt aquae, et operuerunt currus et equites cuncti exercitus Pharaonis, . . . nec unus

quidem superfuit ex eis. Filii autem Israel perrexerunt per medium sicci maris. . . .

19. 9. Ait ei Dominus : Iam nunc veniam ad te, . . . ut audiat me populus loquentem ad te, et credat tibi in perpetuum. . . .

19. 11. Et sint parati in diem tertium. . . .

19. 13. Manus non tanget eum, sed lapidibus opprimetur aut confodietur iaculis ; sive iumentum fuerit, sive homo, non vivet. . . .

19. 16, 18. . . . Ecce coeperunt audiri tonitrua, ac micare fulgura. et nubes densissima operire montem, clangorque buccinae vehementius

blēowan mid swīðlicum drēame; and micel wolcn oferwrēah
ealne ðone munt.   Æ. H. ii. 196.

‖ Ðā . . . wæs gesewen Godes wuldor uppon ānre dūne þe is
gehāten Synay.   Þǣr cōm micel lēoht, and ęgeslic swēg, and
blāwende bӯman.   Æ. H. i. 312.

‖ On ðām munte Synay, þe se Ælmihtiga on becōm, wearð
micel ðunor gehӯred and stemn, and līget gesewen, swā-swā
scīnende lēohtfatu, and þǣr wæs bӯmena drēam hlūde swēgende,
and eal se munt smocigende stōd.   Æ. H. ii. 202.

19. 24. Clypode se Ælmihtiga Drihten Moysen him tō, and cwæð:
Āstīh ęft ādūne. . . . Āstīh nū ęft ūp tō mē, and Aaron
samod.   Æ. H. ii. 196.

20. 7. Ne underfōh ðū ðīnes Drihtnes naman on ӯdelnysse.
     Æ. H. ii. 198, 204.

20. 8. Bēo ðū gemyndig þæt ðū ðone ręstendæg frēolsige.
     Æ. H. ii. 198.

‖ Bēo ðū gemyndig þæt þū ðone ręstendæg gehālgige.
     Æ. H. ii. 206.

20. 11. On six dagum geworhte God ealle gesceafta, and geęndode
hī on ðām seofoðan.   Æ. H. ii. 206.

20. 12. Ārwurða ðīnne fæder and ðīne mōder, þæt ðū lang līf ofer
eorðan wunie.   Æ. H. ii. 36.

‖ Ārwurða þīnne fæder and þīne mōder.   Æ. H. i. 442 ;   cf.
ii. 198, 208.

‖ Ārwurða ðīnne fæder and ēac þīne mōder.   Æ. H. ii. 324.

20. 13. Ne ofslih ðū mannan.   Æ. H. ii. 198.

‖ Ne ofslih ðū mann.   Æ. H. ii. 208.

20. 14. Ne hǣm ðū unrihtlice.   Æ. H. ii. 198.

‖ Ne unrihthǣm ðū.   Æ. H. ii. 208.

20. 15. Ne stala ðū.   Æ. H. ii. 198, 208.

---

perstrepebat. . . . Totus autem mons Sinai fumabat, eo quod descendisset Dominus super eum. . . .

19. 24. Cui ait Dominus: Vade, descende; ascendesque tu, et Aaron tecum. . . .

20. 7. Non assumes nomen Domini Dei tui in vanum. . . .

20. 8. Memento ut diem sabbati sanctifices.

20. 11. Sex enim diebus fecit Dominus coelum et terram, et mare, et omnia quae in eis sunt, et requievit in die septimo. . . .

20. 12. Honora patrem tuum et matrem tuam, ut sis longaevus super terram. . . .

20. 13. Non occides.

20. 14. Non moechaberis.

20. 15. Non furtum facies.

20. 16. Ne bēo ðū lēas gewita. _Æ. H. ii. 198, 208._

20. 17. Ne gewilna ðū ōðres mannes wīfes ; . . . ne gewilna ðū ōðres mannes ǣhta. _Æ. H. ii. 198, 208._

21. 17. Sē ðe wyrigð fæder oððe mōder, oððe hī tyrigð, sē is dēaðes scyldig. _Æ. H. ii. 208._

‖ Sē ðe fæder oððe mōdor mānlice wyrigð, hē sceal dēaðe sweltan. _Æ. H. ii. 324._

24. 12. _See_ Ex. 31. 18.

24. 18. _See Æ. H._ i. 312 ; ii. 100.

25. 8 ff. _See Æ. H._ ii. 198.

31. 18. Þā āwrāt se Ælmihtiga God him twā stǣnene wexbredu mid his āgenum fingre. _Æ. H. ii. 196._

‖ God āwrāt ðā ealdan ǣ mid his fingre on ðām stǣnenum weaxbredum. _Æ. H. ii. 204._

32. 15, 16. _See_ Ex. 31. 18.

34. 20. _See_ Ex. 13. 13.

34. 28. On ðām wǣron āwritene tȳn word, þæt sind tȳn ǣlice beboda. _Æ. H. ii. 196 ; cf._ i. 178, and Ex. 24. 18.

LEVITICUS.

12. 2. _See Æ. H._ i. 134.

12. 6, 8. . . . þæt ðā, þe mihton ðurhtēon, sceoldon bringan ānes gēares lamb mid heora cylde, Gode to lāce, and āne culfre oþþe āne turtlan. Gif þonne hwylc wif tō ðām unspēdig wǣre þæt hēo ðās ðing begytan ne mihte, þonne sceolde hēo bringan twēgen culfranbriddas oððe twā turtlan. _Æ. H._ i. 138, 140 ; cf. i. 134.

13. 2, 46. _See Æ. H._ i. 122, 124.

19. 18. Lufa ðīnne nēxtan swā-swā ðē sylfne. _Æ. H. ii. 340._

20. 9. _See_ Ex. 21. 17.

20. 16. Non loqueris contra proximum tuum falsum testimonium.

20. 17. Non concupisces domum proximi tui, nec desiderabis uxorem eius, non servum, non ancillam, non bovem, non asinum, nec omnia quae illius sunt.

21. 17. Qui maledixerit patri suo vel matri, morte moriatur.

31. 18. Deditque Dominus Moysi ... duas tabulas testimonii lapideas, scriptas digito Dei.

34. 28. . . . Et scripsit in tabulis verba foederis decem.

LEVITICUS.

12. 6, 8. . . . Deferet agnum anniculum in holocaustum, et pullum columbae sive turturem ; . . . quod si non . . . potuerit offerre agnum, sumet duos turtures vel duos pullos columbarum. . . .

19. 18. . . . Diliges amicum tuum sicut teipsum.

NUMBERS.

9. 17. Swā-hwǣr-swā hit ætstōd, þǣr hī wīcodon; and eft, swā-hraðo-swā þæt wolcn styrode, swā stōde samtinges eal sēo fyrd æfter ðām wolcne. *Æ. H. ii. 196.*

17. 1–8. God bebēad Moysen þām heretogan þæt hē genāme twelf drīge gyrda æt þām twelf mǣgðum Israhela ðēoda, and ālēde hī ætforan ðām hālgan scrīne, binnon ðām micclan getelde; and hē wolde ðurh ðā gyrda geswutelian hwǣne hē tō biscope gecoren hæfde. Þā, on ðām ōðrum dæge, wæs Aarones gyrd gemētt grōwende mid bōgum, and blōwende, and berende hnyte. *Æ. H. ii. 8.*

18. 15, 16. God bebēad, on þǣre ealdan ǣ, his folce þæt hī sceoldon him offrian ǣlc frumcenned hysecild, oþþe ālȳsan hit ūt mid fīf scyllingum; ēac on heora orfe, swā-hwæt-swā frum-cenned wǣre, bringan þæt tō Godes hūse, and hit ðǣr Gode offrian. *Æ. H. i. 138.*

18. 26. *See* Æ. H. ii. 224.

20. 26. *See* Æ. H. ii. 212.

21. 6–9. Þā sende hē betwux him fȳrene næddran, þā totǣron ðæs

NUMBERS.

9. 17. Cumque ablata fuisset nubes . . . tunc proficiscebantur filii Israel; et in loco ubi stetisset nubes, ibi castra metabantur.

17. 1–8. Et locutus est Dominus ad Moysen, dicens : Loquere ad filios Israel, et accipe ab eis virgas singulas per cognationes suas, a cunctis principibus tribuum, vir-gas duodecim, et uniuscuiusque nomen superscribes virgae suae. Nomen autem Aaron erit in tribu Levi, et una virga cunctas seorsum familias continebit; ponesque eas in tabernaculo foederis coram tes-timonio, ubi loquar ad te. Quem ex his elegero, germinabit virga eius. . . . Locutusque est Moyses ad filios Israel, et dederunt ei omnes principes virgas per sin-gulas tribus; fueruntque virgae duodecim absque virga Aaron; quas cum posuisset Moyses coram Domino in tabernaculo testimonii, sequenti die regressus invenit ger-minasse virgam Aaron in domo Levi, et turgentibus gemmis eru-perant flores, qui, foliis dilatatis, in amygdalas deformati sunt.

18. 15, 16. Quidquid primum erum-pit e vulva cunctae carnis quam offerunt Domino, sive ex homini-bus sive de pecoribus fuerit, tui iuris erit; ita dumtaxat, ut pro hominis primogenito pretium ac-cipias, et omne animal quod im-mundum est, redimi facias, cuius redemptio erit post unum mensem, siclis argenti quinque, pondere sanctuarii. Siclus viginti obolos habet.

21. 6–9. Quamobrem misit Dominus

folces fela manna, and tō dēaðe gærttrodon. Þa clypode þæt
folc to Moysen ðisum wordum : Wē syngodon ongēan God and
ongēan ðē ; bide for ūs, þæt se Ælmihtiga God þās næddran
fram ūs āfyrsige. Hwæt, ðā Moyses for ðām folce gebæd, and
God þærrihte bebēad Moyse þæt hē geworhte āne ārene næddran,
and sętte ūp tō tācne, and þæt hē manode þæt folc þæt swā-hwā-
swā fram ðām næddrum ābiten wǣre, besāwe ūp tō ðǣre
ārenan næddran, and hē wurde gehǣled. Hit wearð swā gedōn :
ðā næddran hī tōtǣron, and hī besāwon tō ðǣre ārenan næddran,
and hī wurdon gehǣlede fram ðām dēadbǣrum attre þāra
fȳrenra næddryna.   _Æ. H. ii._ 238.

27. 21. *See Æ. H. ii.* 212.

DEUTERONOMY.

4. 13. *See* Ex. 34. 28.

5. 11. *See* Ex. 20. 7.

5. 12. *See* Ex. 20. 8.

5. 16. *See* Ex. 20. 12.

5. 17. *See* Ex. 20. 13.

5. 18. *See* Ex. 20. 14.

5. 19. *See* Ex. 20. 15.

5. 20. *See* Ex. 20. 16.

5. 21. *See* Ex. 20. 17.

6. 4. Drihten þīn God is ān God.   _Æ. H. ii._ 198 ; cf. ii. 204.

8. 3, 4. *See Æ. H. ii.* 196.

9. 9. Moyses ðā wæs wunigende ūp on ðǣre dūne fēowertig daga
and fēowertig nihta tōsǫmne, and hē on eallum ðām fyrste nānes
corðlices bigleofan ne onbyrigde.   _Æ. H. ii._ 198 ; cf. i. 178.

9. 18. *See Æ. H. i.* 178.

10. 6. *See Æ. H. ii.* 212.

in populum ignitos serpentes, ad
quorum plagas et mortes plurimorum, venerunt ad Moysen,
atque dixerunt : Peccavimus, quia
locuti sumus contra Dominum et
te ; ora ut tollat a nobis serpentes.
Oravitque Moyses pro populo, et
locutus est Dominus ad eum : Fac
serpentem aeneum, et pone eum
pro signo ; qui percussus aspex-
erit eum, vivet. Fecit ergo Moyses
serpentem aeneum, et posuit eum
pro signo ; quem cum percussi
aspicerent, sanabantur.

DEUTERONOMY.

6. 4. ... Dominus Deus noster Dominus unus est.

9. 9. ... Perseveravi in monte quadraginta diebus ac noctibus, panem
non comedens, et aquam non
bibens.

10. 9. *See* Æ. H. ii. 225.

22. 21. *See* Æ. H. i. 40, 42, 196.

32. 8. Þa-ða se healica God tōdǣlde and tōstǫncte Adames ofspring, þā sętte hē ðēoda gemǣru æfter getęle his ęngla.   Æ. H. i. 518.

JOSHUA.

1. 1 ff. *See* Æ. H. ii. 212.

3. 16, 17. *See* Æ. H. ii. 212.

4. 18. *See* Æ. H. ii. 212.

5. 2. *See* Æ. H. i. 92.

5. 14. *See* Æ. H. i. 38.

6. 3, 4, 13–16, 20, 21. *See* Æ. H. ii. 212.

9. 27. *See* Æ. H. ii. 222.

10. 11–1?. *See* Æ. H. ii. 212.

11. 23. *See* Æ. H. ii. 214.

12. *See* Æ. H. ii. 214.

JUDGES.

16. 1–3. . . . Se stranga Samson, se hæfde fēohðe tō ðām folce ðe is gehāten Philistei.   Ðā getīmode hit þæt hē becōm tō heora byrig þe wæs Gaza gehāten : þā wǣron ða Philistei swīðe blīðe, and ymbsǣton ða burh.   Ac se stranga Samson ārās on midre nihte, and gelæhte ða burhgeatu, and ābær hī uppon āne dūne, tō bismere his gefaan.   Æ. H. i. 226.

16. 19. *See* Æ. H. i. 488.

1 SAMUEL.

4. 11, 18. *See* Æ. H. ii. 326.

8. 7. *See* Æ. H. ii. 64.

13. 13. *See* Æ. H. ii. 64.

16. 1, 3, 4. Þā spræc God tō his wītegan Samuhele ðisum wordum : Hū lange wilt ðū bewēpan Saules sīð, þonne ic hine āwearp

32. 8. Quando dividebat Altissimus gentes, quando separabat filios Adam, constituit terminos populorum iuxta numerum filiorum Israel.

JUDGES.

16. 1–3. Abiit quoque in Gazam. . . . Quod cum audissent Philisthiim, et percrebruisset apud eos, intrasse urbem Samson, circumdederunt eum, positis in porta civitatis custodibus. . . . Dormivit autem Samson usque ad medium noctis, et inde consurgens apprehendit ambas portae fores cum postibus suis et sera, impositasque humeris suis portavit ad verticem montis. . . .

1 SAMUEL.

16. 1, 3, 4. Dixitque Dominus ad Samuelem : Usquequo tu luges

þæt hē lęng ofer Israhela ðēode ne rīxige? Āfyll ðīn elefæt, and far tō ðǣre byrig Bethleem, tō Isai ; ic forescēawode of his sunum mē gecorenne cyning. Far, and gelaða Isai mid his sunum tō ðīnre onsǣgednysse, and ic geswutelige ðē hwilene ðū tō cyninge gehālgian scealt. Samuhel ðā fērde, be Godes hǣse, tō Bethleem. Æ. H. ii. 64.

16. 7. *See* Æ. H. i. 288.

16. 12–14. And God gecēas Dauid of his seofon gebrōðrum him tō cyninge ofer his folce. Hwæt, ðā Samuhel gehālgode Dauid tō cyninge on middan his gebrōðrum, and Godes Gāst him wæs on wunigende ǣfre of ðām dæge. Witodlice Godes Gāst gewāt fram Saule, and hine āstyrode se āwyrigeda gāst fram Gode. Æ. H. ii. 64.

16. 23. *See* Æ. H. i. 322.

18. 8 ff. *See* Æ. H. ii. 64.

31. 1. *See* Æ. H. ii. 64.

40. 12. *See* Æ. H. i. 8.

2 SAMUEL.

5. 4. *See* Æ. H. ii. 64, 576.

7. 4. *See* Æ. H. ii. 574.

7. 13, 14. . . . þæt his sunu sceolde þæt tempel ārǣran, and hē wolde him bēon for fæder, and him mid mildheortnysse gyrde stȳran, gif hē āhwǣr unrihtlice dyde. Æ. H. ii. 574, 576.

23. 1. *See* Æ. H. i. 322.

Saul, cum ego proiecerim eum ne regnet super Israel? Imple cornu tuum oleo, et veni ut mittam te ad Isai Bethlehemitem ; providi enim in filiis eius mihi regem. . . . Et vocabis Isai ad victimam, et ego ostendam tibi quid facias, et unges quemcumque monstravero tibi. Fecit ergo Samuel, sicut locutus est ei Dominus. Venitque in Bethlehem. . . .

16. 12–14. . . . Et ait Dominus: Surge, unge eum ; ipse est enim. Tulit ergo Samuel cornu olei, et unxit eum in medio fratrum eius ;

et directus est Spiritus Domini a die illa in David, et deinceps. . . . Spiritus autem Domini recessit a Saul, et exagitabat eum spiritus nequam a Domino.

2 SAMUEL.

7. 13, 14. Ipse aedificabit domum nomini meo. . . . Ego ero ei in patrem, et ipse erit mihi in filium, qui si inique aliquid gesserit, arguam eum in virga virorum et in plagis filiorum hominum.

1 KINGS.

2. 11 *See* Æ. H. ii. 64, 576.

2. 46 (Vulg. 3. 1). *See* Æ. H. ii. 576.

3. 3, 4. *See* Æ. H. ii. 576.

3. 5-15. Efne, ðū on þǣre ylcan nihte ǣtēowode him Drihten on swefne, þus cweðende: Bide mē, lōce, hwæs ðū wille, and ic ðē sylle. Đā cwæð Salomon tō Drihtne: Đū cȳddest miccle mildheortnysse ðīnum ðēowan Dauide mīnum fæder, þæt hē on sōðfæstnysse and rihtwīsnysse leofode ætforan ðē; and ðū geūðest his bearne his cynerīces. Nū eom ic cnæpling, and nytende mīnes færes; and ic eom gesęt betwux þīnum folce, þe ne mæg bēon geteald for ðǣre micclan męnigu. Forgif me wīsdōm, þæt ic mage þīn miccle folc gewissian, and ic cunne tōcnāwan betwux gōd and yfel. Đā gelīcode Gode þēos bēn, and cwæð tō Salomone: Đū ne bǣde mē langsum līf, nē miccle welan, nē ðīnra fēonda dēað, ac bǣde mē wīsdōmes; nū forgife ic ðē ēac wīse heortan tō ðān swīðe þæt nān eorðlic man næs ðīn gelīca ǣrðanþe ðū wǣre, nē ēac æfter þē ne bið. And ēac ic ðē forgife þæs ðe ðū ne bǣde, welan and wuldor, swā þæt nān cyning næs ðīn gelīca on ǣrrum dagum. And gif ðū færst on mīnum wegum, and mīne beboda hylst, swā-swā ðīn fæder dyde, ðonne gelęnge ic þīne dagas. Salomon āwōc ðā, and his swefen understōd. *Æ. H. ii. 576.*

1 KINGS.

3. 5-15. Apparuit autem Dominus Salomoni per somnium nocte, dicens: Postula quod vis ut dem tibi. Et ait Salomon: Tu fecisti cum servo tuo David patre meo misericordiam magnam, sicut ambulavit in conspectu tuo in veritate, et iustitia; . . . et dedisti ei filium sedentem super thronum eius. . . . Ego autem sum puer parvulus, et ignorans egressum et introitum meum. Et servus tuus in medio est populi quem elegisti, populi infiniti, qui numerari et supputari non potest prae multitudine. Dabis ergo servo tuo cor docile, ut populum tuum iudicare possit, et discernere inter bonum et malum. . . . Placuit ergo sermo coram Domino, quod Salomon postulasset huiuscemodi rem. Et dixit Dominus Salomoni: Quia . . . non petisti tibi dies multos, nec divitias, aut animas inimicorum tuorum, sed postulasti tibi sapientiam, . . . ecce, . . . dedi tibi cor sapiens et intelligens, in tantum ut nullus ante te similis tui fuerit, nec post te surrecturus sit. Sed et haec, quae non postulasti, dedi tibi, divitias scilicet et gloriam, ut nemo fuerit similis tui in regibus

4. 22, 23. Him becōmon ꝺac swā micele welan tō handa þæt his bigleofa wæs ælce dæg mid his hīrede þrittig mittan clǣnes melowes, and sixtig mittan ōꝺres melowes, twelf fǣtte oxan, and twēntig feldoxan, hundtēontig weꝺera, būton huntoꝺe, and fugoloꝺe and [1] gemæstra fugela.   Æ. H. ii. 576.

4. 29. And him forgeaf ꝺā God swā micelne wīsdōm, and snoternysse, and brādnysse heortan, swā-swā sandceosol on sǣstrande.   Æ. H. ii. 576.

4. 32–34. Þrēo ꝺūsend bigspella hē gesette, and fīf ꝺūsend [2] lēoꝺa. And āsmēade be ǣlcum trēowcynne, fram ꝺām hēagan cederbēame oꝺ-þæt hē cōm tō ꝺǣre lȳtlan ysopan; ꝺac swylce be nȳtenum, and fixum, and fugelum hē smēade. And of eallum lēodum cōmon menn tō gehȳrenne Salomones wīsdōm.   Æ. H. ii. 578.

6. 2, 3. Þæt tempel wæs on lenge sixtig fæꝺma, on wīdnysse twēntig fæꝺma, on hēahnysse ꝺrītig fæꝺma. Þæt ēast portic wæs on lenge twēntig fæꝺma, be þæs temples wīdnysse, and wæs tȳn fæꝺma wīd.   Æ. H. ii. 578.

8. 1 ff., 22–54. *See* Æ. H. ii. 578.

---

cunctis retro diebus. Si autem ambulaveris in viis meis, et custodieris praecepta mea et mandata mea, sicut ambulavit pater tuus, longos faciam dies tuos. Igitur evigilavit Salomon, et intellexit quod esset somnium. . . .

4. 22, 23. Erat autem cibus Salomonis per dies singulos triginta cori similae, et sexaginta cori farinae, decem boves pingues, et viginti boves pascuales, et centum arietes, excepta venatione cervorum, caprearum, atque bubalorum, et avium altilium.

4. 29. Dedit quoque Deus sapientiam Salomoni, et prudentiam multam nimis, et latitudinem cordis, quasi arenam quae est in littore maris.

4. 32–34. Locutus est quoque Salomon tria millia parabolas, et fuerunt carmina eius quinque et mille. Et disputavit super lignis, a cedro quae est in Libano usque ad hyssopum quae egreditur de pariete; et disseruit de iumentis, et volucribus, et reptilibus, et piscibus. Et veniebant de cunctis populis ad audiendam sapientiam Salomonis, et ab universis regibus terrae, qui audiebant sapientiam eius.

6. 2, 3. Domus autem, quam aedificabat rex Salomon Domino, habebat sexaginta cubitos in longitudine, et viginti cubitos in latitudine, et triginta cubitos in altitudine. Et porticus erat ante templum viginti cubitorum longitudinis, iuxta mensuram latitudinis templi, et habebat decem cubitos latitudinis ante faciem templi.

---

[1] Qy. omit 'and'?   [2] An error.

8. 55, 56. Hē āstōd ðā and þæt folc geblētsode, and cwæð: Sȳ ūre Drihten geblētsod, se ðe forgeaf reste and stilnysse his folce Israhel, æfter ðām wordum þe hē ǣr spræc ðurh Moysen his ðēowan. _Æ. H. ii._ 578.

8. 63. Salomon . . . þǣr geoffrode Gode menigfealde lāc. þæt wǣron getealde twā and twēntig þūsend oxena, and hund-twelftig þūsend scēapa. _Æ. H. ii._ 578.

10. 1–10. Sum cwēn wæs on ðām dagum on sūðdǣle[1], Saba gehāten, snoter and wīs. Ðā gehȳrde hēo Salomones hlīsan, and cōm fram ðām sūðernum gemǣrum tō Salomone binnon Hierusalem mid micelre fare; and hire olfendas bǣron sūðerne wyrta, and dēorwurðe gymstānas, and ungerīm goldes. Sēo cwēn ðā hæfde sprǣce wið Salomon, and sǣde him swā-hwæt-swā hēo on hire heortan geðōhte. Salomon ðā hī lǣrde, and hire sǣde, ealra ðǣra worda andgit þe hēo hine āxode. Ðā geseah seo cwēn Saba Salomones wīsdōm, and þæt mǣre templ ðe hē getimbrod hæfde, and ðā lāc þe man Gode offrode, and ðæs cynges menigfealdan ðēnunga, and wæs tō ðān swīðe ofwundrod, þæt hēo næfde furðor nænne gāst, forðanðe hēo ne mihte nā furðor smēagan. Hēo cwæð ðā tō ðām cyninge: Sōð is þæt word þe ic on mīnum earde gehȳrde be ðē and be ðīnum wīsdōme; ac ic nolde gelȳfan ǣrðanðe ic sylf hit gesāwe. Nū hæbbe ic āfandod þæt mē næs be healfan dǣle ðīn mǣrð gecȳdd; māre is þīn wīsdōm and ðīn weorc þonne se hlīsa wǣre þe ic gehȳrde. Ēadige sind þīne ðegnas and ðīne ðēowan, ðe symle ætforan þē standað and ðīnne wīsdōm gehȳrað. Geblētsod sȳ se Ælmihtiga God, þe ðē gecēas and gesette ofer Israhela rīce, þæt ðū dōmas settest and rihtwīs-nysse. Hēo forgeaf ðām cyninge ðā hundtwelftig punda goldes, and ungerīm dēorwurðra wyrta and dēorwurðra gym-stūna. _Æ. H. ii._ 584.

8. 55, 56. Stetit ergo, et benedixit omni ecclesiae Israel voce magna, dicens: Benedictus Dominus, qui dedit requiem populo suo Israel, iuxta omnia quae locutus est; non cecidit ne unus quidem sermo ex omnibus bonis quae locutus est per Moysen servum suam.

8. 63. Mactavitque Salomon hostias pacificas, quas immolavit Domino, boum viginti duo millia, et ovium centum viginti millia. . . .

10. 1–10. Sed et regina Saba, audita fama Salomonis in nomine Do-

---

[1] From Matt. 12. 42, Luke 11. 31, 'Regina austri.' It will be noted that Ælfric understands Saba as her name.

10. 13. Salomon ēac forgeaf þǣre cwēne swā-hwǣs-swā hēo gyrnde æt him, tōforan ōðre cynelican lāce ðe hē hire geaf; and hēo gewęnde ongēan tō hire ēðele mid hire ðegnum. Æ. H. ii. 584.

10. 23–25. Salomon ðā wæs gemǣrsod ofer eallum eorðlicum cynegum, and ealle ðēoda gewilnodon þæt hī hine gesāwon and his wīsdōm gehȳrdon, and hī him męnigfealde lāc brōhton. Æ. H. ii. 584.

10. 26. Fēower hund and ðūsend cræta hē hæfde, and twęlf ðūsend riddena. Æ. H. ii. 578.

11. 42. See Æ. H. ii. 576, 578.

17. 6. See Æ. H. ii. 140.

19. 8. See Æ. H. i. 178; ii. 100.

21. 5–13. See Æ. H. i. 488.

mini, venit tentare eum in aenigmatibus. Et ingressa Ierusalem multo cum comitatu et divitiis, camelis portantibus aromata, et aurum infinitum nimis, et gemmas pretiosas, venit ad regem Salomonem, et locuta est ei universa quae habebat in corde suo. Et docuit eam Salomon omnia verba quae proposuerat; non fuit sermo qui regem posset latere, et non responderet ei. Videns autem regina Saba omnem sapientiam Salomonis, et domum quam aedificaverat, et cibos mensae eius, et habitacula servorum, et ordines ministrantium, vestesque eorum, et pincernas, et holocausta quae offerebat in domo Domini, non habebat ultra spiritum. Dixitque ad regem: Verus est sermo quem audivi in terra mea super sermonibus tuis et super sapientia tua; et non credebam narrantibus mihi, donec ipsa veni, et vidi oculis meis, et probavi quod media pars mihi nuntiata non fuerit; maior est sapientia et opera tua

quam rumor quem audivi. Beati viri tui, et beati servi tui, qui stant coram te semper et audiunt sapientiam tuam. Sit Dominus Deus tuus benedictus, cui complacuisti, et posuit te super thronum Israel, eo quod dilexerit Dominus Israel in sempiternum, et constituit te regem, ut faceres iudicium et iustitiam. Dedit ergo regi centum viginti talenta auri, et aromata multa nimis, et gemmas pretiosas. . . .

10. 13. Rex autem Salomon dedit reginae Saba omnia quae voluit et petivit ab eo, exceptis his quae ultro obtulerat ei munere regio; quae reversa est, et abiit in terram suam cum servis suis.

10. 23–25. Magnificatus est ergo rex Salomon super omnes reges terrae. . . . Et universa terra desiderabat vultum Salomonis, ut audiret sapientiam eius. . . . Et singuli deferebant ei munera. . . .

10. 26. . . . Facti sunt ei mille quadringenti currus, et duodecim millia equitum. . . .

2 KINGS.

2. 11. *See* Æ. H. i. 308 ; ii. 100.

5. 1. Þā cōm him tō sum rīce mann of þām lēodscipe þe is Siria gehāten; his nama wæs Naaman, and hē wæs hrēoflig. Æ. H. i. 400.

5. 14. *See* Æ. H. i. 400.

5. 15, 16. Þā bēad hē ðām Godes menn, for his hǣlðe, dēorwurðe sceattas. Se wītega him andwyrde : Godes miht þē gehǣlde, nā ic. Ne underfō ic ðīn feoh ; ðanca Gode ðīnre gesund-fulnysse, and brūc ðīnra ǣhta. Æ. H. i. 400.

5. 20–27. Þā wæs ðæs wītegan cnapa, Gyezi, mid gītsunge under-cropen, and ofarn, ðone ðegen Naaman ðus mid wordum lic-cetende : Nū fǣrlice cōmon twēigra wītegena bearn tō mīnum lārēowe : āsend him twā scrūd and sum pund. Se ðegen him andwyrde : Wāclic bið him swā lȳtel tō sendenne ; ac genim fēower scrūd and twā pund. Hē ðā gewende ongēan mid þām sceattum, and bedīglode his fær wið þone wītegan. Se wītega hine befrān : Hwanon cōme ðū, Giezi ? Hē andwyrde : Lēof, næs ic on nānre fare. Se wītega cwæð : Ic geseah, ðurh Godes Gāst, þā se ðegen ālyhte of his cræte, and ēode tōgēanes ðē, and ðū nāme his sceattas on fēo and on rēafe. Hafa ðū ēac forð mid ðām sceattum his hrēoflan, ðū and eal ðīn ofspring on ēcnysse. And hē gewende of his gesihðe mid snāwhwītum hrēoflan beslagen. Æ. H. i. 400.

2 KINGS.

5. 1. Naaman, princeps militiae regis Syriae. erat vir magnus apud dominum suum, et honoratus; per illum enim dedit Dominus salutem Syriae; erat autem vir fortis et dives, sed leprosus.

5. 15, 16. . . . Obsecro itaque ut accipias benedictionem a servo tuo. At ille respondit: Vivit Dominus, ante quem sto, quia non accipiam. Cumque vim faceret, penitus non acquievit.

5. 20-27. Dixitque Giezi puer viri Dei : Pepercit dominus meus Naaman Syro isti, ut non acci-peret ab eo quae attulit; vivit Dominus quia curram post eum, et accipiam ab eo aliquid. Et secutus est Giezi post tergum Naaman. . . . Et ille ait : . . . Do-minus meus misit me ad te, dicens: Modo venerunt ad me duo adolescentes de monte Ephraim, ex filiis prophetarum; da eis talentum argenti, et vestes muta-torias duplices. Dixitque Naa-man : Melius est ut accipias duo talenta. Et coegit eum, ligavit-que duo talenta argenti in duobus saccis, et duplicia vestimenta, et imposuit duobus pueris suis, qui et portaverunt coram eo. Cum-que venisset iam vesperi, tulit de manu eorum, et reposuit in domo, dimisitque viros, et abierunt. Ipse autem ingressus, stetit coram do-

18. 13, 17 ff.   *See* Æ. H. i. 568.

18. 29.   Ne bepǣce Ezechias ēow mid lēasum hopan.   Æ. H. i. 568.

18. 35.   Ic gewyllde and oferwann fela ðēoda, and heora godas ne mihton hī gescyldan wið mīnne ðrymm.   Hwæt is se god þe mage ðās burh wið mīnne here bewerian ?   Æ. H. i. 568.

19. 1, 2.   Hwæt, ðā se cyning Ezechias āwearp his purpuran rēaf, and dyde hǣran tō his līce. . . . Ezechias ēac āsende his witan mid hǣran gescrȳdde tō ðām wītegan Isaiam.   Æ. H. i. 568.

19. 4.   Āhefe ðīne gebedu for Israhela ðēode, þæt se Ælmihtiga God gehȳre þā talu ðe Syria cyning āsende tō hospe and tō edwīte his micclan mægenðrymme.   Æ. H. i. 568.

19. 6.   Þā andwyrde se wītega Isaias þām bodum : Secgað ēowrum hlāforde þæt hē unforht sȳ.   Æ. H. i. 568.

19. 14-19.   Ezechias . . . bær ðā gewritu into Godes temple, and āstrehtum limum hine gebæd, þus cweðende : Drihten, weroda God, þū ðe gesitst ofer engla ðrymm, þū eart āna God ealra ðēoda ; þū geworhtest heofonas and eorðan and ealle gesceafta. Āhyld ðīn ēare and gehȳr ; geopena ðīne ēagan and geseoh ðās word, þe Sennacherib āsende tō hospe and tō tāle ðē and þīnum

mino suo. Et dixit Eliseus : Unde venis, Giezi ? Qui respondit : Non ivit servus tuus quoquam. At ille ait : Nonne cor meum in praesenti erat, quando reversus est homo de curru suo in occursum tui ? Nunc igitur accepisti argentum, et accepisti vestes. . . . Sed et lepra Naaman adhaerebit tibi et semini tuo usque in sempiternum. Et egressus est ab eo leprosus quasi nix.

18. 29. . . . Non vos seducat Ezechias. . . .

18. 35. Quinam illi sunt in universis diis terrarum, qui eruerunt regionem suam de manu mea, ut possit eruere Dominus Ierusalem de manu mea ?

19. 1, 2. Quae cum audisset Ezechias rex, scidit vestimenta sua, et opertus est sacco. . . . Et misit Eliacim praepositum domus, et Sobnam scribam, et senes de sacerdotibus

opertos saccis, ad Isaiam prophetam. . . .

19. 4. Si forte audiat Dominus Deus tuus universa verba Rabsacis, quem misit rex Assyriorum dominus suus, ut exprobraret Deum viventem, et argueret verbis, quae audivit Dominus Deus tuus ; et fac orationem pro reliquiis quae repertae sunt.

19. 6. Dixitque eis Isaias : Haec dicetis domino vestro : Haec dicit Dominus : Noli timere. . . .

19. 14-19. Itaque cum accepisset Ezechias litteras de manu nuntiorum, et legisset eas, ascendit in domum Domini, et expandit eas coram Domino. Et oravit in conspectu eius, dicens : Domine Deus Israel, qui sedes super cherubim, tu es Deus solus regum omnium terrae ; tu fecisti coelum et terram. Inclina aurem tuam, et audi ; aperi, Domine, oculos tuos, et

folce. Sōðlice hē tōwēnde þū hǣðenan godas, and hī forbǣrnde, forðanðe hī nǣron godas, ac wǣron manna handgeweorc, trēowene and stǣnene, and hē hī forðī tōbrytte. Ālȳs ūs nū, Drihten, fram his gebēote and mihte, þæt ealle ðēoda tōcnāwon þæt þū āna eart Ælmihtig God. Æ. H. i. 568.

19. 28. Ic geslēa ǣnne wriðan on his nosu, and ǣnne brīdel on his weleras, and ic hine gelǣde ongēan tō his lēode. Æ. H. i. 568.

19. 32. God Ælmihtig cwyð: Ne āscȳtt Sennacherib flān intō ðǣre byrig Hierusalem, nē mid his scylde hī ne gewylt. Æ. H. i. 568.

19. 34. Ic ðā burh gescylde for mē and for mīnum ðēowan Dauid. Æ. H. i. 568, 570.

19. 35–37. Þā on ðǣre nihte fērde Godes ēngel, and ofslōh ðæs Syrian cyninges hēre ān hund þūsend manna, and fīf and hundeahtatig þūsenda. Þæs on merigen ārās Sennacherib, and geseah ðā dēadan līc, and gecyrde mid micelre sceame ongēan tō þǣre byrig Niniue. Hit gelamp ðā þæt hē hine gebæd tō his dēofolgylde, and his twēgen suna hine mid swurde ācwealdon. Æ. H. i. 570.

24. 19. See Æ. H. ii. 64.

25. 1, 4, 7, 9–11, 13 ff. See Æ. H. ii. 66.

1 CHRONICLES.

10. 8. See Æ. H. ii. 64.

29. 27. See Æ. H. ii. 64.

vide; audi omnia verba Sennacherib, qui misit ut exprobraret nobis Deum viventem. Vere, Domine, dissipaverunt reges Assyriorum gentes, et terras omnium, et miserunt deos eorum in ignem; non enim erant dii, sed opera manuum hominum ex ligno et lapide, et perdiderunt eos. Nunc igitur, Domine Deus noster, salvos nos fac de manu eius, ut sciant omnia regna terrae quia tu es Dominus Deus solus.

19. 28. ...Ponam itaque circulum in naribus tuis, et camum in labiis tuis, et reducam te in viam per quam venisti.

19. 32. Quam ob rem haec dicit Dominus de rege Assyriorum:

Non ingredietur urbem hanc, nec mittet in eam sagittam, nec occupabit eam clypeus. ...

19. 34. Protegamque urbem hanc, et salvabo eam propter me, et propter David servum meum.

19. 35–37. Factum est igitur in nocte illa, venit angelus Domini, et percussit in castris Assyriorum centum octoginta quinque millia. Cumque diluculo surrexisset, vidit omnia corpora mortuorum, et recedens abiit, et reversus est Sennacherib rex Assyriorum, et mansit in Ninive. Cumque adoraret in templo Nesroch deum suum, Adramelech et Sarasar filii eius percusserunt eum gladio. ...

2 CHRONICLES.

1. 7-12. *See* 1 Kings 3. 5-15.
9. 30. *See* 1 Kings 11. 42.

EZRA.

1. 1 ff. *See* Æ. H. ii. 66.
3. 2 ff. *See* Æ. H. ii. 66.
5. 2. *See* Æ. H. ii. 66.

JOB[1].

1. 1-5. Sum wer wæs geseten on þām lande þe is gehāten Hus; his nama wæs Iob. Sē wer wæs swīðe bilewite and rihtwīs, and ondrǣdende God and forbūgende yfel. Him wǣron ācennede seofan suna and ðrēo dohtra. Hē hæfde seofon ðūsend scēapa and ðrēo ðūsend olfenda, fīf hund getȳmu oxena and fīf hund assan, and ormǣte micelne hīred. Sē wer wæs swīðe mǣre betwux eallum Ēasternum. And his suna fērdon, and ðēnode ǣlc ōðrum mid his gōdum on ymhwyrfte æt his hūse, and þǣrtō heora swustru gelaðodon. Iob sōðlice ārās on ðām eahteoðan dæge on ǣrnemerigen, and offrode Gode seofonfealde lāc for his seofon sunum, ðȳ-lǣs-ðe hī wið God on heora geðance āgylton. Ðus dyde Iob eallum dagum for his sunum, and hī swā gehālgode. Æ. H. ii. 446.

1. 6-8. Hit gelamp on sumum dæge, ðā-ðā Godes ẹnglas[2] cōmon, and on his gesihðe stōdon, ðā wæs ēac swylce se scucca him

JOB.

1. 1-5. Vir erat in terra Hus, nomine Iob; et erat vir ille simplex et rectus, ac timens Deum, et recedens a malo. Natique sunt ei septem filii, et tres filiae. Et fuit possessio eius septem millia ovium, et tria millia camelorum, quingenta quoque iuga boum, et quingentae asinae, ac familia multa nimis. Eratque vir ille magnus inter omnes Orientales. Et ibant filii eius, et faciebant convivium per domos unusquisque in die suo; et mittentes vocabant tres sorores suas, ut comederent et biberent cum eis. Cumque in orbem transissent dies convivii, mittebat ad eos Iob, et sanctificabat illos, consurgensque diluculo offerebat holocausta pro singulis; dicebat enim: Ne forte peccaverint filii mei, et benedixerint Deo in cordibus suis. Sic faciebat Iob cunctis diebus.

1. 6-8. Quadam autem die cum venissent filii Dei ut assisterent

---

[1] Cf. Grein's *Bibliothek der Angelsächsischen Prosa*, pp. 265-272, where will be found an abridged form of the homily on Job.

[2] Ælfric has a note in the text of his homily: 'Una translatio dicit "filii Dei," et altera dicit "angeli Dei."'

betwux. Tō ðām cwæð Drihten : Hwanon cōme ðū? Se
sceocca andwyrde : Ic fērde geond þās eorðan, and hī beēode.
Drihten cwæð : Ne behēolde ðū, lā, mīnne ðēowan Iob, þæt
nān man nis his gelīca on eorðan, bilewite man and rihtwīs,
ondrǣdende God and yfel forbūgende ? Æ. H. ii. 446.

1. 9–12. Se mānfulla dēofol . . . cwæð tō Drihtne : Ne ondrǣt Iob
on īdel God : þū ymbtrymedest hine and ealle his ǣhta, and
his handgeweorc þū blētsodest, and his ǣhta wēoxon on eorðan.
Ac āstrece hwōn ðīne hand, and getill ealle ðā þing ðe hē āh,
and hē ðē on ansȳne wyrigð. Drihten cwæð tō ðām sceoccan :
Efne, nū ealle ðā ðing ðe hē āh sindon on ðīnre handa, būton
ðām ānum, þæt ðū on him sylfum ðīne hand ne āstrecce. Se
dēofol gewende ðā fram Godes gesihðe. Æ. H. ii. 448, 450 ; cf. i. 6.

1. 14–22. Sum ǣrendraca cōm to Iobe, and cwæð : Þīne syll ēodon,
and ðā assan wið hī lǣswodon ; þā fǣrlice cōmon Sabei, and hī
ealle ūs benāmon, and þīne yrðlingas ofslōgon, and ic āna
ætbǣrst þæt ic ðē þis cȳdde. Mid-þām-ðe se yrðling þis sǣde,
ðā cōm sum ōðer, and cwæð : Fȳr cōm fǣrlice of heofenum,
and forbærnde ealle ðīne scēp, and ðā hyrdas samod, and ic
āna ætwand þæt ic ðē ðis cȳdde. Þā cōm se ðridda ǣrendraca,
and cwæð : Ðā Chaldeiscan cōmon on ðrīm floccum, and ūre
olfendas ealle gelæhton, and ðā hyrdas mid swurde ofslōgon ;
ic āna ætflēah þæt ic ðē þis cȳdde. Efne, ðā-gȳt cōm se fēorða

coram Domino, affuit inter eos
etiam Satan. Cui dixit Dominus :
Unde venis ? Qui respondens,
ait : Circuivi terram, et peram-
bulavi eam. Dixitque Dominus
ad eum : Numquid considerasti
servum meum Iob, quod non sit
ei similis in terra, homo simplex
et rectus, ac timens Deum, et
recedens a malo ?

1. 9–12. Cui respondens Satan ait :
Numquid Iob frustra timet Deum ?
Nonne tu vallasti eum ac domum
eius universamque substantiam
per circuitum, operibus manuum
eius benedixisti, et possessio eius
crevit in terra ? Sed extende
paululum manum tuam, et tange
cuncta quae possidet, nisi in

faciem benedixerit tibi. Dixit
ergo Dominus ad Satan : Ecce,
universa quae habet in manu tua
sunt ; tantum in eum ne extendas
manum tuam. Egressusque est
Satan a facie Domini.

1. 14–22. Nuntius venit ad Iob, qui
diceret : Boves arabant, et asinae
pascebantur iuxta eos, et irrue-
runt Sabaei, tuleruntque omnia,
et pueros percusserunt gladio, et
evasi ego solus ut nuntiarem tibi.
Cumque adhuc ille loqueretur,
venit alter, et dixit : Ignis Dei
cecidit e coelo, et tactas oves
puerosque consumpsit, et effugi
ego solus ut nuntiarem tibi. Sed
et illo adhuc loquente, venit alius,
et dixit : Chaldaei fecerunt tres

ferendraca[1] inn, and cwæð : Ðīne suna and ðīne dohtra æton
and druncon mid heora yldestan brēðer ; and efne, þā fǣrlice
swægde swīðlic wind of ðām wēstene, and tōslōh þæt hūs æt
ðām fēower hwęmmum, þæt hit hrēosende ðīne bearn ofðrihte
and ācwealde ; ic āna ætbærst þæt ic ðē þis cȳdde. Hwæt, ðā
Iob ārās, and tōtær his tunecan, and his loccas foreearf, and
fēol tō eorðan, and cwæð : Nacod ic cōm of mīnre mōdor innoðe,
and nacod ic sceal heonan gewęndan ; Drihten mē forgeaf ðā
æhta, and Drihten hī mē ęft benām ; swā-swā him gelīcode, swā
hit is gedōn ; bēo his nama geblētsod. On eallum ðisum ðingum ne syngode Iob on his welerum, nē nān ðing dyslices
ongēan God ne spræc. Æ. H. ii. 450.

‖ Hē gemacode ðā þæt fȳr cōme ufan, swilce of heofenum,
and forbærnde ealle his scēp ūt on felda, and þā hyrdas samod,
būton ānum þe hit him eyðan sceolde. Æ. H. i. 6.

‖ Nacode wē wǣron ācęnnede, and nacode wē gewītað.
Æ. H. i. 64.

‖ God forgeaf ðā æhta, and God hī ęft ætbrǣd ; sȳ his nama
geblētsod. Æ. H. ii. 328.

‖ Ac se geðyldiga Iob on eallum ðisum ungelimpum ne syngode mid his mūðe, nē nān ðing stuntlices ongēan God ne
spræc, ac cwæð : God mē forgeaf ðā æhta, and hī ęft æt mē
genām ; sȳ his nama geblētsod. Æ. H. i. 472.

‖ On eallum ðisum ðingum ne syngode Iob on his welerum. Æ. H. ii. 452.

2. 1. Ęft siððan on sumum dæge, þā-þā Godes ęnglas stōdon on
his gesihðe, þā wæs ēac se scucca him betwȳnan. Æ. H. ii. 452.

turmas, et invaserunt camelos, et
tulerunt eos, necnon et pueros
percusserunt gladio, et ego fugi
solus ut nuntiarem tibi. Adhuc
loquebatur ille, et ecce alius intravit, et dixit : Filiis tuis et
filiabus vescentibus et bibentibus
vinum in domo fratris sui primo-
geniti, repente ventus vehemens
irruit a regione deserti, et con-
cussit quattuor angulos domus,
quae corruens oppressit liberos
tuos, et mortui sunt, et effugi ego

solus ut nuntiarem tibi. Tunc
surrexit Iob, et scidit vestimenta
sua, et tonso capite corruens in
terram, adoravit, et dixit : Nudus
egressus sum de utero matris
meae, et nudus revertar illuc ;
Dominus dedit, Dominus abstulit ;
sicut Domino placuit, ita factum
est ; sit nomen Domini benedic-
tum. In omnibus his non peccavit
Iob labiis suis, neque stultum quid
contra Deum locutus est.

2. 1. Factum est autem cum quadam

---

[1] Thorpe, ' arendraca.'

2. 3–6. And Drihten him cwæð tō: Hwæt lā, ne behēolde ðū mīnne ðēowan Iob, þæt his gelīca nis on eorðan, and gȳt hē hylt his unscæððignysse? Þū āstyredest mē tōgēanes him, þæt ic ðearflēas hine geswęncte. Se scucca andwyrde: Fel sceal for felle, and swā-hwæt-swā man hæfð hē sylð for his līfe. Āstręce nū þīne hand, and hrępa his bān and his flǣsc, ðonne gesihst ðū þæt hē ðē on ansȳne wirigð. Drihten cwæð tō ðan scuccan: Efne, hē is nū on ðīnre handa, swā-þeah-hwæðere heald his sāwle. Æ. H. ii. 452.

2. 7–10. Ðā gewęnde se dēofol of Drihtnes gesihðe, and slōh Iob mid þǣre wyrstan wunde, fram his hnolle ufewerdan ōð his ilas neoðewerde. Iob sæt ðā sārlice, eal on ānre wunde, ūp on his mixene, and āscræp ðone wyrms of his līce mid ānum crōcscearde. His wīf him cwæð tō: Gȳt ðū þurhwunast on ðīnre bilewitnysse; wyrig God and swelt. Iob hire and-wyrde: Þū sprǣce swā-swā ān stunt wīf. Gif we gōd under-fēngon of Godes handa, hwī ne sceole wē ēac yfel underfōn? On eallum ðisum ðingum ne syngode Iob on his welerum.
Æ. H. ii. 452.

2. 11–13. Witodlice ðā geāxodon þrȳ cyningas, ðe him gesibbe wǣron, eal his ungelimp, and cōmon him tō of heora rīce, þæt hī hine genēosodon. Heora naman wǣron ðus gecīgde: Elifaz, Baldað, Sofar. Hī gecwǣdon þæt hī, samod cumende,

die venissent filii Dei, et starent coram Domino, venisset quoque Satan inter eos, et staret in conspectu eius.

2. 3–6. Et dixit Dominus ad Satan: Numquid considerasti servum meum Iob, quod non sit ei similis in terra, vir simplex et rectus, ac timens Deum, et recedens a malo, et adhuc retinens innocentiam? Tu autem commovisti me adversus eum, ut affligerem eum frustra. Cui respondens Satan, ait: Pellem pro pelle, et cuncta quae habet homo dabit pro anima sua. Alioquin mitte manum tuam, et tange os eius et carnem, et tunc videbis quod in faciem benedicat tibi. Dixit ergo Dominus ad Satan: Ecce in manu tua est, verum-

tamen animam illius serva.

2. 7–10. Egressus igitur Satan a facie Domini, percussit Iob ulcere pessimo, a planta pedis usque ad verticem eius; qui testa saniem radebat, sedens in sterquilinio. Dixit autem illi uxor sua: Adhuc tu permanes in simplicitate tua? benedic Deo et morere. Qui ait ad illam: Quasi una de stultis mulieribus locuta es. Si bona suscepimus de manu Dei, mala quare non suscipiamus? In omnibus his non peccavit Iob labiis suis.

2. 11–13. Igitur audientes tres amici Iob omne malum, quod accidisset ei, venerunt singuli de loco suo: Eliphaz Themanites, et Baldad Suhites, et Sophar Naamathites.

hine geneosodon and gefrōfrodon. Hī ꝺā cōmon, and hine
ne oncnēowon for ꝺǣre ormǣtan untrumnysse, and hrȳmdon
þǣrrihte wēpende. Hī totǣron heora rēaf, and mid dūste
heora hēafod bestrēowodon, and him mid sǣton manega
dagas. Æ. H. ii. 454.

4. 5, **6.** Wīte cōm ofer ꝺē, and ꝺū āteorodest ; sārnys ꝺē hrēpode,
and ꝺū eart geunrōtsod. Hwǣr is nū ꝺīn Godes ege and
ꝺīn strencꝺ ? Hwǣr is ꝺīn geꝺyld and ꝺīnra dǣda fulfrem-
ednys ? Æ. H. ii. 454.

6. 1–3. Iob cwǣꝺ : Ēalā, gif mīne synna, and mīn yrmꝺ þe ic
ꝺolige, wǣron āwogene on ānre wǣgan, þonne wǣron hī swǣrran
gesewene ꝺonne sandcorn on sǣ. Æ. H. ii. 454.

6. 26, 27. Tō ꝺrēagenne gē lōgiaꝺ ēowere sprǣce, and gē ꝺencaꝺ tō
āwendenne ēowerne frēond. Æ. H. ii. 454.

7. 1. Mannes līf is campdōm ofer eorꝺan ; and swā-swā mēdgildan
dagas, swā sind his dagas. Æ. H. ii. 454.

7. 5. Mīn flǣsc is ymscrȳd mid forrotodnysse and mid dūstes
horwum ; mīn hȳd forscarode and is forscruncen. Æ. H. ii. 456.

7. 16. Āra mē, Drihten ; ne sind mīne dagas nāhte. Æ. H. ii. 456.

19. 25–27. Ic gelȳfe þæt mīn Ālȳsend leofaꝺ, and ic sceal on þām
endenēxtan dæge of eorꝺan ārīsan, and eft ic bēo mid mīnum
felle befangen, and on mīnum flǣsce ic gesēo God, ic sylf and
nā ōꝺer. Æ. H. i. 532.

‖ Ic wāt sōꝺlice þæt mīn Ālȳsend leofaꝺ, and ic on ꝺām
endenēxtan dæge of eorꝺan ārīse, and ic bēo eft mid mīnum felle

Condixerant enim ut, pariter ve-
nientes, visitarent eum et con-
solarentur. Cumque elevassent
procul oculos suos, non cognoverunt eum, et exclamantes plora-
verunt, scissisque vestibus spar-
serunt pulverem super caput suum
in coelum. Et sederunt cum eo
in terra septem diebus et septem
noctibus. . . .

4. 5, 6. Nunc autem venit super te
plaga, et defecisti ; tetigit te, et
conturbatus es. Ubi est timor
tuus, fortitudo tua, patientia tua,
et perfectio viarum tuarum ?

6. 1–3. Respondens autem Iob, dixit:
Utinam appenderentur peccata

mea quibus iram merui, et cala-
mitas quam patior, in statera.
Quasi arena maris haec gravior
appareret. . . .

6. 26, 27. Ad increpandum tantum
eloquia concinnatis, . . . et sub-
vertere nitimini amicum vestrum.

7. 1. Militia est vita hominis super
terram ; et sicut dies mercenarii
dies eius.

7. 5. Induta est caro mea putredine
et sordibus pulveris ; cutis mea
aruit et contracta est.

7. 16. . . . Parce mihi, nihil enim
sunt dies mei.

19. 25–27. Scio enim quod Redemptor meus vivit, et in novissimo

befangen, and ic on mīnum flǣsce God gesēo, ic sylf and nā
ōðer; þes hiht is on mīnum bōsme gelēd.　Æ. H. ii. 456.

29. 12–16. Ic ālȳsde hrȳmende þearfan, and ðām stēopbearne þe
būton fultume wæs ic gehēolp, and wydewan heortan ic gefrēfrode.　Ic wæs ymbscrȳd mid rihtwīsnysse; ic wæs blindum
męn ðage, and healtum fōt, and þearfena fæder.　Æ. H. ii. 448.

30. 16, 17. Mē habbað geswęncednysse dagas, and on niht mīn
bān bið mid sārnesse þurhðȳd, and ða ðe mē etað ne
slāpað.　Æ. H. ii. 456.

30. 19. Ic eom lāme wiðmeten, and ȳslum and axum gean-
līcod.　Æ. H. ii. 456.

31. 16, 17. Ic ðearfum ne forwyrnde þæs ðe hī gyrndon; nē ic ne
æt āna mīnne hlāf būton stēopbearne.　Æ. H. ii. 448.

31. 20. Of flȳsum mīnra scēapa wēron gehlȳwde ðearfena
sīdan.　Æ. H. ii. 448.

31. 25. Nē ic ne blissode on mīnum męnigfealdum welum.　Æ. H. ii. 448.

31. 29. Ne fægnode ic on mīnes fēondes hryre.　Æ. H. ii. 448.

31. 32, 33. Ne læg ælðēodig man wiðūtan mīnum hęgum, ac
mīn duru geopenode symle wegfērendum.　Ne behȳdde ic
mīne synna, nē ic on mīnum bōsme ne bedīglode mīne unrihtwīsnysse.　Æ. H. ii. 448.

42. 7, 8. Ac God hī gespræc þā, and cwæð þæt hē him eallum
ðrīm gram wēre, forþanðe hī swā rihtlice ætforan him ne

die de terra surrecturus sum, et
rursum circumdabor pelle mea,
et in carne mea videbo Deum
meum. Quem visurus sum ego
ipse, et oculi mei conspecturi
sunt, et non alius; reposita est
haec spes mea in sinu meo.

29. 12–16. Eo quod liberassem pauperem vociferantem, et pupillum
cui non esset adiutor, . . . et cor
viduae consolatus sum. Iustitia
indutus sum; et vestivi me, sicut
vestimento et diademate, iudicio
meo. Oculus fui caeco, et pes
claudo. Pater eram pauperum. . . .

30. 16, 17. . . . Possident me dies
afflictionis. Nocte os meum per-
foratur doloribus, et qui me come-
dunt non dormiunt.

30. 19. Comparatus sum luto, et
assimilatus sum favillae et cineri.

31. 16, 17. Si negavi quod volebant
pauperibus; . . . si comedi buc-
cellam meam solus, et non comedit pupillus ex ea.

31. 20. Si non . . . latera eius . . . de
velleribus ovium mearum calefac-
tus est.

31. 25. Si laetatus sum super multis
divitiis meis. . . .

31. 29. Si gavisus sum ad ruinam
eius qui me oderat. . . .

31. 32, 33. Foris non mansit pere-
grinus; ostium meum viatori pa-
tuit. Si abscondi quasi homo
peccatum meum, et celavi in
sinu meo iniquitatem meam.

42. 7, 8. . . . Dominus . . . dixit ad

spræcon swā-swā Iob his ðegen. God cwæð him to : Nimað
ēow nū seofon fearras and seofon rammas, and farað ęft ongēan
tō mīnum ðēowan Iobe, and geoffriað ðās lāc for ēow ; Iob
sōðlice, mīn ðēowa, gebit for ēow—and ic his ansỹne underfō—
þæt ēow ne bēo tō dysige geteald, þæt gē swā rihtlice tō mē ne
spræcon swā-swā mīn ðēowa Iob. Æ. H. ii. 456.

42. 9. Elifaz ðā, and Baldað, and Sofar fērdon ongēan tō heora
māege Iobe, and didon swā-swā him God bebēad ; and Drihten
underfēng Iobes ansỹne, and heora synne ðurh his ðingrǣdene
forgeaf. Æ. H. ii. 458.

‖ Ðā ðrȳ cyningas... gewęndon him hām syððan. Æ. H. ii. 456.

42. 10. Drihten ēac ðā gecyrde tō Iobes behrēowsunge, ðā-ðā
hē for his māgum gebæd ; and hine gehǣlde fram eallum
his untrumnyssum, and his ǣhta him ealle forgeald be twȳfealdum. Æ. H. ii. 458.

42. 11. Hwæt, ðā Iobes gebrōðra and geswustru, and ealle ðā þe
hine ǣr cūðon, cōmon him tō, and hine gefrēfrodon, and his
micclum wundrodon, and him gife gēafon. Æ. H. ii. 458.

42. 12, 13. Iob hæfde ǣr his untrumnysse seofon ðūsend scēapa
and ðrēo ðūsend olfenda, fīf hund getȳme oxena and fīf hund
assan ; him wǣron ęft forgoldene fēowertȳne ðūsend scēapa and
syx þūsend olfenda, þūsend getȳme oxena and þūsend assan ;

Eliphaz Themanitem : Iratus est
furor meus in te et in duos amicos
tuos, quoniam non estis locuti
coram me rectum, sicut servus
meus Iob. Sumite ergo vobis
septem tauros et septem arietes,
et ite ad servum meum Iob, et
offerte holocaustum pro vobis ;
Iob autem servus meus orabit
pro vobis—faciem eius suscipiam
—ut non vobis imputetur stultitia ; neque enim locuti estis ad
me recta, sicut servus meus Iob.

42. 9. Abierunt ergo Eliphaz Themanites, et Baldad Suhites, et
Sophar Naamathites, et fecerunt
sicut locutus fuerat Dominus ad
eos, et suscepit Dominus faciem
Iob.

42. 10. Dominus quoque conversus
est ad poenitentiam Iob, cum
oraret ille pro amicis suis. Et
addidit Dominus omnia quaecumque fuerant Iob duplicia.

42. 11. Venerunt autem ad eum
omnes fratres sui et universae
sorores suae, et cuncti qui nove-
rant eum prius, et comederunt
cum eo panem in domo eius, et
moverunt super eum caput, et
consolati sunt eum super omni
malo quod intulerat Dominus
super eum, et dederunt ei unusquisque ovem unam et inaurem
auream unam.

42. 12, 13. Dominus autem benedixit novissimis Iob magis quam
principio eius. Et facta sunt ei
quattuordecim millia ovium, et
sex millia camelorum, et mille

and Drihten hine blētsode swīðor on ęnde ðonne on angynne. Hē hæfde seofon suna and ðrēo dohtra fēr, and siððan ęft eal swā fela. *Æ. H. ii.* 458.

42. 15, 16. Nēron gemētte on ealre eorðan swā wlitige wīmmen swā-swā wēron Iobes dohtra. Hē sōðlice leofode æfter his swingle ān hund gēara and fēowertig gēara, and geseah his bearna bearn ōð ðā fēorðan māgðe. *Æ. H. ii.* 458.

PSALMS.

2. 7. God cwæð tō mē : Ðū eart mīn sunu, nū tō-dæg ic gestrȳnde þē. *Æ. H. ii.* 14.

10. 3. Se synfulla bið gehęrod on his lustum, and se unrihtwīsa bið geblētsod. *Æ. H. i.* 492.

12. 8. Þā ārlēasan turniað on ymbhwyrfte. *Æ. H. i.* 514.

16. 9, 10. Mīn līchama geręst on hihte, forðanþe þū ne forlētst mīne sāwle on hęlle, nō ðū ne geðafast þæt mīn līchama gebrosnige. *Æ. H. ii.* 16.

17. 3. Drihten, ðū āfandodest ūs on ðisum fȳre, and nis on ūs gemētt ǣnig unrihtwīsnys. *Æ. H. ii.* 312.

17. 15. Drihten, ic bēo ætēowed mid rihtwīsnysse on ðīnre gesihðe ; and ic bēo gefylled þonne ðīn wuldor geswutelod bið. *Æ. H. i.* 552.

18. 5, 6. Dēaþes gēomerunga mē bēēodon, and hęlle sārnyssa mē bēēodon ; and ic on mīnre gedrēfednysse Drihten clypode, and hē of his hālgan temple mīne stemne gehȳrde. *Æ. H. ii.* 86.

iuga bovum, et mille asinae. Et fuerunt ei septem filii, et tres filiae.

42. 15, 16. Non sunt autem inventae mulieres speciosae sicut filiae Iob in universa terra. . . . Vixit autem Iob post haec centum quadraginta annis, et vidit filios suos, et filios filiorum suorum usque ad quartam generationem. . . .

PSALMS.

2. 7. Dominus dixit ad me : Filius meus es tu, ego hodie genui te.

10. 3. Quoniam laudatur peccator in desideriis animae suae, et iniquus benedicitur.

12. 8. In circuitu impii ambu-

lant. . . .

16. 9, 10. . . . Caro mea requiescet in spe, quoniam non derelinques animam meam in inferno, nec dabis sanctum tuum videre corruptionem.

17. 3. . . . Igne me examinasti, et non est inventa in me iniquitas.

17. 15. Ego autem in iustitia apparebo conspectui tuo ; satiabor cum apparuerit gloria tua.

18. 5, 6. Dolores inferni circumdederunt me ; praeoccupaverunt me laquei mortis ; in tribulatione mea invocavi Dominum, et ad Deum meum clamavi, et exaudivit de templo sancto suo vocem meam. . . .

19. 1. Heofonas cȳðað Godes wuldor. Æ. H. i. 520.

19. 4. Se swēg heora bodunge fērde geond calle eorðan, and heora word becōmon tō gemǣrum ealles ymbhwyrftes. Æ. H. i. 542.

19. 5. Swā-swā brȳdguma hē gūð forð of his brȳdbeddo. Æ. H. ii. 10; cf. i. 200.

19. 6. Nis nān þe hine behȳdan mæge fram his hǣtan. Æ. H. i. 282; cf. ii. 606.

22. 16. Fela hundas mē ymbe eodon. Æ. H. ii. 114.

Hī ðurhðȳdon mīne handa and mīne fēt. Æ. H. ii. 16.

22. 18. Hī dǣldon mīn rēaf betwux him. Æ. H. ii. 16.

23. 5. Drihten, þū gegearcodest mȳsan on mīnre gesihðe, tōgēanes ðām þe mē gedrǣfdon. Æ. H. ii. 114.

24. 1. Eorðe, and eall hire gefyllednys, and eal ymbhwyrft, and þā ðe on ðām wuniað, ealle hit syndon Godes ǣhta. Æ. H. i. 172.

‖ Sēo eorðe and hire gefyllednys is Godes. Æ. H. ii. 104.

24. 8. Drihten is strang and mihtig on gefeohte. Æ. H. i. 196.

33. 9. Hē hit gecwæð, and þā gesceafta wǣron geworhte; hē bebēad, and hī wǣron gesceapene. Æ. H. i. 122.

34. 1. Ic herige mīnne Drihten on ǣlcne tīman. Æ. H. i. 252.

34. 19. Fela sind þǣra rihtwīsra gedrececednyssa, ac Drihten fram eallum ðysum hī ālȳst. Æ. H. i. 574.

37. 27. Būh fram yfele, and dō gōd. Æ. H. ii. 602.

39. 6. On īdel bið ǣlc man gedrēfed se ðe hordað and nāt hwām hē hit gegaderað. Æ. H. i. 66.

‖ On īdel swincð se ðe goldhordað and nāt hwām hē hit gegaderað. Æ. H. ii. 104.

---

19. 1. Coeli enarrant gloriam Dei....

19. 4. In omnem terram exivit sonus eorum, et in fines orbis terrae verba eorum.

19. 5. ... Ipse tamquam sponsus procedens de thalamo suo. ...

19. 6. ... Nec est qui se abscondat a calore eius.

22. 16. Quoniam circumdederunt me canes multi. ... Foderunt manus meas et pedes meos.

22. 18. Diviserunt sibi vestimenta mea. ...

23. 5. Parasti in conspectu meo mensam, adversus eos qui tribulant me. ...

24. 1. Domini est terra, et plenitudo eius; orbis terrarum, et universi qui habitant in eo.

24. 8. ... Dominus fortis et potens, Dominus potens in praelio.

33. 9. Quoniam ipse dixit, et facta sunt; ipse mandavit, et creata sunt.

34. 1. Benedicam Dominum in omni tempore. ...

34. 19. Multae tribulationes iustorum, et de omnibus his liberabit eos Dominus.

37. 27. Declina a malo, et fac bonum. ...

39. 6. ... Frustra conturbatur;

45. 9. Sēo cwēn stęnt æt ðīnre swīðran on ofergyldum gyrlan, ymbscrȳd mid męnigfealdre fāhnysse. *Æ. H. ii. 586.*

45. 13. Eall hire wuldor is wiðinnan. *Æ. H. ii. 564.*

47. 5. God āstīhð ūp tō heofonum mid micelre myrhðe. *Æ. H. ii. 16.*

49. 12. Se mann, ða-ða hē on wurðmynte wæs, hē hit ne understōd; hē is forðȳ wiðmeten stuntum nȳtenum, and is him gelīc geworden. *Æ. H. i. 96.*

49. 20. *See* Ps. 49. 12.

50. 3. God cymð swutellice, and hē ne suwað; fȳr byrnð on his gesihðe, and on his ymbhwyrfte bið swīðlic storm. *Æ. H. i. 618.*

‖ God cymð swutellice, and hē ne suwað; fȳr byrnð on his gesihðe, and strīðlic hrēohnys bið onbūton him. *Æ. H. ii. 18.*

50. 15. Clypa mē on dæge ðīnre gedrēfednysse; and ic ðē āhrędde, and ðū mērsast mē. *Æ. H. ii. 126.*

50. 16, 17. God cwæð tō ðām synfullum: Hwī bodast ðū mīne rihtwīsnyssa and mīne gecȳðnysse þurh þīnne mūð? Þū sōðlice hatast ðēawfæstnysse, and ðū āwurpe mīne word under-bæc. *Æ. H. ii. 530, 532.*

51. 5. Ealle męn bēoð . . . mid unrihtwīsnysse gēacnode, and mid synnum ācęnnede. *Æ. H. i. 200.*

56. 12. God Ælmihtig, on mē synd þīne behāt, þā ic ðē forgylde ðurh hęrunga. *Æ. H. i. 584.*

58. 1. Gē manna bearn, dēmað rihtlice. *Æ. H. ii. 322.*

59. 17. Mīn gefylsta, ðē ic singe; forðanðe ðū, God, eart mīn andfęnga, mīn God, and mīn mildheortnyss. *Æ. H. ii. 82.*

thesaurizat, et ignorat cui congregabit ea.

45. 9. . . . Astitit regina a dextris tuis in vestitu deaurato, circumdata varietate.

45. 13. Omnis gloria eius . . . ab intus. . . .

47. 5. Ascendit Deus in iubilo. . . .

49. 12. . . . Homo, cum in honore esset, non intellexit; comparatus est iumentis insipientibus, et similis factus est illis.

50. 3. Deus manifeste veniet, Deus noster, et non silebit; ignis in conspectu eius exardescet, et in circuitu eius tempestas valida.

50. 15. Et invoca me in die tribu-

lationis; eruam te, et honorificabis me.

50. 16, 17. Peccatori autem dixit Deus: Quare tu enarras iustitias meas, et assumis testamentum meum per os tuum? Tu vero odisti disciplinam, et proiecisti sermones meos retrorsum.

51. 5. . . . In iniquitatibus conceptus sum, et in peccatis concepit me mater mea.

56. 12. In me sunt, Deus, vota tua, quae reddam laudationes tibi.

58. 1. . . . Recta iudicate, filii hominum.

59. 17. Adiutor meus, tibi psallam;

62. 12. Þū, Drihten, forgyltst ǣlcum be his weorcum. Æ. H. ii. 18.

63. 5. Bēo mīn sāwul gefylled swā-swā mid rysle and mid ungele. Æ. H. i. 522.

68. 33. Singað þām Gode ðe āstāh ofer heofonas tō ēastdǣle. Æ. H. ii. 16.

68. 35. ... on his hālgum, on ðām hē is wundorlic. Æ. H. i. 446.

72. 11. Ealle cyningas onbūgað him, and ealle þēoda him ðēowiað. Æ. H. ii. 18.

73. 28. Mē is gōd þæt ic mē to Gode geðēode, and sętte mīnne hiht on Drihtne. Æ. H. ii. 440.

80. 1. Drihten, ðū ðe sitst ofer cherubin, geswutela ðē sylfne. Æ. H. i. 348.

82. 6. Ic cwæð: Gē sind godas, and gē ealle sind bearn þæs Hēhstan. Æ. H. i. 324 ; cf. i. 366.

‖ Sōðlice męn syndon godas gecīgede. Æ. H. i. 40.

84. 7. Ðā hālgan farað fram mihte tō mihte ; ealra goda God bið gesewen on Sion. Æ. H. ii. 334.

‖ Þā hālgan farað fram mihte tō mihte. Æ. H. i. 602.

86. 1. Ic sōðlice eom wǣdla and þearfa. Æ. H. i. 550 ; cf. Ps. 109. 22.

86. 10. Þū eart mǣre and micel, ðe wundra wyrcst ; þū eart ūna God. Æ. H. ii. 20.

89. 26. Hē sylf clypode tō mē : Þū eart mīn fæder. Æ. H. ii. 16.

89. 27. And ic gesętte hine frumcęnnedne and hēalicne tōforan eallum eorðlicum cynegum. Æ. H. ii. 16.

quia, Deus, susceptor meus es ; Deus meus misericordia mea.

62. 12. ... Domine, ... tu reddes unicuique iuxta opera sua.

63. 5. Sicut adipe et pinguedine repleatur anima mea. ...

68. 33. Qui ascendit super coelum coeli ad orientem. ...

68. 35. Mirabilis Deus in sanctis suis. ...

72. 11. Et adorabunt eum omnes reges terrae ; omnes gentes servient ei.

73. 28. Mihi autem adhaerere Deo bonum est, ponere in Domino Deo spem meam. ...

80. 1. ... Qui sedes super cheru-bim, manifestare.

82. 6. Ego dixi : Dii estis, et filii Excelsi omnes.

84. 7. ... Ibunt de virtute in virtutem ; videbitur Deus deorum in Sion.

86. 1. ... Quoniam inops et pauper sum ego.

86. 10. Quoniam magnus es tu, et faciens mirabilia ; tu es Deus solus.

89. 26. Ipse invocabit me : Pater meus es tu. ...

89. 27. Et ego primogenitum ponam illum excelsum prae regibus terrae.

90. 10. *See* Æ. H. i. 490.

91. 11, 12. God behēad his ęnglum be ðē, þæt hi ðē healdon, and on heora handan hębban, þē-lǣs-ðe ðu æt stāne þinne fōt ætspurne. Æ. H. i. 516; cf. Matt. 4. 1–11.

93. 5. Drihten, ðine gecȳðnyssa sindon swiðe gelēaflice. Æ. H. ii. 42. Drihten, þinum hūse gedafenað hālignys on daga langsumnysse. Æ. H. ii. 582.

94. 18. Gif min fōt āslād, Drihten, ðin mildheortnys geheolp mē. Æ. H. ii. 392.

95. 2. Uton forhradian Godes ansȳne on andetnysse. Æ. H. ii. 124.

106. 17, 18. Sēo eorðe geopenode and forswealh Dathan, and hēo oferwrēah Abiron and his gegaderunge, and heofenlic fȳr barn on heora gesamnunge, and ðā synfullan forbærnde. Æ. H. ii. 420.

109. 22. Ic sōðlice eom wǣdla and þearfa. Æ. H. i. 550; cf. Ps. 86. 1.

110. 1. God cwæð tō minum Drihtne: Site hēr tō minum swiðran. Æ. H. ii. 16; cf. Acts 2. 32 ff.

111. 10. Godes ęge is wisdōmes angynn. Æ. H. i. 550.

112. 1. Ēadig bið se wer se ðe hine ondrǣt God, and āwęnt his willan tō his bebodum. Æ. H. ii. 52.

112. 9. Hē āspende his ðing, and tōdǣlde ðearfum, and his rihtwisnys wunað ā on worulde. Æ. H. i. 254.

116. 15. Eulra gecorenra hālgena dēað is dēorwurðe on Godes gesihðe. Æ. H. i. 48.

118. 22. *See* Æ. H. i. 106.

---

91. 11, 12. Quoniam angelis suis mandavit de te ut custodiant te in omnibus viis tuis. In manibus portabunt te, ne forte offendas ad lapidem pedem tuum.

93. 5. Testimonia tua credibilia facta sunt nimis; domum tuam decet sanctitudo, Domine, in longitudinem dierum.

94. 18. Si dicebam: Motus est pes meus, misericordia tua, Domine, adiuvabat me.

95. 2. Praeoccupemus faciem eius in confessione. . . .

106. 17, 18. Aperta est terra, et deglutivit Dathan, et operuit super congregationem Abiron, et exarsit ignis in synagoga eorum; flamma combussit peccatores.

109. 22. Quia egenus et pauper ego sum. . . .

110. 1. Dixit Dominus Domino meo: Sede a dextris meis. . . .

111. 10. Initium sapientiae timor Domini. . . .

112. 1. Beatus vir qui timet Dominum; in mandatis eius volet nimis.

112. 9. Dispersit, dedit pauperibus; iustitia eius manet in saeculum saeculi. . . .

116. 15. Pretiosa in conspectu Domini mors sanctorum eius.

118. 24. Ðǣs is se dæg þe Drihten worhte; uton blissian and fægnian on ðām dæge. _Æ. H. ii._ 292, 294.

121. 4. Ne slǣpð nō ne hnappað se ðe hylt Israhel. _Æ. II. ii._ 230.

127. 1. Būton Drihten ðā burh gehealde, on ȳdel waciað þā hyrdas ðe hī healdað. _Æ. H. ii._ 230.

127. 2, 3. Ðonne God sylð his lēofum slǣp, þæt is Drihtnes yrfwyrdnys. _Æ. H. ii._ 526.

132. 9. Drihten, þīne sācerdas sind ymbscrȳdde mid rihtwīsnysse. _Æ. H. i._ 210.

135. 15–17. Ðǣra hǣðenra anlīcnyssa sind gyldene and sylfrene, manna handgeweorc; hī habbað dumne mūð and blinde ēagan, dēafe ēaran and ungrāpigende handa, fēt būtan fēðe, bodig būtan līfe. _Æ. H. i._ 366.

138. 6. Se hēalica Drihten scēawað þā ēadmōdan, and þā mōdigan feorran onenāwð. _Æ. H. i._ 128.

139. 16. Mīn Drihten, þīne ēagan gesāwon mine unfulfremednysse, and on þīnre bōc ealle sind āwritene. _Æ. H. i._ 530.

139. 17, 18. Mē sōðlice sind þīne frȳnd, God, swīðe ārwurðe, and heora ealdordōm is swīðe gestrangod. Ic hī gerīme, and hī bēoð gemęnigfylde ofer ðǣre sǣ sandceosol. _Æ. H. ii._ 524.

∥ Ic hī getealde, and heora getęl is māre ðonne sandceosol. _Æ. H. i._ 536.

Ic ārās of dēaðe, and ic eft mid þē eom. _Æ. H. ii._ 16.

141. 2. Drihten, sȳ mīn gebed āsęnd swā-swā byrnende stōr on ðīnre gesihðe. _Æ. II. i._ 118.

118. 24. Haec est dies quam fecit Dominus; exultemus et laetemur in ea.

121. 4. Ecce non dormitabit neque dormiet qui custodit Israel.

127. 1. . . . Nisi Dominus custodierit civitatem, frustra vigilat qui custodit eam.

127. 2, 3. . . . Cum dederit dilectis suis somnum, ecce hereditas Domini, filii. . . .

132. 9. Sacerdotes tui induantur iustitiam. . . .

135. 15–17. Simulacra gentium argentum et aurum, opera manuum hominum: os habent, et non loquentur; oculos habent, et non videbunt; aures habent, et non audient; neque enim est spiritus in ore ipsorum.

138. 6. Quoniam excelsus Dominus, et humilia respicit, et alta a longe cognoscit.

139. 16. Imperfectum meum viderunt oculi tui, et in libro tuo omnes scribentur. . . .

139. 17, 18. Mihi autem nimis honorificati sunt amici tui, Deus; nimis confortatus est principatus eorum. Dinumerabo eos, et super arenam multiplicabuntur. Exsurrexi, et adhuc sum tecum.

141. 2. Dirigatur oratio mea sicut incensum in conspectu tuo. . . .

142. 5. Drihten, þu eart mīn hiht ; bēo mīn dǣl on þǣra lybbendra eorðan. *Æ. H. i. 550.*

146. 3, 4. Nellað gē getrūwian on ealdormannum, nē on manna bearnum, on ðām nis nān hǣl. Heora gāst gewīt, and hī tō eorðan gehwyrfað, and on ðām dæge losiað ealle heora geðōhtas. *Æ. H. i. 410.*

PROVERBS.

1. 28. Þonne hī clypiað tō mē, and ic hī ne gehȳre ; hī ārīsað on ǣrnemerigen, ac hī ne gemētað mē. *Æ. H. ii. 378.*

3. 9. Ārwurða ðīnne Drihten mid þīnum ǣhtum, and of ðīnum frumwǣstmum syle ðearfum. *Æ. H. ii. 102.*

4. 16. Hī blissiað on yfelnysse and on ārlēasum dǣdum, and hī slǣp ne underfōð, būton hī yfel gefremmon. *Æ. H. ii. 322.*

4. 18. And rihtwīsra stōfæt is swilce scīnende lēoht, and weaxende symle ōð sōðre fulfremednysse. *Æ. H. ii. 322.*

5. 22. Ānra gehwilc mann is gewriðen mid rāpum his synna. *Æ. H. i. 208.*

13. 8. Þæs rīcan mannes welan sind his sāwle ālȳsednyss. *Æ. H. i. 204.*

13. 24. Sē ðe sparað his gyrde, hē hatað his cild ; and sē ðe hit lufað, hē lǣrð hit ānrǣdlice. *Æ. H. ii. 324.*

15. 15. Yfele sind ūre dagas. *Æ. H. i. 490.*

16. 32. Sēlre is se geðyldiga wer þonne se stranga ; and sē ðe his mōd gewylt is bētera ðonne se ðe burh oferwinð. *Æ. H. ii. 544.*

17. 3. *See Æ. H. i. 288.*

142. 5. . . . Tu es spes mea, portio mea in terra viventium.

146. 3, 4. . . . Nolite confidere in principibus, in filiis hominum, in quibus non est salus. Exibit spiritus eius, et revertetur in terram suam ; in illa die peribunt omnes cogitationes eorum.

PROVERBS.

1. 28. Tunc invocabunt me, et non exaudiam ; mane consurgent, et non invenient me.

3. 9. Honora Dominum de tua substantia, et de primitiis omnium frugum tuarum da ei.

4. 16. Non enim dormiunt nisi malefecerint, et rapitur somnus ab eis nisi supplantaverint.

4. 18. Iustorum autem semita, quasi lux splendens, procedit et crescit usque ad perfectam diem.

5. 22. . . . Funibus peccatorum suorum constringitur.

13. 8. Redemptio animae viri divitiae suae. . . .

13. 24. Qui parcit virgae, odit filium suum ; qui autem diligit illum, instanter erudit.

15. 15. Omnes dies pauperis mali. . . .

16. 32. Melior est patiens viro forti ; et qui dominatur animo suo, expugnatore urbium.

17. 5. Gif hwā ðearfan forsihð, hē tēlð his Scyppend. *Æ. H. ii. 328.*

19. 11. Þæs mannes wīsdōm bið oncnāwen þurh geðyld. *Æ. H. ii. 544.*

21. 13. Sō ðe āwęnt his nęb fram clypigendum ðearfan, hē sylf clypað ęft tō Gode, and his stemne ne bið gehȳred. *Æ. H. ii. 102.*

21. 20. Gewilnigendlic goldhord līð on ðæs witan mūðe. *Æ. H. i. 116.*

21. 30. Nis nān wīsdōm nē nān rǣd nāht ongēan God. *Æ. H. i. 82.*

23. 14. Stȳr ðīnum cilde, and sleh hit mid gyrde, and ðū swā ālȳst his sāwle fram dēaðe. *Æ. H. ii. 324.*

28. 14. Ēadig bið se man þe symle bið forhtigende; and sōðlice se heardmōda befylð on yfel. *Æ. H. i. 408.*

29. 5. Lyffetyndra tungan gewrīðað manna sāwle on synnum[1]. *Æ. H. i. 494.*

29. 19. Ne bið se stunta mid wordum gerihtlǣced. *Æ. H. ii. 532.*

31. 4. Ne bið nān ðing dīgle þǣr ðǣr druncennys rīxað. *Æ. H. i. 604.*

SONG OF SOLOMON.

4. 11. And unāsęcgendlic brǣð stēmde of hire gyrlum. *Æ. H. i. 444.*

5. 5. Mīne handa drȳpton myrran. *Æ. H. i. 118.*

5. 12. Ic geseah ðā wlitegan swilce culfran āstīgende ofer strēamlicum rīðum. *Æ. H. i. 444.*

6. 10 (Vulg. 9). Hwæt is ðēos ðe hēr āstīhð swilce ārīsende dægrima, swā wlitig swā mōna, swā gecoren swā sunne, and swā ęgeslic swā fyrdtruma? *Æ. H. i. 442.*

17. 5. Qui despicit pauperem, exprobrat Factori eius. . . .

19. 11. Doctrina viri per patientiam noscitur. . . .

21. 13. Qui obturat aurem suam ad clamorem pauperis, et ipse clamabit, et non exaudietur.

21. 20. Thesaurus desiderabilis . . . in habitaculo iusti. . . .

21. 30. Non est sapientia, non est prudentia, non est consilium contra Dominum.

23. 14. Tu virga percuties eum, et animam eius de inferno liberabis.

28. 14. Beatus homo qui semper est pavidus; qui vero mentis est durae corruet in malum.

29. 5. Homo qui blandis fictisque sermonibus loquitur amico suo rete expandit gressibus eius.

29. 19. Servus verbis non potest erudiri. . . .

31. 4. . . . Quia nullum secretum est ubi regnat ebrietas.

SONG OF SOLOMON.

4. 11. . . . Odor vestimentorum tuorum sicut odor thuris.

5. 5. . . . Manus meae stillaverunt myrrham.

5. 12. Oculi eius sicut columbae super rivulos aquarum. . . .

6. 9. Quae est ista, quae progreditur quasi aurora consurgens, pulchra ut luna, electa ut sol, terribilis ut castrorum acies ordinata?

[1] Doubtfully assigned here.

1. 3. Se oxa oncncŏow his hlāford, and se assa his hlāfordes binne.
Æ. H. i. 42.

1. 17–20. Helpaŏ ofsęttum, and stcopcildum dēmaŏ; bewęriaŏ
wydewan wiŏ wælhrēawum ŏhterum, and ŏrēagaŏ mē siŏŏan.
Þis sēde Drihten, and gif cowere synna wǣron wolcnrēade ǣr
ŏan, hī bcoŏ scīnende on snāwes hwītnysse. Gif gē mē
gehȳraŏ, gē etaŏ þǣre eorŏan gōd; gif gē mē geyrsiaŏ, cow
fornimŏ mīn swurd. Æ. H. ii. 322.

5. 7. Sōŏlice Godes wīngeard is Israhela hīwrǣden. Æ. H. ii. 72.

5. 20. Wā ŏām ŏe talaŏ, mid trcowlēasum mōde, yfel tō gōde,
and gōd tō yfele; þcostru tō lcohte, and lēoht tō ŏcos-
trum. Æ. H. ii. 322.

5. 22–24. Wā ŏān ŏe strang biŏ tō swīŏlicum dręncum and tō
gemęncgenne ŏā micclan druncennysse; swilce gerihtwīsiaŏ
þone ārlēasan for sceattum, and þām rihtwīsum ætbrēdaŏ
his rihtwīsnysse swā. Forŏī hī fornimŏ hęlle fȳr swā-swā ceaf,
and heora wyrtruma biŏ swā-swā windige ȳsla. Æ. H. ii. 322.

7. 14. Efne, sceal mǣden gecacnian on hire innoŏe, and ācęnnan
sunu; and his nama biŏ gecīged Emmanuhel. Æ. H. i. 192.

‖ Efne, ān mǣden sceal gecacnian, and ācęnnan sunu; and his
nama biŏ Emmanuhel. Æ. H. ii. 14; cf. Matt. 1. 23.

9. 6, 7. Ūs is cild ācęnned, and ūs is sunu forgifen, and his ealdordōm is on his exlum, and hē biŏ gehāten wundorlic, rǣdbora,

ISAIAH.

1. 3. Cognovit bos possessorem suum,
et asinus praesepe domini sui....

1. 17–20. ... Subvenite oppresso,
iudicate pupillo, defendite vi-
duam. Et venite, et arguite me,
dicit Dominus: si fuerint peccata
vestra ut coccinum, quasi nix
dealbabuntur.... Si ... audieritis
me, bona terrae comedetis. Quod
si ... me ad iracundiam provo-
caveritis, gladius devorabit vos....

5. 7. Vinea enim Domini exercituum domus Israel est. ...

5. 20. Vae qui dicitis malum bonum,
et bonum malum, ponentes tene-

bras lucem, et lucem tenebras....

5. 22–24. Vae qui potentes estis ad
bibendum vinum, et viri fortes
ad miscendam ebrietatem, qui
iustificatis impium pro muneri-
bus, et iustitiam iusti aufertis ab
eo. Propter hoc, sicut devorat
stipulam lingua ignis, et calor
flammae exurit, sic radix eorum
quasi favilla erit, et germen eorum
ut pulvis ascendet. ...

7. 14. ... Ecce virgo concipiet, et
pariet filium; et vocabitur nomen
eius Emmanuel.

9. 6, 7. Parvulus enim natus est
nobis, et filius datus est nobis, et
factus est principatus super hu-

strang God, and fæder þære tōweardan worulde, and sibbe
ealdor ; his rīce and his anweald bið gemęnigfyld, and no bið
nān ęnde his sibbe.   Æ. H. ii. 16.

11. 2, 3. Ðā męn . . . becumað tō seofonfcaldre gife þæs Hālgan
Gāstes : þā sind wīsdōm and andgit, rǣd and stręngð, ingehȳd
and ārfæstnys ; Godes ęge is se seofoða.   Æ. H. ii. 292.

‖ Ān is se Hālga Gāst þe sylð gecorenum mannum ðā seofon-
fealdan gife : þæt is, wīsdōm and andgit, rǣd and stręngð,
ingehȳd and ārfæstnys ; Godes ęge is sōo seofoðe.   Æ. H. ii. 308.

Hē onbryrt ūre mōd mid seofonfcaldre gife : þæt is, mid
wīsdōme and andgyte, mid gecceahte and stręncðe, mid
ingehȳde and ārfæstnysse ; and hē ūs gefylð mid Godes ęge.
     Æ. H. i. 326 ; cf. i. 328, ii. 14.

14. 12, 13. *See* Æ. H. i. 10.

26. 19. Þā dēadan sceolon ārīsan, and þā ðe licgað on byrgenum hī
geedcuciað.   Æ. H. ii. 18.

30. 26. Þonne bið seō sunne be seofonfcaldum beorhtre þonne hēo
nū sȳ, and se mōna hæfð þære sunnan lēoht.   Æ. H. i. 618.

35. 4–6. Sęcgað þām wācmōdum þæt hī bēon gehyrte, and nān
ðing ofdrǣdde ; hēr cymð God sylf, and gehǣlð ūs.   Þonne
bēoð geopenode blindra manna ēagan, and dēaffra manna ēaran
gehȳrað ; þonne hlēapð se healta swā-swā heort, and dumbra
manna tungan bēoð swīðe getinge.   Æ. H. ii. 16.

36. 1. *See* Æ. H. i. 568.

36. 14. *See* 2 Kings 18. 29.

36. 20. *See* 2 Kings 18. 35.

37. 1, 2. *See* 2 Kings 19. 1, 2.

37. 4. *See* 2 Kings 19. 4.

37. 6. *See* 2 Kings 19. 6.

merum eius : et vocabitur nomen eius admirabilis, consiliarius, Deus, fortis, pater futuri saeculi, princeps pacis ; multiplicabitur eius imperium, et pacis non erit finis. . . .

11. 2, 3. Et requiescet super eum spiritus Domini : spiritus sapientiae et intellectus, spiritus consilii et fortitudinis, spiritus scientiae et pietatis ; et replebit eum spiritus timoris Domini. . . .

26. 19. Vivent mortui tui ; interfecti mei resurgent. . . .

30. 26. Et erit lux lunae sicut lux solis, et lux solis erit septempliciter, sicut lux septem dierum. . . .

35. 4–6. Dicite pusillanimis : Confortamini, et nolite timere ; . . . Deus ipse veniet, et salvabit vos. Tunc aperientur oculi caecorum, et aures surdorum patebunt ; tunc saliet sicut cervus claudus, et aperta erit lingua mutorum. . . .

37. 29. *See* 2 Kings 19. 28.

37. 33. *See* 2 Kings 19. 32.

37. 35. *See* 2 Kings 19. 34.

37. 36–38. *See* 2 Kings 19. 35–37.

38. 21. Isaias, þe worhte ðām cyninge Ezechie cliðan tō his dolge, and hine gelācnode. . . .   *Æ. H. i.* 476.

40. 3, 4. Stemn clypigendes on wēstene: Gearciað Godes weig, dōð rihte his paðas. Ǣle dęne bið gefylled, and ǣle dūn bið geēadmēt, and ealle wōhnyssa beoð gerihte, and scearpnyssa gesmēðode [1].   *Æ. H. i.* 360.

‖ Gearciað Godes weig.   *Æ. H. i.* 362.

‖ Gearciað Drihtnes weg, dōð rihte his srōfætu.   *Æ. H. ii.* 530.

40. 6. Ǣle flǣsc is gærs, and þæs flǣsces wuldor is swilce wyrta blōstm.   *Æ. H. i.* 188.

42. 2. He ne flāt, nē ne hrȳmde, ne nān mann his stemne on strǣtum ne gehȳrde.   *Æ. H. i.* 592 ; cf. ii. 44.

44. 17. Męn . . . bugon tō þām ānlīcnyssum þe hī sylfe worhton, and him cwǣdon tō : Þū eart mīn God.   *Æ. H. i.* 208.

53. 4. Sōðlice hē sylf ætbrǣd ūre ādlunga, and ūre sārnyssa hē sylf ābær.   *Æ. H. i.* 122.

53. 7. He is gelǣd tō slęge swā-swā scēp, and hē suwade and his mūð ne ondyde, swā-swā lamb dēð þonne hit man scyrð.   *Æ. H. ii.* 16 ; cf. ii. 40.

57. 15. On hwām geręst Godes Gāst būton on ðām ēadmōdan [2]?   *Æ. H. i.* 362.

---

38. 21. Et iussit Isaias ut tollerent massam de ficis, et cataplasmarent super vulnus, et sanaretur.

40. 3, 4. Vox clamantis in deserto: Parate viam Domini, rectas facite . . . semitas Dei nostri. Omnis vallis exaltabitur, et omnis mons et collis humiliabitur, et erunt prava in directa, et aspera in vias planas.

40. 6. . . . Omnis caro foenum, et omnis gloria eius quasi flos agri.

42. 2. Non clamabit, neque accipiet personam, nec audietur vox eius foris.

44. 17. . . . Curvatur ante illud, et adorat illud et obsecrat, dicens: . . . Deus meus es tu.

53. 4. Vere languores nostros ipse tulit, et dolores nostros ipse portavit. . . .

53. 7. . . . Sicut ovis ad occisionem ducetur, et quasi agnus coram tondente se obmutescet, et non aperiet os suum.

57. 15. . . . Habitans . . . cum contrito et humili spiritu. . . .

---

[1] Probably translated from Luke 3. 4, 5.

[2] Doubtfully assigned here.

58. 1. Clypa, and ne geswīc ðū, āhęfe þīne stemne swā-swā bȳme, and cȳð mīnum folce heora leahtras, and Iacobes hīrede heora synna. *Æ. H. i. 6.*

58. 7. Tōbrec ðīnne hlāf, and syle ðone ōþerne dǣl hungrium męn, and lǣd intō þīnum hūse wǣdlan, and ðā earman ælfręmedan męn, and gefrēfra hī mid þīnum gōdum; þonne ðū nacodne gesēo, scrȳd hine, and ne forseoh ðīn āgen flǣsc. *Æ. H. i. 180.*

60. 8. Hwæt sind þās þe hēr flēogað swā-swā wolcnu, and swā-swā culfran tō heora chōȳrlum? *Æ. H. i. 584.*

62. 2. Þū bist gecīged nīwum naman, þone ðe Godes mūð genęmnode. *Æ. H. i. 96.*

65. 15. God gecīgð his ðēowan ōðrum naman. *Æ. H. i. 96.*

66. 1. Heofon is mīn setl. *Æ. H. i. 520;* cf. Matt. 5. 34–37.

66. 24. Þǣr nǣfre heora wyrm ne swylt, nē heora fȳr ne bið ādwǣsced. *Æ. H. i. 132.*

JEREMIAH [1].

4. 22. Hī sind snotere þæt hī yfel wyrcon, and hī sōðlice ne cunnon nāht tō gōde gewyrcan. *Æ. H. ii. 552.*

8. 7. Storc and swalewe hēoldon ðone tīman heora tōcymes; and þis folc ne oncnēow Godes dōm. *Æ. H. i. 404.*

11. 20. *See* Rom. 9. 29.

58. 1, Clama, ne cesses, quasi tuba exalta vocem tuam, et annuncia populo meo scelera eorum, et domui Iacob peccata eorum.

58. 7. Frange esurienti panem tuum, et egenos vagosque induc in domum tuam; cum videris nudum, operi eum, et carnem tuam ne despexeris.

60. 8. Qui sunt isti qui ut nubes volant, et quasi columbae ad fenestras suas?

62. 2. ...Et vocabitur tibi nomen novum, quod os Domini nominabit.

65. 15. ...Et servos suos vocabit nomine alio.

66. 1. ...Coelum sedes mea....

66. 24. ...Vermis eorum non morietur, et ignis eorum non extinguetur....

JEREMIAH.

4. 22. ...Sapientes sunt ut faciant mala, bene autem facere nescierunt.

8. 7. ...Hirundo et ciconia custodierunt tempus adventus sui; populus autem meus non cognovit iudicium Domini.

---

[1] For passages attributed to Jeremiah, but not found, see Untraced Passages, p. 257.

16. 9. . . . þæt hī sceoldon . . . geswīcan blisse stemne and fægnunge, brȳdguman stemne and brȳde.   *Æ. H. ii. 86.*

16. 16. Ic āsęnde mīne fisceras, and hī gefixiað hī ; mīne huntan, and hī huntiað hī of ǣlcere dūne and of ǣlcere hylle.   *Æ. H. i. 576.*

17. 10. Ic āfandige manna heortan and heora lęndena, and ǣlcum sylle æfter his færelde, and æfter his āgenre āfundennysse.   *Æ. H. i. 114.*

17. 14. Drihten, gehǣl mē, and ic bēo gehǣled ; geheald þū mē, and ic bēo gehealden.   *Æ. H. i. 254.*

23. 24. Ic gefylle mid mē sylfum heofonas and eorðan.   *Æ. H. i. 262.*

29. 10. *See Æ. H. ii. 66.*

31. 15. *See* Matt. 2. 18 (2. 16–18).

LAMENTATIONS.

3. 41. Uton āhębban ūre heortan mid handum tō Gode.   *Æ. H. ii. 124.*

4. 4. Đā lȳtlan cild bǣdon him hlāfes, ac þǣr næs nān mann ðe þone hlāf him betwȳnan tōbrǣce.   *Æ. H. ii. 400.*

EZEKIEL.

1. 10. Ān ðǣra nȳtena wæs on męnniscre ansȳne him ætēowod, ōðer on lēon ansȳne, þridde on cealfes, fēorðe on earnes.   *Æ. H. ii. 430.*

2. 6. Đū mannes bearn, ungelēaffulle and yfel tihtende sind mid þē, and þū wunast mid þām wyrstan wyrmcynne.   *Æ. H. i. 528.*

16. 9. . . . Ego auferam de loco isto . . . vocem gaudii et vocem laetitiae, vocem sponsi et vocem sponsae.

16. 16. Ecce ego mittam piscatores multos, dicit Dominus, et piscabuntur eos : et post haec mittam eis multos venatores, et venabuntur eos de omni monte et de omni colle. . . .

17. 10. Ego Dominus scrutans cor et probans renes ; qui do unicuique iuxta viam suam, et iuxta fructum adinventionum suarum.

17. 14. Sana me, Domine, et sanabor ; salvum me fac, et salvus ero. . . .

23. 24. . . . Numquid non coelum et terram ego impleo ? . . .

LAMENTATIONS.

3. 41. Levemus corda nostra cum manibus ad Dominum. . . .

4. 4. . . . Parvuli petierunt panem, et non erat qui frangeret eis.

EZEKIEL.

1. 10. Similitudo autem vultus eorum : facies hominis et facies leonis a dextris ipsorum quattuor, facies autem bovis a sinistris ipsorum quattuor, et facies aquilae desuper ipsorum quattuor.

2. 6. Tu ergo, fili hominis, . . . increduli et subversores sunt tecum, et cum scorpionibus habitas. . . .

3. 18. Gif þū ne gestentst þone unrihtwīsan, and hine ne manast þæt hē fram his ārlēasnysse gecyrre and lybbe, þonne swelt se ārlēasa on his unrihtwīsnysse, and ic wille ofgān æt ðē his blōd. Æ. H. i. 6.

‖ Būton þū gestande ðone unrihtwīsan, and him his unrihtwīsnysse sęcge, ic ofgā his blōdes gyte æt ðīnum handum. Æ. H. ii. 340.

3. 19. Gif ðū ðonne þone ārlēasan gewarnast, and hē nele fram his ārlēasnysse gecyrran, þū ālȳsdest þīne sāwle mid þǣre mynegunge, and se ārlēasa swylt on his unrihtwīsnysse. Æ. H. i. 6.

3. 26. Ic dō þæt þīn tunge clifað to ðīnum gōman, and þū bist dumb, nā swā-swā ðrēagende wer, forðanþe sēo hīwrǣden is swīðe ðwȳr. Æ. H. ii. 530.

11. 19. Ic ætbrēde him ðā stǣnenan heortan, and ic forgife him flǣscene heortan. Æ. H. ii. 204.

18. 21, 22. Gif se ārlēasa and se synfulla wyrcð dǣdbōte ealra his synna, and hylt ealle mīne beboda, and rihtwīsnysse begǣð, hē leofað, and ne swelt nā yfelum dēaðe; and ic ne gemune nǣnra his synna ðe hē gefręmode. Æ. H. ii. 602.

18. 26, 27. Gif se rihtwīsa gecyrð fram his rihtwīsnysse, and begǣð unrihtwīsnysse ārlēaslice, ealle his rihtwīsnysse ic forgyte; and gif se ārlēasa behrēowsað his ārlēasnysse, and begǣð rihtwīsnysse, ne gemune ic nǣnra his synna. Æ. H. i. 350.

3. 18. Si dicente me ad impium: Morte morieris, non annuntiaveris ei, neque locutus fueris ut avertatur a via sua impia et vivat, ipse impius in iniquitate sua morietur, sanguinem autem eius de manu tua requiram.

3. 19. Si autem tu annuntiaveris impio, et ille non fuerit conversus ab impietate sua, et a via sua impia, ipse quidem in iniquitate sua morietur, tu autem animam tuam liberasti.

3. 26. Et linguam tuam adhaerere faciam palato tuo, et eris mutus, nec quasi vir obiurgans, quia domus exasperans est.

11. 19. . . . Auferam cor lapideum de carne eorum, et dabo eis cor carneum.

18. 21, 22. Si autem impius egerit poenitentiam ab omnibus peccatis suis quae operatus est, et custodierit omnia praecepta mea, et fecerit iudicium et iustitiam, vita vivet, et non morietur; omnium iniquitatum eius, quas operatus est, non recordabor. . . .

18. 26, 27. Cum enim averterit se iustus a iustitia sua et fecerit iniquitatem, morietur in eis; in iniustitia quam operatus est morietur. Et cum averterit se impius ab impietate sua quam operatus

24. 22. Ic dō þæt gē dōð.   Æ. H. ii. 526.

33. 8. *Sec* Ezek. 3. 18.

33. 11. Nylle ic þæs synfullan dēað, ac ic wille þæt hē gecyrre and lybbe.   Æ. H. ii. 124.

|| God cwæð þæt hē nolde þæs synfullan dēað, ac hē wyle swīðor þæt hē gecyrre fram his synnum and lybbe.   Æ. H. ii. 602.

34. 7, 8, 10, 13, 14, 16. Gē hyrdas, gehȳrað Godes word : Mīne scēp sint tōstęncte ðurh ēowre gȳmelēaste, and sind ābitene. Gē cariað embe ēowerne bigleofan, and nū embe þēra scēapa ; forðī ic wille ofgān ðā scēp æt ēowrum handum ; and ic dō þæt gē geswīcað þēre wīcan, and ic wylle āhręddan mīne ēowde wið ēow. Ic sylf wylle gadrian mīne scēp þe wǣron tōstęncte, and ic wylle hī healdan on genihtsumere lǣse. Þæt þæt losode, þæt ic wylle sēcan and ongēan lædan ; þæt þæt ālōfed wæs, þæt ic gehǣle ; þæt untrume ic wylle getrymman, and þæt strange gehealdan, and ic hī lǣswige on dōme and on rihtwīsnysse.   Æ. H. i. 242.

36. 26. *Sec* Ezek. 11. 19.

44. 2. Þis geat ne bið nānum męnn geopenod, ac se Hlāford āna færð inn þurh þæt geat, and ęft ūt færð, and hit bið belocen on ēcnysse.   Æ. H. i. 194.

est, et fecerit iudicium et iustitiam, ipse animam suam vivificabit.

24. 22. Et facietis sicut feci. . . .

33. 11. . . . Nolo mortem impii, sed ut convertatur impius a via sua, et vivat. . . .

34. 7, 8, 10, 13, 14, 16. Propterea, pastores, audite verbum Domini : . . . Facti sunt greges mei in rapinam, et oves meae in devorationem omnium bestiarum agri, eo quod non esset pastor ; neque enim quaesierunt pastores mei gregem meum, sed pascebant pastores semetipsos, et greges meos non pascebant ; . . . ecce ego ipse super pastores requiram gregem meum de manu eorum, et cessare faciam eos ut ultra non pascant gregem, nec pascant amplius pastores semetipsos, et liberabo gregem meum de ore eorum, et non erit ultra eis in escam. . . . Et educam eas de populis, et congregabo eas de terris, et inducam eas in terram suam ; et pascam eas in montibus Israel, in rivis. et in cunctis sedibus terrae ; in pascuis uberrimis pascam eas. . . . Quod perierat requiram, et quod abiectum erat reducam, et quod confractum fuerat alligabo, et quod infirmum fuerat consolidabo. et quod pingue et forte custodiam, et pascam illas in iudicio.

44. 2. . . . Porta haec clausa erit ; non aperietur, et vir non transibit per eam ; quoniam Dominus Deus Israel ingressus est per eam, eritque clausa.

DANIEL.

1. 1 ff. *See* Æ. H. ii. 18, 432.

1. 19. *See* Æ. H. ii. 68.

2. 1 ff. *See* Æ. H. ii. 432.

3. 1, 4-6. Þā arǣrde hē hǣðengyld, and bebēad eallum his folce, be heora līfe, þæt hī sceoldon feallan ādūne, and hī gebiddan tō ðǣre anlīcnysse þe hē arǣrde ; gif hwā hit forsōce, þæt hē sceolde bēon forbærned on hātum ofne. Æ. H. ii. 18.

3. 12. *See* Æ. H. ii. 18.

3. 14-22, 24-29. Þā cwæð se cyning him tō : Hwæt is se God þe mæge ēow āhręddan of mīnum handum? Ðā cwǣdon Annanias, Azarias, Misahel tō ðām cyninge : Se Ælmihtiga God, þe wē wurðiað, is swā mihtig þæt hē ēaðe mæg ūs āhręddan of ðīnum byrnendum ofne, and of ðīnum handum. And wite þū gewiss, þæt wē nǣfre ne būgað tō ðīnum hǣðenscipe. Hē wearð ðā āfylled mid graman, and hēt onǣlan þone ofen swīðe ðearle ; and hēt gebindan ðā cnihtas handum and fōtum, and āwurpan into ðām byrnendum ofne. Þā wæs ðæs cyninges hǣs þǣrrihte gefylled, and hī wǣron āworpene intō ðām byrnendan ofne, and se līg slōh ūt of ðām ofne feorr ūp, and forbærnde tō dēaðe ðā ðe hī inn āwurpon ; and þæt fȳr ne dęrede nāht þām ðrīm cnihtum ðe on God belȳfdon, ac hī wurdon þǣrrihte unbundene, and ēodon orsorhlice

DANIEL.

3. 1, 4-6. Nabuchodonosor rex fecit statuam auream ; . . . et praeco clamabat : . . . Cadentes adorate statuam auream quam constituit Nabuchodonosor rex ; si quis autem non prostratus adoraverit, eadem hora mittetur in fornacem ignis ardentis.

3. 14-22, 24-29 (Vulg. 91-96). Pronuntiansque Nabuchodonosor rex, ait eis : . . . Quis est Deus, qui eripiet vos de manu mea ? Respondentes Sidrach, Misach, et Abdenago, dixerunt regi Nabuchodonosor : . . . Ecce enim Deus noster, quem colimus, potest eripere nos de camino ignis ardentis, et de mani-

bus tuis, o rex, liberare. Quod si noluerit, notum sit tibi, rex, quia deos tuos non colimus, et statuam auream quam erexisti non adoramus. Tunc Nabuchodonosor repletus est furore, . . . et praecepit ut succenderetur fornax septuplum quam succendi consueverat ; et viris fortissimis de exercitu suo iussit ut, ligatis pedibus Sidrach, Misach, et Abdenago, mitterent eos in fornacem ignis ardentis. Et confestim viri illi . . . missi sunt in medium fornacis ignis ardentis, nam iussio regis urgebat ; fornax autem succensa erat nimis. Porro viros illos, qui miserant Sidrach, Misach, et Abdenago, interfecit flamma ignis. . . .

on ðām fȳre, and herodon God. Ðā ēode se cyning tō ðām
ofne, and sceawode geornlice ; þā geseah hē ðǣr fēower menn
gangende binnon ðām fȳre, and hē cwæð ða tō his cnihtum :
Hūlā, ne wurpe wē þrȳ cnihtas intō ðām fȳre ? Hī cwǣdon
him tō : Sōð þū segst, cyning. Þā cwæð se cyning : Ic gesēo
ðǣr fēower weras gangende on middan þām fȳre ungewemmede
and unforswǣlede, and se fēorða is gelīc Godes Bearne. . . .
And hē ðā genēalǣhte ðām ofne, and cwæð tō ðām þrīm
Godes cnihtum : Gē Godes menn, Annania, Azaria, Misahel,
gāð ūt of ðām ofne, and cumað tō mē. Hī þǣrrihte ūtēodon of
ðām byrnendum ofne ætforan eallum ðām folce. Hī sceawodon
heora fex and heora līchaman, and swīðe wundrodon þæt hī
ealswā gehāle and swā gesunde ūtēodon of ðām fȳre, swā hī
inn āworpene wǣron. Þā cwæð se cyning : Geblētsod sȳ ēower
God, se ðe ēow āhredde swā mihtelīce of ðām fȳre. Ic sette
nū ðis gebann on eallum mīnum folce, þæt nān man ne bēo swā
dyrstig, þæt hē ǣnig word oððe ǣnig tāl cweðe ongēan ēowerum
Gode ; gif hit hwā ðonne dēð, hē sceal ðolian his ǣhta and his
āgenes līfes. ᴁ. H. ii. 18, 20.

|| Eft siððan Nabochodonossor, se Chaldeisca cyning, hēt
gebindan handum and fōtum þā ðrȳ gelȳfedan cnihtas, Annanias, Azarias, Missael, and intō ānum byrnendum ofne
āwurpan ; forþanðe hī noldon hī gebiddan tō his dēofolgilde.

Tunc Nabuchodonosor rex obstu-
puit, et surrexit propere, et ait
optimatibus suis: Nonne tres viros misimus in medium ignis com-
peditos ? Qui respondentes regi,
dixerunt : Vere, rex. Respondit,
et ait : Ecce ego video quattuor
viros solutos, et ambulantes in
medio ignis, et nihil corruptionis
in eis est, et species quarti similis
filio Dei. Tunc accessit Nabuchodonosor ad ostium fornacis
ignis ardentis, et ait: Sidrach,
Misach, et Abdenago, servi Dei
excelsi, egredimini, et venite.
Statimque egressi sunt Sidrach,
Misach, et Abdenago de medio
ignis. Et congregati satrapae, et
magistratus, et iudices, et potentes regis contemplabantur viros
illos, quoniam nihil potestatis ha-
buisset ignis in corporibus eorum,
et capillus capitis eorum non
esset adustus, et sarabala eorum
non fuissent immutata, et odor
ignis non transisset per eos. Et
erumpens Nabuchodonosor, ait:
Benedictus Deus eorum, . . . qui
misit angelum suum, et eruit
servos suos qui crediderunt in
eum. . . . A me ergo positum est
hoc decretum, ut omnis populus,
tribus, et lingua, quaecumque
locuta fuerit blasphemiam contra
Deum Sidrach, Misach, et Abdenago, dispereat, et domus eius
vastetur. . . .

. . . Þā sceawode se cyning þǣra ðrēora cnihta feax and
līchaman, þus cweðende : Sȳ geblētsod ᵹower God, se ðe āsęnde
his ęngel, and swā mihtelice his ðēowan of þām byrnendan ofne
ālȳsde. *Æ. H. i. 570.*

3. 47–49 [1] (A. V. Apocrypha : Song of the Three Holy Children
24–26). Ac se Ælmihtiga God, þe hī ānrǣdlice on belȳfdon,
āsęnde his ęngel intō ðām ofne mid þām cnihtum, and hē ðā
tōscēoc þone līg of ðām ofne, swā þæt þæt fȳr ne mihte him
derigan, ac slōh ūt of ðām ofne nigan and fēowertig fæþma, and
forswǣlde þā cwęlleras þe þæt fȳr onǣldon. *Æ. H. i. 570.*

4. 29–37 (Vulg. 26–34.). Æfter ðison ymbe twęlf mōnað ēode se
cyning binnon his healle mid ormǣtre ūpāhęfednysse, hęrigende
his weorc and his mihte, and cwæð : Hū, ne is þis sēo miccle
Babilon ðe ic sylf getimbrode tō cynestōle, and tō ðrymme mē
sylfum, tō wlite and tō wuldre, mid mīnum āgenum mægene
and stręngðe? Ac him clypode þǣrrihte tō swīðe ęgeslic stemn
of heofenum, þus cweðende : Þū Nabochodonosor, þīn rīce
gewīt fram ðē, and þū bist fram mannum āworpen, and ðīn
wunung bið mid wildēorum ; and þū etst gærs swā-swā oxa
seofon gēar, oð-þæt ðū wite þæt se hēalica God gewylt manna
rīcu, and þæt hē forgifð rīce ðām ðe hē wile. Witodlīce on
þǣre ylcan tīde wæs þēos sprǣc gefylled ofer Nabochodonosor,
and hē arn tō wuda, and wunode mid wildēorum, leofode be
gærse swā-swā nȳten, oð-þæt his feax wēox swā-swā wim-
manna, and his næglas swā-swā earnes clāwa. . . . Ic

3. 47–49. Et effundebatur flamma
super fornacem cubitis quadraginta novem, et erupit, et incen-
dit quos reperit iuxta fornacem
de Chaldaeis ; angelus autem Domini descendit cum Azaria et
sociis eius in fornacem, et excus-
sit flammam ignis de fornace.

4. 26–34 [1]. Post finem mensium duodecim in aula Babylonis deambu-
labat. Responditque rex, et ait :
Nonne haec est Babylon magna
quam ego aedificavi in domum
regni, in robore fortitudinis
meae, et in gloria decoris mei ?

Cumque sermo adhuc esset in ore
regis, vox de coelo ruit : Tibi dicitur, Nabuchodonosor rex : Regnum tuum transibit a te, et ab
hominibus eiicient te, et cum
bestiis et feris erit habitatio tua ;
foenum quasi bos comedes, et septem tempora mutabuntur super
te, donec scias quod dominetur
Excelsus in regno hominum, et
cuicumque voluerit det illud.
Eadem hora sermo completus est
super Nabuchodonosor, et ex hominibus abiectus est, et foenum
ut bos comedit, . . . donec capilli

[1] The Vulgate numbering.

Nabochodonosor āhōf mīne ēagan ūp tō heofonum, and mīn andgit mē wearð forgifen, and ic ðā blētsode þone Hēhstan God, and ic hẹrode and wuldrode þone ðe leofað on ēcnysse, forðanðe his miht is ēce, and his rīce stẹnt on mǣgðe and on mǣgðe. Ealle eorðbūgiende sind tō nāhte getealde on his wiðmetenysse; æfter his willan hē dēð ǣgðer ge on heofonan ge on corðan, and nis nān ðing þe his mihte wiðstande, oððe him tō cweðe: Hwī dēst ðū swā? On ðǣre tīde mīn andgit gewẹnde tō mē, and ic becōm tō wurðmynte mīnes cynerīces, and mīn mẹnnisce hīw mē becōm; mīne witan mē sōhton; and mīn mǣrð wearð geēacnod. Nū eornostlice ic mǣrsige and wuldrige ðone heofonlican Cyning, forðanðe ealle his weorc sind sōðe, and his wegas rihtwīse, and hē mæg geēadmettan þā ðe on mōdignysse farað. *Æ. H. ii.* 432, 434.

5. 1–5. On sumere tīde hē feormode ealle his witan, and hēt beran forð þā gyldenan and sylfrenan māðmfatu, þe his fæder on Godes temple binnon Hierusalem genam. Hī druncon ðā of ðām hālgum fatum, and hẹrodon heora hǣðenan godas; ac fǣrrihte wearð gesewen swilce ānes mannes hand wrītende on ðǣre healle wāge, ætforan ðām cyninge. *Æ. H. ii.* 434.

eius in similitudinem aquilarum crescerent, et ungues eius quasi avium. Igitur post finem dierum ego Nabuchodonosor oculos meos ad coelum levavi, et sensus meus redditus est mihi, et Altissimo benedixi, et viventem in sempiternum laudavi et glorificavi, quia potestas eius potestas sempiterna, et regnum eius in generationem et generationem. Et omnes habitatores terrae apud eum in nihilum reputati sunt; iuxta voluntatem enim suam facit tam in virtutibus coeli quam in habitatoribus terrae, et non est qui resistat manui eius, et dicat ei: Quare fecisti? In ipso tempore sensus meus reversus est ad me, et ad honorem regni mei decoremque perveni, et figura mea reversa est ad me; et optimates mei et magistratus mei requisierunt me; . . . et magnificentia amplior addita est mihi. Nunc igitur ego Nabuchodonosor laudo et magnifico et glorifico Regem coeli, quia omnia opera eius vera, et viae eius iudicia, et gradientes in superbia potest humiliare.

5. 1–5. Baltassar rex fecit grande convivium optimatibus suis mille. . . . Praecepit ergo iam temulentus ut afferrentur vasa aurea et argentea, quae asportaverat Nabuchodonosor pater eius de templo quod fuit in Ierusalem; . . . et biberunt in eis, . . . et laudabant deos suos. . . . In eadem hora apparuerunt digiti, quasi manus hominis scribentis . . . in superficie parietis aulae regiae; et rex aspiciebat articulos manus scribentis.

5. 9. Þā wearð se cyning tō ðān swīðe āfyrht þæt hē eal scranc. Æ. H. ii. 436.

5. 13. And him man lǣdde þone wītegan tō, Danihel. Æ. H. ii. 436.

5. 16, 17. Hē cwæð tō ðām wītegan : Rǣd me þis gewrit, and ic ðē forgife eal purpuran rēaf and gyldenne swūrbēah, and þū bist se ðridda mann tō mē on mīnum rīce. Danihel him andwyrde : Gif ðām þe ðū wille ðīne sylene, ðis gewrit ic ðe gerēcce. Æ. H. ii. 436.

5. 22–31. Ðū noldest ðē warnian þurh þīnes fæder ðrēale, ac drunce of Godes māðmfatum, and herodest ðīne hǣðenan godas, dumbe and dēafe. Nū āsende se Ælmihtiga God þē ðis gewrit þe on ðīnre healle wāge stent : MANE, THECHEL, PHARES. MANE, þæt is, God hæfð geteald þīn rīce, and geendod ; THECHEL, þæt is, hē āwæh ðīn rīce on wǣgan, and hē hit āfunde gewanod ; PHARES, þæt is, ðīn rīce is tōdǣled, and forgifen Medum and Persciscum. Þā hēt se cyning syllan ðām wītegan Danihele purpuran rēaf and gyldenne swūrbēah, and hēt cȳðan geond eall þæt hē wǣre se ðridda man tō him. On ðǣre ylcan nihte cōmon Medas, and ofslōgon þone Balthasar, and Darius Meda fēng tō his rīce. Æ. H. ii. 436.

‖ . . . MANE, THECHEL, PHARES. Æ. H. ii. 434, 436.

5. 9. Unde rex Baltassar satis conturbatus est, et vultus illius immutatus est. . . .

5. 13. Igitur introductus est Daniel coram rege. . . .

5. 16, 17. . . . Si ergo vales scripturam legere, et interpretationem eius indicare mihi, purpura vestieris, et torquem auream circa collum tuum habebis, et tertius in regno meo princeps eris. Ad quae respondens Daniel, ait coram rege : Munera tua sint tibi, et dona domus tuae alteri da ; scripturam autem legam tibi, rex, et interpretationem eius ostendam tibi.

5. 22–31. Tu quoque, filius eius Baltassar, non humiliasti cor tuum, cum scires haec omnia, sed adversum dominatorem coeli elevatus es, et vasa domus eius allata sunt coram te ; et tu, et optimates tui, et uxores tuae, et concubinae tuae vinum bibistis in eis ; deos quoque . . . qui non vident neque audiunt . . . laudasti. . . . Idcirco ab eo missus est articulus manus, quae scripsit hoc quod exaratum est. Haec est autem scriptura quae digesta est : MANE, THECEL, PHARES. Et haec est interpretatio sermonis : MANE, numeravit Deus regnum tuum, et complevit illud ; THECEL, appensus es in statera, et inventus es minus habens ; PHARES, divisum est regnum tuum, et datum est Medis et Persis. Tunc iubente rege in-

K

7. 10. Þūsend ðūsenda ðēnodon þām heofonlican Wealdende, and tēn ðūsend sīðan hundfealde ðūsenda him mid wunodon. Æ. H. i. 348.

9. 21–24. Danihel se wītega sętte ēac on his wītegunge þæt se hēahęngel Gabrihel cōm tō flēogende, and him þus tō cwæð : Ic eom cumen tō ðē, Danihel, tō ðī þæt ic sceal ðē tǣcan, and þū understand mīne sprǣce, and understand þās gesihðe. Fēower hund gēara and hundnigontig gēara sind getealde of ðysum dæge ofer ðē and ofer ðīnum folce, and ofer ðǣre byrig Hierusalem ; and þonne bið sēo ealde forgǣgednys geęndod, and synn underfēhð geęndunge, and unrihtwīsnys bið ādylegod, and bið gebrōht ēce rihtwīsnys, and gesihð and wītegunga bēoð gefyllede, and bið gesmyrod ealra hālgena hālga. Æ. H. ii. 14.

10. 13. Efne, nū Michahel, ān ðæra fyrmestra ealdra, cōm mē tō fultume, and ic wunode ðǣr wið þone cyning Persciscre ðēode. Æ. H. i. 518.

10. 20, 21. Mē cōm tō se hēahęngel, Greciscre þēode ealdor, and nis heora nān mīn gefylsta būton Michahel, Ebreisces folces ealdor. Æ. H. i. 518.

13. 6₅[1] (A. V. Apocrypha : Bel and the Dragon 1). *See* Æ. H. i. 570.

14. 27–42[1] (A. V. Apocrypha : Bel and the Dragon 28–42). Ðā Babiloniscan . . . cwǣdon ānmōdlice tō ðām foresǣdan cyninge

dutus est Daniel purpura, et circumdata est torques aurea collo eius, et praedicatum est de eo quod haberet potestatem tertius in regno suo. Eadem nocte interfectus est Baltassar rex Chaldaeus, et Darius Medus successit in regnum. . . .

7. 10. . . . Millia millium ministrabant ei, et decies millies centena millia assistebant ei. . . .

9. 21–24. . . . Ecce vir Gabriel, . . . cito volans, . . . locutus est mihi, dixitque : Daniel, nunc egressus sum ut docerem te ; . . . tu ergo animadverte sermonem, et intellige visionem. Septuaginta hebdomades abbreviatae sunt super

populum tuum, et super urbem sanctam tuam, ut consummetur praevaricatio, et finem accipiat peccatum, et deleatur iniquitas, et adducatur iustitia sempiterna. et impleatur visio et prophetia, et ungatur sanctus sanctorum.

10. 13. . . . Ecce Michael, unus de principibus primis, venit adiutorium meum, et ego remansi ibi iuxta regem Persarum.

10. 20, 21. . . . Apparuit princeps Graecorum veniens, . . . et nemo est adiutor meus in omnibus his nisi Michael princeps vester.

14. 27–42. Quod cum audissent Babylonii, . . . congregati adversum regem, dixerunt : . . . Bel de-

[1] The Vulgate numbering.

Cyrum : Betǣc ūs Daniel, ðe ūrne god Bel tōwearp, and þone dracan ācwealde þe wē on belȳfdon. Gif ðū hine forstent. wē fordȳlegiað þē and ðīnne hȳred. Þā geseah se cyning þæt hī ānmōde wǣron, and nēadunga þone wītegan him tō handum āscēaf. Hī ðā hine āwurpon into ānum sēaðe, on þām wǣron seofan lēon, þām mann scalde dæghwomlīce twā hrȳðeru and twā scēp ; ac him wæs ðā oftogen ǣlces fōdan six dagas, þæt hī ðone Godes mann ābītan sceoldon.

On þǣre tīde was sum ōðer wītega on Iudea lande—his nama wæs Abacuc—se bær his ryfterum mete tō æcere. Þā cōm him tō Godes engel, and ewað: Abacuc, bær ðone mete tō Babilone. and syle Daniele, se ðe sitt on ðǣra lēona sēaðe. Abacuc andwyrde þām engle : Lā lēof, ne geseah ic nǣfre ðā burh, nē ic ðone sēað nāt. Þā se engel gelæhte hine be ðām fexe, and hine bær tō Babilone, and hine sette bufan ðām sēaðe. Ðā clypode se Abacuc : Þū Godes ðēowa. Daniel, nim ðās lāc ðe þē God sende. Daniel ewað: Mīn Drihten Hælend, sȳ ðē lof and wurðmynt þæt þū mē gemundest. And hē ðā ðǣre sande brēac. Witodlīce Godes engel þǣrrihte mid swyftum flihte gebrōhte ðone discðēn, Abacuc, þǣr hē hine ǣr genām.

Se cyning ðā, Cyrus, on ðām seofoðan dæge ēode drēorig tō ðǣra lēona sēaðe, and innbeseah, and efne, ðā Daniel sittende

struxit, draconem interfecit; . . . trade nobis Danielem. alioquin interficiemus te et domum tuam. Vidit ergo rex quod irruerent in eum vehementer. et, necessitate compulsus. tradidit eis Danielem ; qui miserunt eum in lacum leonum ; et erat ibi diebus sex. Porro in lacu erant leones septem. et dabantur eis duo corpora quotidie, et duae oves; et tunc non data sunt eis, ut devorarent Danielem.

Erat autem Habacuc propheta in Iudaea, et ipse coxerat pulmentum, et intriverat panes in alveolo ; et ibat in campum ut ferret messoribus. Dixitque angelus Domini ad Habacuc : Fer prandium quod habes in Babylonem Danieli, qui est in lacu leonum. Et dixit Habacuc : Domine, Babylonem non vidi, et lacum nescio. Et apprehendit eum angelus Domini in vertice eius, et portavit eum capillo capitis sui, posuitque eum . . . supra lacum. . . . Et clamavit Habacuc. dicens : Daniel, serve Dei, tolle prandium quod misit tibi Deus. Et ait Daniel : Recordatus es mei, Deus. . . . Daniel comedit. Porro angelus Domini restituit Habacuc confestim in loco suo.

Venit ergo rex die septimo ut lugeret Danielem; et venit ad lacum, et introspexit, et ecce Daniel sedens in medio leonum.

wæs gesundful on middan þām lēonum.　Þā clypode se cyning
mid micelre stemne : Mǣre is se God þe Daniel on belȳfð.　And
hē ðū mid þām worde hine ātēah of ðām scræfe, and hēt inn-
āwurpan ðā þe hine ǣr fordōn woldon.　Þæs cyninges hās
wearð hrædlice gefremmed, and þæs wītegan ōhteras wurdon
āsceofene betwux ðā lēon, and hī ðǣrrihte mid grǣdigum
ceaflum hī ealle tōtǣron.　Þā cwæð se cyning : Forhtion and
ondrǣdon ealle eorðbūende Danieles God, forðanðe hē is
Alȳsend and Hǣlend, wyrcende tācna and wundra on heofonan
and on eorðan.　Æ. H. i. 570, 572 ; cf. i. 488.

IIOSEA.

4. 8. Hī etað mīnes folces synna.　Æ. H. ii. 536.

6. 6. Ic wylle mildheortnysse, and nā offrunge.　Æ. H. ii. 470 ; cf.
Matt. 9. 13.

11. 1. Of Egypta lande ic geclypode mīnne sunu.　Æ. H. i. 80.

JOEL.

1. 17. Ðā nȳtenu forrotedon on heora meoxe.　Æ. H. i. 118.

2. 28. *See* Acts 2. 1 ff.

2. 32. Ǣlc ðǣra manna þe Godes naman clypað bið gehealden.
Æ. H. ii. 392.

AMOS.

1. 1. *See* Æ. H. i. 322.

5. 13. Hit is āwriten be ðām yfelum tīman, þæt se snotera
sceal suwian, ðonne hē gesihð þæt sēo bodung næfð nænne
forðgang.　Æ. H. ii. 340.

Et exclamavit voce magna rex,
dicens : Magnus es, Domine Deus
Danielis. Et extraxit eum de lacu
leonum. Porro illos qui perdi-
tionis eius causa fuerant intro-
misit in lacum, et devorati sunt
in momento coram eo.　Tunc rex
ait : Paveant omnes habitantes in
universa terra Deum Danielis,
quia ipse est salvator, faciens
signa et mirabilia in terra. . . .

6. 6. . . . Misericordiam volui, et
non sacrificium. . . .

11. 1. . . . Ex Aegypto vocavi filium
meum.

JOEL.

1. 17. Computruerunt iumenta in
stercore suo. . . .

2. 32. . . . Omnis qui invocaverit
nomen Domini salvus erit. . . .

IIOSEA.

4. 8. Peccata populi mei comedent. . . .

AMOS.

5. 13. Ideo prudens in tempore illo
tacebit, quia tempus malum est.

JONAH.

1. 1-5, 7-9, 11, 12, 15-17. God spræc tō ānum wītegan, se wæs
Ionas gehāten: Far tō ðǣre byrig Niniuen, and boda ðǣr ða
word þe ic þē sęcge. Þā wearð se wītega āfyrht, and wolde for-
flēon Godes gesihðe, ac hē ne mihte. Fērde ða tō sǣ, and stāh
on scip. Đā-ða þa scypmęn cōmon ūt on sǣ, þā sęnde him God
tō micelne wind and hrēohnysse, swā þæt hī wǣron orwēne
heora līfes. Hī ða wurpon heora waru oforbord, and se wītega
læg and slēp. Hī wurpon ða tān betweox him, and bǣdon þæt
God sceolde geswutelian hwanon him þæt ungelimp becōme:
þā com ðæs wītegan tā upp. Hī āxodon hine hwæt hē wǣre,
oððe hū hē faran wolde? Hē cwæð þæt hē wǣre Godes ðēow,
se ðe gescēop sǣ and land, and þæt hē flēon wolde of Godes
gesihðe. Hī cwǣdon: Hū dō wē ymbe ðē? Hē andwyrde:
Weorpað mē oforbord, þonne geswīcð þēos gedręccednys.
Hī ða swā dydon, and sēo hrēohnys wearð gestilled, and hī
offrodon Gode heora lāc, and tugon forð. God ða gegearcode
ænne hwæl, and hē forswealh þone wītegan. Æ. H. i. 244, 246.

1. 17. *See* Æ. H. i. 488.

2. 10 (Vulg. 11). And ābær hine tō ðām lande þe hē tō sceolde, and
hine ðǣr ūtāspāw. Æ. H. i. 246.

JONAH.

1. 1-5, 7-9, 11, 12, 15, 16; **2.** 1 [1]. Et
factum est verbum Domini ad
Ionam, ... dicens: Surge, et vade
in Niniven civitatem grandem, et
praedica in ea. ... Et surrexit
Ionas, ut fugeret ... a facie Domini.... Et invenit navem, ... et
descendit in eam ut iret cum eis.
... Dominus autem misit ventum
magnum in mare, et facta est
tempestas magna in mari, et navis
periclitabatur conteri. Et timuerunt nautae, et clamaverunt viri
ad deum suum; et miserunt vasa,
quae erant in navi, in mare, ut
alleviaretur ab eis; et Ionas descendit ad interiora navis, et dormiebat sopore gravi. ... Et dixit
vir ad collegam suum: Venite, et
mittamus sortes, et sciamus quare
hoc malum sit nobis. Et miserunt sortes; et cecidit sors super
Ionam. Et dixerunt ad eum:
Indica nobis cuius causa malum
istud sit nobis: quod est opus
tuum? quae terra tua? et quo
vadis? vel ex quo populo es tu?
Et dixit ad eos: ... Dominum
Deum coeli ego timeo, qui fecit
mare et aridam.... Et dixerunt
ad eum: Quid faciemus tibi? ...
Et dixit ad eos: Tollite me, et
mittite in mare, et cessabit mare
a vobis. ... Et tulerunt Ionam, et
miserunt in mare, et stetit mare
a fervore suo. Et ... immola-
verunt hostias Domino. ... Et
praeparavit Dominus piscem grandem ut deglutiret Ionam. ...
2. 11. ... Et evomuit Ionam in
aridam.

[1] The Vulgate numbering.

3. 1–4, 6, 7. Þā cōm eft Godes word tō ðām wītegan, and cwæð: Ārīs nū, and gā tō ðǣre mycclan byrig Niniuen, and boda swā-swā ic ðē ǣr sǣde. Hē fērde, and bodode þæt him wæs Godes grama onsīgende, gif hī tō Gode būgan noldon. Ðā ārās se cyning of his cynesetle, and āwearp his dēorwyrðe rēaf, and dyde hǣran tō his līce, and axan uppan his hēafod, and bēad þæt ǣlc man swā dōn sceolde, and ǣgðer ge men ge ðā sūcendan cild, and ēac ða nȳtenu, ne onbyrigdon nānes ðinges binnan ðrīm dagum. Æ. H. i. 246.

3. 10. See Æ. H. i. 246.

MICAH.

5. 2. See Matt. 2. 6 (2. 1–15).

5. 5. Þonne bið sib on eorðan, þonne ūre Drihten [sic] cymð tō ūrum lande, and ðonne hē gǣð intō ūrum hūsum. Æ. H. ii. 12.

HABAKKUK.

2. 4. Se rihtwīsa leofað be his geleafan. Æ. H. i. 134.

ZEPHANIAH.

1. 14–16. Se miccla Godes dæg is swiðe gehende and ðearle swyft; biter bið þæs dæges stemn; þǣr bið se stranga gedrēfed. Se dæg is yrres dæg, and gedrēfednysse dæg and angsumnysse, yrmðe dæg and wānunge, þēostra dæg and dimnysse, bȳman dæg and cyrmes. Æ. H. i. 618.

3. 1–4, 6, 7. Et factum est verbum Domini ad Ionam secundo, dicens: Surge, et vade in Niniven civitatem magnam, et praedica in ea praedicationem quam ego loquor ad te. Et surrexit Ionas, et abiit in Niniven; . . . et clamavit, et dixit: Adhuc quadraginta dies, et Ninive subvertetur. . . . Et pervenit verbum ad regem Ninive; et surrexit de solio suo, et abiecit vestimentum suum a se, et indutus est sacco, et sedit in cinere. Et clamavit, et dixit in Ninive ex ore regis et principum eius, dicens: Homines, et iumenta, et boves, et pecora non gustent quidquam, nec pascantur, et aquam non bibant.

MICAH.

5. 5. Et erit iste pax, cum venerit Assyrius in terram nostram, et quando calcaverit in domibus nostris. . . .

HABAKKUK.

2. 4. . . . Iustus autem in fide sua vivet.

ZEPHANIAH.

1. 14–16. Iuxta est dies Domini magnus, iuxta est et velox nimis;

ZECHARIAH.

2. 8. Sē ðe ēow hrepað, hit mē bið swā egle swylce hē hreppe ða
sēo mīnes ēagan. *Æ. H. i.* 390.

Sē ðe ēow hrepað, hit bið mē swā egle swilce hē hreppe mīnes
ēagan sēo. *Æ. H. i.* 516.

9. 9. Þīn cyning cymð tō ðē ēadmōd, and geedstaðelað þē¹.
Æ. H. ii. 14.

13. 9. *See* 1 Pet. 1. 7.

MALACHI.

1. 2, 3. . . . þæt God lufode Iacob, and hatode Esau.   *Æ. H. i.* 110.

4. 2. . . . rihtwīsnysse Sunu.   *Æ. H. ii.* 224.

TOBIT.

11. 15. *See* *Æ. H. ii.* 136.

12. 12. Þā-ðā gē ēow gebædon, ic offrode ēower gebedu ætforan
Gode. *Æ. H. i.* 518.

WISDOM OF SOLOMON.

1. 1. Lufiað rihtwīsnesse, gē ðe on eorðan dēmað; onenāwað
ēowerne God mid gōdnesse symle, and mid heortan ānfealdnysse
sēcað hine georne. *Æ. H. ii.* 320.

1. 7. Godes gāst gefylð ealne ymbhwyrft middangeardes, and hē
hylt ealle ðing, and hē hæfð ingehȳd ǣlces gereordes. *Æ. H. i.* 280.

‖ Godes gāst gefylð ealre eorðan ymbhwyrft.   *Æ. H. ii.* 44.

vox diei Domini amara; tribula-
bitur ibi fortis.   Dies irae dies
illa, dies tribulationis et angus-
tiae, dies calamitatis et miseriae,
dies tenebrarum et caliginis, dies
nebulae et turbinis, dies tubae et
clangoris. . . .

ZECHARIAH.

2. 8. . . . Qui enim tetigerit vos,
tangit pupillam oculi mei.

9. 9. Ecce rex tuus veniet tibi iustus, et salvator; ipse pauper. . . .

MALACHI.

1. 2, 3. . . . Dilexi Iacob, Esau autem
odio habui. . . .

4. 2. . . . Sol iustitiae.

TOBIT.

12. 12. Quando orabas, . . . ego ob-
tuli orationem tuam Domino.

WISDOM OF SOLOMON.

1. 1. Diligite iustitiam, qui iudicatis.
terram; sentite de Domino in
bonitate, et in simplicitate cordis
quaerite illum.

1. 7. Quoniam spiritus Domini replevit orbem terrarum, et hoc
quod continet omnia scientium
habet vocis.

¹ Attributed to Ezekiel by Ælfric.

3. 9. Būton gē hit gelȳfan, ne mage gē hit understandan.
Æ. H. i. 280.

5. 21. Eorðan ymbhwyrft fiht for Gode ongēan þā andgitlēasan.
Æ. H. ii. 540.

ECCLESIASTICUS.

3. 20. Þonne ðū mǣre sȳ, geēadmēd þē sylfne on eallum ðingum.
and ðū gemētst gife and lēan mid Gode.   Æ. H. i. 200.

3. 30 (Vulg. 33). Swā-swā wæter ādwǣscð fyr. swā ādwǣscð sēo
ælmesse synna.   Æ. H. ii. 106.

5. 7 (Vulg. 8, 9). Ne ylca ðū tō gecyrrenne tō Gode, ðȳ-lǣs-þe se
tīma losige þurh ðā sleacan ylcunge.   Æ. H. 282.

7. 36 (Vulg. 40). On eallum ðīnum weorcum bēo ðū gemyndig
þīnes yndenēxtan dæges, and on ēcnysse ðū ne syngast.
Æ. H. i. 408.

|| On eallum ðingum bēo ðū gemyndig þīnes yndenēxtan
dæges, and þū ne syngast on ēcnysse.   Æ. H. i. 482.

25. 16 (Vulg. 23). . . . þæt sēlre wǣre tō wunigenne mid lēon and
dracan þonne mid yfelan wīfe and ofersprǣcum.   Æ. H. i. 486.

27. 6. Lǣmene fatu bēoð on ofne āfandode, and rihtwīse menn on
gedrēfednysse heora costnunge.   Æ. H. i. 554.

34. 24. Þā ælmessan þe of rēaflāce bēoð gesealde sind Gode swā
gecwēme swilce hwā ācwelle ōðres mannes cild, and bringe ðām
fæder þæt hēafod tō lāce.   Æ. H. ii. 102.

50. 8. And, swā-swā on lengctenlicere tīde, rōsena blōstman and
lilian hī ymtrymedon.   Æ. H. i. 444.

---

3. 9. Qui confidunt in illo intelligent veritatem. . . .

5. 21. . . . Pugnabit cum illo (Æ. pro eo) orbis terrarum contra insensatos.

ECCLESIASTICUS.

3. 20. Quanto magnus es, humilia te in omnibus, et coram Deo invenies gratiam.

3. 33. Ignem ardentem extinguit aqua, et eleemosyna resistit peccatis.

5. 8, 9. Non tardes converti ad Dominum; . . . subito enim veniet ira illius, et in tempore vindictae disperdet te.

7. 40. In omnibus operibus tuis memorare novissima tua, et in aeternum non peccabis.

25. 23. . . . Commorari leoni et draconi placebit, quam habitare cum muliere nequam.

27. 6. Vasa figuli probat fornax, et homines iustos tentatio tribulationis.

34. 24. Qui offert sacrificium ex substantia pauperum quasi qui victimat filium in conspectu patris sui.

50. 8. . . . Quasi flos rosarum in diebus vernis, et quasi lilia. . . .

SONG OF THE THREE HOLY CHILDREN.

24–26. *See* Dan. 3. 47–49.

BEL AND THE DRAGON.

1. *See* Dan. 13. 65.

28–42. *See* Dan. 14. 27–42.

MATTHEW.

1. 18–20. Ac ðā-ðā Ioseph undergeat þæt Maria mid cilde wæs. þā wearð hē drēorig, and nolde hire genēalǣcan, ac ðōhte þæt hē wolde hī dīglice forlǣtan. Þā-ðā Ioseph þis smēade, þā cōm him tō Godes engel, and bebēad him þæt sceolde habban gȳmene ǣgðer ge ðǣre mēder ge þæs cildes, and cwæð þæt þæt cild nǣre of nānum men gestrȳned, ac wǣre of þām Hālgan Gāste. Æ. H. i. 196.

1. 21. . . . Iesus, and on ūrum gereorde Hǣlend, forðanðe hē gehǣlð his folc fram heora synnum. Æ. H. i. 94.

1. 23. Efne, sceal mǣden geēacnian on hire innoðe, and ācennan sunu ; and his nama bið gecīged Emmanuhel, þæt is gereht on ūrum geðēode : God is mid ūs. Æ. H. i. 192, 194 ; cf. Isa. 7. 14.

∥ Efne, ān mǣden sceal gēacnian, and ācennan sunu : and his nama bið Emmanuhel, þæt is gereht : God is mid ūs.

Æ. H. ii. 14.

2. 1–15. Þā-ðā se Hǣlend ācenned wæs on þǣre Iudeiscan Bethleem, on Herodes dagum cyninges, efne, ðā cōmon fram ēastdǣle middangeardes þrȳ tungelwītegan tō ðǣre byrig Hierusalem, þus befrīnende : Hwǣr is Iudeiscra lēoda cyning, se ðe

MATTHEW.

1. 18–20. . . . Inventa est in utero habens. . . . Ioseph autem vir eius, cum esset iustus et nollet eam traducere, voluit occulte dimittere eam. Haec autem eo cogitante, ecce, angelus Domini apparuit in somnis ei, dicens : Ioseph fili David, noli timere accipere Mariam coniugem tuam ; quod enim in ea natum est de Spiritu Sancto est.

1. 21. . . . Iesum ; ipse enim salvum faciet populum suum a peccatis corum.

1. 23. Ecce, virgo in utero habebit, et pariet filium ; et vocabunt nomen eius Emmanuel, quod est interpretatum : Nobiscum Deus.

2. 1–15. Cum ergo natus esset Iesus in Bethlehem Iuda, in diebus Herodis regis, ecce magi ab oriente venerunt Ierosolymam, dicentes : Ubi est qui natus est rex Iudae-

ācęnned is? Wē gesāwon sōðlice his steorran on ēastdǣle, and wē cōmon tō ðī þæt wē ūs tō him gebiddon. Hwæt, ðā Herodes cyning, þis gehȳrende, wearð micclum āstyred, and eal sēo burhwaru samod mid him. Hē ðā gesamnode ealle þā ealdorbiscopas and ðæs folces bōceras, and befrān hwǣr Crīstes cęnningstōw wǣre. Hī sǣdon : On ðǣre Iudeiscan Bethleem ; þus sōðlice is āwriten þurh ðone wītegan Micheam : Ēalā þū Bethleem, Iudeisc land, ne eart ðū nāteshwōn wācost burga on Iudeiscum ealdrum ; of ðē cymð se hęretoga se ðe gewylt and gewissað Israhela folc. Ðā clypode Herodes þā ðrȳ tungelwītegan on sundersprǣce, and geornlice hī befrān tō hwilces tīman se steorra him ǣrst ætēowode ; and āsęnde hī tō Bethleem, ðus cweðende : Farað ārdlice, and befrīnað be ðām cilde ; and þonne gē hit gemētað, cȳðað mē, þæt ic mage mē tō him gebiddan. Þā tungelwītegan fērdon æfter þæs cyninges sprǣce ; and efne, ðā se steorra, þe hī on ēastdǣle gesāwon, glād him beforan, oð-þæt hē gestōd bufon ðām gęsthūse þǣr þæt cild on wunode. Hī gesāwon ðone steorran, and þearle blissodon. Ēodon ðā inn, and þæt cild gemētton mid Marian his mēder, and niðerfeallende hī tō him gebǣdon. Hī geopenodon heora hordfatu, and him lāc geoffrodon — gold, and rēcels, and myrram. Hwæt, ðā God on swefne hī gewarnode and bebēad þæt hī eft ne cyrdon tō ðān rēðan cyninge Herode, ac þurh ōðerne weg hine for-

orum ? vidimus enim stellam eius in oriente, et venimus adorare eum. Audiens autem Herodes rex turbatus est, et omnis Ierosolyma cum illo ; et congregans omnes principes sacerdotum et scribas populi, sciscitabatur ab eis ubi Christus nasceretur. At illi dixerunt ei : In Bethlehem Iudae ; sic enim scriptum est per prophetam : Et tu, Bethlehem, terra Iuda, nequaquam minima es in principibus Iuda ; ex te enim exiet dux qui regat populum meum Israel. Tunc Herodes, clam vocatis magis, diligenter didicit ab eis tempus stellae quae apparuit eis ; et mittens illos in Bethlehem, dixit : Ite, et interrogate diligenter de puero ; et cum inveneritis, renuntiate mihi, ut et ego veniens adorem eum. Qui cum audissent regem, abierunt ; et ecce stella quam viderant in oriente antecedebat eos, usque dum veniens staret supra ubi erat puer. Videntes autem stellam gavisi sunt gaudio magno valde. Et intrantes domum, invenerunt puerum cum Maria matre eius, et procidentes adoraverunt eum ; et, apertis thesauris suis, obtulerunt ei munera - aurum, thus, et myrrham. Et responso accepto in somnis ne redirent ad Herodem, per aliam viam reversi sunt

cyrdon, and swā tō heora ēðelo becōmon.   Efne, ðā Godes
ęngel ætēowode Iosepe, ðæs cildes fōsterfæder. on swefnum,
eweðende: Ārīs, and nim þis cild mid þǣre mēder, and flōoh
tō Egypta lande, and bēo þǣr ōð-þæt ic þē ęft sęcge; sōðlice
tōweard is þæt Horodes smēað hū hē þæt cild fordō.   Ioseph
ðā ārās nihtes, and þæt cild mid þǣre mēder samod tō Egypta
lande fęrede, and þǣr wunode ōð-þæt Herodes gewāt; þæt sēo
wītegung wǣre gefylled, þe be ðǣre fare ūr ðus cwæð: Of
Egypta lande ic geclypode mīnne sunu.   Æ. H. i. 78, 80.

|| Þā-ðā se Hǣlend ācęnned wæs on þǣre Iudeiscan Bethleem,
on Herodes dagum cyninges, efne, ðā cōmon fram ēastdǣle
middangeardes ðrȳ tungelwītegan tō ðǣre byrig Hierusalem,
þus befrīnende: Hwǣr is Iudeiscra lēoda cyning, se ðe ācęnned
is?   Æ. H. i. 104.

|| Hwǣr is sē ðe ācęnned is? . . . Iudea cyning.   Æ. H. i. 106.

|| Wē cōmon tō ðȳ ðæt wē ūs tō him gebiddan.   Æ. H. i. 108.

|| Þū Bethleem, Iudeisc land, ne eart ðū wācost burga on
Iudeiscum ealdrum; sōðlice of ðē cymð se lāttēow þe gewylt
Israhela ðēoda.   Æ. H. i. 34.

|| Þā tungelwītegan ēodon intō ðæs cildes gęsthūse, and
hine gemētton mid þǣre mēder.   Hī ðā mid astręhtum līchaman hī tō Crīste gebǣdon, and geopenodon heora hordfatu, and him geoffrodon þrȳfealde lāc—gold, and rēcels, and
myrran.   Æ. H. i. 116.

2. 16–18. Hē . . . geseah þæt hē wæs bepǣht fram ðām tungel-
wītegum, and wearð þā ðearle gegręmod.   Sęnde ðā his
cwelleras, and ofslōh ealle ðā hysecild þe wǣron on þǣre byrig
Bethleem and on eallum hyre gemǣrum, fram twiwintrum
cilde tō ānre nihte, be ðǣre tīde þe hē geāxode æt ðām tungel-
wītegum.   Þā wæs gefylled Hieremias wītegung, þe ðus wītegode: Stemn is gehȳred on hēannysse, micel wōp and ðoterung;

in regionem suam. Qui cum re-
cessissent, ecce, angelus Domini
apparuit in somnis Ioseph, dicens: Surge, et accipe puerum et
matrem eius, et fuge in Aegyptum,
et esto ibi usque dum dicam tibi;
futurum est enim ut Herodes
quaerat puerum ad perdendum
eum.   Qui consurgens accepit
puerum et matrem eius nocte, et
secessit in Aegyptum, et erat ibi
usque ad obitum Herodis; ut
adimpleretur quod dictum est a
Domino per prophetam dicentem:
Ex Aegypto vocavi filium meum.
2. 16–18. Tunc Herodes, videns quoniam illusus esset a magis, iratus
est valde, et mittens occidit omnes pueros qui erant in Bethlehem et in omnibus finibus eius,

Rachel bewēop hire cildru. and nolde bēon gefrēfrod, forðanðe hī ne sind. Æ. H. i. 80.

Rachel bewēop hire cildra. and nolde bēon gefrēfrod, forðanþe hī ne sind. Æ. H. i. 84.

2. 19, 20. Efne. ðā Godes ęngel, æfter Herodes dēaðe. ætēowode Iosepe on swefnum on Egypta lande, þus cweðende : Ārīs. and nim þæt cild and his mōder samod. and gewęnd ongēan tō Israhela lande ; soðlice hī sind forðfarene ðā ðe ymbe þæs cildes feorh syrwdon. Æ. H. i. 88.

" Se ęngel cwæð tō Iosepe : Þā sind forðfarene þe embe ðæs cildes feorh syrwdon. Æ. H. i. 88.

2. 21-23. Hē ðā ārās, swā-swā se ęngel him bebēad, and fęrode þæt cild mid þǣre mēder tō Israhela lande. Þā gefrān Ioseph þæt Archelaus rīxode on Iudea lande æfter his fæder Herode. and ne dorste his nēawiste genēalǣcan. Þā wearð hē ęft on swefne gemynegod þæt hē tō Galilea gewęnde. . . . Þæt cild ðā eardode on þǣre byrig þe is gehāten Nazareth. þæt sēo wītegung wǣre gefylled, þe cwæð þæt hē sceolde bēon Nazarenisc gecīged. Æ. H. i. 88 ; cf. i. 478.

3. 2. Behrēowsiað ēowre synna. and wyrcað dǣdbōte. forðanþe Godes rīce genēalǣhð. Æ. H. ii. 38.

3. 3. See Isa. 40. 3, 4.

3. 4. Eal his rēaf wæs āwefen of olfendes hǣrum ; his bigleofa wæs strðlic ; ne dranc hē wīnes dręnc, ne nānes gemęncgedes

a bimatu et infra. secundum tempus quod exquisierat a magis. Tunc adimpletum est quod dictum est per Ieremiam prophetam dicentem : Vox in Rama audita est, ploratus et ululatus multus ; Rachel plorans filios suos. et noluit consolari. quia non sunt.

2. 19, 20. Defuncto autem Herode, ecce. angelus Domini apparuit in somnis Ioseph in Aegypto, dicens : Surge, et accipe puerum et matrem eius. et vade in terram Israel ; defuncti sunt enim qui quaerebant animam pueri.

2. 21-23. Qui consurgens, accepit puerum et matrem eius, et venit in terram Israel. Audiens autem quod Archelaus regnaret in Iudaea pro Herode patre suo, timuit illo ire ; et admonitus in somnis. secessit in partes Galilaeae. . . . Habitavit in civitate quae vocatur Nazareth. ut adimpleretur quod dictum est per prophetas : Quoniam Nazaraeus vocabitur.

3. 2. . . . Poenitentiam agite ; appropinquavit enim regnum coelorum.

3. 4. Ipse autem Ioannes habebat vestimentum de pilis camelorum. et zonam pelliceam circa lumbas suos ; esca autem eius erat locustae et mel silvestre.

wǣtan nē gebrowenes[1]; ofet hine fēdde and wudehunig, and ōðre wāclice ðigena. Æ. H. i. 352.

‖ Ne dranc hē nāðor nē wīn, nē bēor, nē ealu, nē nān ðǣra wǣtan ðe męnn of drunceniað[1]; ac æt him ofet and þæt þæt hē on wuda findan mihte. Eall his rēaf wæs geworht of oluendes hǣre. Æ. H. ii. 38.

‖ Hē wæs mid olfendes hǣrum gescrȳd, wāclice and strǣlice. Æ. H. i. 330.

3. 12. . . . gegaderað þæt clǣne corn intō his bęrne : . . . þæt ceaf hē forbærnð on unādwǣscendlicum fȳre. Æ. H. ii. 68.

3. 13. Þā cōm hē on ðisum dæge tō Iohannes fulluhte, æt ðǣre ēa þe is gehāten Iordanis, and wolde bēon gefullod æt his handum. Æ. H. ii. 38.

3. 14–17. Hē cwæð þā tō Crīste : Lā lēof, ic sceal bēon gefullod æt ðīnum handum, and þū cymst tō mīnum fulluhte. Crīst ðā him geandwyrde : Lǣt nū ðus, and geðafa ðis ; swā unc gedafenað, þæt wit gefyllon ealle rihtwīsnysse. Iohannes ðā geðafode þæt hē Crīst gefullode. Þā-ðā hē gefullod wæs, þā wearð sēo heofon geopenod bufon his hēafde, and Godes Gāst cōm on ānre culfran hīwe, and gesæt bufon Crīste ; and þæs Fæder stemn clypode of heofonum, and þus cwæð : Ðes is mīn lēofa Sunu, and hē mē wel līcað. Æ. H. ii. 38, 40 ; cf. i. 104, 320, ii. 42, 44.

‖ Þǣr cōm ðā stemn þæs Fæder of heofonum, ðus cweðende : Ðes is mīn lēofa Sunu, ðe mē wel līcað. Æ. H. ii. 42.

‖ Ðes is mīn lēofa Sunu, ðe mē wel līcað. Æ. H. ii. 62 ; cf. Matt. 17. 1–5.

4. 1–11. Se Hǣlend wæs gelǣd fram þām Hālgan Gāste tō ānum wēstene, tō ðȳ þæt hē wǣre gecostnod fram dēofle ; and hē ðā fæste fēowertig daga and fēowertig nihta, swā þæt hē ne on-

3. 12. . . . Congregabit triticum suum in horreum, paleas autem comburet igni inextinguibili.

3. 13. Tunc venit Iesus a Galilaea in Iordanem ad Ioannem, ut baptizaretur ab eo.

3. 14–17. Ioannes autem prohibebat eum, dicens : Ego a te debeo baptizari, et tu venis ad me? Respondens autem Iesus, dixit ei : Sine modo ; sic enim decet nos implere omnem iustitiam. Tunc dimisit eum. Baptizatus autem Iesus, . . . ecce, aperti sunt ei coeli, et vidit Spiritum Dei descendentem sicut columbam, et venientem super se ; et ecce, vox de coelis dicens : Hic est Filius meus dilectus, in quo mihi complacui.

4. 1–11. Tunc Iesus ductus est in desertum a Spiritu, ut tentaretur

---

[1] From Luke 1. 15, 'vinum et siceram non bibet.'

byrigde ǣtes ne wǣtes on eallum þām fyrste ; ac siðð̆an him
hingrode. Þā gentalǣhte se costnere, and him tō cwæð : Gif
ð̆u sȳ Godes Sunu, cweð̆ tō ð̆isum stānum þæt hī bēon āwę̄nde
tō hlāfum. Dā andwearde se Hǣlend, and cwæð̆: Hit is
āwriten : Ne leofað̆ se mann nā be hlāfe ānum, ac lyfað̆ be
eallum ð̆ām wordum þe gāð̆ of Godes mūð̆e. Þā genam se
dēofol hine, and gesę̄tte hine uppan ð̆ām scylfe þæs hēagan
temples, and cwæð̆: Gif ð̆u Godes Sunu sȳ, feall nū ādūn :
hit is āwriten þæt englum is beboden be ð̆ē, þæt hī ð̆e on hira
handum āhę̄bbon, þæt þū furð̆on ne ð̆urfe ð̆īnne fōt ait stāne
ǣtspurnan. Þā cwæð̆ se Hǣlend ę̄ft him tō : Hit is āwriten :
Ne fanda þīnes Drihtnes. Þā genam se dēofol hine ę̄ft, and
gesę̄tte hine uppan ānre swīð̆e hēahre dūne, and ǣtēowde him
ealles middangēardes welan and his wuldor, and cwæð̆ him tō :
Ealle ð̆ās ð̆ing ic forgife ð̆ē, gif ð̆u wilt feallan tō mīnum fōtum
and gebiddan þe tō mē. Dā cwæð̆ se Hǣlend him tō : Gā ð̆u
underbæce, sceocca ! Hit is āwriten : Gehwā sceal hine gebiddan tō his Drihtne ānum, and him ānum ð̆ēowian. Þā
forlēt se dēofol hine ; and him cōmon ę̄nglas tō, and him
ð̆ēnodon. Æ. H. i. 166 ; cf. ii. 100.

∥ Se Hālga Gāst lǣdde þone Hǣlend tō þām wę̄stene, tō ð̆ȳ
ð̆æt hē wǣre þǣr gecostnod. Æ. H. i. 166.

∥ Hwī hingrað̆ þē ? Gif ð̆u Godes Sunu sȳ, wę̄nd þās stānas
tō hlāfum, and et. Æ. H. i. 168.

a diabolo. Et cum ieiunasset
quadraginta diebus et quadraginta noctibus, postea esuriit. Et
accedens tentator dixit ei : Si
Filius Dei es, dic ut lapides isti
panes fiant. Qui respondens dixit :
Scriptum est : Non in solo pane
vivit homo, sed in omni verbo
quod procedit de ore Dei. Tunc
assumpsit eum diabolus in sanctam civitatem, et statuit eum
super pinnaculum templi, et dixit
ei : Si Filius Dei es, mitte te deorsum ; scriptum est enim : Quia
angelis suis mandavit de te, et
in manibus tollent te, ne forte
offendas ad lapidem pedem tuum.
Ait illi Iesus : Rursum scriptum
est : Non tentabis Dominum Deum
tuum. Iterum assumpsit eum diabolus in montem excelsum valde,
et ostendit ei omnia regna mundi,
et gloriam eorum, et dixit ei :
Haec omnia tibi dabo, si cadens
adoraveris me. Tunc dicit ei
Iesus : Vade (Æ. ins. retro [1]),
Satana ; scriptum est enim : Dominum Deum tuum adorabis, et
illi soli servies. Tunc reliquit
eum diabolus ; et ecce, angeli accesserunt, et ministrabant ei.

[1] See Ælfric's discussion, i. 172.

‖ Cweð tō ðysum stānum þæt hī bēon tō hlāfum āwęnde,
and et.   Æ. H. i. 176.

‖ Ne lifað nā se man be hlāfe ānum, ac lifað be ðām wordum
ðe gāð of Godes mūðe.   Æ. H. i. 168.

‖ And hē ðā hine genam, and bær upp on þæt templ, and
hine sętte æt ðām scylfe, and cwæð tō him: Gif ðū Godes
Sunu sȳ, scēot ādūn; forðanþe ęnglum is beboden be ðe,
þæt hī ðē on handum āhębban, þæt þū ne ðurfe ðīnne fōt
æt stāne ætspurnan.   Æ. H. i. 168, 170; cf. Ps. 91. 11, 12.

‖ Ne sceal man fandigan his Drihtnes.   Æ. H. i. 170.

‖ Ne sceal man his Drihtnes fandian.   Æ. H. i. 170.

‖ Þā genam hē hine eft, and ābær hine upp on āne dūne, and
ætȳwde him ealles middangeardes welan and his wuldor, and
cwæð tō him: Ealle ðās ðing ic forgife ðē, gif ðū wilt āfeallan
tō mīnum fōtum, and þē tō mē gebiddan.   Æ. H. i. 170.

‖ Hē cwæð: Þās ðing ic forgife ðē.   Æ. H. i. 172.

‖ Crīst cwæð ðā tō ðām dēofle: Gā ðū underbæcc, sceocca!
Hit is āwriten: Man sceal hine gebiddan tō his Drihtne, and
him ānum ðēowian.   Æ. H. i. 172.

‖ Þā forlēt se dēofol Crīst, and him cōmon ęnglas tō, and
him ðēnodon.   Æ. H. i. 174.

4. 18. Crīst on sumere tīde fērde wið þære Galileiscan sǣ, and
geseah twōgen gebrōðra,—Simonem, se wæs gecīged Petrus,
and his brōðor Andream.   Æ. H. i. 576.

4. 20. Petrus and Andreas, be Crīstes hǣse, ðǣrrihte forlēton
heora nętt, and him fyligdon.   Æ. H. i. 578.

5. 1–3. . . . þæt se Hǣlend . . . gesāwe micele męnigu him fyl-
igende; þā āstāh hē upp on āne dūne. Þā-ðā hē gesæt, þā
genēalǣhton his leorningcnihtas him tō, and hē undyde his
mūð, and hī lǣrde, þus cweðende: Ēadige bēoð þā gāstlican
ðearfan.   Æ. H. i. 548.

‖ Ēadige bēoð þā gāstlican ðearfan, forðanþe heora is heofonan rīce.   Æ. H. i. 550.

---

4. 18. Ambulans autem Iesus iuxta
mare Galilaeae, vidit duos fratres,
– Simonem, qui vocatur Petrus,
et Andream fratrem eius. . . .

4. 20. At illi continuo, relictis reti-
bus, secuti sunt eum.

5. 1–3. Videns autem Iesus turbas,
ascendit in montem. Et cum se-
disset, accesserunt ad eum discipuli eius, et, aperiens os suum,
docebat eos, dicens: Beati pauperes spiritu, quoniam ipsorum
est regnum coelorum.

5. 4. Ēadige bēoð ðā þe hēofiað, forðanðe hī bēoð gefrēfrode. *Æ. H. i. 550.*

‖ Ēadige bēoð þā þe heora synna bewēpað, forðanðe hī bēoð gefrēfrode. *Æ. H. i. 142.*

‖ Ēadige bēoð ðā ðe nū wēpað, forðonðe hī sceolon bēon gefrēfrode.

5. 5. Ēadige bēoð þā līðan, forðanþe hī þæt land geāgniað. *Æ. H. i. 550.*

5. 6. Ēadige bēoð þā þe sind ofhingrode and ofþyrste æfter riht-wīsnysse, forðanðe hī bēoð gefyllede. *Æ. H. i. 550.*

‖ Ēadige bēoð þā þe sind ofhingrode and ofÞyste rihtwīsnysse, forðanðe hī sceolon bēon gefyllede mid rihtwīsnysse. *Æ. H. i. 202.*

5. 7–9. Ēadige bēoð þā mildheortan, forðanþe hī begytað mild-heortnysse. . . . Ēadige bēoð þā clǣnheortan, forðanðe hī gesēoð God sylfne. . . . Ēadige bēoð þā gesibsuman, forðanðe hī bēoð Godes bearn gecīgede. *Æ. H. i. 552.*

‖ Crīst cwæð be gesibsumum mannum, þæt hī sind Godes bearn gecīgede. *Æ. H. i. 604.*

5. 10–12. Ēadige bēoð ðā ðe þoliað ēhtnysse for rihtwīsnysse, forðanðe heora is heofonan rīce. . . . Ēadige gē bēoð þonne man ēow wyrigð, and ēower ēht, and ǣlc yfel ongēan ēow sprecð lēogende, for mē ; . . . blissiað and fægniað, forðanðe ēower mēd is menigfeald on heofonum. *Æ. H. i. 552, 554.*

‖ Blissiað and fægniað ; efne, eower mēd is menigfeald on heofonum. *Æ. H. i. 556.*

5. 13. Gē sind þǣre eorðan sealt. *Æ. H. ii. 536.*

5. 14, 16. Gē sind middangeardes lēoht : scīne ēower lēoht swā

---

5. 5[1]. Beati qui lugent, quoniam ipsi consolabuntur.

5. 4[1]. Beati mites, quoniam ipsi possidebunt terram.

5. 6. Beati qui esuriunt et sitiunt iustitiam, quoniam ipsi satura-buntur.

5. 7–9. Beati misericordes, quoniam ipsi misericordiam consequentur. Beati mundo corde, quoniam ipsi Deum videbunt. Beati pacifici, quoniam filii Dei vocabuntur.

5. 10–12. Beati qui persecutionem patiuntur propter iustitiam, quo-niam ipsorum est regnum coelo-rum. Beati estis cum maledixe-rint vobis, et persecuti vos fuerint, et dixerint omne malum adver-sum vos mentientes, propter me ; gaudete et exultate, quoniam merces vestra copiosa est in coe-lis. . . .

5. 13. Vos estis sal terrae. . . .

5. 14, 16. Vos estis lux mundi. . . . Sic luceat lux vestra coram homi-nibus ut videant opera vestra

[1] This is the order in Ælfric and the Vulgate.

ætforan mannum, þæt hī gescon ꞓowre gōdan weorc, and wuldrian ꞓowerne Fæder þe on heofonum is. Æ. H. i. 542.

¶ Seme ꞓower lēoht ætforan mannum swā þæt hī gescon
ꞓowere gōdan weorc, and wuldrian ꞓowerne Fæder þe on
heofenum is. Æ. H. ii. 564.

¶ . . . þæt ūre gōdan weorc bēon on ðā wīsan mannum cūðe,
þæt hī magon gescon ūre gōdnysse, and þæt hī wuldrian and
hērigan ūrne heofonlican Fæder. Æ. H. i. 180.

5. 17. Ne wēne gē nā þæt ic cōme tō ðī þæt ic wolde tōwurpan
þā ealdan ǣ oððe wītegena gesętnyssa ; ic ne cōm tō ðī þæt
ic hī tōwurpe, ac þæt ic hī gefylde. Æ. H. ii. 198.

Hē ne cōm tō ðȳ þæt hē wolde tōwurpan ðā ealdan ǣ oððe
wītegan, ac wolde hī æfter gāstlicum andgite gefyllan. Æ. H. ii. 58.

Hē cwæð þæt hē ne cōme tō ðȳ þæt hē wolde þā ealdan ǣ
tōwurpan, ac gefyllan. Æ. H. i. 94.

5. 18. Sōð ic ꞓow sęcge : Ān strica oððe ān stæf ðǣre ealdan ǣ ne
bið forgǣged oð-þæt hī ealle gefyllede bēon. Æ. H. ii. 198, 200.

5. 20. Sōð ic ꞓow sęcge : Būton ꞓower rihtwīsnyss māre sȳ þonne
ðǣra Iudeiscra bōcera and sunderhālgena, ne becume gē intō
heofenan rīce. Æ. H. ii. 216.

5. 23, 24. Gif ðū offrast ðīne lāc tō Godes weofode, and þū þǣr
gemyndig bist þæt ðīn brōðor hæfð sum ðing ongēan ðē, forlǣt
ðǣrrihte ðā lāc ætforan ðām weofode, and gang ǣrest tō þīnum
brēðer, and þō tō him gesibsuma ; and, ꞓonne ðū eft cymst tō
ðām weofode, geoffra ðonne ðīne lac. Æ. H. i. 54.

5. 32. Swā-hwā-swā his ǣwe forlǣt, and ōðor genimð, hē bið
þonne ꞓawbrǣce and ꞓac forligr. Éac sē ðe wīfað on ðām for-
lǣtenum wīfe bið unrihthǣmere gehāten fram Gode. Æ. H. ii. 322.

bona, et glorificent patrem vestrum qui in coelis est.

5. 17. Nolite putare quoniam veni
solvere legem aut prophetas ;
non veni solvere, sed adimplere.

5. 18. Amen quippe dico vobis, . . .
iota unum aut unus apex non
practeribit a lege donec omnia
fiant.

5. 20. Dico enim vobis quia nisi
abundaverit iustitia vestra plus
quam scribarum et Pharisaeorum, non intrabitis in regnum

coelorum.

5. 23, 24. Si ergo offers munus tuum
ad altare, et ibi recordatus fueris
quia frater tuus habet aliquid adversum te, relinque ibi munus
tuum ante altare, et vade prius
reconciliari fratri tuo ; et tunc
veniens offeres munus tuum.

5. 32. . . . Quia omnis qui dimiserit
uxorem suam . . . facit eam moe-
chari ; et qui dimissam duxerit
adulterat.

5. 34–37. Ne swera ðū þurh heofenan, forðanðe hēo is Godes
þrymsetl; ne swera ðū þurh eorðan, forðanðe hēo is Godes
fōtsceamol; ne swera þū ðurh ðīn āgen hēafod, forðanðe ðū
ne miht wyrcan ān hǣr þīnes feaxes hwīt oððe blacc.   Ic secge
ēow: Ne swērige gē þurh nān þing, ac bēo ēower sprǣc ðus
geendod: Hit is swā ic secge, oþþe hit nis swā; swā-hwæt-swā
ðǣr māre bið þurh āð, þæt bið of ðām yfelan.   Æ. H. i. 482.

‖ Heofon is his þrymsetl, and eorðe is his fōtsceamul.
Æ. H. i. 262.

‖ Eorðe is gecweden Godes fōtsceamel, and sēo heofen is his
ðrymsetl.   Æ. H. ii. 448; cf. Isa. 66. 1.

5. 43–46. Gē gehȳrdon hwæt gecweden wæs ðām ealdum mannum
on Moyses ǣ: Lufa ðīnne nēxtan, and hata ðīnne fēond.   Ic
sōðlice ēow secge: Lufiað ēowere fȳnd, dōð þām tela ðe ēow
hatiað, and gebiddað for ēowerum ēhterum and ēow tȳnendum,
þæt gē bēon ēoweres Fæder bearn se ðe on heofonum is, se ðe
dēð his sunnan scīnan ofer ðā yfelan and ofer ðā gōdan, and
sylð rēnscūras ðām rihtwīsum and ðām unrihtwīsum.   Gif
gē ðā āne lufiað þe ēow lufiað, hwilce mēde hæbbe gē þonne æt
Gode?   Æ. H. ii. 16.

‖ Hit is þus āwriten on þǣre ealdan ǣ: Lufa ðīnne frēond,
and hata ðīnne fēond.   Æ. H. i. 522.

‖ Ōðre men hatiað heora fȳnd, and yfel mid yfele forgyldað[1];
wē sōðlice lufiað ūre fȳnd, and þām teala dōð þe ūs hatiað.
Æ. H. ii. 484.

‖ Ic bebēode ēow: Lufiað ēowre fȳnd, and dōþ tela þām ðe
ēow hatiað, and gebiddað for ēowre ēhteras, þæt gē bēon bearn

---

5. 34–37. Ego autem dico vobis, non
iurare omnino; neque per coelum,
quia thronus Dei est; neque per
terram, quia scabellum est pedum
eius; ... neque per caput tuum
iuraveris, quia non potes unum
capillum album facere aut ni-
grum. Sit autem sermo vester:
Est, est; Non, non; quod autem
his abundantius est a malo est.

5. 43–46. Audistis quia dictum est:
Diliges proximum tuum, et odio
habebis inimicum tuum.   Ego
autem dico vobis: Diligite inimicos vestros, benefacite his qui
oderunt vos, et orate pro persequentibus et calumniantibus vos,
ut sitis filii Patris vestri qui in
coelis est, qui solem suum oriri
facit super bonos et malos, et
pluit super iustos et iniustos. Si
enim diligitis eos qui vos diligunt,
quam mercedem habebitis? ...

---

[1] From Rom. 12. 17, 'Nulli malum pro malo reddentes'; or 1 Thess. 5. 15; or
1 Pet. 3. 9.

þæs heofonlican Fæder, se ðe læt his sunnan scīnan ofer gōde
and yfele, and hē sylð rēnscūras and wēstmas rihtwīsum and
unrihtwīsum.　Æ. H. i. 522.

‖ Lufiað ꞅowere fȳnd, dōð þām tela þe ꞅow hatiað, þæt gē
bēon ꞅoweres Fæder cild se ðe on heofenum is.　Æ. H. i. 56.

‖ Lufiað ꞅowre fȳnd, dōð þām tela ðe ꞅow hatiað, and gebiddað for ꞅowerum ēhterum and tȳnendum, þæt gē bēon
ꞅowres Fæder bearn se ðe on heofonum is.　Æ. H. ii. 36.

‖ Læt scīnan his sunnan ofer ðā rihtwīsan and unrihtwīsan
gelīce, and sęnt rēnas . . . gōdum and yfelum.　Æ. H. i. 406.

6. 2, 5, 16. Sōð ic ꞅow sęcge: Hī underfēngon heora mēde.　Æ. H. ii. 566.

‖ Hī underfēngon edlēan heora weorca.　Æ. H. i. 412.

6. 8. Ēower heofenlica Fæder wāt hwæs gē behōfiað, ǣrðanðe gē
hine ǣniges ðinges biddan.　Æ. H. i. 158.

6. 9-13. Gebiddað ꞅow mid þisum wordum: . . . Þū, ūre Fæder
þe eart on heofonum, sȳ þīn nama gehālgod.　Cume ðīn rīce.
Sȳ ðīn wylla on eorðan swā-swā on heofonum.　Syle ūs tō-dæg
ūrne dæghwamlīcan hlāf.　And forgyf ūs ūre gyltas, swā-swā
wē forgyfað ðām þe wið ūs āgyltað.　And ne lǣd ðū nā ūs on
costnunge, ac ālȳs us fram yfele.　Sȳ hit swā[1].　Æ. H. i. 258.

‖ Þū, ūre Fæder þe eart on heofenum, sȳ ðīn nama gehālgod.
Gecume ðīn rīce.　Sȳ ðīn willa swā-swā on heofenum swā ēac
on eorðan.　Syle ūs tō-dæg ūrne dæghwomlīcan hlāf.　And forgif
ūs ūre gyltas swā-swā wē forgyfað þām ðe wið ūs āgyltað.　And
ne lǣd þū nā ūs on costnunge, ac ālȳs ūs fram yfele.　Sȳ hit
swā.　Æ. H. ii. 596.

‖ Ūre Fæder þe eart on heofonum.　Æ. H. i. 262 ; cf. i. 54.

‖ Sȳ ðīn nama gehālgod. . . . Cume ðīn rīce. . . . Geweorðe þin
willa on eorðan swā-swā on heofonum. . . . Syle ūs nū tō-dæg
ūrne dæghwamlīcan hlāf. . . . Forgif ūs ūre gyltas swā-swā wē

6. 2, 5, 16. . . . Amen dico vobis:
Receperunt mercedem suam.

6. 8. . . . Scit enim Pater vester quid
opus sit vobis, antequam petatis
eum.

6. 9-13. Sic ergo vos orabitis : Pater
noster qui es in coelis, sanctificetur nomen tuum.　Adveniat

regnum tuum. Fiat voluntas tua.
sicut in coelo et in terra. Panem
nostrum supersubstantialem da
nobis hodie. Et dimitte nobis
debita nostra, sicut et nos dimit-
timus debitoribus nostris. Et ne
nos inducas in tentationem, sed
libera nos a malo. Amen.

[1] See the editor's 'Study of the Lord's Prayer in English,' *American Journal of
Philology*, vol. xii, pp. 59-66.

forgifað þām mannum þe wið ūs āgyltað[1]. . . . Ne geðafa, ðū
God, þæt wē bēon gelǣdde on costnunge. . . . Ac ālȳs ūs fram
yfele.   *Æ. H. i.* 262–270.

6. 14, 15. Gif gē forgyfað þām mannum þe wið ēow āgyltað, þonne
forgyfð ēow ēower Fæder ēowere synna ; gif gē ðonne nellað
forgyfan, nele ēac ēower Fæder ēow forgifan ēowere gyltas.
     Æ. H. i. 52.

‖ Būton gē forgifon mannum heora gyltas, ne forgifð se
heofonlica Fæder ēow ēowere gyltas.   *Æ. H. ii.* 336.

‖ Būton gē forgifon ðām mannum þe ēow āgyltað mid inne-
weardre heortan[2], nele se heofenlica Fæder ēow forgyfan
ēowere gyltas.   *Æ. H. ii.* 604.

‖ Būton gē forgyfon of ēowerum heortum[2] wið ēow āgyl-
tendum. . . .   *Æ. H. ii.* 336.

6. 19–21. Ne behȳde gē ēowerne goldhord on eorðan, þǣr-ðǣr
ōmm and moððan hit āwēstað, and ðēofas ādelfað and for-
stelað ; ac hordiað ēowerne goldhord on heofenum, þǣr ne
cymð tō ne ōm ne moððe, nē þēofas ne delfað nō ne ætbrēdað.
Sōðlice ðǣr-ðǣr þīn goldhord is, þǣr bið þīn heorte.   *Æ. H. ii.* 104.

6. 24–27. Ne mæg nān mann twām hlāfordum samod ðēowian ;
oððe hē ðone ænne hatað and ðone ōðerne lufað, oððe hē hine
tō ðām ānum geðēot and þone ōðerne forsihð. . . . Ne mage gē
Gode ðēowian and ēoweres fēos gestrēone. . . . Bętere is sēo
sāwul ðonne se męte, and se līchama bętera ðonne his scrūd.
. . . Behealdað þūs flēogendan fugelas, ðe ne sāwað nē ne rīpað,
ac ēower heofonlica Fæder hī āfēt. . . . Wē sind miccle rōttran
þonne ðā fugelas. . . . Hwilc ēower mæg gelcan āne ęlne tō his
lęnge ?   *Æ. H. ii.* 460–464.

6. 14, 15. Si enim dimiseritis hominibus peccata eorum, dimittet et
vobis Pater vester coelestis delicta
vestra ; si autem non dimiseritis
hominibus, nec Pater vester dimittet vobis peccata vestra.

6. 19–21. Nolite thesaurizare vobis
thesauros in terra, ubi aerugo et
tinea demolitur, et ubi fures effo-
diunt et furantur. Thesaurizate

autem vobis thesauros in coelo,
ubi neque aerugo neque tinea
demolitur, et ubi fures non effo-
diunt nec furantur. Ubi enim
est thesaurus tuus, ibi est et cor
tuum.

6. 24–27. Nemo potest duobus dominis servire ; aut enim unum
odio habebit et alterum diliget,
aut unum sustinebit et alterum

---

[1] Here may be cited the isolated quotation in Cnut's Laws (Schmid's *Gesetze der
Angelsachsen*, p. 270) : 'And forgyf ūs, Drihten, ūre gyltas, swā wē forgyfað þām þe
wið ūs āgyltað.'

[2] From Matt. 18. 35, 'de cordibus vestris.'

6. 29. *Sce Æ. H. ii.* 464.

6. 31–33. Drihten bēad þæt wē nǣron bysige and carfulle, cweð-ende: Hwæt sceole wē etan, oððe hwæt drincan, oððe mid hwām bēon ymscrȳdde? and cwæð: Witodlice ēower heofenlica Fæder wāt þæt gē þyssera ðinga behōfiað; sēcað ǣrest Godes rīce, and his rihtwīsnysse, and ealle ðās ðing ēow bēoð þǣrtō geēacnode. *Æ. H. ii.* 464.

7. 7. Cnuciað, and ēow bið geopenod.   *Æ. H. ii.* 572.

7. 13, 14. Se weig is swīðe nearu and sticol sē ðe lǣt tō heofonan rīce; and sē is swīðe rūm and smōðe, se ðe lǣt tō helle-wīte. *Æ. H. i.* 162.

  ‖ Se weg se ðe lǣt tō forwyrde is brād and smēðe. *Æ. H. i.* 162, 164.

7. 15. Behealdað ēow wið lēasum wītegum, þe tō ēow cumað on scēapa hīwum.   *Æ. H. ii.* 404.

  ‖ ... forðanþe hī ne sind nā scēp, ac sind wulfas on scēapa hīwum. *Æ. H. ii.* 404.

7. 16–19. Gē oncnāwað hī be heora wǣstmum. ... Hwā gaderað ǣfre wīnberian of ðornum, oþþe fīcæppla of brēmelum? ... Ǣlc gōd trēow wyrcð gōde wǣstmas, and yfel trēow wyrcð yfele wǣstmas. ... Ne mæg þæt gōde trēow wyrcan yfele wǣstmas, nē þæt yfele trēow gōde wǣstmas. ... Ǣlc trēow ðe ne wyrcð gōdne wǣstm bið forcorfen, and on fȳre āworpen. *Æ. H. ii.* 404, 406.

contemnet. Non potestis Deo servire et mammonae. ... Nonne anima plus est quam esca, et corpus plus quam vestimentum? Respicite volatilia coeli, quoniam non serunt, neque metunt, ... et Pater vester coelestis pascit illa. Nonne vos magis pluris estis illis? Quis autem vestrum cogitans potest adiicere ad staturam suam cubitum unum?

6. 31–33. Nolite ergo solliciti esse, dicentes: Quid manducabimus, aut quid bibemus, aut quo operiemur? ... Scit enim Pater vester quia his omnibus indigetis. Quaerite ergo primum regnum Dei, et iustitiam eius, et haec omnia adiicientur vobis.

7. 7. ... Pulsate, et aperietur vobis.

7. 13, 14. ... Lata porta et spatiosa via est quae ducit ad perditionem. ... Quam angusta porta et arcta via est quae ducit ad vitam! ...

7. 15. Attendite a falsis prophetis, qui veniunt ad vos in vestimentis ovium, intrinsecus autem sunt lupi rapaces.

7. 16–19. A fructibus eorum cognoscetis eos. Numquid colligunt de spinis uvas, aut de tribulis ficus? Sic omnis arbor bona fructus bonos facit, mala autem arbor malos fructus facit. Non potest arbor bona malos fructus facere, neque arbor mala bonos

7. 21. Ne færð intō heofonan rīce ǣlc ðǣra ðe cweð tō mē: Drihten, Drihten; ac sē ðe wyrcð mīnes Fæder willan þe on heofonum is, sē færð intō heofonan rīce.   Æ. H. ii. 410.

7. 22, 23. Ic sęcge ēow: Manega cweðað tō mē on ðām micclan dæge: Drihten, Drihten, lā,· hū ne wītegode wē on ðīnum naman, and wē ādrǣfdon dēoflo of wōdum mannum, and wē micele mihta on þīnum naman gefręmedon? Þonne andette ic him: Ne can ic ēow; gewītað fram me, gē unrihtwīse wyrhtan.   Æ. H. i. 306.

8. 1–4. Se Hǣlend niðerēode of ānre dūne, and him filigde micel męnigu. Efne, ðā cōm sum hrēoflig mann, and ālēat wið þæs Hǣlendes, þus cweðende: Drihten, gif þū wilt, þū miht mē geclǣnsian. Se Hǣlend āstręhte his hand, and hine hrępode, and cwæð: Ic wylle; and sȳ ðū geclǣnsod. Þā sōna wearð his hrēofla eal geclǣnsod, and· hē wæs gehǣled [1]. Ðā cwæð se Hǣlend him tō: Warna þæt þū hit nānum męnn ne sęcge; ac far tō Godes temple, and geswutela ðē sylfne ðām sācerde, and geoffra ðīne lāc, swā-swā Moyses bebēad, him on gewitnysse.   Æ. H. i. 120.

‖ Ic wylle; and þū bēo geclǣnsod.   Æ. H. i. 122.

8. 5–13. Drihten fērde æfter ðisum tō ānre byrig þe is gehāten Capharnaum. Þā genēalǣhte him tō sum hundredes ealdor, biddende and cweðende: Drihten, mīn cniht līð æt hām

fructus facere. Omnis arbor quae non facit fructum bonum, excidetur, et in ignem mittetur.

7. 21. Non omnis qui dicit mihi: Domine, Domine, intrabit in regnum coelorum; sed qui facit voluntatem Patris mei qui in coelis est, ipse intrabit in regnum coelorum.

7. 22, 23. Multi dicent mihi in illa die: Domine, Domine, nonne in nomine tuo prophetavimus, et in nomine tuo daemonia eiecimus, et in nomine tuo virtutes multas fecimus? Et tunc confitebor illis: Quia nunquam novi vos; discedite a me, qui operamini iniquitatem.

8. 1–4. Cum autem descendisset de monte, secutae sunt eum turbae multae. Et ecce leprosus veniens adorabat eum, dicens: Domine, si vis, potes me mundare. Et extendens Iesus manum, tetigit eum, dicens: Volo; mundare. Et confestim mundata est lepra eius. Et ait illi Iesus: Vide nemini dixeris; sed vade, ostende te sacerdoti, et offer munus quod praecepit Moyses, in testimonium illis.

8. 5–13. Cum autem introisset Capharnaum, accessit ad eum centurio, rogans eum, et dicens: Domine, puer meus iacet in domo paralyticus, et male torquetur.

---

[1] 'Efne . . . gehǣled' repeated below, Æ. H. i. 120, 122.

bedreda, and is yfele geðrēatod. Drihten him andwyrde : Ic
cume and hine gehǣle. Þā andwyrde se hundredes caldor,
and cwæð : Drihten, ne eom ic wyrðe þæt þū innfare under
mīnum hrōfe ; ac cweð þīn word, and mīn cniht bið gehǣled.
Ic com ān man gesęt under anwealde, hǣbbende under mē
cęmpan ; and ic cweðe tō ðisum : Far ðū, and hē fǣrð ; tō
ōðrum : Cum ðū, and hē cymð ; tō mīnum ðēowan : Dō ðis.
and hē dēð. Þā wundrode se Hǣlend, ðā-ðā hē ðis gehȳrde,
and cwæð tō ðǣre fyligendan męnigu : Sōð ic ēow sęcge, ne
gemētte ic swā micclne gelēafan on Israhela ðēode. Ic sęcge
ēow tō sōðum þæt manega cumað fram ēastdǣle and westdǣle,
and geręstað hī mid Abrahame ðām hēahfædere, and Isaace,
and Iacobe, on heofenan rīce ; þā rīcan bearn bēoð āworpene
intō ðām yttrum þēostrum ; þǣr bið wōp and tōða gebitt. Ðā
cwæð ęft se Hǣlend tō þām hundredes ealdre : Far ðō hām,
and getīmige ðē swā-swā ðū gelȳfdest. And se cniht wearð
gehǣled of ðǣre tīde. Æ. H. i. 126.

‖ Ic cume, and ðīnne cniht gehǣle. Æ. H. i. 128.

‖ Drihten, ne eom ic wyrðe þæt þū innfare under mīne
ðęcene. Æ. H. i. 126.

‖ Drihten, cweð þīn word, and mīn cniht bið hāl.
Æ. H. i. 126, 130.

‖ Ic eom man under anwealde gesętt, hæbbende under mē
cęmpan ; and ic sęcge ðisum : Far ðū, and hē fǣrð ; tō ōðrum :
Cum ðū, and hē cymð ; tō mīnum þēowan : Dō þis, and hē
dēð. Æ. H. i. 130.

‖ Sōð ic ēow sęcge, nā gemētte ic swā micclne gelēafan on
Israhela ðēode. Æ. H. i. 128.

‖ Ic sęcge ēow tō sōðan þæt manega cumað fram ēastdǣle

Et ait illi Iesus : Ego veniam et
curabo eum. Et respondens centurio, ait : Domine, non sum dignus ut intres sub tectum meum ;
sed tantum dic verbo, et sana-
bitur puer meus. Nam et ego
homo sum sub potestate consti-
tutus, habens sub me milites ; et
dico huic : Vade, et vadit ; et
alii : Veni, et venit ; et servo
meo : Fac hoc, et facit. Audiens
autem Iesus miratus est, et se-

quentibus se dixit : Amen dico
vobis, non inveni tantam fidem
in Israel. Dico autem vobis quod
multi ab oriente et occidente venient, et recumbent cum Abraham, et Isaac, et Iacob in regno
coelorum ; filii autem regni eii-
cientur in tenebras exteriores ;
ibi erit fletus et stridor dentium.
Et dixit Iesus centurioni : Vade,
et sicut credidisti fiat tibi. Et
sanatus est puer in illa hora.

and westdǣle, and geręstað hī mid Abrahame þām hēahfædere, and Isaace, and Iacobe, on heofenan rīce.   Æ. H. i. 130.

‖ Manega cumað fram ēastdǣle and fram westdǣle, and sittað mid þām hēahfædere Abrahame, and Isaace, and Iacobe, on heofonan rīce.   Æ. H. i. 336.

‖ Fela cumað fram ēastdǣle and fram westdǣle, and geręstað mid þām hēahfæderum, Abrahame, and Isaace, and Iacobe, on heofonan rīce.   Æ. H. ii. 82.

‖ Þa rīcan bearn bēoð āworpene intō ðām yttrum ðeostrum; þǣr bið wōp and tōða gebitt.   Æ. H. i. 130.

‖ . . . On þā yttran þeostru; . . . þǣr bið wōp and tōða gebitt.   Æ. H. i. 132; cf. Matt. 22. 5–14.

‖ Drihten cwæð tō þām hundredes ealdre: Far ðū hām, and getīmige ðē swā-swā ðū gelȳfdest; and his cniht wearð gehǣled of ðǣre tīde.   Æ. H. i. 132.

8. 20. Dēor habbað hōla, and fugelas habbað nest, hwǣr hī ręstað; and ic næbbe hwǣr ic āhylde mīn hēafod.   Æ. H. i. 160.

8. 23, 24. Ūre Drihten āstāh on scip, and him filigdon his leorning-cnihtas.   Efne, ðā fǣrlice ārās micel styrung and hrēohnys on ðǣre sǣ, swā þæt þæt scip wearð mid ȳðum oferðęht.   Se wind him stōd ongēan mid ormǣtum blǣde; and se Hǣlend wearð on slǣpe on ðām stēorsetle[1].   Æ. H. ii. 378; cf. i. 26.

9. 2. *See* Mark 2. 5.

9. 6. *See* Mark 2. 11.

9. 9. Dā-ðā se Hǣlend fērde on sumere byrig, ðā geseah hē sittan sumne mannan æt tollsetle, Matheus gehāten; and hē cwæð tō him: Folga mē.   Matheus ārās þǣrrihte fram his tolle, and filigde ðām Hǣlende.   Æ. H. ii. 468; cf. i. 324, ii. 288.

‖ Hē hine geseah sittan æt tolle. . . . Folga mē.   Æ. H. ii. 468.

9. 10. *See* Luke 5. 29.

9. 11. *See* Æ. H. ii. 470.

---

8. 20. . . . Vulpes foveas habent, et volucres coeli nidos; Filius autem hominis non habet ubi caput re-clinet.

8. 23, 24. Et ascendente eo in navi-culam, secuti sunt eum discipuli eius.   Et ecce motus magnus fac-tus est in mari, ita ut navicula operiretur fluctibus; ipse vero dormiebat.

9. 9. Et cum transiret inde Iesus, vidit hominem sedentem in te-lonio, Matthaeum nomine.   Et ait illi: Sequere me.   Et surgens secutus est eum.

---

[1] From Mark 4. 38, 'in puppi.'

9. 12. Drihten him cwæð tō : Ne behōfiað ða hālan nānes lǣces, ac ða untruman. *Æ. H. ii.* 470.

9. 13. Hē cwæð : Farað, and leorniað hwæt þæt mǣne : Ic wylle mildheortnysse, and nā offrunge. . . . Ne cōm ic nā tō clypigenne ða rihtwīsan, ac ða synfullan, tō dǣdbōte[1]. *Æ. H. ii.* 470 ; cf. Hos. 6. 6.

9. 37. Drihten cwæð : þæt gerīp is micel, and ða rīfteras fēawa. *Æ. H. ii.* 530.

9. 38. Biddað þæs gerīpes hlāford þæt hē āsende wyrhtan tō his gerīpe. *Æ. H. ii.* 530.

10. 5. Ne fare gē on hǣðenra manna wege, and on Samaritaniscra burgum ne becume gē. *Æ. H. ii.* 212.

10. 8. . . . se forgeaf ūs on his naman ðās mihte þæt wē untrume gehǣlon, and blinde onlihton[2], hrēoflige geclǣnsian, dēoflu āflīan, dēade ārǣran. *Æ. H. i.* 466.

Būtan cēape gē underfēngon ða gife, syllað hī ōðrum būtan cēape. *Æ. H. i.* 412.

10. 22. Sē ðe ǣfre ðurhwunað on ānrǣdum geleafan, sē bið gehealden. *Æ. H. ii.* 330.

10. 28. Ne ondrǣde gē eow ða ðe eowerne līchaman ofslēað, forðanðe hī ne magon eowre sāwle ofslēan ; ac ondrǣdað God, ðe mæg ǣgðer ge sāwle ge līchaman on hellesūsle fordōn. *Æ. H. i.* 554.

10. 32. Ælc ðǣra þe mē andet ætforan mannum, ic andette eac hine ætforan mīnum Fæder se ðe is on heofonum. *Æ. H. ii.* 558.

9. 12. At Iesus audiens ait : Non est opus valentibus medicus, sed male habentibus.

9. 13. Euntes autem discite quid est : Misericordiam volo, et non sacrificium. Non enim veni vocare iustos, sed peccatores.

9. 37. Tunc dicit discipulis suis : Messis quidem multa, operarii autem pauci.

9. 38. Rogate ergo Dominum messis ut mittat operarios in messem suam.

10. 5. . . . In viam gentium ne abieritis, et in civitates Samaritanorum ne intraveritis.

10. 8. Infirmos curate, mortuos suscitate, leprosos mundate, daemones eiicite ; gratis accepistis, gratis date.

10. 22. . . . Qui autem peraeveraverit usque in finem, hic salvus erit.

10. 28. Et nolite timere eos qui occidunt corpus, animam autem non possunt occidere ; sed potius timete eum qui potest et animam et corpus perdere in gehennam.

10. 32. Omnis ergo qui confitebitur me coram hominibus, confitebor et ego eum coram Patre meo qui in coelis est.

---

[1] From Luke 5. 32, 'ad poenitentiam.'

[2] A discrepancy here.

10. 41. Sē ðe wītegan underfēhð, hē hæfð wītogan mēde ; sē ðe rihtwīsne underfēhð, hē hæfð rihtwīses mannes edlēan.

Æ. II. i. 514.

10. 42. Sōð ic ēow sęcge : Swā-hwā-swā sylð ceald wæter drincan ānum þurstigan męnn ðæra ðe on mē gelȳfað, ne bið his mēd forloren. Æ. II. i. 582.

‖ Swā-hwā-swā sylð ānum ðurstigum męnn ceald wæter on mīnum naman, ne forlȳst hē his mēde þære dæde. Æ. H. ii. 106.

11. 2, 3. Hwæt, ðā Iohannes āsęnde of ðām cwearterne twēgen leorningcnihtas tō Crīste, and hine befrān, þus cweðende : Eart ðū sē ðe tōweard is, oþþe wē ōðres andbīdian sceolon ?

Æ. H. i. 480.

11. 4–6. And cwæð syððan tō Iohannes ærendracum : Farað nū tō Iohanne, and cȳðað him þā ðing þe gē gesāwon and gehȳrdon. Efne, nū blinde gesēoð, and ðā healtan gāð, and hreoflige męn synd geclænsode, dēafe gehȳrað, and ðā dēadan ārīsað, and ðearfan bodiað godspel ; and sē bið ēadig þe on mē ne bið geēswicod. Æ. H. i. 480 ; cf. i. 26, and Luke 7. 21–23.

11. 11. Betwux wīfa bearnum ne ārās nān mærra man ðonne is Iohannes se Fulluhtere. Æ. H. i. 356, 542.

‖ Betwux wīfa bearnum ne ārās nān mærra man þonne Iohannes se Fulluhtere. Æ. H. i. 476, 478.

‖ On wīfa bearnum næs nān mærra mann þonne Iohannes se Fulluhtere. Æ. H. ii. 36, 38.

11. 12. Fram Iohannes dagum Godes rīce ðolað nēadunge, and ðā strecanmōd hit gegrīpað. Æ. H. i. 358.

---

10. 41. Qui recipit prophetam in nomine prophetae, mercedem prophetae accipiet ; et qui recipit iustum in nomine iusti, mercedem iusti accipiet.

10. 42. Et quicumque potum dederit uni ex minimis istis calicem aquae frigidae tantum in nomine discipuli, amen dico vobis, non perdet mercedem suam.

11. 2, 3. Ioannes autem . . . in vinculis, . . . mittens duos de discipulis suis, ait illi : Tu es qui venturus es, an alium expectamus ?

11. 4-6. Et respondens Iesus ait illis : Euntes renuntiate Ioanni quae audistis et vidistis. Caeci vident, claudi ambulant, leprosi mundantur, surdi audiunt, mortui resurgunt, pauperes evangelizantur ; et beatus est qui non fuerit scandalizatus in me.

11. 11. . . . Non surrexit inter natos mulierum maior Ioanne Baptista. . . .

11. 12. A diebus autem Ioannis Baptistae usque nunc, regnum coelorum vim patitur, et violenti rapiunt illud.

11. 29. Leorniað æt mē þæt ic eom līðe and swīðe ēadmōd; and gē gemētað rçste ēowrum sāwlum. Æ. H. i. 210.

12. 19. Cf. Isa. 42. 2.

12. 28. Gif ic on Godes Gāste dēofl ādrīefe. . . . Æ. II. ii. 214; cf. Luke 11. 20.

12. 31, 32. Ælc synn and tāl bið forgifen behrēowsigendum mannum, ac þæs Hālgan Gāstes tāl ne bið næfre forgifen. Þeah-ðe hwā cweðe tāllic word ongēan mē, him bið forgifen, gif hē dēð dǣdbōte; sōðlice sē ðe cweð word ongān ðone Hālgan Gāst, ne bið hit him forgifen on ðyssere worulde, nē on ðǣre tōwerdan. Æ. H. i. 498.

12. 42. *See* 1 Kings 10. 1–10, note.

12. 50. Sē ðe wyrcð mīnes Fæder willan sē ðe is on heofonum, he bið mīn brōðer, and mīn mōder, and mīn swēoster. Æ. H. i. 260.

13. 17. Fela wītegan and rihtwīse mçn woldon gescon Crīstes tō-cyme. ac hit næs nā him getīðod. Æ. H. i. 136.

13. 19. Ælc ðǣra ðe gehȳrð þæt heofonlice word, and hē hit ne understçnt, ðonne cymð se yfela, and gelæhð hit. Æ. H. ii. 90.

13. 22. . . . lēase welan. Æ. H. ii. 88.

13. 23. Sum dǣl þæs sǣdes, þe on ðām gōdan lande āsprang, āgeaf ðrītigfealdne wǣstm, sum sixtigfealdne, sum hund-fealdne [1]. Æ. H. ii. 92.

13. 30. On çnde þyssere worulde se sōða Dēma hǣt his çnglas

11. 29. . . . Discite a me, quia mitis sum et humilis corde; et invenietis requiem animabus vestris.

12. 28. Si autem ego in Spiritu Dei eiicio daemones. . . .

12. 31, 32. . . . Omne peccatum et blasphemia remittetur hominibus, Spiritus autem blasphemia non remittetur. Et quicumque dixerit verbum contra Filium hominis, remittetur ei; qui autem dixerit contra Spiritum Sanctum, non remittetur ei neque in hoc saeculo, neque in futuro.

12. 50. Quicumque enim fecerit voluntatem Patris mei qui in coelis est, ipse meus frater, et soror, et mater est.

13. 17. Multi prophetae et iusti cupierunt videre quae videtis, et non viderunt.

13. 19. Omnis qui audit verbum regni, et non intelligit, venit malus, et rapit quod seminatum est in corde eius. . . .

13. 22. . . . Fallacia divitiarum. . . .

13. 23. Qui vero in terram bonam seminatus est, hic est qui . . . fructum affert, et facit aliud quidem centesimum, aliud autem sexagesimum, aliud vero trigesimum.

13. 30. . . . In tempore messis dicam messoribus: Colligite primum zi-

[1] Ælfric attributes this to 'Se öðer godspellere,' by whom, on p. 88, he means Matthew; the order of the words, however, is that in Mark.

gadrian þone coccel byrþenmǣlum, and āwurpan intō ðām
unādwǣscendlicum fȳre. . . . And se clǣna hwǣte bið gebrōht
intō Godes berne. Æ. H. i. 526.

13. 41. Mannes Bearn āsent his englas, and gegaderað of his rīce
ealle æswicunga. Æ. H. ii. 562.

13. 43. Þonne scīnað ðā rihtwīsan swā-swā sunne on heora Fæder
rīce. Æ. H. i. 218.

14. 3, 4. *See* Æ. H. i. 478.

14. 6, 7. *See* Æ. H. i. 480.

14. 10. *See* Æ. H. i. 478, 488.

14. 19. Hē tōbræc ðā fīf hlāfas, and sealde his leorningcnihtum.
and hēt beran ðām folce. Æ. H. i. 186 ; cf. John 6. 1-14.

14. 22. Þā hēt hē his leorningcnihtas faran tō scipe, and oferrōwan
þone brym, oð-þæt hē ðā menigu forlǣtan mihte. Æ. H. ii. 384.
See also John 6. 15, 16, 19.

14. 23. Crīst āna āstāh ūp tō ðǣre dūne, þæt hē hine gebǣde.
Æ. H. ii. 384.

   ‖ Hē āstāh āna ūp tō ðǣre dūne, hine tō gebiddenne.
Æ. H. ii. 388.

14. 25-28. Drihten cōm tō his leorningcnihtum þǣr-ðǣr hī on
rēwette gedrēfede wǣron, on ðǣre feorðan wæccan. . . . Ðā-ðā
Drihten ðām scipe genēalǣhte, ðā wurdon hī āfyrhte, wēndon
þæt hit sum gedwimor wǣre. Drihten cwæð him tō : Habbað
ēow trūwan ; ic hit eom, ne bēo gē ofdrædde. . . . Petrus him
andwyrde : Drihten, gif ðū hit sȳ, hāt mē gān tō ðē bufon ðām
wætere. Æ. H. ii. 388.

   ‖ Drihten, hāt mē gān tō ðē ūpon ðām wætere. Æ. H. ii. 388, 390.

zania, et alligate ea in fasciculos
ad comburendum, triticum autem
congregate in horreum meum.

13. 41. Mittet Filius hominis angelos
suos, et colligent de regno eius
omnia scandala. . . .

13. 43. Tunc iusti fulgebunt sicut
sol in regno Patris eorum. . . .

14. 19. . . . Fregit, et dedit discipulis
panes, discipuli autem turbis.

14. 22. Et statim compulit Iesus
discipulos ascendere in navicu-
lam, et praecedere eum trans
fretum, donec dimitteret turbas.

14. 23. . . . Ascendit in montem
solus orare. . . .

14. 25-28. Quarta autem vigilia
noctis, venit ad eos ambulans
super mare. Et videntes eum super
mare ambulantem, turbati sunt.
dicentes : Quia phantasma est. . . .
Statimque Iesus locutus est eis,
dicens : Habete fiduciam ; ego
sum, nolite timere. Respondens
autem Petrus dixit : Domine, si
tu es, iube me ad te venire super
aquas.

14. 29–31. Drihten cwæð : Cum tō mē. And Petrus þærrihte, būton ælcere twȳnunge, ēode of ðām scipe, swīðe gebyld þurh Drihtnes hǣse, and ēode ūpon ðām wætere, swā-swā his Drihten. ... Đā geseah hē fǣrlice þone strangan wind, and begann hine tō ondrǣdenne, and, mid-þām-ðe hē dēaf, clypode tō his Drihtne : Drihten, gehelp mīn. ... Ne forlēt Drihten Petrum, ðēah-ðe hē ðurh his twȳnunge bedufe, ac āstrehte his hand, and hine gehēold. ... Drihten ðrēade Petrum, and cwæð : Þū lȳtles gelēafan, hwī twȳnode þū ? *Æ. H. ii. 390, 392.*

14. 36. Drihten, ðā-ðā hē tō lande becōm, gehǣlde ealle ðā untruman þe him tō gelǣdde wǣron, þurh his rēafes hrepunge.

Æ. H. ii. 394.

15. 4. *See* Exod. 20. 12, 21. 17.

15. 14. Gif se blinda man bið ōðres blindan lāttēow, þonne befeallað hī bēgen on sumum blindum sēaðe. *Æ. H. ii. 320.*

15. 21, 22. Đā fērde hē ðanon tō ðǣre burhscīre þe is gehāten Tyrus. and tō ðǣre ōðre þe is gehāten Sidon. Efne, ðā fērde ān Chananeisc wīf of ðām gemǣrum tōgēanes ðām Hǣlende, and him tō clypode, þus cweðende. ... Hēo clypode : Dauides bearn, gemiltsa mē ; mīn dohtor is yfele fram dēofle gedreht. *Æ. H. ii. 110.*

‖ Dauides bearn, gemiltsa mīn. *Æ. H. ii. 110.*

‖ Sum wif wæs ðe cōm tō Crīste, and bæd for hire dehter, þe læg on wōdum drēame. *Æ. H. ii. 50.*

15. 23–25. Crīstes leorningcnihtas tō him genēalǣhton, and ðām wīfe tō him geðingodon, þus cweðende : Lā lēof, forlǣt hī, forðanðe hēo clypað æfter ūs. ... Drihten andwyrde his apostolum mid þisum wordum, and cwæð : Ne eom ic āsend būton

14. 29–31. At ipse ait : Veni. Et descendens Petrus de navicula, ambulabat super aquam ut veniret ad Iesum. Videns vero ventum validum, timuit : et cum coepisset mergi, clamavit dicens : Domine, salvum me fac. Et continuo Iesus, extendens manum, apprehendit eum, et ait illi : Modicae fidei, quare dubitasti ?

14. 36. Et rogabant eum ut vel fimbriam vestimenti eius tangerent ; et quicumque tetigerunt, salvi facti sunt.

15. 14. ... Caecus autem si caeco ducatum praestet, ambo in foveam cadunt.

15. 21, 22. Et egressus inde Iesus secessit in partes Tyri et Sidonis. Et ecce mulier Chananaea a finibus illis egressa clamavit, dicens ei : Miserere mei, Domine, fili David ; filia mea male a daemonio vexatur.

15. 23–25. ... Et accedentes discipuli eius rogabant eum dicentes : Dimitte eam, quia clamat post nos. Ipse autem respondens ait :

tō ðām scēapum Israhela hīwrǣdene þe losedon. . . . Þæt wīf
cōm, and hī āstrẹhte ætforan Drihtne, þus cweðende : Drihten
lēof, help mīn.　Æ. H. ii. 112, 114.

15. 26–28. Þā cwæð Crīst tō hire þæt hit nǣre nā rihtlic þæt man
nāme his cildra hlāf, and wurpe hundum.　Hēo ðā andwyrde :
Gēa, lēof Drihten, and þēah-hwæðere oft ðā hwelpas gelæccað
þā cruman þe feallað of þæs hlāfordes bēode.　Ðā andwyrde se
Hǣlend, and cwæð : Ēalā ðū wīf, micel is ðīn gelēafa :
getīmige ðē swā-swā ðū wilt.　Hire dohtor wearð þǣrrihte
gewittig.　Æ. H. ii. 50.

‖ Drihten cwæð tō ðām wīfe : Nis nā gōd þæt man nime his
bearna hlāf, and wurpe hundum. . . . Þæt wīf cwæð tō Crīste :
Gēa, lēof Drihten, swā-ðēah ðā hwelpas etað of ðām crumon þe
feallað of heora hlāfordes mȳsan. . . . Drihten andwyrde þām
Chananeiscum wīfe, and cwæð : Ēalā ðū wīf, micel is ðīn
gelēafa ; getīmige ðē swā-swā ðū wylt.　And hire dohtor wearð
þā gehǣled of ðǣre tide.　Æ. H. ii. 114. 116.

15. 30, 31. *See* Mark 8. 1, 2, note.

15. 32–38. *See* Mark 8. 1 ff.

16. 13–19. Drihten cōm tō ānre burhscīre ðe is gecīged Cesarea
Philippi, and befrān his gingran hū mẹnn be him cwyddedon.
Hī andwyrdon : Sume mẹnn cweðað þæt ðū sȳ Iohannes se
Fulluhtere, sume sẹcgað þæt ðū sȳ Helias, sume Hieremias,
oððe sum ōðer wītega.　Se Hǣlend ðā cwæð : Hwæt sẹcge gē
þæt ic sȳ ?　Petrus him andwyrde : Þū eart Crīst, ðæs lifigendan
Godes Sunu.　Drihten him cwæð tō andsware : Ēadig eart ðū,
Simon, culfran bearn, forðanðe flǣsc and blōd þē ne onwrēah

Non sum missus nisi ad oves quae
perierunt domus Israel. At illa
venit, et adoravit eum, dicens :
Domine, adiuva me.

15. 26–28. Qui respondens ait : Non
est bonum sumere panem filiorum,
et mittere canibus. At illa dixit :
Etiam, Domine, nam et catelli
edunt de micis quae cadunt de
mensa dominorum suorum. Tunc
respondens Iesus ait illi : O mulier,
magna est fides tua ; fiat tibi
sicut vis. Et sanata est filia eius
ex illa hora.

16. 13–19. Venit autem Iesus in
partes Caesareae Philippi, et interrogabat discipulos suos, dicens :
Quem dicunt homines esse Filium
hominis ? At illi dixerunt : Alii
Ioannem Baptistam, alii autem
Eliam, alii vero Ieremiam, aut
unum ex prophetis. Dicit illis
Iesus : Vos autem quem me esse
dicitis ? Respondens Simon Petrus
dixit : Tu es Christus, Filius Dei
vivi. Respondens autem Iesus
dixit ei : Beatus es, Simon Bar
Iona, quia caro et sanguis non

ðisne gelēafan, ac mīn Fæder se ðe on heofonum is. Ic ðē
sęcge þæt þu eart stǣnen, and ofer ðysne stān ic timbrige
mīne cyrcan, and hęlle gatu nāht ne magon ongēan hī. Ic
betǣce ðē heofonan rīces cǣge; and swā-hwæt-swā ðū bintst
on eorðan, þæt bið gebunden on heofonum; and swā-hwæt-
swā ðū unbintst ofer eorðan, þæt bið unbunden on heofonum.   Æ. H. i. 364.

‖ His apostoli him andwyrdon : Sume męn cwyddiað þæt ðū
sȳ Iohannes se Fulluhtere, sume sęcgað þæt ðū sȳ Helias,
sume Hieremias, oððe ān ðæra wītegena.   Drihten ðā befrān :
Hwæt sęcge gē þæt ic sȳ ?   Æ. H. i. 366.

‖ Syððan āxode hī : Hū cwoðe gē be mē ?   Þā cwæð Petrus :
Þū eart Crīst, þæs lifigendan Godes Sunu.   Æ. H. ii. 388.

‖ Him andwyrde se gehȳrsuma Petrus : Ðū eart Crīst, þæs
lifigendan Godes Sunu.   Æ. H. i. 366 ; cf. i. 190.

‖ Þū eart Crīst, ðæs lifigendan Godes Sunu.   Æ. H. i. 76, 366, 580.

‖ Drihten cwæð tō Petre : Ēadig eart ðū, culfran sunu. . . .
Ne onwrēah ðē flǣsc nē blōd þisne gelēafan, ac mīn Fæder se
ðe on heofenum is. . . . Þū eart stǣnen. . . . And ic timbrige
mīne cyrcan uppon ðisum stāne. . . . Ne magon hęlle gatu nāht
tōgēanes mīnre cyrcan.   Æ. H. i. 368.

‖ Ic sęcge þē : Þū eart Petrus, and ofer ðisne stān ic getimbrige
mīne cyrcan.   Æ. H. ii. 390.

‖ Þū eart stǣnen, and ofer ðisne stān . . . ic getimbrige mīne
cyrcan.   Æ. H. ii. 390.

‖ Ic ðē betǣce heofonan rīces cǣge. . . . And swā-hwæt-swā
ðū bintst ofer eorðan, þæt bið gebunden on heofonum ; and
swā-hwæt-swā ðū unbintst ofer eorðan, þæt bið unbunden on
heofenan.   Æ. H. i. 368, 370 ; cf. Matt. 18. 18.

16. 26. *See* Luke 9. 25.

17. 1–5. Moyses and Elias ēac swilce sǣdon his ðrōwunge[1] on ǣr,
uppon ānre dūne ðe se Hǣlend āstāh mid ðrīm leorning-

revelavit tibi, sed Pater meus qui
in coelis est. Et ego dico tibi
quia tu es Petrus, et super hanc petram aedificabo ecclesiam meam,
et portae inferi non praevalebunt
adversus eam. Et tibi dabo claves
regni coelorum ; et quodcumque
ligaveris super terram erit liga-
tum et in coelis ; et quodcumque
solveris super terram erit solutum
et in coelis.

17. 1–5. Et post dies sex assumit
Iesus Petrum, et Iacobum, et
Ioannem fratrem eius, et ducit

[1] From Luke 9. 31, 'et dicebant excessum eius.'

cnihtum ; and his ansȳn ætforan him eal scēan swā-swā sunne, and his gewæda scinon on snāwes¹ hwītnysse. Þā wolde Petrus slēan sōna ðrēo geteld for ðǣre gesihðe, ac ðǣr swēgde ða stemn ðæs heofonlican Fæder hēalice of wolcne : Ðes is mīn lēofa Sunu, on ðām mē wel līcað ; gehȳrað hine. _Æ. H. ii. 242._

‖ Þes is mīn lēofa Sunu, þe mē wel līcað ; gehȳrað him ². _Æ. H. i. 104._

17. 24–27. Ðæs cāseres tolleras āxodon Petrus ðone apostol, ðā-ðā hī geond ealne middangeard ðām cāsere toll gegaderodon ; hī cwǣdon : Wyle ēower lārēow Crīst ǣnig toll syllan ? Þā cwæð Petrus þæt hē wolde. Þā, mid-þām-ðe Petrus wolde befrīnan þone Hǣlend, þā forscēat se Hǣlend hine, ðe ealle ðing wāt, þus cweðende : Hwæt ðincð þē, Petrus ? Æt hwām nimað eorðlice cynegas gafol oððe toll,—æt heora gesiblingum, oþþe æt ælfrǫmedum ? Petrus cwæð : Æt ælfrǫmedum. Se Hǣlend cwæð : Hwæt lā, synd heora siblingas frige. Þē-lǣs-ðe wē hī ǣswicion, gā tō ðǣre sǣ, and wurpe ūt ðīnne angel, and þone fisc ðe hine hraðost forswelhð, geopena his mūð, þonne fintst þū ðǣron ænne gyldenne węcg ; nim ðone, and syle tō tolle for mē and for ðē. _Æ. H. i. 510, 512._

‖ Syle for mē and for ðē. _Æ. H. i. 512._

18. 1, 2. Drihtnes leorningcnihtas tō him genēalǣhton, þus cweðende : Lā lēof, hwā is fyrmest manna on heofenan rīce ? Se Hǣlend him ðā tō clypode sum gehwǣde cild. _Æ. H. i. 510._

illos in montem excelsum seorsum, et transfiguratus est ante eos. Et resplenduit facies eius sicut sol ; vestimenta autem eius facta sunt ☐☐☐ sicut nix. Et ecce apparuerunt illis Moyses et Elias cum eo loquentes. Respondens autem Petrus, dixit ad Iesum : ... si vis, faciamus hic tria tabernacula.... Et ecce vox de nube, dicens : Hic est Filius meus dilectus, in quo mihi bene complacui ; ipsum audite.

Et cum intrasset in domum, praevenit eum Iesus, dicens : Quid tibi videtur, Simon ? Reges terrae a quibus accipiunt tributum vel censum,—a filiis suis, an ab alienis ? Et ille dixit : Ab alienis. Dixit illi Iesus : Ergo liberi sunt filii. Ut autem non scandalizemus eos, vade ad mare, et mitte hamum, et cum piscem qui primus ascenderit tolle, et, aperto ore eius, invenies staterem ; illum sumens, da eis pro me et te.

17. 24–27. ... Accesserunt qui didrachma accipiebant ad Petrum, et dixerunt ei : Magister vester non solvit didrachma? Ait : Etiam.

18. 1, 2. In illa hora accesserunt discipuli ad Iesum, dicentes : Quis, putas, maior est in regno coelorum ? Et advocans Iesus

¹ From Mark 9. 3 (Vulgate, 2), 'velut nix.'   ² By error for Matt. 3. 17.

‖ Þā apostolas . . . āxodon ðā ðone Hǣlend hwā wǣre fyrmest manna on heofonan rīce. Æ. H. i. 512.

18. 3. Sōð ic ēow sęcge : Ne becume gē tō heofonan rīce būton gē bēon āwęnde, and gewordene swā-swā lyttlingas. Æ. H. i. 512.

‖ Būton gē bēon swā bilewite on unscæððignysse swā-swā cild, næbbe gē infær tō heofonan rīce. Æ. H. ii. 336.

18. 4-5. Swā-hwā-swā hine sylfne geēadmēt, swā-swā ðis cild, hē bið fyrmest on heofonan rīce. . . . Sē ðe underfēhð ænne swilcne lyttling on mīnum naman, hē underfēhð mē sylfne.

  Æ. H. i. 512, 514.

‖ Sē ðe underfēhð ænne lȳtling on mīnum naman, hē under-fēhð mē sylfne. Æ. H. ii. 286.

18. 6-8. Sē ðe geǣswicað ānum ðyssera lyttlinga ðe on mē gelȳfað, sēlre him wǣre þæt him wǣre getīged ān ormǣto cwyrnstān tō his swūran, and hē swā wurde on dēoppre sǣ besęnced. . . . Wā middangearde for ǣswicungum. . . . Nēod is þæt ǣswicunga cumon, ðēah-hwæðere wā ðām męnn ðe hī of cumað. . . . Gif ðīn hand oððe ðīn fōt þē ǣswicige, ceorf of þæt lim, and āwurp fram ðē. . . . Æ. H. i. 514, 516.

18. 10. Behealdað þæt gē ne forsēon ænne of þysum lȳtlingum.

  Æ. H. i. 516.

Ic sęcge ēow þæt heora ęnglas symle gesēoð mīnes Fæder ansȳne se ðe on heofonum is. Æ. H. i. 516.

18. 18. And swā-hwæt-swā hī bindað ofer eorðan, þæt bið on heofonum gebunden ; and swā-hwæt-swā hī unbindað ofer eorðan, þæt bið unbunden on heofonum. Æ. H. i. 542 ; cf. Matt. 16. 1 -19.

parvulum, statuit eum in medio eorum.

18. 3. Et dixit : Amen dico vobis : Nisi conversi fueritis, et efficia-mini sicut parvuli, non intrabitis in regnum coelorum.

18. 4-5. Quicumque ergo humilia-verit se sicut parvulus iste, hic est maior in regno coelorum. Et qui susceperit unum parvulum talem in nomine meo, me suscipit.

18. 6-8. Qui autem scandalizaverit unum de pusillis istis qui in me credunt, expedit ei ut suspendatur mola asinaria in collo eius, et demergatur in profundum maris. Vae mundo a scandalis. Necesse est enim ut veniant scandala, verumtamen vae homini illi per quem scandalum venit. Si autem manus tua vel pes tuus scandalizat te, abscinde eum, et proiice abs te . . . .

18. 10. Videte ne contemnatis unum ex his pusillis ; dico enim vobis quia angeli eorum in coelis sem-per vident faciem Patris mei qui in coelis est.

18. 18. . . . Quaecumque alligaveri-tis super terram erunt ligata et

18. 20. Swā-hwǣr-swā bēoð twēgen oððe ðrȳ gegadrode on mīnum naman, þǣr ic sylf bēo him tōmiddes. Æ. H. ii. 284.

18. 35. *See* Matt. 6. 14, 15.

19. 13, 14. Hē cwæð, þā-ðā him man tō bǣr cild tō blētsigenne, and his gingran þæt bemǣndon : Geðafiað þæt ðās cild tō mē cumon ; swilcera is sōðlice heofonan rice. Æ. H. i. 512.

‖ . . . swā-swā God sylf gecwæð, ðā-ðā hē blētsode ðā gebrōhtan cild, and sǣde his gyngrum : Swilcra is Godes rīce. Æ. H. ii. 326.

19. 17–19. *See* Luke 18. 20–22, notes.

19. 27. On ðǣre tīde cwæð Petrus se apostol tō ðām Hǣlende : Efne, wē forlēton ealle woruldðing, and ðē ānum fyligað ; hwæt dēst ðū ūs þæs tō lēane ? Æ. H. i. 392.

‖ Wē forlēton ealle ðing. . . . Wē fyligað ðē. Æ. H. i. 394.

‖ Efne, wē forlēton ealle ðing, and ðē folgiað. Æ. H. ii. 96.

‖ Hwæt sceal ūs getīmian ? . . . Hwæt dēst ðū ūs tō edlēane ? Æ. H. i. 394.

19. 28. Se Hǣlend andwyrde : Sōð ic ēow secge þæt gē ðe mē fyligað sceolon sittan ofer twelf dōmsetl on ðǣre edcynninge, ðonne ic sitte on setle mīnes mægenðrymmes ; and gē ðonne dēmað twelf Israhela mǣgðum. Æ. H. i. 394.

‖ On ðām ǣriste sittað þā twelf apostoli mid Crīste on heora dōmsetlum, and dēmað þām twelf mǣigðum Israhela ðēode. Æ. H. i. 394, 396.

‖ . . . þæt hī on ðām micclum dōme ofer twelf dōmsetl sittende bēoð, tō dēmenne eallum mannum þe ǣfre on līchaman līf underfēngon. Æ. H. i. 542.

19. 29. Ǣlc ðǣra ðe forlǣt, for mīnum naman, fæder oððe mōder,

in coelo; et quaecumque solveritis super terram erunt soluta et in coelo.

18. 20. Ubi enim sunt duo vel tres congregati in nomine meo, ibi sum in medio eorum.

19. 13, 14. Tunc oblati sunt ei parvuli, ut manus eis imponeret, et oraret. Discipuli autem increpabant eos. Iesus vero ait eis : Sinite parvulos . . . ad me venire ; talium est enim regnum coelorum.

19. 27. Tunc respondens Petrus, dixit ei : Ecce nos relinquimus omnia, et secuti sumus te ; quid ergo erit nobis ?

19. 28. Iesus autem dixit illis : Amen dico vobis quod vos qui secuti estis me, in regeneratione cum sederit Filius hominis in sede maiestatis suae, sedebitis et vos super sedes duodecim, iudicantes duodecim tribus Israel ?

19. 29. Et omnis qui reliquerit domum, vel fratres, aut sorores,

gebrōðru oððe geswystru, wīf oððe bearn, land oððe gebytlu[1], be hundfealdum him bið forgolden, and hē hæfð ðær-tō-ēacan þæt ēce līf. *Æ. H. i. 396.*

20. 1. . . . þæt heofenan rīce wǣre gelīc sumum hīredes ealdre, se ðe fērde on ǣrnemerigen, and wolde hȳrian wyrhtan intō his wīngearde. *Æ. H. ii. 74.*

20. 2–6. Witodlice ðæs hīredes ealdor gehȳrde wyrhtan intō his wīngearde on ǣrnemerigen, eft on undern, and on midne dæg, on nōntīde, and on ðære endlyftan tīde. . . . Tō hwī stande gē hēr ealne dæg ȳdele? *Æ. H. ii. 74 ; cf. ii. 76, 78.*

20. 7. Hī cwǣdon : Forðanþe nān man ūs ne hȳrde. *Æ. H. ii. 76.*

20. 9. Witodlice fram ðām endenēxtan ongann se hīredes ealdor tō āgyldenne þone penning. *Æ. H. ii. 78.*

20. 12. . . . bǣron ðā byrðene and ðæs dæges hǣtan. *Æ. H. ii. 80.*

20. 14–16. Ic wille syllan ðisum endenēxtum eal swā micel swā ðē. . . . Lā, hū ne mōt ic dōn þæt ic wille ? . . . Oððe ðīn ēage is yfel, forðanþe ic eom gōd ? . . . Þus bēoð þā endenēxtan fyrmeste, and þā fyrmestan endenēxte. . . . Fela sind gelaðode, and fēawa gecorene. *Æ. H. ii. 80, 82.*

20. 17. *See* Luke 18. 31–43, note 4.

20. 22, 23. . . . se ðe cwæð tō his twām apostolum, Iacobum et

aut patrem, aut matrem, aut uxorem, aut filios, aut agros, propter nomen meum, centuplum accipiet, et vitam aeternam possidebit.

20. 1. Simile est regnum coelorum homini patrifamilias, qui exiit primo mane conducere operarios in vineam suam.

20. 2–6. Conventione autem facta cum operariis ex denario diurno, misit eos in vineam suam. Et egressus circa horam tertiam, vidit alios, . . . et dixit illis : Ite et vos in vineam meam. . . . Illi autem abierunt. Iterum autem exiit circa sextam et nonam horam, et fecit similiter. Circa undecimam vero exiit, et invenit

alios stantes, et dicit illis : Quid hic statis tota die otiosi ?

20. 7. Dicunt ei : Quia nemo nos conduxit. . . .

20. 9. Cum venissent ergo qui circa undecimam horam venerant, acceperunt singulos denarios.

20. 12. . . . qui portavimus pondus diei et aestus.

20. 14–16. . . . Volo autem et huic novissimo dare sicut et tibi. Aut non licet mihi quod volo facere ? an oculus tuus nequam est, quia ego bonus sum ? Sic erunt novissimi primi, et primi novissimi ; multi enim sunt vocati, pauci vero electi.

20. 22, 23. Respondens autem Iesus dixit : . . . Potestis bibere calicem

[1] Note the arrangement in pairs, and the transposition of 'gebytlu' for this purpose.

Iohannem [1] : Mage gē drincan þone cālic þe ic drincan sceall ?
Hī sǣdon þæt hī mihton.   Drihten sǣde : Witodlice, gē drincað
mīnne cālic. · Æ. H. ii. 544.

21. 1, 2. Se Hǣlend fērde tō ōðre byrig Hierusalem, and ðā-ðā hē
genōalǣhte ðǣre dūne Oliueti, þā sęnde hē his twēgen leorningcnihtas, þus cweðende : Gað tō ðǣre byrig þe ēow ongēan is,
and gē gemētað þǣrrihte getīgedne assan, and his folan samod ;
untȳgað hī, and lǣdað tō mē.   Æ. H. i. 206.

21. 3. Se Hlāford behōfað þēra assena ; and sęnt hī ęft ongēan. . . .
        Æ. H. i. 208, 210.

21. 5. *See* Æ. H. ii. 242.

21. 7–9. Crīstes leorningcnihtas lēdon hyra rēaf uppan þān assan.
. . . Þæt folc ðe heora rēaf wurpon under þæs assan fēt. . . .
Þā ðe ðǣra trēowa bōgas hēowon, and mid þām Crīstes weig
gedæfton. . . . Þæt folc ðe Crīste beforan stōp, and þæt ðe him
fyligde, ealle hī sungon : Osanna filio Dauid, þæt is on ūrum
geðēode : Sȳ hǣlo Dauides bearne. . . . Geblētsod is se ðe cōm
on Godes naman. . . . Sȳ hǣlo Dauides bearne on hēahnyssum.
        Æ. H. i. 210, 212, 214.

‖ Geblētsod is sē ðe cōm on Godes naman.   Æ. H. i. 60.

21. 14. Him ðā tō genðalǣhton blinde and healte, and hē hī
gehǣlde.   Æ. H. i. 406.

21. 41. Ic sęcge ēow þæt Godes rīce bið ēow ætbrōden, and bið
forgyfen ðǣre ðēode þe his wǣstmas wyrcað.   Æ. H. ii. 74.

22. 1–4. Drihten wæs sprecende on sumere tīde tō his apostolum

quem ego bibiturus sum ? Dicunt
ei : Possumus. Ait illis : Calicem
quidem meum bibetis. . . .
21. 1, 2. Et cum appropinquassent
Ierosolymis, et venissent Beth-
phage ad montem Oliveti, tunc
Iesus misit duos discipulos, dicens
eis : Ite in castellum quod contra
vos est, et statim invenietis asinam
alligatam, et pullum cum ea ; solvite, et adducite mihi.
21. 3. . . . Dominus his opus habet ;
et confestim dimittet eos.
21. 7–9. . . . Imposuerunt super
eos vestimenta sua. . . . Plurima

autem turba straverunt vestimenta
sua in via ; alii autem caedebant
ramos de arboribus, et sternebant
in via. Turba autem quae praece-
debant, et quae sequebantur, clamabant dicentes : Hosanna filio
David ; benedictus qui venit in
nomine Domini ; hosanna in
altissimis.
21. 14. Et accesserunt ad eum caeci
et claudi, . . . et sanavit eos.
21. 41. . . . Vineam suam locabit
aliis agricolis, qui reddant ei
fructum temporibus suis.
22. 1–4. Et respondens Iesus, dixit

[1] From Mark 10. 35, ‘Iacobus et Ioannes.’

mid bigspellum, þus cweðende: Heofonan ríce is gelíc sumum
cyninge þe worhte his suna gyfte. Þā sęndo hō his bydelas tō
gelaðigenne his underðeoddan. . . . Þā-ðā hī noldon cuman tō
ðǣm giftum, ðā sęnde hō ęft, þus cweðende: Sęcgað ðǣm gelað-
odum: Efne, ic gegearcode mīne gōd, ic ofslōh mīne fearras and
mīne gemǣstan fugelas, and ealle mīne ðing ic gearcode; cumað
tō þǣm giftum. Æ. H. i. 522.

‖ Mīne fearras sind ofslagene, and mīne gemǣstan fugelas.
Æ. H. i. 524.

22. 5-14. Hī hit forgȳmeleāsodon, and fērdon, sume tō heora
tūnum, sume tō heora cēape. . . . Sume hī gelǣhton þā bydelas,
and mid tēonan gewǣhton, and ofslōgon. Ac se cyning, ðā-ðā
hē þis geāxode, sęnde his hęre tō, and þā manslagan fordyde,
and heora burh forbǣrnde. . . . Se cyning cwað ða tō his
þegnum: Ðās gyfta sind gearowe, ac þā ðe ic þǣrtō gelaðode
nǣron his wyrðe. Farað nū tō wega ūtscytum, and swā-hwylce-
swā gē gemētað laþiað tō þǣm gyftum. . . . Hwæt, ðā ðæs
cyninges ǣrendracan fērdon geond wegas, gadrigende ealle þā
ðe hī gemētton, ǣgðer ge yfele ge gōde; and gesętton þā gifta
ęndemes. . . . Se cyning ðode inn, and gescēawode þā gebēoras;
þā geseah hē þǣr ǣnne mann þe næs gescrȳd mid gyftlicum
rēafe. . . . Þū frēond, hūmeta dorstest ðū gān tō mīnre gearc-
unge būton gyftlicum rēafe? . . . Hē þǣrrihte ādumbode. . . .
Se cyning cwæð tō his ðegnum: Bindað þone misscrȳddan
handum and fōtum, and wurpað intō ðǣm yttrum þēostrum;
þǣr bið wōp and tōða gebitt. . . . Fela sind gecīgede, and fēawa
gecorene. Æ. H. i. 524, 526, 528, 530, 532.

iterum in parabolis eis, dicens: Simile factum est regnum coelorum homini regi, qui fecit nuptias filio suo. Et misit servos suos vocare invitatos ad nuptias, et nolebant venire. Iterum misit alios servos, dicens: Dicite invitatis: Ecce prandium meum paravi, tauri mei et altilia occisa sunt, et omnia parata; venite ad nuptias.

22. 5-14. Illi autem neglexerunt, et abierunt, alius in villam suam, alius vero ad negotiationem suam. Reliqui vero tenuerunt servos eius, et contumeliis affectos occiderunt. Rex autem cum audisset, iratus est, et, missis exercitibus suis, perdidit homicidas illos, et civitatem illorum succendit. Tunc ait servis suis: Nuptiae quidem paratae sunt, sed qui invitati erant non fuerunt digni. Ite ergo ad exitus viarum, et quoscumque inveneritis vocate ad nuptias. Et egressi servi eius in vias, congregaverunt omnes quos invenerunt, malos et bonos; et impletae

22. 21. . . . . þæt hwā sceolde āgildan ðām cāsere þæt him gebyreð, and Gode þæt him gebyreð. Æ. H. ii. 68.

22. 30. *See* Luke 20. 35, 36.

22. 37-40. Lufa ðīnne Drihten mid ealre ðīnre heortan, and mid eallum mōde; þis is þæt mǣste bebod. Is eft ōðer bebod ðisum swīðe gelīc: Lufa ðīnne nēxtan swā-swā ðē sylfne. Þās twā bebodu belūcað ealle bēc. Æ. H. ii. 314; cf. i. 232, and Luke 18. 20-22, notes.

23. 3. Gif se lārēow wel tǣce and yfele bȳsnige, dōð swā-swā hē tǣcð, and nā be ðām þe hē bȳsnað. Æ. H. i. 242.

‖ Gif se lārēow riht tǣce, dō gehwā swā-swā hē tǣcð; and gif hē yfel bȳsnige, ne dō gē nā be his gebȳsnungum, ac dōð swā-swā hē tǣcð. Æ. H. ii. 48.

‖ Dōð swā-swā hī tǣcað, and ne dō gē swā-swā hī dōð. Æ. H. ii. 68.

23. 8, 9. Gē ealle sind gebrōðra, and ænne Fæder habbað, se ðe on heofonum is hēalice sittende. Æ. H. ii. 318.

23. 12. *See* Luke 18. 12-14.

23. 27, 28. Wā ēow hīwerum; gē sind gelīce gemōttum ofergeweorcum, þe bēoð wiðūtan wlitige mannum ætēowode, and sēo byrgen ðēah bið āfylled mid dēadum bānum and forrotodnysse; swā sind gē ēac ætēowode wiðūtan rihtwīse on manna gesihðum, and gē sind wiðinnan āfyllede mid hīwunge and unrihtwīsnysse. Æ. H. ii. 404.

sunt nuptiae discumbentium. Intravit autem rex ut videret discumbentes, et vidit ibi hominem non vestitum veste nuptiali. . . . Amice, quomodo huc intrasti non habens vestem nuptialem? At ille obmutuit. Tunc dixit rex ministris: Ligatis manibus et pedibus eius, mittite eum in tenebras exteriores; ibi erit fletus et stridor dentium. Multi enim sunt vocati, pauci vero electi.

22. 21. . . . Reddite ergo quae sunt Caesaris Caesari, et quae sunt Dei Deo.

22. 37-40. . . . Diliges Dominum Deum tuum ex toto corde tuo, et in tota anima tua, et in tota mente tua; hoc est maximum et primum mandatum. Secundum autem simile est huic: Diliges proximum tuum sicut teipsum. In his duobus mandatis universa lex pendet, et prophetae.

23. 3. Omnia ergo quaecumque dixerint vobis servate et facite; secundum opera vero eorum nolite facere. . . .

23. 8, 9. . . . Omnes autem vos fratres estis. . . . Unus est enim Pater vester qui in coelis est.

23. 27, 28. Vae vobis, . . . hypocritae; quia similes estis sepulcris dealbatis, quae a foris parent hominibus speciosa, intus vero plena sunt

24. 5. Manega lēase Crīstas [1] cumað on mīnum naman, cweðende : Ic eom Crīst, and wyrcað fela tācna and wundra [1] tō bepǣcenne mancynn. Æ. H. i. 4.

24. 7. *See* Luke 21. 10, 11.

24. 12, 13. And ðonne genihtsumað sēo unrihtwīsnys, and bið forðī manegra manna lufu ācōlod ; ac sē ðe þurhwunað oð ęnde on gelēafan, sē bið gehealden. Æ. H. ii. 542.

‖ Sē ðe ǣfre ðurhwunað on ānrǣdum gelēafan, sē bið gehealden. Æ. H. ii. 330.

24. 21. Ðonne bcoð swilce gedręccednyssa swilce nǣron nǣfre ǣr fram frymðe middangeardes. Æ. H. i. 4.

24. 22. *See* Mark 13. 20.

24. 24. *See* Matt. 24. 5, note.

24. 29, 30. Þǣrrihte æfter ðǣre micclan gedrēfednysse bið sēo sunne āðȳstrod, and se mōna ne sylð nān lēoht, and steorran feallað of heofonum. and heofonan mihta bēoð āstyrode ; and ðonne bið ætēowed Crīstes rōdetācn on heofonum and ealle eorðlice mǣgða hēofiað. Æ. H. i. 610.

24. 31. Drihten āsęnt his ęnglas mid bȳman and micelre stemne, and hī gaderiað his gecorenan fram fēower windum, of eallum eorðlicum gemǣrum oð ðā hēalican heofonan [2]. Æ. H. i. 616.

24. 36. Nāt nān man ðone dæg nē ðone tīman ðȳsre worulde geęndunge, nē ęnglas, nē nān hālga, būton Gode ānum.
 Æ. H. i. 298.

ossibus mortuorum et omni spurcitia ; sic et vos a foris quidem paretis hominibus iusti, intus autem pleni estis hypocrisi et iniquitate.

24. 5. Multi enim venient in nomine meo, dicentes : Ego sum Christus ; et multos seducent.

24. 12, 13. Et quoniam abundavit iniquitas, refrigescet charitas multorum ; qui autem perseveraverit usque in finem, hic salvus erit.

24. 21. Erit enim tunc tribulatio magna, qualis non fuit ab initio mundi usque modo. . . .

24. 29, 30. Statim autem post tribulationem dierum illorum sol obscurabitur, et luna non dabit lumen suum, et stellae cadent de coelo, et virtutes coelorum commovebuntur ; et tunc parebit signum Filii hominis in coelo, et tunc plangent omnes tribus terrae. . . .

24. 31. Et mittet angelos suos cum tuba et voce magna, et congregabunt electos eius a quattuor ventis, a summis coelorum usque ad terminos eorum.

24. 36. De die autem illa et hora nemo scit, neque angeli coelorum, nisi solus Pater.

[1] From Matt. 24. 24, 'Pseudochristi . . . dabunt signa magna et prodigia.'

[2] Perhaps influenced by Mark 13. 27, 'a summo terrae usque ad summum coeli.'

25. 1, 2. . . . . þæt heofenan rīce wǽre gelīc tȳn mǽdenum, þe genāmon heora lēohtfatu, and ēodon tōgēanes ðām brȳdguman and þǽre brȳde.　Þǽra mǽdena wǽron fīf stunte, and fīf snotore.　Æ. H. ii. 562.

‖ Ðā mǽdenu woldon gān tōgēanes ðām brȳdguman mid heora lēohtfatum.　Æ. H. ii. 566.

25. 4–10. Ðā snoteran mǽdenu nāmon ðone ele on heora lēohtfatum. . . . Ac hē ęlcað his tōcymes, and on ðǽre anbīdunge þā mǽdenu hnappiað and slāpað. . . . On middre nihte wearð clypung gehȳred: Efne, hēr cymð se brȳdguma; gāð him tōgēanes. . . . Þā ārison ealle ðā mǽdenu, and gegearcodon heora lēohtfatu. . . . Þā stuntan mǽdenu cwǽdon tō ðām snoterum: Syllað ūs sumne dǽl ēoweres eles, forðanþe ūre lēohtfatu sind ācwęncte. . . . Ðā snoteran mǽdenu andwyrdon ðām stuntum, and cwǽdon: Þī-lǽs-ðe hit ne genihtsumige ūs and ēow, farað tō ðām syllendum, and bicgað ēow ele. . . . Þā, mid-ðām-þe hī fērdon ymbe ðone cēap, ðā cōm se brȳdguma; and ðā fīf mǽdenu, ðe mid þām lēohte gearwe wǽron, fērdon mid him in tō ðām giftum; and þæt geat wearð belocen.
　　　Æ. H. ii. 564, 566, 568, 570.

‖ Þæt geat wǽs belocen.　Æ. H. ii. 572.

25. 11. Ðā æt nēxtan cōmon ðā stuntan mǽdenu, and clypodon tō ðām brȳdguman: Hlāford, hlāford, hāt geopenian þæt geat.　Æ. H. ii. 572.

‖ Ðā stuntan mǽdenu clypodon: Hlāford, hlāford, hāt geopenian ūs þæt geat.　Æ. H. ii. 572.

---

25. 1, 2. Tunc simile erit regnum coelorum decem virginibus, quae, accipientes lampades suas, exierunt obviam sponso et sponsae. Quinque autem ex eis erant fatuae, et quinque prudentes.

25. 4–10. Prudentes vero acceperunt oleum in vasis suis cum lampadibus. Moram autem faciente sponso, dormitaverunt omnes et dormierunt. Media autem nocte clamor factus est: Ecce sponsus venit; exite obviam ei. Tunc surrexerunt omnes virgines illae, et ornaverunt lampades suas.

Fatuae autem sapientibus dixerunt: Date nobis de oleo vestro, quia lampades nostrae extinguuntur. Responderunt prudentes, dicentes: Ne forte non sufficiat nobis et vobis, ite potius ad vendentes, et emite vobis. Dum autem irent emere, venit sponsus; et quae paratae erant intraverunt cum eo ad nuptias; et clausa est ianua.

25. 11. Novissime vero veniunt et reliquae virgines, dicentes: Domine, Domine, aperi nobis.

25. 12, 13. And se hláford andwyrde : Sōð ic ēow sęcge : Ne cann
ic ēow. . . . Waciað eornostlice, forðanþe gē nyton þone dæg nē
ðā tīd. *Æ. H. ii. 572, 574.*

25. 14, 15. Sum rīce man wolde faran on ælðēodigne eard. Þā
clypode hē his ðēowan him tō, and betæhte him his gōd.
Sumon hē betæhte fīf pund, sumum twā pund, sumum ān.
ǽlcum be his āgenre mihte, and hēt hī mid þām fēo him māre
gestrýnan ; and fērde siððan on ælðēodignysse, swā-swā hē
gemynt hæfde. *Æ. H. ii. 548 ; cf. ii. 550.*

25. 16. Se gōda ðēowa, þe ðā fīf pund underfēng, gestrýnde his
hláforde þǽrtō ōðre fīf. *Æ. H. ii. 550.*

25. 18. Se lýðra ðēowa, se ðe þæt ān pund underfēng, fērde
and bedealf hit on eorðan, and swā his hláfordes feoh behýdde. *Æ. H. ii. 552.*

25. 21. Ðonne cweð hē tō ðām gōdum ðēowan : . . . Ēalā, ðū
gōda ðēowa and getrýwe, þū wǽre getrýwe on lýtlum ðingum,
ic wylle ðē sęttan ofer māran ; far nū intō ðīnes hláfordes
gefēan. *Æ. H. ii. 552.*

25. 24–30. Se āsolcena ðēowa, þe nolde tilian nān ðing his hláforde
mid ðām befæstum punde, cōm him tō mid belādunge, and
cwæð : Lā lēof, ic wāt þæt ðū eart swīðe styrne mann, and wilt
niman þæt ðū ǽr ne sealdest, and wilt rīpan þæt þū ǽr ne
sēowe ; þā wearð ic forðī āfyrht, and behýdde ðīn pund on
eorðan ; efne, þū hæfst nū ðīn āgen. . . . Se hláford cwæð tō
þām lýðran ðēowan : Ðū yfela ðēowa and sleac, þē gedafenode
þæt ðū befæstest mīn feoh myneterum tō slēanne, and ic wolde

25. 12, 13. At ille respondens ait :
Amen dico vobis : Nescio vos.
Vigilate itaque, quia nescitis diem
neque horam.

25. 14, 15. Sicut enim homo peregre
proficiscens, vocavit servos suos,
et tradidit illis bona sua. Et uni
dedit quinque talenta, alii autem
duo, alii vero unum, unicuique
secundum propriam virtutem, et
profectus est statim.

25. 16. Abiit autem qui quinque
talenta acceperat, et operatus est
in eis, et lucratus est alia quinque.

25. 18. Qui autem unum acceperat,
abiens fodit in terram, et abscondit
pecuniam domini sui.

25. 21. Ait illi dominus ejus : Euge,
serve bone et fidelis, quia super
pauca fuisti fidelis, super multa te
constituam ; intra in gaudium
domini tui.

25. 24–30. Accedens autem et qui
unum talentum acceperat, ait :
Domine, scio quia homo durus es,
metis ubi non seminasti, et con-
gregas ubi non sparsisti ; et timens
abii, et abscondi talentum tuum
in terra ; ecce, habes quod tuum
est. Respondens autem dominus
ejus, dixit ei : Serve male et piger,
. . . oportuit . . . te committere

mīn āgen ofgān mid ðām gafole. . . . Nimað þæt pund of ðām
yfelan ðēowan, and syllað þām ðe mē brōhte tȳn pund. Hī
cwǣdon : Lā lēof, hē hæfð tȳn pund[1]. . . . Ic secge ēow tō
sōðan : Ǣlc þēra ðe hæfð, him bið māre geseald, and hē
genihtsumað. Sē ðe næfð, him bið ætbrōden þæt þæt hē hæfð.
. . . Se unholda ðēowa wearð ðā āworpen on þām yttrum
þēostrum. Æ. H. ii. 552, 554, 556.

25. 31–46. Witodlīce mannes Bearn cymð on his mægenðrymme,
and ealle englas samod mid him tō ðām micclum dōme ; þonne
sitt hē on ðām setle his mægenðrymnysse, and bēoð gegaderode ætforan him ealle ðēoda ; and hē tōscǣt hī on twā, swā-
swā scēphyrde tōscǣt scēp fram gātum. Þonne gelōgað hē ðā
scēp on his swīðran hand, and ða gǣt on his wynstran. . . .
Þonne cwyð se Cyning Crīst tō ðām þe on his swīðran hand
standað : Cumað, gē blētsode mīnes Fæder, and gēagniað þæt
rīce ðe ēow gegearcod wæs fram frimðe middaneardes. Mē
hingrode, and gē mē gereordodon ; mē ðyrste, and gē mē
scencton ; ic wæs cuma, and gē mē underfēngon on ēowerum
gesthūsum ; ic wæs nacod, and gē mē scrȳddon ; ic wæs geuntrumod, and gē mē genēosodon ; ic wæs on cwearterne, and gē
cōmon tō mē and mē gefrēfrodon. Ðonne andswariað þā rihtwīsan Crīste, and cweðað : Drihten, hwænne gesāwe wē ðē
hungrine, and wē ðē gereordodon ? oððe þurstigne, and wē ðē

pecuniam meam numulariis, et
veniens ego recepissem utique
quod meum est cum usura. Tollite
itaque ab eo talentum, et date ei
qui habet decem talenta. Omni
enim habenti dabitur, et abunda-
bit ; ei autem qui non habet, et
quod videtur habere auferetur ab
eo. Et inutilem servum eiicite
in tenebras exteriores. . . .

25. 31–46. Cum autem venerit Filius
hominis in maiestate sua, et omnes
angeli cum eo, tunc sedebit super
sedem maiestatis suae, et con-
gregabuntur ante eum omnes
gentes ; et separabit eos ab invicem, sicut pastor segregat oves

ab haedis. Et statuet oves quidem a dextris suis, haedos autem
a sinistris. Tunc dicet Rex his
qui a dextris eius erunt : Venite,
benedicti Patris mei, possidete
paratum vobis regnum a constitu-
tione mundi. Esurivi enim, et
dedistis mihi manducare ; sitivi,
et dedistis mihi bibere ; hospes
eram, et collegistis me ; nudus,
et cooperuistis me ; infirmus, et
visitastis me ; in carcere eram, et
venistis ad me. Tunc respondebunt ei iusti, dicentes : Domine,
quando te vidimus esurientem, et
pavimus te ? sitientem, et dedimus
tibi potum ? quando autem te

[1] From Luke 19. 25, 'Et dixerunt ei : Domine, habet decem mnas.'

scęncton? oððe hwænne wǣre ðū cuma, and wē ðē underfēngon? oððe hwænne gesāwe wē ðē untrumne oþþe on
cwearterne, and wē ðē genēosodon? Þonne andwyrd se Cyning
ðām rihtwīsum þisum wordum : Sōð ic ēow sęcge : Swā lange
swā gē dydon ānum, þisum lǣstan, on mīnum naman, gē hit
dydon mē sylfum. Þonne cweð hē eft tō ðām synfullum, þe
on his wynstran healfe standað : Gewītað fram mē, gē āwyrigedan, intō ðām ēcan fȳre, þe is gegearcod ðām dēofle and his
āwyrigedum gāstum. Mē hingrode, and gē mē ǣtes forwyrndon ; mē ðyrste, and gē mē drincan ne sealdon ; ic wæs cuma,
and gē mē underfōn noldon ; ic wæs nacod, nolde gē mē wǣda
tīðian ; ic wæs untrum and on cwearterne, nolde gē mē genēos-
ian. Þonne andswariað ðā unrihtwīsan mānfullan : Lā lēof,
hwænne gesāwe wē ðē hungrine, oððe ðurstine, oððe cuman,
oþþe nacodne, oððe geuntrumodne, oþþe on cwearterne, and wē
ðē noldon ðēnian? Þonne andwyrd se Cyning him, and cwyð :
Sōð ic ēow sęcge : Swā lange swā gē forwyrndon ānum of ðisum
lȳtlum, and noldon him on mīnum naman tīðian, swā lange gē
mē sylfum his forwyrndon. Þonne farað ðā uncystigan and
ðā unrihtwīsan intō ēcere cwicsūsle, mid dēofle and his āwyrigedum ęnglum ; and ðā rihtwīsan gecyrrað fram ðām dōme intō
ðām ēcan līfe. Æ. H. ii. 106, 108.

‖ Cumað, gē geblētsode mīnes Fæder, and gehabbað þæt
rīce þæt ēow gegearcod wæs fram aginne middangeardes.
    Æ. H. i. 264.

‖ Cumað tō mē, gē geblētsode mīnes Fæder, and onfōð

vidimus hospitem, et collegimus te, aut nudum, et cooperuimus te? aut quando te vidimus infirmum aut in carcere, et venimus ad te? Et respondens Rex dicet illis : Amen dico vobis: Quamdiu fecistis uni ex his fratribus meis minimis, mihi fecistis. Tunc dicet et his qui a sinistris erunt : Discedite a me, maledicti, in ignem aeternum, qui paratus est diabolo et angelis eius. Esurivi enim, et non dedistis mihi manducare ; sitivi, et non dedistis mihi potum ; hospes eram, et non collegistis me ; nu-dus, et non cooperuistis me ; infirmus et in carcere, et non visitastis me. Tunc respondebunt ei et ipsi, dicentes ; Domine, quando te vidimus essurientem, aut sitientem, aut hospitem, aut nudum, aut infirmum, aut in carcere, et non ministravimus tibi? Tunc respondebit illis dicens : Amen dico vobis : Quamdiu non fecistis uni de minoribus his, nec mihi fecistis. Et ibunt hi in supplicium aeternum, iusti autem in vitam aeternam.

þæt rīce ðe ēow is gegearcod fram frymðe middangeardes.
Æ. H. i. 396.

‖ Mē hingrode, and gē mē gereordodon; mē ðyrste, and gē mē scęncton; ic wæs nacod, and gē mē scrȳddon. Æ. H. i. 336.

‖ Ic wæs cuma, and gē mē underfēngon. Æ. H. ii. 286.

‖ Þæt þæt gē dōð ānum ðearfan on mīnum naman, þæt gē dōð mē sylfum. Æ. H. i. 258.

‖ Þæt þæt gē dōð þearfum on mīnum naman, þæt gē dōð mē sylfum. Æ. H. i. 336.

‖ Swā-hwæt-swā gē dōð on mīnum naman ānum ðām lǣstum, þæt gē dōð mē sylfum. Æ. H. ii. 438.

‖ Gewītað fram mē, gē āwyrigedan, intō ðām ēcum fȳre, þe is gegearcod dēofle and his āwyrgedum gāstum. Æ. H. i. 396.

‖ Gewītað fram mē, gē āwyrigedan, intō ðām ēcan fȳre, þe ðām dēofle is gegearcod and his āwyrigedum ęnglum.
Æ. H. ii. 572, 592.

26. 14. *See* Luke 22. 3–5, and Æ. H. i. 26.

26. 15. *See* Luke 22. 3–5, note.

26. 20–25. Hē ēode ęft sittan siððan mid his ðegnum. And on his gereorde hē geunrōtsode[1], cwæð þæt heora ān hine belǣwan wolde. Hī ðā ealle mid angsumum mōde ǣnlīpige cwǣdon: Eom ic hit, Drihten? Þā andwyrde se Hǣlend him sōna ðus: Sē ðe bedȳpð on disce mid mē his hlāf on lǣpeldre, hē is mīn lǣwa. Wā ðām męn þe mē belǣwð! bętere him wǣre þæt hē geboren nǣre. Þā befrān Iudas gif hē hit wǣre. Ðā cwæð se Hǣlend: Ðū hit sǣdest. Æ. H. ii. 242, 244.

‖ . . . þæt him sēlre wǣre þæt hē geboren nǣre. Æ. H. ii. 244.

26. 26–28. Hē genam ðā hlāf, and hine līflice gehālgode, tōdǣlde his ðegnum, and hī ðicgan hēt; cwæð þæt hit wǣre his āgen līchama. . . . Ęft swā gelīce gelæhte ænne cālic, sēnode mid swīð-

26. 20–25. . . . Discumbebat cum duodecim discipulis suis. Et edentibus illis, dixit: Amen dico vobis quia unus vestrum me traditurus est. Et contristati valde coeperunt singuli dicere: Numquid ego sum, Domine? At ipse respondens ait: Qui intingit mecum manum in paropside, hic me tradet. . . . Vae autem homini illi per quem Filius hominis tradetur; bonum erat ei, si natus non fuisset homo ille. Respondens autem Iudas, qui tradidit eum, dixit: Numquid ego sum, Rabbi? Ait illi: Tu dixisti.

26. 26–28. . . . Accepit Iesus panem, et benedixit, ac fregit, deditque

---

[1] From John 13. 21, 'turbatus est spiritu.'

ran, and scalde his gingrum, of tō sūpenne æfter gereorde ; sǣde
þæt hit wǣre sōðlice his blōd ðǣre nīwan gecȳðnysse, þæt hē for
mannum āgēat on synna forgyfennysse. Æ. H. ii. 244.

He hālgode hlāf ǣr his ðrōwunge, and tōdǣlde his discipulum,
þus cweðende : Etað þisne hlāf, hit is mīn līchama ; and dōð
þis on mīnum gemynde [1].   Eft hē blētsode wīn on ānum cālice,
and cwæð : Drincað ealle of ðisum ; þis is mīn blōd, þæt ðe bið
for manegum āgoten on synna forgifenysse.   Æ. H. ii. 266, 268.

‖ Þis is mīn līchama and mīn blod.   Æ. H. ii. 274.

26. 31-35. Eft se Hǣlend sǣde sōðlice his gingrum : Ealle gē
mē ǣswiciað on ðissere ānre nihte. Hit is sōðlice āwriten :
Ic ofslōa ðone hyrde, and ðā scēp siðððan sōna bēoð tōstencte.
Æfter-ðan-ðe ic ārīse of dēaðe gesund, ic ēow eft gemēte on
Galileiscum earde.   Þā andwyrde Petrus āna mid gebēote :
Ic ðē nǣfre ne ǣswicige, ðēah-ðe ealle ōðre dōn.   Drihten
eft andwyrde ānrǣdlice Petre : Þū mē wiðsæcst ðriwa on
ðissere nihte, ǣrðanðe se hana hafitigende crāwe.   Petrus
cwæð þæt hē nolde hine nǣfre wiðsacan, ðēah-ðe hē sceolde
samod mid him sweltan ; and ealle ðā ōðre ealswā cwǣdon.

      Æ. H. ii. 244, 246.

26. 39. Fæder mīn, gif hit gewurðan mæg, āfyrsa þisne cālic fram
mē.   Æ. H. ii. 544.

26. 48, 49. Þā cwæð se lǣwa tō ðām lāðum flocce : Swā-hwilcne-
swā ic cysse, cōpað his sōna.   And hē ðā mid cosse Crīst
belǣwde.   Æ. H. ii. 246.

discipulis suis, et ait : Accipite et
comedite ; hoc est corpus meum.
Et accipiens calicem gratias egit,
et dedit illis, dicens : Bibite ex
hoc omnes ; hic est enim sanguis
meus novi testamenti, qui pro
multis effundetur in remissionem
peccatorum.

26. 31-35. Tunc dicit illis Iesus :
Omnes vos scandalum patiemini
in me in ista nocte. Scriptum
est enim : Percutiam pastorem,
et dispergentur oves gregis. Postquam autem resurrexero, praecedam vos in Galilaeam. Respondens autem Petrus ait illi : Et si
omnes scandalizati fuerint in te,
ego nunquam scandalizabor. Ait
illi Iesus : Amen dico tibi quia
in hac nocte, antequam gallus
cantet, ter me negabis. Ait illi
Petrus : Etiamsi oportuerit me
mori tecum, non te negabo. Similiter et omnes discipuli dixerunt.

26. 39. . . . Pater mi, si possibile
est, transeat a me calix iste. . . .

26. 48, 49. Qui autem tradidit eum
dedit illis signum, dicens : Quemcumque osculatus fuero ipse est ;
tenete eum. . . . Et osculatus est
eum.

----

[1] From Luke 22. 19, 1 Cor. 11. 24, 'hoc facite in meam commemorationem.'

26. ₅₁₋₅₄. Đā ābrǣd Petrus[1] bealdlice his swurd, and geslōh heorn ānum þæt swīðre[2] ēare of. Ac Crīst him stȳrde mid stīðum wordum, and hēt hine hȳdan þæt hearde īsen ; cwæð þæt hē mihte ðā mā ðonne twelf ēoroda heofenlicra engla æt his Fæder ābiddan, gif hit weorðan ne sceolde swā-swā wītegan cwǣdon.
    Æ. H. ii. 246.

26. ₅₇. *See* Æ. H. ii. 248.

26. ₅₈. Ac Petrus him filigde feorran.   Æ. H. ii. 248.

26. ₆₃₋₆₇. Þā āxode hine se ealdorbiscop, and mid āðe gehālsode, þæt hē openlice sǣde gif hē Godes Sunu sōðlice wǣre. Se Hǣlend him cwæð tō : Ic eom swā ðū sǣdest ; and ic sittende bēo æt mīnes Fæder swīðran, and on wolcnum ic cume on ðissere worulde geendunge. Đā cwæð se ealdorbiscop mid orgel-worde : Hwæt ðincð ēow nū be ðissere segene ? Hī ealle andwyrdon mid ānre stemne þæt hē scyldig wǣre witodlice tō dēaðe. And hī hine bospætton, hūxlice sprecende.   Æ. H. ii. 248.

26. ₆₇, ₆₈. Iudei . . . mid ānum wǣfelse his neb bewundon[3], slēande mid handbredum hūxlice and gelōme, and hēton hine rǣdan hwā hine hreopode.   Æ. H. ii. 248.

26. ₆₉₋₇₅. Petrus stōd ofcalen on ðām cauertūne, æt micclum

26. ₅₁₋₅₄. Et ecce unus ex his qui erant cum Iesu, extendens manum, exemit gladium suum, et, percutiens servum principis sacerdotum, amputavit auriculam eius. Tunc ait illi Iesus : Converte gladium tuum in locum suum. . . . An putas quia non possum rogare Patrem meum, et exhibebit mihi modo plusquam duodecim legiones angelorum ? Quomodo ergo implebuntur Scripturae, quia sic oportet fieri ?

26. ₅₈. Petrus autem sequebatur eum a longe. . . .

26. ₆₃₋₆₇. . . . Et princeps sacerdotum ait illi : Adiuro te per Deum vivum ut dicas nobis si tu es Christus, Filius Dei. Dicit illi Iesus : Tu dixisti ; verumtamen dico vobis, amodo videbitis Filium hominis sedentem a dextris virtutis Dei, et venientem in nubibus coeli. Tunc princeps sacerdotum scidit vestimenta sua, dicens : . . . Quid vobis videtur ? At illi respondentes dixerunt : Reus est mortis. Tunc exspuerunt in faciem eius, et colaphis eum ceciderunt. . . .

26. ₆₇, ₆₈. . . . Alii autem palmas in faciem eius dederunt, dicentes : Prophetiza nobis, Christe, quis est qui te percussit ?

26. ₆₉₋₇₅. . . . Accessit ad eum una ancilla, dicens : Et tu cum Iesu Galilaeo eras. At ille negavit.

---

[1] From John 18. 10, 'Simon ergo Petrus.'
[2] From Luke 22. 50, John 18. 10, 'auriculam eius dexteram.'
[3] From Mark 14. 65, 'coeperunt . . . velare faciem eius,' or Luke 22. 64, 'velaverunt eum.'

fȳre¹ mid manegum ōðrum.   Ðā cwæð him ān wyln tō, þæt hē
wǣre mid Crīste ; ac hē sōna wiðsōc þæt hit swā nǣre.   Þā eft
ymbe hwīle cwæð sum ōðer wyln þæt hē mid ðām Hǣlende
on hȳrede wǣre ; and hē eft wiðcwæð þæt hē hine ne cūðe.
Þā genēalǣhton mā hine meldigende ; ac Petrus wiðsōc gȳt
ðriddan sīðe.   And se hana sōna hlūdswēge sang.   Ðā becyrde
se Hǣlend and beseah tō Petre², and hē sōna gemunde his
micclan gebēotes, and mid biterum wōpe his wiðersæc behrēow-
sode.   Æ. H. ii. 248.

27. 3. Iudas ðā geseah ðone rēðan dōm, and gebrōhte þæt feoh,
þe hē mid fācne genam, tō ðām ealdorbiscopum, gebolgen
swīðe.   Æ. H. ii. 250.

27. 5. And hine sylfne āhēng sōna mid grīne.   Æ. H. ii. 250.

27. 6, 7, 9. Ðā noldon ðā Iudei þæt feoh gelęcgan on heora fǣtels-
um, swilce hī fācne nǣron ; ac gebohton ænne æcer ælðeodigum
tō byrgelsum, þæt ðæs wītegan word wurdon gefyllede, þe ǣr
be ðām fēo ealswā wītegode.   Æ. H. ii. 250.

27. 11. Se Hǣlend ðā stōd on ðām dōmęrne gelǣdd.   Þā āxode
Pilatus hine orgollice gif hē Iudeiscre ðēode cyning on eornost
wǣre.   Ðā andwyrde se Hǣlend : Ðū hit sǣdest.   Æ. H. ii. 250.

27. 15–17. Ðā hēoldon ðā Iudei on hēalicum gewunan þæt hī ǣlce

... Vidit eum alia ancilla, et ait
his qui erant ibi : Et hic erat
cum Iesu Nazareno. Et iterum
negavit : ... Quia non novi hominem. Et post pusillum accesserunt qui stabant, et dixerunt
Petro : Vere et tu ex illis es. ...
Tunc coepit detestari et iurare
quia non novisset hominem. Et
continuo gallus cantavit. Et recordatus est Petrus verbi Iesu
quod dixerat : Prius quam gallus
cantet, ter me negabis. Et egressus foras flevit amare.

27. 3. Tunc videns Iudas, qui eum
tradidit, quod damnatus esset,
poenitentia ductus retulit triginta
argenteos principibus sacerdotum
et senioribus.

27. 5. ... Et abiens laqueo se sus-
pendit.

27. 6, 7, 9. Principes autem sacerdotum, acceptis argenteis, dixerunt : Non licet eos mittere in
corbonam, quia pretium sanguinis
est. Consilio autem inito, emе-
runt ex illis agrum figuli, in sepulturam peregrinorum. ... Tunc
impletum est quod dictum est per
Ieremiam prophetam. ...

27. 11. Iesus autem stetit ante
praesidem, et interrogavit eum
praeses, dicens : Tu es rex Iudaeorum ? Dicit illi Iesus : Tu dicis.

27. 15–17. Per diem autem solen-
nem consueverat praeses populo

¹ Probably from John 18. 18, 'Stabant autem servi et ministri ad prunas, quia
frigus erat, et calefaciebant se ; erat autem cum eis et Petrus stans, et calefaciens se.'
² From Luke 22. 61, 'Et conversus Dominus respexit Petrum.'

gēare ænne scyldigne ābǣdon æt ðām ealdormęnn tō heora
Ēastertīde.   And hæfdon ðā on bęndum ænne bealdne ðēof,
Barraban gecīgedne, for manslihte tō slęge ¹.   Þā befrān
Pilatus þæs folces męnigu hwæðerne hī gecuron, Hǣlend oððe
Barraban ?   Æ. H. ii. 252.

27. 21–25, 27–29, 31. Þæt folc him tō cwæð þæt hī gecuron Barraban.
Ðā āxode Pilatus ęft æt ðām folce, hwæt hē be Drihtne gedōn
sceolde ?   Þā cwǣdon hī ealle mid ānre stemne : Sȳ hē āhangen
on hēalicere rōde.   Ðā geseah Pilatus ðǣra Iudeiscra gehlȳd,
and āðwōh his handa on heora gesihðe, cwæð þæt hē unscyldig
his slęges wǣre.   Þā cwǣdon ðā Iudei him tō andsware : Bēo
his blōdes gyte ofer ūrum bearnum, and eal sēo wracu on ūs
wunigende.   Ðā hēt Pilatus ðone Hǣlend beswingan, and
betǣhte hine ðā tō heora bēnum, swā þæt hē wælhrēawlice
wurde āhangen.   Hwæt, ðā his cęmpan hine gelæchton on ðām
dōmęrne mid dyrstigum anginne, and hine unscrȳddon his
āgenum gyrelum, and mid wolcnrēadum wǣfelse hine bewǣfdon,
and mid þyrnenum helme his hēafod befēngon, and for cyne-
gyrde him hrēod forgēafon, bīgende heora cnēowu, and cweðende
mid hospe : Sȳ ðū hāl, lēof, Iudeiscre lēode cyning.   IIr ðā
hrǣdlice ęft hine unscrȳddon þām rēadan wǣfelse, and his
rēaf him on dydon, and woldon þǣrrihte tō rōde gelǣdan.
       Æ. H. ii. 252.

27. 32, 34. Hwæt, ðā cęmpan hine gelǣddon tō ðǣre cwealmstōwe,

dimittere unum vinctum, quem
voluissent.   Habebat autem tunc
vinctum insignem, qui dicebatur
Barabbas. Congregatis ergo illis,
dixit Pilatus : Quem vultis dimittam vobis, Barabbam, an Iesum
qui dicitur Christus ?

27. 21–25, 27–29, 31. . . . At illi
dixerunt : Barabbam. Dicit illis
Pilatus : Quid igitur faciam de
Iesu qui dicitur Christus ? Dicunt omnes : Crucifigatur. . . .
Videns autem Pilatus quia . . .
tumultus fieret, . . . lavit manus
coram populo, dicens : Innocens
ego sum a sanguine iusti huius.
. . . Et respondens universus popu-

lus, dixit : Sanguis eius super nos
et super filios nostros. . . . Iesum
autem flagellatum tradidit eis ut
crucifigeretur. Tunc milites prae-
sidis suscipientes Iesum in prae-
torium. . . . Et, exuentes eum,
chlamydem coccineam circumdederunt ei, et, plectentes coronam
de spinis, posuerunt super caput
eius, et arundinem in dextera
eius. Et, genu flexo ante eum,
illudebant ei, dicentes : Ave, rex
Iudaeorum. . . . Et postquam illu-
serunt ei, exuerunt eum chlamyde,
et induerunt eum vestimentis eius,
et duxerunt eum ut crucifigerent.

27. 33, 34. Et venerunt in locum

_____
¹ From Mark 15. 7, 'qui . . . fecerat homicidium.'

þǣr man cwealde sceaðan, and him budon drincan gebitrodne
wīndrẹnc, ac hē hit āscēaf sōna fram his mūðe. *Æ. H. ii. 254.*

27. 35. *See* John 19. 23.

27. 37, 38. *See* John 19. 18–20.

27. 42, 43. Gif hē sȳ Israhela cyning, þonne āstīge hē nū of ðǣre
rōde. and wē gelȳfað on hine. *Æ. H. i. 226.*

  ‖ Gif ðū Godes Sunu sȳ, gā of ðǣre rōde, and wē siððan swā
on ðē gelȳfað. *Æ. H. ii. 256.*

27. 45. Hwæt, ðā ymbe midne dæg wearð middaneard āðēostrod,
and sēo sunne behȳdde hire hātan lēoman oð ðā nigoðan tīde,
ðo wē nōn hātað. *Æ. H. ii. 256;* cf. i. 108.

27. 48. Eft ðā cwæð se Hǣlend þæt him hearde ðyrste. Ðā arn
tō ðǣm ẹcede sum ārlēas cẹmpa, and bedȳpte āne spinegan, and
bær tō his mūðe[1]. *Æ. H. ii. 256.*

27. 50–53. Ðā clypode Drihten, and cwæð tō his Fæder : Ic betǣce,
Fæder, þē nū mīnne gāst[2]. And hē, āhyldum hēafde[3], hine
sōna āgeaf. Efne, ðā tōbærst þæs temples wāhryft fram ðǣre
fyrste ufan oð ðā flōr neoðan ; and eal eorðe bifode, and tōburston
stānas ; byrgenu openodon mid dēadum bānum, and hālgena
līchaman lēohtlice ārison, cōmon tō ðǣre byrig, cūðlice ætēowode
manegum mannum. *Æ. H. ii. 256, 258 ;* cf. i. 108, 224, 226.

  ‖ Þæs temples wāhryft ēac wearð tōborsten. *Æ. H. ii. 258.*

27. 54. Se hundredes ealdor sōðlice clypode, æfter ðisum tācnum :
Þēs is sōð Godes Bearn. *Æ. H. ii. 258.*

qui dicitur Golgotha, quod est
Calvariae locus. Et dederunt ei
vinum bibere cum felle mistum.
Et cum gustasset, noluit bibere.

27. 42, 43. . . . Si rex Israel est, de-
scendat nunc de cruce, et credi-
mus ei. . . . Dixit enim : Quia
Filius Dei sum.

27. 45. A sexta autem hora tenebrae factae sunt super universam
terram usque ad horam nonam.

27. 48. Et continuo currens unus
ex eis, acceptam spongiam implevit aceto, . . . et dabat ei
bibere.

27. 50–53. Iesus autem iterum clamans voce magna, emisit spiritum.
Et ecce, velum templi scissum est
in duas partes a summo usque
deorsum ; et terra mota est, et
petrae scissae sunt ; et monu-
menta aperta sunt, et multa corpora sanctorum, qui dormierant,
surrexerunt, et exeuntes de monumentis post resurrectionem eius,
venerunt in sanctam civitatem, et
apparuerunt multis.

27. 54. Centurio autem, et qui cum
eo erant, custodientes Iesum, viso
terrae motu et his quae fiebant,

---

[1] From John 19. 28, 29, ‘Iesus . . . dixit: Sitio ; . . . obtulerunt ori eius.’
[2] From Luke 23. 46, ‘Pater, in manus tuas commendo spiritum meum.’
[3] From John 19. 30, ‘inclinato capite.’

N

27. 57, 58. Þā sum rīce ðegen ðearle wæs gelȳfed dearnunge[1] on Drihten for ðām dyrstigum folce, his nama wæs Ioseph ; and hē genēalǣhte ðā hrǣdlice on ǣfen tō ðām ealdormęn, bæd þæt hē mōste Drihtnes līc bebyrian. Þā . . . Pilatus . . . geðafode ðām ðegene þæt hē hine behwurfe. Æ. H. ii. 260.

27. 62–66. Hwæt, ðā Iudei ēodon tō Pilate, bǣdon þæt hē bude ðā byrgene besęttan mid wacelum weardum, þæt hē ne wurde forstolen, and ðām folce gesǣd þæt hē sylf ārȳse. Þā geðafode Pilatus þæt hī hine besǣton mid ymtrymminge, and ðā ðrūh geinnsegelodon. Æ. H. ii. 262.

‖ Þā-ðā Crīst bebyrged wæs, þā cwǣdon þā Iudeiscan tō heora ealdormęnn Pilate : Lā lēof, se swica ðe hēr ofslegen is cwæð gelōmlice, þā-þā hē on līfe wæs, þæt hē wolde ārīsan of dēaðe on þām ðriddan dæge. Æ. H. i. 220.

28. 2. *See* Æ. H. i. 108.

28. 3. His wlite wæs swilce līget, and his rēaf swā hwīt swā snāw. Æ. H. i. 222.

28. 5, 6. Se ęngel gehyrte ðā wīf, þus cweðende: Ne bēo gē āfyrhte. . . . Gē sēcað þone Hǣlend ; hē ārās ; nis hē hēr.
Æ. H. i. 222, 224.

28. 19, 20. Farað, and lǣrað ealle ðēoda, and fulliað hī on naman þæs Ælmihtigan Fæder, and his Suna, and þæs Hālgan

timuerunt valde, dicentes: Vere Filius Dei erat iste.

27. 57, 58. Cum autem sero factum esset, venit quidam homo dives ab Arimathaea, nomine Ioseph, qui et ipse discipulus erat Iesu ; hic accessit ad Pilatum, et petiit corpus Iesu. Tunc Pilatus iussit reddi corpus.

27. 62–66. Altera autem die, quae est post Parasceuen, convenerunt principes sacerdotum et Pharisaei ad Pilatum, dicentes: Domine, recordati sumus quia seductor ille dixit adhuc vivens: Post tres dies resurgam. Iube ergo custodiri sepulcrum usque in diem tertium, ne forte veniant discipuli eius, et furentur eum, et dicant plebi: Surrexit a mortuis ; et erit novissimus error peior priore. Ait illis Pilatus: Habetis custodiam, ite, custodite sicut scitis. Illi autem abeuntes, munierunt sepulcrum, signantes lapidem, cum custodibus.

28. 3. Erat autem aspectus eius sicut fulgur, et vestimentum eius sicut nix.

28. 5, 6. Respondens autem angelus dixit mulieribus: Nolite timere vos ; scio enim quod Iesum, qui crucifixus est, quaeritis ; non est hic ; surrexit enim. . . .

28. 19, 20. Euntes ergo docete omnes gentes, baptizantes eos in nomine Patris, et Filii, et Spiritus sancti ; docentes eos servare omnia

---

[1] From John 19. 38, 'occultus autem, propter metum Iudaeorum.'

Gāstes ; and lǣraðs̆ hī þæt hī healdon ealle ðā ðing þe ic ẻow bebēad. Æ. H. ii. 112.

‖ Faraðs̆ geond ealne middangeard, and lǣraðs̆ ealle ðẻoda, and fulliaðs̆ hī on naman þæs Fæder, and þæs Suna, and þæs Hālgan Gāstes ; and bẻodaðs̆ þæt hī healdon ealle ðā beboda þe ic ẻow tǣhte. Æ. H. i. 208.

‖ Ūre Drihten bebēad his discipulum þæt hī sceoldon lǣran and tǣcan eallum þẻodum ðā ðing þe hē sylf him tǣhte.
Æ. H. i. 6.

Ic bẻo mid ẻow eallum dagum, ōðs̆ þisre worulde geẹnd-unge. Æ. H. i. 310.

‖ Efne, ic bẻo mid ẻow eallum dagum, ōðs̆ þissere worulde gefyllednysse. Æ. H. i. 611.

‖ Efne, ic bẻo mid ẻow eallum dagum, ōðs̆ gefyllednysse ðyssere worulde. Æ. H. ii. 368.

MARK.

1. 3. *See* Isa. 40. 3, 4.

1. 6. *See* Matt. 3. 4.

1. 9. *See* Matt. 3. 13.

1 10. *See* Æ. H. i. 104.

1. 16. *See* Matt. 4. 18.

1. 18. *See* Matt. 4. 20.

1. 24. Þū eart Godes Sunu ; forðī ðū cōme þæt ðū woldest ūs for-dōn. Æ. H. i. 304.

2. 5. Mīn bearn, ðē synd þīne synna forgifene. Æ. H. i. 472.

2. 11. Ārīs nū, and ber hām ðīn legerbed. Æ. H. i. 472.

2. 17. *See* Matt. 9. 12.

4. 3. *See* Luke 8. 4-6.

4. 20. *See* Matt. 13. 23, and note.

4. 38. *See* Matt. 8. 23, 24, note.

5. 1-4. Hī ðā oferrẻowon ðone brym, and gelẹndon on ðām lande

quaecumque mandavi vobis; et ecce, ego vobiscum sum omnibus diebus, usque ad consummatio-nem sacculi.

MARK.

1. 24. . . . Venisti perdere nos ? scio qui sis, Sanctus Dei.

2. 5. . . . Fili, dimittuntur tibi pec-cata tua.

2. 11. . . . Surge, tolle grabatum tuum, et vade in domum tuam.

5. 1-4. Et venerunt trans fretum maris in regionem Gerasenorum. Et exeunti ei de navi, statim oc-currit de monumentis homo in

þe is gehāten Gerasenorum. Efne, ðā-ðā hī ūpēodon, arn ān wōd man tōgēanes ðām Hǣlende, se hæfde wununge on hǣðenum byrgenum, and hine ne mihte nān man mid racenteagum nē mid fōtcopsum gehæftan.   Æ. H. ii. 378.

5. 11 ff. *See* Æ. H. ii. 380.

5. 25, 27, 28. Wē rǣdað be sumon wīfe, þe wæs twelf gēar geuntrumod ðurh blōdes ryne. Ðā ēode hēo betwux þǣre menigu ðe se Hǣlend onfērde, and cwæð tō hire sylfre: Gif ic hūru his rēafes gefnædu[1] hreppe, ic bēo sōna hāl.   Æ. H. ii. 394.

5. 29 ff. *See* Luke 8. 44–48.

5. 41. *See* Luke 8. 54, 55, note.

6. 17. Se wælhrēowa cyning Herodes hine gehæfte, and on cwearterne sette, for his brōðor wīfe Herodiaden.   Æ. H. i. 476; cf. i. 478.

6. 18, 21–23. *See* Æ. H. i. 478, 480.

6. 27. *See* Æ. H. i. 478, 488.

6. 41. *See* Matt. 14. 19.

6. 45 ff. *See* Matt. 14. 22 ff.

6. 56. *See* Matt. 14. 36.

7. 25–30. *See* Matt. 15. 21 ff.

8. 1, 2. On sumere tīde wæs micel menigu mid þām Hǣlende on ānum wēstene metelēas. Þā clypode se Hǣlend his leorningcnihtas him tō, and cwæð: Mē ofhrēowð þissere menigu, . . . forðanðe hī nū for ðrīm dagum hēr mīn andbīdodon, and hī nabbað hwæt hī etað.   Æ. H. ii. 396.

‖ Þæt folc andbīdode ðrȳ dagas mid ðām Hǣlende for hǣlðe heora untrumra[2].   Æ. H. ii. 396.

spiritu immundo, qui domicilium habebat in monumentis, et neque catenis iam quisquam poterat eum ligare; quoniam saepe compedibus et catenis vinctus, dirupisset catenas, et compedes comminuisset, et nemo poterat eum domare.

5. 25, 27, 28. Et mulier, quae erat in profluvio sanguinis annis duodecim, . . . cum audisset de Iesu, venit in turba retro; . . . dicebat enim: Quia si vel vestimentum eius tetigero, salva ero.

6. 17. Ipse enim Herodes misit, ac tenuit Ioannem, et vinxit eum in carcere propter Herodiadem uxorem Philippi fratris sui. . . .

8. 1, 2. In diebus illis iterum cum turba multa esset, nec haberent quod manducarent, convocatis discipulis, ait illis: Misereor super turbam, quia ecce iam triduo sustinent me, nec habent quod manducent.

[1] From Matt. 9. 20, Luke 8. 44, 'fimbriam vestimenti eius.'
[2] From Matt. 15. 30, 31 ?'

8. 3. Gif ic hı forlǣte fæstende hām gecyrran, þonne āteoriað hı
be wege. . . . Sume hı cōmon feorran. *Æ. H. ii.* 396.

8. 6. Crīst hı hēt sittan uppon ðǣre corðan. . . . Drihten ðancode
ǣrðanðe hē ða hlāfas tōbrǣc. . . . Se Hǣlend ða tōbrǣc ða
hlāfas, and sealde his leornerum, þæt hı hit ðām folce dǣlan
sceoldon. *Æ. H. ii.* 398, 400.

8. 8, 9. Þæt folc æt, and hı wurdon ealle gefyllede. . . . Of ðǣre
lāfe wǣron gefyllede seofan spyrtan. . . . Þǣr wǣron gereordode fēower þūsend manna. *Æ. H. ii.* 400, 402.

8. 36. *See* Luke 9. 25.

9. 3 (Vulg. 2). *See* Matt. 17. 1–5, note.

9. 37 (Vulg. 36). *See* Matt. 18. 4, 5.

9. 44 (Vulg. 43). Þǣr nǣfre heora wyrm ne swylt, nē heora fȳr
ne bið ādwǣsced. *Æ. H. i.* 132.

10. 11, 12. Swā-hwā-swā his ǣwe forlǣt, and ōðer genimð, hē bið
þonne ćawbrǖce and ēac forligr. . . . Eft, gif wīf āwyrpð
hire āgenne wer, and ōðerne gecȳst, hēo bið sōð ćawbrǖce.
  Æ. H. ii. 322, 324.

10. 13, 14. *See* Matt. 19. 13, 14.

10. 17. *See* Luke 18. 18, note 2.

10. 19. *See* Exod. 20. 12.

10. 38, 39. *See* Matt. 20. 22, 23.

11. 25, 26. Þonne gē standað on ćowrum gebedum, forgyfað swā-
hwæt-swā gē habbað on ćowrum mōde tō ǣnigum men, and
ćower Fæder þe on heofonum is forgyfð ćow ćowre synna. Gif
gē þonne nellað forgyfan mid inweardre heortan þām þe ćow
gremiað, þonne ēac ćower Fæder ðe on heofonum is nele ćow
forgyfan ćowre synna. *Æ. H. i.* 266.

---

8. 3. Et si dimisero eos ieiunos in
domum suam, deficient in via;
quidam enim ex eis de longe
venerunt.

8. 6. Et praecepit turbae discumbere super terram. Et accipiens
septem panes, gratias agens fregit,
et dabat discipulis suis ut appo-
nerent . . . turbae.

8. 8, 9. Et manducaverunt, et satu-
rati sunt; et sustulerunt quod
superaverat de fragmentis septem
sportas. Erant autem qui manducaverant quasi quattuor millia. . . .

9. 43. Ubi vermis eorum non mori-
tur, et ignis non extinguitur.

10. 11, 12. . . . Quicumque dimiserit uxorem suam, et aliam
duxerit, adulterium committit
super eam. Et si uxor dimiserit
virum suum, et alii nupserit, moe-
chatur.

11. 25, 26. Et cum stabitis ad oran-
dum, dimittite si quid habetis
adversus aliquem, ut et Pater

12. 17. *See* Matt. 22. 21.

12. 25. *See* Luke 20. 35, 36.

12. 31. Cf. Matt. 19. 19 (19. 17–19).

12. 41–44. Æt sumum sǣle gesæt se Hǣlend binnan ðām temple on Hierusalem, ætforan ðām māðmhūse, and beheold hū þæt folc heora ælmyssan wurpon intō ðām māðmhūse, and ðā fela rīcan brōhton micele ðing. Þā cōm ðǣr ān earm wudewe, and geoffrode Gode ænne feorðling. Drihten ðā cwæð tō his leorningcnihtum : Ic secge eow tō sōðan þæt þēos earme wydewe brōhte māran lāc þonne ænig ðyssera ricera manna. Hī ealle sealdon þone dǣl heora spēda þe him geðūhte. ac ðeos wydewe ealne hire bigleofan mid ēstfullum mōde geoffrode. Æ. H. i. 582.

‖ Witodlice sum earm wydewe nǣfde ealra ǣhta būton ænne feorðling, þone hēo brōhte tō Godes weofode on Crīstes andwerdnysse ; and hū hī ðǣrrihte mid his hālgan mūðe geherode. and cwæð : Sōð ic eow secge þæt ðeos earm wydewe brōhte māran lāc ðonne ænig ōðer mann on ðisum dæge, forðanðe hēo brōhte eal þæt hēo hæfde mid ēstfullum mōde. Æ. H. ii. 106.

13. 6. *See* Matt. 24. 5.

13. 8. *See* Luke 21. 10, 11.

13. 13. *See* Matt. 24. 12, 13.

13. 20. And būtan se Ælmihtiga God ðā dagas gescyrte, eall mennisc forwurde ; ac for his gecorenum hē gescyrte þā dagas. Æ. H. i. 4.

13. 22. *See* Matt. 24. 5.

13. 27. *See* Matt. 24. 31, note.

13. 32. *See* Matt. 24. 36.

---

vester qui in coelis est dimittat vobis peccata vestra. Quod si vos non dimiseritis, nec Pater vester qui in coelis est dimittet vobis peccata vestra.

12. 41–44. Et sedens Iesus contra gazophylacium, aspiciebat quomodo turba iactaret aes in gazophylacium, et multi divites iactabant multa. Cum venisset autem vidua una pauper, misit duo minuta, quod est quadrans. Et convocans discipulos suos, ait illis : Amen dico vobis quoniam vidua haec pauper plus omnibus misit qui miserunt in gazophylacium. Omnes enim ex eo quod abundabat illis miserunt ; haec vero de penuria sua omnia quae habuit misit, totum victum suum.

13. 20. Et nisi breviasset Dominus dies, non fuisset salva omnis caro; sed propter electos, quos elegit, breviavit dies.

13. 37. Þæt þæt ic tō ēow gecweðe, þæt ic cweðe tō eallum mannum. _Æ. II. ii. 524._

14. 10. _See Æ. II. i. 26._

14. 18–21. _See Matt. 26. 20–25._

14. 22–24. _See Matt. 26. 26–28._

14. 27–31. _See Matt. 26. 31–35._

14. 44. _See Matt. 26. 48, 49._

14. 61–65. _See Matt. 26. 63–67, and note._

15. 2. _See Matt. 27. 11._

15. 7. _See Matt. 27. 15–17, note._

15. 20. _See Matt. 27. 21–25, 27–29, 31._

15. 22, 23. _See Matt. 27. 33, 34._

15. 27. _See John 19. 18–20._

15. 33. _See Matt. 27. 45._

15. 36. _See Matt. 27. 48._

15. 39. _See Matt. 27. 54._

15. 44. _See John 19. 38–42, note._

16. 5. Se engel sæt on ða swīðran healfe ðære byrgene ; . . . se bydel wæs ymbscrȳd mid scīnendum rēafe. _Æ. H. i. 222._

16. 6. _See Matt. 28. 5, 6._

16. 14. _See Æ. H. i. 300._

16. 15–18. Þā cwæð se Wealdend tō his gingrum : Farað geond ealne middangeard, and bodiað godspel eallum gesceafte. Sē ðe gelȳfð and bið gefullod, sē bið gehealden ; sē ðe ne gelȳfð. hē bið genyðerod. Ðās tācnu fyligað þām mannum þe gelȳfað : . . . On mīnum naman hī ādrǣfað dēoflu ; hī sprecað mid nīwum gereordum ; hī āfyrsiað næddran ; and ðeah-ðe hī unlybban drincan, hit him ne deraþ ; hī settaþ heora handa ofer ādlige men, and him bið tela. _Æ. II. i. 300, 304._

¶ Faraþ geond ealne middangeard, and bodiað godspel eallum gesceafte. . . . Sē ðe gelȳfð and bið gefullod, hē bið gehealden ; and sē ðe ne gelȳfð, hē bið geniðerod. _Æ. H. i. 302 ; cf. i. 26._

13. 37. Quod autem vobis dico, omnibus dico. . . .

16. 5. Et introeuntes in monumentum viderunt iuvenem sedentem in dextris, coopertum stola candida. . . .

16. 15–18. Et dixit eis : Euntes in mundum universum praedicate evangelium omni creaturae. Qui crediderit et baptizatus fuerit, salvus erit ; qui vero non crediderit, condemnabitur. Signa autem eos qui crediderint haec sequentur : In nomine meo daemonia eiicient ; linguis loquentur novis ; serpentes tollent ; et si

16. 19. *See* Æ. H. .308 ; cf. i. 306.

16. 20. Fordon and bodedon gehwǣr, Drihtne samod wyrcend-
um, and ðā sprǣce getrymmendum mid æfterfyligendum
tācnum.   Æ. H. i. 310.

LUKE.

1. 5–7. Sum ēawfæst Godes ðegen wæs gehāten Zacharias ; his
gebędda wæs gecīged Elisabeth.   Hī būtū wǣron rihtwīse
ætforan Gode, on his bebodum and rihtwīsnyssum forðstæp-
pende būtan tāle.   Næs him cild gemǣne.   Æ. H. i. 352.

|| Elisabeth, sēo wæs Zacharian wif.   Hī būtū wǣron riht-
wīse, and hēoldon Godes beboda untǣllice.   Ðā wǣron hī
būtan cilde, oð-þæt hī wǣron forwęrede męnn.   Æ. H. i. 200, 202.

1. 11. *See* Æ. H. i. 202.

1. 13. Se ylca engel . . . cȳdde þæt hē sceolde be his ealdan wīfe
sunu habban, Iohannem ðone Fulluhtere.   Æ. H. i. 202.

1. 14. Manega blissiað on his gebyrdtīde.   Æ. H. i. 354.

1. 15. *See* Matt. 3. 4.

1. 17. . . . þæt hē forestōpe ðām Hǣlende on gāste and on mihte
þæs wītegan Helian.   Æ. H. i. 356.

1. 19. *See* Æ. H. i. 24.

1. 20. Nū ðū nylt gelȳfan mīnum wordum, bēo ðū dumb oð-þæt
þæt cild bēo ācęnned.   Æ. H. i. 202.

1. 22. *See* Æ. H. i. 202.

1. 26, 27. Godes hēahęngel, Gabrihel, wæs āsęnd fram Gode tō

mortiferum quid biberint, non
eis nocebit ; super aegros manus
imponent, et bene habebunt.

16. 20. Illi autem profecti praedi-
caverunt ubique, Domino cooperante, et sermonem confirmante
sequentibus signis.

LUKE.

1. 5–7. Fuit . . . sacerdos quidam
nomine Zacharias ; . . . et uxor
illius, . . . nomen cius Elisabeth.
Erant autem iusti ambo ante
Deum, incedentes in omnibus
mandatis et iustificationibus Domini sine querela.   Et non erat

illis filius, . . . et ambo processis-
sent in diebus suis.

1. 13. Ait autem ad illum angelus :
. . . Uxor tua Elisabeth pariet tibi
filium, et vocabis nomen eius
Ioannem.

1. 14. . . . Et multi in nativitate eius
gaudebunt.

1. 17. Et ipse praecedet ante illum
in spiritu et virtute Eliae. . . .

1. 20. Et ecce eris tacens, et non
poteris loqui, usque in diem quo
haec fiant, pro eo quod non credidisti verbis meis. . . .

1. 26. 27. . . . Missus est angelus
Gabriel a Deo in civitatem

ðǣre Galileiscan byrig Nazareth, tō ðām mǣdene þe wæs Maria
gehāten ; and hēo āsprang of Dauides cynne, þæs māran
cyninges ; and hēo wæs bewęddod þām rihtwīsan Iosepe.
Æ. H. i. 194 ; cf. i. 460.

|| Maria wæs bewęddod Iosepe ðām rihtwīsan. Æ. H. i. 190.

1. 28. Se ęngel grētte Marian, and cwæð þæt hēo wǣre mid Godes
gife āfylled. and þæt hyre wæs God mid, and hēo wæs geblētsod
betwux wīfum. Æ. H. i. 196 ; cf. i. 198.

1. 31. Efne, ðū scealt gecāenian on ðīnum innoðe, and þū ācęnst
sunu. Æ. H. i. 198 ; cf. i. 24.

His nama wæs Hiesus. Æ. H. i. 198.

1. 32. Þēs bið mǣre, and hē bið gecīged Sunu þæs Hēxstan.
Æ. H. i. 198.

Crīst hēold Dauides cynesetl. Æ. H. i. 198.

1. 34. Þā cwæð Maria tō ðām ęngle : Hū mæg þæt bēon þæt ic
cild hæbbe, forðanðe ic nānes weres ne brūce ? Æ. H. i. 198.

1. 35. Þā andwyrde se ęngel ðām mǣdene : Se Hālga Gāst cymð
ufen on ðē, and miht ðæs Hȳhstan ofersceadewað ðē. . . .
Þæt Hālige, þe of ðē bið ācęnned, bið gecīged Godes Sunu.
Æ. H. i. 198, 200.

1. 36. See Æ. H. i. 202.

1. 38. Ðā cwæð Maria tō ðām ęngle : Ic eom Godes ðīnen ; getīmige mē æfter ðīnum worde. Æ. H. i. 200.

1. 40–45. Nū cōm ðā sēo ēadige Maria tō his hūse, and grētte his
wīf, hyre māgan, Elisabeth. Ðā, mid-þām-þe þæt wīf gehȳrde
þæs mǣdenes grētinge, ðā blissode þæt cild Iohannes on his

Galilaeae cui nomen Nazareth, ad
virginem desponsatam viro cui
nomen erat Ioseph, de domo
David ; et nomen virginis Maria.

1. 28. . . . Angelus ad eam dixit :
Ave, gratia plena ; Dominus tecum ; benedicta tu in mulieribus.

1. 31. Ecce concipies in utero, et
paries filium, et vocabis nomen
eius Iesum.

1. 32. Hic erit magnus, et Filius
Altissimi vocabitur, et dabit illi
Dominus Deus sedem David patris
eius. . . .

1. 34. Dixit autem Maria ad angelum :
Quomodo fiet istud, quoniam virum non cognosco ?

1. 35. Et respondens angelus dixit
ei : Spiritus sanctus superveniet
in te, et virtus Altissimi obum-
brabit tibi. Ideoque et quod
nascetur ex te sanctum vocabitur
Filius Dei.

1. 38. Dixit autem Maria : Ecce
ancilla Domini ; fiat mihi secundum verbum tuum. . . .

1. 40–45. Et intravit in domum
Zachariae, et salutavit Elisabeth.
Et factum est, ut audivit saluta-
tionem Mariae Elisabeth. exul-

mōdor innoðe ; and sēo mōder wearð āfylled mid þām Hālgan
Gāste, and hēo clypode tō Marian mid micelre stemne, and
cwæð: þū eart geblētsod betwux wīfum, and geblōtsod is se
wæstm þīnes innoðes. Hū getīmode mē þæt mīnes Drihtnes
mōder wolde cuman tō mē? Efne, mid-þām-þe sēo stefn ðīnre
grētinge swēgde on mīnum ēarum, ðā blissode mīn cild on
mīnum innoðe, and hoppode ongēan his Drihten, þe þū berst on
ðīnum innoðe. . . . Ēadig eart ðū, Maria, forðonðe þū gelȳfdest þām wordum ðe þē fram Gode gebodode wǣron, and hit
biðˀ gefremmed swā-swā hit ðē gecȳdd wæs. Æ. H. i. 202 ; cf. i. 352.

1. 46. Mīn sāwul mǣrsað Drihten. Æ. II. i. 202.

1. 52–55. God āwearp ðā rīcan of setle. . . . And hū āhōf ðā ēadmōdan.   God gefylð þā hingrigendan mid his gōdum. . . .
Hū forlēt ðā rīcan īdele. . . . God underfēng his cnapan
Israhel. . . . Swā-swā hē spræc tō ūrum fæderum, Abrahame,
and his ofspringe on worulda.   Æ. H. i. 202, 204.

1. 60, 63. *See* Æ. H. i. 354.

1. 64. *See* Æ. H. i. 352.

2. 1–20. On ðām tīman se Rōmanisca cāsere Octauianus sętte
gebann þæt wǣre on gewritum āsętt eall ymbhwyrft. Þēos
tōwritennys wearð ārǣred fram ðām ealdormęn Cyrino, of
Sirian lande, þæt ǣlc man oferhēafod sceolde cęnnan his
gebyrde and his āre on ðǣre byrig þe hē tō gehȳrde. Þā fērde
Ioseph, Crīstes fōsterfæder, fram Galileiscum earde, of ðǣre
byrig Nazareð, tō Iudeiscre byrig, sēo wæs Dauides, and wæs
gecīged Bethleem ; forðanðe hē wæs of Dauides mǣgðe, and

tavit infans in utero eius; et
repleta est Spiritu sancto Elisabeth, et exclamavit voce magna,
et dixit : Benedicta tu inter mulieres, et benedictus fructus ventris tui. Et unde hoc mihi, ut
veniat mater Domini mei ad me ?
Ecce enim ut facta est vox salu-
tationis tuae in auribus meis,
exultavit in gaudio infans in utero
meo. Et beata quae credidisti,
quoniam perficientur ea quae
dicta sunt tibi a Domino.

1. 46. . . . Magnificat anima mea
Dominum.

1. 52–55. Deposuit potentes de sede,

et exaltavit humiles. Esurientes
implevit bonis, et divites dimisit
inanes. Suscepit Israel puerum
suum. . . . Sicut locutus est ad
patres nostros, Abraham, et semini eius in saecula.

2. 1–20. Factum est autem in diebus
illis, exiit edictum a Caesare
Augusto ut describeretur universus orbis. Haec descriptio prima
facta est a praeside Syriae Cyrino.
Et ibant omnes ut profiterentur
singuli in suam civitatem. Ascendit autem et Ioseph a Galilaea
de civitate Nazareth in Iudaeam
in civitatem David, quae vocatur

wolde andettan mid Marian hire gebyrde, þe wæs þā gȳt bearn-
eaca. Ðā gelamp hit, þā-ðā hī on þǣre byrig Bethleem
wīcodon, þæt hire tīma wæs gefylled þæt hēo cennan sceolde ;
and ācende ðā hyre frumcennedan sunu, and mid cildclāðum
bewand, and ālēde þæt cild on heora assena binne, forþanþe ðǣr
næs nān rȳmet on þām gesthūse. Þā wǣron hyrdas on þām
earde waciende ofer heora Ꞇowede ; and efne, ðā Godes engel
stōd on emn hī, and Godes beorhtnys hī besꞆēan ; and hī
wurdon micclum āfyrhte. Ðā cwæð se Godes engel tō ðām
hyrdum : Ne ondrēdað Ꞇow ; efne, ic Ꞇow bodige micelne
gefēan, þe becymð eallum folce ; forðanþe nū tō-dæg is Ꞇow
ācenned Hǣlend Crīst on Dauides ceastre. Gō gesēoð þis
tācen : Gō gemētað þæt cild mid cildclāðum bewunden, and
on binne gelēd. Þā fǣrlice, æfter þæs engles sprǣce, wearð
gesewen micel menigu heofenlices werodes God herigendra.
and singendra : Gloria in excelsis Deo, et in terra pax hominibus bone uoluntatis ; þæt is on ūrum gereorde : Sȳ wuldor
Gode on hēannyssum, and on eorðan sibb mannum, þām
ðe bēoð gōdes willan. And ðā englas ðā gewiton of heora
gesihðe tō heofonum. Hwæt, ðā hyrdas þā him betwēonan
sprǣcon : Uton faran tō Bethleem, and gesēon þæt word þe
ūs God æteowde. Hī cōmon ðā hrædlice, and gemētton
Marian, and Ioseph, and þæt cild gelēd on ānre binne, swā-

Bethlehem ; eo quod esset de
domo, et familia David, ut pro-
fiteretur cum Maria desponsata
sibi uxore praegnante. Factum
est autem, cum essent ibi, impleti sunt dies ut pareret ; et
peperit filium suum primogenitum, et pannis eum involvit, et
reclinavit eum in praesepio, quia
non erat eis locus in diversorio. Et
pastores erant in regione eadem
vigilantes, et custodientes vigi-
lias noctis super gregem suum ;
et ecce. angelus Domini stetit
iuxta illos, et claritas Dei circumfulsit illos ; et timuerunt timore
magno. Et dixit illis angelus :
Nolite timere ; ecce enim, evan-
gelizo vobis gaudium magnum,

quod erit omni populo ; quia
natus est vobis hodie Salvator,
qui est Christus Dominus, in civitate David. Et hoc vobis signum :
Invenietis infantem pannis invo-
lutum, et positum in praesepio.
Et subito facta est cum angelo
multitudo militiae coelestis lau-
dantium Deum, et dicentium :
Gloria in altissimis Deo, et in
terra pax hominibus bonae volun-
tatis. Et factum est, ut disces-
serunt ab eis angeli in coelum,
pastores loquebantur ad invicem :
Transeamus usque Bethlehem, et
videamus hoc verbum quod factum est, quod Dominus ostendit
nobis. Et venerunt festinantes,
et invenerunt Mariam, et Ioseph,

swā him se ęngel cȳdde. Þā hyrdas sōðlice oncnēowon be þām worde þe him gesǣd wæs be ðām cilde. And ealle wundrodon þe þæt gehȳrdon, and ēac be ðām ðe þā hyrdas him sǣdon. Maria sōðlice hēold ealle þās word, āræfniende on hire heortan. Ðā gecyrdon þā hyrdas ongēan, wuldrigende and hęrigende God on eallum ðām ðingum þe hī gehȳrdon and gesāwon, swā-swā him fram þām ęngle gesǣd wæs.   Æ. H. i. 28. 30, 32 ; cf. ii. 86.

‖ Maria ācęnde ðā hire frumcęnnedan sunu, . . . and hine mid cildclāðum bewand, and for rȳmetlēaste on ānre binne gelēde.   Æ. H. i. 34.

‖ Ne bēo gē āfyrhte ; efne, ic bodige ēow micelne gefēan, ðe eallum folce becymð ; forðanþe nū tō-dæg is ācęnned Hǣlend Crīst on Dauides ceastre.   Æ. H. i. 36.

‖ Nū tō-dæg is ēow ācęnned Hǣlend Crīst on Dauides ceastre.   Æ. H. i. 36.

‖ Sȳ wuldor Gode on hēannyssum, and on eorðan sibb þām mannum þe bēoð gōdes willan.

‖ Sȳ wuldor Gode on hēannyssum, and on eorðan sibb mannum, ðām ðe bēoð gōdes willan.   Æ. H. i. 38.

‖ Sȳ wuldor Gode on hēannyssum, and on eorðan sibb ðām mannum ðe synd gōdes willan.   Æ. H. i. 582.

‖ Gode wuldor on hēannyssum.   Æ. H. i. 56.

‖ Þā hyrdas ðā sprǣcon him betwēonan, æfter ðǣra ęngla framfærelde : Uton gefaran tō Bethlcem, and gescēon þæt word þe geworden is, and God ūs geswutelode.   Æ. H. i. 40.

‖ Uton gescēon þæt word þe geworden is.   Æ. H. i. 40.

‖ Hrædlice ðā cōmon þā hyrdas, and gemētton Marian, and Ioseph, and þæt cild gelēd on ðǣre binne.   Æ. H. i. 40.

‖ Maria sōðlice hēold ealle ðās word, āræfniende on hire heortan.   Æ. H. i. 42.

‖ And þā hyrdas gecyrdon ongēan, wuldrigende and hęrigende God on eallum ðām ðingum ðe hī gehȳrdon and gesāwon, swā-swā him gesǣd wæs.   Æ. H. i. 42.

---

et infantem positum in praesepio. Videntes autem cognoverunt de verbo quod dictum erat illis de puero hoc. Et omnes qui audierunt mirati sunt, et de his quae dicta erant a pastoribus ad ipsos.

Maria autem conservabat omnia verba haec, conferens in corde suo. Et reversi sunt pastores glorificantes et laudantes Deum in omnibus quae audierant et viderant, sicut dictum est ad illos.

2. 21. Æfter-þan-ðe wǣron gefyllede ehta dagas Drihtnes ācennednysse þæt hē ymbsniden wǣre, þā wæs his nama geetged Iesus, þæt is Hǣlend, ðām naman hē wæs gehāten fram ðām ęngle, ǣrðāmþe hē on innoðe geēacnod wǣre. Æ. H. i. 90 ; cf. ii. 68.

2. 22–24. See Æ. H. i. 134, ii. 68.

2. 24. Geoffrode hire lāc Gode, . . . swā hit on Godes ǣ gesęt wæs : . . . twēgen culfranbriddas, oððe twā turtlan. Æ. H. i. 138, 140.

2. 25–32. Ðā wæs þǣr binnan þǣre byrig Hierusalem sum Godes mann, and his nama wæs Symeon ; hē wæs swȳðe rihtwīs, and hæfde micelne Godes ęge, and hē geandbīdode ðone frōfer ðe behāten wæs þām folce Israhel, þæt is Crīstes tōcyme. Se Hālga Gāst wæs wunigende on ðǣm Symeone. . . . Ðā cōm him andswaru fram þām Hālgan Gāste, þæt hē ne sceolde dēaðes onbyrigan ǣr-þām-ðe hē Crīst gesāwe. And hē wæs þā blīðe þæs behātes, and cōm tō Godes temple, þurh myngunge ðæs Hālgan Gāstes. . . . Hē hine genam ðā on his earmas, . . . and þancode georne Gode. . . . Hē cwæð ðā : Mīn Drihten, ðū forlǣtst mē nū mid sibbe of þisum līfe, æfter þīnum worde ; forðonþe mīne ēagan gesāwon þīnne Hālwęndan, ðone ðū gearcodest ætforan ansȳne ealles folces,—lēoht tō onwrigennysse þēoda, and wuldor þīnum folce Israhele. Æ. H. i. 134, 136.

‖ Drihten, þū forlǣtst mē nū on sibbe of ðysum līfe, forðonþe mīne ēagan habbað gesewen ðīnne Hālwęndan, . . . ðone þū gearcodest ætforan gesihðe ealles folces. . . . Hē is lēoht tō onwrigennysse ðēoda, and wuldor þīnum folce Israhel.
Æ. H. i. 142, 144.

2. 33, 34. Þā Maria, þæt hālige mǣden, and þæs cildes fōstorfæder,

2. 21. Et postquam consummati sunt dies octo ut circumcideretur puer, vocatum est nomen eius Iesus, quod vocatum est ab angelo prius quam in utero conciperetur.

2. 24. Et ut darent hostiam, secundum quod dictum est in lege Domini, par turturum, aut duos pullos columbarum.

2. 25–32. Et ecce homo erat in Ierusalem, cui nomen Simeon ; et homo iste iustus et timoratus, expectans consolationem Israel ; et Spiritus sanctus erat in eo. Et responsum acceperat a Spiritu sancto, non visurum se mortem nisi prius videret Christum Domini. Et venit in spiritu in templum. . . . Et ipse accepit eum in ulnas suas, et benedixit Deum, et dixit : Nunc dimittis servum tuum, Domine, secundum verbum tuum, in pace, quia viderunt oculi mei salutare tuum, quod parasti ante faciem omnium populorum,—lumen ad revelationem gentium, et gloriam plebis tuae Israel.

2. 33, 34. Et erat pater eius et mater mirantes super his quae

Ioseph, wæron ofwundrode þæra worda þe se ealda Symeon clypode be ðām cilde. And se Symeon him ðā sealde blētsunge, and wītegode gȳt māre be þām cilde. and cwæð : Þis cild is gesętt manegum mannum tō hryre, and manegum tō æriste and tō tācne, and þām bið wiðcweden. Æ. H. i. 144.

‖ Tō tācne cōm Crīst, and þām is wiðcweden. Æ. H. i. 144.

2. 35. His swurd sceal ðurhgān ðīne sāwle. Æ. H. i. 146.

2. 36–40. Þā cōm þær sum wuduwe, sēo wæs Anna gehāten. Sēo leofode mid hire were seofon gēar, and syððan hēo wæs wuduwe fēower and hundeahtatig gēara, and þēowode Gode on fæstenum, and on gebedum, and on clǣnnysse ; and wæs on eallum þām fyrste wunigende binnan þām Godes temple ; and cōm ðā tō þām cilde, and wītegode be him, and andette Gode. . . . Sēo ēadige Maria, and Ioseph, ðæs cildes fōsterfæder, gecyrdon tō þære byrig Nazareth mid þām cilde ; and þæt cild wēox, and wæs gestrangod, and mid wīsdōme āfylled ; and Godes gifu wæs on him wunigende. Æ. H. i. 146, 148, 158.

3. 1–4. On ðām fīftēoðan gēare ðæs cāseres rīces Tyberii cōm Godes word ofer Iohannem on ðām wēstene ; and hē fērde tō folces nēawiste, and bodade Iudeiscum folce fulluht on synna forgyfenysse, swā-swā hit āwriten is on Isaies wītegunge. Æ. H. i. 352 ; cf. i. 478.

3. 4, 5. *See* Isa. 40. 3, 4.

3. 17. *See* Matt. 3. 12.

3. 19. *See* Æ. H. i. 478.

dicebantur de illo. Et benedixit illis Simeon, et dixit ad Mariam matrem eius: Ecce, positus est hic in ruinam et in resurrectionem multorum in Israel, et in signum cui contradicetur.

2. 35. Et tuam ipsius animam pertransibit gladius. . . .

2. 36–40. Et erat Anna prophetissa, . . . et vixerat cum viro suo annis septem a virginitate sua. Et haec vidua usque ad annos octoginta quattuor ; quae non discedebat de templo, ieiuniis et obsecrationibus serviens nocte ac die. Et haec, ipsa hora superveniens, con-

fitebatur Domino. . . . Reversi sunt in Galilaeam in civitatem suam Nazareth. Puer autem crescebat, et confortabatur, plenus sapientia ; et gratia Dei erat in illo.

3. 1–4. Anno autem quintodecimo imperii Tiberii Caesaris . . . factum est verbum Domini super Ioannem, Zachariae filium, in deserto ; et venit in omnem regionem Iordanis, praedicans baptismum poenitentiae in remissionem peccatorum, sicut scriptum est in libro sermonum Isaiae prophetae. . . .

3. 22. *See* Æ. H. i. 104.

4. 10, 11. *See* Ps. 91. 11, 12.

4. 29, 30. Đā Iudei lǣddon Crīst ǣt sumum sǣle tō ānum clife, and woldon hine niđer āscūfan ; ac hē đodo betwēonan heora handum āweg, swā þæt heora nān nyste hwǣr hē becōm.
Æ. II. ii. 236.

4. 34. *See* Mark 1. 24.

5. 6. *See* Æ. H. ii. 290.

5. 29. Matheus [1] þā gearcode micel gereord þām Hǣlende, and hine tō his hūse gelađode. Æ. H. ii. 468.

5. 31. *See* Matt. 9. 12.

5. 32. *See* Matt. 9. 13, note.

6. 25. Wā đow þe nū hlihgað ; gē sceolon hēofian and wēpan.
Æ. II. i. 180.

6. 36. Bēoð mildheorte, swā-swā đower Fæder is. Æ. H. ii. 322.

6. 37, 38. Forgyfað, and đow bið forgyfen. Syllað, and đow bið geseald. Æ. H. ii. 100.

Ēow bið āmeten swā-swā gē āmǣton, on đām ylcan gemete đe gē mannum dōð. Æ. II. ii. 322.

‖ Gif gē forgyfað, đow bið forgyfen. Æ. H. i. 52.

7. 11–15. Ūre Drihten fērde tō sumere byrig sēo is gehāten Naim, and his gingran samod, and genihtsum menigu. Þā-đā hē genēalǣhte þām portgeate, þā ferede man ānes cnihtes līc tō byrgene. . . . Se cniht wæs āncenned sunu his mēder. . . . Se Hǣlend wearð āstyred mid mildheortnysse ofer đǣre mēder. . . . Hē genēalǣhte and hreopode þā bǣre, and þā bǣrmenn ætstōdon. . . . Drihten cwæð tō đām cnihte : Ic secge đē : Ārīs ; and hē đǣrrihte gesæt and spræc. And se Hǣlend betǣhte hine his mēder. Æ. H. i. 490, 492, 494.

4. 29, 30. . . . Duxerunt illum usque ad supercilium montis, . . . ut praecipitarent eum. Ipse autem transiens per medium illorum, ibat.

5. 29. Et fecit ei convivium magnum Levi in domo sua. . . .

6. 25. . . . Vae vobis qui ridetis nunc, quia lugebitis et flebitis.

6. 36. Estote ergo misericordes, sicut et Pater vester misericors est.

6. 37, 38. . . . Dimittite, et dimittemini. Date, et dabitur vobis. . . . Eadem quippe mensura qua mensi fueritis, remetietur vobis.

7. 11–15. Et factum est, deinceps ibat in civitatem quae vocatur Naim ; et ibant cum eo discipuli

---

[1] From Matt. 9. 9.

‖ Mid·þām-ðe Drihten hrepode ðā bǣre, ðā ætstōdon ðā bǣr-męnn. _Æ. II. i. 494._

‖ Þu cniht, ic sęcge ðē : Ārīs. _Æ. H. i. 498._

7. 16. Þæt folc wearð mid micclum ęge āblicged. . . . Þæt folc cwæð : Þæt mǣre wītega ārās betwux ūs, and þæt God his folc genēosode. _Æ. H. i. 494._

7. 19. _See_ Matt. 11. 2, 3.

7. 21–23. Hwæt, ðā se Hǣlend on ðǣre ylcan tīde . . . gehǣlde manega untruman fram mislicum coðum, and wōdum mannum gewitt forgeaf, and blindum gesihðe. And cwæð syððan tō Iohannes ǣrendracum : Farað nū tō Iohanne, and cȳðað him þā ðing þe gē gesāwon and gehȳrdon. Efne, nū blinde gesēoð, and ðā healtan gāð, and hrēoflige męn synd geclǣnsode, dēafe gehȳrað, and· ðā dēadan ārīsað, and ðearfan bodiað godspel ; and sē bið ēadig þe on mē ne bið geēswicod. _Æ. H. i. 480_ ; cf. i. 26, and Matt. 11. 4–6.

7. 28. _See_ Matt. 11. 11.

8. 4–6. On sumere tīde, ðā-ðā micel męnigu samod cōm tō ðām Hǣlende, and fram gehwilcum burgum tō him genēalǣhton, þā sǣde hē him þis bigspel : Sum sǣdere fērde tō sāwenne his sǣd. . . . Þæt sǣd þe fēoll be ðām wege mid twȳfealdre dare losode, ðā-ðā wegferende hit fortrǣdon, and fugelas tōbǣron. . . . Wē sprǣcon be ðām sǣde þe betwux þām ðornum sprang, and mid heora wǣstme forðrysmod wearð. . . . Þæt sǣd þe

eius, et turba copiosa. Cum autem appropinquaret portae civitatis, ecce defunctus efferebatur filius unicus matris suae. . . . Quam cum vidisset Dominus, misericordia motus super eam. . . . Et accessit, et tetigit loculum. Hi autem qui portabant steterunt. Et ait : Adolescens, tibi dico : Surge. Et resedit qui erat mortuus, et coepit loqui. Et dedit illum matri suae.

7. 16. Accepit autem omnes timor, . . . dicentes : Quia propheta magnus surrexit in nobis, et quia Deus visitavit plebem suam.

7. 21–23. (In ipsa autem hora multos

curavit a languoribus, et plagis, et spiritibus malis ; et caecis multis donavit visum.) Et respondens dixit illis : Euntes renuntiate Ioanni quae audistis et vidistis : Quia caeci vident, claudi ambulant, leprosi mundantur, surdi audiunt, mortui resurgunt, pauperes evangelizantur ; et beatus est quicumque non fuerit scandalizatus in me.

8. 4–6. Cum autem turba plurima convenirent, et de civitatibus properarent ad eum, dixit per similitudinem : Exiit qui seminat, seminare semen suum ; et dum seminat, aliud cecidit secus viam,

bufon ðām stǣnigum lande fēol sprytte hwæthwega, ac, ðā-ðā
sēo hǣte cōm, ðā forscranc hit, forðanðe hit næfde nænne
wǣtan. *Æ. H. ii. 88, 90.*

8. 11, 12, 14, 15. Þæt sǣd is Godes word. . . . Þonne ætbrēt se flēog-
enda sceocca ðǣrrihte þæt hālige sǣd of swilcera gedwolena
heortan. . . . Ðā sind þe Godes word gehȳrað, ac hī sind gebys-
gode mid heora welum, and mid heora lifes lustum forsmorode,
and ne berað nænne wǣstm. . . . Se dǣl þæs sǣdes ðe on gōdre
eorðan befēol, þæt sind ðā ðe Godes word on gōdre heortan
healdað, and bringað wǣstm on geðylde. *Æ. H. ii. 90, 92.*

8. 41 ff. *See Æ. H. i. 496.*

8. 43, 44. *See* Mark 5. 25, 27, 28.

8. 44-48. Hēo crēap ðā betwux ðām mannum, bæftan þām Hǣlende,
and forstæl hire hǣlu, swā þæt hēo hrepode his rēafes fnædu ;
and hire blōdes gyte sōna ætstōd. Þā cwæð se Hǣlend : Hwā
hreopode mē ? Petrus him andwyrde : Lā leof, þeos menigu
ðē ofðrincð, and ðū āxast hwā ðe hreopode. Drihten cwæð :
Sum man mē hreopode ; witodlice ic gefrēdde þæt ðǣre hǣlðe
miht of mē ēode. . . . Hēo geseah ðā þæt hit dīgele næs, and
fēol bifigende tō ðæs Hǣlendes fōton, and sǣde ætforan eallum
ðām folce hwī hēo hine hrepode, and hū hēo ðǣrrihte gehǣled
wearð. Drihten hire cwæð tō : Dohtor, ðīn gelēafa þe gehǣlde ;
gang ðē nū on sibbe. *Æ. H. ii. 394.*

et conculcatum est, et volucres
coeli comederunt illud. Et aliud
cecidit supra petram ; et natum
aruit, quia non habebat humorem.
Et aliud cecidit inter spinas,
et simul exortae spinae suffoca-
verunt illud.

8. 11, 12, 14, 15. . . . Semen est
verbum Dei. . . . Deinde venit
diabolus, et tollit verbum de corde
eorum. . . . Quod autem in spinas
cecidit hi sunt qui audierunt, et
a sollicitudinibus et divitiis et
voluptatibus vitae euntes suffocantur, et non referunt fructum.
Quod autem in bonam terram hi
sunt qui in corde bono et optimo
audientes verbum retinent, et
fructum afferunt in patientia.

8. 44-48. Accessit retro, et tetigit
fimbriam vestimenti eius ; et confestim stetit fluxus sanguinis
eius. Et ait Iesus : Quis est
qui me tetigit ? . . . Dixit Petrus :
. . . Praeceptor, turbae te com-
primunt et affligunt, et dicis :
Quis me tetigit ? Et dixit
Iesus : Tetigit me aliquis ; nam
ego novi virtutem de me exiisse.
Videns autem mulier quia non
latuit, tremens venit, et procidit
ante pedes eius ; et ob quam
causam tetigerit eum, indicavit
coram omni populo, et quemadmodum confestim sanata sit. At
ipse dixit ei : Filia, fides tua
salvam te fecit ; vade in pace.

8. 49. See Æ. H. i. 496.

8. 54, 55. Ðā genam hē hī be ðǣre handa, and cwæð : Þū mǣden, ic
secge ðē¹, Ārīs. And hēo ðǣrrihte ārās, and metes bǣd. Æ. H. i. 496.
‖ Þū mǣden, ārīs. Æ. H. i. 498.

9. 16. See Matt. 14. 19.

9. 25. Hwæt fremað ǣnigum men, ðeah-ðe hē ealne middaneard tō
his anwealdum gebīge, gif hē āna losað ? Æ. H. ii. 328.

9. 31. See Matt. 17. 1–5, note.

9. 58. See Matt. 8. 20.

9. 59, 60. Be swylcum cwæð se Hǣlend tō ānum his gecorenan,
ðā-ðā hē wolde his fæder līc bebyrian ; hē cwæð : Geðafa þæt
ðā dēadan bebyrion heora dēadan ; far ðū, and boda Godes
rīce. Æ. H. i. 492, 494.

10. 1. Se Hǣlend gecēas him, tōēacan þām twelf apostolum, twā
and hundseofontig leorningcnihta, and sende hī twām and twām
ætforan him tō ǣlc þēra byrig and stōwe þe hē sylf tōweard
wæs. Æ. H. ii. 528 ; cf. i. 26.

10. 2–7. Drihten cwæð : Þæt gerīp is micel, and ðā rifteras fēawa.
. . . Biddað þæs gerīpes hlāford þæt hē āsende wyrhtan tō
his gerīpe. . . . Farað ; efne, ic sende ēow swā-swā lamb
betwux wulfum. . . . Ne bere gē mid ēow pusan, oððe codd,
nē gescȳ. . . . Ne gecyrre gē nænne mann be wege. . . . On
swā hwilcum hūse swā gē incumað, cweðað ǣrest : Wunige
sib on ðisum hūse. And gif þǣr bið sibbe bearn, ēower sib
wunað ofer ðām hūse ; gif on ðām hūse ne bið sibbe bearn,
ēower sibb gewent eft tō ēow. . . . Wuniað on þām hūse ðe
gē tō cumað, etende and drincende þæt þæt hī habbað
ēow tō syllenne. . . . Sōðlice se wyrhta is wurðe his
mēde. Æ. H. ii. 530, 532, 534.

---

8. 54, 55. Ipse autem tenens manum
eius clamavit, dicens : Puella,
surge. Et reversus est spiritus
eius, et surrexit continuo. Et
iussit illi dari manducare.

9. 25. Quid enim proficit homo, si
lucretur universum mundum, se
autem ipsum perdat ? . . .

9. 59, 60. Ait autem ad alterum :
Sequere me. Ille autem dixit :
Domine, permitte mihi primum

ire, et sepelire patrem meum.
Dixitque ei Iesus : Sine ut mortui
sepeliant mortuos suos ; tu autem
vade, et annuntia regnum Dei.

10. 1. Post haec autem designavit
Dominus et alios septuaginta
duos, et misit illos binos ante
faciem suam in omnem civitatem
et locum, quo erat ipse venturus.

10. 2–7. Et dicebat illis : Messis
quidem multa, operarii autem

¹ From Mark 5. 41, 'tibi dico.'

10. 16. Sē ðe ēow gehȳrsumað, hē gehȳrsumað mē ; and sē ðe ēow forsihð, hē forsihð mē.   Æ. H. ii. 50.

‖ Sē ðe ēow gehȳrð, hē gehȳrð mē ; and sē ðe ēow forsihð, hē forsihð mē.   Æ. H. ii. 310.

10. 27. See Luke 18. 20-22.

10. 38-42. Se Hǣlend becōm intō sumere cāðelican byrig ; and ān wīf, Martha gehāten, gelaðode hine tō hire gereorde. . . . Martha wæs swīðe bysig ymbe Drihtnes ðēnunge ; and hire swuster Maria sæt stille æt Drihtnes fōtum, heorcnigende his lāre. Martha swanc, and Maria sæt ǣmtig. . . . Martha spræc cūðlice tō ðām Hǣlende, wolde þæt hē hēte hire swuster hire fylstan æt ðǣre ðēnunge, þe hēo micclum ymbhogode. Þā belādode Drihten Marian, and cwæð : Martha, Martha, þū eart carful and bysig ymbe fela ðing ; witodlice ān ðing is nȳdbehōf. . . . Maria gecēas þone sēlestan dǣl, se ðe ne bið hire nǣfre ætbrōden.   Æ. H. ii. 438, 440.

11. 1. Þā cwǣdon hī tō ðām Hǣlende : Lēof, tǣce ūs hū wē magon ūs gebiddan.   Æ. H. i. 258.

11. 2-4. See Matt. 6. 9-13.

11. 5. Se Hǣlend cwæð tō his leorningcnihtum : Hwilc ēower is þe hæfð sumne frēond, and gǣð him tō on middere nihte, and cwyð. . . .   Æ. H. i. 246.

pauci. Rogate ergo dominum messis ut mittat operarios in messem suam. Ite ; ecce ego mitto vos sicut agnos inter lupos. Nolite portare sacculum, neque peram, neque calceamenta, et neminem per viam salutaveritis. In quamcumque domum intraveritis, primum dicite : Pax huic domui. Et si ibi fuerit filius pacis, requiescet super illum pax vestra ; sin autem, ad vos revertetur. In eadem autem domo manete, edentes et bibentes quae apud illos sunt ; dignus est enim operarius mercede sua. . . .

10. 16. Qui vos audit, me audit ; et qui vos spernit, me spernit. . . .

10. 38-42. . . . Ipse intravit in quoddam castellum ; et mulier quaedam, Martha nomine, excepit illum in domum suam. Et huic erat soror nomine Maria, quae etiam sedens secus pedes Domini, audiebat verbum illius. Martha autem satagebat circa frequens ministerium ; quae stetit, et ait : Domine, non est tibi curae quod soror mea reliquit me solam ministrare ? dic ergo illi ut me adiuvet. Et respondens dixit illi Dominus : Martha, Martha, sollicita es et turbaris erga plurima ; porro unum est necessarium. Maria optimam partem elegit, quae non auferetur ab ea.

11. 1. . . . Dixit unus ex discipulis eius ad eum : Domine, doce nos orare. . . .

11. 5. Et ait ad illos : Quis vestrum habebit amicum, et ibit ad illum media nocte, et dicet illi. . . .

11. 8, 9. Gif hŏ ðurhwunað cnucigende, þonne ārīst se hīredes
ealdor for ðæs ōðres onhrōpe, and him getrŏað þæs ðe hē bitt,
nā for frēondrǣdene, ac for his unstilnysse. . . . Biddað, and
ēow bið forgifen ; sēcað, and gē gemētað ; cnuciað, and ēow bið
geopenod.   Æ. H. i. 248, 250.

∥ Cnuciað, and ēow bið geopenod.   Æ. H. ii. 572.

11. 11–1?. Hwilc fæder wile syllan his cilde stān, gif hit hine
hlāfes bitt? oþþe næddran, gif hit fisces bitt? oððe þone wyrm
ðrōwend, gif hit ǣges bitt?   Gif gē cunnon, þā ðe yfele sind,
syllan ðā gōdnysse ēowrum bearnum, hū micele swīðor wile
ēower heofonlica Fæder forgyfan gōdne gāst him bidden-
dum?   Æ. H. i. 250, 252.

∥ Gē ðe sind (synt) yfele. . . .   Æ. H. i. 254.

11. 20. Gif ic on Godes fingre dēofla ādrǣfe. . . .   Æ. H. ii. 204 ; cf.
Matt. 12. 28.

11. 27. Ēadige sind þā innoðas þe hī gebǣron, and ðā brēost þe
swylce gesīhton.   Æ. H. i. 84.

11. 41. Syllað ðone oferēacan ēow to ælmesdǣdum, and efne, ealle
ðing ēow bēoð geclǣnsode.   Æ. H. ii. 328.

12. 4, 5. Ic secge ēow mīnum frēondum : Ne bēo gē āfǣrede for
ðām ehterum ðe þone līchaman ofslēað, and siððan nabbað
hwæt hī māre dōð.   Ic ætēowige ēow hwæne gē sceolon ēow
ādrǣdan : ondrǣdað ēow þone ðe mæg þone līchaman ofslēan,
and siððan ðā sāwle on hellesūsle āsendan.   Æ. H. ii. 542.

11. 8, 9. Et si ille perseveraverit
pulsans, dico vobis, etsi non dabit
illi surgens eo quod amicus eius
sit, propter improbitatem tamen
eius surget, et dabit illi quotquot
habet necessarios. . . . Petite, et
dabitur vobis ; quaerite, et invenietis ; pulsate, et aperietur
vobis.

11. 11–13. Quis autem ex vobis
patrem petit panem, numquid
lapidem dabit illi? aut piscem,
numquid pro pisce serpentem
dabit illi? aut si petierit ovum,
numquid porriget illi scorpionem?
Si ergo vos cum sitis mali, nostis
bona data dare filiis vestris,
quanto magis Pater vester de
coelo dabit spiritum bonum pe-
tentibus se ?

11. 20. Porro si in digito Dei eiicio
daemonia. . . .

11. 27. . . . Beatus venter qui te
portavit, et ubera quae suxisti.

11. 41. Verumtamen quod superest
date eleemosynam, et ecce, omnia
munda sunt vobis.

12. 4, 5. Dico autem vobis amicis
meis : Ne terreamini ab his qui
occidunt corpus, et post haec non
habent amplius quid faciant.
Ostendam autem vobis quem
timeatis : timete eum qui, postquam occiderit, habet potestatem
mittere in gehennam. . . .

12. 16–21. Sum welig mann wæs on worulde, and his wæstmas
genihtsumlice þugon. Þā smēade se rīca, and cwæð: Hwæt
dō ic lā, nū ic næbbe hwǣr ic mæge ealle mīne wæstmas
gegaderian? Eft hē cwæð: Ic wille rȳman mīnne bęrtūn, and
mīne bęrnu getācnian, and ðider gegadrian ealle mīne wæstmas,
and cweðan tō mīnre sāwle: Mīn sāwul, ðū hæfst fela gōd
tō manegra gēara brice; gerest ðē nū, and et, and drinc, and
gewistfulla. Þā cwæð God tō ðām rīcan: Dū stunta, nū tō-
niht ðū scealt ðīn līf ālǣtan; hwæs bēoð þonne þīne teolunga?
Swā bið se ðe him sylfum goldhordað, and nis on Gode
welig. Æ. H. ii. 104.

12. 23–25. *See* Matt. 6. 24–27.

12. 27. *See* Æ. H. ii. 464.

12. 35. Bēon ēower lęndena ymbgyrde, and ēower lēohtfatu byrnende. Æ. H. ii. 564.

12. 37. . . . þæt hē dēð his hālgan sittan, and hē sylf farende him
ðēnað. Æ. H. ii. 442.

12. 47. Se ðēowa ðe wāt his hlāfordes willan, and nele hine gefręm-
man, sceal bēon gewītnod mid micclum wītum. Æ. H. ii. 338.

12. 49. Ic com tō ðī þæt ic wolde sęndan fȳr on eorðan, and ic
wylle þæt hit byrne. Æ. H. i. 322.

13. 6–9. Sum hīredes hlāford hæfde āplantod ān fīctrēow binnon
his wīngearde, and cōm æfter fyrste tō ðām trēowe, sōhte
wæstm ðǣron, and nænne ne gemētte. Hē cwæð ðā tō þæs
wīngeardes biggęngan: Efne, nū ðrēo gēar ic sōhte wæstm on

12. 16–21. . . . Hominis cuiusdam
divitis uberes fructus ager attulit.
Et cogitabat intra se dicens: Quid
faciam, quia non habeo quo con-
gregem fructus meos? Et dixit:
Hoc faciam: Destruam horrea
mea, et maiora faciam; et illuc
congregabo omnia quae nata sunt
mihi, et bona mea. Et dicam
animae meae: Anima, habes multa
bona posita in annos plurimos; re-
quiesce, comede, bibe, epulare.
Dixit autem illi Deus: Stulte, hac
nocte animam tuam repetunt a te;
quae autem parasti, cuius erunt?
Sic est qui sibi thesaurizat, et non
est in Deum dives.

12. 35. Sint lumbi vestri praecincti,
et lucernae ardentes. . . .

12. 37. . . . Faciet illos discumbere,
et transiens ministrabit illis.

12. 47. Ille autem servus, qui cognovit voluntatem domini sui, et non
praeparavit, et non fecit secundum voluntatem eius, vapulabit
multis.

12. 49. Ignem veni mittere in terram,
et quid volo nisi ut accendatur?

13. 6–9. . . . Arborem fici habebat
quidam plantatam in vinea sua,
et venit quaerens fructum in illa,
et non invenit. Dixit autem ad
cultorem vineae: Ecce anni tres
sunt ex quo venio quaerens

ðisum frctrēowe, and nænne ne funde; forceorf hit; tō hwī hręmð hit ðisne stęde?　Se biggęnga him andwyrde: Hlāford, lǣt hit standan gēarlanges, oð-þæt ic hit bedelfe, and mid meoxe bewurpe, and hit witodlice wēstm wyrcð; gif hit ðonne beran nele, ðū cymst and forcyrfst hit.　Æ. H. ii. 406, 408.

14. 11. *See* Luke 18. 12–14.

14. 16. Sum man gearcode micele feorme, and ðǣrtō manega gelað-ode.　Æ. H. ii. 370.

14. 17, 18. Ealle mīne ðing sind gegearcode. . . . Hī ealle samod hī belādiað.　Se forma cwæð: Ic bohte ænne tūn, and mē is nēod tō farenne, and ðone gesēon; ic bidde ðē, belāda me.　Æ. H. ii. 372.

14. 19. Sum ōðer cwæð: Ic bohte fīf getȳmu oxena, and ic wille faran fandian ðǣra. . . . Ic bidde ðē þæt ðū mē lādige.　Æ. H. ii. 372, 374.

14. 20–24. Se ðridda cwæð: Ic hæbbe nū gewīfod, and forðī tō ðǣre feorme cuman ne mæg. . . . Se ðēowa gecyrde hām, and sǣde his hlāforde ðǣra gelaðodra forsewennysse.　Se hlāford ðā gelāthyrt cwæð tō his ðēowan: Far ārdlice geond þās strǣta and wīc, and gegadera ðearfan and ālēfede, blinde and healte, and gelǣd hider inn. . . . Se ðēowa cwæð: Hlāford, hit is gedōn swā ðū hēte, and hēr gȳt is rȳmet ǣmtig. . . . Be ðām cwæð se hlāford tō ðān ðēowan: Far nū geond wegas and hęgas, and nȳd hī inn tō farenne, þæt mīn hūs bēo gefylled. . . . Ic sęcge ēow tō sōðan þæt nān ðǣra wera ðe, gelaðode, cuman noldon, ne onbirigð mīnes gereordes.　Æ. H. ii. 374, 376.

fructum in ficulnea hac, et non invenio; succide ergo illam; ut quid etiam terram occupat? At ille respondens, dicit illi: Domine, dimitte illam et hoc anno, usque dum fodiam circa illam, et mittam stercora, et siquidem fecerit fructum; sin autem, in futurum succides eam.

14. 16. . . . Homo quidam fecit coenam magnam, et vocavit multos.

14. 17, 18. . . . Iam parata sunt omnia. Et coeperunt simul omnes excusare. Primus dixit ei: Villam emi, et necesse habeo exire, et videre illam; rogo te, habe me excusatum.

14. 19. Et alter dixit: Iuga boum emi quinque, et eo probare illa; rogo te, habe me excusatum.

14. 20–24. Et alius dixit: Uxorem duxi, et ideo non possum venire. Et reversus servus nuntiavit haec domino suo.　Tunc iratus pater-familias dixit servo suo: Exi cito in plateas et vicos civitatis, et pauperes, ac debiles, et caecos, et claudos introduc huc. Et ait servus: Domine, factum est ut

14. 26. Sꝺ ðe tō mē cymð, ne mæg hē bēon mīn leorningcniht, būton hē his wīf hatige.   Æ. H. i. 308.

15. 1–7. Gerēfan and synfulle men genēalǣhton ðām Hǣlende, and woldon his lāre gehȳran.   Þā ceorodon ða sunderhālgan and ða bōceras Iudeiscre ðēode, forðanðe se Hǣlend underfēng ða synfullan, and him mid gereordode.   Þā sǣde se Hǣlend ðām Iudeiscum bōcerum ðis bigspel : Hwilc ēower hæfð hundtēontig scēapa. . . . Hwilc ēower hæfð hundtēontig scēapa, and gif hē forlȳsð ān ðǣra scēapa, ðonne forlǣt hē ða nigon and hundnigontig on wēstene, and gǣð sēcende þæt ān ðe him losode?
. . . Ðā-ða hē hit gemētte, hē hit bær on his exlum tō ðǣre ēowde blissigende. . . . Hē gelaðode his frȳnd and his nēhgebūras. . . . Hē cwæð : Blissiað mid mē, forðanðe ic gemētte mīn forlorene scēap. . . . Ic secge ēow, māre bliss bið on heofonum be ānum synfullan men, gif hē his synna mid dǣdbōte behrēowsað, ðonne sȳ be nigon and hundnigontig rihtwīsum ðe nānre behrēowsunge ne behōfiað.   Æ. H. i. 338, 340.

15. 8. *See* Æ. H. i. 342.

15. 10. . . . þæt micel blis wǣre on heofonum be ānum dǣdbōtan.   Æ. H. i. 350.

16. 9. Tiliað ēow frēonda on Godes ðearfum, þæt hī on ēowrum geendungum onfōn ēow intō ēcum eardungstōwum.   Æ. H. i. 337.

imperasti, et adhuc locus est.   Et ait dominus servo : Exi in vias et sepes, et compelle intrare, ut impleatur domus mea. Dico autem vobis quod nemo virorum illorum qui vocati sunt gustabit coenam meam.

14. 26. . . . Si quis venit ad me, et non odit . . . uxorem, non potest meus esse discipulus. . . .

15. 1–7. Erant autem appropinquantes ei publicani et peccatores, ut audirent illum.   Et murmurabant Pharisaei et scribae, dicentes : Quia hic peccatores recipit, et manducat cum illis.   Et ait ad illos parabolam istam, dicens : Quis ex vobis homo qui habet centum oves, et si perdiderit unam ex illis, nonne dimittit nonagin-

ta novem in deserto, et vadit ad illam quae perierat, donec inveniat eam?   Et cum invenerit eam, imponit in humeros suos gaudens ; . . . convocat amicos et vicinos, dicens illis : Congratulamini mihi, quia inveni ovem meam quae perierat.   Dico vobis quod ita gaudium erit in coelo super uno peccatore poenitentiam agente, quam super nonaginta novem iustis qui non indigent poenitentia.

15. 10. . . . Gaudium erit coram angelis Dei super uno peccatore poenitentiam agente.

16. 9. . . . Facite vobis amicos de mammona iniquitatis, ut, cum defeceritis, recipiant vos in aeterna tabernacula.

16. 13. *See* Matt. 6. 24–27.

16. 15. Gē rihtwīsiað ēow ætforan mannum ; and God cann ēowere heortan.   Æ. H. ii. 404.

16. 16. Sēo ealde ǣ and wītegan wǣron ōð Iohannes tōcyme ; s   iððan ongann godspelbodung.   Æ. H. i. 354.

16. 19, 20. Sum welig man wæs mid purpuran and godewebbe geglenged, and dæghwamlice mǣrlice leofode. Þā læg sum wǣdla æt[1] his geate, and his nama wæs Lazarus, se wæs līc-ðrōwere.   Æ. H. i. 328.

‖ Sum rīce man wæs. . . . Sum ðearfa wæs gehāten Lazarus.

     Æ. H. i. 330.

16. 21, 22, 24–28. Ðā genēalǣhton ðā hundas, and his wunda gelic-cedon. . . . Þā gelamp hit þæt se wǣdla gewāt, and englas ferodon his sāwle tō ðæs hēahfæderes wununge Abrahames ; and ðæs rīcan gāst æfter forðsīðe wearð on helle besenct. . . . Hē bæd þā Abraham mid earmlicre stemne þæt Lazarus mōste his tungan drȳpan. . . . Se hēahfæder Abraham him cwæð tō : Ðū, mīn bearn, bēo ðē gemyndig þæt ðū underfēnge welan on ðīnum līfe, and Lazarus yrmðe. . . . Betwux ūs and ēow is gefæstnod micel ðrosm ; þeah hwā wille fram ūs tō eow, hē ne mæg, ne ēac fram ēow tō ūs. . . . Ðā bearn him on mōd his gebrōðra gemynd, . . . and gyrnde forð þæt Lazarus hī mōste warnigan, þæt hī ne becōmon tō his sūsle.   Æ. H. i. 330, 332, 334.

16. 15. . . . Vos estis qui iustificatis vos coram hominibus ; Deus autem novit corda vestra. . . .

16. 16. Lex et prophetae usque ad Ioannem ; ex eo regnum Dei evangelizatur. . . .

16. 19, 20. Homo quidam erat dives, qui induebatur purpura et bysso, et epulabatur quotidie splendide. Et erat quidam mendicus, nomine Lazarus, qui iacebat ad ianuam eius, ulceribus plenus.

16. 21, 22, 24–28. . . . Canes venie-bant, et lingebant ulcera eius. Factum est autem ut moreretur mendicus, et portaretur ab angelis in sinum Abrahae. Mortuus est autem et dives, et sepultus est in inferno. . . . Et ipse clamans dixit : Pater Abraham, miserere mei, et mitte Lazarum, ut intingat ex-tremum digiti sui in aquam, ut refrigeret linguam meam. . . . Et dixit illi Abraham : Fili, recordare quia recepisti bona in vita tua, et Lazarus similiter mala ; . . . et in his omnibus inter nos et vos chaos magnum firmatum est, ut hi, qui volunt hinc transire ad vos non possint, neque inde huc trans-meare. Et ait : Rogo ergo te, pater, ut mittas eum in domum patris mei—habeo enim quinque fratres—ut testetur illis, ne et ipsi veniant in hunc locum tormen-torum.

[1] Thorpe, 'at.'

16. 31. Se hēahfæder him andwyrde : Gif hī forscōð Moyses ᚢ and ðǣra wītegena bodunga, nellað hī gelȳfan, þēah hwā of dēaðe ārīse. *Æ. H. i. 334.*

18. 9–11. Drihten sǣde þis bigspel be sumum mannum þe on him sylfum trūwodon þæt hī rihtwīse wǣron, and ōðre forsāwon, þus cweðende : Twēgen men ēodon intō Godes temple hī tō gebiddenne ; ān wæs sunderhālga, and ōðer wæs openlīce synful. . . . Hē cwæð : God ! ic ðancige ðē þæt ic ne eom nā swilce ōðre menn. *Æ. H. ii. 426, 428.*

‖ Ic ne com swilce swā [1] ōðre men. *Æ. H. ii. 428.*

18. 12–14. Ic fæste twēgen dagas on ðǣre wucan, and ic tēoðie ealle mīne ǣhta. . . . Se synfulla stōd feorran, gecnǣwe his misdǣda, and ne dorste his ēagan ūpāhebban, ac slōh his brēost, þus cweðende : . . . God Ælmihtig, gemiltsa mē synfullum. . . . Sōð ic ēow secge : Hē ēode hām gerihtwīsod fram ðām ōðrum. . . . Ælc ðǣra ðe hine onhefð bið gecādmēt, and sē ðe hine sylfne gecādmēt, sē bið āhafen. *Æ. H. ii. 428, 430, 432.*

‖ Ælc ðǣra þe hine onhefð, hē sceal bēon gecādmēt ; and sē ðe hine geēadmēt, hē sceal bēon āhafen. *Æ. H. i. 202.*

‖ Ælc ðǣra ðe hine onhefð bið gecādmēt, and sē ðe hine geēadmēt bið geuferod. *Æ. H. i. 362.*

‖ Ælc ðǣra ðe hine onhefð bið gecādmēt, and sē ðe hine gecādmēt, hē bið āhafen. *Æ. H. i. 512.*

18. 15, 16. *See* Matt. 19. 13, 14.

18. 18. Sum welig mann cōm tō ðām Hǣlende, and fēoll tō his fōtum [2], ðus cweðende : Ēalā ðū gōda lārēow, hwæt sceal ic dōn þæt ic hæbbe þæt ēce līf ? *Æ. H. ii. 400.*

16. 31. Ait autem illi : Si Moysen et prophetas non audiunt, neque si quis ex mortuis resurrexerit credent.

18. 9–11. Dixit autem et ad quosdam qui in se confidebant tamquam iusti, et aspernabantur ceteros, parabolam istam : Duo homines ascenderunt in templum ut orarent : unus Pharisaeus, et alter publicanus. Pharisaeus ... haec apud se orabat : Deus, gratias ago tibi quia non sum sicut ceteri hominum. . . .

18. 12–14. Ieiuno bis in sabbato ; decimas do omnium quae possideo. Et publicanus a longe stans, nolebat nec oculos ad coelum levare, sed percutiebat pectus suum, dicens : Deus, propitius esto mihi peccatori. Dico vobis : Descendit hic iustificatus in domum suam ab illo ; quia omnis qui se exaltat humiliabitur : et qui se humiliat exaltabitur.

18. 18. Et interrogavit eum quidam

----

[1] Thorpe, 'swilceswā.'   [2] From Mark 10. 17, 'genu flexo ante eum.'

18. 19. Nis nān man gōd būtan Gode ānum.   Æ. H. i. 254.

18. 20–22. Gif ðū wylt becuman tō ðān ēcan līfe, heald þās
bebodu[1] : Ne ofslih ðū mann[2] ; Ne unrihthǣm ðū ; Ne stala
ðū ; Ne bēo ðū lēas gewita ; Ārwurða þīnne fæder and ðīne
mōdor ; and, Lufa ðīnne nēxtan swā-swā ðē sylfne[3].   Đā andwyrde se rīca, and cwæð : Ealle ðās þing ic hēold symle fram
mīnum geogoðhāde.   Him andwyrde eft se Hǣlend, and cwæð :
Anes ðinges ðē is wana : far nū, and becēapa wið fēo ealle
ðīne ǣhta, and dǣl ðearfum, and þū hæfst ðonne þīnne goldhord on heofonan rīce ; and cum, and filig mē.   Æ. H. ii. 400 ;
cf. Exod. 20. 12 ff.

∥ Lufa ðīnne nēxtan swā-swā ðe sylfne.   Æ. H. ii. 340.

18. 31–43. . . . ðæt se Hǣlend genāme onsundron his twelf
leorningcnihtas[4], and cwæð tō him : Efne, wē sceolon faran
tō ðǣre byrig Hierusalem, and þonne bēoð gefyllede ealle
ðā ðing þe wǣron be mē āwritene þurh wītegan.   Ic sceal
bēon belǣwed ðēodum, and hī doð mē tō bysmore, and be-
swingað, and syððan ofslēað ; and ic ārīse of dēaðe on þām
ðriddan dæge.   Þā nyston his leorningcnihtas nān andgit
þyssera worda.   Đā gelamp hit þæt hī genēalǣhton ānre byrig
þe is gehāten Hiericho, and ðā sæt þǣr sum blind man be
ðām wege ; and, þā-þā hē gehȳrde þæs folces fær mid þām

princeps, dicens : Magister bone,
quid faciens vitam aeternam pos-
sidebo ?
18. 19. . . . Nemo bonus nisi solus
Deus.
18. 20–22. . . . Non occides ; Non
moechaberis ; Non furtum facies ;
Non falsum testimonium dices ;
Honora patrem tuum et matrem.
Qui ait : Haec omnia custodivi
a iuventute mea.   Quo audito,
Iesus ait ei : Adhuc unum tibi
deest : omnia quaecumque habes
vende, et da pauperibus, et habebis thesaurum in coelo ; et veni,
sequere me.

18. 31–43. Assumpsit autem Iesus
duodecim, et ait illis : Ecce, ascen-
dimus Ierosolymam, et consum-
mabuntur omnia quae scripta sunt
per prophetas de Filio hominis.
Tradetur enim gentibus, et illude-
tur, et flagellabitur, et conspuetur ;
et, postquam flagellaverint, occident eum ; et tertia die resurget.
Et ipsi nihil horum intellexerunt,
et erat verbum istud absconditum
ab eis, et non intelligebant quae
dicebantur.   Factum est autem,
cum   appropinquaret   Iericho,
caecus   quidam   sedebat   secus
viam ; . . . et cum audiret turbam

---

[1] From Matt. 19. 17, 'Si autem vis ad vitam ingredi, serva mandata.'
[2] The order from Matt. 19. 18, 'Non homicidium facies ; Non adulterabis.'
[3] From Matt. 19. 19, 'Diliges proximum tuum sicut teipsum.'
[4] From Matt. 20. 17, 'duodecim discipulos secreto.'

Hǣlende, ðā ācsode hē hwā þǣr fērde. Hī cwǣdon him tō
þæt þæt wǣre ðæs Hǣlendes fǣr. Þā begann hē tō hrȳmenne,
and cwæð : Hǣlend, Dauides bearn, gemiltsa mīn. Ðā męn
þe beforan þām Hǣlende fērdon cīddon ongēan ðone blindan,
þæt hē suwian sceolde. Hē clypode þā miccle swīðor : Hǣlend,
Dauides bearn, gemiltsa mīn. Þā stōd se Hǣlend, and hēt
lǣdan þone blindan tō him. Þā-ðā hē genēalǣhte, þā ācsode
se Hǣlend hine : Hwæt wylt ðū þæt ic þē dō? Hē cwæð:
Drihten, þæt ic mage gesēon. And se Hǣlend him cwæð tō :
Lōca nū ; þīn gelēafa hæfð ðē gehǣled. And hē ðērrihte
geseah, and fyligde þām Hǣlende, and hine mǣrsode. Þā
eal þæt folc, þe þæt wundor geseh, herede God mid micelre
onbryrdnysse. Æ. H. i. 152.

‖ Ic ārīse of dēaðe on þām ðriddan dæge.   Æ. H. i. 152.

‖ Hǣlend, Dauides bearn, gemiltsa mīn.   Æ. H. i. 156.

‖ Hwæt wilt ðū þæt ic ðē dō ?   Æ. H. i. 158.

‖ Lā lēof, dō þæt ic mæge gesēon.   Æ. H. i. 158.

‖ Lōca nū ; þīn gelēafa ðē gehǣlde.   Æ. H. i. 158.

19. 2–6. Zacheus wæs sum rīce mann ; and cēpte þæs Hǣlendes
fǣr, and wolde gesēon hwilc hē wǣre, ac hē ne mihte for
ðǣre męnigu ðe him mid fērde, forðanðe hē wæs scort on
wǣstme. Þa forarn hē ðām Hǣlende, and stāh uppon ān
trēow, þæt hē hine gesēon mihte. Crīst ðā beseah upp wið
þæs rīcan, and cwæð : Zachee, stīh ārdlice ādūn, forðanðe mē
gedafenað þæt ic nū tō-dæg þē gecyrre. Zacheus ðā swyftlice
of ðām trēowe ālihte, and hine blissigende underfēng. Æ. H. i. 580.

praetereuntem, interrogabat quid
hoc esset. Dixerunt autem ei
quod Iesus Nazarenus transiret.
Et clamavit, dicens : Iesu, fili
David, miserere mei. Et qui
praeibant increpabant eum ut
taceret. Ipse vero multo magis
clamabat : Fili David, miserere
mei. Stans autem Iesus iussit
illum adduci ad se. Et cum
appropinquasset,   interrogavit
illum, dicens : Quid tibi vis
faciam ? At ille dixit : Domine,
ut videam. Et Iesus dixit illi :
Respice ; fides tua te salvum fecit.

Et confestim vidit, et sequebatur
illum, magnificans Deum. Et
omnis plebs, ut vidit, dedit laudem
Deo.

19. 2–6. Et ecce vir nomine
Zachaeus ; et hic princeps erat
publicanorum, et ipse dives ; et
quaerebat videre Iesum quis esset,
et non poterat prae turba, quia
statura pusillus erat. Et prae-
currens ascendit in arborem sy-
comorum ut videret eum. . . .
Suspiciens Iesus vidit illum, et
dixit ad eum : Zachaee, festinans
descende, quia hodie in domo tua

19. 8–10. Ðā āstōd hē ætforan him, and him ānmōdlice tō cwæð: Drihten, efne, ic tōdǣle healfne dǣl mīnra gōda ðearfum; and swā-hwæt-swā ic mid fācne berȳpte, þæt ic wylle be fēower-fealdum forgyldan. Drihten him tō cwæð: Nū tō-dæg is ðisum hīrede hǣl gefremmed, forðanðe hē is Abrahames ofspring. Ic cōm tō sēcenne and tō gehǣlenne þæt þe on mancynne losode. _Æ. H. i._ 582.

‖ . . . Zacheus, se ðe healfe his ǣhta þearfum dǣlde, and mid healfum dǣle forgeald be fēowerfealdum swā-hwæt-swā hē ǣr on unriht be ānfealdum rēafode. . . . _Æ. H. i._ 130, 132.

19. 25. _See_ Matt. 25. 24–30.

19. 41, 42. Ðā-ðā hē genēalǣhte þǣre ceastre, and hē hī geseah. Ðā wēop hē ofer hī. . . . Drihten cwæð tō ðǣre byrig: Gif þū wistest hwæt þē tōweard is, þonne wēope ðū mid mē[1]. Witod-lice on ðisum dæge þū wunast on sibbe; ac ðā tōweardan wraca sind nū bedīglode fram ðīnum ēagum. _Æ. H. i._ 402, 404.

‖ On ðysum dæge þū wunast on sibbe; ac sēo tōwearde wracu is nū bedīglod fram ðīnum ēagum. _Æ. H. i._ 408.

19. 43, 44. Se tȳma cymð þæt ðīne fȳnd ðē ymbsittað mid ymbtrymminge, and ðē on ǣlce healfe genyrwiað, and tō eorðan þē āstreccað, and ðīne bearn samod ðe on ðē sind. . . . And hī ne forlǣtað on ðē stān ofer stāne. _Æ. H. i._ 408, 410.

‖ Forðanþe ðū ne oncnēowe ðone tīman ðīnre genēo-sunge. _Æ. H. i._ 404.

19. 45, 46. Drihten ādrǣfde of ðām temple ðā cȳpmen, þus cweð-

oportet me manere. Et festinans descendit, et excepit illum gaudens.

19. 8–10. Stans autem Zachaeus, dixit ad Dominum: Ecce dimi-dium bonorum meorum, Domine, do pauperibus; et si quid aliquem defraudavi, reddo quadruplum. Ait Iesus ad eum: Quia hodie salus domui huic facta est, eo quod et ipse filius sit Abrahae. Venit enim Filius hominis quae-rere et salvum facere quod pe-rierat.

19. 41, 42. Et ut appropinquavit,

videns civitatem flevit super illam. dicens: Quia si cognovisses et tu. et quidem in hac die tua, quae ad pacem tibi; nunc autem ab-scondita sunt ab oculis tuis.

19. 43, 44. Quia venient dies in te, et circumdabunt te inimici tui vallo, et circumdabunt te, et co-angustabunt te undique, et ad terram prosternent te, et filios tuos qui in te sunt; et non relin-quent in te lapidem super lapi-dem, eo quod non cognoveris tempus visitationis tuae.

19. 45, 46. Et ingressus in templum,

---

[1] Note the curious exegesis.

ende : Hit is āwriten þæt mīn hūs is gebedhūs ; and gē hit habbað gedōn sceaðum tō scrœfe.   Æ. H. i. 406.

‖ Mīn hūs is gebedhūs ; and gē hit habbað gedōn sceaðum tō scrœfe.   Æ. H. i. 410.

19. 47. Hē . . . wæs lǣrende þæt folc dæghwomlice binnan ðām temple.   Æ. H. i. 406.

‖ And hē wæs tǣcende dæghwomlice binnan ðām temple.   Æ. H. i. 412.

20. 25. *See* Matt. 22. 21.

20. 35, 36. Nān wer ne wīfað, nē wīf ne ceorlað, nē tēam ne bið getȳmed ; nē hī dēaðes ne ābyrigað siððan ; ac bēoð englum gelīce.   Æ. H. i. 238.

21. 9. Ðonne gē gehȳrað on middanearde gefeoht and sace, ne bēo gē āfyrhte ; þās ðing sceolon ǣrest cuman, ac ne bið swā-ðēah þǣrrihte sēo geendung.   Æ. H. ii. 538.

‖ Þās frēcednyssa sceolon ǣrest cuman, ac ne bið swā-ðēah þǣrrihte sēo geendung. . . .   Æ. H. ii. 538.

21. 10, 11. Þēod ārīst ongēan þēode, and rīce winð ongēan rīce. . . . Micele eorðstyrunga bēoð geond stōwa. . . . Coða becumað. . . . Hunger bið. . . . Ōgan of heofenum, and micele tācna.   Æ. H. ii. 538.

‖ Ðēod ārīst ongēan ðēode, and rīce ongēan rīce, and micele eorðstyrunga bēoð gehwǣr, and cwealm, and hunger.   Æ. H. i. 608.

21. 12–19. Swā-ðēah ǣrðanþe ðās ðing gelimpað, man ēht ēower, belǣwende on gesamnungum, and tēonde tō cynegum, and tō ealdormannum, and tō cwearternum, for mīnum naman. . . . Þis ēow gelimpð sōðlice on gewitnysse. . . . Settað eornostlice on ēowerum heortum, þæt gē ne þurfon āsmēagan hū gē

coepit eiicere vendentes in illo et ementes, dicens illis: Scriptum est quia domus mea domus orationis est ; vos autem fecistis illam speluncam latronum.

19. 47. Et erat docens quotidie in templo. . . .

20. 35, 36. Illi vero . . . neque nubent, neque ducent uxores ; neque enim ultra mori poterunt ; aequales enim angelis sunt. . . .

21. 9. Cum autem audieritis praelia et seditiones, nolite terreri ; oportet primum haec fieri, sed nondum

statim finis.

21. 10, 11. Tunc dicebat illis: Surget gens contra gentem, et regnum adversus regnum. Et terraemotus magni erunt per loca, et pestilentiae, et fames, terroresque de coelo, et signa magna erunt.

21. 12–19. Sed ante haec omnia iniicient vobis manus suas, et persequentur tradentes in synagogas et custodias, trahentes ad reges et praesides, propter nomen meum ; continget autem vobis in testimonium. Ponite ergo in cor-

andwyrdan sceolon. Ic sōðlice sylle ēow mūð and wīsdōm, þām ne magon wiðstandan nē wiðcweðan ealle ēowere wiðerwinnan. . . . Gē bēoð belǣwede fram fæderum, and gebrōðrum, and fram māgum, and hī ēow tō dēaðe gewrǣcað. . . . Gē bēoð andsǣte eallum mannum for mīnum naman ; and swā-ðēah ne losað ān hǣr of ēowerum hēafde. . . . On ēowerum geðylde gē geūhniað ēow ēowere sāwla.　Æ. H. ii. 540, 542, 544

‖ Ne sceal ēow bēon forloren ān hǣr of ēowrum hēafde.
　Æ. H. i. 236.

‖ On ēowrum geðylde gē habbað ēowere sāwla.　Æ. H. ii. 92.

21. 25. Tācna bēoð on sunnan, and on mōnan, and on steorrum ; and on eorðan ðēoda ofðriccednys, for gemęncgednysse sǣlicra ȳða and swēges.　Æ. H. i. 608.

‖ Tācna gewurðað on sunnan, and on mōnan, and on steorrum ; and on eorðan bið þēoda ofðryccednyss.　Æ. H. i. 608.

21. 26-33. Męnn forsēariað for ōgan, and andbīdunge ðǣra ðinga þe becumað ofer ealne middangeard ; witodlice heofonan mihta bēoð āstyrode. . . . Þonne wē gesēoð mannes Bearn cumende on wolcnum, mid micelre mihte and mægenðrymme. . . . Þonne ðās wundra ongynnað, āhębbað þonne ēowre hēafda, and behealdað, forðanðe ēower ālȳsednyss genēalǣhð. . . . Drihten cwæð : Behealdað þās fīctreowa, and ealle ōðre trēowa ; þonne hī spryttað, ðonne wite gē þæt hit sumorlǣhð. Swā ēac gē magon witan, ðonne gē ðās foresǣdan tācna gesēoð, þæt Godes rīce genēalǣhð. . . . Sōð ic ēow sęcge : Ne gewīt ðēos mǣgð ōð-þæt ealle ðās ðing gewurðað. . . . Heofen and eorðe gewītað ; and mīne word nǣfre ne gewītað.　Æ. H. i. 610, 612, 614, 616.

dibus vestris non praemeditari quemadmodum respondeatis. Ego enim dabo vobis os et sapientiam, cui non poterunt resistere et contradicere omnes adversarii vestri. Trademini autem a parentibus, et fratribus, et cognatis, et amicis, et morte afficient ex vobis. Et eritis odio omnibus propter nomen meum ; et capillus de capite vestro non peribit. In patientia vestra possidebitis animas vestras.

21. 25. Et erunt signa in sole, et luna, et stellis ; et in terris pressura gentium, prae confusione sonitus maris et fluctuum.

21. 26-33. Arescentibus hominibus prae timore, et expectatione quae supervenient universo orbi ; nam virtutes coelorum movebuntur. Et tunc videbunt Filium hominis venientem in nube cum potestate magna et maiestate. His autem fieri incipientibus, respicite, et levate capita vestra, quoniam appropinquat redemptio vestra. Et dixit illis similitudinem : Videte

21. 34. Beoð wære þæt ꝥowere heortan ne beon gehefgode mid oferfylle, and druncennysse, and mid woruldcarum, and se fǽrlica deað becume ofer eow. *Æ. H. ii. 22.*

22. 3–5. Hwæt, ðā se deofol intō Iudan bestōp, ān ðǣra twelfa Drihtnes ðegena. And hē sōna eode tō ðǣra Iudeiscra rǣde, and openlice befrān hwæt hī him feos geūðon, gif hē ðone Hǽlend him belǽwan mihte[1]. Hī ðā þæs fægnodon, and þæt feoh gesetton on ðrittig scillingum[1]. *Æ. H. ii. 242; cf. i. 26.*

22. 19. *See* Matt. 26. 26–28, note.

22. 38. Þǣr wǣron twā swurd stōlice gebrōhte tō ðām wiðerstealle, gif hit swā Crīst wolde. *Æ. H. ii. 248.*

22. 50. *See* Matt. 26. 51–54, note 2.

22. 51. *See Æ. H. ii. 246.*

22. 61. *See* Matt. 26. 69–75, note 2.

22. 63–65. *See* Matt. 26. 67, 68, and note.

23. 3. *See* Matt. 27. 11.

23. 7–9. Þā gemunde se ealdormann þæt Herodes wæs on ðǣre scīre ðā, and āsende Crīst him tō. Herodes sōðlice wæs swīðe geblissod mid ðǣre gesihðe, for his swīðlicum tācnum, and wolde gesēon sum wundor fram him; ac Crīst him nolde nān ðing tō gecweðan. *Æ. H. ii. 250.*

23. 11–16. Ðā forseah Herodes hine swīðe mid his hīrede, and be his hwītum rēafum hūxlice spræc, and āsende hine sōna tō ðām

ficulneam, et omnes arbores; cum producunt iam ex se fructum, scitis quoniam prope est aestas. Ita et vos cum videritis haec fieri, scitote quoniam prope est regnum Dei. Amen dico vobis quia non praeteribit generatio haec donec omnia fiant. Coelum et terra transibunt; verba autem mea non transibunt.

21. 34. Attendite autem vobis, ne forte graventur corda vestra in crapula et ebrietate, et curis huius vitae, et superveniat in vos repentina dies illa.

22. 3–5. Intravit autem Satanas in Iudam, . . . unum de duodecim.

Et abiit, et locutus est cum principibus sacerdotum et magistratibus. . . . Et gavisi sunt. . . .

22. 38. At illi dixerunt: Domine, ecce duo gladii hic. At ille dixit eis: Satis est.

23. 7–9. Et ut cognovit quod de Herodis potestate esset, remisit eum ad Herodem, qui et ipse Ierosolymis erat illis diebus. Herodes autem, viso Iesu, gavisus est valde; . . . audierat multa de eo, et sperabat signum aliquod videre ab eo fieri. . . . Ipse nihil illi respondebat.

23. 11–16. Sprevit autem illum Herodes cum exercitu suo, et illusit

---

[1] From Matt. 26. 15, 'Et ait illis: Quid vultis mihi dare, et ego vobis eum tradam? At illi constituerunt ei triginta argenteos.'

foresǣdan Pilate ; and hī wurdon ðā gefrȳnd for ðǣre dǣde, swā-swā hī nǣron nǣfre ǣr on līfe. Þā clypode Pilatus eft tō ðām folce, cwæð be ðām Hǣlende þæt hē unscyldig wǣre, forðanðe Herodes nē hē eac ne mihte nænne gylt on him tō dēaðe āfindan : cwæð þæt hē wolde hine beswingan, and tō līfe ālǣtan. Æ. H. ii. 252 ; cf. i. 478.

23. 32. Ðǣr wǣron gelǣdde mid ðām lifigendan Drihtne twēgen scyldige sceaðan, for heora synnum tō hōnne. Æ. H. ii. 254.

23. 34. Mīn heofenlica Fæder, ic ðē nū bidde, forgif ðās dǣde þisum gedwolmannum, forðanðe hī nyton hwæt hī nū dōð.
.Æ. H. ii. 256 ; cf. ii. 258.

‖ Mīn Drihten, miltsa him ; nyton hī hwæt hī dōð. Æ. H. ii. 34.

23. 39-43. Ān ðǣra sceaðena eac swilce clypode : Gif ðū Hǣlend Crīst sȳ, gehǣl ðē and ūs. Þā andwyrde se ōðer, hine ðrēagende : Hwæt ðū lā, earming, ne ondrǣtst ðū ðē God ? Wit synd gewītnode for wælhrēawum dǣdum, and þes hālga Hǣlend hangað hēr unscyldig. Eft ðā se ylca clypode tō Crīste : Gemun ðū mīn, Drihten, þonne ðū mihtig becymst tō ðīnum āgenum rīce, roderes Wealdend[1] ! Se Hǣlend him cwæð tō mid sōðum behāte : Nū tō-dæg ðū bist on neorxena wange mid mē. Æ. H. ii. 256.

‖ Drihten, geðenc mīn þonne ðū tō þīnum rīce becymst. Crīst him andwyrde : Sōð ic þē secge : Nū tō-dæg þū bist mid mē on neorxnawanges myrhðe. Æ. H. i. 576.

‖ Drihten, bēo mīn gemyndig þonne ðū cymst tō ðīnum rīce. Drihten him andwyrde : Sōð ic ðē secge : Nū tō-dæg þū bist mid mē on neorxena wange. Æ. H. ii. 78.

indutum veste alba, et remisit ad Pilatum. Et facti sunt amici Herodes et Pilatus in ipsa die ; nam antea inimici erant ad invicem. Pilatus autem, convocatis principibus sacerdotum, et magistratibus, et plebe, dixit ad illos : ... Nullam causam inveni in homine isto ex his in quibus eum accusatis. Sed neque Herodes ; nam remisi vos ad illum, et ecce nihil dignum morte actum est ei.

Emendatum ergo illum dimittam.
23. 32. Ducebantur autem et alii duo nequam cum eo, ut interficerentur.

23. 34. Pater, dimitte illis ; non enim sciunt quid faciunt. ...

23. 39-43. Unus autem de his qui pendebant latronibus blasphemabat eum, dicens : Si tu es Christus, salvum fac temetipsum et nos. Respondens autem alter, increpabat eum, dicens : Neque

---

[1] A poetical epithet ; indeed the speech might be printed as two lines of alliterative verse.

23. 44. *See* Matt. 27. 45.

23. 46. *See* Matt. 27. 50–53, note 2.

23. 48. And sēo ōðer menigu ðe ðǣr mid stōdon bēoton heora brēost, būgende tō Gode. .Æ. H. ii. 258.

23. 56. *See* Æ. H. i. 220.

24. 1. *See* .Æ. H. i. 220.

24. 13, 14. Ēodon twēgen Drihtnes leorningcnihtas tō ānre byrig, sēo wæs fīf mīla fram Hierusalem, Emmaus gehāten; þā ēodon hī, sprecende ymbe þæs Hǣlendes þrōwunge him betwȳnan. .Æ. H. ii. 284.

24. 25 ff. *See* Æ. H. ii. 284, 286.

24. 36–39. Þā æt nēxtan cōm se Hǣlend tō his leorningcnihtum, þǣr hī gegaderode wǣron, and cwæð him tō: Sȳ sibb betwux ēow; ic hit eom, ne bēo gē nā āfyrhte. Þā wurdon hī āfǣrede, and wēndon þæt hit sum gāst wǣre. Ðā cwæð hē him tō: Hwī sind gē āfǣrede, and mislice ðencað be mē? Scēawiað mīne handa and mīne fēt, þe wǣron mid næglum þurhdrifene. Grāpiað and scēawiað; gif ic gāst wǣre, ðonne næfde ic flǣsc and bān. .Æ. H. i. 220.

24. 42, 43. . . . þæt Crīst ǣte æfter his ǣriste gebrǣdne fisc and hunies bēobrēad. .Æ. H. ii. 292; cf. i. 206.

24. 50, 51. And hē lǣdde hī ðā ūt of ðǣre byrig ūp tō ānre dūne

---

tu times Deum, quod in eadem damnatione es? Et nos quidem iuste, nam digna factis recipimus; hic vero nihil mali gessit. Et dicebat ad Iesum: Domine, memento mei cum veneris in regnum tuum. Et dixit illi Iesus: Amen dico tibi: Hodie mecum eris in paradiso.

23. 48. Et omnis turba eorum qui simul aderant ad spectaculum istud, et videbant quae fiebant, percutientes pectora sua revertebantur.

24. 13, 14. Et ecce, duo ex illis ibant ipsa die in castellum, quod erat in spatio stadiorum sexaginta ab Ierusalem, nomine Emmaus; et ipsi loquebantur ad invicem de his omnibus quae acciderant.

24. 36–39. Dum autem haec loquuntur, stetit Iesus in medio eorum, et dicit eis: Pax vobis: ego sum; nolite timere. Conturbati vero et conterriti, existimabant se spiritum videre. Et dixit eis: Quid turbati estis, et cogitationes ascendunt in corda vestra? Videte manus meas et pedes, quia ego ipse sum; palpate, et videte; quia spiritus carnem et ossa non habet, sicut me videtis habere.

24. 42, 43. At illi obtulerunt ei partem piscis assi, et favum mellis. Et cum manducasset coram eis. . . .

24. 50, 51. Eduxit autem eos foras in Bethaniam, et, elevatis manibus suis, benedixit eis. Et factum est,

ðe is gecweden Mons Oliueti[1], and hī geblētsode upāhafenum handum.　Þā mid þǣre blētsunge fērde hē tō heofonum.

　　Æ. H. i. 294, 296 ; cf. Acts 1. 9–15.

24. 52. *See* Acts 1. 9–15, note.

JOHN.

1. 1–3. On frymðe wæs Word, and þæt Word wæs mid Gode, and þæt Word wæs God. Þis wæs on frymðe mid Gode. Ealle ðing sind þurh hine geworhte ; and nis nān þing būton him gesceapen.　Æ. H. i. 70 ; cf. i. 280.

　‖ On frymðe wæs Word, and þæt Word wæs mid Gode, and þæt Word wæs God.　Æ. H. i. 40, 358.

1. 9. *See* Æ. H. i. 294.

1. 14. Þæt ylce Word wæs geworden flǣsc, and wunode on ūs, þæt wē hine gescon mihton.　Æ. H. i. 40.

1. 18. Hē wæs ǣfre on ðæs Fæder bōsme.　Æ. H. i. 280, 282.

1. 23. *See* Isa. 40. 3, 4.

1. 29, 30. Ðā-ðā Iohannes hine geseah cumende tō him, þā cwæð hē be him : Hēr gǣð Godes Lamb, se ðe ætbrȳt and ādȳlegað middaneardes synna.　Be ðysum ic sǣde ēow ǣr : Sē ðe æfter mē cymð, hē is beforan me ; forðanðe hē wæs ǣr ic gewurde.

　　Æ. H. ii. 38.

　‖ Lōca nū ! Efne, hēr gǣð Godes Lamb, se ðe ætbrēt middangeardes synna.　Æ. H. i. 358.

　‖ Þū Godes Lamb, ðe ætbrētst middaneardes synna.　Æ. H. ii. 264.

　‖ . . . þæt hē wǣre Godes Lamb, se ðe ætbrūde middaneardes synna.　Æ. H. ii. 40.

1. 32. *See* Æ. H. i. 104.

2. 1, 2. Gifta wǣron gewordene on ānum tūne ðe is gecīged

dum benediceret illis, recessit ab eis, et ferebatur in coelum.

JOHN.

1. 1–3. In principio erat Verbum, et Verbum erat apud Deum, et Deus erat Verbum. Hoc erat in principio apud Deum. Omnia per ipsum facta sunt ; et sine ipso factum est nihil quod factum est.

1. 14. . . . Verbum caro factume st,

et habitavit in nobis. . . .

1. 18. . . . Qui est in sinu Patris. . . .

1. 29, 30. Altera die vidit Ioannes Iesum venientem ad se, et ait : Ecce Agnus Dei, ecce qui tollit peccatum mundi. Hic est de quo dixi : Post me venit vir qui ante me factus est ; quia prior me erat.

2. 1, 2. Et die tertia nuptiae factae sunt in Cana Galilaeae ; et erat

---

[1] From Acts 1. 12, 'a monte, qui vocatur Oliveti.'

Chana, on ðām Galileiscan earde; and ðǣr wæs Maria, þæs Hǣlendes mōder. Se Hǣlend wæs ꝥac gelaðod tō þām giftum. Æ. H. ii. 54 : cf. i. 58.

2. 3. Wīn ātꝥorode æt ðām giftum. Æ. H. ii. 54.

‖ Þā gelamp hit þæt æt ðām giftum wīn wearð ātꝥorod. Æ. H. i. 58.

2. 4. Drihten cwæð tō hjs mōder : Fǣmne, hwæt is mē and ðē tō ðān? Æ. H. ii. 54.

2. 6. Æt þām giftum wǣron gesætte six stǣnene wæterfatu, æfter ðǣra Iudeiscra clǣnsunge, healdende ǣnlīpige twȳfealde gemetu, oððe þrȳfealde. Æ. H. ii. 56 ; cf. i. 58.

2. 7 ff. See Æ. H. i. 58, 168.

2. 10, 11. Se drihtealdor cwæð tō ðām brȳdguman : Ælc man sylð on forandæge his gōde wīn, and þæt wacrre þonne ðā gebꝥoras drunciað : þū sōðlice hꝥolde þæt gōde wīn ōð ðiss. . . . Þis tācn worhte se Hǣlend on angynne his wundra, on ðām Galileiscan Chana, and geswutelode his wuldor : and his leorningcnihtas on hine gelȳfdon. Æ. H. ii. 70, 72 ; cf. i. 26.

2. 14. Ðǣr sǣton myneteras. and ðǣr wǣron gecȳpe hrȳðeru, and scꝥp, and culfran. Æ. H. i. 406.

‖ Ðǣr wǣron gecȳpe oxan, and scꝥp, and culfran, and þǣr sǣton myneteras. Æ. H. i. 412.

2. 15. Hꝥ worhte āne swipe of rāpum, and hī ealle mid gebꝥate ūtāscynde. Æ. H. i. 406.

‖ Mid swype ðā cȳpan ūtādrǣfde. Æ. H. i. 410.

3. 3. Būton gehwā bꝥo tuwa ācænned, ne mæg hꝥ nā faran intō heofonan rīce. Æ. H. ii. 10.

mater Iesu ibi. Vocatus est autem et Iesus . . . ad nuptias.

2. 3. Et deficiente vino. . . .

2. 4. Et dicit ei Iesus : Quid mihi et tibi est, mulier ? . . .

2. 6. Erant autem ibi lapideae hydriae sex positae secundum purificationem Iudaeorum, capientes singulae metretas binas vel ternas.

2. 10, 11. Et dicit ei : Omnis homo primum bonum vinum ponit ; et, cum inebriati fuerint, tunc id quod deterius est ; tu autem servasti bonum vinum usque adhuc. Hoc fecit initium signorum Iesus in Cana Galilaeae, et manifestavit gloriam suam ; et crediderunt in eum discipuli eius.

2. 14. Et invenit in templo vendentes boves, et oves, et columbas, et numularios sedentes.

2. 15. Et cum fecisset quasi flagellum de funiculis, omnes eiecit de templo. . . .

3. 3. . . . Nisi quis renatus fuerit denuo, non potest videre regnum Dei.

3. 5. Būton gehwā bēo geedcęnned of wætere and of ðān Hālgan Gāste, ne mæg hē faran intō Godes rīce. *Æ. H. ii. 12.*

‖ Būton gehwā bēo geedcęnned of wætere and of þām Hālgum Gāste, ne mæg hē faran intō heofenan rīce. *Æ. H. i. 94.*

3. 13. Nān man ne āstīhð tō heofonum būton sē ðe of heofenum āstāh, mannes Bearn se ðe is on heofenum. *Æ. H. ii. 386.*

‖ Mannes Bearn þe of heofenum āstāh, and on heofenum is. *Æ. H. ii. 386.*

3. 14, 15. Swā-swā Moyses āhōf ðā næddran on ðām wēstene, swā gedafenað þæt ic bēo āhafen, þæt ælc ðæra þe on mē gelyfð ne losige, ac þæt hē hæbbe þæt ēce līf. *Æ. H. ii. 238.*

3. 16. Swā swīþe lufode God þysne middangeard, þæt hē his āncęnnedan Sunu scalde for ūs. *Æ. H. i. 528.*

3. 29. Sē ðe brȳde hæfð, hē is brȳdguma. *Æ. H. ii. 10.*

3. 30. Crīste gedafenað þæt hē weaxe, and mē þæt ic wanigende bēo. *Æ. H. i. 356.*

4. 21. Gelȳf mē. *Æ. H. i. 482.*

4. 34. Mīn męte is þæt ic wyrce mīnes Fæder willan, þæt is rihtwīsnys. *Æ. H. i. 552.*

4. 46, 47, 50-53. Sum undercyning cōm tō Crīste, and hine bæd þæt hē hām mid him sīðode, and his sunu gehælde ; forðanþe hē læig æt forðsīðe. Þā cwæð se Hælend tō ðām undercyninge : Gewęnd þē hām, þīn sunu leofað. Hē gelȳfde þæs Hælendes sprǣce, and hām sīðode. Ðā cōmon his ðegnas him tōgēanes, and cȳddon þæt his sunu gesund wǣre. Hē ðā befrān on hwilcere tīde hē gewyrpte. Hī sǣdon : Gyrstandæg ofer midne dæg hine forlēt se fēfor. Þā oncnēow se fæder þæt hit wæs sēo tīd on ðǣre ðe se Hælend him tō cwæð : Far ðē hām, þīn sunu leofað. Se cyning gelȳfde ðā on God, and eal his hīred. *Æ. H. i. 128.*

3. 5. . . . Nisi quis renatus fuerit ex aqua et Spiritu sancto, non potest introire in regnum Dei.

3. 13. Et nemo ascendit in coelum nisi qui descendit de coelo, Filius hominis qui est in coelo.

3. 14, 15. Et sicut Moyses exaltavit serpentem in deserto, ita exaltari oportet Filium hominis, ut omnis qui credit in ipsum non pereat, sed habeat vitam aeternam.

3. 16. Sic enim Deus dilexit mundum, ut Filium suum unigenitum daret. . . .

3. 29. Qui habet sponsam, sponsus est. . . .

3. 30. Illum oportet crescere, me autem minui.

4. 21. . . . Crede mihi. . . .

4. 34. . . . Meus cibus est ut faciam voluntatem eius qui misit me. . . .

4. 46, 47, 50-53. . . . Et erat quidam

5. 14. Efne, nū ðū eart gehǣled ; ne synga ðū heononforð, þȳ-lǣs-ðe ðe sum ðing wyrse gelimpe.   Æ. H. i. 350.

5. 17. Mīn Fæder wyrcð dæghwomlice oð þis, and ic wyrce.
Æ. H. ii. 206.

5. 28, 29. Se tīma cymð þæt ealle ðā þe on byrgenum bēoð, gehȳrað Godes Suna stemne, and hī forð gāð: þā ðe gōd worhton tō līfes ǣriste ; þā sōðlice þe yfel worhton tō geniðe-runge ǣriste.   Æ. H. ii. 568.

6. 1–14. Se Hǣlend fērde ofer ðā Galileiscan sǣ, þe is gehāten Tyberiadis ; and him filigde micel menigu, forðonþe hī be-hēoldon ðā tācna þe hē worhte ofer ðā untruman men.   Þā āstāh se Hǣlend ūp on āne dūne, and þǣr sæt mid his leorning-cnihtum.   And wæs ðā swīðe gehende sēo hālige Easter-tīd.   Þā beseah se Hǣlend ūp, and geseah þæt ðǣr wæs mycel mennisc tōweard, and cwæð tō ānum his leorningcnihta. se wæs gehāten Philippus: Mid hwām mage wē bicgan hlāf ðisum folce?   Þis hē cwæð tō fandunge þæs leorningcnihtes : hē sylf wiste hwæt hē dōn wolde.   Ðā andwyrde Philippus : Þeah hēr wǣron gebohte twā hund peningwurð hlāfes, ne mihte

regulus. . . . Abiit ad eum, et roga-bat eum ut descenderet et sanaret filium eius ; incipiebat enim mori. . . . Dicit ei Iesus: Vade, filius tuus vivit.   Credidit homo sermoni quem dixit ei Iesus, et ibat. Iam autem eo descendente, servi oc-currerunt ei, et nuntiaverunt di-centes quia filius eius viveret. Interrogabat ergo horam ab eis in qua melius habuerit.   Et dix-erunt ei : Quia heri hora septima reliquit eum febris.   Cognovit ergo pater quia illa hora erat in qua dixit ei Iesus: Filius tuus vivit.   Et credidit ipse, et domus eius tota.

5. 14. . . . Ecce, sanus factus es ; iam noli peccare, ne deterius tibi aliquid contingat.

5. 17. . . . Pater meus usque modo operatur, et ego operor.

5. 28, 29. . . . Venit hora in qua omnes qui in monumentis sunt audient vocem Filii Dei, et pro-cedent : qui bona fecerunt in resurrectionem vitae ; qui vero mala egerunt in resurrectionem iudicii.

6. 1–14. . . . Abiit Iesus trans mare Galilaeae, quod est Tiberiadis ; et sequebatur eum multitudo magna, quia videbant signa quae faciebat super his qui infirma-bantur.   Subiit ergo in montem Iesus, et ibi sedebat cum disci-pulis suis.   Erat autem proximum pascha, dies festus Iudaeorum. Cum sublevasset ergo oculos Iesus, et vidisset quia multitudo maxima venit ad eum, dixit ad Philippum : Unde ememus panes, ut mandu-cent hi ?   Hoc autem dicebat tentans eum ; ipse enim sciebat quid esset facturus.   Respondit ei Philippus: Ducentorum de-nariorum panes non sufficiunt eis, ut unusquisque modicum quid

furðon hyra ǽlc ānne bitan of ðām gelæccan. Þā cwæð ān his leorningcnihta, se hātte Andreas, Petres brōðor : Hēr byrð ān cnapa fīf berene hlāfas and twēgen fixas ; ac tō hwān mæg þæt tō swā micclum werode ? Þā cwæð se Hǣlend : Dōð þæt þæt folc sitte. And þǣr wæs micel gærs on ðǣre stōwe, myrige on tō sittenne. And hī ðā ealle sǣton, swā-swā mihte bēon fīf ðūsend wera. Ðā genam se Hǣlend þā fīf hlāfas ; and blētsode, and tōbræc, and tōdǣlde betwux ðām sittendum ; swā gelīce ēac þā fixas tōdǣlde ; and hī ealle genōh hæfdon. Þā-ðā hī ealle fulle wǣron, ðā cwæð se Hǣlend tō his leorningcnihtum : Gaderiað þā lāfe, and hī ne losion. And hī ðā gegaderodon ðā bricas, and gefyldon twelf wilian mid ðǣre lāfe. Þæt folc ðā, ðe ðis tācen geseah, cwæð þæt Crīst wǣre sōð wītega, se ðe wæs tōweard tō ðisum middangearde. Æ. H. i. 180, 182 ; cf. ii. 396.

|| Dōð þæt þæt folc sitte. Æ. H. i. 184.

|| Se Hǣlend hēt þā gegadrian þā lāfe, þæt hī losian ne sceoldon ; and hī ðā gefyldon twelf wilion mid þām bricum.
Æ. H. i. 190.

|| Hī ðā gegaderodon twelf wilian fulle mid þām bricum.
Æ. H. i. 190.

|| Þæt folc ðā, þe þæt wundor geseah, cwǣdon be Crīste þæt hē wǣre sōð wītega ðe tōweard wæs. Æ. H. i. 190.

|| Þæt folc cwæð ðā be Crīste, þæt hē wǣre sōð wītega.
Æ. H. i. 190.

6. 15, 16, 19. Þæt folc rǣdde be him þæt hī woldon hine gelæccan, and āhebban tō cyninge. . . . Þā-þā Crīst ongeat ðæs

accipiat. Dicit ei unus ex discipulis eius, Andreas frater Simonis Petri : Est puer unus hic qui habet quinque panes hordeaceos et duos pisces ; sed haec quid sunt inter tantos ? Dixit ergo Iesus : Facite homines discumbere. Erat autem foenum multum in loco. Discubuerunt ergo viri, numero quasi quinque millia. Accepit ergo Iesus panes ; et cum gratias egisset, distribuit discumbentibus ; similiter et ex piscibus quantum volebant. Ut autem impleti sunt, dixit discipulis suis :

Colligite quae superaverunt fragmenta, ne pereant. Collegerunt ergo, et impleverunt duodecim cophinos fragmentorum ex quinque panibus hordeaceis, quae superfuerunt his qui manducaverant. Illi ergo homines, cum vidissent quod Iesus fecerat signum, dicebant : Quia hic est vere propheta, qui venturus est in mundum.

6. 15, 16, 19. Iesus ergo cum cognovisset quia venturi essent, ut raperent eum et facerent eum regem, fugit iterum in montem

folces willan, ðā flēah hē anstandende tō ānre dūne, and his
gefēran gewendon tō sǣ. . . . Dā on niht ꝥode se Hǣlend ūpon ðām wætere mid drīum fōtum, oð-þæt hē cōm tō his leorningcnihtum, ðǣr-ðǣr hī wǣron on rēwute. Æ. H. i. 162 ; cf.
i. 26, 108. See also Matt. 14. 22 ff.

6. 29. Þæt is Godes weorc, þæt gē on ðone gelȳfan þe hē āsende.
Æ. H. ii. 412.

6. 49. Fela manna ǣton of ðām heofenlican mete on ðām wēstene,
and druncon þone gāstlican drenc [1], and wurdon swā-ðēah
dēade. Æ. H. ii. 274.

6. 50. Sē ðe of ðām hlāfe geett, ne swylt hē on ꝥenysse. Æ. H. i. 34.

6. 51. Ic eom se līflica hlāf þe of heofenum āstāh ; and swā-hwā-
swā of ðām hlāfe geett, hē leofað on ꝥenysse ; and se hlāf ðe ic
sylle for middaneardes līfe is mīn līchama. Æ. H. ii. 202.

|| Ic eom se līflica hlāf, þe of heofenum āstāh. Æ. H. i. 34 ; cf.
ii. 292.

6. 53, 54, 58 (Vulg. 54, 55, 59). Sōð, sōð, ic ꝥow secge : Nabbe gē
līf on ꝥow, būton gē eton mīn flǣsc and drincon mīn blōd. Sē
ðe et mīn flǣsc, and mīn blōd drincð, hē wunað on mē, and ic
on him, and hē hæfð þæt ēce līf, and ic hine ārǣre on ðām
endenēxtan dæge. Ic eom se līflica hlāf ðe of heofonum āstāh.
Nā swā-swā ēowere forðfæderas ǣton þone heofenlican mete
on wēstene, and siððan swulton ; se ðe et ðisne hlāf, hē leofað
on ꝥenysse. Æ. H. ii. 266.

|| Sē ðe et mīn flǣsc, and drincð mīn blōd, hē hæfð ēce
līf. Æ. H. ii. 274.

ipse solus. Ut autem sero factum est, descenderunt discipuli
eius ad mare. . . . Cum remigassent
ergo, . . . vident Iesum ambulantem supra mare, et proximum
navi fieri. . . .

6. 29. . . . Hoc est opus Dei, ut credatis in eum quem misit ille.

6. 49. Patres vestri manducaverunt
manna in deserto, et mortui sunt.

6. 50. . . . Si quis ex ipso manduca-
verit, non moriatur.

6. 51. Ego sum panis vivus qui de
coelo descendi. Si quis mandu-

caverit ex hoc pane, vivet in
aeternum ; et panis quem ego
dabo caro mea est pro mundi
vita.

6. 54, 55, 59. Dixit ergo eis Iesus :
Amen, amen, dico vobis : Nisi
manducaveritis carnem Filii hominis, et biberitis eius sanguinem,
non habebitis vitam in vobis. Qui
manducat meam carnem, et bibit
meum sanguinem, habet vitam
aeternam ; et ego resuscitabo eum
in novissimo die. . . . Hic est panis
qui de coelo descendit. Non

[1] From 1 Cor. 10. 4, 'et omnes eundem potum spiritalem biberunt.'

6. 69. *Sec* Æ. H. i. 190.

7. 38. Swā-hwām-swā ðyrste, cume tō mē and drince, and of his innoðe flēowð līflic wæter. Æ. H. ii. 274.

8. 12. Ic eom lēoht ealles middangeardes; sē ðe mē fyligð, ne cymð hē nā on þȳstrum, ac hē hæfð līfes lēoht. Æ. H. i. 144.

 ‖ Ic eom middangeardes lēoht; se ðe me fyligð, ne gǣð hē on þēostrum, ac hē hæfð līfes lēoht. Æ. H. i. 530.

8. 34. Sōð, sōð, ic eow secge: Ælc ðæra ðe synne wyrcð, hē bið þonne ðǣre synne ðēow. Æ. H. ii. 228.

8. 44. Gē sind dēofles bearn, and gē willað ēoweres fæder willan wyrcan; hē wæs manslaga fram frymðe, and hē ne wunode on sōðfæstnysse, forðanðe nān sōðfæstnys nis on him. Æ. H. ii. 226.

8. 46. Hwilc ēower ðrēað mē be synne? Gif ic sōð secge, hwī nelle gē mē gelȳfan? Æ. H. ii. 226.

 ‖ Hwilc ēower ðrēað mē for synne? . . . Gif ic sōð secge, hwī nelle gē mē gelȳfan? Æ. H. ii. 226.

8. 47. Sē ðe fram Gode is, hē gehȳrð Godes word; forðī gē nellað gehȳran, forðanðe gē ne sind fram Gode. Æ. H. ii. 226, 228.

 ‖ Sē ðe is fram Gode, he gehȳrð Godes word. . . . Forðī gē nellað gehȳran, forðanðe gē ne sind fram Gode. Æ. H. ii. 228.

8. 48. Þā Iudeiscan cwædon be Crīste þæt hē wǣre Samaritanisc, and hæfde dēofol on him. Æ. H. ii. 228.

8. 49. Ic ārwurðige mīnne Fæder, and gē unārwurðiað mē. Æ. H. i. 442; ii. 230.

8. 50. Ne sēce ic mīn wuldor; sē is ðe sēcð and tōscǣt. Æ. H. ii. 230.

 ‖ Ic ne sēce mīn wuldor; is swā-ðēah se ðe sēcð and tōscǣt. Æ. H. ii. 232.

sicut manducaverunt patres vestri manna, et mortui sunt; qui manducat hunc panem vivet in aeternum.

7. 38. Qui credit in me, . . . flumina de ventre eius fluent aquae vivae.

8. 12. . . . Ego sum lux mundi; qui sequitur me non ambulat in tenebris, sed habebit lumen vitae.

8. 34. . . . Amen, amen, dico vobis quia omnis qui facit peccatum servus est peccati.

8. 44. Vos ex patre diabolo estis, et desideria patris vestri vultis facere. Ille homicida erat ab initio, et in veritate non stetit, quia non est veritas in eo. . . .

8. 46. Quis ex vobis arguet me de peccato? Si veritatem dico vobis, quare non creditis mihi?

8. 47. Qui ex Deo est verba Dei audit. Propterea vos non auditis, quia ex Deo non estis.

8. 48. Responderunt ergo Iudaei, et dixerunt ei: Nonne bene dicimus nos quia Samaritanus es tu, et daemonium habes?

8. 49. . . . Honorifico Patrem meum, et vos inhonorastis me.

8. 50. Ego autem non quaero glo-

8. 51-55. Sōð, sōð, ic ēow secge : Swā-hwā-swā mīn word hylt, ne
gesihð hē dēað on ēcnysse. . . . Þā Iudeiscan cwǣdon : Nū wē
oncnāwað þæt ðū eart wōd. Abraham forðfērde, and wītegan ;
and ðū segst : Swā-hwā-swā mīn word hylt, ne onbyrigð hē
dēaðes on ēcnysse. . . . Hwilcne wyrcst ðū ðē sylfne ? . . .
Drihten andwyrde : Gif ic mē sylfne wuldrige, þonne bið mīn
wuldor nāht. Mīn Fæder is ðe mē wuldrað, be ðām gē secgað
þæt hē ēower God sȳ ; and gē hine ne oncnēowon. . . . Ic hine
cann, and gif ic secge þæt ic hine ne cunne, þonne bēo ic lēas,
ēow gelīc. Æ. H. ii. 232, 234.

‖ Gē secgað þæt hē ēower God sȳ ; and gē hine ne oncnēowon. Æ. H. ii. 234.

8. 56. Abraham, ēower fæder, blissode þæt hē mīnne dæg gesāwe,
and hē geseah, and þæs fægnode. Æ. H. ii. 234.

8. 57, 58. Hwæt. ðā Iudeiscan yrsigende cwǣdon tō Crīste : Hwæt
lā, gīt ðū ne eart fīftig gēara, and gesāwe ðū Abraham ? Drihten
him andwyrde : Sōð, sōð, ic ēow secge : Ærðanðe Abraham
gewurde, ic eom. Æ. H. ii. 236.

‖ Ærðanþe Abraham gewurde, ic eom. Æ. H. ii. 236.

8. 59. Hī ðā nāmon stānas, þæt hī hine torfodon. . . . Se Hǣlend
sōðlice hine behȳdde, and ēode of ðām temple. Æ. H. ii. 236.

9. 2, 3. His leorningcnihtas hine āxodon, for hwæs synnum se
mann wurde swā blind ācenned. Þā cwæð se Hǣlend þæt hē
nǣre for his āgenum synnum, ne for his māga, blind geboren,

riam meam ; est qui quaerat et
iudicet.

8. 51-55. Amen, amen, dico vobis :
Si quis sermonem meum servave-
rit, mortem non videbit in aeternum. Dixerunt ergo Iudaei :
Nunc cognovimus quia daemonium habes. Abraham mortuus
est, et prophetae ; et tu dicis :
Si quis sermonem meum serva-
verit, non gustabit mortem in
aeternum. . . . Quem te ipsum
facis ? Respondit Iesus : Si ego
glorifico meipsum, gloria mea
nihil est ; est Pater meus qui
glorificat me, quem vos dicitis
quia Deus vester est ; et non
cognovistis cum. Ego autem novi

eum ; et si dixero quia non scio
eum, ero similis vobis, mendax. . . .

8. 56. Abraham pater vester exultavit ut videret diem meum ;
vidit, et gavisus est.

8. 57, 58. Dixerunt ergo Iudaei ad
eum : Quinquaginta annos nondum habes, et Abraham vidisti ?
Dixit eis Iesus : Amen, amen, dico
vobis : Antequam Abraham fieret,
ego sum.

8. 59. Tulerunt ergo lapides, ut
iaccrent in eum. Iesus autem
abscondit se, et exivit de templo.

9. 2, 3. Et interrogaverunt eum discipuli eius : Rabbi, quis peccavit,
hic, aut parentes eius, ut caecus
nasceretur ? Respondit Iesus :

ac forðī þæt Godes wundor þurh hine geswutelod wǣre. *Æ. H. i. 474.*

9. 6, 7. *See Æ. H. i. 474.*

10. 11, 12. Ic eom gōd hyrde; se gōda hyrde sylð his āgen līf for his scēapum. Se hȳra, se ðe nis riht hyrde, hē gesihð þone wulf cuman, and hē forlǣt ðā scēp, and flȳhð; and se wulf sum gelǣcð, and ðā ōðre tōstęncð. *Æ. H. i. 238.*

  ‖ Se gōda hyrde sylð his āgen līf for his scēapum. *Æ. H. i. 238.*

  ‖ Se hȳra flīhð, þonne hē ðone wulf gesihð. *Æ. H. i. 240.*

10. 13. He flȳhð, forðanðe hē is hȳra, and nā hyrde. *Æ. H. i. 240.*

10. 14–16. Ic eom gōd hyrde, and ic oncnāwe mīne scēp, and hī oncnāwað mē. . . . Swā-swā mīn Fæder oncnāwð mē, and ic oncnāwe hine; and ic sylle min āgen līf for mīnum scēapum. . . . Ic hæbbe ōðre scēp, þe ne sind nā of ðisre ēowde; and ðā ic sceal lǣdan, and hī gehyrað mīne stemne; and sceal beon ān eowd, and ān hyrde. *Æ. H. i. 242, 244.*

  ‖ Ic hæbbe ōðre scēp, þā ðe ne sind of ðyssere ēowde; and ðā ic sceal lǣdan, and hī gehyrað mīne stemne. *Æ. II. ii. 114.*

10. 18. Mihte ic hæbbe mīne sāwle tō syllenne, and ic ēaðelice mæg hī ęft geniman. *Æ. H. ii. 244.*

10. 34. Ic cwæð: Gē sind godas. *Æ. II. i. 324; cf. i. 366.*

  ‖ Sōðlice męn syndon godas gecīgede. *Æ. H. i. 40.*

11. 5. *See Æ. H. ii. 438.*

11. 21. Drihten, gif ðū hēr andwerd wǣre, nǣre ūre brōðer forð-faren. *Æ. H. i. 130.*

11. 25, 26. Ic eom ǣrist and līf; se ðe gelȳfð on mē, þeah-ðe hē

Neque hic peccavit, neque parentes eius, sed ut manifestentur opera Dei in illo.

10. 11, 12. Ego sum pastor bonus; bonus pastor animam suam dat pro ovibus suis. Mercenarius autem, et qui non est pastor, cuius non sunt oves propriae, videt lupum venientem, et dimittit oves, et fugit; et lupus rapit, et dispergit oves.

10. 13. Mercenarius autem fugit, quia mercenarius est. . . .

10. 14–16. Ego sum pastor bonus, et cognosco meas, et cognoscunt me meae. Sicut novit me Pater,

et ego agnosco Patrem; et animam meam pono pro ovibus meis. Et alias oves habeo, quae non sunt ex hoc ovili; et illas oportet me adducere, et vocem meam audient; et fiet unum ovile, et unus pastor.

10. 18. . . . Potestatem habeo ponendi eam, et potestatem habeo iterum sumendi eam. . . .

10. 34. . . . Ego dixi: Dii estis.

11. 21. . . . Domine, si fuisses hic, frater meus non fuisset mortuus.

11. 25, 26. . . . Ego sum resurrectio et vita; qui credit in me, etiam si mortuus fuerit, vivet; et omnis

dĕad bĕo, hē leofaᵭ; and ǣlc ᵭǣra þe leofaᵭ, and on mē gelȳfᵭ, ne swelte hē on ēcnysse. .Æ. H. ii. 240.

11. 33, 35. Dā gedrēfde hē hino sylfne, and tēaras āgēat. .Æ. H. i. 408.

11. 39. *See* .Æ. H. i. 206, 406.

11. 43. And mid micclre stemne clypode: Lazare, gā forᵭ. .Æ. H. i. 408.

11. 44. Tōlȳsaᵭ his bendas, þæt hē gān mæge. .Æ. H. i. 234.

11. 53. Dā Iudeiscan ealdras geornlice smēadon hū hī Hǣlend Crīst ācwęllan mihton. .Æ. H. ii. 242.

12. 10, 11. Þā hēafodmęnn þæs folces smēadon betwux him þæt hī woldon ofslēan þone Lazarum, þe Crīst of dēaᵭe āwręhte; forᵭan-ᵭe manega ᵭæs folces męnn gelȳfdon on þone Hǣlend, þurh ᵭæs dēadan mannes ǣrist. .Æ. H. i. 206.

12. 26. Sō ᵭe mē þēnige, fylige hē mē. .Æ. H. i. 160.

Þǣr-þǣr ic sylf bĕo, þǣr biᵭ mīn ᵭēn. .Æ. H. ii. 386, 440.

12. 31. . . . þæt hē wǣre middangeardes caldor, and hē scoolde bĕon ūtādrǣfed. .Æ. H. i. 172.

13. 4, 5, 12, 14, 15. Þā ārās Drihten of ᵭām gereorde, and āwearp his rēaf swīᵭe ricene; wearᵭ þā bewǣfed mid ānre wæter-scȳtan. And his gingrena fēt ēadmōdlice āᵭwōh. And eft his rēaf ǣrdlice genam, and hī sittende ᵭisum wordum gesprǣc: Ic gesętte ēow nū sōᵭe gebȳsnunge, þæt ēower ǣlc sceole ōᵭres fēt āᵭwēan, swā-swā ic lārēow ēow hrēclīg āᵭwōh. .Æ. H. ii. 242.

13. 21. *See* Matt. 26. 20-25, note.

13. 35. Be ᵭām oncnāwaᵭ ealle męn þæt gē sind mīne folgeras, gif gē habbaᵭ lufe ēow betwȳnan. .Æ. H. ii. 522.

---

qui vivit, et credit in me, non morietur in aeternum. . . .

11. 33, 35. . . . Turbavit scipsum, . . . et lacrymatus est Iesus.

11. 43. . . . Voce magna clamavit: Lazare, veni foras.

11. 44. . . . Solvite eum, et sinite abire.

11. 53. Ab illo ergo die cogitaverunt ut interficerent eum.

12. 10, 11. Cogitaverunt autem principes sacerdotum ut et Lazarum interficerent; quia multi propter illum abibant ex Iudaeis, et credebant in Iesum.

12. 26. Si quis mihi ministrat, me sequatur; et ubi sum ego, illic et minister meus erit. . . .

12. 31. . . . Nunc princeps huius mundi ciicietur foras.

13. 4, 5, 12, 14, 15. Surgit a coena, et ponit vestimenta sua; et, cum accepisset linteum, praecinxit se. . . . Et coepit lavare pedes discipulorum. . . . Accepit vestimenta sua; cum recubuisset iterum, dixit eis: . . . Vos debetis alter alterius lavare pedes. Exemplum enim dedi vobis. . . .

13. 35. In hoc cognoscent omnes quia discipuli mei estis, si dilectionem habueritis ad invicem.

14. 2. On mīnes Fæder hūse sind fela wununga.   Æ. H. i. 350.

  ‖ Drihten cwæð . . . þæt on his Fæder hūse sindon fela wununga.   Æ. H. i. 446.

14. 6. Ic eom weig, and sōðfæstnys, and līf.   Æ. H. i. 154, 156.

  ‖ Ic eom sōðfæstnys.   Æ. H. i. 484.

14. 23. Sō ðe me lufað, hē hylt mīn bebod; and mīn Fæder hine lufað, and wit cumað tō him, and mid him wuniað.   Æ. H. i. 362.

  ‖ Sō ðe mē lufað, hē hylt mīn bebod; and mīn Fæder hine lufað for ðǣre hȳrsumnysse, and wit cumað him tō, and him mid wuniað.   Æ. H. ii. 314.

  ‖ Sō ðe mē lufað, hē hylt mīn bebod.   Æ. H. ii. 314.

14. 24. Sō ðe mē ne lufað, ne hylt hē mīn bebod.   Æ. H. ii. 316.

14. 26. Hē ēow tiht and gewissað tō eallum ðām ðingum ðe ic ēow sǣde.   Æ. H. i. 298; cf. i. 550.

14. 27. Ic forlǣte ēow sibbe; and ic forgife ēow mīne sybbe.   Æ. H. ii. 580.

15. 5. Ne mage gē nān ðing dōn būtan mē.   Æ. H. i. 310.

  ‖ Ne mage gē nān ðing tō gōde gedōn būton mē.   Æ. H. ii. 432.

15. 12–16. Ðis is mīn bebod, þæt gē lufion ēow betwȳnan, swā-swā ic ēow lufode. Nǣfð nān man māran lufe þonne hē sylle his sāwle for his frēondum. Gē sind mīne frȳnd, gif gē dōð swā-swā ic ēow bebēode. Ne hāte ic ēow þēowan, forðanðe se þēowa nāt hwæt his hlāford dēð; ic hēt ēow mīne frȳnd, forþanðe ic cȳdde ēow swā-hwæt-swā ic æt mīnum Fæder gehȳide. Ne gecure gē mē, ac ic gecēas ēow, and ic sette eow þæt gē faron, and beron wǣstm, and ēower wǣstm

---

14. 2. In domo Patris mei mansiones multae sunt. . . .

14. 6. . . . Ego sum via, et veritas, et vita. . . .

14. 23. . . . Si quis diligit me, sermonem meum servabit; et Pater meus diliget eum, et ad eum veniemus, et mansionem apud eum faciemus.

14. 24. Qui non diligit me, sermones meos non servat. . . .

14. 26. . . . Ille vos docebit omnia, et suggeret vobis omnia, quaecumque dixero vobis.

14. 27. Pacem relinquo vobis; pacem meam do vobis. . . .

15. 5. . . . Sine me nihil potestis facere.

15. 12–16. Hoc est praeceptum meum, ut diligatis invicem, sicut dilexi vos. Maiorem hac dilectionem nemo habet, ut animam suam ponat quis pro amicis suis. Vos amici mei estis, si feceritis quae ego praecipio vobis. Iam non dicam vos servos, quia servus nescit quid faciat dominus eius; vos autem dixi amicos, quia omnia quaecumque audivi a Patre meo, nota feci vobis. Non vos me elegistis, sed ego elegi vos, et posui vos ut eatis, et fructum

þurhwunige ; and swā-hwæt-swā gē bidda% æt mīnum Fæder
on mīnum naman, hē sylð ēow.   Æ. II. ii. 522.

‖ Gē bēoð mīne frȳnd, gif gē wyrcende bēoð ðā ðincg ðe ic
bebēode ēow tō gehealdenne.   Æ. II. ii. 316.

‖ Gē bēoð mīne frȳnd, gif gē ðā þing dōð þe ic ēow
bebēode.   Æ. II. ii. 522.

‖ Ne hāte ic ēow ðēowan, forðanðe se þēowa nāt hwæt his
hlāford dēð.   Æ. II. ii. 522.

‖ Ic hēt ēow mīne frȳnd, forðanðe ic eow cȳdde ealle ðā ðing
þe ic æt mīnum Fæder gehȳrde.   Æ. II. ii. 524.

‖ Gē sind mīne frȳnd, and ic cȳðe ēow swā-hwæt-swā ic æt
mīnum Fæder gehȳrde.   Æ. II. i. 542.

‖ Ne gecure gē mē, ac ic gecēas ēow.   Æ. II. ii. 524.

‖ Éower wæstm ðurhwunað. . . . Swā-hwæt-swā gē biddað
æt mīnum Fæder on mīnum naman, hē sylþ ēow.   Æ. II. ii. 526.

15. 18. Gif ðēs middangeard ēow hatað, wite gē þæt hē mē hatode
ær ēow.   Æ. II. i. 556.

15. 19. Ic ēow gecēas of middanearde.   Æ. II. ii. 366.

15. 20. Gif hī mīn ēhton, þonne ēhtað hī ēac ēower.   Æ. II. i. 556.

15. 26. Se Frōforgāst, þe ic ēow āsendan wille, Gāst ðære sōðfæstnysse, ðe of mīnum Fæder gǽð, hē cȳð gecȳðnysse be
mē.   Æ. II. i. 280.

16. 20. Gē bēoð geunrōtsode on þisum līfe, ac eower unrōtnys bið
āwend tō ēecre blisse.   Æ. II. i. 142.

16. 23. Sōð ic ēow secge : Swā-hwæt-swā gē biddað on mīnum
naman æt mīnum Fæder, hit bið ēow getīðod.   Æ. II. i. 466.

17. 1–11. Se Hǽlend cwæð tō his Fæder, ūpāhafenum ēagum tō
heofenum : Fæder mīn, se tīma cōm ; mǽrsa ðīnne Sunu, þæt

afferatis, et fructus vester maneat;
ut quodcumque petieritis Patrem
in nomine meo, det vobis.

15. 18. Si mundus vos odit, scitote
quia me priorem vobis odio
habuit.

15. 19. . . . Ego elegi vos de
mundo. . . .

15. 20. . . . Si me persecuti sunt, et
vos persequentur. . . .

15. 26. Cum autem venerit Para-
clitus, quem ego mittam vobis
a Patre, Spiritum veritatis, qui

a Patre procedit, ille testimonium
perhibebit de me.

16. 20. . . . Vos autem contristabi-
mini, sed tristitia vester vertetur
in gaudium.

16. 23. . . . Amen, amen, dico vobis :
Si quid petieritis Patrem in nomine meo, dabit vobis.

17. 1–11. Haec locutus est Iesus, et,
sublevatis oculis in coelum, dixit :
Pater, venit hora ; clarifica Filium
tuum, ut Filius tuus clarificet te.
Sicut dedisti ei potestatem omnis

ðīn Sunu þē mǣrsige. ... Swā-swā ðū forgēafe him andweald
ealles flǣsces, þæt hē forgife ēce līf ðām eallum ðe ðū him
forgēafe. ... Þis is sōðlice ēce līf, þæt hī ðē ænne oncnāwon
sōðne God, and ðone ðe ðū āsęndest Hǣlend Crīst. ... Ic
mǣrsode ðē ofer eorðan; ic gefylde þæt weorc ðe þū mē
forgēafe tō wyrcenne. ... Mǣrsa mē nū, Fæder, mid þǣre
mǣrsunge þe ic mid ðē hæfde ǣrðanþe middaneard gewurde.
... Ic geswutelode ðīnne naman mannum, ðām þe ðū mē
forgēafe of middanearde. ... Þīne hī wǣron, and ðū hī mē
forgēafe. ... Hī hēoldon ðīne sprǣce, and hī oncnēowon þæt
ealle ðing þe ðū mē forgēafe sind fram þē; forðanðe ic forgeaf
him ðā word ðe ðū mē forgēafe; and hī hī underfēngon, and
oncnēowon þæt ic fram ðē fērde, and hī gelȳfdon þæt ðū mē
sęndest. ... Ic bidde for hī; ne bidde ic for middanearde, ac
for ðā ic bidde þe ðū mē forgēafe.... Ealle mīne ðing sindon
ðīne, and ðīne ðing sindon mīne; ic eom gemǣrsod on him.
And ic on middanearde ne eom; hī sindon on middanearde,
and ic cume tō ðē. Æ. H. ii. 360, 362, 364, 366, 368.

∥ Fæder, se tīma cōm; mǣrsa ðīnne Sunu, þæt ðīn Sunu ðē
mǣrsige. Æ. H. ii. 360.

∥ Þæt is ēce līf, þæt hī ðē oncnāwon sōðne God, and ðone ðe
þū āsęndest Hǣlend Crīst. Æ. H. i. 42.

17. 20. Ne bidde ic nā for ðisum ānum, ac ēac swilce for ðā ðe on
mē gelȳfað þurh heora word. Æ. H. ii. 368.

17. 24. Fæder mīn, ic wille þæt ðā þe ðū mē forgēafe bēon mid
mē ðǣr-ðǣr ic bēo, þæt hī mīne mǣrðe gescēon, ðe ðū mē

carnis, ut omne quod dedisti ei,
det eis vitam aeternam. Haec
est autem vita aeterna, ut cog-
noscant te, solum Deum verum,
et quem misisti Iesum Christum.
Ego te clarificavi super terram;
opus consummavi quod dedisti
mihi ut faciam. Et nunc clarifica me tu. Pater, apud temetipsum, claritate quam habui prius
quam mundus esset apud te.
Manifestavi nomen tuum hominibus quos dedisti mihi de mundo.
Tui erant, et mihi eos dedisti;
et sermonem tuum servaverunt.
Nunc cognoverunt quia omnia
quae dedisti mihi abs te sunt;
quia verba quae dedisti mihi
dedi eis; et ipsi acceperunt, et
cognoverunt vere quia a te exivi,
et crediderunt quia tu me misisti.
Ego pro eis rogo; non pro mundo
rogo, sed pro his quos dedisti
mihi. ... Et mea omnia tua sunt,
et tua mea sunt; et clarificatus
sum in eis. Et iam non sum in
mundo, et hi in mundo sunt, et
ego ad te venio. ...

17. 20. Non pro eis autem rogo tantum, sed et pro eis qui credituri
sunt per verbum eorum in me.

17. 24. Pater, quos dedisti mihi, volo

forgeafe ; forðanðe ðu lufadest me ǣr middaneardes gesętnysse. Æ. H. ii. 368.

18. 3. Iudas se swicola swīðe hraðe ðodo to ðām ārleasum ðhterum þe he ǣr gespræc, and genam him fultum æt ðām Phariseum ; and hī ðā eodon ealle gewǣpnode and mid leohtfatum. Æ. H. ii. 246.

18. 4–8. Hwæt, ðā se Hǣlend him togeanes stop, and unforht āxode hwæne hī sōhton. Hī ðā ewǣdon þæt hī Crīst sōhton. Dā sǣde he him : Ic hit sōðlice eom. Hī ðā mid þām worde węndon underbæc, feallende to eorðan, mid fyrhte fornumene. Ęft ðā siððan āxode se Hǣlend hwæne hī sōhton swā swīðe gewǣpnode. Hī ęft andwyrdon mid þām ǣrran worde ; ewǣdon þæt hī ðone Hǣlend habban woldon. Þā andwyrde he mid þām ylcan worde : Ic eow sǣde ǣr þæt ic se eom ; gif ge me sēcaðŏ, lǣtað mine gyngran āweg. Æ. H. ii. 246.

18. 10. *See* Matt. 26. 51–54, notes 1 and 2.

18. 18. *See* Matt. 26. 69–75, note.

19. 18–20. Þā hengon ðā cęmpan Crīst on æle middan, and þā twēgen sceaðan him on twā healfa. And Pilatus āwrāt þæs wītes intingan on ānre tabelan mid þrīm gereordum, Ebreiscum, and Greciscum, and Ledenum samod : Þes is se Hǣlend, Iudeiscra Cyning. And āsętte ðis gewrit sōna to ðǣre rōde.
Æ. H. ii. 254.

19. 23–27. Þā dǣldon ðā ewęlleras Crīstes reaf on feower, heora ǣlcum his dǣl, swā him demde seo tā ; and heoldon his

---

ut ubi sum ego et illi sint mecum, ut videant claritatem meam, quam dedisti mihi ; quia dilexisti me ante constitutionem mundi.

18. 3. Iudas ergo cum accepisset cohortem, et a pontificibus et Pharisaeis ministros, venit illuc cum laternis, et facibus, et armis.

18. 4-8. Iesus itaque ... processit, et dixit eis : Quem quaeritis ? Responderunt ei : Iesum Nazarenum. Dicit eis Iesus : Ego sum.... Ut ergo dixit eis : Ego sum, abierunt retrorsum, et ceciderunt in terram. Iterum ergo interrogavit eos : Quem quaeritis ? Illi autem

dixerunt : Iesum Nazarenum. Respondit Iesus : Dixi vobis quia ego sum ; si ergo me quaeritis, sinite hos abire.

19. 18-20. Ubi crucifixerunt eum, et cum eo alios duos hinc et hinc, medium autem Iesum. Scripsit autem et titulum Pilatus, et posuit super crucem. Erat autem scriptum : Iesus, ... Rex Iudaeorum. ... Et erat scriptum Hebraice, Graece, et Latine.

19. 23-27. Milites ergo cum crucifixissent eum, acceperunt vestimenta eius (et fecerunt quattuor partes, unicuique militi partem),

tunecan untōslitene, forðanðe hēo wæs eal būton scame. . . .
Se hālige Maria, þæs Hǣlendes mōder, stōd wið ða rōde
ðearle drēorig, and Iohannes samod, hire swuster bearn.　Ða
clypode Drihten tō his drēorian mēder : Efne, hēr hangað nū
ðīn sunu, fǣmne. . . . Hē cwæð tō Iohanne : Hēr stænt ðīn
mōdor.　Þā hæfde Iohannes hire siððan gȳmene mid geswǣsum
ðēnungum, ā on ðisum līfe.　_Æ. H._ ii. 256.

‖ Ðā cwæð hē tō his āgenre mēder : Ðū fǣmne, efne, hēr is
þīn sunu.　Eft hē cwæð tō Iohanne : Lōca nū, hēr stent þīn
mōdor.　Syððan, of þām dæge, hæfde se godspellere Iohannes
gȳmene þǣre hālgan Marian, and mid carfulre þēnunge, swā-
swā āgenre mēder, gehȳrsumode.　_Æ. H._ i. 438 ; cf. i. 58.

19. 28, 29. _See_ Matt. 27. 48, note.

19. 30. _See_ Matt. 27. 50–53, note 3.

19. 31–34. Ðā wælhrēowan Iudei noldon geðafian, for ðām
symbeldæge, þæt hī swā hangodon cuce on ðām rōdum, ac
woldon hī ācwellan, and bǣdon Pilate þæt man heora sceancan
tōbrǣce ǣr þǣre Eastertīde, and of ðām rōdum āwurpe.　Þā
cōmon ðā cempan mid cwylmbǣrum tōlum, and sōna ðǣra
sceaðena sceancan tōbrǣcon, ðe ðā-gȳt cwylmigende cuce
hangodon.　Hī gemētton ðā Crīst middanearde dēadne, and
his hālgan sceancan scǣnan ne dorston ; ac ān ðǣra cempena
mid cwealmbǣrum spere his sīdan geopenode, and of ðǣre
ūtflēow blōd and wæter samod.　_Æ. H._ ii. 260 ; cf. i. 216, ii. 282.

19. 37. _See Æ. H._ ii. 282.

19. 38–42. Þā sum rīce ðegen ðearle wæs gelȳfed dearnunge on
Drihten, for ðām dyrstigum folce ; his nama wæs Ioseph ; and

et tunicam.　Erat autem tunica
inconsutilis, desuper contexta per
totum. . . . Miserunt sortem. . . .
Stabant autem iuxta crucem Iesu
mater eius. . . . Cum vidisset ergo
Iesus matrem, et discipulum stantem quem diligebat, dicit matri
suae : Mulier, ecce filius tuus.
Deinde dicit discipulo : Ecce
mater tua.　Et ex illa hora accepit eam discipulus in sua.

19. 31–34.　Iudaei ergo (quoniam
Parasceve erat), ut non remane-
rent in cruce corpora sabbato

(erat enim magnus dies ille sabbati), rogaverunt Pilatum ut fran-
gerentur eorum crura, et tolle-
rentur.　Venerunt ergo milites,
et primi quidem fregerunt crura,
et alterius qui crucifixus est cum
eo.　Ad Iesum autem cum venissent, ut viderunt eum iam mor-
tuum, non fregerunt eius crura ;
sed unus militum lancea latus
eius aperuit, et continuo exivit
sanguis et aqua.

19. 38–42.　Post haec autem rogavit
Pilatum Ioseph ab Arimathaea

hē genēalǣhte ðā hrædlice on ǣfen tō ðām ealdormęn, bæd þæt
hē mōste Drihtnes līc bebyrian. Þā wundrode Pilatus þæt
hē swā hraðo gewāt[1], and geðafode ðām ðegene þæt hē hine
behwurfe. Da cōm ēac Nichodemus mid gemęngedre sealfe
of myrran and alwan, manegra punda gewyht. And hī bewundon his līc mid linenre scȳtan, gedęced mid wyrtum, swā-
swā heora gewuna wæs. Þā stōd on ðǣre stōwe sum stǣnen
ðrūh, on ðǣre nǣfre ne læg nān corðlic mann. Da lēdon ðā
þegenas ðone Hǣlend ðǣron. Æ. H. ii. 260, 262.

‖ Þā cōmon twēgen gelȳfede męn, Ioseph and Nichodemus,
and bebyrigdon his līc ǣr ǣfene on nīwere ðrȳh, mid dēor-
wyrðum rēafum bewunden. Æ. H. i. 216.

20. 12. See Æ. H. i. 222.

20. 19. Æfter ðæs Hǣlendes ǣriste wǣron his discipuli belocene
on ānum hūse for ðæs Iudeiscan folces ōgan. . . . Se Hǣlend
cwæð tō him : Bēo sibb betwux ēow. Æ. H. i. 232.

‖ Hī sǣton beclȳsede, for ōgan Iudeisces folces, on ānum
hūse. Æ. H. i. 232.

20. 21, 22. Swā-swā min Fæder sęnde mē, swā sęnde ic ēow. . . .
Crīst blēow on ðā apostolas, and cwæð : Onfōð Hāligne
Gāst. Æ. H. i. 232.

‖ Crīst āblēow ðone Hālgan Gāst ūpon ðā apostolas ǣr his
ūpstige, ðus cweðende : Onfōð Hāligne Gāst. Æ. H. i. 324.

. . . ðā-ðā hē him on āblēow, ðus cwæðende : Onfōð Hāligne
Gāst. Æ. H. i. 370.

20. 23. Þǣra manna synna þe gē forgyfað, þǣra bēoð forgifene ;
and ðām ðe gē oftēoð þā forgifenysse, ðām bið oftogen. Æ. H. i. 232.

‖ Dǣra manna synna þe gē forgyfað bēoð forgyfene ; and

(eo quod esset discipulus Iesu,
occultus autem propter metum
Iudaeorum), ut tolleret corpus
Iesu. Et permisit Pilatus. . . .
Venit autem et Nicodemus, . . .
ferens mixturam myrrhae et aloes,
quasi libras centum. Acceperunt
ergo corpus Iesu, et ligaverunt
illud linteis cum aromatibus, sicut
mos est Iudaeis sepelire. Erat
autem in loco . . . monumentum
novum, in quo nondum quisquam
positus erat. Ibi ergo . . . posuerunt Iesum.

20. 19. Cum . . . fores essent clausae,
ubi erant discipuli congregati
propter metum Iudaeorum, venit
Iesus, . . . et dixit eis : Pax vobis.

20. 21, 22. . . . Sicut misit me Pater,
et ego mitto vos. . . . Insufflavit,
et dixit eis : Accipite Spiritum
sanctum.

20. 23. Quorum remiseritis peccata,
remittuntur eis ; et quorum reti
nueritis, retenta sunt.

[1] From Mark 15. 44, 'Pilatus autem mirabatur si iam obiisset.'

ðām ðe gē forgifenysse ofunnon, him bið oftogen sēo forgyfenys. Æ. H. i. 370.

20. 27. *See* Æ. H. i. 234, 300, 302.

20. 29. Hē cwæð tō Thomas: Þū gelȳfst, forðanðe ðū mē gesāwe. . . . Gesǣlige bēoð þā þe mē ne gesāwon, and þēah on mē gelȳfað. Æ. H. i. 234.

‖ Ēadige bēoð þā þe mē ne gesēoð, and hī hwæðere gelȳfað on mē. Æ. H. i. 190.

20. 30, 31. Se Hǣlend worhte fela ōðre tācna on gesihðe his leorningcnihta, þe nǣron gesętte on Crīstes bēc. Þās wundra sind āwritene tō ðī þæt gē sceolon gelȳfan þæt se Hǣlend is Godes Sunu ; and gē sceolon habban þæt ēce līf þurh ðone gelēafan. Æ. H. i. 230.

21. 1, 2. Se Hǣlend hine geswutelode æfter his ǣriste æt ðǣre sǣ Tyberiadis his seofon leorningcnihtum. Æ. H. ii. 288 ; cf. ii. 292.

21. 6. Hē hēt wurpan þæt nęt on ðā swīðran healfe þæs rēwetes. Æ. H. ii. 290.

21. 9. Hī gemētton fȳr, and fisc on uppon, and hlāf on em, ðā-ðā hī tō lande cōmon.

21. 11. *See* Æ. H. ii. 290.

21. 17. Drihten him tō cwæð ðriwa æt ðisum ylcan gereorde ; hē cwæð: Petrus, lufast ðū mē? Hē cwæð: Drihten, ðū wāst ealle ðing, and þū wāst þæt ic ðē lufige. Drihten cwæð him tō : Gif ðū mē lufige, lǣswa mīne scēp. Æ. H. ii. 290.

ACTS.

1. 3–8. Se Hǣlend. middangeardes Ālȳsend, ætēowde hine sylfne cucenne his gingrum, æfter his þrōwunge and his ǣriste, on

20. 29. Dixit ei Iesus : Quia vidisti me, Thoma, credidisti ; beati qui non viderunt. et crediderunt.

20. 30, 31. Multa quidem et alia signa fecit Iesus in conspectu discipulorum suorum, quae non sunt scripta in libro hoc. Haec autem scripta sunt ut credatis quia Iesus est Christus Filius Dei ; et ut credentes vitam habeatis in nomine eius.

21. 1, 2. Postea manifestavit se iterum Iesus discipulis ad mare Tiberiadis. . . .

21. 6. . . . Mittite in dexteram navigii rete. . . .

21. 9. Ut ergo descenderunt in terram viderunt prunas positas, et piscem superpositum, et panem.

21. 17. Dicit ei tertio : Simon Ioannis, amas me ? . . . Petrus . . . dixit ei : Domine, tu omnia nosti ; tu scis quia amo te. Dixit ei : Pasce oves meas.

ACTS.

1. 3–8. Quibus et praebuit seipsum vivum post passionem suam in

manegum ðrafungum, geond fēowertig daga, and him tō
sprǣc ymbe Godes rīce, samod mid him reordigende. And
bebēad him þæt hī of ðǣre byrig Hierusalem ne gewiton, ac þæt
hī ðǣr anbīdedon his Fæder behātes (hē cwæð) þe gē of mīnum
mūðe gehȳrdon; forðanðe Iohannes se Fulluhtere gefullode on
wætere, and gē bēoð gefullode on ðām Hālgan Gāste nū æfter
fēawum dagum. Eornostlice, sēo gegaderung his leorningenihta
cwæð ðā ānmōdlice: Drihten lēof, wilt ðū nū gesęttan ęnde
þysre worulde? Hē him andwyrde: Nis nā ēow tō gewitenne
ðā tīd oððe ðā handhwīle þe mīn Fæder gesętte þurh his mihte;
ac gē underfōð þæs Hālgan Gāstes mihte, and gē bēoð mīne
gewitan on Iudea lande, and on eallum middangearde, ōð-þæt
ęndenēxte land. Æ. H. i. 294; cf. i. 28, 296.

‖ Se hālga hēap befrān Crīst hwæðer hē wolde on ðām tīman
þisne middangeard geęndian. Hē ðā cwæð him tō andsware:
Nis nā ēower mǣð tō witenne þone tīman þe mīn Fæder þurh
his mihte gesętte. Æ. H. i. 298.

1. 8. *See* Æ. H. i. 318.

1. 9-15. Þā . . . fērde hē tō heofonum, him on lōcigendum; and
þæt heofonlice wolcen lēat wið his, and hine genam fram heora
gesihðum. Dā-ðā hī ūp tō heofonum starigende stōdon, ðā
gesāwon hī ðǣr twēgen ęnglas on hwītum gęrelan, þus cweðende:
Gē Galileisce weras, hwī stande gē ðus starigende wið heofenas
weard? Se Hǣlend, þe is nū genumen of ēowrum gesihðum
tō heofonum, swā hē cymð ęft swā-swā gē gesāwon þæt hē tō

multis argumentis, per dies quadraginta apparens eis, et loquens
de regno Dei. Et convescens
praecepit eis ab Ierosolymis ne
discederent, sed expectarent promissionem Patris, quam audistis
(inquit) per os meum; quia
Ioannes quidem baptizavit aqua,
vos autem baptizabimini Spiritu
sancto non post multos hos dies.
Igitur qui convenerant interroga-
bant eum, dicentes: Domine, si
in tempore hoc restitues regnum
Israel? Dixit autem eis: Non
est vestrum nosse tempora vel
momenta quae Pater posuit in sua
potestate; sed accipietis virtutem

supervenientis Spiritus sancti in
vos, et eritis mihi testes . . . in
omni Iudaea, . . . et usque ad
ultimum terrae.

1. 9-15. Et, . . . videntibus illis,
elevatus est; et nubes suscepit
eum ab oculis eorum. Cumque
intuerentur in coelum euntem
illum, ecce duo viri astiterunt
iuxta illos in vestibus albis, qui
et dixerunt: Viri Galilaei, quid
statis aspicientes in coelum? Hic
Iesus, qui assumptus est a vobis
in coelum, sic veniet quemadmodum vidistis eum euntem in
coelum. Tunc reversi sunt Ierosolymam. . . . Et cum introissent

heofonum āstāh. Hī ðā gecyrdon tō ðǣro byrig Hierusalem mid micclre blisse[1], and āstigon upp on āne ūpflēringe, and þǣr wunodon . . . on gebedum and on Godes herungum. . . . On ðyssere geferrǣdene wǣron Petrus and Iohannes. Iacob and Andreas, Philippus and Thomas, Bartholomeus and Matheus, se ōðer Iacob and Simon, se ōðer Iudas, and Maria þæs Hǣlendes mōdor, and gehwilce ōðre, ǣgðer ge weras ge wīf. Eal sēo menigu wæs ān hund manna and twēntig, ānmōdlice on gebedum wunigende. Æ. H. i. 294, 296 ; cf. i. 2-8, 220, 228, and Luke 24. 50, 51, note.

[Se hālga hȳred wæs wunigende ānmōdlice on gebedum on ānre ūpflōra, anbīdigende his behātes[2]. Æ. H. i. 314.

1. 18. Iudas . . . tōbærst on emtwā, and his innoð tōflēow. Æ. H. ii. 250.

2. 1-7, 7, 8, 11-17, 19. On ðisum dæge, þe is Pentecostes gecweden, cōm fǣrlice micel swēg of heofonum, and gefylde ealle ðā ūpflēringe mid fȳre. And wæs ætēowed bufon heora ǣlcum swylce fȳrene tungan ; and hī wurdon ðā ealle gefyllede mid þām Hālgum Gāste, and ongunnon tō sprecenne mid mislicum gereordum, be ðām þe se Hālga Gāst him tǣhte. Þā wǣron gegaderode binnan ðǣro byrig Hierusalem ēawfæste weras of ǣlcere ðēode ðe under heofonum cardiað ; and þā apostoli sprǣcon tō ðæs folces gegaderunge, and heora ǣlc onenēow his āgen gereord. Dā wearð sēo menigu swīðe āblicged, and mid wundrunge cwǣdon : Lā, hū ne sind þās ðe hēr sprecað Gali-

in coenaculum, ascenderunt ubi manebant Petrus et Ioannes, Iacobus et Andreas, Philippus et Thomas, Bartholomaeus et Matthaeus, Iacobus Alphaei et Simon Zelotes, et Iudas Iacobi. Hi omnes erant perseverantes unanimiter in oratione cum mulieribus, et Maria matre Iesu, et fratribus eius. . . . Erat autem turba hominum simul, fere centum viginti.

1. 18. ... Crepuit medius, et diffusa sunt omnia viscera eius.

2. 1-5, 7, 8, 11-17, 19. Et cum complerentur dies Pentecostes, . . .

factus est repente de coelo sonus tamquam advenientis spiritus vehementis, et replevit totam domum ubi erant sedentes. Et apparuerunt illis dispertitae linguae tamquam ignis, seditque supra singulos eorum ; et repleti sunt omnes Spiritu sancto, et coeperunt loqui variis linguis, prout Spiritus sanctus dabat eloqui illis. Erant autem in Ierusalem habitantes Iudaei, viri religiosi ex omni natione quae sub coelo est. . . . Stupebant autem omnes, et mirabantur, dicentes : Nonne ecce

[1] Cf. Luke 24. 52, 'cum gaudio magno.'　　　[2] See Acts 1. 4.

leisce? And ūre ǣle gehȳrde hū hī sprǣcon ūrum gereordum, on ðām ðe wē ācęnnede wǣron! Wē gehȳrdon hī sprecan Godes mǣrða mid ūrum gereordum. Lā, hwæt þis bēon sceole? Þā cwǣdon ðā Iudeiscan mid hospe: Þās men sindon mid muste fordręnete. Þā andwyrde Petrus: Hit is underntīd; hū mihte wē on ðysre tīde bēon fordręnete? Ac ðæs wītegan cwyde Ioheles is nū gefylled: God cwæð þurh ðæs wītegan mūð þæt hē wolde his Gāst āsęndan ofer męnnisc flǣsc; and manna bearn sceolon wītigian: and ic sylle mine forebēacn ufan of heofonum, and mīne tācna niðer on eorðan. Æ. H. i. 314; cf. i. 232, 318, 330: ii. 44, 280, 472, 474.

‖ Þā cōm se Hālga Gāst on fȳres hīwe tō ðām hālgum hȳrede on þām endleoftan dæge Crīstes ūpstiges, and hī ealle onǣlde mid undergendlicum fȳre; and hī wurdon āfyllede mid þǣre heofonlican lāre, and cūðon ealle woruldlice gereord, and bodedon unforhtlice gelēafan and fulluht rīcum and rēðum. Æ. H. i. 308.

2. 21. *See* Joel 2. 32.

2. 27. *See* Ps. 16. 9, 10.

2. 32–35. 37. 38. 41. 42. 45. Wite gē sōðlice þæt Crīst ārās of dēaðe, and on ūre gewitnysse āstāh tō heofonum, and sitt æt his Fæder swīðran, swā-swā Dauid be him wītegode, þus cweðende: Drihten cwæð tō mīnum Drihtne: Site tō mīnre swīðran, oð-þæt ic ālęcge ðīne fȳnd under þīnum fōtsceamele. Þā þæt folc ðis gehȳrde, ðā wurdon hī onbryrde, and cwǣdon tō ðām aposs-tolon: Lā lēof, hwæt is ūs tō dōnne? Þā andwyrde Petrus:

omnes isti qui loquuntur. Galilaei sunt? Et quomodo nos audivimus unusquisque linguam nostram in qua nati sumus? . . . Audivimus eos loquentes nostris linguis magnalia Dei. . . . Quidnam vult hoc esse? Alii autem irridentes dicebant: Quia musto pleni sunt isti. . . . Petrus . . . locutus est eis: . . . Non enim, sicut vos aestimatis, hi ebrii sunt, cum sit hora diei tertia; sed hoc est quod dictum est per prophetam Ioel: Et erit in novissimis diebus (dicit Dominus) effundam de Spiritu meo super omnem carnem; et prophetabunt filii vestri; . . . et dabo prodigia in coelo sursum, et signa in terra deorsum. . . .

2. 32 35, 37, 38, 41, 42, 45. Hunc Iesum resuscitavit Deus, cuius omnes nos testes sumus. Dextera igitur Dei exaltatus. . . . David . . . dixit autem: . . . Dixit Dominus Domino meo: Sede a dextris meis, donec ponam inimicos tuos scabellum pedum tuorum. . . . His antem auditis, compuncti sunt corde, et dixerunt ad Petrum et ad reliquos apostolos: Quid faciemus, viri fratres? Petrus vero ad illos:

Behrēowsiað ēowre synna, and underfōð fulluht on Crīstes naman, and ēowre synna bēoð ādȳlegode, and gē underfōð þone Hālgan Gāst. Þā underfēngon hī his lāre, and bugon tō fullulte on ðām dæge ðrēo ðūsend manna. Þā wǣron ealle on ānnysse mid þām apostolum ; and becēapodon heora ǣhta, and þæt feoh betǣhton ðām apostolum, and hī dǣldon ǣlcum be his nēode.   *Æ. H. i.* 314, 316.

3. 14. *See Æ. H. ii.* 252.

4. 32, 34, 35. Wearð eall sēo gelēaffulle menigu swā ānmōd swilce hī ealle hæfdon āne heortan and āne sāwle ; nō heora nān næfde synderlice ǣhta, ac him eallum wæs gemǣne heora ðing. Nō ðǣr næs nān wǣdla betwux him. Þā ðe landāre hæfdon, hī hit becēapodon, and þæt wurð brōhton tō ðǣra apostola fōtum ; hī ðā dǣldon ǣlcum be his nēode.   *Æ. H. i.* 316 ; *cf. i.* 326.

     [Hī wǣron on swā micelre ānnysse, swilce him eallum wǣre ān sāwul and ān heorte.   *Æ. H. ii.* 276.

5. 1–11. Þā wæs sum ðegen, Annanias gehāten, and his wīf Saphira ; hī cwǣdon him betwēonan þæt hī woldon būgan tō ðǣra apostola gefērrǣdene. Nāmon ðā tō rǣde þæt him wǣrlicor wǣre þæt hī sumne dǣl heora landes wurðes ǣthæfdon, weald him getīmode. Cōm ðā se ðegen mid fēo tō ðām apostolum. Þā cwæð Petrus : Annania, dēofol bepǣhte ðīne heortan, and ðū hæfst ālogen þām Hālgan Gāste. Hwī woldest ðū swician on ðīnum āgenum ? Ne luge ðū nā mannum, ac Gode.

Poenitentiam (inquit) agite, et baptizetur unusquisque vestrum in nomine Iesu Christi in remissionem peccatorum vestrorum ; et accipietis donum Spiritus sancti. ...Qui ergo receperunt sermonem eius baptizati sunt ; et appositae sunt in die illa animae circiter tria millia. Erant autem perseverantes in doctrina apostolorum. . . . Possessiones et substantias vendebant, et dividebant illa omnibus, prout cuique opus erat.

4. 32, 34, 35. Multitudinis autem credentium erat cor unum et anima una ; nec quisquam eorum quae possidebat aliquid suum esse dicebat, sed erant illis omnia

communia.... Neque enim quisquam egens erat inter illos. Quotquot enim possessores agrorum aut domorum erant, vendentes afferebant pretia eorum quae vendebant, et ponebant ante pedes apostolorum. Dividebatur autem singulis prout cuique opus erat.

5. 1–11. Vir autem quidam nomine Ananias, cum Saphira uxore sua, vendidit agrum, et fraudavit de pretio agri, conscia uxore sua ; et afferens partem quamdam, ad pedes apostolorum posuit. Dixit autem Petrus : Anania, cur tentavit Satanas cor tuum, mentiri te Spiritui sancto, et fraudare de pretio agri ? Nonne manens tibi

þā hē þas word gehȳrde, þā fēol hē ādūne and gewāt. Þa-ða hē
bebyrged wæs, þā cōm his wīf Saphira, and nyste hū hire were
gelumpen wæs. Ða cwæð Petrus : Sege mē, becēapode gē ðus
micel landes? Hēo andwyrde : Gēa, lēof, swā micel. Eft ða
cwæð Petrus : Hwī gewearð inc swā, þæt gyt dorston fandian
Godes? Hēo fēoll ðērrihte and gewāt, and hī man bebyr-
igde tō hyre were. Þā wearð micel ege on Godes gelaðunge,
and on eallum þe þæt geāxodon.   Æ. II. i. 316, 318 ; cf. i. 398.

5. 12, 15, 16. Þā worhte God fela tācna on ðām folce ðurh ðæra
apostola handa, swā þæt hī gelōgodon ðā untruman be ðære
strǣt þǣr Petrus forð ēode ; and swā hraðe swā his sceadu hī
hreopode, hī wurdon gehǣlede fram eallum untrumnyssum. Þā
arn micel menigu tō of gehendum burgum, and brōhton heora
untruman and ðā dēofolsēocan ; and hī ealle wurdon gehǣlede
æt ðæra apostola handum.   Æ. H. i. 316.

5. 17–23. Wurdon ðā Iudeiscan mid andan āfyllede ongēan his
apostolas, and gebrōhton hī on cwearterne. On ðǣre ylcan
nihte Godes engel undyde þā locu ðæs cwearternes, and hī ūt-
ālǣdde, þus cweðende : Gāð tō ðām temple, and bodiað þām
folce līfes word. And hī swā dydon. Hwæt, ða Iudeiscan þæs
on merien ðeahtodon embe ðæra apostola forwyrd, and sendon

manebat, et venundatum in tua erat potestate? Quare posuisti in corde tuo hanc rem? Non es mentitus hominibus, sed Deo. Audiens autem Ananias haec verba, cecidit et expiravit. . . . Surgentes autem iuvenes amoverunt eum, et efferentes sepelierunt. . . . Uxor ipsius, nesciens quod factum fuerat, introivit. Dixit autem ei Petrus : Dic mihi, . . . si tanti agrum vendidistis? At illa dixit: Etiam, tanti. Petrus autem ad eam : Quid utique convenit vobis tentare Spiritum Domini? . . . Confestim cecidit ante pedes eius, et expiravit. . . . Iuvenes . . . sepelierunt ad virum suum. Et factus est timor magnus in universa ecclesia, et in omnes qui audierunt haec.

5. 12, 15, 16. Per manus autem apostolorum fiebant signa et prodigia multa in plebe. . . . Ita ut in plateas eiicerent infirmos, . . . ut, veniente Petro, saltem umbra illius obumbraret quemquam illorum, et liberarentur ab infirmitatibus suis. Concurrebat autem et multitudo vicinarum civitatum Ierusalem, afferentes aegros, et vexatos a spiritibus immundis ; qui curabantur omnes.

5. 17–23. Exsurgens autem princeps sacerdotum, et omnes qui cum illo erant, . . . repleti sunt zelo, et iniecerunt manus in apostolos, et posuerunt eos in custodia publica. Angelus autem Domini per noctem aperiens ianuas carceris, et educens eos, dixit : Ite, et stantes loquimini in templo plebi

tō ðām cwearterne, þæt hī man gefętte. Þā cwęlleras ða geopenodon þæt cweartern, and nænne ne gemētton. Hī ða cȳddon
heora ealdrum : Þæt cweartern wē fundon fæste beclȳsed, and
ðā weardas wiðūtan standende, ac wē ne gemētton nænne
wiðinnan. Æ. H. i. 572.

‖ Þā hēafodmęn Iuleisces folces gebrōhton Crīstes apostolas
on cwearterne. Þā on niht cōm him tō Godes ęngel, and lǣdde
hī ūt of ðām cwearterne ; and stōd on merigen þæt cweartern
fæste belocen. Æ. H. i. 230.

6. 5–7. 1. Þǣra diacona wæs se forma Stephanus. . . . Hē wæs
swīðe gelēafful, and mid þām Hālgum Gāste āfylled. Þā ōðre
six wǣron gecīgede ðisum namum : Stephanus wæs se fyrmesta,
ōðer Philippus, þridda Procorus, fēorða Nicanor, fīfta Timo-
theus, sixta Parmenen, seofoða Nicolaus. Ðās seofon hī
gecuron and gesętton on ðǣra apostola gesihðe, and hī ða
mid gebedum and blētsungum tō diaconum gehādode wurdon.
Wēox ðā dæghwonlice Godes bodung, and wæs gemęnigfylld
þæt getęl crīstenra manna þearle on Hierusalem. Þā wearð
se ēadiga Stephanus mid Godes gife and mid micelre stręncðe
āfylled, and worhte forebēacena and micele tācna on ðām folce.
Ðā āstōdon sume ðā ungelēaffullan Iudei, and woldon mid
heora gedwylde þæs ēadigan martyres lāre oferswīðan ; ac hī
ne mihton his wīsdōme wiðstandan, nē ðām Hālgum Gāste
ðe ðurh hine spræc. Þā sętton hī lēase gewitan, ðe hine

omnia verba vitae huius. Qui
cum audissent, intraverunt diluculo in templum, et docebant.
Adveniens autem princeps sacerdotum, et qui cum eo erant, con-
vocaverunt concilium, et omnes
seniores filiorum Israel, et miserunt ad carcerem ut adducerentur.
Cum autem venissent ministri, et,
aperto carcere, non invenissent
illos, reversi nuntiaverunt, dicentes : Carcerem quidem invenimus
clausum cum omni diligentia, et
custodes stantes ante ianuas ;
aperientes autem, neminem intus
invenimus.

6. 5–7. 1. . . . Et elegerunt Stephanum, virum plenum fide et

Spiritu sancto, et Philippum, et
Prochorum, et Nicanorem, et
Timonem, et Parmenam, et Nico-
laum. . . . Hos statuerunt ante
conspectum apostolorum, et
orantes imposuerunt eis manus.
Et verbum Domini crescebat, et
multiplicabatur numerus discipulorum in Ierusalem valde. . . .
Stephanus autem, plenus gratia
et fortitudine, faciebat prodigia
et signa magna in populo. Surrexerunt autem quidam de synagoga, . . . disputantes cum Ste-
phano ; et non poterant resistere
sapientiae et Spiritui qui loquebatur. Tunc summiserunt viros
qui dicerent se audivisse cum

forlugon, and cwǣdon þæt hē tāllice word sprǣce be Moyse
and be Gode. Þæt folc wearð ðā micelum āstyred, and þā
hēafodmenn, and þā Iudeiscan bōceras; and gelæhton Stephanum, and tugon tō heora geþeahte. And ðā lēasan gewitan
him on besǣdon: Ne geswīcð ðes man tō sprecenne tāllice
word ongēan þās hālgan stōwe and Godes ǣ; wē gehȳrdon
hine secgan þæt Crīst tōwyrpð þās stōwe, and tōwent ðā
gesetnysse ðe ūs Moyses tǣhte. Þā behēoldon ðā hine ðe on
þām geðeahte sǣton, and gesāwon his nebwlite swylce sumes
engles ansȳne. Ðā cwæð se ealdorbiscop tō ðām ēadigan
cyðere: Is hit swā hī secgað? Æ. H. i. 44, 46.

7. 2–50. *See* Æ. H. i. 46.

7. 8. *See* Æ. H. ii. 190.

7. 49. *See* Matt. 5. 34–37.

7. 51–60. Gē wiðstandað þām Hālgum Gāste mid strðum swūran
and ungeleaffulre heortan; gē sind meldan and manslagan, and
gē ðone rihtwīsan Crīst nīðfullice ācwealdon; gē underfēngon
ǣ on engla gesetnysse, and gē hit ne hēoldon. Hwæt, ðā
Iudeiscan þā wurdon þearle on heora heortan āstyrode, and
biton heora tēð him tōgēanes. Se hālga Stephanus wearð þā
āfylled mid þām Hālgum Gāste, and behēold wið heofonas
weard, and geseah Godes wuldor, and þone Hǣlend standende
æt his Fæder swīðran; and hē cwæð: Efne, ic gesēo heofenas
opene, and mannes Sunu standende æt Godes swīðran. Iudei

dicentem verba blasphemiae in
Moysen et in Deum. Commove-
runt itaque plebem, et seniores, et
scribas; et concurrentes rapuerunt
eum, et adduxerunt in concilium.
Et statuerunt falsos testes, qui
dicerent: Homo iste non cessat
loqui verba adversus locum sanctum, et legem; audivimus enim
eum dicentem quoniam Iesus
Nazarenus hic destruet locum
istum, et mutabit traditiones quas
tradidit nobis Moyses. Et intuentes eum omnes qui sedebant
in concilio, viderunt faciem eius
tamquam faciem angeli. Dixit
autem princeps sacerdotum: Si
haec ita se habent?

7. 51-60. Dura cervice et incir...um-
cisis cordibus . . . vos semper
Spiritui sancto resistitis. . . .
Quem prophetarum non sunt persecuti patres vestri? Et occiderunt eos qui praenuntiabant
de adventu Iusti, cuius vos nunc
proditores et homicidae fuistis;
qui accepistis legem in disposi-
tione angelorum, et non custo-
distis. Audientes autem haec
dissecabantur cordibus suis, et
stridebant dentibus in eum. Cum
autem esset plenus Spiritu sancto,
intendens in coelum, vidit gloriam
Dei, et Iesum stantem a dextris
Dei; et ait: Ecce video coelos
apertos, et Filium hominis stantem

ða, mid micelre stemne hrȳmende, hēoldon heora ēaran, and ānmōdlice him tō scuton, and hī hine gelæhton, and of ðēre byrig gelæddon tō stānenne. Þā lēasgewitan ðā lēdon heora hacelan ætforan fōtum sumes geonges cnihtes, se wæs gecīgod Saulus. Ongunnon ðā oftorfian mid heardum stānum ðone ēadigan Stephanum ; and hē clypode, and cwæð : Drihten Hǣlend, onfōh mīnne gāst. And gebīgde his cnēowu, mid micelre stemne clypigende : Mīn Drihten, ne sęte ðū ðūs dǣda him tō synne. Æ. H. i. 46, 48.

‖ Se forma martyr Stephanus cwæð þæt hē gesāwe heofonas opene, and ðone Hǣlend standan on his Fæder swīðran.
    Æ. H. i. 308, 310 ; cf. i. 306.

‖ Crīst, onfōh mīnne gāst.   Æ. H. ii. 26.

‖ Drihten, ne sęte ðū ðūs dǣda him tō synne.   Æ. H. i. 50 (bis).

‖ Drihten mīn, ne sęte þū him ðūs dǣda tō synne.   Æ. H. ii. 34.

8. 3. See Æ. H. i. 324.

8. 17. Hī sętton heora handa ofer gelȳfede męn, and hī underfēngon þone Hālgan Gāst.   Æ. H. i. 316.

9. 1–11, 13–26. Hē nam ðā gewrit æt ðām ealdorbiscopum tō ðēre byrig Damascum, þæt hē mōste gebindan ðā crīstenan ðe hē on ðēre byrig gemētte, and gelǣdan tō Hierusalem. Þā gelamp hit on þām sīðe þæt him cōm fǣrlice tō micel lēoht. And hine āstręhte tō eorðan, and hē gehȳrde stemne ufan þus cweðende : Saule, Saule, hwī ēhtst ðū mīn ? Yfel bið ðē sylfum þæt ðū spurne ongēan ðā gāde [1]. Hē ðā mid micelre fyrhte [1] andwyrde

a dextris Dei. Exclamantes autem voce magna continuerunt aures suas, et impetum fecerunt unanimiter in eum, et eiicientes eum extra civitatem lapidabant. Et testes deposuerunt vestimenta sua secus pedes adolescentis, qui vocabatur Saulus. Et lapidabant Stephanum invocantem, et dicentem : Domine Iesu, suscipe spiritum meum. Positis autem genibus, clamavit voce magna, dicens : Domine, ne statuas illis hoc peccatum. . . .

8. 17. Tunc imponebant manus

super illos, et accipiebant Spiritum sanctum.

9. 1–11, 13–26. . . . Accessit ad principem sacerdotum, et petiit ab eo epistolas in Damascum, . . . ut si quos invenisset huius viae viros ac mulieres, vinctos perduceret in Ierusalem. Et cum iter faceret, contigit ut . . . subito circumfulsit eum lux de coelo. Et, cadens in terram, audivit vocem dicentem sibi : Saule, Saule, quid me persequeris ? Qui dixit : Quis es, Domine ? Et ille : Ego sum Iesus quem tu persequeris ;

---

[1] A transposition.

þǣre stemne : Hwæt eart ðū, lēof Hlāford ? Him andwyrde
sēo clypung þǣre godcundan stemne : Ic eom se Hǣlend þe
ðū ēhtst ; ac ārīs nū, and far forð tō ðǣre byrig ; þǣr ðē bið
gesǣd hwæt ðū gedafenige tō dōnne. Hē ārās ðā, āblendum
ēagum, and his gefēran hine swā blindne tō ðǣre byrig gelǣddon. And hē ðǣr andbīdigende ne onbyrigde ǣtes nū wǣtes
binnan ðrēora daga fæce.

Wæs ðā sum Godes ðegen binnan ðǣre byrig ; his nama wæs
Annanias. Tō ðām spræc Drihten ðysum wordum : Annania,
ārīs, and gecum tō mīnum ðēowan Saulum, se is biddende
mīnre miltsunge mid eornestum mōde. Hē andwyrde ðǣre
drihtenlican stemne : Mīn Hǣlend, hū mæg ic hine gesprecan,
se ðo is ēhtere ðīnra hālgena, ðurh mihte ðǣra ealdorbiscopa ?
Drihten cwæð : Far swā ic ðē sǣde, forðanðe hē is mē gecoren
fǣtels, þæt hē tōbere mīnne naman ðēodum, and cynegum, and
Israhela bearnum ; and hē sceal fela ðrōwian for mīnum naman.
Annanias ðā becōm tō ðām gecorenan cempan, and sette his
handa him onuppan mid þisre grētinge : Saule, mīn brōðor, se
Hǣlend, þe ðū be wege gespræc, sende mē wið ðīn, þæt þū
gesēo, and mid þām Hālgan Gāste gefylled sȳ. Þā, mid ðisum
wordum, fēollon swylce fylmena of his ēagum, and hē ðǣrrihte
gesihðe underfēng, and tō fulluhte bēah.

durum est tibi contra stimulum
calcitrare. Et tremens ac stu-
pens dixit. . . : Et Dominus ad
eum : Surge, et ingredere civitatem, et ibi dicetur tibi quid te
oporteat facere.... Surrexit autem
Saulus de terra, apertisque oculis
nihil videbat ; ad manus autem
illum trahentes, introduxerunt
Damascum. Et erat ibi tribus
diebus non videns, et non man-
ducavit neque bibit.

Erat autem quidam discipulus
Damasci, nomine Ananias. Et
dixit ad illum in visu Dominus :
Anania, . . . surge, ... et quaere
. . . Saulum ; . . . ecce enim
orat. . . . Respondit autem Ananias : Domine, audivi a multis de
viro hoc, quanta mala fecerit

sanctis tuis in Ierusalem ; et hic
habet potestatem a principibus
sacerdotum alligandi omnes qui
invocant nomen tuum. Dixit
autem ad eum Dominus : Vade,
quoniam vas electionis est mihi
iste, ut portet nomen meum coram
gentibus, et regibus, et filiis Israel ;
ego enim ostendam illi quanta
oporteat eum pro nomine meo
pati. Et abiit Ananias, et introivit in domum ; et, imponens ei
manus, dixit : Saule frater, Dominus misit me Iesus, qui apparuit
tibi in via qua veniebas, ut videas,
et implearis Spiritu sancto. Et
confestim ceciderunt ab oculis
eius tamquam squamae, et visum
recepit ; et, surgens, baptizatus
est. . . .

Wunode ðā sume fēawa daga mid þām Godes ðēowum binnan ðǣre byrig; and mid micelre bylde þām Iudēiscum bodade þæt Crīst, ðe hī wiðsōcon, is ðæs ælmihtigan Godes Sunu. Hī wurdon swīðlice āblicgede, and cwǣdon: Lā, hū ne is ðes se wælhrēowa ēhtere crīstenra manna? hūmeta bodað hē Crīstes gelēafan? Saulus sōðlice micclum swȳðrode, and ða Iudēiscan gescęnde, mid ānrǣdnysse sēðende þæt Crīst is Godes Sunu.

Hwæt, ðā æfter manegum dagum gerēonodon ðā Iudēiscan hū hī ðone Godes cęmpan ācwęllan sceoldon, and sętton ðā weardas tō ǣlcum geate ðǣre ceastre. Paulus ongeat heora syrwunge, and ðā crīstenan hine genāmon, and on ānre wilian ālēton ofer ðone weall. And hē fērde ongēan tō Hierusalem, and hine gecnēðlǣhte tō ðām hālgan hēape Crīstes hīredes. Æ. H. i. 386, 388.

‖ Saule, hwī ēhtst ðū mīn? Æ. H. i. 390.

‖ Hwī ēhtst ðū mīn? Æ. H. i. 390.

‖ Hwæt eart ðū, Hlāford? Æ. H. i. 390.

‖ Dęrigendlic bið ðē þæt þū spurne ongēan þā gāde. Æ. H. i. 390.

‖ Gā inn tō ðǣre ceastre, and ðǣr þū bið gesǣd hwæt þē gedafenað tō ðōnne. Æ. H. i. 124.

‖ Þrȳ dagas hē wunode būtan gesihðe. Æ. H. i. 390.

9. 17, 18. *See* Æ. H. i. 390.

9. 25. *See* Æ. H. i. 390.

10. 41. *See* Æ. H. i. 206.

12. 1–21, 23. Herodes cyning wolde, æfter Crīstes ūpstige tō heofenum, geswęncan sume of ðǣre gelaðunge, and sęnde werod

Fuit autem cum discipulis qui erant Damasci per dies aliquot; et continuo in synagogis praedicabat Iesum, quoniam hic est Filius Dei. Stupebant autem omnes qui audiebant, et dicebant: Nonne hic est qui expugnabat in Ierusalem eos qui invocabant nomen istud, et huc ad hoc venit, ut vinctos illos duceret ad principes sacerdotum? Saulus autem multo magis convalescebat, et confundebat Iudaeos qui habitabant Damasci, affirmans quoniam hic est Christus.

Cum autem implerentur dies multi, consilium fecerunt in unum Iudaei ut eum interficerent. Notae autem factae sunt Saulo insidiae eorum. Custodiebant autem et portas die ac nocte, ut eum interficerent. Accipientes autem eum discipuli nocte, per murum dimiserunt eum, submittentes in sporta. Cum autem venisset in Ierusalem, tentabat se iungere discipulis.

12. 1–21, 23. Eodem autem tempore misit Herodes rex manus, ut affligeret quosdam de ecclesia;

ymbe þæt. Þā ofslōh hē Iacobum, Iohannes brōðor þæs god-
spelleres. And geseah þæt hit gelīcode þām Iudeiscum, and
wolde gelæccan Petrum. Hē ðā hine gefōng, and on cwearterne
gebrōhte, and betǣhte hine on ðām hæfte sixtȳne cęmpum tō
healdenne ; hit wæs ðā Ēastertīd, and forðī hē ęleode his
slęges. Petrus ðā wæs gehæfd on ðām cwearterne ; and eal
sōo gelēaffulle gelaðung būton tōforlǣtennysse him fore bǣdon.
Þā læg Petrus, on ðǣre nihte þe Herodes wolde hine on merigen
forðlǣdan, betwux twām cęmpum slāpende, mid twām racentēagum getīged ; and ðā weardas hēoldon þæs cwearternes
duru, swā-swā him geboden wæs. Efne, ðā cōm Godes ęngel
scīnende, and þæt blinde cweartern eal mid lēohte āfylde ;
hē cnyste ðā Petres sīdan, and cwæð : Ārīs hraðe ; and þā
racentēagan fēollon ðǣrrihte of Petres handum. Se ęngel
cwæð : Begyrd þē, and scēo þē, and fylig mē. Petrus ðā him
filigde ; and ðūhte him swilce hit swefen wǣre. Hī ðā oferēodon
ðā twā weardsetl, oð-þæt hī becōmon tō ðām īsenan geate, and
þæt tōsprang þǣrrihte him tōgēanes. Hī ēodon forð oð-þæt
hī cōmon tō ānre wīc ; and se ęngel him gewāt fram. Petrus
ðā beðōhte hine sylfne, and cwæð : Nū ic wāt tō sōðan þæt
Drihten āsęnde his ęngel, and mē āhrędde fram Herodes
handum, and fram ælcere anbīdunge Iudeisces folces. Hē

occidit autem Iacobum fratrem
Ioannis. . . . Videns autem quia
placeret Iudaeis, apposuit ut ap-
prehenderet et Petrum. . . .
Quem cum apprehendisset, misit
in carcerem, tradens quattuor
quaternionibus militum custodi-
endum, volens post Pascha pro-
ducere eum populo. Et Petrus
quidem servabatur in carcere ;
oratio autem fiebat sine intermis-
sione ab ecclesia ad Deum pro eo.
Cum autem producturus eum esset
Herodes, in ipsa nocte erat Petrus
dormiens inter duos milites, vinctus catenis duabus ; et custodes
ante ostium custodiebant carcerem. Et ecce, angelus Domini
astitit, et lumen refulsit in habitaculo ; percussoque latere Petri,
excitavit eum, dicens : Surge velo-
citer ; et ceciderunt catenae de
manibus eius. Dixit autem angelus
ad eum : Praecingere, et calcea
te caligas tuas, . . . et sequere me.
Et exiens sequebatur eum ; existi-
mabat autem se visum videre.
Transeuntes autem primam et se-
cundam custodiam, venerunt ad
portam ferream, . . . quae ultro
aperta est eis. Et exeuntes pro-
cesserunt vicum unum ; et continuo discessit angelus ab eo. Et
Petrus, ad se reversus, dixit : Nunc
scio vere quia misit Dominus
angelum suum, et eripuit me de
manu Herodis, et de omni exspec-
tatione plebis Iudaeorum. . . .
Venit ad domum, . . . ubi erant
multi congregati. . . . Pulsante

becōm ða tō his geferum, and cnucode æt ðære dura. Him
arn tō sum mēden þæs geleaffullan weredes ; hire nama wæs
gecīged Rode ; and ða-ða hēo onenēow Petres stemne, ne mihte
for ðære blisse ða duru geopenian, ac cyrde ongēan, sǣde þæt
Petrus þær stōde. Þā geleaffullan cwǣdon þæt hit nǣre
Petrus, ac wǣre his engel. Petrus cnucode forð, oð-þæt hī
hine inn lēton ; and micclum his wundrodon. Hē rehte ða
him hū God hine āhredde þurh his engel of ðām cwearterne,
and cwæð : Cȳðað þis Iacobe and ūrum gebrōðrum. And ēode
ða tō sumere ōðre stōwe. Hwæt, ða on merigen wearð micel
styrung betwux ðām cempum þe hine healdan sceoldon. And
Herodes gewende tō Cesaream, and ðǣr hæfde gemōt wið
Tyrum and Sidoniscum. Ða mid-þām-ðe hē swīðost mōtode,
on his dōmsetle sittende, mid cynelicum rēafe gescrȳd, þā stōp
him tō Godes engel, and hine ofslōh, forðanðe hē ne sealde
Gode nænne wurðmynt ; and hē ðǣrrihte, mid wyrmum for-
numen, gewāt of līfe.   Æ. H. ii. 380, 382 ; cf. i. 402, 524.

‖ Eft siððan Herodes, Iudea cyning, sette ðone apostol
Petrum on cwearterne mid twām racentēagum gebundenne,
and weardas wiðinnan and wiðūtan gesette ; ac on ðære nihte
þe se ārleasa cyning hine on merigen ācwellan wolde, cōm
Godes engel scīnende of heofonum, and gelǣdde hine ūt ðurh
ða īsenan gatu.   Æ. H. i. 574.

‖ Þā-ða se engel hine of ðām cwearterne gelǣdde, and hē tō
his gefērum becōm, and cnucigende inganges bæd, þā cwǣdon
þā geleaffullan : Nis hit nā Petrus þæt ðǣr cnucað, ac is his
engel.   Æ. H. i. 516, 518.

autem eo ostium ianuae, processit puella ad audiendum, nomine Rhode ; et ut cognovit
vocem Petri, prae gaudio non
aperuit iannam, sed intro currens nuntiavit stare Petrum ante
ianuam. . . . Illi autem dicebant : Angelus eius est. Petrus
autem perseverabat pulsans. Cum
autem aperuissent, viderunt eum,
et obstupuerunt. . . . Narravit
quomodo Dominus eduxisset eum
de carcere, dixitque : Nuntiate
Iacobo et fratribus haec.   Et
egressus abiit in alium locum.
Facta autem die, erat non parva
turbatio inter milites quidnam
factum esset de Petro. Herodes
autem, . . . descendensque a Iudaea
in Caesaream, ibi commoratus est.
Erat autem iratus Tyriis et Sido-
niis. . . . Statuto autem die Herodes, vestitus veste regia, sedit pro
tribunali, et concionabatur ad eos.
Confestim autem percussit eum
angelus Domini, eo quod non
dedisset honorem Deo ; et, con-
sumptus a vermibus, expiravit.

13. 2, 3. Sẏððan ... cōm clypung of ðām Hālgan Gāste tō ðām
gelēaffullan weroðe, þus cweðende : Āsęndað Paulum and
Barnaban tō ðām weorce ðe ic hī gecoren hæbbe. Se hālga
hēap ðā, be Godes hǽse and gecorennysse, hī āsęndon to
lǽrenne eallum lēodscipum.   *Æ. H. i.* 388.

13. 33. *See* Ps. 2. 7.

13. 35. *See* Ps. 16. 9, 10.

14. 19. *See Æ. H. i.* 392.

15. 11. Wē gelȳfað þæt wē bēon gehealdene þurh Cristes gife.
swā-swā hī.   *Æ. H. i.* 214.

15. 35–39. *See Æ. H. i.* 388.

18. 3. Paulus, ... se ðe wæs on woruldcræfte teldwyrhta.   *Æ. H. i.* 392.

20. 34. *See Æ. H. i.* 392.

22. 4. *See Æ. H. i.* 324.

22. 20. *See Æ. H. ii.* 82.

26. 11. *See Æ. H. i.* 324.

28. 3, 5. *See Æ. H. i.* 574.

ROMANS.

1. 4. Sē ðe is forestiht Godes Sunu.   *Æ. H. ii.* 364.

1. 17. *See* Hab. 2. 4.

2. 6. God forgylt ǣlcum męn be his dǣdum.   *Æ. H. ii.* 340.

2. 12. Ðā ðe būtan Godes ǣ syngodon, hī ēac losiað būtan
ǣlcere ǣ.   *Æ. H. i.* 396.

‖ Þā ðe Godes ǣ ne cunnon, and būton Godes ǣ syngiað, hī
ēac būton Godes ǣ losiað.   *Æ. H. ii.* 52.

‖ Þā ðe būton Godes ǣ syngiað, ðā losiað ēac būton
Godes ǣ.   *Æ. H. ii.* 442.

5. 3–5. Gelēaffullum gedafenað þæt hī wuldrion on gedrēfed-
nyssum, forðanðe sēo gedrēfednys wyrcð geðyld, and þæt
geðyld āfandunge, and sēo āfandung hiht. Se hiht sōðlice

---

13. 2, 3. ... Dixit illis Spiritus sanctus: Segregate mihi Saulum et
Barnabam in opus ad quod as-
sumpsi eos. Tunc ... dimiserunt
illos.

15. 11. Sed per gratiam Domini Iesu
Christi credimus salvari, quemadmodum et illi.

18. 3. Et quia eiusdem erat artis ...
(erant autem scenofactoriae artis).

ROMANS.

1. 4. Qui praedestinatus est Filius
Dei. ...

2. 6. Qui reddet unicuique secundum opera eius.

2. 12. Quicumque enim sine lege pec-
caverunt, sine lege peribunt. ...

5. 3–5. ... Gloriamur in tribula-
tionibus, scientes quod tribulatio

ne biꝺ næfre gescynd, forꝰanþe Godes lufu is āgoten on ūrum heortum þurh ꝰone Hālgan Gāst se ꝰe ūs is forgifen. Æ. H. i. 554

8. 9. Witodlice, sē ꝰe Crīstes Gāst on him næfꝺ, nis sē his. Æ. H. ii. 202.

8. 18. Ne sind nā tō wiꝺmetenne ꝰā þrōwunga þyssere tīde ꝰām tōweardan wuldre þe biꝺ on ūs geswutelod. Æ. H. i. 486.

8. 30. Dā ꝰe hē forestihte, þā hē ꝫac clypode him tō; and ꝰā ꝰe hē him tō clypode, ꝰā hē gerihtwīsode; and ꝰā ꝰe hē gerihtwīsode, þā hē gemǣrsode. Æ. H. ii. 366.

8. 32. God Fæder ne sparode his āgenum Bearne, ac for ūs eallum hine tō dēaꝰe scalde. Æ. H. ii. 62.

9. 13. God lufode Iacob, and hatode Esau. Æ. H. i. 110.

9. 29. Dominus Sabaoꝺ, þæt is: Hęres Illāford, oꝰꝰe, Weroda Drihten. Æ. H. i. 526.

10. 13. *See* Joel 2. 32.

12. 1. And hē bebēad þæt wē sceolon gearcian ūre līchaman līflice onsægednysse, and hālige, and Gode andfęnge. Æ. H. i. 482.

12. 4, 5. *See* Eph. 5. 23, 30.

12. 17. *See* Matt. 5. 43–46.

13. 1. Ælc sāwul sȳ underꝰēod hēalicrum anwealdum. Æ. H. ii. 362.

13. 9. *See* Luke 18. 20–22.

13. 10. Sēo sōꝰe lufu is gefyllednys Godes ǣ. Æ. H. i. 346.

∥ Hēo is fulfręmednys Godes ǣ. Æ. II. ii. 522.

13. 11–14. . . . Nū is tīma ūs of slǣpe tō arīsenne; ūre hǣl is gehęndre þonne wē gelȳfdon. Sēo niht gewāt, and se dæg

patientiam operatur, patientia autem probationem, probatio vero spem. Spes autem non confundit, quia charitas Dei diffusa est in cordibus nostris per Spiritum sanctum qui datus est nobis.

8. 9. . . . Si quis autem Spiritum Christi non habet, hic non est eius.

8. 18. . . . Non sunt condignae passiones huius temporis ad futuram gloriam quae revelabitur in nobis.

8. 30. Quos autem praedestinavit, hos et vocavit; et quos vocavit, hos et iustificavit; quos autem iustificavit, illos et glorificavit.

8. 32. Qui etiam proprio Filio suo non pepercit, sed pro nobis omnibus tradidit illum. . . .

9. 13. . . . Iacob dilexi, Esau autem odio habui.

9. 29. . . . Dominus sabaoth. . . .

12. 1. Obsecro itaque . . . ut exhibeatis corpora vestra hostiam viventem, sanctam, Deo placentem. . . .

13. 1. Omnis anima potestatibus sublimioribus subdita sit. . . .

13. 10. . . . Plenitudo ergo legis est dilectio.

13. 11–14. . . . Hora est iam nos de somno surgere; nunc enim propior est nostra salus quam cum credidimus. Nox praecessit, dies

genēalǣhte; uton āwurpan ðēostra weorc, and bēon ymbscrȳdde mid lēohtes wǣpnum, swā þæt wē on dǣge ārwurðlice faron ; nā on oferǣtum and druncennyssum, nā on forligerbęddum and unclǣnnyssum, nā on geflite and andan ; ac bēoð ymbscrȳdde þurh Drihten Hǣlend Crīst. Æ. H. i. 600, 602.

‖ . . . Nū is tīma ūs of slǣpe tō ārīsenne. Æ. II. i. 602.

‖ Ūre hǣl is gehęndre þonne wē gelȳfdon. Æ. II. i. 602.

‖ Sēo niht gewāt, and se dæg genēalǣhte. Æ. H. i. 602.

‖ Uton āwurpan þēostra weorc, and bēon ymbscrȳdde mid lēohtes wǣpnum, swā þæt wē on dǣge ārwurðlice faron. Æ. H. i. 604.

‖ Ac bēoð ymbscrȳdde ðurh Drihten Hǣlend Crīst. Æ. H. i. 606.

14. 10. Ealle wē sceolon standan æfter ðisum līfe ætforan Crīstes dōmsetle. Æ. H. ii. 328.

15. 1. Wē strange sceolon beran ðǣra unstręngra byrðene. Æ. H. ii. 390.

1 CORINTHIANS.

1. 24. Crīst is Godes miht, and Godes wīsdōm. Æ. H. i. 520.

1. 27. God gecȳst ðā untruman þises middaneardes, þæt hē ðā strangan gescynde. Æ. H. ii. 376.

1. 31. Sē ðe wuldrige, wuldrige on Gode. Æ. H. i. 578.

2. 9. Ne mæg nān ēage on ðisum līfe gesēon, nē nān ēare gehȳran, nē nānes mannes heorte āsmēagan, ðā ðing ðe God gearcað þām ðe hine lufiað. Æ. H. ii. 588.

3. 9. Wē sind Godes gefylstan. Æ. H. i. 8.

3. 11. Ne mæg nān man lęcgan ōþerne grundweall on ðǣre hālgan gelaðunge būton ðone þe ðǣr gelēd is, þæt is Hǣlend Crīst. Æ. H. ii. 588.

autem appropinquavit ; abiiciamus ergo opera tenebrarum, et induamur arma lucis. Sicut in die honeste ambulemus ; non in comessationibus et ebrietatibus ; non in cubilibus et impudicitiis ; non in contentione et aemulatione ; sed induimini Dominum Iesum Christum. . . .

14. 10. . . . Omnes enim stabimus ante tribunal Christi.

15. 1. Debemus autem nos firmiores imbecillitates infirmorum sustinere. . . .

1 CORINTHIANS.

1. 24. . . . Christum Dei virtutem, et Dei sapientiam.

1. 27. . . . Infirma mundi elegit Deus, ut confundat fortia.

1. 31. . . . Qui gloriatur, in Domino glorietur.

2. 9. . . . Oculus non vidit, nec auris audivit, nec in cor hominis ascendit, quae praeparavit Deus iis qui diligunt illum.

3. 9. Dei enim sumus adiutores. . . .

3. 11. Fundamentum enim aliud

3. 12–15. Swā-hwā-swā getimbrað ofer ðisum grundwealle gold, oððe seolfor, oððe dēorwurðe stānas, oþþe trēowa, strēaw oþþe ceaf, ānes gehwilces mannes weorc bið swutel. Godes dæg hī geswutelað, forðanðe hē bið on fȳre ætēowod ; and þæt fȳr āfandað hwilc heora ǣlces weorc bið. Gif hwæs getimbrung ðurhwunað, and ðām fȳre wiðstent, þonne underfēhð se wyrhta edlēan æt Gode his weorces. Gif hwæs weorc forbyrnð, hē hæfð þone hearm, and bið swā-ðēah gehealden ðurh fȳr.
Æ. H. ii. 588.

3. 16. Nyte gē þæt ēowere lima syndon þæs Hālgan Gāstes tempel, se ðe on ēow is ? Æ. H. ii. 580.

3. 17. Sē ðe gewęmð Godes tempel, God hine fordēð. Æ. H. i. 212.
Godes tempel is hālig ; þæt gē sind. Æ. H. i. 412 ; ii. 580.

4. 7. Þū mann, hwæt hæfst ðū þæs ðe ðū fram Gode ne under-fēnge ? Hwī wuldrast ðu, swilce ðū nān ðing ne underfēnge ?
Æ. H. ii. 432.

5. 7. Crīst is ūre Ēastertīd. Æ. H. ii. 278.

5. 8. Wē sceoldon wistfullian. nā on yfelnysse beorman, ac on þeorf-nyssum sȳfernysse and sōðfæstnysse. Æ. H. ii. 278.

5. 13. Āfyrsiað þone yfelan fram ēow. Æ. H. i. 124.

6. 9, 10. Dyrne forligeras oððe dēofolgyldan, sceaðan and rēaferas, oððe rēðe manslagan, gȳtseras and drinceras, þe dollice lybbað, nabbað Godes rīce on rodorlicere heofonan. Æ. H. ii. 330.

. . . ðæt ðā wyrigendan Godes rīce ne geāgniað. Æ. H. ii. 34.

nemo potest ponere praeter id quod positum est, quod est Christus Iesus.

3. 12–15. Si quis autem superaedi-ficat super fundamentum hoc aurum, argentum, lapides preti-osos, ligna, foenum, stipulam, uniuscuiusque opus manifestum erit. Dies enim Domini declarabit, quia in igne revelabitur ; et uni-uscuiusque opus quale sit ignis probabit. Si cuius opus manserit quod superaedificavit, mercedem accipiet. Si cuius opus arserit, detrimentum patietur ; ipse autem salvus erit, sic tamen quasi per ignem.

3. 16. Nescitis quia templum Dei estis, et Spiritus Dei habitat in vobis ?

3. 17. Si quis autem templum Dei violaverit, disperdet illum Deus. Templum enim Dei sanctum est, quod estis vos.

4. 7. . . . Quid autem habes quod non accepisti ? Si autem acce-pisti, quid gloriaris quasi non acceperis ?

5. 7. . . . Pascha nostrum . . . est Christus.

5. 8. Itaque epulemur, non . . . in fer-mento malitiae et nequitiae, sed in azymis sinceritatis et veritatis.

5. 13. . . . Auferte malum ex vobis ipsis.

6. 9, 10. . . . Neque fornicarii, neque

6. 19. *See* Æ. H. i. 262.

6. 20. Gē sind gebohte mid micclum wurðe; wuldriað forðī, and beraðGod on ᵹowrum līchaman. Æ. H. i. 210.

7. 29. Þa ðe wīf habbað, bēon hī swilce hī nān nabbon. Æ. H. i. 148.

9. 11. Gif wē ᵹow þā gāstlican sēd sāwað, hwōnlic bið þæt wē ᵹowere flǣsclican ðing rīpon. Æ. H. ii. 534.

9. 25. Ǣlc ðǣra þe on gecampe winð, forhæfð hine sylfne fram eallum ðingum. Æ. H. ii. 86.

10. 1–4. Ealle ūre forðfæderas wǣron gefullode on wolcne and on sǣ; and ealle hī ǣton þone ylcan gāstlican mete, and ealle hī druncon þone ylcan gāstlican drenc. Hī druncon sōðlice of æfterfiligendum stāne; and se stān wæs Crīst. Æ. H. ii. 272, 274.

‖ Hī ealle ǣton ðone gāstlican mete, and ðone gāstlican drenc druncon. Æ. H. ii. 202; cf. John 6. 49, note.

‖ Hī druncon of ðām gāstlican stāne; and sē stān wæs Crīst. Æ. H. ii. 202.

‖ Se stān sōðlice wæs Crīst. Æ. H. i. 98.

10. 11. Wē sind ðā ðe worulda geendunga on becōmon. Æ. H. ii. 372.

10. 17. Wē manega sindon ān hlāf and ān līchama. Æ. H. ii. 276.

11. 23–25. *See* Matt. 26. 26–28.

12. 8–11. Sumum men hē forgifð wīsdom and sprǣce, sumum gōd ingehȳd, sumum micelne gelēafan, sumum mihte tō gehǣlenne untruman, sumum wītegunge, sumum tōscēad gōdra gāsta and yfelra; sumum hē forgifð mislice gereord, sumum gereccednysse mislicra sprǣca. Ealle ðās ðing dēð se Hālga Gāst, tōdǣlende ǣghwilcum be ðām ðe him gewyrð. Æ. H. i. 322.

idolis servientes, neque adulteri, neque molles, neque masculorum concubitores, neque fures, neque avari, neque ebriosi, neque maledici, neque rapaces, regnum Dei possidebunt.

6. 20. Empti enim estis pretio magno; glorificate, et portate Deum in corpore vestro.

7. 29. ... Qui habent uxores tamquam non habentes sint.

9. 11. Si nos vobis spiritualia seminavimus, magnum est si nos carnalia vestra metamus?

9. 25. Omnis autem qui in agone

contendit, ab omnibus se abstinet. ...

10. 1–4. ... Patres nostri omnes.... baptizati sunt in nube et in mari; et omnes eamdem escam spiritalem manducaverunt, et omnes eumdem potum spiritalem biberunt. Bibebant autem de spiritali, consequente eos, petra; petra autem erat Christus.

10. 11. ... Nostram, in quos fines sacculorum devenerunt.

10. 17. ... Unus panis, unum corpus multi sumus. ...

12. 8–11. Alii quidem per Spiritum

12. 12, 20, 21. *See* Eph. 5. 23, 30.

12. 26. Gif ān lim bið untrum, ealle ðā ōðre ðrōwiað mid þām ānum. *Æ. H. i.* 274.

12. 27. Gē sōðlice sindon Crīstes līchama and leomu. *Æ. H. ii.* 276 ; cf. i. 368, 390.

|| Gē sind Crīstes līchama and his lyma. *Æ. H. ii.* 386 ; cf. i. 368, 390.

13. 2, 3. Ðēah se mann hæbbe fullne gelēafan, and ælmessan wyrce, and fela tō gōde gedō, eal him bið ȳdel, swā-hwæt-swā hē dēð, būton hē hæbbe sōðe lufe. *Æ. H. i.* 528.

|| Þēah-ðe ic āspende ealle mīne æhta on ðearfena bigleofan, and ðēah-ðe ic mīnne āgenne līchaman tō cwale gesylle, swā ðæt ic forbyrne on martyrdōme ; gif ic næbbe ðā sōðan lufe, ne fremað hit me nān ðing. *Æ. H. i.* 54.

14. 20. Ne bēo gē cild on andgite, ac on yfelnyssum ; bēoð on and-gite fulfremede. *Æ. H. i.* 512.

14. 26. Þonne gē ēow tō gereorde gaderiað, hæbbe ēower gehwilc halwende lāre on mūðe, and sealmbōc on handa. *Æ. H. i.* 604.

14. 38. Se mann þe God forgyt, God forgyt ēac hine. *Æ. H. ii.* 52.

|| Sē ðe ne cann, hine man ēac ne cann. *Æ. H. ii.* 442.

15. 24. Þonne hē betǣcð rīce his Fæder. *Æ. H. i.* 264.

15. 52. On ānre prēowthwīle, on ðǣre endenēxtan bȳman ; sēo bȳme sōðlice blǣwð, and ðā dēadan ārīsað ungebrosnode, and wē bēoð awende. *Æ. H. ii.* 568.

datur sermo sapientiae ; alii autem sermo scientiae secundum eumdem Spiritum ; alteri fides in eodem Spiritu ; alii gratia sanitatum in uno Spiritu ; alii operatio virtutum, alii prophetia, alii discretio spirituum, alii genera linguarum, alii interpretatio sermonum. Haec autem omnia operatur unus atque idem Spiritus, dividens singulis prout vult.

12. 26. Et si quid patitur unum membrum, compatiuntur omnia membra. . . .

12. 27. Vos autem estis corpus Christi, et membra de membro.

13. 2, 3. . . . Si habuero omnem fidem, . . . et si distribuero in

cibos pauperum omnes facultates meas, et si tradidero corpus meum ita ut ardeam, charitatem autem non habuero, nihil mihi prodest.

14. 20. . . . Nolite pueri effici sensibus, sed malitia parvuli estote ; sensibus autem perfecti estote.

14. 26. . . . Cum convenitis, unusquisque vestrum psalmum habet, doctrinam habet, apocalypsim habet, linguam habet, interpretationem habet. . . .

14. 38. Si quis autem ignorat, ignorabitur.

15. 24. . . . Cum tradiderit regnum Deo et Patri. . . .

15. 52. In momento, in ictu oculi, in novissima tuba ; canet enim

16. 13. Bēoð wacole, and standað on gelēafan, and onginnað wer-
lice, and bēoð gehyrte.   Æ. H. i. 188.

2 CORINTHIANS.

1. 12. Ūre wuldor is sēo gecȳðnys ūres ingehȳdes.   Æ. H. ii. 564.

5. 10. Ealle wē sceolon standan æfter ðisum līfe ætforan Crīstes
dōmsetle, þæt ǣlc ðǣr underfō swā-hwæt-swā hē on līchaman
ādrēah, oððe gōd oþþe yfel.   Æ. H. ii. 328 ; cf. ii. 12.

6. 10. Swā-swā nāht hæbbende, and ealle ðing geāgniende.
    Æ. H. i. 550.

9. 9. See Ps. 112. 9.

10. 17. Sē ðe wuldrige, wuldrige on Gode.   Æ. H. i. 578.

11. 2. Ic bewęddode ēow ānum were, þæt gē sceoldon gearcian
clǣne mǣden Crīste.   Æ. H. ii. 10.

‖ Ic bewęddode ēow ānum were, þæt gē gearcian Crīste ān
clǣne mǣden.   Æ. H. ii. 54.

‖ Ic bewęddode ēow ānum were, þæt gē gearcian ān clǣne
mǣden Crīste.   Æ. H. ii. 566.

11. 23. See 2 Cor. 11. 26, 27, note.

11. 25. . . . þæt hē ænne dæg and āne niht on sǣgrunde ādruge.
    Æ. H. i. 574.

11. 26, 27. Hē wæs gelōmlice on mycelre frēcednysse, ǣgðer ge on
sǣ ge on lande, on wēstene, betwux sceaðum, on hungre and on
ðurste, and on manegum wræccum, on cyle, and on nacednysse,
and on manegum cwearternum [1].   Æ. H. i. 392.

tuba, et mortui resurgent incor-
rupti, et nos immutabimur.

16. 13. Vigilate, state in fide, viriliter
agite, et confortamini.

2 CORINTHIANS.

1. 12. Nam gloria nostra haec est,
testimonium   conscientiae   nostrae. . . .

5. 10. Omnes enim nos manifestari
oportet ante tribunal Christi, ut
referat unusquisque propria cor-
poris, prout gessit, sive bonum
sive malum.

6. 10. . . . Tamquam nihil habentes,
et omnia possidentes.

10. 17. Qui autem gloriatur, in
Domino glorietur.

11. 2. Despondi enim vos uni viro
virginem castam exhibere Christo.

11. 25. . . . Nocte et die in profundo
maris fui.

11. 26, 27. In itineribus saepe, periculis fluminum, periculis latronum, periculis ex genere, periculis ex gentibus, periculis in
civitate, periculis in solitudine,
periculis in mari, periculis in

[1] From 2 Cor. 11. 23, 'in carceribus.'

11. 33. *See* Æ. H. i. 390.

12. 2, 4. Ic wāt ðone mann on Crīste, þe wæs gegripen nū for fēowertȳne gēarum, and gelǣd oð ðā þriddan heofonan. And eft hē wæs gelǣd tō neorxnawange ; and ðǣr gehȳrde ðā dīgelan word, þe nān eorðlic mann sprecan ne mōt. *Æ. H. ii. 332.*

‖ Hē wæs gelǣd tō heofonan oð ðā ðriddan flēringe ; and þǣr hē geseh and gehȳrde Godes dīgelnysse, ðā hē ne mōste nānum men cȳðan. *Æ. H. i. 392.*

12. 7–9. Mē is geseald sticels mīnes līchaman, and se sceocca me gēarplæt [1], þæt sēo micelnys Godes onwrigenyssa mē ne onhebbe. Forðan ic bæd þriwa mīnne Drihten þæt hē āfyrsode þæs sceoccan sticels fram mē ; ac hē mē andwyrde : Paule, ðē geniht-sumað mīn gifu ; sōðlice mægen bið gefremod on untrumnysse. Nū wuldrige ic lustlice on mīnum untrumnyssum, þæt Crīstes miht on mē wunige. *Æ. H. i. 474.*

GALATIANS.

3. 11. *See* Hab. 2. 4.

3. 29. Gif gē sind Crīstes, þonne sind gē Abrahames sǣd, and æfter behāte yrfenuman. *Æ. H. i. 98.*

‖ Witodlice, gif gē crīstene synd, þonne bēo gē Abrahames ofspring, and yrfenuman æfter behāte. *Æ. H. i. 204.*

‖ Eornostlice, gif gē Crīstes sind, þonne sind gē Abrahames sǣd, and æfter behāte yrfenuman. *Æ. H. ii. 62.*

4. 4, 5. Þā-þā ðǣra tīda gefyllednys cōm, ðā sende God Fæder his Sunu tō mancynnes ālȳsednysse. *Æ. H. i. 194.*

falsis fratribus ; in labore et aerumna, in vigiliis multis, in fame et siti, in ieiuniis multis, in frigore et nuditate.

12. 2, 4. Scio hominem in Christo ante annos quattuordecim, . . . raptum huiusmodi usque ad tertium coelum. . . . Raptus est in paradisum ; et audivit arcana verba, quae non licet homini loqui.

12. 7–9. Et ne magnitudo revelationum extollat me, datus est mihi stimulus carnis meae, an-gelus Satanae qui me colaphizet. Propter quod ter Dominum rogavi ut discederet a me ; et dixit mihi : Sufficit tibi gratia mea ; nam virtus in infirmitate perficitur. Libenter igitur gloriabor in infirmitatibus meis, ut inhabitet in me virtus Christi.

GALATIANS.

3. 29. Si autem vos Christi, ergo semen Abrahae estis, secundum promissionem heredes.

4. 4, 5. At ubi venit plenitudo tem-

---

[1] For 'ēarplæt,' or 'geēarplæt.'

4. 10, 11. Ic wēne þæt ic swunce on ȳdel, ðā-ðā ic ēow tō Gode gebīgde; nū gē cēpað dagas and mōnðas mid ydelum wīglung·um.   Æ. H. i. 102.

4. 19. Gē synd mīne bearn, ðā ðe ic nū ōðre sīðe gecācnige, ōð-þæt Crīst bēo on ēow geednīwod.   Æ. H. i. 492.

5. 14. *See* Matt. 19. 19.

EPHESIANS.

1. 4. Swā-swā hē ūs gecēas on Crīste ǣr middaneardes gesętnysse.   Æ. H. ii. 366.

1. 10. . . . þæt sceoldon ealle heofonlice ðing and eorðlice bēon geedstaðolode on Crīste.   Æ. H. i. 214.

2. 14. Hē is ūre sibb, se ðe dyde ǣgðer tō ānum, tōwurpende [1] ðā ǣrran fēondscipas on him sylfum.   Æ. H. i. 106.

‖ Sē is ūre sib, se ðe dyde ǣgðer tō ānum.   Æ. H. ii. 580.

2. 17. Se Hǣlend bodade on his tōcyme sibbe ūs ðe feorran wǣron, and sibbe þām ðe gehęnde wǣron.   Æ. H. ii. 106.

3. 14, 17–19. Ic bīge mīne cnēowu tō ðām ælmihtigan Fæder for ēow, þæt gē bēon on sōðre lufe gewyrtrumode, þæt gē magon underfōn mid eallum hālgum hwæt sȳ brādnyss, langnyss, hēahnyss, and dēopnyss on Godes gesętnyssum; and tōcnāwan ēac ðā oferstīgendan sōðan lufe Drihtnes Crīstes, þæt gē bēon gefyllede on ealre Godes gefyllednysse.   Æ. H. ii. 408.

poris, misit Deus Filium suum, . . . ut eos, qui sub lege erant, redime-ret. . . .

4. 10, 11. Dies observatis, et menses, et tempora, et annos; timeo vos, ne forte sine causa laboraverim in vobis.

4. 19. Filioli mei, quos iterum parturio, donec formetur Christus in vobis.

EPHESIANS.

1. 4. Sicut elegit nos in ipso ante mundi constitutionem. . . .

1. 10. . . . Instaurare omnia in Christo, quae in coelis, et quae in terra sunt. . . .

2. 14. Ipse enim est pax nostra, qui fecit utraque unum, et . . . solvens inimicitias in carne sua.

2. 17. Et veniens evangelizavit pacem vobis qui longe fuistis, et pacem iis qui prope.

3. 14, 17–19. Huius rei gratia flecto genua mea ad Patrem Domini nostri Iesu Christi. . . . In charitate radicati et fundati, ut possitis comprehendere cum omnibus sanctis quae sit latitudo, et longitudo, et sublimitas, et profundum; scire etiam supereminentem scientiae charitatem Christi, ut impleamini in omnem plenitudinem Dei.

[1] Possibly translates the 'evacuans' of *v.* 15.

4. 3. *See* Æ. H. ii. 276.

5. 16. Yfele sind ūre dagas.   Æ. H. i. 490.

5. 22. Wīf sceolon gehȳrsumian heora werum gedafenlice, and hī symle ārwurðian swā-swā āgene hlāfordas.   Æ. H. i. 322.

5. 23. *See* Æ. H. i. 260, 272.

5. 27. Ealle ðā þe tō Godes rīce gebyrigað, nabbað nāðor nē wǫmm nē āwyrdnysse on heora līchaman.   Æ. H. i. 236.

5. 30. *See* Æ. H. i. 260, 272.

6. 2. *See* Exod. 20. 12.

6. 11, 12, 14, 16, 17. Ymbscrȳdað ēow mid Godes wǣpnunge, þæt gē magon standan ongēan dēofles syrwungum ; forðanðe ūs nis nūn gecamp ongēan flǣsc and blōd, ac tōgēanes dēofellicum ealdrum and gāstlicum yfelnyssum.   Standað, eornostlice, mid begyrdum lęndenum on sōðfæstnysse, and ymbscrȳdde mid rihtwīsnysse byrnan ; and nymað þæs gelēafan scyld, and ðæs hihtes helm, and þæs Hālgan Gāstes swurd, þæt is Godes word.   Æ. H. ii. 218.

PHILIPPIANS.

2. 8. Hē wæs gehȳrsum his Fæder ǣfre ōð dēað.   Æ. H. ii. 6.

2. 15, 16. Gewuniað betwux þwȳrum mancynne ; scīnað betwux þām swā-swā steorran, līfes word healdende.   Æ. H. i. 528.

3. 19. Heora wamb is heora God, and heora ęnde is forwyrd, and heora wuldor on gescyndnysse.   Æ. H. i. 604.

3. 21. *See* Æ. H. i. 236.

5. 16. . . . Dies mali sunt.

5. 22. Mulieres viris suis subditae sint, sicut Domino.

5. 27. Ut exhiberet ipse sibi gloriosam ecclesiam, non habentem maculam aut rugam. . . .

6. 11, 12, 14, 16, 17. Induite vos armaturam Dei, ut possitis stare adversus insidias diaboli ; quoniam non est nobis collucatio adversus carnem et sanguinem, sed adversus principes et potestates, adversus mundi rectores tenebrarum harum, contra spiritualia nequitiae. . . . State, ergo, succincti lumbos vestros in veritate, et induti loricam iustitiae . . . in omnibus sumentes scutum fidei ; . . . et galeam salutis assumite, et gladium Spiritus, quod est verbum Dei.

PHILIPPIANS.

2. 8. . . . Factus obediens usque ad mortem. . . .

2. 15, 16. Ut sitis . . . in medio nationis pravae et perversae ; inter quos lucetis sicut luminaria in mundo, verbum vitae continentes. . . .

3. 19. Quorum finis interitus, quorum Deus venter est, et gloria in confusione ipsorum. . . .

COLOSSIANS.

2. 9. On him wunað eal gefyllednys þǣre godcundnysse. *Æ. H. i.* 150.

2. 14. Mid his upstige is ādȳlegod þæt cyrographum ūro geniðer-
unge. *Æ. H. i.* 300.

3. 5. Se gītscre . . . bið . . . þām gelīc þe deofolgyld begǣð.
Æ. H. i. 326.

3. 12, 14-17. Ymbscrȳdað ̄eow, swā-swā Godes gecorenan, mid
mildheortnysse and mid welwillendnysse, mid ̄eadmōdnysse,
mid gemetfæstnysse, mid geðylde ; and habbað ̄eow, tōforan
eallum ðingum, ðā sōðan lufe, sēo ðe is bend ealra fulfremed-
nyssa ; and Crīstes sib blissige on ̄eowrum heortum, on ðǣre
gē sind gecīgede on ānum līchaman. Bēoð þancfulle, and
Godes word wunige betwux ̄eow genihtsumlice on eallum wīsdōme ; tǣcende and tihtende ̄eow betwȳnan on sealmsangum
and gāstlicum lofsangum, singende mid gife Godes on ̄eowrum
heortum. Swā-hwæt-swā gē dōð on worde oððe on weorce, dōð
symle on Drihtnes naman, þancigende ðām ælmihtigan Fæder
ðurh his Bearn. *Æ. H. i.* 606.

|| Swā-hwæt-swā gē dōð on worde oððe on weorce, dōð symle
on Drihtnes naman, þancigende þām ælmihtigan Fæder þurh his
Bearn. *Æ. H. i.* 102.

3. 18. *See* Eph. 5. 22.

3. 19. Lufiað, gē weras, ̄eowere wīf on ̄ewe ; ne bēo gē bitere him
ungebeorhlice. *Æ. H. ii.* 322.

3. 22-24. Ēalā, gē ðēowan, bēoð gehȳrsume ̄eowerum hlāfordum ;

COLOSSIANS.

2. 9. . . . In ipso inhabitat omnis
plenitudo divinitatis. . . .

2. 14. Delens quod adversus nos
erat chirographum decreti. . . .

3. 5. . . . Avaritiam, quae est simulacrorum servitus.

3. 12, 14-17. Induite vos ergo, sicut
electi Dei, . . . viscera miseri-
cordiae, benignitatem, humilita-
tem, modestiam, patientiam ; . . .
super omnia autem haec, charitatem habete, quod est vinculum
perfectionis ; et pax Christi ex-
ultet in cordibus vestris, in qua
et vocati estis in uno corpore ; et
grati estote. Verbum Christi
habitet in vobis abundanter in
omni sapientia, docentes et com-
monentes vosmetipsos psalmis,
hymnis, et canticis spiritualibus,
in gratia cantantes in cordibus
vestris Deo. Omne quodcumque
facitis in verbo aut in opere,
omnia in nomine Domini Iesu
Christi, gratias agentes Deo et
Patri per ipsum.

3. 19. Viri, diligite uxores vestras,
et nolite amari esse ad illas.

3. 22-24. Servi, obedite per omnia
dominis carnalibus ; non ad ocu-

swā-hwæt-swā [1] gē wyrcað, wyrcað mid mōde, swā-swā Gode
sylfum, and hē sylð ēow mēde. Ne ðēowige gē tō ansȳne,
ac mid ānfealdre heortan, nē swilce beforan mannum, ac mid
Godes ōgan. Æ. H. ii. 326.

1 THESSALONIANS.

2. 9. *See* Æ. H. i. 392.

4. 13 (Vulg. 12). Mīne gebrōðra, ic nelle þæt gē nyton be ðām
slāpendum. Æ. H. ii. 566.

4. 16–18 (Vulg. 15–17). Drihten sylf āstīhð of heofonum on stemne
þæs hēahengles, and mid Godes bȳman ; and ðā dēadan ærest
ārīsað ; syððan wē ðe lybbað, and on līchaman bēoð gemētte,
bēoð gelæhte forð mid þām ōðrum on wolcnum tōgēanes Crīste ;
and wē swā symle syððan mid Gode bēoð. Frēfriað ēow mid
þisum wordum. Æ. H. i. 616.

5. 2. Drihtnes dæg cymð swā-swā ðēof on niht.   Æ. H. ii. 568.

5. 15. *See* Matt. 5. 43–46.

2 THESSALONIANS.

3. 8. *See* Æ. H. i. 392.

1 TIMOTHY.

5. 6. Sēo wuduwe þe lyfað on ēstmettum, hēo ne lyfað nā, ac hēo
is dēad. Æ. H. i. 146.

5. 18. *See* Luke 10. 2–7.

lum servientes, quasi hominibus
placentes, sed in simplicitate
cordis, timentes Deum. Quodcumque facitis, ex animo operamini, sicut Domino, et non
hominibus, scientes quod a Domino accipietis retributionem
hereditatis. ...

1 THESSALONIANS.

4. 12. Nolumus autem vos ignorare,
fratres, de dormientibus. ...

4. 15–17. Quoniam ipse Dominus...
in voce archangeli, et in tuba Dei,

descendet de coelo ; et mortui ...
resurgent primi ; deinde nos qui
vivimus, qui relinquimur, simul
rapiemur cum illis in nubibus
obviam Christo in aera; et sic
semper cum Domino erimus. Itaque consolamini invicem in verbis
istis.

5. 2. ... Dies Domini sicut fur in
nocte, ita veniet.

1 TIMOTHY.

5. 6. Nam quae in deliciis est, vivens
mortua est.

6. 7. Ne brōhte wē nān ðing tō ðisum middangeardo, nō wē nān ðing heonon mid ūs lǣdan ne magon.   Æ. H. i. 256.

6. 10. Sēo grǣdignys is . . . wyrtruma ūlces yfeles.   Æ. H. ii. 410.

‖ . . . gȳtsunge, sēo ðe is wyrtruma ūlces yfeles.   Æ. H. ii. 462.

6. 15. Hē is ealra cyninga Cyning, and ealra hlāforda Hlāford.   Æ. H. i. 8.

6. 17, 18. Bebēodað þām rīcum þæt hī ne mōdigan, nō hī ne hopian on heora ungewissum welan; ac bēon hī rīce on gōdum weorcum, and syllan Godes ðearfum mid cystigum mōde.   Æ. H. i. 256.

HEBREWS.

1. 3. . . . þæt hē wǣre his Fæder wuldres beorhtnys.   Æ. H. ii. 606; cf. i. 28.

1. 5. See Ps. 2. 7; 89. 26.

1. 13. See Ps. 110. 1.

1. 14. Englas bēoð tō ðeninggāstum fram Gode hider on worulde āsende, þæt hī bēon on fultume his gecorenum, þæt hī ðone ēcan ēðel onfōn mid him.   Æ. H. i. 570.

5. 5. See Ps. 2. 7.

10. 38. See Hab. 2. 4.

11. 6. Gelēafa, . . . būton þām ne mæg nān mann Gode līcian.   Æ. H. i. 134.

12. 5, 6. Ne forgȳm ðū, mīn bearn, þīnes Drihtnes stēore, nō ðū bēo gewǣht þonne hē ðē þrēað; ðone ðe Drihten lufað, þone hē ðrēað, and sōðlice beswingð ǣlcne sunu ðe hē underfēhð.   Æ. H. ii. 328.

‖ God þrēað and beswingð ǣlcne ðe hē underfēhð tō his rīce.   Æ. H. i. 486; cf. Rev. 3. 19.

6. 7. Nihil enim intulimus in hunc mundum; haud dubium quod nec auferre quid possumus.

6. 10. Radix enim omnium malorum est cupiditas. . . .

6. 15. . . . Rex regum, et Dominus dominantium.

6. 17, 18. Divitibus huius saeculi praecipe non sublime sapere, neque sperare in incerto divitiarum; . . . divites fieri in bonis operibus, facile tribuere, communicare.

HEBREWS.

1. 3. Qui cum sit splendor gloriae... eius. . . .

1. 14. Nonne omnes sunt administratorii spiritus, in ministerium missi propter eos qui hereditatem capient salutis?

11. 6. Sine fide autem impossibile est placere Deo. . . .

12. 5, 6. . . . Fili mi, noli negligere disciplinam Domini, neque fati-

12. 29. God is . . . fornymende fȳr. Æ. H. i. 322.

13. 1, 2. Wunige betwux ēow lufu sōðre brōðerrǣdene, and ne forgȳmelēasige gē cumlīðnysse. Æ. H. ii. 286.

JAMES.

1. 2. Ēalā, gē mīne gebrōðra, wēnað ēow ælcere blisse, þonne gē bēoð on mislicum costnungum. Æ. H. i. 554.

2. 8. *See* Matt. 17. 49.

2. 13. Sē ðe dōm gesęt būton mildheortnysse, him bið ęft gedōmed būton mildheortnysse. Æ. H. ii. 322.

2. 14. Hwæt fręmað þē þæt ðū hæbbe gelēafan, gif ðū næfst ðā gōdan weorc? Æ. H. i. 304.

2. 17. Se gelēafa ðe bið būtan gōdum weorcum, sō bið dēad.
  Æ. H. i. 302.

  ‖ Se gelēafa þe bið būtan gōdum weorcum, sō is dēad.
  Æ. H. i. 236.

2. 19. Dēoflu gelȳfað, ac hī forhtiað. Æ. H. i. 304.

2. 23. *See* Æ. H. i. 558.

2. 20, 26. *See* Jas. 2. 17.

3. 10. Ne magon wē mid ānum mūðe blōtsian and wyrian.
  Æ. H. ii. 36.

4. 4. Swā-hwā-swā wile bēon frēond þisre worulde, sō bið geteald Godes fēond. Æ. H. i. 162.

  ‖ Swā-hwā-swā wile bēon frēond þyssere worulde, hē bið Godes fēond geteald. Æ. H. i. 612.

geris dum ab eo argueris; quem enim diligit Dominus, castigat; flagellat autem omnem filium quem recipit.
12. 29. Etenim Deus noster ignis consumens est.
13. 1, 2. Charitas fraternitatis maneat in vobis, et hospitalitatem nolite oblivisci.

JAMES.

1. 2. Omne gaudium existimate, fratres mei, cum in tentationes varias incideritis.
2. 13. Iudicium enim sine miseri-

cordia illi qui non fecit misericordiam. . . .
2. 14. Quid proderit . . . si fidem quis dicat se habere, opera autem non habeat? . . .
2. 17. Sic et fides, si non habeat opera, mortua est in semetipsa.
2. 19. . . . Daemones credunt, et contremiscunt.
3. 10. Ex ipso ore procedit benedictio et maledictio. Non oportet, fratres mei, haec ita fieri.
4. 4. . . . Quicumque ergo voluerit amicus esse saeculi huius, inimicus Dei constituitur.

4. 7, 8. Wiðstandaþ þām dēofle, and hē flihð fram ēow; genēalǣc-að Gode, and hē genēalǣhð tō ēow.   Æ. H. i. 604.

∥ Genēalǣcað tō Gode, and God genēalǣhð tō ēow.   Æ. H. ii. 52.

5. 4. *See* Rom. 9. 29.

5. 16-20. . . . þæt wē sceolon andettan ūre synna gelōme, and ǣlc for ōðerne gebiddan, þæt wē bēon gehealdene. Helias se wītega wæs ūs mannum gelīc, ðrōwiendlic swā-swā wē; and hē swā-ðēah ābæd þæt rēn wæs forwyrned ðām wiðerweardum folce tō ðrēora gēara fyrste, and syx mōnða fæce. Hē ābæd eft siððan æt ðām sōðan Gode þæt hē rēnas forgeaf, and eorðlice wæstmas.   Gif hwilc man gebīgð ōðerne fram ge-dwylde, hē ālȳst his sāwle sōðlice fram dēaðe, and fela synna ādȳlegað þurh ðæs gedwolan rihtinge.   Æ. H. ii. 330.

1 PETER.

1. 1. *See* Æ. H. i. 268.

1. 5. Þurh Godes gife gē sind gehealdene on gelēafan.   Æ. H. i. 114.

∥ Gē sind on Godes gife gehealdene þurh gelēafan.   Æ. H. ii. 524.

1. 7. Forðanþe sēo āfandung ēowres gelēafan is miccle dēorwurðre þonne gold þe bið ðurh fȳr āfandod.   Æ. H. i. 554; cf. i. 6, 268, 544.

1. 24. Ǣlc flǣsc is gærs, and þæs flǣsces wuldor is swilce wyrta blōstm.   Æ. H. i. 188.

2. 4, 5. Genēalǣcað tō ðām lybbendum stāne, se ðe is fram mannum āworpen, and fram Gode gecoren and geārwurðod; and bēoð gē sylfe ofer ðām stāne getimbrode, swā-swā lybbende stānas on gāstlicum hūsum.   Æ. H. ii. 580.

4. 7, 8. . . . Resistite autem diabolo, et fugiet a vobis; appropinquate Deo, et appropinquabit vobis. . . .

5. 16-20. Confitemini ergo alteru-trum peccata vestra, et orate pro invicem ut salvemini. . . . Elias homo erat similis nobis passibilis; et oratione oravit ut non plueret super terram, et non pluit annos tres et menses sex. Et rursum oravit, et coelum dedit pluviam, et terra dedit fructum suum. . . . Si quis . . . erraverit a veritate, et converterit quis eum, scire debet quoniam qui converti fecerit pec-catorem ab errore viae suae,

salvabit animam eius a morte, et operiet multitudinem peccatorum.

1 PETER.

1. 5. . . . In virtute Dei custodimini per fidem in salutem. . . .

1. 7. Ut probatio vestrae fidei multo pretiosior auro quod per ignem probatur. . . .

1. 24. . . . Omnis caro ut foenum, et omnis gloria eius tamquam flos foeni. . . .

2. 4, 5. Ad quem accedentes lapidem vivum, ab hominibus quidem re-probatum, a Deo autem electum et honorificatum; et ipsi tam-

2. 21. Crīst ðrōwode for ūs, and sealde us bȳsne þæt wē sceolon fyligan his fōtswaðum. _Æ. H._ i. 164.

3. 1. _See_ Eph. 5. 22.

3. 6. Swā-swā Sarra gehȳrsumode Abrahame, and hine hlāford hēt ; ðǣre dōhtra gē sind, wel dōnde and nā ondrǣdende ǣnige gedrēfednysse. _Æ. H._ i. 98.

3. 9. _See_ Matt. 5. 43–46.

3. 18. _See_ Æ. H. ii. 276.

3. 20. _See_ Æ. H. ii. 60.

4. 9. Bēoð cumlīðe ēow betwȳnan, būton ceorungum. _Æ. H._ ii. 286.

5. 8, 9. Bēoð sȳfre and wacole, forðanðe se dēofol, ēower wiðer-winna, færð onbūtan swā-swā grymetende lēo, sēcende hwǣne hē ābīte ; wiðstandað þām strange on gelēafan. _Æ. H._ ii. 448.

1 JOHN.

2. 4. Sē ðe cwyð þæt hē God cunne, and his beboda ne hylt, hē is lēas. _Æ. H._ i. 302.

‖ Gif hwā cwyð þæt hē lufige þone lifigendan God, and his beboda ne hylt, hē bið lēas ðonne. _Æ. H._ ii. 314 ; cf. i. 236.

2. 6. Sē ðe cweð þæt hē on Crīste wunige, hē sceal faran swā-swā Crīst fērde. _Æ. H._ ii. 468.

2. 15. Ne lufige gē middangeard, nē ðā ðing ðe him on wuniað ; forðan swā-hwā-swā middangeard lufað, næfð hē Godes lufe on him. _Æ. H._ i. 614.

‖ Ne lufige gē ðisne middaneard, nē ðā ðing ðe on mid-danearde sind. _Æ. H._ ii. 340.

3. 14. Sē ðe his brōðor ne lufað, hē wunað on dēaðe. _Æ. H._ i. 54.

quam lapides vivi superaedifica-mini, domus spiritualis. . . .

2. 21. . . . Christus passus est pro nobis, vobis relinquens exemplum ut sequamini vestigia eius.

3. 6. Sicut Sara obediebat Abrahae, dominum eum vocans; cuius estis filiae, benefacientes et non perti-mentes ullam perturbationem.

4. 9. Hospitales invicem sine mur-muratione.

5. 8, 9. Sobrii estote, et vigilate, quia adversarius vester diabolus tamquam leo rugiens circuit, quaerens quem devoret ; cui

resistite fortes in fide. . . .

1 JOHN.

2. 4. Qui dicit se nosse eum, et mandata eius non custodit, men-dax est. . . .

2. 6. Qui dicit se in ipso manere, debet, sicut ille ambulavit, et ipse ambulare.

2. 15. Nolite diligere mundum, neque ea quae in mundo sunt ; si quis diligit mundum, non est charitas Patris in eo.

3. 14. . . . Qui non diligit, manet in morte.

3. 15. Ǣlc ðǣra þe his bróðor hata‏ð is manslaga.   ÆE. II. i. 54.

3. 16. Wē oncnēowon Crīstes lufe on ūs þurh þæt, þæt hē scalde hine sylfne for ūs ; and wē sceolon syllan ūs sylfe for gebróðrum.   Æ. II. ii. 318.

4. 9. Dā geswutelode God hū miccle lufe hē hæfde and hæfð tō ūs, þā-ðā hē āsҽnde his āgen Bearn tō slҽge for ūs.   Æ. H. ii. 6.

4. 20. Sē ðe ne lufað his bróðor þone ðe hē gesihð, hū mæg hē lufian God, þone ðe hē ne gesihð līchamlice ?   Æ. H. i. 232, 326.

5. 16. Sum synn is ðe bringð tō dēaðe ; ic bidde þæt nān man for þēre ne gebidde.   Æ. H. ii. 528.

REVELATION.

1. 7. *See* Æ. H. i. 28.

1. 9. *See* Æ. H. i. 58.

1. 10. *See* Rev. 19. 6.

3. 4. *See* Æ. H. i. 88.

3. 19. Þā ðe ic lufige, ðā ic ðrēage and beswinge.   Æ. H. i. 470.

‖ Ic ðrēage and swinge þā ðe ic lufige.   Æ. H. ii. 328.

‖ Se ælmihtiga God beswingð and þrēað þā ðe hē lufað.   Æ. H. ii. 548 ; cf. Heb. 12. 5, 6.

3. 20. Ic stande æt ðēre dura cnucigende ; and swā-hwā-swā mīne stemne gehȳrð, and ðā duru mē geopenað, ic gange in tō him, and mid him gereordige, and hē mid mē.   Æ. H. ii. 468, 470.

5. 5. Hē is Lēo gecīged of Iudan mǣgðe, Dauides wyrtruma.   Æ. H. i. 358.

7. 9–12. Ic geseah swā miccle mҽnigu swā nān man gerȳman ne mæg, of eallum ðēodum and of ælcere mǣgðe, standende ætforan Godes þrymsetle, ealle mid hwītum gyrlum gescrȳdde,

3. 15. Omnis qui odit fratrem suum homicida est. . . .

3. 16. In hoc cognovimus charitatem Dei, quoniam ille animam suam pro nobis posuit ; et nos debemus pro fratribus animas ponere.

4. 9. In hoc apparuit charitas Dei in nobis, quoniam Filium suum unigenitum misit Deus in mundum, ut vivamus per eum.

4. 20. . . . Qui enim non diligit fratrem suum quem videt, Deum, quem non videt, quomodo potest diligere ?

5. 16. . . . Est peccatum ad mortem ; non pro illo dico ut roget quis.

REVELATION.

3. 19. Ego quos amo, arguo et castigo. . . .

3. 20. Ecce sto ad ostium, et pulso ; siquis audierit vocem meam, et aperuerit mihi ianuam, intrabo ad illum, et coenabo cum illo, et ipse mecum.

5. 5. . . . Leo de tribu Iuda, radix David. . . .

7. 9–12. . . . Vidi turbam magnam, quam dinumerare nemo poterat,

healdende palmtwigu on heora handum, and sungon mid
hluddre stemne : Sȳ hǣlu ūrum Gode þe sitt ofer his þrymsetle.
And ealle englas stōdon on ymbhwyrfte his ðrymsetles, and
āluton to Gōde, þus cweðende : Sȳ ūrum Gode blōtsung and
beorhtnys, wīsdom and þancung, wurðmynt and strengð, on
ealra worulda woruld.   Amen.   Æ. H. i. 538.

‖ And hī standað ætforan his ðrymsetle, hæbbende heora
palmtwigu on handa.   Æ. H. i. 90.

14. 3. And singað þone nīwan lofsang.   Æ. H. i. 90.

14. 4. Hī sind ðā ðe Crīste folgiað on hwītum gyrlum, swā-hwider-
swā hē gāð.   Æ. H. i. 88, 90.

19. 6. *See* Æ. H. ii. 86.

19. 10. Beheald þæt ðū ðās dǣde ne dō ; ic eom ðīn efenðēowa,
and ðīnra gebrōðra ; gebide ðē tō Gode ānum.   Æ. H. i. 38.

‖ Ne dō þū hit nā, þæt þū tō mē ābūge : ic eom Godes
þēowa, swā-swā ðū and þīne gebrōðra ; gebide ðē tō Gode
ānum.   Æ. H. i. 174.

19. 16. *See* 1 Tim. 6. 15.

21. 1. Þonne bið nīwe heofon and nīwe eorðe.   Æ. H. i. 618.

22. 9. *See* Rev. 19. 10.

22. 11. Sē ðe derað, derige hē gȳt swȳðor ; and sē ðe on fūl-
nyssum wunað, befȳle hine gȳt swȳðor ; . . . sē ðe hālig is, bēo
hē gȳt swȳðor gehālgod.   Æ. H. i. 484.

UNTRACED PASSAGES.

Sȳ ðām ārlēasan ætbrōden sēo gesihð Godes wuldres.   Æ. H. i. 300.
Þonne hē bið mid īdelum hlīsan and lyffetungum befangen,

ex omnibus gentibus, et tribubus, et populis, et linguis, stantes ante thronum, . . . amicti stolis albis, et palmae in manibus eorum ; et clamabant voce magna, dicentes : Salus Deo nostro qui sedet super thronum. . . . Et omnes angeli stabant in circuitu throni, . . . et adoraverunt Deum, dicentes : . . . Benedictio, et claritas, et sapientia, et gratiarum actio, honor, et virtus, et fortitudo Deo nostro in saecula saeculorum. Amen.

14. 3. Et cantabant quasi canticum novum. . . .

14. 4. . . . Hi sequuntur Agnum quocumque ierit. . . .

19. 10. . . . Vide ne feceris ; conservus tuus sum, et fratrum tuorum . . . Deum adora. . . .

21. 1. Et vidi coelum novum et terram novam. . . .

22. 11. Qui nocet, noceat adhuc ; et qui in sordibus est, sordescat adhuc ; . . . et sanctus, sanctificetur adhuc.

UNTRACED PASSAGES.

Tollatur impius ne videat gloriam Dei.

þonne bið hit swylce hū sȳ mid sumere moldhȳpan of hroren.
     Æ. H. i. 492.

Se wītega Hieremias cwæð be ðām Hǣlende : Ðes is ūre God,
and nis nān ōðer geteald tō him.   Hē ārǣrde and gesętte stōore
and þēawfæstnysse his folce Israhel.   Hē wæs siððan gesewen
ofer eorðan, and mid mannum hē drohtnode.   Æ. H. ii. 12.

. . . Wītegode Hieremias tō þǣre byrig Hierusalem, þus cweðende :
Tō ðe cymð þīn Ālȳsend, and þis bið his tācn : Hē geopenað
blindra manna ēagan, and dēadum hē forgifð heorcnunge, and
mid his stemne hē ārǣrð þā dēadan of heora byrgenum.
     Æ. H. ii. 16.

. . . þæt se hēalica God hatað unrihtwīsra gife.   Æ. II. ii. 338.

God gecwæð þæt ǣlc synn ðe nǣre ofer eorðan gebōt sceolde bēon
on ðissere worulde gedēmed.   Æ. H. ii. 338.

Sē ðe wēnð þæt hē hāl sȳ, sē is unhāl.   Æ. H. ii. 470.

INDEX OF BIBLICAL PASSAGES

INDEX OF PRINCIPAL WORDS

[The words excluded from this list are such as the commoner conjunctions, prepositions, pronouns, and numerals; the nouns Dryhten, God, mọnn(a); the adjectives eall, micel, mọnig; the verbs bēon (wesan), cuman, cunnan, cweðan, dōn, gān, habban, magan, mōtan, sculan, sẹcgan, sprecan, weorðan, willan (nellan), witan (nytan); and the adverbs ēac, gȳt, hēr, hwǣr, hwonne, nā (nō), nū, swā, ðā, ðǣr (and compounds), ðonne, and ðus. Of others it is intended that all the instances shall be given, unless otherwise indicated.]

[The references in this Index refer to the page and line.]

ā, 19. 13; 21. 16; 67. 16; 114. 22; 224. 7; 249. 22.

Aaron (Aron), 6. 25; 7. 3; 8. 14; 85. 16; 90. 11; 92. 8.

Abacuc, 131. 10, 11, 13, 16, 20.

Abel, 3. 3.

āberan, 42. 15; 80. 3; 94. 19; 120. 20; 133. 19; 144. 12.

ābiddan, 174. 5; 176. 1.

Abiron, 114. 12.

ābisgian, 51. 5; 54. 11.

ābītan, 93. 7; 124. 8; 131. 8; 253. 8, 9; 254. 13.

āblāwan, 225. 22, 24.

āblẹndan (āblǣndan), 67. 18; 73. 15; 235. 4.

āblicgan, 192. 4; 228. 24; 236. 4.

Abner, 12. 3, 6.

Abraham, 81. 15, 24, 25; 82. 21; 83. 11, 14, 15, 18, 22, 25; 84. 5; 151. 12; 152. 1, 4, 7; 186. 15; 200. 14, 16, 17; 204. 5; 217. 3, 13, 16, 17, 19; 246. 17, 19, 21; 254. 4; Habraham, 41. 4.

Abram, 81. 25.

ābrecan, 20. 12.

ābrēdan, 174. 1.

ābūgan, 256. 15.

ābyrian, 205. 11.

ācẹnnan, 103. 8; 105. 16; 112. 20; 118. 18, 20, 22; 137. 13, 16, 19; 138. 1; 139. 10, 13, 15; 184. 21; 185. 9, 19; 187. 4, 12; 188. 9, 13, 15; 211. 26; 217. 23; 219. 2.

ācẹnnednyss, 83. 6; 189. 1.

ācēosan, 58. 1.

ācōlian, 167. 6.

ācsian. *See* āxian.

ācwelan, 65. 20.

ācwẹllan, 67. 17; 88. 14; 102. 18; 105. 5; 131. 2; 136. 20; 219. 9; 224. 17; 233. 17; 236. 9; 238. 21.

ācwẹncan, 168. 14.

Adam, 76. 7; 77. 10, 12, 14, 16, 17; 78. 23; 94. 3.

ādelfan, 5. 13; 64. 14; 148. 16.

ādeorcian, 27. 9.

ādlig, 183. 29.

ādlung, 120. 19.

ādōn, 13. 15; 29. 15; 35. 15; 46. 15.

ādrǣdan, 196. 23.

ādrǣfan, 11. 23; 79. 3; 150. 6; 155. 4; 183. 26; 196. 14; 204. 25.

ādrẹncan, 80. 10.

ādrēogan, 245. 6, 18.

ādrifan, 22. 5; 36. 1; 59. 7.

U

geðrōwian, 48. 12.

geðyld, 20. 18; 41. 14; 49. 1; 53. 7; 58. 18; 107. 8; 117. 3; 193. 10; 206. 6, 10; 239. 28, 29; 249. 8.

geðyldeg (-ig), 20. 9; 22. 15; 49. 2; 105. 20; 116. 21.

geðyldelice, 55. 13.

geðyncan, 68. 13; 182. 11.

geuferian, 201. 21.

geunclǣnsian, 36. 5, 6.

geunnan, 96. 9.

geunrōtsian, 4. 23; 107. 7; 172. 20; 221. 23.

geuntrumian, 50. 11 (2); 170. 19; 171. 15; 180. 6.

gewǣcan, 165. 12; 206. 4; 251. 23.

gewǣde, 160. 2.

gewǣpnian, 50. 2; 223. 5, 12.

gewǣtan, 41. 5.

gewǟld. *See* geweald.

gewanian, 129. 15.

gewarnian, 123. 8; 138. 23.

geweald (gewǟld), 11. 13, 23, 24; 18. 11; 45. 6; 63. 1, 5.

gewealdan, 102. 11; 116. 22; 127. 20; 138. 9; 139. 18.

gewealden, 54. 16.

gewęmman, 242. 12.

gewęndan, 23. 19; 78. 21, 22; 82. 20; 99. 3; 100. 14, 21; 104. 13; 105. 8; 106. 10; 109. 11; 128. 9; 140. 7, 16; 194. 26; 212. 23; 215. 2; 238. 12.

geweorðan (gewurðan), 9. 10(2); 11. 4; 29. 5; 71. 16; 76. 1, 2; 86. 13; 112. 7; 147. 28; 161. 4; 173. 21; 188. 26, 27; 206. 14, 26; 210. 12, 19, 27; 217. 18, 19; 222. 7; 231. 5; 243. 26.

geweorðian, 16. 20.

gewęrian, 20. 14; 63. 19; 65. 12.

gewifian, 198. 17.

gewil, 67. 8.

gewildan, 20. 11.

gewilnian, 54. 1, 2; 91. 2 (2); 99. 5.

gewilnigendlic, 117. 5.

gewi(o)ta, 44. 1; 58. 9; 91. 1; 201. 4; 227. 12; 232. 24; 233. 4.

gewiss, 125. 14.

gewissian, 85. 19; 96. 12; 138. 10; 220. 13.

gewistfullian, 197. 8.

gewit(t), 48. 13; 53. 10; 192. 10.

gewitan, 227. 9.

gewītan, 38. 6; 40. 8; 54. 5; 71. 15; 95. 12; 105. 16; 116. 4; 127. 18; 139. 7; 150. 8; 171. 7; 172. 12, 14; 187. 19; 200. 13, 26; 206. 25, 26, 27; 225. 3; 227. 3; 231. 1, 6; 237. 19; 238. 17; 240. 25; 241. 8.

gewitness (-nyss), 61. 13; 65. 20, 21; 67. 6; 150. 18; 205. 26; 229. 21.

gewitnian, 197. 19; 208. 16.

gewittig, 158. 10.

gewrit, 53. 15; 101. 14; 129. 4, 7, 12; 186. 20; 223. 22; 234. 19.

gewriðan, 116. 15; 117. 11.

gewuna, 44. 16, 18; 175. 21; 225. 7.

gewundian, 39. 17; 64. 17.

gewunelic, 86. 20.

gewunian, 45. 10; 66. 5; 248. 19.

gewurðan. *See* geweorðan.

gewyht, 225. 5.

gewyrc(e`an, 6. 15; 24. 16; 37. 19; 61. 8; 75. 3; 76. 5, 9, 15; 77. 8, 15; 90. 19; 93. 5; 101. 17; 111. 17; 121. 18; 141. 5; 210. 7.

gewyrpan, 212. 26.

gewyrtrumian, 247. 17.

geyppan, 22. 8.

geyrsian, 118. 7.

gids-. *See* gits-.

giefa, 50. 10. *See also* gifan, gifu.

gī(e)man, 19. 11; 35. 4; 54. 14.

gīemelēas, 67. 11.

gīemelist (gȳmelēast), 17. 10; 37. 24; 124. 8.

gīcning, 41. 16.

gierd (gyrd), 14. 9; 46. 10; 88. 21; 92. 5, 7, 8; 95. 21; 116. 18; 117. 7.

gierness, 63. 5.

gierwan, 40. 15.

giesthūs. *See* gęsthūs.

Giethro, 5. 6.

gietsere. *See* gitsere.

Giezi (Gyezi), 100. 9, 16.

gifan, 99. 2; 109. 18; 129. 7. *See also* giefa, giofol.

gift (gyft), 62. 15; 165. 2, 4, 7, 15, 17, 19; 168. 19; 210. 27; 211. 3, 4, 5, 9. *See also* gyftlic.

wẹcg, 160. 19.

wẹdd, 19. 2; 66. 20; 80. 6, 9; 81. 22; 82. 1, 4, 5, 12, 13, 19.

weg (weig), 17. 17; 26. 23; 35. 17; 37. 10; 52. 6; 59. 1; 96. 20; 120. 7, 11, 12; 128. 13; 138. 24; 149. 9, 12; 153. 11; 164. 14; 165. 16, 18; 181. 2; 192. 21; 194. 22; 198. 24; 202. 22; 220. 4; 235. 19.

wegan, 6. 23.

wegfarende, 192. 22.

wegfērend, 108. 19.

weig. See weg.

wel, 9. 2; 11. 23; 12. 14; 19. 19; 33. 7; 35. 1; 52. 13; 53. 3; 55. 2; 141. 22, 24, 25; 166. 9; 254. 5.

wela, 14. 11; 17. 22; 39. 11; 55. 3; 96. 15, 18; 97. 1; 108. 16; 116. 17; 142. 14; 143. 13; 155. 19; 193. 7; 200. 18; 251. 8.

welig (-eg), 39. 4; 40. 14; 55. 1; 67. 13; 197. 1, 11; 200. 6; 201. 25.

welor (-er), 14. 19; 17. 1; 32. 9; 102. 7; 105. 11, 24; 106. 18.

welwillendnyss, 249. 7.

wēnan, 11. 4; 14. 10; 26. 6; 29. 16; 85. 22; 38. 1; 40. 1; 49. 6, 7; 145. 9; 156. 22; 209. 15; 247. 1; 252. 4; 257. 15.

wẹndan, 67. 8; 142. 23; 223. 10.

wẹnian, 26. 20.

weofod (weobud, wiofud), 30. 5, 7; 34. 19, 22; 63. 6; 145. 21, 23, 25; 182. 15.

weorc, 13. 14; 14. 11; 20. 17; 26. 18, 21; 33. 4; 34. 15; 41. 22; 47. 1; 54. 1, 8; 58. 16; 59. 8, 9; 63. 14; 76. 9, 11, 13; 78. 13, 17; 98. 24; 113. 1; 127. 12; 128. 12; 136. 11; 145. 1, 4, 6; 147. 12; 215. 6; 222. 5; 239. 3; 241. 1, 9; 242. 3, 5, 7 (2); 249. 15, 18; 251. 9; 252. 10, 11, 13.

weorld (world, woruld), 17. 4; 22. 7; 39. 11; 41. 8, 17, 22; 56. 3, 15; 57. 19; 114. 22; 119. 1; 155. 10, 23; 167. 22; 174. 13; 179. 10, 12, 15; 186. 16; 197. 1; 227. 9; 243. 18; 251. 15; 252. 20, 22; 256. 6 (2); 257. 14. See also world-, woruld-.

weoroldgōd, 73. 1.

weorpan (wurpan), 34. 11; 126. 4; 133. 7, 8, 14; 158. 5, 12; 160. 17; 164. 13; 165. 25; 182. 6; 226. 16.

weorð (wurð), 62. 16; 64. 18; 230. 13, 20; 243. 2.

weorðian (wurðian), 10. 11; 34. 16, 17; 37. 6; 56. 11; 68. 15; 125. 12.

weorðmynd (wurðmynt, wyrðmynt), 17. 22; 20. 7; 112. 5; 128. 9; 131. 18; 238. 16; 256. 5.

weorðscipe, 18. 9; 52. 10; 54. 19.

weotuma, 62. 17; 66. 4.

wēpan, 32. 3; 39. 5; 47. 25 (2); 107. 3; 144. 5; 191. 13; 204. 13, 14.

wer, 8. 10; 17. 3; 20. 10; 22. 15; 43. 2; 47. 7, 11, 12; 64. 4, 8; 69. 1, 9; 77. 19; 78. 8; 103. 6, 7, 11; 114. 19; 116. 21; 123. 13; 126. 6; 181. 17; 185. 16; 190. 9; 198. 26; 205. 10; 214. 7; 228. 7, 21; 231. 2, 7; 245. 11, 13, 15; 248. 3; 249. 22.

wered. See werod.

wẹrgan. See wiergan.

wẹrian, 66. 20.

wērig, 56. 8.

werlic, 245. 1.

werod (-ed), 89. 10; 101. 15; 187. 15; 214. 4; 236. 26; 238. 2; 239. 2; 240. 13.

westdǣl, 151. 11; 152. 1, 3, 6.

wēsten, 5. 1; 9. 7; 85. 19; 89. 22; 105. 3; 120. 7; 141. 27; 142. 21; 180. 22; 190. 19; 199. 10; 212. 9; 215. 8, 23; 245. 21.

weðer, 97. 4.

wexan. See we(a)xan.

wīc, 24. 22; 198. 21; 237. 19.

wicca, 66. 6.

wīce, 124. 11.

wīcian, 9. 7; 92. 1; 187. 3.

wīd, 79. 10; 97. 17.

wīdfaran, 25. 12.

wīdgill, 35. 17.

wīdnyss, 97. 14, 16.

wiergan (wẹrgan, wyrian), 19. 22; 46. 23; 63. 11; 66. 24; 91. 4, 6; 104. 10; 106. 7, 15; 144. 21; 242. 24; 252. 18.

wi(e)ta, 39. 1; 64. 10; 101. 7; 117. 5; 128. 10, 15.

ERRATA

Page 6, l. 5 from bottom,—*for* gōdwębbe *read* godwębbe.

,, 13, l. 10,—*for* oferhelede *read* oferhęlede.

,, 24, l. 8 from bottom,—*for* gēworhte *read* geworhte.

,, 41, ll. 3 and 9 from bottom,—*for* grin *read* grīn.

,, 47, l. 3,—*for* Fulga *read* Fulgā.

,, 65, ll. 6 and 12 from bottom,—*for* twȳfealdum *read* twyfealdum.

,, 83, l. 4 from bottom,—*for* sandcĕōsol *read* sandceosol.

,, 84, l. 5 from bottom,—*for* sandcĕōsol *read* sandceosol.

,, 96, l. 11,—*for* me *read* mē.

,, 109, l. 9 from bottom,—*for* twȳfealdum *read* twyfealdum.

,, 139, l. 9 from bottom,—*for* þrȳfealde *read* þryfealde.

,, 154, bottom line,—*for* streçanmōd *read* strecanmōd.

,, 192, l. 4 from bottom,—*for* twȳfealdre *read* twyfealdre.

,, 205, l. 8 from bottom,—*add* :—cf. ii. 568.

,, 211, l. 10,—*for* twȳfealde *read* twyfealde.

,, 211, l. 11,—*for* þrȳfealde *read* þryfealde.

,, 239, l. 9,—*for* Cristes *read* Crīstes.

,, 250, after l. 6 from bottom,—*insert* :—5. 5.   *See* Æ. II. ii. 292.

,, 254, after l. 13,—*insert* :—2 PETER. 2. 22.   *See* Æ. II. ii. 602, cf. ii. 380.

www.ingramcontent.com/pod-product-compliance
Lightning Source LLC
Chambersburg PA
CBHW030823110726
47900CB00006B/1727